BEWARE OF KLINGONS
WEARING SMILES...

The screen lit up, giving a view of the slowly turning gas giant. Suddenly the intruder seemed to leap forward, to show an irregular artificial shape clearly outlined against the brilliant hues of the planet's dense atmosphere.

"That's a Klingon cruiser, Jim," McCoy declared.

"I can see that, Bones," Kirk muttered. "Mr. Sulu, sound red alert. Mr. Arex, align phasers to..."

"Receiving transmission from the Klingon ship, Captain," Uhura interrupted.

"Acknowledge their signal, Lieutenant."

The Klingon who appeared on the viewscreen was seated in the counterpart of Kirk's command chair. His attitude was one of relaxed attention. Except for the tight set of his lips, he appeared almost friendly.

And when the image had fully resolved at both ends of the transmission, he even smiled...

That could only mean one thing... TROUBLE!

Also in Pocket Books

STAR TREK LOGS 1 - 3
STAR TREK LOGS 4 - 6

STAR TREK
Volumes 68 - 73

STAR TREK: THE NEXT GENERATION
Volumes 29 - 34

STAR TREK: DEEP SPACE NINE
Volumes 1 - 10

STAR TREK: VOYAGER
Volume 1

Plus

STAR TREK: PROBE
STAR TREK: BEST DESTINY
STAR TREK: SAREK
STAR TREK: SHADOWS ON THE SUN

STAR TREK: THE NEXT GENERATION: RELICS
STAR TREK: THE NEXT GENERATION: REUNION
STAR TREK: THE NEXT GENERATION: DEVIL'S HEART
STAR TREK: THE NEXT GENERATION: IMZADI
STAR TREK: THE NEXT GENERATION: DESCENT

STAR TREK©

LOG SEVEN
LOG EIGHT
LOG NINE
LOG TEN

Alan Dean Foster

POCKET BOOKS

LONDON · SYDNEY · NEW YORK · TOKYO · SINGAPORE · TORONTO

First published in Great Britain by Pocket Books, 1995
An imprint of Simon & Schuster Ltd

STAR TREK LOG SEVEN
Copyright© Paramount Pictures Corporation, 1976, 1993
STAR TREK LOG EIGHT
Copyright© Paramount Pictures Corporation, 1976, 1993
STAR TREK LOG NINE
Copyright© Paramount Pictures Corporation, 1977, 1993
STAR TREK LOG TEN
Copyright© Paramount Pictures Corporation, 1978, 1993

Star Trek is a Registered Trademark of Paramount Pictures

This book is copyright under the Berne Convention.
No reproduction without permission.
All rights reserved.

Simon & Schuster Ltd
West Garden Place
Kendal Street
London W2 2AQ

Simon & Schuster of Australia Pty Ltd
Sydney

A CIP catalogue record for this book is
available from the British Library
ISBN 0-671-85405-4

This book is a work of fiction. Names, characters, places and incidents are either the product of the author's imagination or are used fictitiously. Any resemblance to actual events or locales or persons, living or dead, is entirely coincidental.

Printed in Great Britain by
HarperCollins*Manufacturing,*
Glasgow

Contents

Log Seven 1

Log Eight 177

Log Nine 359

STAR TREK
LOG SEVEN

For all the fans of Star Trek,
everywhere . . . ignore the ignorant
and stick to your phasers!

STAR TREK LOG SEVEN

Log of the Starship *Enterprise*
Stardates 5536.3–5536.9 Inclusive

James T. Kirk, Capt., USSC, FS, ret.
Commanding

transcribed by
Alan Dean Foster

At the Galactic Historical Archives
on S. Monicus I
stardated 6111.5

For the Curator: JLR

THE COUNTER-CLOCK INCIDENT

(Adapted from a script by John Culver)

1

A warm light seemed to suffuse April's face as he stared at the drawings. Soft, caressing, intense—the kind of gentle radiance Rembrandt used to edge his portraits with.

The works hanging on the wall before him, which had inspired such a reverent gaze, would never hang in any museum, would never raise the brow of the lowliest art critic. Yet April's mind applied a critic's terminology to them. Masterpieces—exquisite, sensuous, drawn with unsurpassed skill and vivid realization—they were.

True, the drawings had no depth beyond the minimally necessary. There was no attempt to give body to the colossal conception so skeletally sketched. The use of color was minimal, every drawing done in unrelieved blue on white.

But that didn't matter. His mind filled in the myriad colors that would be added later.

"Magnificent, isn't she?" the old man standing on April's left murmured. "Even in the preliminary blueprints. The soundness of Franz Joseph's original design holds up well. You know, there was a time when people thought he designed these ships only for amusement, that they'd never have any practical application."

"Hard to believe," April agreed. "Still, they were well ahead of their time." He peered harder at the wall full of drawings. "NCC-1701, Class One . . . that's a heavy cruiser, right?"

"Sure is," Commodore van Anling admitted. "Her major components are being put together out in the San Francisco yards right now. I could take you out there, but"—he nodded toward the wall—"there's much more to be seen in those prints than in a few irregular masses of metal and plastic.

9

Free-space assembly won't begin for another eight months yet."

"I see." April turned to the smaller, deceptively frail-looking man. "But why tell me all this, sir? Why call me away from my regular duties?" The light in his eyes deepened to an expectant gleam. "Am I going to be assigned to her?"

The commodore nodded, unable to suppress a slight smile.

April's voice rose like a small boy's. "What section, sir? If you have any idea, if it wouldn't be against regulations to tell me . . . !"

"I do and it isn't," van Anling told him, moving to a chair facing the wall.

"Engineering?" April prompted.

"No."

"Communications, then? Surely communications." The commodore shook his head. "Sciences . . . a security post?"

"No . . . no." Under the pencil-thin white mustache the older officer cracked an irrepressible grin.

"For heaven's sake, sir, give me to the Klingons, send me up for disobedience . . . but *tell* me! I've got to restudy whatever section it is, got to prepare. . . ."

"You sure do," van Anling informed him somberly, "because you're going to be in all of them." At April's blank stare, he added, "Because she's going to be your ship . . . *Captain* April."

"My . . . ship?"

"You're going to be her captain . . . her first captain," the commodore continued. April eyed him uncertainly, but there was no tag to the incredible pronouncement. Therefore it had to be true.

Slowly April turned, to stare anew at the wall filled with diagrams and blueprints. His gaze traveled from one to another, but all at once the regular lines seemed wavy, the precision gone. Lines clashed crazily, ran blindly into adjoining ones. The gleam in his eyes was gone, replaced suddenly by signs of another emotion.

Fear. Fear and a thrill so overwhelming he felt as though the combination would shove his heart right out through his chest. All of a sudden Robert April was the happiest man in the world . . . and he was scared to death.

"I . . . I'm not ready for this, sir," he finally managed to confess.

"That's all right," van Anling replied benignly. "You've got a whole year to make yourself ready. Better get to it, son."

In the harsh, gray shadows of the moon, beneath hills of devastated ash and pumice, an unlimited-range, high-resolution navigational computer finished digesting a gigantic body of minutiae. The results of many days of intense electronic cogitation were regurgitated in the form of a tiny printout on an insignificant little shard of tape.

The tape was carefully routed from the computer processor through an intermediary to the person in charge of the installation, who then relayed it to the captain of the small vessel resting in orbit high above the station. The captain passed it on, together with the requisite orders, to his own navigator. That worthy conferred with his two associates—one mechanical, the other only partly so.

The thing, he explained, would have to be aligned so and so at a speed of such and such, to achieve the optimum eventual impact. From time to time the ship's gunnery officer nodded knowingly or added a comment or correction of his own. Eventually everyone agreed. The results of the discussion were transmitted to the captain, who gave his approval and issued the formal order, which the gunnery officer executed.

Although the projector mounted on the small ship looked unimpressive, its efficiency was astounding. There was no flash, no concussive aftershock, no rumbling boom, of course, but the projector did its job nonetheless. Sensors immediately took over, announcing unemotionally that the projectile was on course at the proper speed. It would reach its target in approximately two weeks, four days, sixteen hours and assorted minutes.

The captain of the small ship eyed the tiny blip until it had faded completely from the sensitive tracking screen. More than anything else, he wished he could be there when the projectile impacted on its target. Destiny, however, had ordered more mundane activities for him on that distant day. He sighed. If he were lucky, they might be able to pick up the results on the tracking monitors—if they were still in the area.

Construction of the battle cruiser was proceeding smoothly. More smoothly, in fact, than had the construction of any similar vessel in some time. Possibly the Vulcan foreman had something to do with it. But whether through causes superhuman or supernatural, it began to be whispered among the construction crew and Starfleet personnel that this was going to be an especially blessed ship, a lucky ship. . . .

The projectile possessed no power units of its own. It had no sensing equipment, no detectors, no screens—nothing that could be sensed by any type of sophisticated energy-detection equipment. There was nothing to spoil the eventual surprise of its arrival, and it had to be perfectly aligned when fired. Divergence of even a hundredth of a degree could cause it to miss its intended target entirely. So its planners, both electronic and human, had been careful. It held to its course and flew silently on its way.

The United Federation of Planets Starfleet assembly station swung in majestic orbit around Earth. It resembled a bombed toy factory.

Gigantic preassembled sections of ships were boosted to this spot from half a hundred points on Earth's surface; special components from as many more deep-space cargo containers were unloaded. Thousands of elements were manufactured nearby, in dozens of enormous drifting factories, their production facilitated by zero gravity and total vacuum. Each of several million parts had to fit into sisters and brothers within a thousandth of a millimeter. Humanoid minds had conceived the project, but none of it would have been possible without the aid of machines.

One section was devoted to assembling two massive warp-drive engines. Construction crews working in triple shifts seamed the yawning sections together, work continuing around the clock.

An unusual pause in the work rhythm accompanied the placing of shielding from Tashkent. Assembly totally halted as the second-shift engineer-in-charge slowly turned his flexible armored worksuit to face the glowing Earth below. He arranged his suit carefully, moving the upper part in a particular way. His motions were directed toward a distant point on the planet's surface. They were as accurate as he could make them without benefit of detailed instrumentation. A slight divergence would not matter. His thoughts exceeded the actual movements in importance.

He quickly resumed directing the shielding installation. Below, Mecca had rotated past, turning majestically with the rest of the world.

In bits and pieces the huge ship began to form, sections of a white puzzle taking shape against a chill black background. Each crew, each shift, prided itself on being more accurate than its predecessor. Every coterie of seamers drifted on tethers and tried to outdo its counterparts for smoothness of joining and accuracy of component integration. The technicians and constructors and fabricators who set the lanes for the ship's bowling alley in place did their job with no less care and finesse than did the cybernetics crew responsible for locking the central computer into the ganglion of electronic nerves which stretched the length and breadth of the steadily maturing ship.

While construction proceeded with remarkable speed and efficiency, a tiny projectile continued toward a preselected point in space.

Eventually the day came when no more massive boosters lifted from the Earth's surface. No components required a last recheck; every bit of instrumentation had been certified operational. Everything was in place, from photon torpedos to potted philodendrons.

Several thousand strong, the construction crews began to assemble around the finished ship. Individuals in worksuits drifted in, as did crews of two or three manning engineering lighters—several hundred looking on from the orbital assembly stations that boxed in the construction area. All looked on as the first crew finally took official possession of their ship.

The engineering staff alone did not proceed at once to assigned quarters. Starship engineers seldom used their on-board personal cabins. They lived in jeffries tubes and cramped accessways and in the free spaces between computer housings.

April barely had time to check out the glistening chronometer in his quarters. Luxuriating in the comparative spaciousness of the captain's cabin would have to wait. He had a ship to command.

It was a short turbolift ride to the bridge. His first-shift officers awaited him there. Slowly, appraisingly, he looked them over one at a time. Were they all as nervous as he was, he wondered? Some had had more time in Starfleet than he did, albeit in noncommand ratings. Did any of them feel the same overpowering mix of fear and exultation, terror and expectancy, that had been building in him since that day the commodore had shown him this ship, at the time only a smattering of diagrams spread on a wall outside the San Francisco naval yard?

To April's relief, it was First Officer Shundresh who smoothly broke the silence.

"Ready to get under way, Captain."

"Very well, Mr. Shundresh. All stations stand by."

Suddenly his fear was gone, replaced by a strange calmness. It all seemed so natural somehow, as if he had been doing this for years. Walking forward, he assumed his position in the command chair. His body melted easily into the deceptively blunt contours. The chair was comforting beyond imagination, in a way that bordered on the erotic.

Leaning over, April pressed the proper button and spoke with a reassurance that sprang from just-tapped regions. "Engineering?"

"Chief Engineer Kursley," the thick voice filtered back. "Standing by for orders, sir."

"Activate warp-drive engines, Chief."

"Activating warp-drive, Captain." Kursley turned to the prime engineering board. She eyed her subordinates, then muttered a silent liturgy. It might have been a prayer, might have been something else. She engaged the energies of a sun.

Hitherto quiescent monitors awoke on the bridge. Blank-eyed circlets winked on, needles sprinted ahead, bands ascended on gauges, and a tiny shock ran through every member of the bridge crew.

"All systems," April ordered firmly, "final checkout. Report."

Response came from around the bridge, from speakers at the freshly painted communications station, and finally from Navigation.

"Visual contact, sir. Object approaching on collision course, bearing dead ahead."

"Acknowledged, Lieutenant Po." April addressed the general intercom. "All hands, stand by."

Other, distant hands were standing by in a small room beneath the lunar surface. Other eyes checked chronometers and predictors as they watched the distant Earth-ball, fighting to find a minute speck outlined against that brilliant blue-white globe. The drama begun on a small stage several weeks before was approaching the final curtain.

"Contact in thirty seconds, Captain," Lieutenant Po reported, with an irrepressible shiver of excitement.

"Thank you, Lieutenant."

In suits and ships and stations, thousands of men and women of several races watched their fully formed offspring and waited expectantly.

"Four . . . three . . . ," the navigator counted off tensely, "two . . . one . . . interdiction. . . ."

Head-on, the tiny projectile struck the completed cruiser, exploded, and burst into a small but rapidly expanding ball of brilliance. Tiny reflective fragments caught the morning sunlight and turned the diffusing globe into a spray of diamonds.

Thousands of watching eyes saw the distant explosion and reacted. From electronic pickups set strategically around the assembly area, billions more on Earth and on other globes also saw it—and all reacted.

On billions of speakers, the aged but enormously respected voice of the Federation president, Samuel Solomon Qasr, sounded from a chamber on the moon: "In the name of the United Federation of Planets, for the United Nations of Earth, the Planetary Confederation of Forty Eridani, the United Planets of Sixty-one Cygni, the Star Empire of Epsilon Indii, the Alpha Centauri Concordium of Planets, and all other peace-loving, space-going peoples, I christen thee *Enterprise*!"

Those on board the just-commissioned ship heard those words, but not the cheering of the construction crews gathered around them, or the comments and smiles and expressions of satisfaction on the world below. Though each crew member might have permitted himself a silent observation, of varying content and intensity, these were not voiced aloud.

There was too much to do now.

The Federation Exploration Territory was enormous beyond comprehension, and it was but a minuscule portion of this tiny section of the galaxy. Battle cruisers were too expensive, their personnel too valuable to be tied up on anything as wasteful as a shakedown cruise.

It seemed there was a certain world on the present fringe of Federation expansion which desperately required the know-how and capabilities of a major-class vessel. April had his orders. The initial cruise of the *Enterprise* would be fully operational.

Ceremony concluded, April leaned back in his chair, already a part of him, and called firmly to his helmsman.

"Ahead warp-factor three, Lieutenant Nobis."

It was four decades, forty long years since he had given that first order, April thought. He was still on the bridge of the *Enterprise*, only this day and this place in time he found himself behind the captain's chair, instead of sitting in it.

Still odd, he mused to himself. Odd to be standing here, staring at the familiar—and always overpowering—panorama of stars depicted on the viewscreen ahead and listening to someone else making the entry into the official log.

"Captain's log," the voice was saying, "Stardate 5536.3. The *Enterprise* is on course to the planet Babel, where an inter-Federation ambassadorial gathering is scheduled. Highlight of the conference is to be a ceremony honoring the *Enterprise*'s distinguished passenger."

Kirk paused and glanced behind him to see April still staring quietly at the main screen. The commodore's mind appeared to be elsewhere, but his eyes sparkled as he stared intently at the perfectly ordinary starfield ahead. There was an enthusiasm there that was often absent in officers a third his age. The superstructure might be aged and wrinkled, but

Kirk knew the mind it housed was as keen and fascinated with the universe as ever.

Every so often Uhura, Arex, or Sulu would steal a surreptitious glance at their honored guest when they were sure no one was looking. Kirk smiled. A little hero worship would not affect ship efficiency. Besides, he had to admit he wasn't wholly immune to it himself. He turned his attention back to the log. After all, it wasn't every day one had a living legend for an after-dinner chess partner.

"Commodore Robert April," Kirk continued recording, "was the first captain of the U.S.S. *Enterprise* and, for the past twenty years, the Federation ambassador-at-large. Now seventy-five years old, Commodore April has reached mandatory retirement age." Kirk pressed one switch, activated another.

"Captain's log, supplemental to entry of 5536.3. Said retirement age being a bureaucratic abberation—arbitrarily decided on by a cluster of smug civil servants without regard to individual capability or overall Starfleet efficiency—and a regulation badly in need of overhaul." He clicked off.

"Nice of you to add that, Jim," April approved in soft, almost small-boy tones. "Do you really think anyone will ever pay any attention to it?"

Kirk shook his head. "They had to pick a number, Commodore. How they arrived at seventy-five for everyone human is something I'll never understand. Instead of basing the figure on individual ability and performance, they simply—"

April cut him off smoothly, soothingly. "Oh well. If they didn't have a number, Jim, then there'd be a blank spot on a form some place. And you know what *that* would mean."

Kirk grumbled sarcastically. "The end of Starfleet, I suppose."

"That is hardly likely, Captain. Nor is it logical," Spock observed from across the bridge.

"I guess not, Mr. Spock, but neither is the mandatory retirement setup."

"I never claimed it was, Captain. On Vulcan such things are determined with rather more regard to reason."

"Perhaps it will all change in Starfleet someday, Mr. Spock," April mused hopefully. "Too late for me, I'm afraid." He turned his gaze forward again and was silent for a minute.

"You know, no matter where I've traveled through this galaxy, Jim, this bridge is more home to me than anywhere else. I can't count the number of times these past twenty years when I've turned to give an order to someone and found myself seated across from some utterly bemused diplomat I was negotiating with. It's a wonder I accomplished anything for the Federation." He chuckled. "Most diplomats don't take orders very well—or even suggestions."

"Probably intentional," Kirk observed. "If every one of you behaved reasonably and intelligently at all times, why then all our problems would be quickly solved, and you'd all be out of a job. No more diplomatic corps." April smiled knowingly.

"But as far as this bridge being home," Kirk continued, "yes, I know the feeling myself, Commodore."

"The *Enterprise* has always been like my own child, in a way," April went on. "I was there in San Francisco when her basic components were being built. I consulted with her chief construction engineer, Franz Joseph IV, on her internal configuration. I was present at the orbital assembly plant when they put her innards together.

"When they tested out each newly installed component, whether warp-drive or swimming pool, I was there. The additions and modifications she's taken since are good ones. A ship-of-the-line has to be kept up to date, but . . ." He shrugged. "I miss some of the old-fashioned touches."

"Nostalgia is notoriously inefficient," Spock commented, but so softly no one could hear. He knew an emotional observation when he heard one.

The elevator doors parted to admit Dr. McCoy. He was accompanied by an attractive little woman who projected an air of supreme self-confidence and contentment. Her attire was current high fashion, all emerald green and black and bearing no relationship to Starfleet uniforms. Gray hair, unabashedly untouched, was done up in long taffylike swirls and twists. Even the single flower she carried seemed designed only to complement her. The colorful blossom had petals that wound in and about themselves in an intricate, delicately engineered manner.

The last person in the room she resembled was her husband. Only one thing, besides age, linked them inseparably—both wore that same aura of composure and confidence like a coat of jewels.

For his part, Dr. McCoy wore his standard on-duty uniform and an air of what could best be described as bemused pleasure.

"Jim," he began admiringly, "I didn't realize until now how many of the instruments I use in Sick Bay were originally designed and first used by Sarah. Did you know that she cribbed the first version of the standard cancer monitor together out of some old medical components and phaser-monitor units?"

The woman smiled demurely. "As the first medical officer aboard a ship equipped with warp-drive, it was always necessary for us to come up with new ideas."

"Your modesty is unnecessary, Ms. April," Kirk observed honestly. "Your achievements as a pioneer Starfleet physician are well known and extensively documented. There are many doctors who cannot do what a medical engineer does, and a corresponding number of medical engineers who are ill-prepared to administer treatment. You're one of the few people in Starfleet medicine who ever managed to master the requirements of both professions."

"And it's nice to know," McCoy added, "that the doctor is as beautiful as she is accomplished. A beauty that's reflected by the flower she carries."

"If your medical ability is as accomplished as your flattery, Dr. McCoy, then I know Captain Kirk has no worries in that area of *Enterprise* operations. I won't be impolite and ask if that's a quote—I'll assume you made it up on the spur of the moment." She smiled a youngish smile. "Please feel free to insert such comments wherever you think they fit into the conversation."

Her smile faded as she looked down at the delicate growth in her hands. "I'm afraid, though, that my flower is dying."

So many references to the flower prompted Kirk to turn to get a better look at it. "Let's see . . . botanical text, the Reddin catalog . . . volume six, which sector . . . ?" Mumbling to himself, he thumbed the text. He located it quickly. "A native of Capella Four, isn't it?"

She nodded. "The mature blossom has a lifespan of only a few hours. If you recognize it, Captain, you'll recall how brief the growing period is on that world.

"This is an extreme example even for Capella Four, I'm told. When it was given to me this morning it was a bud barely out of seed. Within a few hours it will be dead." She paused. "It's one of the most beautiful growths in the galaxy, and one of the shortest-lived. What a pity." She looked up. "I know people like that, too, Captain."

"Excuse me, sir," Spock said in the ensuing silence. "You asked to be notified when we made visual contact with the Beta Niobe Nova."

"Yes . . . thank you, Mr. Spock." Kirk glanced backward. "Ms. April, you're about to see another of the galaxy's most beautiful—and, in astronomical terms, short-lived— sights. Its remnants, though, will last a lot longer than the petals of your flower. The Beta Niobe Nova. Mr. Spock?"

"A moment, Captain, some precision focusing is required." They waited while the first officer made final adjustments at his console. The forward viewscreen blurred, then cleared, to show a monstrous eruption in space, an explosion of primal energy, of raw power—and only incidentally of blazing color.

Yellow and white gases, mutilated matter, glowed at its heart, while at its edges erratic and undisciplined streamers of brilliant red and orange charged blindly into indifferent emptiness. In this isolated section of space, the depressing darkness of the universe was suffused with wild color and wilder energies.

"Magnificent," Sarah April gushed.

"Magnificent and deadly," Spock echoed, "but we are traveling at a safe distance from the nova, Ms. April."

"Beta Niobe, Niobe . . . I've heard that name in connection with the *Enterprise* before." She looked up at the commodore. "Bob, didn't you read me a report some years ago . . . ?"

"Yes . . . you were present when the star first exploded, weren't you, Jim?" he asked.

"We were, Commodore," Kirk replied. "I wasn't aware that in addition to handling all your duties and activities as ambassador-at-large you managed to keep track of such trivia as our day-to-day operations."

April looked at once flattered and embarrassed. "It's not trivia to me, Jim. A part of me will always be on this ship, and the rest of me is intensely interested in what happens to it. Some of your reports to Starfleet headquarters read as anything but uninteresting trivia. As you know, your ship's log is always available to me—a courtesy Starfleet extends to former starship captains. I know what's happening aboard the *Enterprise* as soon as headquarters does.

"If I recall this particular report correctly, you were trapped in a planet's past, about to be tried as a witch just before this star started to go nova."

Kirk nodded. "One of our narrower escapes. For Dr. McCoy and Mr. Spock as well as for me."

"I'll say it was narrow!" McCoy added fervently. "I was trapped in that world's ice age at the time. The only other time in my life I've ever been that cold was when our computer went berserk a little while back and turned the Recreation Chamber into subarctic snowpack."

"Captain . . . ?" A hesitant query from the region of the helm. Kirk looked over absently.

"What is it, Mr. Sulu? Important?"

"I don't know, sir." He looked puzzled. "I've got something moving toward us, at extreme range right now."

Kirk swiveled. "Mr. Spock?"

"No basis for identification as yet, Captain," the first officer replied, staring into the gooseneck viewer. "Vessel is no longer at extreme range, however."

Now it was Kirk's turn to appear confused. "*That* was a quick change. Are you sure, Spock?"

Both curved eyebrows sank as Spock analyzed several readouts at once. "Captain, the object is traveling at a speed nothing short of incredible. Presently on collision course with the *Enterprise*."

Kirk didn't hesitate. "Sound red alert, Lieutenant Uhura. 'Nothing short of incredible' doesn't tell me much, Spock. Spock?"

Crimson warning lights blinked on, accompanied by the appropriate aural blarings.

"Excuse me, Captain," the first officer finally muttered.

"You'll have to ascribe my hesitation to sheer incredulity. This object is traveling at a rate theoretically impossible for matter to achieve.

"More specifically—bear in mind I have to override the standard settings, Captain—it is moving at a speed on the order of warp-thirty-six."

The numbers cut through Kirk like a scalpel. "You're right," he finally confessed, "it *is* impossible. Mr. Spock, nothing can travel that fast."

"I fear, Captain, that in this case you must redefine that observation. It is nothing, less one."

"No natural object," April put in, "has ever been recorded as traveling at that speed—or at anything close to it."

"Preliminary sensor reports, Captain," Spock continued, "lead me to an even more astonishing conclusion." He looked up from his instruments. "The object is an artificial construct. I *must* assume it is some kind of ship."

Kirk pondered the information. When he spoke again, his voice was unconsciously hushed. "Who has the technology to build a vessel that can move at that velocity?"

"Obviously, no known race, Captain," Spock pointed out. "Impossible or not, it will make contact with us in one point four minutes."

There was nothing theoretical about the order Kirk gave them. "Hard over, helmsman, change course to a new heading, two full degrees to starboard."

Even as he gave the order he knew that if this ridiculously rapid visitor turned out to be inimical, there was no way they could dodge or outrun it.

The same thought evidently was running through his first officer's mind, because a second later Spock commented, "It is apparently nonbelligerent, Captain. It appears a collision was not intended, as the vessel has not altered its course to match ours.

"If it continues in its present direction, it will plunge directly into the center of the Beta Niobe Nova."

Was that it, then, Kirk thought quickly—a hurried rush to extinction, to suicide? Or was an unknown crew injured, its ship damaged?

"Lieutenant Uhura," he called over his shoulder, "open

hailing frequencies. I want to talk to that ship's captain—if it has one."

A long pause while Uhura worked at her console. Finally she turned, spoke discouragingly. "I'm sorry, Captain. I've sent everything in its direction except carrier pigeons. If there's anyone on board capable of responding, they've elected not to."

Kirk pondered. "Have you tried all the emergency frequencies, Lieutenant?"

"Sir, I've broadcast on every possible frequency for every listed race, and a few that are only hypothetical. No response."

"Vessel is nearing a parallel course, Captain," Sulu reported uneasily—uneasily because their brief course change was now taking them toward the raging nova instead of past it.

"Increase speed to warp-seven, Mr. Sulu, try to stay with it as much as possible."

"Aye, sir."

"Despite our best efforts, the alien vessel will shoot past us very shortly, Captain," Spock declared.

"I realize that, Spock." His voice dropped to a murmur. "It may be that they can't communicate—maybe their communications equipment's been damaged. Perhaps the entire crew is injured. We've got to find out, somehow."

"It'll have to be soon, sir," Sulu noted. "She'll go right out of range as soon as she parallels us."

"Then we'll have to slow her down. Mr. Sulu, put our forward tractor beam on that ship as soon as it comes within range. Full power."

"Is that advisable, Captain?" Spock wondered aloud.

"It's more advisable than letting a possibly friendly crew burn to a crisp in the nova, Mr. Spock. If I were injured and aboard that vessel, I'd want any stranger to lend a hand. If they know what they're doing and insist on committing suicide . . . well, let's evaluate that possibility last of all."

"It is not that, Captain," Spock protested. "I agree with you completely on the possibility that the crew may be incapacitated or that their broadcast instrumentation is damaged beyond use. If that is the case, then naturally we must do everything in our power to aid them. My worry is that we may overextend ourselves in doing so. I am particularly concerned about the aftereffects of locking a tractor beam on an object moving at such a velocity. To understate the matter, there could be severe physical repercussions. Such a thing has never been tried before."

"Naturally not, Mr. Spock, the opportunity never arose before. It'll be history in a few seconds, whatever the result. Mr. Sulu?"

"Forward tractor beam energized, Captain." A pause; then, "Contact achieved . . . locked on."

"Any effect?"

"Sir," Sulu responded after a quick check of his readouts, "I'm running it at maximum power, but the alien is still moving on the same course."

"Tractor beam monitors report no damage to components or tractor bracing," Spock reported evenly. "No sign of dangerous stress apparent yet."

It was Arex's turn to speak up. The quiet navigator made his first comment on the proceedings. "We are apparently having some effect on the vessel's mobility, Captain, if not its course. Using the parameters employed by Mr. Spock, it would appear that the other ship's speed has dropped to the equivalent of warp-twenty-seven."

"Darn well froze it in its tracks," Kirk muttered. "That's *some* ship."

That was when Uhura's excited voice commanded all the attention on the bridge.

"Captain, we're being beamed!"

II

"I can't be certain—the message is terribly scrambled, and like nothing I've ever seen before—but I *think* it's a request to open intership communications," Uhura declared.

"So much for the disability and damage theory," Kirk observed tautly. "That means they're probably healthy—just antisocial. Switch on the screen, Uhura."

The communications officer appeared to be struggling with her instrumentation, but eventually the view of the grand nova vanished. It was replaced by a portrait of a more composed subject, but one in its own way no less fascinating.

As usual, Kirk awaited this first view of an unknown race without preconceived imagery. Even so, the first sight of a representative of supreme warp-drive technology was at once disappointing and shocking. Disappointing because its manipulator was no wizened alien genius, and shocking because the reality tended to the other extreme. In fact, the young woman who appeared on the screen was so human that she could have traded uniforms with Uhura or any of the *Enterprise*'s female complement and moved freely about the ship.

When she spoke, however, her speech was anything but familiar. Nothing sounded normal; even the inflections seemed intentionally misplaced.

"Demood eb yam I ro ecno ta pihs ym esaeler, ssergorp ym gniwols si maeb ruoy, noissim ytiroirp a no mI."

Following this urgent stream of decidedly incomprehensible alien chatter, the viewscreen once again went dark. It was replaced automatically by the view forward—the steadily growing magnificence of the Beta Niobe Nova.

"Human, certainly," Kirk ventured, "unless her race is a shape-changer."

"It would have to be more than that, Captain," Spock observed, "to mimic so precisely without ever having contacted us."

"Possibly even a direct human analog," the captain continued, "though the likeness appears too exact to be true. The only thing that doesn't match up is her language. Never heard anything like that before. Yet somehow it sounds vaguely familiar. I could swear she referred to herself as 'I' at least once."

"It might merely have been the 'aye' sound, Jim," April suggested from behind him. "I didn't recognize the language, either. I haven't heard speech like that, not in all my travels throughout the galaxy. But as you say, it did have something familiar about it. Strange."

"Let's see if the ship's translator can come up with identification, Lieutenant Uhura," ordered Kirk.

"All right, sir."

As she ran the tape of the woman's brief speech through that intricate portion of the *Enterprise*'s computer system, she also allowed the sounds to play over the bridge speakers. Once again everyone listened to that oddly pitched, weirdly modulated, yet faintly familiar babble. Repetition failed to produce enlightenment; no one could make any more sense out of the situation this time than before.

A pause after it trailed off, then, "Negative response, Captain," she finally reported. "Whatever it is, it's no known language in our section of the galaxy."

"Implement decoding procedures," came the command. "Might be a coded variant of some little-known humanoid speech."

The woman on the screen hadn't delivered her message as if it were in code, Kirk thought as Uhura worked. She had delivered her sentence—if that's what it was—rapidly and without apparent effort, as though it were her natural, everyday speech. Furthermore, she had done so in a fashion suggesting that her listeners would understand instantly.

There was surprise and just a hint of embarrassment in Uhura's voice when she spoke again. "I've got the answer, Captain. I should have recognized the pattern right away, but it was a little too close to home. The woman was speaking our own language, only in reverse."

"Reverse," Arex echoed from the navigation station. "No wonder it sounded so familiar, like a tape played backward."

"Correct," Kirk agreed sourly—he should have identified it himself—"only without the distortions one would expect of such a playback.

"All right, Uhura, let's hear that tape again, only backward this time—that should sound forward to us. And put the visual tape on screen again, too."

Uhura nodded. Once more they saw the anxious face of the woman, once more listened to her tense message. Only this time it was easily understandable, even though her words failed to match her mouth movements.

"I'm on a priority mission," the words tumbled out, "your beam is slowing my progress. Release my ship at once or I may be doomed."

"Short and to the point. Open hailing frequency again, Lieutenant, matching ours to her broadcast. Tell her she's endangering her life if she continues on her present course, and explain why. Tape it and then broadcast it in reverse, so she'll understand. Though it's beyond me," he continued puzzledly, "how anyone could head for the heart of a nova and not have an inkling there just might be a bit of danger involved. Something doesn't make sense here." A sudden thought intervened.

"Mr. Spock, we should be close enough to obtain a decent internal sensor scan. How many life forms aboard that vessel?"

"I have just concluded a check of our first readings, Captain. The result is conclusive: There is only one. The woman we saw on the screen."

"No response, sir," Uhura broke in. "She's incapable of replying—or else is just refusing to."

Kirk was about to suggest another approach when a demanding buzz from his armchair intercom caught his attention.

"Engineering to bridge. Engineering to bridge."

"Yes, Scotty, what is it?"

"Captain, I'm gettin' severe stress reports from all over the ship. The *Enterprise* wasn't meant to travel at such a speed."

What speed, Kirk wondered.

Scott rushed on. "If we keep on like this, we'll break up, Captain."

"Just a minute, Scotty." Kirk looked ahead. "Sulu, are we still holding on with that tractor?"

The helmsman checked his readouts. "Holding firm, Captain."

That explained it, then. "Lieutenant Arex, we are apparently being towed. What is our present speed?"

"Warp-eleven, sir," the Edoan replied incredulously, after a frantic check of his instrumentation.

"No wonder Scotty's having trouble. Mr. Spock, how long before the alien vessel impinges on the outermost danger zone, the first lethal radiation?"

Spock made a quick check and performed some rapid calculations. "Three minutes, forty-two seconds plus, Captain. There may be some local variance in field strength, but generally speaking . . ."

Kirk spoke hurriedly to the chair pickup again. "Scotty?"

"I heard, Captain."

"We'd burn up in the nova before our superstructure went. I'm trying to stop that ship from destroying itself."

"Well and noble, Captain," the chief engineer agreed, "but speakin' of destroyin' oneself, keep in mind we can't travel like this much longer."

"Three and half minutes, Scotty, that's all. Give me that. Kirk out."

And he cut off, leaving the chief to oversee some frenzied emergency bracing of the warp-drive engines.

"Speed still increasing, Captain," Arex reported. "Warp-fourteen, warp-fifteen . . ."

Seconds before, they were traveling at warp-eleven, and even that was putting a severe strain on the ship. It also meant that the engines on board that tiny suicidal craft were even more powerful than first imagined—they were slowly overcoming the drag effect of the *Enterprise*'s tractor.

Kirk had no choice but to release that beam. There was a point beyond which he wasn't willing to go to rescue the confused or misguided pilot of the other ship, and that point had been reached. The *Enterprise* must not be risked.

"Cancel the tractor, Mr. Sulu. Lieutenant Uhura, continue beaming our message at the other ship until they acknowledge or . . ."—he hesitated—". . . until they become incapable of acknowledging. That gives you about three minutes. When she hits those first radiation belts, her instrumentation's going to fry. Maybe she'll at least change course a little."

"Yes, sir," Uhura said doubtfully. "I'll beam it, sir, but . . ."

"Captain . . . ?" There was a strained note in Sulu's voice. It brought Kirk's head around quickly. "I can't release the tractor."

"Explain, Mr. Sulu. Fast."

Sulu stared helplessly at his console. "All controls appear inoperative—the ship isn't responding as she should."

"Take it easy, Lieutenant. Go to manual override."

The helmsman's hands flashed over the console, repeated the necessary manipulations again, then a third time. "Still no response, sir. We're locked tight." A touch of panic was creeping into his voice now.

"We've got to break that beam," Kirk said tightly.

"Our speed is now warp-twenty," Spock announced quietly. "Alien vessel will contact first lethal radiation in one minute, fifty seconds."

"Never mind that now," Kirk shouted. "Mr. Spock, see if you can aid Mr. Sulu." The first officer moved rapidly to the helm. "Lieutenant Uhura, contact Security and have them break out a phaser rifle. I want the tractor-beam components melted into a tin puddle!"

Even as he gave the order he knew there was no way Security could break out the necessary equipment, set up, and perform the required destruction before they passed the point of no return. They needed those three and a half minutes again, and now they didn't have even half that.

He swiveled in the chair, resigned. "I'm sorry, Commodore, Dr. April. It looks as if we're not going to make this conference."

He saw that further words were unnecessary. The commodore and his wife were probably the most relaxed people on the bridge. It was a serenity derived from having faced death a dozen times before. Anyone who served on a far-ranging starship knew that life was at best a transitory business.

"Captain," April told him, "as Starfleet personnel we were always prepared to give up what small sentience life has granted us. I was ready for the end before I ever set foot on my first ship."

"We're still starship personnel, Captain," Sarah April added softly, holding tight to the now wilting flower.

"We do have one chance left," a grim-faced Kirk explained. "After it enters the first zone of strong radiation, the alien ship should burn up rapidly. With nothing to lock onto, our tractor beam will be freed." He turned toward the science station.

"Mr. Spock, will we have enough time to apply full braking power and execute the necessary course change?"

Spock considered the question in light of the constantly changing information the ship's sensors supplied. "We're up to warp-twenty-four and still increasing speed rapidly, Captain. But I calculate that we will have forty-two point eight five seconds to effect a significant course change following destruction of the alien vessel. That is assuming, of course, that it does not possess radiation screens as advanced as its engines."

Kirk had no time to reflect on that possibility. "Mr. Sulu, I want a course implemented at warp-eight the moment our tractor is released."

"Yes, sir. Bearing, sir?"

"Whatever will get us clear of here the quickest—this is no time to be choosy."

Sulu nodded, then punched the necessary information into the *Enterprise*'s helm. Kirk hit the intercom again.

"Mr. Scott, we're going to try to slow our speed a little. Stand by to apply full braking power in fifty seconds."

"Standing by, Captain," Scott acknowledged. "A good thing, too."

"Fifty-two seconds to contact for the other ship, Captain," Spock declared.

Kirk studied the view on the screen ahead. Detectors still showed the tail end of the tiny alien craft. It seemed incapable of mounting engines equipped to drive it at such incredible velocities. It was almost lost against the now frighteningly near blaze of red, orange-yellow, and white fluorescing gases.

"Eighteen . . . twelve, eleven," the first officer was counting off.

"Stand by to execute course change, Mr. Sulu. No time to spare. Apply maximum braking power."

"Braking," Sulu announced. The fading silhouette of the alien ship had vanished now, subsumed by a licking tongue of orange phosphorescence.

"Now, Sulu," Kirk snapped, unable to restrain giving the verbal command even though he knew the *Enterprise*'s electronic nerves were prekeyed to perform the necessary maneuver.

"Something's wrong, Captain!" Sulu yelled immediately. "We're still being pulled by the alien ship!"

"Impossible, impossible," Kirk murmured. "There shouldn't be anything left for the tractor beam to lock onto. By now that tiny craft and its enigmatic pilot should have been reduced to cinders."

"We're still connected by tractor to something, Captain," announced Arex, "and we're still building speed."

"Contact with destructive energy levels in thirty-five seconds," declared a dispassionate Spock, eyes never straying from his instruments.

"Incredible engineering," Kirk mumbled. "A ship that small capable of warp-thirty-six. If her people can build engines like that, maybe they *have* invented shielding sufficient to permit a ship to survive the heat and radiation of a nova. But the *Enterprise* can't."

He knew the answer, but decided there was nothing to be lost by a last check. "Mr. Scott, we are receiving full braking power, aren't we?"

"Aye, sir," the answer came back, "but we're as bad off as before. As long as we're locked to that little skiff, or whatever it is, I canna do nothin' with the engines."

"Contact in twenty seconds," Spock informed him solemnly.

"Mr. Sulu . . . ?"

"Still no change, sir. We're still locked in. Warp-speed . . . warp-thirty-five."

Kirk was out of the command chair and at the helmsman's side in a second, keying controls himself. It was a last, desperate hope. Even the most experienced officer could overlook . . . overlook what? What could he hope to find that both Sulu and Spock had missed?

Some minuscule calculation, some fail-safe forgotten, ignored.

"It's *got* to work," he muttered to himself as he furiously manipulated useless controls.

"Fourteen seconds," counted Spock inexorably. "Thirteen, twelve . . ."

Kirk returned to his seat, turning slowly as he sat. At least they would not die in darkness. The awesome, overpowering glory of the nova's heart was sucking them in at incredible speed.

"No use. It's finished."

Behind him, Robert April had unobtrusively slipped an arm around his wife's shoulders. Her hands clutched a little tighter around the nearly dead blossom.

"Three . . . two . . . one . . . ," Spock concluded.

Something picked the *Enterprise* up and heaved it forward, bounced it off a rubbery surface, and threw it once more. Those on the bridge bobbed about like rubber toys in a bathtub. A dizzying assortment of color swirled about the ship, but no one had the time or inclination to notice—everyone was too busy trying to keep from being tossed against a bulkhead or neighbor as the ship rode out a tremendous buffeting.

Kirk reflected on the fact that there shouldn't have been any buffeting, let alone anyone still alive to feel it. By now the *Enterprise* should have been nothing but a rapidly diffusing field of ruptured molecules melting into the raging energies of Beta Niobe.

The ship slowly ceased its violent shaking. And yet, Kirk mused as he rose slowly to his feet from where he had been thrown, they were still here, still alive, and, from the looks of the bridge, still functioning. He saw his shocked surprise mirrored in the faces of the other officers as they found themselves intact. Slowly, stations were resumed by dazed personnel.

"What happened?" Uhura finally wondered aloud.

"A great many things, Lieutenant," Spock declared. He was working at his station with an intenseness unusual even for him.

Uhura was unable to request a more specific explanation, because Kirk had called for damage reports. They came in immediately and constituted another surprise. All decks reported no damage, no injuries other than a few minor bumps and scrapes to personnel from being violently thrown about.

Kirk's amazement grew. Everyone still alive, and healthy as well.

Of course, he still had no idea what had happened to them, or where they were cruising at the moment. At any instant the ship might come apart at the seams, as should have happened several minutes before. He shrugged mentally. No point in dwelling on that. Maybe they would at least be spared enough time to figure out what had happened to them.

"Lieutenant Uhura, can you get us any external visuals?"

"I'll try, sir." Some very peculiar static rippled across the main viewscreen, then cleared without warning.

Or had it?

Kirk blinked, but the image that had appeared on the screen was still there, unwavering, unchanged, unbelievable. It was as impressive as it was impossible, in its own bizarre way. What Kirk and Spock and everyone else saw was a normal-looking universe, normal except for one slight change.

It was a universe of pure white, speckled with stars of varying intensities of black.

"Where are we?" April whispered in amazement.

"I don't . . ." Kirk paused, noticing a new aberration. The starfield on the screen was shrinking away, not moving past. A quick check of instrumentation confirmed his observation. The *Enterprise* was traveling back-end first through this perverse vacuum.

"I believe, Captain," Spock hypothesized aloud as he stared at the negative panorama ahead, "that we have somehow passed into an alternate universe, normal in every respect—but normal in reverse of what we know to be real. We have entered a universe where everything is the opposite of our own."

"Black stars in a white void," Kirk murmured. "It looks frightening, somehow."

"Physics are never frightening, Captain. Merely hard work sometimes."

"Mr. Sulu," Kirk asked firmly, "what's our present situation?"

"Still apparently locked onto the alien ship, Captain."

Kirk turned to his first officer. "Radiation?"

"Nothing, Captain," Spock announced after a moment's check of his gauges. "It seems we're no longer in any danger. I wonder if we ever were."

Kirk thought of one more detail to be checked. "Bridge to Engineering . . . Scotty, how are we holding up?"

"It was hectic for a few minutes, sir. What's going on? Everything's workin' properly—but in reverse. We're havin' to learn how to run the ship all over again, backward. Takes a minute to get used to it. Not the instrumentation adjustments; it's the goin' against years of experience, pushin' *off* when you want *on*, turnin' to maximum when you want to shut somethin' down. I know when I adjust the engine flux backward now that everythin's goin' to be all right, but I canna keep from feelin' in my bones that I'm goin' to blow us to kingdom come."

"Take your time and do the best you can, Scotty," Kirk sympathized. "Speaking of the engines . . . ?"

"They shouldn't still be with us, Captain, but they are. Don't ask me how or why. They should have torn free of their pylons a long time ago, considerin' the strain on them."

"Thank you, Scotty. Keep a close watch and let me know if our status changes."

"Aye, sir. Engineering out."

"Now then, Lieutenant Uhura, we're going to contact our closed-mouthed alien-human friend again." The firmness in his tone indicated that this time silence wouldn't be accepted. "We need some answers, and a universe-sized explanation. That pilot is the only one around who can provide them for us."

"Captain Kirk!"

He spun, to see a wide-eyed Dr. April gesturing with something in her hands.

"I'm sure Captain Kirk has other problems to consider at the moment besides the state of your gift, dear," the commodore observed.

"Then he'd better consider this new one, Bob. Look at it. You too, Captain—everyone."

Somehow in the midst of the dire emergency it seemed only proper to find herself staring at a flower. But Dr. April's concern was well-founded.

"Before we entered this negative universe, extra dimension or whatever this is, this bloom was on the verge of dying. Now look at it—it's in full bloom again!"

Indeed, a glance was sufficient to show the brilliant blossom bursting forth with apparently new, waxy petals and glistening young stamen. It had regained the color it had when the Aprils had boarded the *Enterprise* . . . and more.

"It doesn't make sense," Kirk finally commented, "which only makes sense here, I suppose. If everything else is backward . . ."

"It's more than a regeneration, Captain," she went on. "It's almost as if it were growing younger again. I can feel the regeneration as I'm holding it."

"Feel it . . . you can see it," Sulu declared.

Even as they watched the blossom began to shrink again, the petals pulling in on themselves, as the flower commenced its return toward the small, hard bud from which it had originally sprung.

"Captain," Spock put in, "I suspect that Dr. April's flower is not the only thing on board that is growing younger."

"What do you mean, Mr. Spock?"

"To start, Captain, you might note that the ship's chronometers are running backward."

Kirk stared down at his own wrist instrument. He watched the second hand methodically tick off time in a counterclockwise direction. As he watched, he could see the minute hand slowly edging backward as well.

The full alienness of the situation in which they found themselves was driven home more powerfully by this simple alteration of an everyday event—the measuring of time—than by the view of black stars spotted across white space.

"Time as well as physics is apparently reversed here, Captain," the first officer concluded.

"One crisis at a time, Spock."

Uhura called to him. "The alien ship is finally responding to our call, Captain. I have visual contact established, ready to put on the screen."

"Please do so, Lieutenant."

Once more the portrait of the alien pilot appeared before them. Only this time, when she spoke, the words sounding on the speakers matched her mouth movements, and Kirk found he could understand her perfectly.

"Your actions almost cost me my life, and your own as well." She was obviously still confused as to why the *Enterprise* had interfered. "Why didn't you release my ship as I asked?"

"This poses an interesting physical and semantic question, Captain," mused Spock. "Are we understanding her speech because she is speaking backward but our thought processes are reversed?"

"We can debate it later, Mr. Spock. At the moment, the only thing I'm interested in reversing for sure is our presence here."

But the alien pilot *had* posed a question.

"I'm Captain James T. Kirk, commanding the U.S.S. *Enterprise*. We tried to prevent you from entering the Beta Niobe Nova because it has been our experience in the past that vessels which enter novas are never heard from again. We thought that you might have been injured, or your ship's navigation helm crippled. We had no reason to believe," he continued drily, "that your vessel was equipped to withstand such forces. For that matter, we didn't expect our own ship could, either. We attempted to disengage our tractor beam at the last minute, but were unable to do so."

"I see. Your gesture was gallant and well-meaning, but wholly unnecessary. I had to return to my own universe, Captain Kirk. In order to do so, it was necessary for my ship to pass through the distortion fields and stress energies of what you call the Beta Niobe Nova, in order to emerge into my universe from the new star, Amphion."

"New star? Mr. Spock, check our readings aft."

Spock looked up a moment later and nodded in confirmation of the pilot's claim. "It seems to be so, Captain. Instead of a nova, retracing our course leads us back into what appears to be a very new, very black star."

"Who are you," Kirk asked the flat, solemn face on the screen, "and how did you come to be in our universe in the first place?"

"I am a solitary explorer—Karla Five, I am called. I was caught unawares when Amphion, previously a dead star, abruptly went nova and came to life. I was pulled in by the explosively expanding gravitational field. Instead of burning up, I passed into a universe where everything operates in reverse of my own."

"Our universe," Kirk said.

"I wandered helplessly for several months, but never losing track of the place where I had emerged into your universe," she continued. "Endless calculations led me to a single conclusion: The only chance I had of returning home was to pass back at maximum acceleration through the exploding star, your nova. And then at that last moment, you happened on a ship you thought was in distress, and were drawn in with me. I am sorry."

"You mentioned your calculations," Spock reminded her. "What is your explanation for this transuniverse effect?"

"Tentative, certainly," Karla Five explained. "It would appear that the forces at the heart of a nova generate sufficient spatial stress to create a bridge between our two universes. A vessel moving toward this shifting bridge at a sufficient speed will pass from universe to universe rapidly enough to avoid the dangerous energies which exist in such centers."

Behind Kirk, Commodore April listened to Karla Five's theory with astonishment and admiration. "In her universe, then, a nova is a dead star which comes to life, whereas in ours it's one which is going through its death throes in a violent manner. When these two differently defined events take place at a particular point in space, it is possible to travel between the two. This discovery could revolutionize cosmology."

"*If* we can get back to tell it to anyone," Kirk reminded him. "And the way to do that seems pretty obvious. We have to go back the way we came, through the double nova."

Karla Five looked troubled. "Would that I could be sure such a thing was possible, Captain Kirk. Amphion was not a full-sized burning sun when I was drawn into it. That has changed. I would not think it possible to dive into the heart of a live sun and survive."

"We'd think the same thing of a full-sized nova, which is what Beta Niobe is," Kirk countered.

"True, Captain. Even so, the question of our return is apparently not a simple matter of retracing our steps. We must examine the alternatives more intensely."

"What would you suggest, Mr. Spock?"

"Some additional time to consider the physics of the matter, and if possible to study the information produced by Karla Five's computer."

"Naturally I'll give all the aid I can, as will my people," the alien pilot told them. "I am now proceeding to my home world of Arret, Captain Kirk. I suggest you set a course to follow my ship."

"That shouldn't be difficult," Kirk replied, "seeing as how we're still attached to you by our tractor beam." She looked grim, shook her head.

Of course, that undoubtedly constituted a friendly gesture here, Kirk reminded himself. Unless she was concerned about something else. Unless his own optic nerves were also working in reverse, feeding him backward information. Or . . .

He shook his head. There were ramifications to their present situation that could drive a man mad.

"Mr. Sulu, plot a following course. And keep trying to disengage that tractor beam. Meanwhile call off the security detail—no point in destroying the tractor mechanism now."

"Aye aye, sir."

"Mr. Spock, get with your people in Life Sciences and see if they can verify that everyone on board is growing younger. Also the rate at which such reverse aging is taking place—if in fact that's what's happening to us."

It didn't take long for the efficient instruments and technicians of the great cruiser to verify that that was precisely what was happening.

Kirk considered the news calmly, finally glancing up from his command position. "Well, there you have it, everyone. I'm sure none of us minds growing younger instead of older for a change."

Silence.

"It pleases me anyway, Jim," April finally said. "If we could remain in this universe long enough, I'd no longer be at the mandatory retirement age."

"Let's not lose sight of our present position, Commodore. We must return home. I'm open to suggestions. Spock?"

"There seems only one reasonably sure way, Captain," he explained quietly. "We must reproduce, as exactly as possible, the conditions which carried Karla Five's ship from her universe into ours. Two novas must occupy the same space in both universes in order to create the proper gateway. The difficulty here has already been pinpointed by Karla Five.

"We must locate a star in the process of being born, which must also coincide with a nova in our own galaxy. As she has pointed out, Amphion is now a raging furnace, a growing star. We cannot chance returning via the same route."

April was shaking his head. "The chances of our doing that even if we had time to scan this whole negative galaxy . . . no, Mr. Spock, the odds are too high to compute."

"I must disagree with your evaluation of our chances, Commodore. I have already computed the odds. They are on the order of fifty-two million to one."

Kirk grinned tightly . . . or did he frown, and have it reversed here? No way of knowing. "At least we have a chance."

Heated discussion followed, which included most of the engineering officers and astrophysics technicians. Various suggestions were made; one was to detach the *Enterprise*'s saucer and main living quarters and use the warp-drive engines to overload, thus generating a new star in this universe.

Scott vetoed the idea, pointing out vociferously that they were not in the business of making stars, that the physics were doubtful, that there was no way they could be certain of aligning their artificially generated sun with an existing nova in the positive universe—and besides, without the warp-drive engines they might not get up enough speed to make the dangerous passage in time to prevent total destruction.

The suggestion, along with the others, was tabled. Most were more fantastic than reasonable, requiring gigantic amounts of energy beyond the *Enterprise*'s ability to produce.

Nevertheless, discussions continued throughout the ship, even as they entered orbit around Karla Five's home world of Arret.

"Message coming in, Captain," Uhura announced. "Karla Five is asking if you're prepared to beam down to her world."

"Indicate that we'll be down shortly. Commodore April, Mr. Spock, and I will comprise the landing party."

Kirk rose from his chair and headed for the turbolift, April following. They arrived in the Transporter Room to find Scott waiting for them, prepared to handle the transporter chores himself. But the chief engineer could not disguise a worried frown.

"Something the matter, Scotty? Karla Five *has* given us coordinates to beam down?"

"Aye, sir, she has that."

The three officers moved to the transporter alcove. "Well," Kirk prompted, "why the hesitation, Scotty? I know when something's on your mind."

"It's just, Captain, that . . . well, she identifies the location as her son's laboratory."

Kirk's forehead furrowed. He considered the obvious youth of Karla Five, his ship's desperate situation, and understood the cause of Scott's concern.

"I see what you mean, Scotty. We don't have time for kid games right now. But these people live in a peculiar universe. Their sense of humor might be somewhat backward, too. Anyhow, those are the coordinates she gave. I suspect we're going to need her help to get out of this. Let's not give unnecessary offense. Beam us down, Mr. Scott."

"Aye, sir," Scott acknowledged, looking unhappy. He moved the appropriate levers and dials.

A high whine sounded in the chamber, shrill and familiar. But the corresponding sensation of molecular dissolution was absent. Kirk glanced down, saw himself still standing, solid as ever, on the transporter disk. He looked questioningly at the transporter console, but Scott seemed equally puzzled.

"I dinna understand it, Captain. I'm running through the usual sequence. Everything checks out operational, but—"

Spock interrupted. "The key word is 'usual,' Mr. Scott. Reverse the procedure. Beam us *up* from the provided coordinates."

"But you're already . . . ach, of course! I should know by now."

Reversing the standard transporter sequence produced three properly glittering pillars of light within the alcove.

III

Kirk, Spock, and Commodore April materialized on the steps of a two-story modern structure. A short glance around indicated that they were located on the outskirts of a fair-sized metropolis.

The buildings around them, and in the distant urban area, were decidedly different. Not unattractively so, Kirk noted approvingly. They were clearly designed for normal-sized, normally proportioned humanoids. Only the aesthetic approach was different.

Leaning back, Kirk squinted at the sky. It was blue, but with an alien suggestion of bright green. Somewhere above it, he knew, it faded into a white canopy against which an orphaned *Enterprise* orbited forlornly.

"Good evening, gentlemen."

Karla Five was standing in the entrance to the building, squinting at them and smiling. "I'm sorry you had to arrive on Arret in the middle of the night."

Kirk began to wonder if his mind was running in circles now as well as in reverse. "Middle of the night?" he echoed. "The sun is shining in our faces."

"I beg your pardon, Captain?" Karla Five looked amused. "What a funny thing to say. The moon is quite visible. See?" And she indicated the dark purple orb which dominated the sky.

Kirk stared. "You'll have to excuse me, I'm still not used to reversing everything. It takes some getting used to."

"No need to explain, Captain Kirk," she replied. "I know exactly what you're going through. At least you have the company of others to help you. When I was thrown unexpectedly into your universe I nearly went mad. Imagine seeing brightly colored stars against *black* space. Horrible, unnatural sight!

"Anyway," she assured them, "the sun will come up soon and it will be dark again. Please come into my son's laboratory. I've awakened him, and he's already hard at work on your problem."

The interior of the house was as pleasant as the exterior, filled with many full-grown plants undoubtedly growing younger. Karla Five led them to a large, spacious chamber. The walls were lined with star-maps—all black on white, of course.

They proceeded to a small, rectangular construct set in the far corner of the vast, domed room. Closer inspection revealed its identity. There was nothing mysterious about it, and since it was exactly what it appeared to be, Kirk thought it utterly out of place in the extensively equipped lab.

It was a playpen, and it was occupied now by a small child. The infant was surrounded by toys, a plastic bottle of liquid, and numerous other less readily identifiable items.

At the moment the child was on its unsteady, stubby legs, playing with a rattling attachment secured to the side of the crib.

Kirk noticed a man in his fifties working nearby. He nodded on noticing Kirk's gaze, then adjusted his lab coat and went back to realigning the chart slides he was projecting on a far section of wall.

"With all respect," April commented, also noticing the busy adult, "how can a woman as young as you have a son old enough to be accomplished in the sciences?"

Karla Five's surprise seemed genuine. "I'm astonished that a young man like yourself would ask such a question, Commodore April. Allow me to introduce my son, Karl Four."

Kirk was beginning to wonder if he was expected to shake hands with the infant, when the older man approached them.

"I'm honored to meet you, gentlemen," he began. "I've read my mother's tapes of her encounter with you in the other universe, and how you come to be here. I hope I can help."

Spock was explaining even as Kirk tried once more to readjust his thinking.

"Eminently logical, you see. Since the flow of time is

reversed here, then it is natural for one to be born at an advanced age and to die in infancy. Your descendants," he said to Karl Four, "are born before you, and your ancestors after. I should like to see some local obstetrical—"

"Please, Mr. Spock," Kirk interrupted, a mite desperately, "let's stick to physics."

"If this is your son," April inquired, "then who is the chap in the playpen?"

"Karl Six, of course," she explained easily. "My father. He's led a long and healthy life, made many contributions to our people in the sciences." She shook her head—happily? Sadly, Kirk corrected himself.

"I'm afraid most of his knowledge is gone now. He has entered senile infancy."

"You mean he no longer has it?" wondered Kirk.

Karla Five made a gesture. "I mean our society no longer has it. As our race evolves, all knowledge is lost . . . the natural order of things."

"More and more fascinating," declared a thoroughly enchanted Spock. "A race begins with all the knowledge it will ever have, and as it evolves, the knowledge is progressively lost. Progressive regression."

"We could remain eternally awed at the differences between our universes and civilizations," Kirk snapped briskly, "but we have to find a method of returning to our own universe."

"Exactly what I've been devoting all my time to since Karla Five beamed me the details of your difficulty," Karl Four told them. He gestured. "If you'll direct your attention to the far wall. . . ."

As they turned, he moved to a small panel and adjusted the switches on it. The wall across the chamber seemed to vanish. In its place was a three-dimensional cube looking for all the world like a gigantic block of glassy chocolate-chip ice cream.

"This is an in-depth map of our galaxy—at least, the portion of it we have explored," Karl Four explained. "Our home system, and Arret, is here."

As he spoke, one of the black flecks near the cube's center brightened—or was it darkened?

"And you entered our universe through the new star, the

Amphion Nova . . . here." A minuscule distance away from the first, a second black fleck pulsed noticeably.

Kirk studied the exquisite detail of the map carefully. "Somehow we have to coordinate this with our own charts, match the location of known novas in our universe to potential birthing stars here. Mr. Spock?"

"I foresee no difficulty, Captain. All physical laws appear to operate uniformly here, only in opposition to those we know. Therefore, distances and speeds in this universe should conform to our own. Karl Four, if I could have a look at the workings of your chart projector, and an explanation . . ."

"At your service, sir," the Arretian scientist responded.

Several hours of study and numerous exchanges of information with the Engineering Department brought results in the form of several specially modified chart-spools beamed down from the orbiting starship.

They should have functioned, according to Spock's design, in the Arretian navigational computer, but they did not. They failed even to activate it.

It was April who suggested the solution. "How soon we forget. Try running your computer in reverse, Karl Four. It should accept our information then."

And so it was. Everything went smoothly after that.

"Incredible, the degree of parallel," Karl Four murmured continually. "I wonder which universe will meet its end first. Yours, which is aging, or ours, which becomes progressively more youthful. I wonder if the nova-nova bridge is the only physical interrelation between our universes. I wonder," he mused, "what the theological relationships might be?"

"Maybe someday we'll have time to find out," ventured Kirk. "Right now, it's the nova-nova bridge I'm interested in."

"Assuming Beta Niobe and the Amphion sun here do match up on the two charts, Mr. Spock," wondered April aloud, "*can* we locate similar potential occurrences in both universes?"

Spock replied thoughtfully. "I believe so, Commodore, provided the Arretian navigational equipment will continue to process *Enterprise* information as efficiently as it has thus far."

Karl Four adjusted the chart projector once again. Kirk

started in spite of himself when the huge map shifted suddenly to a black cube with colored stars hung within. Nor could he fail to notice the way Karl Four jumped at the appearance of the, to him, perverse sight—one which contradicted all his own laws of nature.

"A direct match-up," said Spock, indicating the second still-pulsing pinpoint. "Beta Niobe . . . Amphion on the negative-universe chart. Plotting from there . . . have you some kind of probe, sir?"

Karl Four hunted in a cabinet until he produced a long, thin metal rod. He handed it to Spock, who inserted it into the black cube, moving it slowly forward through space and stars with equal facility, until the tip stopped near a small star.

"This should be Vulcan."

The Arretian pressed a switch, and the system Spock had located glowed brightly. Again the pointer moved, slightly.

"And here, Earth."

"Amazing," Karla Five said. She nodded to her son, who switched back to the Arretian chart. "It corresponds exactly to Arret." Back to the color-on-black universe of the Federation. Kirk found himself growing a little dizzy as they switched universes by the minute.

"I would like to visit my Vulcan analog," Spock declared, studying the glowing points within the cube projection. "Perhaps someday it will be possible."

"If we don't get out of here, Mr. Spock, you'll have a chance to do more visiting than you want."

"That anxious I am not, Captain." The first officer turned his attention back to the chart, gesturing with the long pointer for all the world like a schoolmaster lecturing a class of youngsters.

"It is now possible to determine with reasonable accuracy the position of simultaneous novas in the two universes, with more ease than I thought would be the case. If . . . ," and he looked back at Karl Four, "you can coordinate both maps at the same time."

The Arretian thought hard a moment, then shook his head slowly. "Yes, I think the projector can handle two spools at once. I won't vouch for what it will look like, though."

He worked at the controls. The result was a chart that was

neither black nor white, but a faded gray. The density of the chart was tremendously increased, filled as it was with nearly twice the number of stars and systems.

"A touch here," Karl Four murmured, "and we should see something interesting."

Twenty-odd points on the chart turned red. Spock studied them, then walked over and had a brief, tense conversation with the astronomer.

"The red glows indicate where two stars occupy the same space in both universes," he explained to the onlookers. "The difficulty is that while several are novas in our universe, none is sufficiently youthful to be birthing stars here.

"The star material here which will birth soonest, Karl Four tells me, is this point," and he indicated one of the pulsing lights. "It will spring to life in roughly three hundred fifty of our years . . . give or take a decade or two."

"And we haven't got three hundred fifty years—give or take anything," Kirk declared. "Though it's not a question of age." His mouth twisted slightly. "We'd all have returned to infancy and been long gone by then."

Spock inhaled deeply. "Unfortunately correct, Captain."

"There's the chance of keying one of these potential new novas into life here, gentlemen. Locate the best possible combination of swirling gases and concurrent pressure, and ignite the first thermonuclear reaction. An overloaded ship engine could conceivably do it," Karl Four said.

"We thought of that," Kirk told him, "but we can't use our warp-drive engines—that would leave us relatively helpless, our speed curtailed severely."

"How about one of our vessels?" the Arretian suggested.

"If you think it might work. I don't see us trying anything else."

"There is one other problem." They turned to look at Karla Five. "In order to avoid destruction, I had to pass through the nova at maximum velocity. I understand that your vessel, Captain Kirk, is not capable of such speeds."

"A good point, Captain," Spock agreed. "To which I see no immediate solution."

"Of course, you're welcome to use my ship, Captain Kirk.

It is the most advanced of its type . . . we have no others capable of reaching such speeds, either."

"Then I'm afraid that won't do us much good, Karla," Kirk replied sadly. "Thanks for the offer . . . but I have a crew of four hundred thirty, and your ship is suitable for only a few people, at most."

"Captain," Spock said, suddenly brightening, "there is a chance Karla Five's vessel *could* solve all these problems. We require another, powerful vessel to go to overload, to initiate the new star. We can use hers both as an unmanned projectile, to accomplish this, and as a tug to aid us in achieving the necessary speed. We need merely keep our tractor beam attached. We gained the velocity required to pass into this universe in this fashion. I do not see why we cannot use the same method to pass out from it."

"Spock, you may be right. You'd better be, because I don't see that we've got another choice," he finished grimly.

"Of course, any miscalculation . . ." He paused meaningfully. "If the reaction isn't sufficient to set off the new star in this universe, we may run through a murderous field of superhot plasma. Or if speed alone is enough to carry us through, the proper distortion may not be created. In that event, we could emerge right in the heart of an unstressed nova."

"In which case," April observed succinctly, "we won't have time to consider our mistake . . . having already ceased to exist."

Preparations proceeded smoothly, thanks to the aid of the sympathetic Arretians. Some of Arret's top physicists reworked the mathematics, to insure that everything would perform as required. For example, it was felt that merely overloading the extremely advanced engines which powered Karla Five's exploratory skiff would be insufficient to spark the necessary thermonuclear reaction in the center of the star-to-be. So the Arretian military loaded the smaller craft with compact but immensely powerful fusion weaponry, to provide a proper catalyst.

Linkages were established which would permit the *Enterprise*'s helm to control Karla Five's vessel as precisely as a living pilot could. Eventually, the two ships left Arretian orbit together, traveling at rapidly increasing speed and with the best wishes of Arret's scientific community. The prognosis was only slightly in favor of success, but both sides concealed their true feelings and concerns under a mask of empirical assurance.

"Captain's log, Stardate 5536.6," Kirk was reciting, days later. "Time continues to flow backward for us. We have set our course for a dead star aborning in this universe which corresponds to the nova Minerva in ours.

"There appears to be a new, correlating factor between the flow of time and our increasing speed, but as yet this has presented no difficulty. We are on course, and all instrumentation is operating at maximum efficiency, including the devices linking the *Enterprise* to the Arretian scout ship."

He concluded the entry and turned a gaze as yet only mildly concerned toward the science station. "Mr. Spock, any indication as to what the possible effects of the accelerated time-flow might be?"

"Theoretical only, thus far, Captain," his first officer replied. Then he added the obvious, "Anyhow, we must proceed with the programmed course and velocity regardless of all side effects. It is our only chance."

Kirk nodded, looking over his shoulder, and smiled at the pacing figure of Commodore April. He had been walking his destinationless path ever since they had left Arret.

"You may as well relax, sir. As Mr. Spock says, our course of action is committed, unalterable. And that patch of brown in your hair is very becoming."

April stopped, grinned a lopsided grin at Kirk. "Thank you, Captain. You're looking rather on the youngish side yourself, lately. Don't let my aimless meandering worry you . . . I *am* relaxing." The grin vanished, and he looked disappointedly at the deck.

"I have mixed feelings about the remainder of our journey, no matter what its outcome. Oh, I'll be glad to get home, all right, but not necessarily to Babel. That only means the official end of my career. Of my usefulness. . . ."

Kirk was spared the necessity of a reply as Spock broke in with an announcement. "I have visual contact with the region of the potential new star, Captain."

Kirk mentally thanked his first officer for the interruption—the conversation was beginning to make him uncomfortable. His tone turned businesslike.

"Let's see what we're heading into, Mr. Spock."

The *Enterprise*'s forward sensors leaped ahead, finally slowing to focus on still another rectangle of this fantastic, cream-colored universe with its black suns and feathery gray nebulae.

"I don't see anything, Mr. Spock."

"A moment, Captain. We are headed directly for it, but it is denser white matter in white space. I will superimpose an outline."

Adjustments at the science console produced a rough black circle in the center of the screen.

"If I didn't know better, Mr. Spock, I'd suspect it was another white hole."

"No, Captain, preliminary sensor readings indicate it's nothing like the one we encountered near the Milky Way's Shapely Center.

"There is considerable stress, shifting gravitational potential, and other unusual phenomena present, but nowhere near the extreme distortions of the spatial matrix we encountered in the white hole."

"Just as well," Kirk murmured. "I've no desire to repeat that trip again." Uhura called over to him, cutting off his thoughts in midremembrance.

"Message coming in from Arret, Captain. Karla Five making contact."

"Put her through, Lieutenant."

Transmission all the way from Arret was no longer crystal-clear, but the resolution was sufficient to show the aged yet youthful scout standing before the star-chart projector in her son's laboratory.

"I want to wish you luck, Captain Kirk," she said, her voice filtered and distorted with distance. "I was present at the official farewell, but I applied for and received permission to make this final broadcast. As I was, in a way, personally responsible for bringing you here, the government felt I was entitled to wish you on your way personally. The pity of it is that after all we've done, no matter what the astrophysicists tell me, I'll never know if you fail or succeed."

"Just keep in mind that you've done all you could for us, Karla," replied Kirk truthfully. "And perhaps you will know someday. Someday when a way is found of crossing the barriers between our universes in safety and comfort. When that day comes, we'll thank you personally for your help . . . in *our* universe, next time. The important thing is that you've shown such a journey is possible. We thank you also for the sacrifice of your vessel. You see, I know that your government couldn't force you to turn it over to us, and that you volunteered it freely."

"A small sacrifice, Captain," the fading, emotional voice declared. "The information I was able to bring back is worth more to my people than any number of such vessels. Indeed, the information your computer library supplied made up the loss of one scout many times over.

"I only hope that it proves to be a worthwhile sacrifice. Success to you, Captain Kirk, Mr. Spock, Commodore April, and all . . ."

The screen blanked. "Transmission ended from Arret, sir," Uhura reported dutifully.

"Thank you, Lieutenant. Mr. Spock?" The view of space forward resumed. "Mr. Sulu, how's the tractor link holding up?"

Sulu checked his read-outs. To ensure that the invisible bond joining the *Enterprise* and the smaller Arretian ship didn't break at a crucial juncture, every tractor beam on board that could be brought to bear was locked on the superfast scout.

"Still holding firm, Captain. The original tractor link as well as all subsequent holds."

"Very good, Lieutenant. Let me know immediately if the bonds show any sign of weakening."

Sulu nodded as Arex reported from navigation. "Speed increasing steadily, Captain. We're holding on course."

That left one last section to check. "Bridge to Engineering . . . Scotty, are you there?"

"Standin' by, Captain."

"What's our situation?"

"Stable so far, sir," the chief engineer reported. "Of

course, I've some idea what to expect this time around, and we've prepared for it—I hope. That new bracin' installed by the Arretians seems to be doin' what they claimed it would. If it holds up under this passage it's goin' to cause some heavy thinking on the part of the engineers responsible for designin' warp-drive supports. Not to mention what a sensation those diagrams of that scout ship's engines are goin' to be."

"Don't get too excited about that, Scotty," Kirk reminded him. "Remember, the element that powers those engines is found only in the Arretian's universe. We'll have to work out the difficulties of interuniversal transport and travel before we can think of a cruiser traveling at warp-thirty or so."

"I know, Captain," Scott replied, trying not to sound as disappointed as he was. "Ah, but wouldn't it be a darlin' surprise for our friends the Klingons!"

It was hours later, when they had more than doubled their speed, that Kirk noticed the at once marvelous, ominous change creeping through the *Enterprise*.

He had been so involved in last-minute course calculations, in monitoring the status of the Arretian scout, that he had failed to see the startling alterations taking place all around him. In fairness, though, so had everyone else. The gradualness of the first changes—and their uniformity—were responsible for the oversight.

Metamorphosis was proceeding so rapidly now, however, that it struck Kirk like a blow to the belly. The subtle sensation that something was drastically different was concretized when McCoy and Sarah April reappeared on the bridge. The shift was most apparent in their faces.

The deep lines caused by too many patients lost through the unavailability of the necessary drugs, too many needless deaths incurred on hostile worlds, were missing from McCoy's visage. He was noticeably younger.

As was Dr. Sarah April, paragon of Starfleet medical technology, who was now a very unvenerable fortyish beauty devoid of white hair, lines around the eyes, and all other indications of advanced age.

Abruptly Kirk saw the bridge staff through clear eyes and a clear mind. Sulu and Uhura, he now noticed, had regained the appearance of teenagers. Spock showed the least amount of change, which was only natural as Vulcans aged more slowly than humans. It was hardest to tell when he looked at Arex, since adolescent Edoans often look exactly like their wizened elders.

"Mr. Spock, I think we have passed the point of needing theoretical opinions on the effects of the increased time-flow."

"I had noticed it before now, Captain," the first officer said somberly, "but as we have no alternative course of action, I saw no point in needlessly distressing anyone."

Kirk wasn't sure he agreed with Spock's reasoning, but he had no time to argue with it. He wasn't sure how much time he had left, period.

"I suppose the first crucial minute will be when our youngest crew member returns to . . . to the moment of birth," he ventured.

Spock concurred. "That will take place, taking into account a rapid increase in our regression corresponding to our increasing speed, in approximately eighteen minutes, thirty-five seconds, Captain. However, that will not be the *most* crucial time."

"Explain, Mr. Spock."

"Before that point is reached, we will all have returned to infantilism. And," he concluded, "this means we are losing our knowledge concomitant with our years, and both at an alarming rate. It is possible that we will be too young, mentally, to operate the *Enterprise* at the crucial stage in our interuniversal passage. . . ."

IV

Kirk pondered the problem for long minutes, then broke off when he found himself staring with a little too much fascination at the sixteen-year-old boy sitting before the now massive-looking helm console.

"How's our present course, Mr. Sulu?"

The youth started to reply, hesitated, and stared blankly at the now bewildering array of instrumentation spread before him. "I . . . I'm not sure," he finally confessed in a shockingly altered tenor. "What am I doing here, anyway? What are all these dials and gauges and lights?" He turned and stared with rising confusion at Kirk.

"And you . . . you're . . . ? Who are you, mister?"

"He's too young, Captain," Spock interrupted. "Far younger than he was when he entered Starfleet. Not only has he regressed beyond the point of knowing how to operate *Enterprise* instrumentation, his youthful mind is beginning to doubt its far larger store of memories. Look at Lieutenant Uhura."

Kirk turned and saw a puzzled young girl running her hands uncertainly over winking telltales.

"They are turning into children, Captain," Spock concluded.

"But they just can't lose all their acquired knowledge, Mr. Spock. Our physical makeup isn't the same as the Arretians."

"I suspect all the knowledge is still there, Captain," his first officer explained, "locked away deep within their minds. But the mechanism for retrieving such information is degenerating as they grow younger."

"We'll cope, somehow," countered Kirk tightly. "Mr.

Arex, take over helm functions for Mr. Sulu. I want a full status report from all sections, Lieutenant Uhura. Lieutenant Uhura?"

"I beg your pardon, mister?" she replied dazedly.

"Never mind. Spock, you can fill in for her temporarily. Their replacements would only be as young and ineffective as they. You and Mr. Arex are the only longer-lived crew members on board."

"True, Captain," admitted Spock. "We will manage as long as we are able. But who will fill in for you?"

Kirk gave him a peculiar look. "What do you mean, 'fill in for me'?"

Spock explained patiently something Kirk knew but refused to believe. "You are a deal older than Lieutenant Sulu or Uhura, but at what age did you become a starship captain? How old were you when you entered Starfleet Academy? When did you take advanced navigation, or command mechanics?"

Kirk chewed that over, then finally nodded reluctant agreement. "We'll lose control rapidly, all right. By the time we reach the vicinity of the potential star, I'm not going to know what we have to do, let alone how to do it."

"As a Vulcan, I age the slowest, true," Spock commented. There was no hint of pride or racial arrogance in that statement. It was merely fact. Merely Spock. "I will be capable of retaining my effectiveness longer than anyone else.

"But I fear even I will become too young to know what to do at the crucial moment. It will be close . . . very close." He glanced at his controls, wondering idly at what moment they would become only glassed-in numbers for him. He wished he could divorce himself from his body to study the no doubt intriguing phenomenon at leisure.

"Ten minutes, fourteen seconds," he announced finally. "We may just make it, Captain, according to the final computer projection. At the appropriate moment it will be vital to activate the weaponry on board the Arretian scout. That must be handled by someone other than myself."

Kirk blinked at the strange words. He saw things plainly, but his thoughts were masked by thicker and thicker layers of uncertainty. Nothing related to anything else. He found he could describe but not explain, see without understanding, perceive but not evaluate.

Children surrounded him, at the helm, at Communications. And at the navigation console, even Arex was beginning to look decidedly cuddly.

"Captain," a demanding voice said, "do you think you will be able to handle the Arretian engine overload functions?"

"Overload . . . engine overload? How do we do that, Mr. Spock?"

The first officer inhaled deeply. In his still-exacting mind, their chances dropped a few percentage points. "I fear I must assume control, Captain. You are no longer able to command the *Enterprise*."

Kirk retained enough maturity to readily agree. "Whatever you say, Spock. What shall I do?"

A new voice spoke up. Its master had just now appeared on the bridge, had only taken stock of the recent developments.

He was tall, straight, supremely confident. The voice was new and at the same time familiar. A bit softer now, perhaps, its timbre sharp and precise. Kirk thought he recognized it, thought he recognized the stranger as well.

"I'm sorry, Mr. Spock," the voice said commandingly. "As long as I'm aboard, I'm still senior officer here. My subsequent appointment as ambassador-at-large does not supersede my Starfleet ranking, it only complements it. I hate to pull rank, but I'd guess that in another five minutes even you will become incapable of command, much less of performing intricate operations." He checked his madly revolving watch, noting the speed with which the hands were spinning in reverse.

"That's not soon enough to execute the few but vital maneuvers essential to our hope of return."

Spock did not argue; there was no reason to. The commodore's logic was unassailable. "You are correct, of course, Commodore April. I had forgotten all but regular crew under the stress of the moment. I would be grateful if you would assume command."

"I hereby do so officially, Mr. Spock." He sounded

slightly bemused now. "But why the 'commodore'? It's Captain . . . Captain April."

"Who?" muttered Spock.

"Bob . . . ?"

The young commodore-captain turned.

"We seem to be the only adults left on the bridge," Sarah April observed. "They're all children now, or teenaged."

Her husband nodded. "Make sure they don't hurt themselves, Sarah." He turned his attention to the instruments at the helm. "If we're going to go home, instead of to blazes, we have to ignite this star at just the right moment. Mr. Spock, I realize your reasoning powers are now impaired, but how are you at still following orders?"

Spock strained visibly. "Information . . . is vanishing rapidly, sir. For the moment . . . yes, I can function. The sensation is somewhat akin to submitting to anesthesia."

"Right. Assume the navigator's position." The adolescent Vulcan proceeded to do so, gently moving a squawking, feathered protester out of the chair.

"Report, Mr. Spock," April said from the helm.

"The potential star is directly ahead, Captain." The first officer's manner and inflection were steady as ever. Only a close acquaintance would have noted the lighter, slightly less serious tone in his speech. "Bearing, mark," and he strenuously recited the readings, unsure of their meaning. But observation did not require as much knowledge as interpretation, and another pair of eyes was what April needed now.

"Activate the weaponry on board the Arretian ship."

That almost . . . almost defeated Spock. Knowledge was draining from him like water from a cracked pitcher. It took a long minute of painful thought before he was able to key the relatively simple command required to arm the awesome energies packed into the tiny scout.

"Activated, Captain," he finally acknowledged.

"Nine seconds to ignition," April recited, staring at the helm readouts. "Seven, six . . ." His gaze rose to the main screen, as did Sarah April's and Spock's.

A black flower blossomed before them, its stretching petals tinged with violent and royal blue. The unnatural colors were startling against the pure white background of space.

April spared a split second for a survey of the bridge. No

longer did it resemble the hub of one of the Federation's most storied, most efficient ships. Instead it had taken on the appearance of an undisciplined interspecies nursery.

Children and in some cases infants now babbled and struggled within the confines of baggy clothing grown monstrously large for their tiny forms. Naturally, the inorganic materials had not shrunk along with the crew members. If anything, April noted with alarm, the rate of reverse was accelerating. Surely the first officer now fumbling confusedly at the navigation console was no older than seven. He was past following even simple commands.

There was, however, still one other person on the bridge who could perform the remaining crucial maneuvers. One whose ability matched if not exceeded his own. He looked over his shoulder at the radiantly beautiful woman watching him.

"Sarah, do you remember any of your basic navigation?"

"Like it was yesterday, Bob." She moved to the navigation console while the commodore-captain assumed the command chair.

"Keep us on course, whatever else happens, whatever might happen to me," April told her. She studied the instrumentation briefly, moved her hands over the dials and switches. It seemed like only yesterday she was tested on similar boards to pass her basic command functions classes at the Academy.

A small adjustment was called for here. The computer identified the deviation and brought it to the attention of its human masters. It could do no more. It needed an organic mind to order the necessary shift in course. Sarah April moved almost automatically to provide that command.

Satisfied, the navigation computer realigned the *Enterprise*. Once more it was on the course prescribed for its eventual salvation . . . or destruction.

Tail first, the great cruiser plunged into the center of a rapidly heating mass of pressurized gases and particles. The tremendous release of energy produced by the volatized Arretian ship had kindled strange reactions among the mass of already unstable material.

As a tremendous shaking suddenly gripped the *Enterprise*, fusion began.

Sarah April felt like a pebble in a tin can as she clung tightly to the navigation console. But Commodore-Captain April locked himself into the command chair and exulted in the glory conveyed by the main viewscreen.

For what seemed like hours, but was mere seconds, they rode the shock wave of ruptured space.

Abruptly, without warning, the buffeting ceased. There was only the soft hum of monitors, the quiet beeps and mutters of unstressed instruments.

April became aware that he was still frozen to his seat. Slowly he relaxed his muscles, let his body slump. He became aware of something else: His eyes were closed tight enough to hurt.

He opened them slowly, and as usual his eyes registered the view forward before his mind comprehended.

Black space flecked with colored suns.

They were home again.

Sarah April left the navigation console and moved slowly to his side. "The computer can hold us steady here. I didn't have enough navigation to be able to reprogram us from wherever we are, Bob. That may be a problem."

She nodded to where the seven-year-old Spock was sitting near the navigation station, staring back at them with precocious, wide eyes.

April's attention was still focused on the screen. "I never thought pure blackness could look so lovely." Finally he looked away, down, and embraced her as hard as he had the rocking command chair only moments before.

"We did it. We're back in our own universe again," he finally sighed, releasing her. Now he could turn his attention to Spock and the rest of the ship's youthful crew.

"The reverse aging process seems to have stopped, but I see no signs of rapid aging beginning. The effect apparently operates only in the negative universe."

"Does that mean they're all going to remain children?" Sarah asked.

"No . . . no, that doesn't make sense, either," he said thoughtfully. He gestured at Spock, who amiably gestured back. "I have no doubt that Spock, Captain Kirk, and the others will return to their normal ages naturally—but at our universe's normal speed.

"That would mean, for example, that Mr. Spock will have to grow up all over again. Unless . . ."

"The transporter records!" Dr. April exclaimed. "It retains the records of their original molecular structure. It *could* return them to the age they were when they last transported."

"It could," he agreed. "But the entire ship's crew . . . it will take some time. We're going to be busy for a while, my love."

"You think it will work, too, Bob?" She appeared uncertain now. "Hasn't it been tried before, and found not to? I seem to recall experiments. If it worked, everyone could have near immortality, simply by having their youthful selves recorded for transporting and then, upon aging, entering transporters to be reintegrated according to their preserved youthful records."

"Yes to everything you said, Sarah," April concurred. "But one exception should—*has* to—make a difference. Remember, the molecular structure of everyone on board has been altered by unnatural, extrauniversal forces. Those fountain-of-youth experiments with transporters weren't carried out on people who'd been exposed to the accelerated time-flow and radiations and who-knows-what of the negative universe.

"It's those molecular changes that should be reversible, Sarah. At least, the theory seems sound, if I remember my transporter mechanics correctly." He smiled. "As you say, it seems like yesterday. But we don't have to use the transporter, Sarah. We can remain young, live our lives over again. To be able to do that, have a second life—it was worth the trip to the negative universe and the difficulties of returning. We've found a true fountain of youth, Sarah—in mathematics and spatial physics, instead of an obscure plot of mythical topography."

"And all anyone has to do to make use of it," she said sadly, "is to have a great amount of daring and a ship that can travel at warp-thirty-five. I'm afraid that our experience is going to prove unique."

"I'm afraid you're right, Sarah. Actually, we're not going to live our lives over again, are we? We're going to live a second life. That's good." He smiled, warm, loving, a together-understanding smile. "I wouldn't want to live the other one over again. I don't see how we could ever improve on what we've had already. No, Sarah, we've been blessed beyond any other people, been granted a special privilege. We mustn't abuse it."

"We didn't abuse it the first time around Bob. I'm not at all worried about a repeat performance."

April's theory about the action of negative-universe forces turned out to be correct. They started with the bridge crew, and breathed sighs of relief when the adult analogs reappeared to take the place of the children who had entered the transporter.

Each member of the crew exited from the alcove with a splitting headache. This was the only noticeable side effect—headache, and a uniform sometimes badly askew. Both ailments were easily treated.

It was slow going at first, carefully reprogramming according to old records and then reintegrating with equal care. But once the engineering officers had been brought back to true maturity, they were able to take over the task and proceed with greater speed and efficiency.

So it didn't take overlong for the *Enterprise* to return to normal strength, experientially as well as in numbers.

Kirk leaned back in the command chair and reflected on his brief but profound reentry into childhood. Everyone on board had reacted differently to the experience, and not a few were undergoing psychiatric outpatient treatment for traumas incurred as a result.

"I don't think we have any serious cases, Jim," McCoy had informed him. "But if you see any of the younger ensigns walking around sucking their thumbs, try not to be too harsh on them."

Once again it was McCoy whose easy humor had shattered a tense, potentially nerve-racking situation. Any lingering worries among the crew vanished in laughter as the good doctor's comment passed around the ship.

Most of the experience had faded to the memory of a distant dream for Kirk, but there was one resurrected bit of personal history that had stuck with him.

He had a picture of a small, feisty boy in preschool, with the instructor hovering over his computer terminal, bawling him out for running mock battles with the math keys instead of practicing computation tables.

"Jimmy Kirk, I've told you and told you," she scolded. "If you keep wasting your time with such nonsense you'll never amount to anything!"

"Something amusing, Captain Kirk?"

"Hmmm . . . what?" Kirk started, then glanced back and up at a youthful Robert April. "No, Commodore, I was just thinking that among your other numerous distinctions, you're now going to be regarded as the youngest commodore in the fleet. But of course, you're not. Let's see, extrapolating from your present recorded age, as opposed to your new actual one, I'd estimate that you can probably retire at the natural age of one hundred and thirty. That should give you over a hundred years in the service, Commodore.

"I'd give a lot to see what Starfleet accounting's going to do with *those* figures! Either they'll have to refigure the basis for computing pensions, or else you can retire tomorrow with a full commodore's pension and a whole lifetime to enjoy it in."

"There is a host of fascinating ramifications, Captain," April agreed. "But as you can guess, financial considerations are not foremost in my mind." He looked downcast.

"The Minerva Nova's not far from Babel. And we'll be there shortly. I know that should make me happy, Jim, but it doesn't any more. I don't care much about money." He looked up, and his sorrowful eyes bore into Kirk's own, the same light of deep space glowing in their depths.

"You, of all people, can understand what does."

Under pressure of that pleading stare, Kirk couldn't hold back any longer.

"Well then, I might as well tell you that we've been in contact with Starfleet ever since we regained control of the *Enterprise*. Naturally, they were most interested in the details of our journey into the negative universe. *All* the details, Commodore."

April looked at him unsurely. There was something in the captain's voice. "What do you mean, Jim?"

"Nothing . . . just that we received a reply from Starfleet headquarters, relayed all the way to us, which might cheer you up a bit. I'd intended waiting to reveal its contents until we were in orbit around Babel, but"—he shrugged—"I couldn't stand to see a young man cry.

"Lieutenant Uhura, would you repeat the message to Commodore and Dr. April?"

Uhura nodded happily. Like everyone else on board, she had come to regard the Aprils as fellow crew members rather than as distinguished passengers. So it gave her pleasure equal to Kirk's own to be able to read, "In view of Commodore Robert April's heroic actions aboard the U.S.S. *Enterprise* this stardate, the senior command is reviewing mandatory retirement regulations with special regard to the unusual circumstances surrounding Commodore April's present physical status.

"His earlier requests to remain in active service will be given priority reevaluation. End communiqué." She looked back across the bridge and smiled.

April said nothing, but Sarah's left hand slid smoothly into his right. His palm enveloped hers as naturally and reassuringly as a snowbank settles around a sleeping sled-dog.

"And I have more time to continue my research," she murmured. "Perhaps this time I can accomplish one or two things."

"Well, bravo," April finally exclaimed confidently. "Maybe now I can talk them into doing away with that idiot mandatory retirement age altogether." His voice rose with the zeal of renewed youth.

"Retirement shouldn't be a function of abstract statistics. By God, the Federation's got to realize that a person's ability isn't automatically invalidated on a specific date."

"I'll support you on that, Bob," Kirk agreed, "and would even if I didn't see myself repeating your complaint a number of years from now."

"Insertion into Babel orbit in one hour fifteen minutes, Captain," Sulu reported from the helm. April looked resigned.

"Sarah and I had better get our things together, Jim. I may have to have some emergency alterations performed on my dress uniform."

"And I can't wait to perform some on *mine*," Dr. April added vivaciously.

April half-whispered the next words, but Kirk heard them

clearly. "And, Jim, even if it wasn't too pleasant for the rest of you, thanks for the opportunity to be a starship captain again."

They turned to leave the bridge, and as they did so Kirk noticed that Sarah April was holding the brilliant, revived Capellan flower.

"Bob always did say that the *Enterprise* had the best crew in Starfleet. I see it's as true today as it was thirty years ago. Thank you for everything, Captain Kirk."

"Doctor April," he acknowledged softly. Then his tone brightened. "I always wanted to be a kid again. After having the chance, I can see I wasn't missing much." He gestured at the blossom. "I see your flower's bloomed again."

She was staring up at the contented face of the commodore, but she heard him. "Everything has, Captain," she murmured.

Kirk watched them until they had left the bridge. He turned and settled back into the chair. There was still a little time left before he would have to go through the rigors of donning a full-dress uniform and making inane conversation with boring but important people.

For now he could spend a number of pleasant hours doing nothing but staring at the exhilarating, lush blackness of the *real* universe.

As they neared Babel, he noticed Spock staring into apparent nothingness. Such abstract concentration was not unusual for the first officer, however. Often his thoughts were his own best friend. But Kirk detected a hint of a peculiar expression crossing Spock's face from time to time.

Idly, he asked, "What did you think of your temporary return to the joys of childhood, Spock? You didn't age down to a squalling babe like most of us, so your memory of those minutes is probably stronger."

"Joys of childhood, Captain?" the first officer echoed diffidently. He assumed a firm, no-nonsense tone. "Childhood is a time of indiscipline, insecurity, and instability, both emotional and logical. From a physiological and informational point of view the experience was somewhat intriguing, but it was otherwise nonbeneficial. I would hardly call it a 'joy,' and I surely have no special desire to repeat it."

"Naturally, of course," Kirk muttered, taken a bit aback

by his friend's logical appraisal of what, for him, had been a warm if confusing experience. "I suppose I agree with you. After all, that's the only rational way to look at it."

"Quite."

"By the way, what were you thinking of just now?"

"Captain?"

"A moment ago. You were wandering."

"I was . . . analyzing the experience in question and culling its scientific values."

Kirk seemed disappointed. "Of course, though it almost appeared once that you might have been talking to yourself."

"A not impossible phenomenon, Captain. I am not immune to subliminal vocalizations. It is merely rare in Vulcans. But I am interested. What did you think you heard?"

"Nothing that made sense," the Captain replied, repeating it slowly. "Ee-chiya—that's all."

"You are correct, Captain, nothing that makes sense." He returned his attention to his multitude of instruments, his readouts and gauges and illumined lists of scientific minutiae.

"It vaguely resembled an obscure Vulcan scientific term, nothing more. Nothing more. . . ."

The astounding metamorphosis of the Aprils was the highlight of the ambassadorial gathering at Babel. Expecting to honor an aged, white-haired couple, the conferees were shocked when the youthful pair presented themselves at function after stunned function.

All they met were shocked, stunned, and envious. Hopes did not fall even when inquiries into the transformation by friends old and new revealed the methodology necessary to achieve the radical alteration. None present regarded the dangers of diving into a nova seriously—old men have nothing to lose. It made some of them bolder than the rawest recruit.

The devolution of the Aprils would have one side effect. It would speed, with the aid of the charts provided by Arretian scientists, research into warp-drive technology.

Now immortality had become a question of getting rapidly from place to place, in order to get from time to time . . .

V

As it turned out, Kirk was spared the enervating agony of attending endless speeches, parties, and conferences. A Federation cruiser not on planned layover could not be permitted to languish unengaged at an idle port of call. Their job had been to deliver Commodore April and his wife to the conference. This done, it was only a matter of time before new orders were received.

Kirk kept a reluctant smile on his face as he took leave of various representatives on Babel.

"Emergency priority signal received aboard, Captain," Spock whispered to him. Kirk frowned, then reapplied the reluctant smile he had been artfully employing all afternoon.

"Sorry to have to run, Ambassador Werthel, Admiral M'aart, Dame M'arrt," he explained hastily to the little group. "Duty runs on its own timetable."

"Arr, yes," the ample mate of the Caitian admiral purred in remembrance. "How clearrly I myself rrememberr the time only a few yearrs ago when—"

"Yes, well, you'll have to tell me all about it, in full detail, the next time we can get together," Kirk assured her, backing smoothly toward the doorway. "Let's get out of here, Mr. Spock," he said feelingly, "before this smile cracks my face."

"A physiological impossibility, Captain, though the meaning is clear."

With mixed feelings Kirk reentered the bridge: relief at the return to comfortable surroundings (how that admiral's wife could whine!), but apprehension at what would prompt Starfleet to break in on a diplomatic conference.

"You're certain this was an emergency priority call, Lieutenant?" he asked Uhura.

"Yes, sir. I keyed the proper response code the moment I heard that you and Mr. Spock were back on board. The message should be coming through any second."

"All right, Lieutenant." Tap, tap, click, tap . . . He forced his fingers to freeze on the command-chair armrest, forced himself to listen to the quiet. "Mr. Spock, has the science section noted anything out of the ordinary in this region?"

"Negative, Captain. I ran a standard query through all subsections the moment I arrived back on board. Everything in this sector reports in normal and undisturbed."

"Call coming through, Captain."

"Um. Put it on the main screen, Lieutenant."

Kirk swiveled slightly as the screen cleared. Crisp with power, it showed the slight form of an aged Oriental seated behind a gleaming chrome desk devoid of ornamentation. Long white shoulder-length hair was combed straight back, and the creases in that young-old face seemed as fresh and as neatly cut as the lines of her uniform. Only the eyes of polished hazel revealed an intensity inspired by something other than age. They hinted at heavy burdens borne by generations. Only in the last few had those burdens changed from physical to mental.

A hand came up in casual, knowing wave. Three stripes decorated the sleeve.

"Greetings, Captain Kirk," a surprisingly strong voice said over the speakers and across parsecs.

Kirk's reply was one of respectful surprise. This he hadn't expected. "Hello, Commodore Sen. How are things at Starfleet Security?"

The commodore smiled wistfully. "Interesting, as always, Captain Kirk. Interesting and perpetually worrisome. And, as always, people rather than events cause the most trouble. For example, how do the names Van and Char Delminnen strike you?"

"At a vague angle, Commodore. Sorry, but I—"

"Excuse me, Captain, but I believe I am familiar with the persons in question. If memory serves me—"

"Doesn't it always?" Uhura murmured. Spock favored her with a mildly reproving glance.

"If memory serves, Van Delminnen was a Fellow of the London Institute for Theoretical Physics some years ago. A research Fellow. His specialty lay on the fringe of what was known about the specific gravity of heavy elements.

"Apparently his brilliance was exceeded only by his unorthodox methodology, which was in turn matched by the volatility of his temperament. He withdrew from the institute amid a storm of accusations and counteraccusations. Dropped from sight . . . I recall the tape well."

"Nothing heard of them since?"

"The only information I have encountered, Captain, were rumors that he and his sister were living on an otherwise uninhabited moon in the Theta Draconis system."

"Your opinion of him . . . from the information you've encountered?"

The first officer paused thoughtfully for a moment. "Arrogant and harmless . . . a crippled genius, Captain, possibly mentally unstable."

"You are partially correct, First Officer Spock," the serious voice called from the screen. "Brilliant—decidedly. Unorthodox—yes. Mentally unstable . . . perhaps. But we have reason to doubt the 'harmless.' " She reached off-screen and consulted several sheets of plastic. After a cursory glance, she turned back to the visual pickup.

"Captain Kirk, a prospecting vessel whose specialty is searching out marginal deposits of valuable metals passed through the limits of the Theta Draconis system ten standard days ago. They were returning to mine a small deposit of polonium reported by the original drone survey of the system as existing on a continent of the ninth planet." She leaned forward.

"Instead of the ninth world, they found a previously unreported asteroid cluster of considerable mass. A similar cluster had also taken the place of the system's eighth planetary body. Simple calculations by the ship's computer indicated what you must already have suspected: The mass of the two asteroidal groupings very nearly equaled that of the two missing worlds.

"As you might imagine, they left the system without pursuing these unusual developments more closely, straining their engines to their limits.

"I am told," she continued, as the bridge crew listened in amazement, "that normal spatial phenomena can in no way account for this dual disaster. We must therefore assume that abnormal forces are at work. Combine this information with the detection of highly unusual, very powerful radiation emanating from the system's largest moon, which circles its fifth world—well, I hardly think I need to draw you a diagram, Captain Kirk.

"You see, Mr. Spock, the rumors were correct. The Delminnens have taken up residence in the Theta Draconis system. They have also seemingly taken to making small planetoids out of big planets.

"Starfleet is very worried. *I* am very worried. And since the *Enterprise* is the Federation ship nearest the Theta Draconis system, you too should be worried, Captain Kirk.

"You will proceed immediately to the system in question and establish contact with the Delminnens. You will invite Van Delminnen to return to Terra, where he is to be granted a permanent appointment to Starfleet Research at a generous annual stipend."

"Suppose," Kirk ventured, "Delminnen declines our invitation? He has no reason to hold any love for Federation institutions."

"In that unfortunate event," the commodore replied, "you are authorized to utilize whatever means you deem necessary to entice him and his sister aboard ship. Good luck, Captain Kirk."

The image vanished. "Transmission concluded, Captain," Uhura reported. "Standard recording procedures were in operation."

"Thank you, Lieutenant. I want that blanket authorization made part of the formal record." He turned to his first officer. "Mr. Spock . . . opinions?"

"A device capable of producing the effect described by the commodore seems beyond the capability of modern technology, Captain. Total annihilation of a planetary mass, yes. Selective disintegration, no."

"And yet it appears that Delminnen can do just that. No wonder Starfleet is concerned." Kirk turned to the helm. "Mr. Sulu, set course for Theta Draconis Five. Warp-five.

Mr. Arex, sound yellow alert. All stations will remain on same until the Delminnens are secured on board."

"You make those two sound like a dangerous weapon, Captain," Sulu observed solemnly.

"That's exactly how the commodore described them, Lieutenant. And that's exactly how we're going to treat them—at least until we find out what's been going on in the Draconis system . . ."

Great bands of orange, red, and yellow turned Theta Draconis Five into a monstrous ball of poisoned softness. Its hostile surface lay swathed in a fuzzy cloak of ammonia and methane, and it howled at the ether with wild, undisciplined radiations.

Records indicated that it was attended by seven satellites, one of which the *Enterprise* was currently orbiting. It was not the largest or the smallest, but it was surely unique, for it possessed a breathable atmosphere.

". . . and little else," Spock intoned, his eyes fixed to the gooseneck viewer. "Other than the livable atmosphere, there is nothing of interest on the moon, nothing to make it attractive to settlers. It has neither commercial nor military value."

"All of which makes it ideal for a would-be hermit like Delminnen," Kirk observed as he stared at the rust-colored globe and its startlingly white miniature icecaps. He touched a switch on the command-chair arm.

"Captain's log, Stardate 5536.8. We have arrived at Theta Draconis and established orbit around the habitable moon of the fifth planet, where we are hoping to encounter the elusive Delminnens and their mysterious weapon . . . if indeed it is a weapon, if it indeed exists.

"Personally, I am skeptical as to the existence of said device. But Mr. Spock has verified the appearance of two unreported asteroid clusters in the positions formerly occupied by planets eight and nine, so some immensely powerful force *has* been at work in this system." The captain closed down the log and looked to his left. "Initial report, Mr. Spock?"

The first officer looked across, his attention turned from his readouts. "Mostly desert, tundra or hot, with little free water. No indication of life more developed than the lower invertebrates. It's easy to see why the Delminnens selected this particular satellite. It offers nothing of interest to the most bored traveler."

"Then perhaps they won't mind leaving it so much. Lieutenant Uhura, see if you can raise the Delminnens. Try near the edge of the north polar cap—that appears to be the most hospitable section of this moon."

"Aye, sir." She turned to her instrumentation and responded after a surprisingly short pause. "Captain, I have made some kind of aural-visual contact already."

"They must have some detection equipment, then," Kirk noted. "Very well, flash the image on the main screen." He threw Spock a quick glance. "Get a fix on the transmitter's location and relay it to Transporter Control."

Spock moved to comply as Uhura struggled with her equipment. "The signal is weak but clear . . . there."

The figure that appeared was that of a shockingly young man: rail-thin, pale-skinned, with too-large eyes bordering a shark-hook of a nose. Straight sandy hair fell in hirsute drips across his face, and he brushed constantly, nervously at the strands.

"Who the devil are you and what do you want?"

Spock had moved to stand next to the command chair. "Sociable fellow, isn't he?" Kirk whispered to him, before turning to the screen and assuming his most pleasant tone.

"Good day to you, Professor Delminnen. I am James Kirk, Captain of the starship *Enterprise*, currently in orbit around your charming worldlet. I come at the urgent request of Starfleet Command."

"I'll bet." Delminnen smirked, smiling at some private joke.

"I have been instructed to offer you, in the name of the Federation, a permanent research position in advanced physical theory at the Starfleet Institute itself, with all the honors thereunto attached." He kept a straight face as he added, "There has been considerable renewed interest in some of your early theories, you see."

And the later developments, Kirk added, but to himself only.

"May I have the pleasure of conveying your acceptance to Starfleet headquarters?"

"Just . . . just a minute, Captain," Delminnen said. "I need a moment to consider."

Those aboard the *Enterprise* waited while the figure disappeared from the screen. The lift doors slid apart, and Dr. McCoy entered the bridge. He looked from the now blank screen to Kirk. The captain put a finger to his lips as Delminnen reappeared.

"I have considered your words, Captain Kirk," he said, "and find I don't believe a one of them." His voice rose angrily. "Why should those scientific cretins at Starfleet suddenly have the desire, or the sense, to request my services? Why should they now wish to subject me to honor instead of ridicule?"

Kirk took a deep breath. "I think you know the answer to that, Delminnen. Evidence of your . . . experimentation in this system has reached command levels. Naturally, everyone is anxious to admire the development which—"

"I thought as much," Delminnen said. His smirk turned into a wide, unfriendly smile. "I just wanted to hear it out loud. *Admire* pagh! They want to steal my knowledge! They always take what they can't understand." He all but snarled into the pickup.

"You can tell those mathematical morons what they can do with their honors, Captain. And if you don't leave me and my sister alone, you'll find yourself the recipient of a demonstration of just how *admirable* my work here is."

Kirk stared quietly at the suddenly blank screen. "So much," he murmured softly, "for diplomacy. What do you think of our reluctant guest, Mr. Spock?"

The first officer considered. "A difficult speciman. I can understand how such a psychological type could produce peculiar theories, but it eludes me completely as to how he could translate those theories into anything practical. Yet it seems he has. We must handle him the same way one would store a photon torpedo with a sensitive detonator—forcefully but with great care."

"I concur. Order a security landing party to stand by in the Main Transporter Room."

"Armed, Captain?"

"Armed."

Spock rose and turned to leave, adding, "Then I think it

best that I instruct those chosen myself, so that everyone is fully cognizant of the difficulties involved."

As the lift doors closed behind the science officer, Kirk turned to the still-silent McCoy. "What's your professional opinion of Delminnen, Bones?"

"You mean, does he appear sane?"

Kirk gave a twisted smile. "Nothing so obvious. What I want to know is . . . is he sane enough? Or is he likely to go off the deep end when we knock on his front door and ask him to accompany us?"

"Well, he's arrogant, suspicious, and possibly a borderline paranoid, but I don't think he's homicidal, Jim. And his arrogance is rather reassuring."

Kirk frowned in puzzlement.

"He's too certain of his own importance to be suicidal," McCoy explained.

"I hope you're right. In any case, you'll have an opportunity to make a firsthand diagnosis any minute. You're coming down with Spock and me."

"Me? What for?"

"Our orders say to utilize all necessary means to bring Delminnen and his sister back with us. If he becomes violent and we have to be less than tactful with him, I want you along to pick up the pieces." Kirk pushed against the arms of the chair and sighed resignedly. "Let's get it over with."

"Captain!"

Kirk turned from the lift to look sharply back at the helm. "What is it, Mr. Sulu?"

The helmsman was working hastily with a bank of instruments that had been silent the entire journey from Babel. They were all suddenly active.

"Detectors indicate another vessel emerging from the planet's shadow."

Kirk rushed back to his seat. "Identification?"

"Not possible yet."

"Mr. Arex, have you a fix on her?"

"Yes, Captain," came the gentle, whistling reply. "It is a capital ship, apparently non-Federation in origin."

"Full magnification on the forward scanners, Mr. Sulu."

The screen lit up, giving a view of the slowly turning gas giant. Suddenly the intruder seemed to leap forward, to show an irregular, though clearly artificial, shape outlined against the brilliant hues of the planet's dense atmosphere.

"That's a Klingon cruiser, Jim," McCoy declared.

"I can see that, Bones," Kirk muttered. "Mr. Sulu, sound red alert. Mr. Arex, align phasers to—"

"Receiving transmission from the Klingon ship, Captain," Uhura interrupted.

"Acknowledge their signal, Lieutenant." He turned an expectant gaze to the viewscreen.

The Klingon who appeared there was seated in his counterpart of Kirk's command chair, but his height was evident nonetheless. His attitude was one of relaxed attention—in fact, he very nearly slouched. Except for the tight set of his lips and the churning one might detect beneath unusually bushy brows, he appeared almost friendly. And when the image had fully resolved at both ends of the transmission, he even smiled.

"Well, well . . . it is true what is said about the false size of the universe. I have been expecting and dreading such a meeting for many years.

"How have you been, Jim?"

A soft sigh of air on the bridge came as several jaws dropped simultaneously.

"He called you 'Jim,' " McCoy finally whispered in astonishment. "You two *know* each other?" But Kirk continued to stare at the screen, ignoring the question.

"Hello, Kumara. It *is* you?"

"It is indeed none other, old friend. A strange place, after so many years, for a reunion, is it not?"

"Jim!" McCoy was fairly dancing with curiosity.

"Not now, Bones," Kirk replied firmly. His voice rose as he addressed the attentive figure on the screen. "Yes, it's a strange place for a reunion, Commander . . . it is 'Commander' now, isn't it?"

The figure smiled again and nodded.

"In fact, it's such a strange place that I wonder what you're doing here. This system is far off Imperial patrol routes."

The Klingon commander shifted in his seat. "A reasonable question, Jim. One which I might equally well ask of you. But since you inquired first . . . I have been instructed by the Imperial Resources Bureau to survey this system with regard to locating salvageable resources. While I will concede its greater proximity to the Federation sphere, you will recognize that it has not been formally claimed by your government. Therefore, we have as much right here as you.

"You are welcome to whatever you may find, though. With the slight exception of the sun-forsaken bit of sand you now orbit, our explorations have proven singularly unprofitable. There is practically nothing here worthy of Imperial attention . . . doubly true when one considers the distance to the nearest Imperial world.

"But enough of business!" The smile widened. "It is good to see you again, Jim. I invite you to share a container of Gellian *vitz* with me. Would you do me the honor of joining me aboard, say, ten of your minutes from now? Or, if you prefer, I can come aboard the *Enterprise*."

Kirk smiled in return. "No, your ship will be fine. The honor is mine, Kumara. I accept."

"I am gratified. Till then . . ."

Kirk's smile held until the Klingon commander's image had vanished. His expression turned grim, and he snapped at the chair pickup.

"Transporter Room—stand by to transport landing party. Mr. Spock?"

"Here, Captain," the reply came.

"Red alert was sounded because there's a Klingon cruiser in the area. All personnel are to transport down with one hand on their sidearms."

"Very good, Captain."

Kirk clicked off, and McCoy had to run to reach the elevator with him. "Why the rush, Jim? You can't possibly expect to get Delminnen and his sister off-moon in time to make your appointment with this Kumara."

Kirk's tone was low, curt. "Listen, Bones, Kumara may just be the best starship commander the Klingons have. You can bet your precision nerve welder the Emperor didn't send him this far from base to play prospector! I'll also bet that hypothetical bottle of Gellian *vitz* he mentioned that he's here because Klingon intelligence got wind of that Federation prospector's report. They're prospecting, all right—and if they get their hands on Delminnen, they'll mine him for all he's worth and they won't be too concerned about putting him back together when they've finished with him."

McCoy hesitated momentarily. "Jim, I asked you if you knew this Kumara . . . personally, I meant. You waved me off. Where do you know each other from so well that you immediately call each other by first names?"

"Is it that important, Bones?"

"Well, now, I don't know, Jim," McCoy said evenly. "When two enemy captains display a certain degree of familiarity unheard of in previous—"

"All right," Kirk broke in, turning to face the doctor. "Yes, Kumara and I know each other on an informal basis. Did you ever hear of the FEA, Bones?"

McCoy considered. "No . . . no, wait a second. The Friendship Exchange Action, wasn't it?"

Kirk nodded. "Remember what it was about?"

"Sure—it was well documented in all the psychology journals. Was set up during one of those brief friendly periods between the Federation and the Klingon Empire. Some bright medical theorist thought it might promote understanding between peoples if academy cadets from both cultures spent some time in close contact with one another. The program was limited to command candidates, if I remember right."

"It was and you do," Kirk acknowledged as the lift doors slid apart.

"Do what?" Spock inquired politely, and Kirk was forced to explain as he and McCoy entered the Transporter Room.

"Gentlemen, Kumara is one of the sharpest, smartest individuals I've ever met, and we can be thankful the Empire hasn't another dozen like him. He's also the only Klingon I've encountered who wasn't so puffed up with his own importance that he ignored his opponent's capabilities. And he expects us to believe he's here for casual 'exploration'!"

"Begging your pardon, Captain," Spock commented, "but this still doesn't explain how you come to address each other in so familiar a fashion."

"Oh, that. We were roommates, Mr. Spock." He led them into the transporter alcove.

Five armed crew members were already there, each standing at the ready on his respective disk. One small, dark-skinned man saluted as the three officers stepped up into the alcove.

"Ensign Gemas and landing party reporting ready, sir."

"Very good, Ensign." Kirk looked at the waiting group. "We may have to move fast . . . be prepared for anything."

Short, confident nods; a few muffled "ayes."

Kirk turned to face the console. "Scotty, I want you to stay with us at all times. Keep the transporter energized. If I'm right about our obliging visitor, we may have to come aboard in a hurry."

"No need to worry, Captain. I'm not movin' until you're all back right where you are now."

"Good. Try to set us down about fifty meters from the surface transmitter coordinates . . . in some cover, if information is sufficient to permit it."

Scotty manipulated the instrumentation, and Kirk saw him waver and disappear. He wondered if an armed Klingon would replace the tense figure of his chief engineer.

The security-team members were already drawing their phasers as they materialized. They landed light-footed, owing to the weak gravity, breathing short and fast in the thin air. A few stars shone through the violet sky, and the immense globe of Theta Draconis Five hung like a baleful candy eye above the far horizon.

A few scraggly, ground-hugging shreds of greenish-brown resembling dying kelp shivered in the lee of well-worn boulders, offering the only defiance to the terribly-near sterility of naked space.

Sixteen eyes studied the unimpressive surroundings until they were satisfied as to its harmlessness. McCoy pointed to the east.

"There it is, Jim."

A low, rambling group of single-story interconnecting building modules thrust out of the sand nearby. They clustered near a huge metallic bubble like termites around a bloated queen.

Kirk sniffed at the odd, unsatisfying atmosphere. "Maybe I'm wrong," he muttered. "I hope so." He took a step toward the buildings.

Displaced air let out a soprano scream as a blue beam passed near his right shoulder. It struck a boulder behind, sending rock splinters flying. One crewman clutched at his shoulder as he spun to the sand.

"Take cover! Spread out and return fire!" Kirk yelled, even as he dove for the nearest clump of rocks. Spock was at his side, his phaser out and firing as he hit the ground. McCoy had hold of the injured crewman's legs and was pulling him to shelter, analyzing the man's surface wound at the same time.

Kirk peered around the left side of a hunk of basalt. The source of the beams was the near bank of a dry streambed. Silhouettes of the beam-wielders were readily identifiable. Phaser beams began to strike the edge of the bank, fusing sand and gravel and sending rock fragments flying. The Klingon landing party was well protected.

"It would appear that your initial estimate of Commander Kumara was correct, Captain," Spock observed as his beam singed the hair of a too-anxious Klingon.

"Yes. Still, it's not like him to assume a formal defensive position like this and slug it out. More likely we surprised him just as his party set down. Spock, if this fight goes against him, I don't think he would hesitate to destroy the Delminnens to keep them and their device from falling into non-Imperial hands. I'm going to try to get them clear of that complex before the Klingons decide to blow it to bits. Give me all the covering fire you can."

There was a pause while the instructions were relayed to the other members of the landing party. Then they unleashed a furious burst of phaser firepower as Kirk dashed for the nearest wall of the modular cluster.

Something warm went by his right ear, humming like a wasp. He dove, rolled, and came up behind the wall of the outermost structure. A quick glance around the edge revealed that the Klingons were fully occupied with the rest of the *Enterprise*'s landing party.

Reaching up, Kirk felt his ear. A blister was beginning to form, so near had the beam been. But he still had all of him.

Sliding along the wall in an attempt to remain concealed from those inside as well as everyone outside, he finally reached a thick window. It took a moment to make the proper adjustment to his hand phaser. Then, using it like a torch, he carefully melted down the window plastic.

A cautious peek showed the interior of a comfortable, den-like room. It was dark and deserted. Resetting his phaser on stun, he put one leg over the sill and eased himself into the room. It was empty.

Kirk took out his communicator and flipped it open. Suddenly someone screamed.

Sound, left; door, closed; reaction—that which is quickest rather than that which is planned.

The door opened easily. At the far end of the half-laboratory, half-living quarters, Kumara was supporting an unconscious Van Delminnen while wrestling with a struggling woman. Her features were softer, less aquiline than Delminnen's, but the resemblance was unmistakable.

Kumara was juggling his communicator along with the two bodies. Looking up, he saw Kirk framed in the doorway and froze.

Thawing was rapid. "Up, fool," he shouted into his communicator. "Beam us up or it's your head! Beam—" He was forced to drop his communicator in order to hold on to Char Delminnen.

Kirk was running toward the trio as they began to fade. "Scotty—up!" was all he had time to yell into his own communicator.

On board the *Enterprise*, Scott heard the brief command and spoke to his assistant. "Don't stand there like you've seen Loch Nessie, mon—let's get him up!" Sure hands commenced rapid manipulation of precision controls.

The figure of Kirk began to scintillate at the edges. At the same time, he threw himself, arms outstretched toward the three figures. Confused energies interacted in a brilliant display of condensed high-power pyrotechnics.

The reaction on board the *Enterprise* was smaller but no less spectacular. Lights that should have remained dark flashed brightly on the transporter console. Gauges which ought to have stayed quiescent suddenly danced as if afflicted by a mechanical Saint Vitus' dance. Sparks arched indecently from switch to closed contact and back again.

Scott's mind was in turmoil, but he held himself steady as he adjusted, realigned, and compensated, glancing nervously from the console to the still-vacant transporter alcove.

"Come on, Captain," he whispered tightly, "come *on*."

He shoved one switch forward another notch. Four jumbled, indistinct shapes began to form within the alcove. They flickered in and out like boat lights in a fog.

"Engineering," he called to the open directional pickup, "Main Transporter Room, Chief Scott speaking. I want all the power transporter circuits will carry—or you'll be carryin' it with your hands next time!"

He shoved the crucial control into the red. As he did so, the four shapes grew more distinct, almost materialized.

The control hit the far end of the slot.

Metal ran like water, and intricate components turned to blobs of expensive slag. Tiny popping sounds came from within the console's base.

Kirk and a young woman solidified. Simultaneously, the other two indistinct images abruptly disappeared. Kirk wavered, his leg muscles rippling uncontrollably; then he collapsed to the floor, rolling out of the alcove. The woman fell on top of him.

"Captain!" Waving at the acrid smoke which now curled about the ruined console, Scott staggered around its edge, moving to a wall intercom. "Sick Bay . . . corpsman to the Main Transporter Room, on the double! Chief Kyle?"

"Here, sir," came the reply.

"Stand by second-level transporter . . . we've still got a landing party on the surface."

"Standing by, sir."

Spock studied the ravine ahead, turned, and called back to the rest of the team. "Cease firing . . . they've transported clear." He turned his attention toward the cluster of structures as a figure wriggled up alongside him.

"You think they've given up the fight, Spock?" wondered McCoy, his attention likewise riveted on the buildings.

"The fight . . . yes," commented Spock unsurely. "The war . . . I don't know. I wish I knew as much about this Klingon Kumara as the captain seems to. He may already be back on board . . . someone used a communicator a little while ago."

A tremendous explosion caused both men to bury their heads in the sand. Bits of metal and plastic and other nonmetallic debris, mixed with sand and rock, rained down on them.

They looked up. When the dust and smoke cleared, they saw a small crater where the metal bubble and its attendant structures had stood.

McCoy looked questioningly at Spock. "If the captain's *not* already on board . . ."

Spock merely nodded, flipped open his communicator. "Spock to *Enterprise* . . . beam us up. What"—he stumbled over the words, an indication of how he felt—"what word on the captain?"

"He's aboard and all right, Mr. Spock," came the filtered burr of Chief Engineer Scott, much to the relief of both men. "But somethin' . . . I dinna know what yet . . . went wrong with the transporter. Nurse Chapel is treatin' him. Stand by to beam up."

They materialized in a room different from the one they had left. Disorientation lasted only a moment; then Spock addressed the security team. "Ensign Gemas, dismiss your people. You," he said to the injured crewman, "report to Sick Bay and have that shoulder treated."

"Tell whoever's on duty to use the extractor, son," McCoy added. "You've still got some stone shrapnel imbedded in the muscle." The man nodded, wincing painfully.

McCoy, was the first to enter the rubble of the still-smoke-filled Transporter Room, saw the two seated figures propped against the wall flanking the alcove.

"Jim!" He hurried over to the captain, knelt, and looked at Nurse Chapel.

"Nervous shock, Doctor," she explained in a professional tone, "complicated by extended trauma of unknown origin."

"Thank you, Chapel. I'll take over here. Help her." He indicated the blank-eyed woman slumped against the wall, and Chapel moved to do so. Spock bent to study the woman also.

McCoy examined Kirk hurriedly, pulled a hypo from a kit Chapel had brought, and administered it. While he waited for the drug to take effect, he glanced curiously back toward the transporter console, where Scott and his assistant were busily examining its cauterized innards.

"What happened, Mr. Scott?"

The chief engineer stared a moment longer at the intricate circuit board—its fluid-state switches a mass of thin goo, its hundreds of microchips forming metal stalactites on its edge—and he shook his head dolefully.

"I dinna know, Doctor. One minute there were four figures beamin' in, then they'd fade almost to nothing, then grow solid again. In an' out, in an' out, no matter how fine we calibrated the resolution or how much power we poured into materialization. I finally decided to pull 'em in with everythin' we had. The captain came through all right and so did the young lady, but the other two, whoever they were, disappeared. Dinna ask me where to."

McCoy would have pressed for details, but Kirk was groaning and moving his head.

"Doctor," Spock declared with concern, "this one is not responding to stimuli." Chapel indicated agreement.

"Get a stretcher detail up here, Chapel, and have her moved to Sick Bay."

"Yes, Doctor." She moved to issue the necessary order. Spock leaned close to Kirk and looked up at McCoy.

"He's coming around. I don't know what happened to them when the transporter went crazy, but the effects were just this side of overpowering."

A pair of medical techs appeared with a wheelabout between them, and McCoy watched as the woman was gently placed on the mobile bed and rolled from the room.

Kirk let out a loud moan, diverting their attention.

"Captain, can you reason?" inquired Spock anxiously. "Do you know where you are?"

Kirk only groaned again.

Spock looked worriedly at McCoy. "What are the possible effects on someone held in transport for too long, Doctor?"

McCoy shrugged slightly. "No one knows for certain what happens to the mind in extended transport, Spock. Transporters used under normal conditions are foolproof. Under abnormal conditions, we just don't know enough about what actually takes place. There are two known cases of people who were in transport when there was an all-systems power failure, backups included. They were finally brought in, but in a coma from which they never emerged."

He looked back to Kirk, just as the captain opened his eyes and blinked. "Where are the others?"

At the sound of Kirk's voice, Scott left analysis of the ruined transporter console to his assistant. "Thank the saints you're all right, Captain."

"Thank *you*, Scotty." Kirk stood up, rubbing at his forehead. "You've heard of locking someone in a water-filled, lightless tank so that they experience near-total sensory deprivation, Bones?"

"I'm familiar with the therapy, Jim."

"Well, I just experienced the opposite extreme." He looked around the room. "Am I the only one who came through?"

"No, Captain," Scott informed him. "There was a young lady as well. And there appeared to be at least two other figures, but for some reason the transporter malfunctioned and we couldn't hold them." He looked at the deck. "I fear they've gone to where no one can find them."

"No, Scotty, and don't blame yourself. Your transporter didn't fail. Our friend Kumara was all set to have himself and the Delminnens beamed back to his ship while we supposedly sat around and waited for the big reunion. I inconveniently barged in on him as he was preparing to do just that.

"As soon as he saw me he ordered his techs to beam himself and the Delminnens up. I didn't have time to do anything but make the same request of you, Scotty, and take a dive for the three of them, hoping our transporter could overpower theirs. Looks like it ended up a tie." He glanced over at Spock. "I see you got back safely Spock. Casualties?"

"One injured, Captain," the first officer reported. "Not seriously."

"Good. Maintain red alert. Where's the girl . . . Char Delminnen?"

"In Sick Bay by now, Jim," McCoy explained. "She's suffering from shock also. I ran a quick test on her, and I suppose your shock was induced by the same thing. Some of your blood got switched around in all the transporting confusion—veins to arteries and vice versa. Your shock was induced by temporary oxygen starvation." He shook his head. "Wait till they read about that in the *Starfleet Medical Journal*."

"Will she be all right?"

"I expect so. She's probably coming out of it even as we're talking."

"Captain . . . ?" Scott looked pensive.

"Yes, what is it, Scotty?"

"You'll pardon me for sayin' so, but you took the devil of a chance intersectin' transporter fields like that. No wonder everythin' went overload. You could've had a lot more than your hemoglobin switched around."

"I know, Scotty," Kirk replied solemnly. "I knew it at the time. But there was nothing else to do. At least Char Delminnen's safe."

"Wonderful for her," McCoy noted bitterly, "but the one we came for is either dead or, more likely, on board the Klingon cruiser."

"A situation we're going to have to rectify, Bones."

"Message from the bridge, sir," came a call from an ensign standing by the wall intercom. Kirk hurried to take his position.

"Transporter Room, Kirk here."

Sulu's voice was excited, tense. "Captain, the Klingon cruiser appears to be picking up speed. Indications are she's retracing her original approach."

"Lay in a tracking course, Mr. Sulu. Don't let her slow speed fool you—Kumara's trying to get into the shadow of the gas giant. If he can do that, he'll move to maximum speed immediately, before we can get a fix on him. Don't let him out of detector range."

"Yes, *sir*!"

Kirk moved to rejoin McCoy and Spock.

"What is it, Jim?"

"Van Delminnen's on board the Klingon ship all right. Kumara's now trying to sneak out of the system and run for cover. We're going after him, Bones."

"Was that indicated in the orders, Captain?" wondered Spock.

Kirk threw his first officer a hard look. "The orders were

to bring back the Delminnens, Mr. Spock, utilizing whatever methods were necessary."

"A blanket authorization with regard to the persons of the Delminnens, Captain," Spock persisted, "but does that justify pursuit of an enemy ship?"

"They can quibble over the semantics later, Mr. Spock," Kirk declared. "*After* Van Delminnen is safely delivered to the nearest Starfleet base." He stalked toward the lift.

A sudden surge rocked them as the lift opened onto the bridge. Kirk moved immediately to his command position while Spock took his place at the science station. McCoy hovered nearby, feeling helpless as usual, despite the benefits his presence always brought to a tense bridge.

"Report, Mr. Sulu."

"Captain, as soon as we started to move, they increased their speed slightly. I adjusted our own to match, at which point they accelerated again. Thanks to your warning, Mr. Arex and I anticipated it and matched velocity once more. We are still within detector range, traveling at warp-six." He checked a readout. "But we are not making up any distance on them."

"I didn't expect we would be, Mr. Sulu," replied Kirk. "They're certain to be traveling at their maximum safe speed . . . for now. That's going to have to change. Mr. Spock?"

"Yes, Captain?"

"Did you discover anything in the Delminnen complex which might have been the weapon?"

"Unfortunately, we never had the opportunity to look. Do not look alarmed, Captain—neither did the Klingons."

Kirk relaxed visibly.

"The Delminnen residence, laboratories, and any conceivable weapon were completely destroyed by a timed device planted by the Klingons soon after you entered the outer structure. We were unable to prevent the destruction. Considering the manner in which the Klingons departed, it seems reasonable to assume that the device was intended to detonate with all of us inside the complex. It seems rather wasteful. I am surprised the Klingons did not attempt to recover the device itself."

"I'm not, Spock. Kumara never liked to take chances. Having captured one major piece, he opted to blow up the board. Obviously, he's convinced Delminnen can be persuaded to give him the plans for the device." He stared grimly at the starfield displayed on the main screen. "The Klingons can be most persuasive."

He paused, mulling multiples of light over in his mind. "Spock, what is the nearest Klingon military base of importance in this region?"

"A moment, Captain." Spock bent over the library computer and reported quickly. "According to what information we have, there is a naval base of considerable size on Shahkur Nine."

"Do we have coordinates for said world?"

"Yes, Captain. They are imprecise, however."

"*Hmm.*" Kirk turned to the helm. "Mr. Arex, assuming Shahkur lies at the closest possible point given by those imprecise stats, compute the time we can expect to have before ships from that world could be expected to rendezvous with Kumara—and with the *Enterprise*."

Arex's triple hands worked busily at the navigation console, extrapolating from a simple yet crucial series of numbers. He expressed no worry, no excitement over the results. That was the Edoan way. Emotions were subdued, but not supressed as they were among the inhabitants of Vulcan.

"Assuming both vessels maintain their current velocity, Captain, I give us no more than forty-eight standard hours."

"Maximum?"

"Given the restrictions of questionable coordinates for Shahkur . . . yes. That figure is for vessels of the *Enterprise*'s class out from Shahkur. Lesser classes would take longer, of course."

"But we can't assume they'll send lesser-class ships." He glanced back at Spock. "This Shahkur Nine is supposed to be a *major* base, Mr. Spock?"

"Yes, Captain."

Kirk looked resigned. "Then we'd better assume Kumara will meet additional cruisers in a couple of days. That gives us very little time to rescue Delminnen."

"Or to kill him, Captain," reminded Spock quietly.

Kirk's voice was flat. "Or to kill him."

* * *

It was silent on the bridge for several of those forty-eight hours. Silent, but far from inactive, as Kirk and Spock considered the options open to them in the shrinking time available.

The stillness was too much for McCoy, finally. He had checked half a dozen times on the condition of the injured security specialist and paid an equal number of visits to Char Delminnen—all a waste of time, as the specialist's injury was minor and Nurse Chapel had the woman under mild sedation.

"Well, what are we going to do, Jim? We could call for help ourselves, but that would bring a Federation fleet into contact with a Klingon force of possibly equal size. Then we'd have a nice little interstellar war on our hands."

"I know, Bones. That's why we're going to have to resolve this one alone, without help."

"If we run into three or four Klingon cruisers, it'll be resolved all right," McCoy observed sardonically.

"Captain," Spock began, "if I may suggest the obvious . . . ?"

Both men turned to look at him.

"If we go to emergency power, we should be able to get within phaser range."

"All we need for that to work, Spock, is to have a normal, belligerent, cocky commander on board the Klingon ship. Instead, we have to contend with Kumara. I tell you, Spock, we can't apply the usual standards here!

"If we go to emergency power, you know what will happen? Kumara will laugh fit to split his collar. He would love to see us burn out our nacelles trying to get within phaser range. The moment we got close enough to tickle his tail, *he'd* go on emergency power and keep right on running until overload. Then we'd both drift along on impulse power with charred converters—straight toward Shahkur Nine and the oncoming Klingon relief force."

"As much faith as I have in Scotty and his engineers, I can't risk that." Kirk's brow furrowed. "But Bones is right. We can't continue on like this without trying something. Let me know, Mr. Spock, how this sounds to you . . ."

VI

There was quiet jubilation on the bridge of the Klingon cruiser. Everyone on board knew that the mission had been partly successful. And if the presence of the peculiar human on board wasn't proof enough, the presence of the trailing Federation cruiser was.

A certain amount of grumbling among the elder officers followed the commander's refusal to turn and engage their pursuer. Running away was alien to the soul of any Klingon warrior. But the younger officers harbored no such feelings, though they were as brave as their superiors. They realized that Commander Kumara's orders were best for the Empire, best for the ship and best for themselves.

So they contented themselves with the knowledge that their pursuer was traveling under the impetus of mounting frustration.

"Commander," the helmsman reported smartly, "the Federation ship is remaining constant relative to our position. Should we utilize emergency power to increase the distance between us?"

"I'm rather fond of our present distance, Lieutenant Kritt, and see no reason to change it. We will maintain our present speed unless we are *compelled* to do otherwise, and we will maintain it without straining our resources. Restrain from public exhibition of your foolishness, and think."

"I abase myself, Honored Commander," the helmsman replied as he strove to comprehend Kumara's point.

For his part, the commander continued his idle study of the viewscreen. His rear scanners showed the pursuing *Enterprise*, only a distant, barely moving dot against the blackness of space—space which one day would be a part of the Empire, as the Great Gods intended it should be.

"Lieutenant, there is a game humans play, a game Vulcans play. It is called chess. Ever hear of it?"

Kritt turned from his console, confident that the heathen Federation ship was still a safe distance behind, and succeeded in looking earnestly puzzled.

"A human game? Hardly, Commander. Why do you ask?"

"I suspected you had not. Few of us have, preferring to languish in contempt of anything not Klingon; and that is much to be deplored. You might look it up in the archives sometime. The knowledge would do you good.

"Were Captain Kirk and I presently to be engaged in such a game, I would say I have him dangerously in check, with the next move being his."

"Ah," observed Kritt, brightening, "it is something like *bagap*, then?"

Kumara considered, then indicated approval. "There are similarities, yes, though *bagap* is a much faster game. And chess is played with little wooden idols on a plastic or celluloid field, instead of with live slaves."

"It sounds very dull."

"Be assured, it is not." Kumara's manner shifted abruptly from one of casual camaraderie and introspection to that of the complete dictator. "Under no circumstances are we to engage emergency power unless the *Enterprise* does so first! Make certain all concerned understand this implicitly!"

"At once, Commander," Kritt shot back, relaxing now that his superior was once more the model of Klingon leadership . . .

"Kumara," Kirk explained to the attentive Spock as McCoy listened in, "is difficult to surprise, but there's no reason to suppose that his subordinates are anything other than the usual Klingon ratings. That means they'll be contemptuous, secure in their present tactical position—and overconfident. I'm hoping that will also make them just lazy enough."

"Lazy enough for what, Jim?" McCoy wondered.

"You'll see. Mr. Spock, have the shuttlecraft readied for departure."

Spock's eyebrows lifted in surprise. "The *shuttlecraft*, Captain?"

"That's right. Make certain it's fully fueled."

Spock moved to his library-science station and directed his words to the intercom pickup. "First Officer Spock to Shuttle Bay. Prepare Shuttle One for immediate flight." He looked back across at Kirk.

"Pilot and course, Captain?"

"There will be no pilot, Spock. The shuttle will run on automatics which will be guided by the *Enterprise*'s battle computer."

"Now I'm thoroughly confused, Jim," McCoy muttered.

"With luck, the Klingons will be too, Bones. Mr. Arex, set a course for the shuttle: zero degrees inclination to plane of present course." Then he recited a plot which even McCoy was able to recognize.

"But . . . that's *our* present course, Jim."

Kirk smiled back at him. "I'm not fooling anyone, you see. The simplest device is often the best. Everyone keeps an eye out for the least obvious." He addressed the chair pickup. "Engineering?"

"Engineering, Scott here. Are we goin' to make a run at them finally, Captain?"

"After a fashion, Scotty. I'm going to want every milligram of push you can coax out of those engines in a few minutes. We're going to have to push them right to the limit."

"You'll have whatever you need, Captain."

At the rear of the *Enterprise*, twin clamshell doors slid back to reveal a high, well-lit chamber—the shuttlecraft hangar. Tiny wisps of frozen air, missed by the recyclers, puffed out from the crack which appeared between the doors.

Spock listened for a moment, then turned to report, "Shuttlecraft One ready for launch, Captain."

Kirk took a deep, hopeful breath. "All right. Ready, everyone. Mr. Sulu, I want full emergency power."

"Aye, sir." Sulu activated the necessary controls. A steady, rarely heard whine began to build on the bridge as the *Enterprise*'s immense engines labored to comply.

* * *

On board the Klingon cruiser, Lieutenant Kritt suddenly bent close over his console and stared intently at the readouts from the rear-facing scanners.

"Commander, the Federation ship is closing on us!" He paused to check the information with the helmsman. "Reports confirmed—they are increasing speed rapidly."

Kumara frowned slightly, and peered at the growing dot on the viewscreen. He searched his mind for possibilities, but found nothing but groundless conjecture.

"I had expected something more elaborate from James Kirk. Even so, he *is* pressed for time. He must know we will contact Shahkur Base and request reinforcement soon." He barked an order at Kritt. "Prepare to go on emergency power."

Sulu was busy studying the information his own scanners were sending back to him. "We're gaining on them, sir."

"Speed, Mr. Sulu?"

"Warp-seven . . . coming up on warp-eight, maximum speed."

"Push her as far as she'll stand, Lieutenant."

Sulu shoved down the final switch, pressed the last button, and turned his attention to a bank of small dials. All were creeping steadily into the red at the end of each scale.

"Definitely closing on the Klingon ship, Captain," Arex reported with a touch of excitement.

"Engine temperature rising rapidly, Captain," Spock reported.

On board the Klingon cruiser, Kumara examined the flow of information and muttered into a pickup. "Stand by, Engineering. Not yet, Kritt," he added, noticing one of the navigator's hands hovering tensely over a control. "Learn patience and attain permanence."

"Converter temperature is nearing the melting point, Captain," Spock reported, not looking up from his instrumentation. "Coming up on phaser range. Shall I prepare to fire?"

"Negative, Mr. Spock." There was a beep at his arm. "What is it, Scotty?"

The chief engineer's worried voice sounded distantly over the speaker, distorted by the now deafening whine of the engines.

"Captain, we canna keep this up much longer without melting something critical!"

"Hold steady a bit longer, Scotty."

"A bit is all it'll be. Captain. Engineerin' out."

"Exalted Commander," a worried Kritt said, looking anxiously from his console back at Kumara, "they'll be within phaser range any minute."

"Gently, Lieutenant, gently."

Spock's tone never changed, only the information was modulated. "Engine temperature nearing the critical point, Captain." He turned and looked at Kirk, with an expression that said more lucidly than words, Do now whatever you've got a mind to do.

Kirk hesitated no longer.

"Launch shuttlecraft!"

Spock gave the order and reported promptly, "Shuttlecraft away and locked on course."

"Cut emergency power . . . reduce speed to warp-six."

"Reducing speed," Sulu responded.

"Engine temperature dropping rapidly, Captain," Spock announced. As he did so, the temperature on the bridge also seemed to drop noticeably.

"Engineering, report," Kirk said into the pickup. There was a long moment before Scott's tired voice replied.

"Engineerin' . . . We almost lost one of the dilithium chambers. You cut it mighty near, Captain."

"Sorry, Scotty. Had to. Congratulate everyone back there for me. For all of us."

"I will, Captain . . . as soon as they stop tremblin'. Engineering out." Scott clicked off, moved to the central console, and planted a wet kiss of gratitude on a certain gauge which had yet again moved him one minute nearer a comfortable retirement.

"What now, Jim?" McCoy wondered aloud, staring at the viewscreen. Their quarry was no longer a distant glowing pinpoint, but now a definite inimical silhouette.

"I'd estimate about five minutes, Bones." Kirk chewed his lower lip and tried to see deeper than the ship's scanners . . .

***

On board the Klingon cruiser, Lieutenant Kritt leaned back in his stiff, unyielding seat and spoke with satisfaction. "Commander, the Federation ship's position is once again constant with respect to ours. They are no longer closing distance."

If he expected his exalted superior to look pleased, he was disappointed. Sometimes Kumara could be as impassive as a Vulcan. The commander gave every sign of having expected the good news.

"I thought they couldn't maintain that speed much longer, Lieutenant," he commented easily, before turning his attention to the intercom. "Engineering, stand down. Emergency power will not be required." He looked back at the screen, murmuring half to himself, "Nice bluff, James Kirk, but you should know better than to try to panic me."

"Pardons, Commander," Kritt wondered, "but aren't we going to utilize emergency power to reopen the distance between our ships? They are extremely close now."

"Extremely, but not dangerously so, Lieutenant. Have you learned nothing? They could only have hoped to prod us into straining our own resources—something," he added smugly, "we will not do. So long as we remain out of phaser range, they might as well be a dozen system-units behind, for all the harm they can do us. Nor do I believe their vessel has the capacity to repeat that maneuver again before we are contacted by relief ships from Shahkur Base." He looked well pleased with himself.

"Then there is the delicious irony of the situation."

Kritt looked confused. "Irony, Commander?"

"Do you not see it? Fah! I am assisted by blind men. Not only has their attempt to pressure us failed completely, Lieutenant, but now they must bear the additional torment of following us at much closer range. Close enough for their scanners to read our registration numbers—close enough for them to sense our smiles, you see."

Kritt turned back to his readouts and studied them, his gaze shifting thoughtfully from the tiny unemotional figures back to the main screen with its portrait of the pursuing *Enterprise*. "I think I do, Commander. I think . . ."

***

Spock noted the latest readings of separation and reported, "The enemy vessel is maintaining course and speed, Captain."

"No evidence of increasing her speed?"

"No, Captain. Apparently they are content to remain at this distance."

"Good. Mr. Spock, prepare for remote converter override of the shuttlecraft's engine. Remove safeties and cancel failsafes. Mr. Sulu, *now* you can energize the forward phasers."

Realization dawned on the helmsman's face, and he bent to the task gleefully. The purpose was slower in coming to McCoy; Spock had already guessed it.

"An excellent idea, Captain," the first officer commented approvingly. "It requires only that the Klingons act as Klingons. Given that, the possibilities for success are substantial."

"So *that's* it!" McCoy declared. "You really think it will change the status quo, Jim?"

"I'm hopeful, Bones. A lot depends on their instrumentation being so tied up with monitoring our every sneeze that they'll overlook an object the size of the shuttle. They know we're well out of photon-torpedo range—but the shuttle's engine is capable of covering a good deal more space.

"Of course, it would be a useless effort if Kumara's ship was undertaking defensive maneuvers. But it's not. They're simply cruising along an unwavering course."

"Shuttle closing on enemy vessel, sir," Arex reported.

Everyone on the bridge stared at the screen, trying to spot the minute spark that would be the shuttle. Detectors tracked it easily, though, where the naked eye failed.

At one end of the *Klathas*'s bridge an officer suddenly squinted, staring hard and uncertainly at an unexpectedly active screen, noting a small but potentially significant reading. It might be nothing. Probably was, in which case he risked exposing himself to embarrassment and ridicule.

On the other hand, if the instrumentation was doing its job . . . and mechanicals were immune to insult.

"Commander?" he finally said, electing to tempt the gods.

"Yes? What is it, Korreg?"

"Exalted One, I wish you would give your opinion of

this. It appears to be a very oddly formed meteoric body which—"

Kumara barely had time to look startled before dashing down to stare over the scanner-control officer's shoulder. When he saw the activated screen and matched it against the reading nearby, he turned a light purple.

"IDIOT!"

Korreg winced, not sure whether he'd exercised the proper option.

Kumara didn't have time to enlighten him. That would come soon enough . . . perhaps lethally.

"Engineering!" he roared into the intercom. "Full emergency power—maximum thrust!"

"But, Commander," a hesitant voice replied, "you just said—"

"I want full emergency thrust immediately or I'll personally pull your eyes from your head, Kanndad!"

"Ye—yes, Commander! At once!"

"Captain," Sulu cried, "the Klingon ship is increasing her speed. They appear to be going on emerg—"

"Present shuttlecraft position, Lieutenant!" Kirk barked, cutting the helmsman off.

"Shuttle is nearing critical radius, Captain," Sulu reported, more in control of himself now, though the tenseness remained in his voice. "Wait . . . distance is increasing. Klingon cruiser beginning to pull—"

"Spock! Exercise engine override—*now*!"

The first officer touched a switch. Kilometers of circuitry sent a single, brief signal to the racing shuttle, still traveling ahead of the now slowed *Enterprise* at her launch speed of warp-eight. The on-board shuttlecraft computer was simple compared to the massive machine mind on board the starship, but it was fully capable of interpreting that concise command.

A few relays opened, protesting controls were ignored, normal modifiers were shunted aside as the shuttle obediently self-destructed. As it did so, a stunning flash of white radiance momentarily blinded the *Enterprise*'s forward scanners.

The effects of that silent explosion on the *Klathas* were somewhat more extreme.

"Report, Mr. Sulu," Kirk demanded, mentally crossing his fingers. "Status of Klingon cruiser?"

The helmsman double-checked his instrumentation to be certain before announcing, "She's losing speed, Captain . . . dropping below warp-seven . . . below warp-six. We're moving into phaser range."

"It worked, Jim," McCoy observed, a note of satisfaction and admiration in his voice.

Kirk didn't sound enthusiastic. "We don't know how well it worked, Bones. The range was extreme, and expanding even as I gave Spock the order. We've obviously disabled her, damaging her engines, but her offensive weaponry may still be intact and fully operational. Now comes the difficult part."

"You mean attacking?"

"No. Trying to convince Kumara that he's got to surrender. Stand by forward phasers and torpedo banks. Mr. Sulu."

"Standing by, sir," replied the helmsman firmly.

Emergency ventilators were rapidly clearing the *Klathas*'s bridge of smoke and dangerous freed gases. The sounds of coughing and the crew's gasps for decent air provided an unnerving accompaniment to Kumara's efforts to regain the command seat. He had been ungently thrown from that position when the shuttlecraft's engine exploded.

Painfully, he hauled himself to a sitting position in the chair, favoring the arm he had fallen on. A careful yet rapid survey showed that the bridge was still operational and casualties were minor.

What it was like at the rear of the *Klathas*, the place that had borne the brunt of the concussion caused by superheated gases and vaporized solids, he could well imagine.

"Speed . . . speed is still falling, Commander," a battered Kritt reported slowly, feeling his bruised jaw with one hand. Kumara activated the intercom and was gratified to find that it worked perfectly.

"Engineering, damage report." Silence shouted back at him from the stern of the ship. He tried again. "Engineering, this is your commander. Kanndad, what's the difficulty back there? I need this ship back up to speed in ten *aines* or I'll have you all fed to the converters!"

A worn, rasping voice finally replied. It was tinged with a vaguely insubordinate sarcasm. "Kanndad here Captain. We've sustained major damage to both engine nacelles. This ship won't make good cruising speed for several hundred *aines*, *if* the damage is repairable at all, and *if* most of my key personnel haven't been too seriously injured. What happened?"

"Never mind that now," Kumara told him irritably. He did not take note of his engineer's sarcastic response. He didn't have time for such luxuries. "Other than the drive, what is our power status?"

Kanndad turned silent again, apparently consulting someone out of pickup range.

"Eighty percent, Commander," he finally reported. Kumara took some comfort from that announcement. They were crippled but still armed.

Kritt spoke into the nearly clear atmosphere. "Federation ship closing to battle range, Commander." A pause; then, "They are transmitting."

Kumara could guess the nature of that transmission. Well, if Kirk thought the *Klathas* was drifting helplessly, he had an unpleasant surprise in store.

"I can see that she's closing, offspring of a worm's slave. As to the transmission, we'll answer it all right. Arm all rearward projectors and fire at will. And, Korreg, for once in your misbegotten life, see if you can hit something smaller than a blue star. Full power to the defensive screens." He stared at the viewscreen, which now clearly showed the ominous form of the approaching *Enterprise*.

"It is just," he muttered, too softly for anyone to hear, "that a ship of fools be commanded by a fool."

But if they survived the coming fight, he vowed, Kirk would not fool him again . . .

VII

Sulu carefully noted the sliding dial which indicated battle position relative to their quarry. "Inside range, Captain."

Kirk hesitated. He had no idea how badly the *Klathas* was damaged or how many serious injuries her crew had already suffered. "Uhura, any response to our transmission?"

"Not yet, Captain. Possibly their own communications have been damaged."

"Possibly. Or Kumara could be—"

A dull *crump* sounded, and the bridge was rocked by a wave of energy. Lights flickered momentarily before steadying.

"We've absorbed a full attack from the Klingons' rear projector banks, Captain," Spock informed them. "Our screens are holding tight."

"Returning fire, Captain," said Sulu, adjusting massive instruments of destruction with delicate fingers.

Kirk half smiled. "That's our answer. I should have known Kumara would choose to open negotiations in his own way. What's their speed, Lieutenant?"

Sulu checked a different set of readouts. "Holding at about warp-five, Captain."

"We have to reduce their speed still further," Kirk instructed everyone. "Otherwise, we'll simply fight a running battle until the ships from Shahkur meet up with Kumara. We have to weaken him significantly, weaken him to the point where he'll have no choice but to surrender. We have slightly more mobility, Mr. Sulu. Use it."

"Doing my best, sir," the thoroughly occupied helmsman responded. "We'll cut them down."

That section of space was filled for the next hour with a

hellish display of barely controlled energies, beams of blue and red piercingly brilliant through the stark blackness. Occasional eruptions of lambent cloud appeared on the exterior of each vessel whenever offensive probing beams contacted the argumentative energies of a defensive screen.

Sulu used the *Enterprise*'s superior speed carefully, teaming with the ship's battle computer to confuse the Klingons' retaliatory efforts while optimizing the *Enterprise*'s own attacks. There was little the Klingons could do to compensate. If they lowered their speed to throw off the *Enterprise*'s attacks, they conceded even more mobility to the Federation ship, gave her battle computer another chip to play . . . and, most important, lengthened the time between themselves and the Shahkur rendezvous.

At 62.24 minutes into the running battle, a phaser beam partially penetrated a severely strained defensive screen to strike one of the *Klathas*'s engine nacelles a glancing blow. That glancing blow killed twenty technicians and wounded as many others. The local damage was extreme.

Kumara knew they had taken a considerable hit from the wrench it communicated to the bridge. This time he managed to hold his position.

"Kanndad . . . Kanndad!" he yelled into the intercom. It gave back only a threatening crackle.

"Communications to that part of the ship temporarily out," Kritt reported. "Working to reestablish. Secondary engineering reports left converter potential critically damaged by phaser fire. We're going to lose more than half our remaining speed. Engineering reports that unless total engine shutdown occurs within five *du-aines*, to permit repairs, all light-multiple drive capability will be lost."

"When primary engineering communications are reestablished, instruct Engineer Kanndad to do his utmost, Lieutenant."

"Yes, sir," a disgruntled Kritt acknowledged. "Maintaining fire. Shifting to compensate for weakened screen."

Kumara heard the words, looked at the faces of his immediate subordinates, and knew that unless they effected a drastic reversal of the present battle conditions, he would be forced to surrender or ship-suicide.

Undoubtedly, Kirk would be prepared for any new tricks. Very well, then . . . he would try an old one.

"Attention, all stations."

Harried, dispirited faces turned to look at him as he activated general intership intercom, sending his voice throughout the battle-weary vessel.

"Attention. Burial details and all nonoffensive-action personnel. You will begin a complete canvass of the ship and gather all nonessential items—repeat, gather all nonessential items. Strip your cabins, the corridors, storage chambers of anything and everything not integral to life support or ship operations." His voice darkened.

"I am being generous in not including certain personnel in this classification. However, if this order is not efficiently complied with, that may change.

"All items are to be collected and transferred to the Auxiliary Landing Craft Hangar. Life Support Station: You will prepare to vent surplus atmosphere through surface vents in conjunction with the ejection of surplus material via the landing-craft hangar." He checked his wrist chronometer, reading it through the scratches which now covered its face.

"Ejection of material and atmosphere is to take place in . . . three-quarters *du-aines*. It will include any personnel remaining in the lock, so I strongly suggest you move rapidly. Your commander and officers salute you, warriors of Klingon!"

He switched off and turned, to see the bridge complement hard at their stations, continuing the fight. All but Kritt, who was eyeing him expectantly.

"We cannot outrun them any more, Lieutenant," Kumara explained, "nor does it appear we will be able to make contact with the relief force in time. Therefore, everything on this vessel except the crew is going to commit suicide. My own private stock of Gellian *vitz* included."

Kritt almost asked, "To what end," then decided that it would become evident. The predatory gleam in the commander's eyes, however, was more encouraging than any words could have been.

The time arrived. "Auxiliary Landing Craft Hangar reporting," came a voice from one of the bridge speakers. "Ejection of material accomplished."

"Surplus atmosphere discharged," came the word from Life Support Control.

"Now," Kumara said to the general intercom, "all power to everything but minimal life-support systems is to be shut down."

"But, Commander," Korreg protested as the lights on the bridge began to dim, "what about our projectors, our defenses?"

"I said *everything*, Lieutenant." He turned his gaze to the main screen. "I only hope they don't decide to take the easy way out. I am depending on Captain Kirk to act like a human . . ."

Spock's eyebrows twitched once as the new information appeared on his readouts. "Captain, detectors indicate that the Klingons are losing their internal power. Defensive screens fading."

"I'll say," said an exuberant Sulu. "That last burst went right through her starboard-crew section."

"Cease fire, Mr. Sulu!" Kirk ordered quickly. "I'll not fire on a helpless ship . . . not even a Klingon's."

"It could be a trick, Jim," McCoy commented cautiously.

"Yes, it could, Bones." Kirk studied the small image of the *Klathas* thoughtfully. "But you heard what Sulu just said . . . apparently, we can penetrate her weakened screens at will. Though I wonder if—"

"Sir!" There was an undercurrent of excitement in the helmsman's voice. "Detectors indicate the *Klathas* is trailing a large amount of metallic and plastic debris."

"Confirmed, Captain," Spock announced. "I have also noted a steady stream of frozen atmosphere leaking from several locations on the cruiser's exterior."

Elation reigned on the bridge, mingled with exclamations of satisfaction. Only Kirk—and Spock, naturally—betrayed no sign of pleasure.

"Well, what are we hesitating for, Jim?" McCoy finally asked. "They're in no condition to argue surrender terms."

Kirk shook his head slowly. "I don't like it, Bones. It's too sudden, too easy. One minute they're fighting with everything they have, and the next, without being struck a severe blow, they seem to be coming apart."

"We can't tell how much running damage they've suffered, Jim."

"Maybe not, Bones." He made a decision. "Lieutenant Uhura, try to raise the Klingon bridge." Uhura moved to comply. She looked back and shrugged slightly several moments later.

"Negative, Captain. Their communications are dead. I can't find evidence of any activity, not even on-board closed transmissions, not a hand communicator . . . nothing. That ship's as mute as a coffin."

Which it could very well be by now, Kirk mused. But to be *certain* . . . how to be certain . . .

"The *Klathas* is losing speed rapidly, Captain," Arex indicated. "Dropping below warp-five . . . warp-four . . . continuing to lose speed, sir."

"Stop looking so glum, Jim," McCoy said. "They're the ones experiencing all the trouble, not us."

"It certainly looks that way, Bones." He sighed. "All right. Take us in close, Mr. Sulu. Keep your phasers trained on her bridge and bring us in just outside of transporter range."

The *Enterprise* promptly cut her own speed to match that of the rapidly slowing *Klathas*. The eyes studying this gradual shift were equally intent on both sides, but the glint of eagerness lay in those on board the Klingon cruiser.

"That's right, Captain Kirk," Kumara was murmuring softly, watching as the dim screen showed the *Enterprise* edging cautiously nearer, "come close . . . a bit more, that's right. No need to hurry. We'll have our reunion yet . . . minus the *vitz*, I fear."

Spock abruptly did something that he did only on rare occasions: He raised his voice. "Captain, preliminary analysis of the debris from the Klingon ship."

"Go ahead, Mr. Spock."

The first officer paused to recheck his information. It was nonspecific, general, but, for all that, of dangerous significance. "Sensors indicate that the detritus consists of personal possessions, supplies, spare fabricating material, and assorted other non-vital equipment."

"So?" an uncomprehending McCoy blurted.

"Not only is there nothing of vital concern to ship operations present, Doctor, but the drifting material appears to be wholly intact and undamaged."

Fact and reason formed critical mass in Kirk's whirling mind. "Mr. Sulu, initiate full evasive maneuvers, and fire at—"

Sulu's hand never reached the helm controls. Something loud and unyielding threw him sideways, slamming him into Arex's station. The Edoan navigator, thanks to triple limbs, managed to remain in his seat. Few of his companions succeeded in doing likewise.

Further explosions rocked the bridge, sending unsecured reports flying and tumbling the crew about like quicksilver on glass.

Quite without warning, the awesome barrage ceased.

Slowly, positions were regained. Reports began to come in from various stations around the bridge. They were not encouraging. The bridge illumination had dimmed considerably.

Other concerns were uppermost in Kirk's mind, however. "Mr. Sulu, Mr. Spock, report on disposition of enemy vessel."

Sulu had to compensate for several no longer usable instruments. Eventually he reported, "They have continued to drop speed, Captain. Apparently they are moving to operate on impulse power alone. Indications are that near-normal internal power has returned."

"Odd. Comments, Mr. Spock?"

"Sensors indicate that they have failed to reestablish other than minimal defensive screens, Captain. No sign of projector activity. This would seem to indicate that they have sustained major engine damage and have been compelled to shut down their drive to effect repairs. Our own speed is, however, dropping even more rapidly than theirs."

"At least they're not leaving us," Kirk muttered. "That's something, anyway. I concur with your assessment of the damage they must have suffered, Spock. Otherwise we wouldn't be here talking about it now. Kumara must have exhausted his power reserves with that last attack."

"Excuse me, sir," Uhura broke in. "Damage reports are beginning to come in from all levels. Decks Four through

Seven indicate extensive though minor instrumentation damage. Firecontrol reports heavy damage to all phaser banks and photon-torpedo banks. Rear phasers are marginally operative, but the firecontrol computer has sustained major damage. Dr. McCoy reports . . ."

Kirk looked around at that. He hadn't even seen Bones leave the bridge.

". . . numerous minor injuries, mostly abrasive and concussive in nature. Several serious cases. He reports that he's preparing to supervise surgery."

"What about your own station, Lieutenant?"

Uhura checked her telltales and finally declared, "All deep-space Starfleet frequencies are inoperative due to broadcast-antenna damage combined with power loss. Local and on-board communications systems functional . . . if we don't get hit like that again."

"I don't expect we will, Lieutenant," he told her tightly, blinking as full illumination was restored to the bridge. He turned to study the battered shape of the *Klathas*. It seemed as though he could detect laughter drifting across the intervening space, floating right through the screen. That was impossible, of course. He told himself that as he waited for the most important report of all, the one which would determine their subsequent actions and options . . . if indeed they had any of the latter remaining.

The laughter refused to go away.

Even the beep of the chair intercom was a relief, though he knew he couldn't expect any good news. He was right.

"That you, Scotty?"

"Aye, Captain." The chief engineer was standing at an auxiliary intercom station, watching busy specialists wrestling with battered components. His own previously sterile suit was laden with grime and colored liquid from fluid-state switches that now conducted only his disgust.

"D'ye want it all at once, or in installments?"

"Let's have the worst of it, Scotty." Kirk readied himself.

"That last projector hit was the worst, sir. Played hell with and damaged—never mind the details. I'll have a list of damaged components and material—and personnel—transferred forward soon as I get the chance.

"Simply put, we've got no warp-drive capability. Impulse

power, yes, but we canna go nowhere verra fast for sometime. That's a minimum estimate. I hope you haven't got any pressin' engagements, Captain."

In spite of the grim report, Kirk managed a smile. "I'll send my regrets where necessary, Scotty. Do the best you can. If it's any consolation, the Klingons are apparently as badly damaged as we are. They're not going anywhere either. How's ship power?"

"Adequate for anythin' you want to try, Captain," the chief engineer declared reassuringly. "I heard about what happened up in Firecontrol. Too bad. The rear phasers'd work, if we had anythin' to work 'em with. Cut up the Klingons like veal on a butcher's block."

"We're not going to cut even that with those phasers for a good while, Scotty," Kirk reminded him. "Right now I'll settle for some mobility."

"Give it to you as soon as we can, Captain."

"I know you will, Scotty. Bridge out." Kirk searched his thoughts for a course of action, aware of the concerned glances the bridge personnel surreptitiously threw him . . . and found nothing.

"Summary and suggestions, Mr. Spock?"

The first officer replied smoothly, as though the consequences of near annihilation were an everyday event. "Engines dead, phasers inoperable, life-support systems sufficient. We can't run, we can't fight, but we are going to continue to exist . . . unless repairs to the *Klathas* outstrip our own. Until then . . ."

"Stalemate," Kirk decided, staring at the viewscreen.

On board the *Klathas*, Engineer Scott's counterparts were working furiously to remove twisted bits of metal, to cut away burned out components and circuitry so that the arduous task of replacing them could begin.

Kumara was there himself, surveying the damage. He moved easily among the destruction, accompanied by Engineer Korreg and Lieutenant Kritt, offering a word of encouragment here, a blistering insult there—whatever seemed appropriate to accelerate the work.

He thought of Kirk, and worried as he fumed. "It's not going fast enough, Korreg."

"I abase myself, Exalted Commander. My head is yours . . . but my technicians are working as fast as they are able. There is much structural damage. It must be removed, cut away, before actual repair can begin."

"I'll cut off some extremities if replacement of damaged instrumentation doesn't commence within a hundred *aines*, Engineer. Tell them that. Perhaps it will stimulate their muscles, if not their minds."

"I will tell them, Commander," and Korreg hastily departed from the vicinity of the commander.

Kumara turned suddenly on the attentive Lieutenant Kritt. Kritt cringed—needlessly, as it developed. The commander had started at a sudden thought, not from any desire to heap abuse on his subordinate.

"Have the human Delminnen brought from the restraining chamber to the bridge. I'll meet you there."

"At once, Commander." The lieutenant turned to go, then hesitated. "It may take a few moments to . . . ah . . . restore the human to presentability."

"So long as he's coherent and will remain so. And for the *Sequa*'s sake, tell those in charge of him that this is no ordinary human. He is a valuable property and is to be treated as such . . . or I will match their living conditions and treatment on board with his."

"Yes, Commander." Kritt hurried down the corridor while Kumara made his thoughtful way back to the bridge.

As it turned out, Van Delminnen appeared well able to manipulate both body and mind, though the former was not undamaged. But Kumara's warning had been delivered. The two husky guards who half carried, half dragged the slight human onto the bridge handled him with appropriate care.

Delminnen shook himself free of his captors, who gladly let him go—the feel of the soft human being difficult to stomach. He glanced around the bridge, his head moving rapidly, quickly, like a bird hunting for an especially ripe bug in the bark of a tree. His gaze settled contemptuously on Kumara, who gazed back with interest.

Kritt moved angrily from his station to stand next to Delminnen. "Bow in the presence of the commander, weak one!"

Delminnen's head went back slightly, prompting Kritt to raise a furious fist.

But Kumara waved the lieutenant off. "No, no, no, Kritt! How many times must I tell you to utilize your head for something other than shoulder ballast? Leave the poor creature alone. In your justifiable anger you might accidentally mortally damage it. Then how would we obtain the information we seek? One cannot coerce a corpse. Return to your position and continue to monitor the *Enterprise*. That is where my concern lies—not with this single human."

"As you command, Exalted One," Kritt muttered disappointedly. "But the disrespect—" Throwing the imperturbable Delminnen a vicious smile, he turned and stalked back to his station.

Kumara waited until the lieutenant was seated. Then he clasped his hands together around one knee, leaned back slightly, and struggled to execute an earnest grin—which for a Klingon was no mean feat.

"Now then, Van Delminnen . . . It has come to the attention of the Empire that you have developed a device based on new scientific principles which seems capable of reducing normal worlds to collections of drifting debris. I hardly need impress upon you that we would regard the possession of such a device by a government unfriendly to ours as threatening in the extreme."

"Whereas," Delminnen countered sarcastically, "if it were given into your protection, everyone could rest assured that it would be used for the benefit of all."

"Naturally."

"You're a liar—and worse, an unimaginative one."

There was a violent bang as of flesh on metal and some loud murmurings behind Kumara at that unpardonable insult. The commander turned and barked sharply, "Officers of the *Klathas*, attend to your duties!" Then he turned back to Delminnen and continued to smile amiably.

"Very well, since you doubt our motives . . ."

"I don't doubt them one bit," Delminnen sneered.

". . . let me rephrase the situation. You must concede that the Federation would utilize your device for similar purposes should they gain control of it. They will offer you little in return. On the other hand, you are my prisoner. Rather than be disagreeable, if you turn over the plans for your device to us, I will swear on my ancestors that you and your sister will be safely—"

That promise brought a sign of concern from the human, whose steel exterior showed the first indications of cracking slightly.

"Char . . . she's on board too?"

"Why, certainly," Kumara admitted, with commendable swiftness. "You don't think we'd separate the two of you, did you?"

Delminnen looked understandably suspicious. "She wasn't with us when we materialized in your transporter."

"Naturally not," Kumara agreed, his mind working as fast as only Kirk knew it could. "The *Enterprise* tried to snatch both of you from us. To compensate, we had to use two transporters. Your sister boarded the *Klathas* in the other one."

"Then why haven't I seen her?"

"She experienced some minor injuries when materializing in an awkward position. At the moment she is resting quietly and comfortably in our infirmary chambers. My chief medical officer informs me that she can have visitors in another day.

"Of course, I don't *want* to keep you apart any longer than that, Van Delminnen. But if you insist on being obstinate, you'll discover that I am a master of obstinacy.

"Should you decide, logically, to cooperate, you will be provided with a luxurious and private abode in an environment of your own choosing. You will have the facilities of a fully equipped laboratory, all the materials you require, and a free hand to spend the rest of your lives carrying out any kind of research you desire. Your privacy will be guarded and assured, and within the limits of the Empire you can come and go as you wish. Anything else you desire you have only to request." His voice rose in an excellent imitation of hearty good fellowship.

"Come, come, man . . . would your own government offer you as much? Or would they put you off with a modest stipend and a warning to take care with what you study? What say you?"

Delminnen locked eyes with the commander. His reply

was jerky, nervous, as was all of his speech, but there was a firmness to it nonetheless.

"I say it's mighty peculiar for you to be so accommodating and generous to the helpless prisoner from a race you despise. And if you were as confident of eventually obtaining the information you want, by one means or another, you wouldn't be so anxious to secure my agreement. I know the *Enterprise* has been following your ship." He crossed his arms with an air of finality. "I think I'll wait a bit before agreeing to anything. There are developments yet to be seen."

That was too much for Kritt. Despite Kumara's order, he was out of his chair, all but snarling at this infuriating example of a lower order.

"Let me have him for a few *aines* in the persuasion chambers, Most Exalted. I'll show him the folly of attempting to dictate to a Klingon commander."

"Please, Lieutenant." Kumara sighed irritably. "I am conducting the interrogation. While I might agree with your desires, emotionally, your suggestion is premature. Have you not studied this creature? I have done so, while he has been babbling.

"While possibly a veritable genius, he is obviously, like so many of this kind, mentally unstable. Torture might send him into a catatonic state from which his mind—and the secrets locked therein—might never emerge.

"In that case, I would find it necessary to have the questioner—yourself, for example—executed. I should prefer not to. At times you have shown yourself to perform somewhat less incompetently than your compatriots. Do return to your station."

Thoroughly disgusted both with the situation and with the commander's attitude toward it, Kritt returned once again to his position. He sat there fuming quietly and thinking of what he would do to the human if he were in Kumara's place.

"Van Delminnen," Kumara said, "I cannot understand your attitude. Even for a human, it is exceptionally obtuse. Let us try this—a communication between yourself and Captain Kirk which we monitored earlier showed you emphatically refusing him even permission to land. If you hate him and the Federation he stands for, which has so grievously and wrongly mistreated you, why not spite them all by turning your knowledge over to us?"

Delminnen drew himself up in a self-conscious pose of pride and arrogance—a very Klingon thing to do, in fact. "My genius," he informed Kumara, "is not for sale to the highest bidder. You all desire my knowledge, yet none of you is sufficiently intelligent to know how to ask for it." He smiled in a strange way—strange even for him.

Kumara was mildly amused, but not by the smile. "You have a novel way of rationalizing your insanity, Delminnen. Too novel for me. I haven't the time to probe it just now. Rest assured that there will be time for everything." He looked to the guard on the scientist's left.

"Convey him to Karau in Humanoid Psychology—perhaps they can figure this one out. And tell them not to damage him beyond what is absolutely necessary."

"It shall be as you say, Commander," the guard replied. The guards took hold of Delminnen, despite his protests, and escorted him from the bridge.

Kumara turned thoughtfully back to the main viewscreen. He hadn't really expected the human to be sensible and agree to the inevitable. The only time his demeanor had altered was when his sibling had been mentioned. If she were on board now, it would be a simple matter to use her as a lever with which to topple Delminnen's stubbornness.

But she wasn't on board. She was out there, somewhere in the bowels of Kirk's ship, and Kumara did not think Kirk would be so foolish as to permit him access to her.

Still, he had Delminnen. It might take longer, be a bit messier, but eventually they would pry the information out of him—provided they all weren't vaporized first.

With his mind he tried to bridge the gap between ships, reach across to the tiny bump at the apex of the cruiser's saucer which he knew housed the ship's bridge. He reached out and tried to penetrate a single mind therein.

What are you thinking, acquaintance of my youth, he mused to himself. How will you proceed? We are even with our guesswork now. Whatever happens next could be decisive. Whence will it come, and when it does, will the gods permit me to escape again?

The trouble is, James Kirk, I know you too well—and you know me. How does one fool a mirror . . . ?

"I wonder what Kumara's thinking now, Bones." Kirk's gaze remained fixed on the screen, which still showed the image of the damaged Klingon cruiser.

McCoy's reply was bitter: "Probably laughing himself silly over the way he suckered us into that last barrage. Sitting in his command chair, watching us bleed and snickering to himself."

"How are things in Sick Bay?" Kirk asked, aware that the anger was directed more at the result of Klingon bellicosity—the casualties the ship had suffered—than at Kumara himself.

"Better than we deserve, Jim. If the one projector that did most of the engine damage had struck at a broader angle instead of slant-on, we could have suffered a blood bath back there. As it is, there are half a dozen specialists and one ensign who'll be lucky to pull through."

"If they're not dead already, they never will be, Bones. Not with you hovering over them."

"I wish I had your confidence in me, Jim." He glanced down at his wrist chronometer. "She ought to be here by now. I told—"

"Captain . . . Dr. McCoy?" Both men turned to face the elevator.

Two people had just emerged. One was a medical specialist. The other was Char Delminnen. She looked pale but otherwise none the worse for her wrestling match with transporter energies. The resemblance to her brother, Kirk noted, was amazing. A few slight changes in bone structure here, a movement of skin, and they could have been twins.

She was looking with interest around the bridge. Eventually her gaze settled on Kirk, and she inspected him with the same thoroughness with which he had regarded her.

The specialist marched her over, saluted, and waited for McCoy's instructions.

"Report, Mendez."

"All vital signs strong, body functions normal. No evidence to indicate delayed-time reactions. Mental condition stable."

"All right, you can go, Mendez," McCoy told him. "Tell

Nurse Chapel to keep me posted if any of the casualties on critical show signs of deterioration."

"Yes, sir." The specialist saluted again and left the bridge, leaving Kirk and McCoy free to appraise Char Delminnen for the first time.

And they were in for a hard time, Kirk reflected, if she was anything like her brother.

"How do you feel, Ms. Delminnen?" McCoy ventured. Her gaze rested briefly on the doctor, then turned immediately to Kirk. He found her voice unexpectedly light, almost musical. But it was as adamantine as her brother's.

"Captain, where is Van?"

Kirk glanced for approval to McCoy, who nodded once. "She's as sound as I can make her, Jim. You might as well tell her."

Her attention shifted confusedly from McCoy to Kirk and back again. "What is this . . . what are you talking about? Isn't . . . isn't Van on board this ship?"

Kirk raised a placating hand and turned to indicate the screen. "I'm afraid I have to tell you he is not, Ms. Delminnen. Unless we're much mistaken, he's on that one."

They waited, McCoy watching her anxiously while she stared silently at the disabled Klingon cruiser. There was no scream, no violent outburst, not the slightest hint of hysteria. But her next words were whispered.

"I see. The Klingons got Van and you got me." She turned abruptly to look accusingly at Kirk. "Have you been in contact with them? Do you know if he's all right?"

"We've been in contact all right," Kirk explained patiently. "We've been fighting a running battle with them for much too long. Both our ship and the *Klathas* have been disabled. At the moment it's a race to see who can repair their engines first.

"As to your brother, we've had no word from the Klingons. They haven't volunteered any information, and we haven't had time to request any—not that they'd be inclined to make comments about anything other than our theoretical ancestry at the moment."

Char Delminnen turned her eyes to the deck and sighed. "Ever since our parents died and we were farmed out to foster parents, Van and I have never been separated for very long. We see things too much the same, too well, to look elsewhere for companionship." Her eyes turned up to him, and they were haunted.

"I don't know how he'll react if we're kept apart very long. In many ways Van is still a child. You've got to find a way to return him to me, Captain Kirk!"

The fury behind her request took both men aback. Though he had no reason to be ashamed of their efforts thus far, Kirk found himself squirming under that demanding gaze.

"We've been risking the ship and our lives to do just that, Ms. Delminnen. I don't think you need worry too much. Your brother's extremely important to the Klingons as well as to us. You can bet they're being careful not to harm him."

He did not think it would be diplomatic to discuss the ultimate steps they were prepared to take to keep Van Delminnen and his device from falling into the Empire's hands.

Char Delminnen relaxed physically at Kirk's assurance, but her words, as she turned away slightly, were still filled with fury . . . and bitterness.

"And all this has happened because of that stupid discovery of his. I told him some interloper might discover evidence of its use. I *told* him! But would he listen?" She shook her head slowly. "That child—the universe is his playpen." Her head snapped around, and Kirk found himself confronted by that accusing stare again.

"That's the only reason you're interested in us, isn't it? You're no better than the Klingons."

Kirk bridled. "I think we, and the Federation—*your* Federation, Ms. Delminnen, whether you like it or not—are entitled to better than that. As for personal concern, comparing us with the Klingons is akin to—"

"Yes, that is the reason," Spock interrupted. Kirk threw his first officer a look of reproach.

"Thank you, Mr. . . . Spock, isn't it? I appreciate your honesty. At least I'm sure of where I stand."

"We could express more concern for you," Spock continued, looking up from the library computer console, "but you and your brother make it exceedingly difficult for anyone else to be interested in anything *but* your work."

Kirk's look of reproach vanished, and he saw that Char

Delminnen had no reply to Spock's accusation. All she could do was shrug.

"So Van and I are jealous of our privacy. We didn't ask for visitors. We didn't inflict ourselves on you. It was the other way around."

"So it was," Kirk agreed firmly, "but you invited this visitation whether you'll admit it or not. Yes, our primary concern is the device—and why shouldn't it be? Do you realize what the Klingons will do, what they'll be able to demand, if they gain possession of a weapon so destructive that—"

"Oh, for heaven's sake, don't you understand?"

Kirk and McCoy looked at her askance. "What do you mean?"

"The device . . . it's not a weapon."

VIII

Clearly, there were those on the bridge whose attention was not focused solely on their tasks of the moment, for the general shock this comment produced spread beyond Kirk and McCoy.

"Wait . . . I think I understand you," Kirk finally began, speaking in a soothing, calming manner. "It's all a matter of semantics. Very possibly your brother did not regard his invention as a weapon. You must see, however, that to an outsider any device which is capable of obliterating an entire world . . ."

"Yes, yes . . . but you have to know, Captain Kirk, it was never conceived as a weapon. For all his intransigence, Van could no more develop a weapon of destruction than he could moderate a diplomatic conference."

"If destroying planets isn't an offensive gesture," wondered McCoy, "then what was this machine's intended purpose?"

"You know that this system is exceptionally poor in usable metals? That was a major reason why it was never colonized, not even outposted."

McCoy looked blank. "So?"

"Van got the idea for a device which would enable orbiting vessels to mine such metals at depths previously thought impossible, and from great distances. It involved the calculus of stress in ways I don't pretend to understand. I'm not sure anyone but Van could understand them.

"It sounded like a grandiose absurdity at first, but Van became obsessed with the thought. He neglected all our other projects, threw himself wholly into this one. You have no idea, gentlemen, what Van becomes when he is obsessed with an idea."

"I can imagine," ventured McCoy.

"He doesn't eat, he doesn't sleep—he exists to work. He exists *on* work. And eventually he produced the concepts needed to make the device a reality." Her grim visage lightened in remembrance. "How excited he was, how thrilled, how expectant! This was the discovery which was going to refute his critics. This was to bring him the recognition forever denied by petty, less talented men." She slumped.

"What else is there to say? You saw the results for yourselves. We tried the finished machine out on kilometers-deep nickel-iron deposits in the mantle of the ninth planet. The result was destructive beyond all imagining. Van was appalled, then furious . . . at the machine and at himself. He reworked, recalculated everything. He found no mistake. By his calculations, the machine should have worked as it was.

"I tried to dissuade him from making another test." She laughed disconsolately. "Try to extinguish a sun. So we aimed the machine at iridium deposits on the eighth world . . . with identical results.

"Do you wonder, Captain Kirk, Dr. McCoy, at the manner in which he greeted you? It was his failure infuriating him, not your presence. The latter he could stand, but not the first. That's why he refused to cooperate.

"But you've got to believe that Van intended no harm to anyone. He's no world-smashing monster. He wanted to produce something that would vindicate him, yes, but also to create something which would benefit Federation peoples." Abruptly the hard shell splintered and she was pleading.

"Get him back, Captain Kirk, please get him back! Without me he's no danger to anyone, except himself."

"Ms. Delminnen, while it may come as a shock to you, we *are* concerned about you and your brother in ways other than mercenary. As Federation citizens, and as individuals, it's our duty to protect you. Even if your brother had produced nothing of value, the mere fact that he's a Federation citizen would probably have impelled us along the same course of action we're following now."

"And after you've got him back, assuming you can do that . . . ?" she asked, in control of herself again.

"That will have to be decided by the Federation Council. I'm only a starship captain, you know—not the all-powerful manipulator of others' lives you seem to think I am."

She stared at him a moment longer. "Though I have absolutely no reason to do so, I find myself believing you, Captain Kirk. I realize, however, that you'll be forced to destroy the Klingon ship—and my brother—if you fail to recapture him."

Kirk looked surprised—he thought he had avoided the need to mention that final, fatal possibility altogether. He hadn't counted on this woman's perceptiveness—it was almost as if she'd read his mind.

"We don't intend . . ." he started to mumble, and then decided to be as forthright as she was. "You understand, then, that we simply cannot . . . *cannot* permit the Klingons to rebuild your brother's device."

Char Delminnen's reaction was unexpected. She was momentarily speechless with shock. "Oh, but don't you see . . . didn't you know?" she finally explained. "They *can't*."

Now it was Kirk's turn to be shocked. The rest of the bridge was equally stunned. "Maybe you ought to elaborate," he said slowly.

She began to pace excitedly back and forth, waving one hand animatedly as she spoke. "I thought you had done your research, studied us thoroughly. It seems in your haste and anxiety to recover the weapon, both you and the Klingons neglected to trouble yourselves much with its creators. Yes," she half shouted, forestalling McCoy's unvoiced comment, "I said *creators*. You've no idea how Van worked, do you?"

Kirk glanced over at Spock, who looked blank and shook his head negatively, once. Char Delminnen turned smug.

"Van couldn't build a toy truck, let alone anything as complicated as that machine. I told you how close we are. We always work together. Don't you remember me telling you that he was neglecting our projects? *Ours!* Van gets an idea into his head, spins it around, clarifies the theory—and then I draw the diagrams and execute the finished product. He conceives, I construct. It has always been like that.

"After all, I'm the one with the degree in practical engineering."

"Mr. Spock?" Kirk eyed his first officer expectantly, but

Spock was already working at the library computer. Shortly he turned and spoke softly.

"Historical records confirm the body of Delminnen's report."

"I see." He turned his attention back to the still-pacing woman. "What you're saying, then, is that your brother is incapable of duplicating the machine?"

"Duplicating! They couldn't construct a primitive crystal set from Van's instructions! I'm the only one who can understand his verbal and mathematical shorthand. The two of us make one genius, Captain. Separated, we're merely two competent technicians."

Kirk turned thoughtfully to the viewscreen and studied the still driveless *Klathas*. Soon he began to chuckle. The sound rose, concurrent with Spock's eyebrows, became a chortle, than a laugh.

"Jim!" McCoy stared at his friend. Spock was equally puzzled.

"Really, Captain. I hardly consider the information the young lady has recently imparted of such a nature as to—"

"I'm . . . sorry, Spock . . . Bones." He regained control of himself. "Forgive me, Ms. Delminnen. I wasn't laughing at your brother's plight, or at your concern. It's just so . . . so . . . I can't help but visualize Commander Kumara's expression when he pulls what you've just told us out of your brother, when he discovers that in all this haste and confusion, he's the one who should be chasing *us*!"

The situation they were now in suddenly dawned on McCoy. He too chuckled. Spock reguarded this display of emotion coolly.

Almost as coolly as did Char Delminnen: "I'll be in the cabin Dr. McCoy assigned to me, Captain. If and when you have additional questions, or have rescued my brother, you'll find I'm available."

She turned and marched pompously to the elevator. Kirk turned to McCoy.

"You're going to leave her to herself, Bones?"

"She's as healthy as I can make her, Jim. She and her brother may both need treatment, but not of a physical variety." He shook his head slowly. "What a family . . . so much talent enveloped in so many neuroses."

Kirk turned and saw the rest of the bridge crew listening attentively. "What are you all staring at? Don't you have stations to man? In case some of you aren't aware of it, this ship is on red alert and in the midst of an ongoing battle. Or perhaps there are some among you who . . ."

The level of activity on the bridge rose rapidly.

"Mr. Spock, your estimation of how soon repairs to the *Klathas* will be completed?" The first officer bent to his console. He looked up calmly several moments later.

"It is difficult to evaluate the damage to the enemy vessel with much accuracy, Captain. Judging from the information available through the library, combined with that obtained by our sensors, however, I should say that they will complete minimally necessary repairs to their engines well ahead of us."

Kirk double-checked with Engineering and found that Scott confirmed Spock's analysis.

"All right, Scotty, do what you can. Kirk out." The captain sat back and considered their situation. If the *Klathas* were allowed to run under warp-drive for even a short time while the *Enterprise* remained comparatively immobile, they would lose contact with her completely. There had to be some way to prevent that. Phasers and photon-torpedo banks were inoperable owing to the damaged firecontrol computer; impulse power would be useless . . . they had to stick with the *Klathas* somehow.

Stick with . . .

"Mr. Arex."

"Yes Captain?" The Edoan navigator responded promptly.

"I need a report on the status of the tractor beams."

"Just a moment, sir." Arex checked his console, tried a few switches, and found they responded as programmed. "Instruments indicate that all tractor units are intact and capable of full function, sir. Power leads to Engineering are undamaged, and all other subsidiary instrumentation appears functional."

"Thank you, Mr. Arex." Down went the intercom button. "Scotty . . ."

"Aye, Captain, what now?" the chief engineer wondered. "If it's about the drive . . ."

"Not this time, Scotty. How would it affect your repair work back there if I had to request maximum, sustained power to the tractor beams?"

"The tractors?" Scott hesitated only long enough to mentally retrace one diagram out of several thousand locked and filed securely in the manual of his mind. "Not at all, Captain. That's an independent power link. I can give you all the attractive force you want."

"I'll hold you to that, Scotty," Kirk told him thankfully. "We may need it all." He clicked off and snapped an order to the helm. "Mr. Sulu! Prepare to engage the *Klathas* with all forward tractors. Use near full power, one unit below maximum."

"Aye, sir," Sulu responded. "Should I attempt to close the distance between us?"

"Negative, Mr. Sulu. Maintain present disposition. We're close enough for effective tractor work. I don't want to move in to where Kumara can use portable weaponry against us. Since we can't go anywhere until Mr. Scott's people have repaired the drive, I just want to make sure the Klingons can't go anywhere without us."

"Prepared to lock onto enemy vessel, Captain," Sulu reported. "All forward tractors powered and standing by."

"Engage, Mr. Sulu."

The helmsman gave the necessary electronic order. There was the briefest pause before a slight quiver was felt on the bridge.

A jolt was felt on the bridge of the *Klathas*. Kumara looked up as Kritt reported, "Commander, sensors indicate that the Federation vessel has—"

"Locked onto us with her tractor beams," Kumara finished for him. "I don't require mechanicals to confirm that for me. It was an obvious desperation move." He eyed the drifting *Enterprise*. "I only wonder why it took them so long."

Five *aines* passed before Kumara's chair intercom buzzed for attention. "Report yourself," he said to the pickup.

"Engineering here, Exalted Commander." There was a touch of exultation in Korreg's exhausted voice. "I am pleased to report that we have restored partial drive capability."

A shrill battle cry broke out on the bridge at these words. For once Kumara decided to ignore the breach of discipline. The men could do with a little enthusiasm.

"Remember, Commander, we have only partial capability. Our speed and maneuverability are still severely limited."

"I understand, Korreg. It will be enough, I think. My commendation to you and your personnel. At the successful completion of this mission there will be honors for all. I salute you."

He turned from the intercom to an uncertain Kritt. "But, Exalted One, there is still the problem of the *Enterprise*'s tractors."

"Must I constantly be afflicted with reminders of the obvious?" Kumara moaned. "Am I forever to be oppressed by relentless idiocy? Worm's offspring, product of a misaligned mating, can you see no solution to anything save what is written already? Prepare to get under way!"

"At once, Commander!" a rejuvenated Kritt responded. The rest of the bridge crew bent to their own tasks happily, secure in the confidence expressed by their commander's renewed good mood.

Sulu's attention was caught by the sudden activation of long-quiescent readouts. "Captain," he announced anxiously, "the *Klathas* appears to be increasing speed."

"Confirmed, Captain," Spock declared evenly. "They are approaching velocity beyond the ability of impulse power. It would seem that they have their warp-drive working again."

"Mr. Sulu," Kirk inquired, "report on the status of all tractor linkages."

The helmsman hurriedly checked the appropriate telltales and reported steadily, "Tractors all holding firm, sir. No sign of weakening, and all instrumentation operating efficiently."

"Mr. Spock, compute energy output of the *Klathas* and compare with her rate of acceleration." Spock did the necessary figuring and announced a figure. Kirk relaxed a little. "They've regained only partial use of their drive, Spock. By the time they can complete their repairs, according to your estimates of the damage they've suffered, Mr. Scott should have restored our own engines back to equal operation. That means full use of our weapons systems as well, since the firecontrol computer is expected to be fixed at the same time." He looked satisfied.

"Then we can restart this argument on an equal basis again . . ."

Lieutenant Kritt looked up from his console, some of his initial enthusiasm at the return of drive capability now dampened by what his readouts told him.

"We are approaching warp-speed, Commander, but we cannot exceed it by much until further repairs have been completed by Engineering. We do not have enough power to break the *Enterprise*'s tractor lock on us."

Kumara remained relaxed, confident. "Not with sheer speed we do not, Lieutenant."

"Your pardon, Exalted One?"

"Pay attention, Kritt." Kumara's voice rose to reach every attentive ear on the bridge. "Pay attention, all of you. We will execute the following course changes, and execute them with utmost precision. And in so doing, we will finish this absurd contest once and for all . . ."

There was no panic on the *Enterprise*'s bridge when evidence of the initial Klingon maneuver was reported by her detectors.

"Captain," Sulu declared promptly, "the Klingons are shifting strongly to starboard, running at a considerable angle now to their previous course."

I wonder what Kumara is up to, Kirk thought.

"It seems strange, Captain," Spock announced, obviously puzzled. "They have the benefit, however temporary, of warp-drive capability. I should think their proper course of action would be to make as much distance toward their base at Shahkur as possible before we regain use of our own drive and weapons."

"I agree, Spock. That's my thought too. Possibly Kumara is trying to trick us again, trying to convince us there's Klingon aid closer but in a different direction." He began to be concerned. It wasn't like Kumara to try anything so transparent.

"Mr. Spock, you're certain the Klingons have no military facilities nearer than Shahkur?"

Spock utilized the library briefly. "Absolutely nothing, Captain. Shahkur is at the extreme fringe of the Empire. And the Klingons do not normally patrol this region in force, so I think it extremely unlikely they have contacted another ship."

"He's up to something," Kirk muttered.

At that moment a slight quiver ran through the bridge. "*Klathas* has executed another radical course change, Captain," Sulu reported. "Approximately forty-five degrees to port of their new course."

"Tractor status?"

"Still holding tight, Captain," Arex announced quietly. "We're staying with them. No change in disposition."

Another quiver rattled the bridge. It was slightly stronger this time.

Sulu's voice rose slightly. "Now they're shifting to starboard again."

On the screen Kirk saw the *Klathas* nearly vanish to the right before scanner compensators realigned her in the center of the screen. Simultaneously, a strong jolt rocked the bridge so hard that Uhura had to grab the arms of her chair to keep from being thrown free.

"Shifting again, Captain!"

"Steady, Mr. Sulu." He was on the intercom instantly. Now it was obvious what Kumara was up to. The question was . . . could they do anything about it?

"Scotty, have you restored any drive capability yet? Anything at all?"

"No, Captain," the chief engineer replied. "And"—his voice was momentarily drowned out as the next shock rocked the *Enterprise* and forced Kirk to brace himself against the arm of the chair—"we're not goin' to have any if this infernal shakin' gets any worse. What the devil's goin' on up there?"

"It's the Klingon ship. Kumara knows he hasn't regained enough power to break free of our tractors, so he's playing crack-the-whip . . . with us on the snapping end."

"The colloquial identification is obscure, Captain," Spock

firmly declared, "but the physical theory cannot be quarreled with. If this continues, the centripetal force will soon be sufficient to overpower our tractor beams and break the *Klathas* free."

Kirk didn't have to cut the intercom—the next shock did that. This one was severe enough to send sparks flying from several consoles and knock two momentarily unbraced specialists to the deck.

McCoy stumbled over to the command chair and grabbed the back for support. "Jim, we can't go on like this. If it gets any worse, it won't matter whether the Klingons break free or not. I'm receiving injury reports already, from all over the ship." Another jolt sent him spinning to the floor, despite his hold on the chair back.

"Captain, I must concur with the doctor," Spock insisted, struggling to retain his own position. "Calculations indicate that much additional stress will begin to affect the ship's hull. Even the strongest seams cannot take—"

"All right, Spock!" Kirk's mind churned furiously. There was no time for careful consideration of possible alternatives, no time to judge possible reciprocal effects of his idea.

Besides, it was his only idea. The trouble was, it could affect them as severely as it did the Klingons.

Another shock struck as the *Klathas* slammed over to a new heading once more. The tractors still held, a credit to their designers. Unfortunately, human beings were not nearly so solidly constructed.

Kirk climbed painfully back into the command chair, every millimeter of his body bruised and strained. Only Arex, with his triple limbs, had succeeded in retaining his position during that last shock, but even he appeared shaken.

Lights flickered momentarily, then came on strong. The next time they might not. "Mr. Spock, I want a half-second countdown to the *Klathas*'s next projected course change. They have to maintain a set pattern of changes for maximum effectiveness."

"Fifteen, fifteen, fourteen, fourteen . . ." Spock recited in a monotone, not questioning the reasoning behind the command.

"Mr. Arex, on command you will disengage tractor beams

for the minimum amount of time possible, then reengage. Do you understand?"

"No, sir . . . but standing ready." One finger hovered over the button in question, still with inhuman control.

". . . Nine, nine, eight, eight . . ." The first officer continued to count, his voice never wavering.

"Stress on the exterior plates is nearing the danger point, sir," the ensign at the engineering station reported tensely. Kirk ignored him, his gaze locked on the screen, where the *Klathas* was sliding rapidly to starboard again, his attention focused on Spock's count to the exclusion of all else.

". . . Four, four, three, three, two, two . . ."

"Whatever you're going to do, Jim, *do* it!" yelled McCoy.

". . . One, o—"

"Now, Arex!"

The Edoan's finger descended, firmly depressed the switch controlling the forward tractors, allowed it to rise, then depressed it again. The action was almost too fast for a human eye to follow.

Several things happened at once. A tiny dial on Arex's console barely quivered. A tremendous force wrenched at the *Enterprise*. It sounded as though every bit of metal—every plate, beam, wire, down to the fillings in Scott's back teeth—vibrated in protest. This time the lights stayed out. The only illumination on the bridge was provided by the brilliant display of sparks which arced from one outraged console to another.

Transparent facings on gauges and dials shattered, and everyone, including Arex, was thrown heavily to the deck.

Kirk had only a glimpse of the screen as he was thrown clear of the command chair. It dimmed but didn't wink out entirely. It showed the *Klathas* whipping around like a top, to stop facing the *Enterprise* bow-on.

The lights came back on slowly, but with none of the usual crispness of emergency backups snapping in. Groans and mild curses, indicative of pain incurred, formed a slowly rising murmur on the bridge.

Kirk had to pull himself bodily back into his chair. "Mr. Arex, report," he said, wincing and clutching at his right shoulder. "Report on the status of the Klingon vessel. Disposition and speed relative to our own."

There was a long pause. This time not even Arex had escaped the pounding, and it took a few minutes for the Edoan's jarred mind to settle enough so that he could make sense of what his instruments were telling him—those that were still operative.

"Instruments show . . . instruments show . . ." His soulful eyes widened slightly in surprise. "Sir, all engine activity, including impulse power, has ceased aboard the *Klathas*!"

"Mr. Spock, confirmation." *Please,* he added silently.

"Correct, Captain," the first officer reported. "The *Klathas* shows no evidence of internal power beyond what is required to maintain vital life-support systems. She shows no signs of drive activity."

"And what about ourselves?"

Spock studied his instrumentation a moment longer. "We have apparently sustained additional damage as well, Captain. We are in little better shape than the *Klathas*."

"Damage reports starting to come in, Captain," Uhura announced. Her left cheek was swollen and badly discolored, but her voice was as crisp and precise as ever.

"Make note of them, Lieutenant," Kirk responded, "and I'll review them at first opportunity. Meanwhile, get me Engineering."

Uhura worked her console, then explained, "Sorry, sir . . . that portion of intership communications is presently inoperative. Lieutenant M'ress has checked in to say that she is working on the breakdown with communications personnel and Engineering Maintenance."

"It may be just as well, Jim," McCoy suggested. "I'm not sure I'd care to listen to Scotty just now—not after what that last shock must have done to his half-finished repairs. What *did* happen, anyway?"

"It worked is what happened, Bones, although it worked on both of us—on the *Enterprise* as well as on the *Klathas*." He tried to slip into a comfortable position, discovered that his battered body found no position comfortable, and tried to take his mind off the throb in his shoulder by explaining.

"Did you ever play crack-the-whip when you were a kid, Bones? On any kind of skates?"

"Sure." He grimaced. "I always seemed to end up on the outside end."

"What would happen if that outside end suddenly grabbed hold of something immovable, like a fixed post or other solid object, and held on—even if only for a second?"

McCoy's brows drew together in thought. Then he smiled and nodded slowly. "Of course . . . The shock would be transmitted all the way down the line, to the inner end. If it were done to a line of skating kids, the ones at the other end would be shaken off . . . although everyone would experience the shock to some degree." His eyes suddenly moved to the screen. "So that's what happened to the *Klathas*." He gestured at the now completely immobile alien ship. "It spun them completely around. And I thought *we'd* taken the worst of it."

"Jubilation is pleasant but only temporary, Doctor," Spock suggested unexcitedly, calmly—rationally. He turned his gaze to Kirk. "What do we do now, Captain?"

"Now?" Kirk spread his upturned palms in an age-old gesture. "I'm afraid I didn't have much time to think about that, Mr. Spock. We had to cope somehow, and it seems we have. Do now?" He looked up at the screen.

"We wait to see who can repair his engines or phasers first. Until then, both vessels will continue to drift along exactly as we are—eye to eye, nose to nose—calling each other bad names."

"A most unprofitable apportionment of mental resources, Captain," the first officer observed disapprovingly.

"What was that, Spock?"

"Pay no attention, Jim," McCoy advised him. "Spock's just jealous because Vulcans are culture-conditioned against swearing."

"Word inebriation," Spock countered, slightly miffed. But that was the end of it . . .

IX

"Captain's log, supplemental." Kirk paused, took a long breath, and regarded the *Klathas*. Its position had not changed since Kumara's ploy to break free of the *Enterprise*'s tractors had been so joltingly countered. It still faced the *Enterprise* nose-on, the lights on its bridge glaring at the starship's scanners.

"We have been drifting below warp-speed together with the *Klathas* for several standard days now. Events have devolved into a race between the engineering complements of both vessels, to see which can be the first to effect repairs to their respective drives and offensive-weapons systems.

"Since phaser instrumentation requires considerably more time and effort, we are concentrating our efforts on repairing the warp-drive, with reasonable assurance that the Klingons are doing the same . . . or so Mr. Spock assures me, based on evidence of detectable activity on board the Imperial cruiser." He paused.

"My only consolation in all of this," he finally concluded, "is the knowledge that Commander Kumara of the *Klathas* is probably more frustrated than I . . ."

He finished the log entry and switched the recorder off, then took the moment of relative quiet to survey the bridge. Spock was engaged in some esoteric research of his own, his instruments set to alert him to any hint of unusual activity on board the Klingon ship. Sulu was replaying a game of trifence on an auxiliary monitor, his own telltales quiet. Uhura was half asleep at her console.

Only Arex appeared alert and absorbed. Come to think of it, the navigator had remained attentive to something for several hours now.

"What do you find so interesting, Mr. Arex?" Kirk asked.

"Hmmm?" The delicate head with its jutting bony ridges turned, limpid eyes gazed back at Kirk. "I have been engrossed in the approach of an impossibility, Captain."

Spock showed that he wasn't all that buried in research by turning to listen curiously. "Elucidate, Lieutenant."

"I have been debating whether to do precisely that, sir," Arex replied. "I wished to be certain of my findings first. It grows more extraordinary as we near. Even so, because of the uncertain situation with regard to the enemy vessel, I have hesitated before mentioning it."

"Before mentioning what, Mr. Arex?" wondered Kirk in puzzlement.

"Captain, my instruments indicate that we are approaching an object of planetary mass. Furthermore—and this is most exciting—it appears to possess free water in oceanic quantities and a breathable atmosphere."

Slowly the rest of the bridge began to stir from somnolence, began to utilize long-inactive instrumentation.

"Spock, the charts for this area—"

"Show it as an empty region, Captain. No stars, most certainly no planets." He bent to his gooseneck viewer, adjusted controls, made demands on exterior scanners and sensors. "Yet I must confirm Mr. Arex's observations." He looked up again, his eyes glowing with the fervor of a scientist who has just made a discovery as spectacular as it was unexpected.

" 'Extraordinary' is an understatement, Captain. It is unique."

"What's unique?" McCoy asked, strolling from the elevator. He had just concluded his tour of all the patients remaining in Sick Bay and satisfied himself as to their condition.

Kirk's voice was hushed with wonder. "We're apparently going to encounter a habitable world, Bones."

McCoy's gaze went to the viewscreen. It still showed only the *Klathas*, floating against a background of thinly sprinkled stars. And since the warp-drive was still out . . .

"A world . . . where, Jim? If we're approaching a sun, the scanners seem to be ignoring it."

"That's just it, Bones. There is no sun. We're going to meet a wanderer."

McCoy was properly startled. "A wanderer? An inhabitable wanderer? I thought such a thing was impossible, Jim."

"So did I, Bones. Any reasonable astronomer will tell you that the odds of encountering a planet which has broken free of its parent sun are . . . well, astronomical. I know of only two such encounters in Federation history, and both are well documented. This is a new discovery.

"But the chances of finding a wandering world with a breathable atmosphere, and free water on the surface . . ."

"Are beyond computation, Captain," Spock concurred. "I would not have believed it possible."

"To spot a non-system object of less than solar mass in free space, Bones, a ship has to be traveling below warp-one, on impulse power or less. No one travels like that . . . unless they've had an accident. Even then, with such incredible odds . . . Bones, this discovery is nearly as important as freeing Delminnen from the Klingons."

"I'm not sure Char Delminnen would agree with you, Jim," McCoy murmured softly.

Days passed. The *Enterprise* and the *Klathas*, locked together in mutual impotence, drifted closer to the wanderer. It grew from a statistic in Arex's computer to a ball, then to a globe, and finally to a massive, real world with continents and oceans and clouds.

Those clouds were the key to its habitability, for they were just thick enough to retain the heat the planet appeared to produce, yet not thick enough to produce a radical, suffocating greenhouse effect.

"According to sensors, the wanderer is about the same size as Earth," Spock was reporting, studying his readouts, "though its gravity is slightly stronger. Both the *Klathas* and the *Enterprise* have already been drawn into orbit around it."

"It's rich in heavy metals and radioactives, too," Kirk mused. "We already know it produces energy. At least we'll have the chance to inspect a unique spatial phenomenon at close range."

"And be carried a little bit farther from the Klingon base

at Shahkur Nine while we're inspecting," McCoy pointed out with satisfaction.

"There's . . . there's something else, Captain," Spock reported. There was an odd note in the first officer's voice that made Kirk turn quickly.

"What is it, Mr. Spock?"

"Incredible as it may seem," he informed the bridge, his expression as close to stunned amazement as it was possible for it to be, "this wanderer appears to be not merely habitable, but inhabited."

Spock's astonishment was instantly transmitted to everyone on the bridge.

"Spock . . . you're certain?" Kirk finally managed to mumble.

"I don't think there is any question of it, Captain. There is too much evidence for it to be denied, despite the uncertainty of high-resolution sensors. Roads, population density . . . all appear present, though in very limited fashion. It suggests a well-populated world, though a technologically impoverished one. Actual surface survey may reveal otherwise, of course."

McCoy was staring at the brilliant, glistening cloud layer against which the *Klathas* was outlined. "What must they be like, Jim, a people who have developed never knowing a sun or a moon—never even knowing the stars? If Spock's assessment of their progress is correct, they can't possibly have telescopes capable of piercing their protective cloud layer."

"I can't imagine a civilization maturing under these conditions, Bones. And yet"—Kirk gestured at the screen—"we're confronted with the actuality. What," he wondered, "should we call it?"

"That's easy, Jim. There's only one name for it—Gypsy."

For a change, Spock and the doctor were in perfect agreement.

Detailed charting of the wanderer began, under the auspices of Spock's science staff. At no time did anyone forget that a battle for survival could erupt with the *Klathas* at any moment, but Kirk could see no reason why nonessential personnel should not take the opportunity to make a thorough study of the wanderer, at least until hostilities resumed. Undoubtedly, the Klingons' science section was occupied by similar activities.

"Final estimates show gravity as one point fourteen Earth normal, atmosphere point ninety-six Earth-Vulcan normal at the surface, temperature in the temperate zones varying between one hundred eighty and two hundred five degrees K."

"Why would it vary?" McCoy asked. "There's no sun to warm any part of the globe more than another."

"The atmosphere is slightly heavier at the planet's equator, thinner at its poles," Spock explained, "although nowhere as extreme climatically as on Earth. There are no ice caps, for example. Other than that," the first officer finished, "this world is a near duplicate of Earth or Vulcan."

"What about light?" McCoy persisted. "How could any civilization develop in the total absence of light?"

"I could make a case for several such civilizations, Doctor, but for this remarkable world it is unnecessary. The dense atmosphere contains an extremely high proportion of ionized gases and natural fluorescents, which are excited by the abundance of radioactives in the surface. If anything, these people must be afflicted with perpetual illumination, and not darkness."

"I see." McCoy nodded. "They live under the granddaddy of all auroras."

"As to what the inhabitants are like, Doctor," Spock continued, "there is evidence—evidence which can be confirmed only by on-surface inspection—that they are at least roughly humanoid in appearance and build. We've sent down a few drone probes for close-in study. Superficially, at least, the resemblance to the normal Vulcan-human pattern is astounding."

"Absolutely no chance of their being advanced enough to help in repairing the *Enterprise*, or in countering the Klingons?" a hopeful Kirk queried.

"I'm afraid not, Captain," Spock replied drily. "First impressions have only just been confirmed by the probes. There are no centers of population larger than a good-sized town. Settlement appears to be primarily rural, with even villages isolated and scattered. I would say they are in the process of emerging from a medieval era into one of primitive middle-class capitalism. I'd place their level of technology no higher than fifteenth-century Earth or fifth-epoch Vulcan."

"Then we're not likely to encounter warp-drive technicians awaiting our call for assistance," Kirk observed. "Even so, the fact that they've achieved any kind of civilization at all—the very fact of their existence—is incredible. What a pity that we're too busy fighting the Klingons to remain to study them."

Spock agreed sadly. "Most unfortunate, Captain. We can plot this world's position and a probable trajectory for it, but it will still be extremely difficult to locate again."

"Excuse me, Captain." Kirk turned his attention to Uhura. "We're being beamed from the *Klathas*."

"They've got their communications working again, then. Put it on the screen, Lieutenant."

Surprisingly, Kirk found he felt no particular animosity toward the figure who appeared. There were signs of strain on the man's face: indications of fatigue induced by too much worry and too little sleep.

Kirk wondered if he looked as bad.

"Good day to you, James Kirk," Kumara began pleasantly. "I trust you are feeling well?"

"I'm getting by, Kumara. Yourself?"

The Klingon commander frowned, appeared petulant. "I've been rather restless lately, I'm afraid. For one thing, I am still rearranging my quarters. That little trick of yours in cutting your tractors and then reestablishing contact after we had changed our course drastically realigned that section of the *Klathas*."

"Sorry to hear it," Kirk replied, in a tone which indicated he wasn't sorry at all. "I'll bet that's not the only thing that's had to be rearranged." For some reason, Kirk found this falsely jovial atmosphere quite irritating. Maybe it was the memory of the faces he had seen in Sick Bay these past days.

"All right, Kumara, you didn't break battle silence for the first time in days to apprise me of the state of your bedroom. What do you want?"

Kumara's outward demeanor wasn't shaken. He remained unruffled. "You are quite correct, Jim. You see, a new development has caused me to reconsider our position.

"I have only just discovered that the man Delminnen is

utterly incapable of building, designing, or instructing my technicians in how to duplicate his awesome device. It appears only his female sibling can do that."

"You damned torturer!" McCoy exploded. "How did you pry that out of him, Kumara? I know the Klingons are noted for their inventiveness with—"

Kumara waved him to silence. "Please, ah,"—he peered harder at his own screen—"Doctor, I believe. Am I a barbarian, to resort to the primitive physical intimidation of helpless prisoners? Besides, I would not risk losing forever the knowledge held in the human Delminnen's mind.

"No, to be quite truthful, the human bragged about it all over the *Klathas* as soon as he became convinced his sibling was not on board. It was hardly necessary to pry anything out of him." The Klingon commander's expression twisted. "Needless to say, I viewed his revelation with considerable dismay."

Kirk was growing impatient. "All this unnatural courtesy and politeness must be upsetting your liver, Kumara. Why did you beam me? What is it you want?"

Kumara looked back at Kirk with exaggerated surprise. "Why, the same thing you do, Jim. An end to all this suspense and a final disposition of our . . . um . . . mutual interests."

"We'll settle that as soon as my chief engineer informs me our drive is repaired—which should be any minute now."

"Perhaps," Kumara admitted, smiling easily. "Then again, it may be some time yet before the damage to either of our ships is rectified. I have thought of another way."

"Careful, Jim," McCoy whispered.

"What *other* way, Kumara?"

"I propose a contest."

"A contest?" Kirk echoed warily. "What kind of contest?"

"One that is simple and effective." Kumara leaned forward. "It should appeal to you, Jim."

"Go on."

"It's simple, really. You wish the man Delminnen returned to you. I need his sibling. Separately, they are useless to both of us."

"I disagree," countered Kirk. "They're both still alive

... something they probably wouldn't be if you had both of them for very long."

"You question my morality, too, but never mind," Kumara continued. "Here is what I propose. I am sure you have been studying the extraordinary world below us intensively these past days. Each of us will assume the attire of the inhabitants. We will take one officer with us from our respective crews. You will also take the girl with you, while I shall bring the man.

"We will take nothing but these clothes, our communicators, and some local means of exchange, and we will beam down to the planet. There are methods of insuring that each side descends with the correct number of people, the right people, and nothing in the way of modern weapons. Neither side can attempt to unexpectedly beam the other aboard his ship, since we will both have transporters locked on us at all times. And you will recall what interlocking transporter fields did the *last* time."

"Jim, he's crazy," McCoy whispered anxiously. "You can't possibly be thinking of—"

"Go on, Kumara," Kirk said slowly.

"Each group of three will beam down at opposite ends of the largest town on the main continent, the one bordering the central sea where the two rivers meet. We will then allow ourselves three time periods under the local conditions to . . . ah . . . effect a determination of our conflict, one way or the other. If at the conclusion of that period a solution has not been achieved, each party will beam back up to its ship and we will try something else.

"Even if my group proves successful, it may still be that your ship will regain its drive and weapons capabilities first. Then my success will have been for naught. Naturally the reverse may occur. So in any case this may not necessarily be the resolution of our situation.

"What do you think?"

McCoy was stunned, for it seemed that Kirk was actually seriously considering the Klingon's proposal. "Jim, you're not thinking of going along with this madness, are you? Don't you see what he's up to? It's you he's worried about, not the *Enterprise*. He's thought up this entire bizarre scheme as a way of eliminating *you*."

"Quiet, Bones" was all Kirk said. To Kumara he explained, "I agree that we can insure through various means that no advanced weapons are transported down, that the number of personnel is limited to a single assisting officer, and so on. But even the best of such guarantees can be circumvented. I want something more."

Kumara looked like a man forced to play his last ace instead of holding it in reserve. "Very well." He rose from his command chair and lifted both arms in a peculiar salute that was half military, half religious in origin.

"I swear as commander of a warship of the Imperial Fleet, as a Klingon lord, by the sacred warrior's soul of his Imperial Majesty Emperor Karhammur the Fortieth, and by the God of Gods, Great Kinkuthanza, to abide by the terms of the contest I have just set before us and before witnesses."

He lowered his arms and resumed his seat. "Furthermore, I agree to exchange ships' *nadas*. They will be able to oversee the actual transporting of each group to the surface, besides acting as hostages."

Kirk considered, ignoring McCoy's silent entreaties. The stalemate was unnerving. Should the Klingons finish their repairs first, he would be at a decided disadvantage. He looked across at Spock and saw his first officer waiting patiently.

"What's your opinion, Mr. Spock?"

"I am not qualified to offer an opinion where a superior officer's life is at stake, Captain. However, I believe the commander's suggestion could be turned to our advantage."

Kirk nodded. "My thoughts exactly, Spock."

McCoy looked angrily over at the first officer. "You're crazy too, Spock! What makes you think a Klingon's going to adhere to any kind of rules?"

"Two things, Bones. First of all, Spock, can you recall any instance of a Klingon officer's breaking an oath sworn on the Emperor's soul and on Kinkuthanza?"

"Never, Captain. To do so would be the equivalent of murdering one's honor, and the honor of one's line back to the first generation. It is one of the few things I can think of which would be binding on a Klingon."

"Kumara," Kirk said curtly, turning back to the screen, "I accept your proposal."

"Excellent! I will beam down with one assisting officer to the eastern end of the town, the sector known to the inhabitants as 'Gray Shadow,' in one hour, your time, from the cessation of this conversation. You were always first in classes at the FEA in Adaptive Ecology, Jim. You will be a challenge. Rest assured the human Delminnen will be with me."

His arms came up and crossed again in that peculiar fashion.

"Good hunting, Jim."

The screen blanked. "Transmission ended, Captain," Uhura reported.

Kirk activated the intercom. "Alien Ecology and Sociology, attention. This is the captain speaking. I will require in forty minutes suitable attire for myself, Science Lieutenant Bresica Celli, and Ms Char Delminnen for a stay on the surface of Gypsy. Nothing fancy—you should aim for clothing appropriate for members of the lower noble classes. Also an ample supply of the local medium of exchange. Simulations must be accurate enough to fool the locals."

As he broke off and rose from the chair, McCoy stepped between Kirk and the elevator. "You're not going through with this, Jim. There are more sensible ways to get yourself killed!"

"What makes you think I'm the one who's going to get killed, Bones? I'm afraid I've got to take the risk. Kumara's gambling too. This may be our only chance to rescue Van Delminnen. If we finish engine and weapons repairs first, you know they're going to kill him rather than risk the Federation's obtaining the device. But if we conclude our repairs first *and* have both Delminnens safely on board . . . no, I can't pass up that chance."

McCoy looked desperately over at the science station. "Spock, you reason with him!"

Spock left his position and confronted Kirk, who looked back at him in surprise. "I fear the doctor is correct, Captain. I must object. As it stands now, this scheme is inadvisable, highly dangerous, and illogical."

"There, you see?" McCoy looked satisfied.

"What's the matter, Spock?" a puzzled Kirk wondered. "A moment ago you declared the contest could be to our advantage. What's made you change your mind?"

"He's seen reason, that's all, Jim."

Spock's brows arched as he glanced at McCoy. "I always see reason, Doctor." Spock turned to face Kirk. "It is your present choice of personnel, Captain, which prompts my objection."

Kirk frowned. The frown turned into a grin, and he walked back to the command chair and activated the intercom. "Sciences? Inform Lieutenant Celli his services will not be required on this expedition. The second set of native clothing should conform to the uniform specifications of First Officer Spock." He cut off and smiled back over his shoulder.

"Mr. Spock?"

Not a sign of a smile cracked that stolid visage, not a hint of a chuckle modulated the reply, but Kirk sensed both nonetheless.

"I withdraw my objection, Captain. Subsequent modifications now indicate that participation in the contest is logical."

"Spock!"

The first officer turned a reproving gaze on McCoy. "As the captain is determined to go, Doctor, it is only sensible that the best-qualified support accompany him. I am the best-qualified support. Therefore, I am going too. Really, you complicate things unnecessarily."

Spock brushed by a dazed McCoy, following Kirk into the elevator.

Alien Sociology was in constant communication with the engineers in Nonmetallic Fabrication, with the result that Kirk had hardly entered his cabin when a specialist, laden with an armload of clothing, buzzed for admittance.

Kirk accepted the bundle, dismissed the man, and set about examining all the camouflage he would have on the strange world below. Sciences had assured him that, with a few minor changes, he, Spock, and Char Delminnen would be indistinguishable from the "Gypsies" they would soon move among.

The clothes were unremarkable, that being remarkable in itself. To look closely at them one would have guessed that they had been produced on a primitive hand loom instead of in the bowels of a matrix synthesizer. Kirk tried on the boots, the simple long pants and loose upper garment, the fur vest, and he finished by closely inspecting the carefully "aged" necklace with its concealed universal translator. The matching earpiece would appear to an uncertain observer as nothing more than a minor deformity—nothing sufficient to arouse anyone's interest.

Local currency was concealed in a sort of pouch-belt and consisted of a collection of small, heavy metal squares. Fortunately, the native coins were dull and poorly stamped. There were limits even to the *Enterprise*'s ultra-high-powered sensors.

Another buzz sounded insistently at the door.

"Come," Kirk said, for the door's benefit as much as that of his visitor. Responding to his verbal command, the single wedge slid aside.

Kirk examined himself in his mirror and turned to greet McCoy. "Well, Bones, do I look like a native?"

"You look like a fool," McCoy shot back tautly, "which I suppose is appropriate, since you're going on a fool's errand."

Kirk didn't reply, but waited for the doctor to finish.

"You don't mean to go through with this, Jim. This isn't a game being played with plastic pieces on some rec-room board. Kumara wants only two things out of this—Char Delminnen alive and you dead." He looked across at his friend, expression and voice straining for comprehension. "How can you possibly trust that—that—his very concepts of right and wrong are alien to ours!"

"Bones," Kirk began softly, "I knew Kumara when both of us were green, unspaced cadets. I know that was a long time ago, but from what I've seen these past days, he hasn't changed, and I don't think I have. He might steal you blind at the first opportunity, stab you in the back if he thought he could get away with it, lie, cheat—anything for an advantage."

McCoy was nodding knowingly. "Sounds like a Klingon gentleman all right."

"But he won't go back on that oath. He'll abide because he set the guidelines, Bones, not me. Yes, he'd do all those other things, given the chance, but he won't go back on that oath. And you're right—that *is* alien to us." Carefully he smoothed the pouch-belt around his waist, so that no tempting bulges would show.

"Besides, there's no way he could go back on his word after we've exchanged *nadas*."

McCoy momentarily forgot his anger in puzzlement. "Exchange *nadas*? Didn't that have something to do with the hostage exchange you two were talking about?"

"That's right," confirmed the captain. "Another alien tradition, and another of the very few agreements binding on a Klingon. I hope you'll be comfortable during your visit to the *Klathas*, Bones."

It took much less than a minute for McCoy to digest the import of that statement. "*Me?* I'm going to the *Klathas*? But why me, Jim?"

"Because you're our resident servant and high priest of *Nada*, the Klingon god-patron of medicine. There have been reports of Klingons entering a hospital on board ship or on-planet and massacring the patients . . . but they have never touched a physician. It's part of their warrior-tainted cultural pattern. Your status on the *Klathas* will be that of a saint, Bones."

"Saint to a bunch of Klingons—I can't think of a less welcome honor."

"You'd better be grateful for it. It guarantees your immunity . . . and for that reason you're the only one I can trust the Klingons *not* to massacre if the contest goes against them. Naturally, while you're on board the *Klathas*, your Klingon counterpart will be here on the *Enterprise*."

"But it's all unnecessary, Jim," McCoy objected one last time. "Kumara's set the whole thing up. He's called the rules, the place, everything. And another thing . . . How can you risk something as potentially dangerous as the Delminnen device on a two-man expedition?"

Kirk sighed. "I told you, Bones, it's our best chance for rescuing Van Delminnen." He started for the door.

McCoy put a restraining hand on his shoulder, still angry and still unconvinced. When he spoke again, his tone was low and almost accusing.

"Blast it, Jim, are you sure you're going through with this because you believe that—or because you're as vain about your ability to outmaneuver Kumara on a strange world as he thinks you are?"

Kirk glared at the doctor, and for a long moment what

passed between them was as eloquent as it was unspoken. Finally: "You think Kumara's appealing to my vanity, then?"

"Is he, Jim?"

"I . . . I don't know. Maybe he is, Bones. Maybe he has already outmaneuvered me before the game's even started. But I do know this . . ." His voice rose.

"Besides keeping the weapon from the Klingons, there's also Char Delminnen to think of. It's our duty to save her brother, because he's a Federation citizen, because he's a human being. If I pass up a chance to do that to protect my own neck, Bones, then my commission's worthless.

"In addition, I'm going crazy waiting around while our engineering section races theirs to see who can fix their engines first. Don't you think Kumara's nervous? He's so nervous, *he's* the one who's proposed something to resolve part of our problem, given us the chance to do something besides sit around and wait for our fingernails to dissolve in our mouths.

"By all that's worth salvaging in this bizarre galaxy, Bones, I'm going to make the most of that opportunity."

Neither man moved until McCoy seemed to slump in on himself a little. He looked away. "All right. If I can't talk you out of it, at least I can accompany you to the transporter room."

"Sure you don't want to take anything with you, Bones," Kirk wondered, "to make your visit on the *Klathas* more bearable?"

"The only thing that could do that would be a Class Four phaser," the doctor grunted, "suitable for performing large-scale surgery on massed Klingon bodies. Let's go . . ."

X

"Captain's log, supplemental," Kirk recited, addressing the wall intercom in the Transporter Room. It was keyed by verbal command to the ship's log.

"Char Delminnen, Mr. Spock, and myself are preparing to beam down to the wandering world we have named Gypsy to commence a contest with our Klingon counterparts. We hope this contest will favorably resolve the stalemate in which we presently find ourselves with regard to her brother and the Imperial cruiser *Klathas*.

"In consequence of this, an exchange of ships' chief physicians has been effected, thus forcing a solemn bind upon the Klingons not to deviate from the rules set down for the competition . . . with appropriate sensors and scanners also monitoring the terms of the contest.

"Doctor McCoy is now aboard the *Klathas*, and his Klingon doppelgänger, Surgeon-in-Battle Kattrun dek Prenn, has arrived aboard the *Enterprise*." He paused for a second, finally adding, "I only hope that my evaluation of the incipient action turns out to be more accurate than Dr. McCoy's."

The entry ended, Kirk turned and walked past the transporter console to join a waiting Spock and Char Delminnen in the activated alcove. Briefly he noted the disposition of their native garb, the quality and detail of their facial makeup, and found everything satisfactory, if not visually pleasing.

"Ready, Mr. Spock?"

"Quite ready, Captain." He rubbed at the thick cap pulled low on his head. "Though this wig and attendant headgear are more than a little irritating."

"You'll get used to them, Spock. They're necessary—our Gypsies don't have acute hearing organs."

"An unfortunate evolutionary defect," the first officer commented drily.

Kirk smiled, then turned a more solemn, appraising gaze on the stiff figure at his right. "And you, Ms. Delminnen, are you sure you want to go through with this? Our success hinges on you, you know. I can't order you to participate."

Her reply was impatient. "I've already consented to it, Captain, as has my brother. The sooner we stop brooding about possible consequences and get on with it, the sooner Van and I will be reunited. Isn't that right?"

"That is very right." Convinced that the slight, hypertense woman would be an asset rather than a burden, Kirk turned to face back into the room. After a quick check of the chronometer disguised as a ring, he said pleasantly, "Energize when ready, Mr. Scott."

"Aye, Captain."

The chief engineer adjusted the necessary instrumentation, and in a moment the ship's population decreased by three. At the same time, two beings of differing temperament and physical makeup lay in unfamiliar surroundings and began counting the minutes. There were a great many to pass until the end of three days, and none could say whether Dr. Leonard McCoy or SIB Kattrun dek Prenn counted harder . . .

A good deal of planning and examination of long-range sensor reports had gone into determining exactly where the party from the *Enterprise* should set down. Ideally, the place should offer temporary concealment without being too isolated, and without immediately exposing the strangers to the new world—or the new world to the strangers—before either had a chance to be acclimated.

So the three ministers in mufti materialized in the middle of a deserted alleyway. Faint people noises could be heard nearby, just loud enough for all three to properly adjust their necklace translators.

Even more than the damp alleyway with its claustrophobic high stone walls, even more than the always mind-tingling sound of a new tongue, Kirk was drawn to the sky overhead. The light was dimmer than was usual on Earth, but more spectacular than the meteorologists had predicted.

No one color dominated a sky that was aflame with auroral blaze: Reds, greens, blues and golds and violent purple shifted and writhed in an atmosphere of perpetual excitation. Whenever a particularly brilliant display occurred, they would acquire a new phenomenon—a shadow. And the shadows changed constantly, according to the varying intensity of the sky. To look at one's own shadow was to be subject to a stroboscopic display of peculiarly personal dimensions.

A final check insured that no one had observed their unorthodox method of arrival. "Everyone all right?" Kirk whispered. His words sounded strange and tickled his brain, voiced as they were through the translator in the local tongue and then retranslated back through the tiny device implanted in his left ear.

"Quite, Captain . . . ," "Yes, Captain . . . ," came the replies.

"Okay, our first step is to obtain some local weapons. I don't expect Kumara to waste any time in local sight-seeing, so we'd better not either." He turned to face the open end of the alley. "If Scotty dropped us where the cartographers indicated he should, we ought to be next to a fair-sized marketplace."

The group moved cautiously down the alleyway and out into a strange new world of noise and movement and color. The alley fronted on an extensive bazaar. One old woman saw them emerge from the alley. If she found it extraordinary, she chose not to publicize the discovery. Kirk already suspected from the sociologists' preliminary reports that this was a world where one minded one's own business.

They began to stroll down the long lanes between stalls. The bazaar was a weird combination of old Earth Arabian and medieval Edoan.

One thing that was never in doubt from the moment they appeared was the efficacy of their disguises. They were immediately besieged by hawkers and vendors offering wares and goods and services as colorful as they were enigmatic. There were many offered which even Spock could make no sense of, and others which seemed to conflict with laws natural and otherwise.

Their objectives now were too practical to be disguised by alien rhetoric, however. Kirk adopted what he hoped was just the right degree of imperious indifference, ignoring bargains and luxuries alike.

"Something about this all strikes me as very strange, Captain," Spock commented, his gaze moving from one stall to the next.

"That's hardly surprising, Mr. Spock," replied Kirk, fending off a proffered armload of aromatic meat. "This whole world is very strange, from its very existence on down."

"Captain Kirk." He turned his attention to the booth Char Delminnen was pointing at.

It was a tightly sealed, smallish shop, its narrow tables replete with lethal-looking medieval-style weaponry, some faintly familiar, some less so. None was beyond utilization by the new arrivals. There are only so many ways to change the appearance of metal designed to penetrate another person without impairing its efficiency.

Hands clasped over a well-cultivated paunch, the proprietor stood staring pensively at the entrance to his stall.

Kirk said, "Excuse me, we need to buy some weapons." The translator, bearing in mind Kirk's assumed social station on this world, translated it as:

"Bestir thyself, o lazy one! We would purchase arms from your pitiful stock."

The stall owner started and nearly fell over his own legs in his haste to get to his feet. His eyes glittered nearly as much as the false jewels in Kirk's necklace.

"Ten thousand genuflections, noble sir! The gods' blessings on you and your offspring, may they be many. You desire weapons? Rest content you have come to the finest armory in the city. My most magnificent steels and swords, knives and daggers, are unmatched—and available especially to you, my lords and lady, at prices so modest as to make one blush the color of her cheeks. Were you to search a thousand years through a hundred—"

"Enough, grandfather of loquacity! You have convinced us," Kirk declared, the translator once again having embellished his simple reply. He made a pretense of inspecting the stock. "We shall require two swords of your best metal and temper—sabers, not rapiers. And two dirks, short and tough enough to penetrate leather without turning." He hesitated. "And your most delicately honed stiletto for the lady."

Char Delminnen eyed him with satisfaction.

The owner was bowing and abasing himself to the point of embarrassing both Kirk and Spock, though it was more to conceal the mercenary gleam in his eyes than to honor his customers.

"At once, noble lords! You shall have the finest only. I do not keep the very best here exposed to the sky, and to thieves. Pray grant me a moment." Still bowing obsequiously, he backed into the depths of the stall.

Spock's attention had remained focused on the constantly moving, surrounding crowd. The first officer had been quite content to leave the purchasing to Kirk, who now turned to him, whispering.

"Any sign of Kumara or anyone who might be his accompanying officer?"

Spock shook his head. "If they are in our immediate vicinity, Captain, they are too well disguised for me to discover. I think we are still reasonably safe. Even at a fast run, it is still a fair distance to the other side of this town."

They separated as the owner, puffing heavily, appeared with the five weapons.

"As you requested, lords," he beamed, setting them out carefully on red velvet. "The apex of my humble craft. Notice the color in the metal, the superb honing!" He rambled on as Kirk and Spock hefted the swords, removing them from their matching scabbards. They made a few practice passes at each other with them, keeping the movements simple. Modern fencing might very well be an eye-catching anomaly here, and one thing they didn't desire was suspicious attention from the locals.

"I suppose they'll do," Kirk agreed, the words coming out in a bored and slightly petulant tone. He slid his saber into the scabbard, which attached easily to his pouch-belt. The thick, triangular dirks went through a belt loop on the opposite side from the sword. Char Delminnen found a secretive place for the narrow stiletto.

"I know you will be pleased, noble lords." His eyes narrowed and he leaned forward, lowering his voice. "It is plain you are not of Ghuncha Town, and are strangers here. Might I make so bold as to inquire—"

"As to the cost, which can be excessive for those who are too curious," Spock interrupted. His brows rose slightly at the way the translator interpreted his prosaic sentence.

"Certainly, yes," the proprietor babbled hastily. "I did not mean to pry, I did not . . . fifty *pahds*, noble sirs, will be more than sufficient."

"Since it is more than sufficient, it is doubtless more than we should pay," Kirk rumbled, reaching into the lining of his pouch-belt. "However, I have no time to haggle." He brought out a handful of brown metal squares. The shopkeeper's eyes nearly joined an unsold sword on the red velvet as Kirk counted out five of the largest squares and handed them to the man.

"Thank you, noble lords . . . blessings forever upon you," he called as they turned and began walking away. "Blessings a thousand times!"

"I'd trade a thousand blessings for a place to rest, Captain Kirk," Delminnen ventured many hours later. "Isn't it time to stop? There's no real night here, so we'll have to decide on our own."

"Innkeeping must be a round-the-clock business on Gypsy, Captain," Spock added. "We should have no difficulty in locating a busy one. Ms. Delminnen is correct. We must pace ourselves carefully or risk exhaustion at a crucial moment. The slightly greater gravity here does tend to weary one rapidly. I could use a meal myself."

"All right," Kirk agreed, wiping his forehead. The strain of trying to locate a Klingon under every curious face was beginning to tire him also. "It would be a good idea to establish some kind of local base of operations while we still have time for such things. Any sign of a likely prospect, Mr. Spock?"

The first officer was standing on tiptoe, staring ahead and slightly to their left. "I have already addressed myself to the problem, Captain. There appears to be an inn of some sort directly ahead of us."

A short walk brought them to the front of the establishment. They couldn't read the lettering on its front, but a quick, unobtrusive survey of the structure's exterior and the clientele carefully moving in and out through the oddly hinged multiple swinging—or was it folding—doors seemed to confirm Spock's initial appraisal. Furthermore, the appearance of those entering and leaving suggested a moderately high-class business.

That was enough for Kirk. They would have enough trouble remaining incognito without inviting conflict with the less savory elements of the native population. After watching the operation of the strange doors long enough to insure they wouldn't get pinched by them, he led Spock and Delminnen inside.

A system of mirrors and high windows admitted plenty of light. The interior wasn't much dimmer than the alley they had materialized in. To their left was a series of low tables at which some natives, mostly male, reclined while drinking and eating. To the right was a circular desk.

Between the two a long, paved walkway ran slightly above floor level until it met a branching stairway at the far end of the big room. This led up to a series of interior balconies before terminating in a large skylight three stories up.

A few patrons looked up, casually inspected the newcomers, and returned to their meals. Kirk noted the relative cleanliness of the place with satisfaction and moved to address the single opening in the high circular desk.

There was no one behind it. A small gong hung under a curved support to one side. Kirk lifted the tiny metal stick and hit the gong once, twice.

A tall, aged, cadaverous native appeared from an unsuspected doorway at the back of the concealed area. He wore an interesting arrangement of bloomers and overlapping vests, together with what would pass on Earth for a mournful expression. He looked more like a mortician than a concierge . . . a fact which led Kirk to wonder about the perhaps deceptive peacefulness of the inn.

Nevertheless, they were here, and it was unlikely they would encounter any place better.

"What," the native asked tiredly, "do my lords require?"

"Food and lodging for this night and maybe several more. Your best room, on the second floor, one entrance only."

The native glanced at Char Delminnen, then back at Kirk. "One room, my lord, for the three of you?"

The translator turned Kirk's mild impatience into anger. "Yes, *one* room! Are you deaf—or do you wish to be? There must be sufficient individual bedding for all. You will see to it personally that suitable arrangements are made."

Either this native was made of stronger stuff than the weapons seller or he simply didn't care. "Whatever my lords require. I shall see to it."

Kirk turned as if to leave, then hesitated. "There is one more thing, innkeeper."

"My lord?"

"Have you yourself seen, or heard tell of, two men . . . strangers like ourselves, with strong jaws and exceptional arrogance? They have a slightly foppish, tremendously arrogant younger man with them?" Kirk noticed Char Delminnen bridle at that description of her brother, but, if anything, the translators would only enlarge on his characterization of Van Delminnen's natural obstinacy.

The innkeeper paused thoughtfully. " 'Arrogance' is a strange word to use in identifying a man, my lord. I am sorry, but I am not in any way familiar with the persons you describe."

"I see," replied a disappointed Kirk. "Should you hear tell of such a group, inform us at once." He jiggled his pouch-belt significantly, so that the native could hear the clink of currency within.

The innkeeper merely bowed politely. "I shall do so, my lords." He gestured at the double stairway at the far end of the room. "Stairway on your right, second floor, third door down." A peculiarly shaped key was handed over. "Rest well. The room is already prepared as you desire."

Kirk frowned momentarily but then, why shouldn't such a room be readily available? He took the key, and they started for the stairs.

It was fortunate that the native's directions had been so explicit, since the carved squiggles on each door meant nothing to any of them. Kirk tried the door and found it unlocked, and they entered.

The room was spacious but dim, despite the large window. Spock moved to inspect it. He noted with a mutter of gratification that it was a sheer drop to the street below, and that the building facing them had no window directly opposite. They would have nothing to worry about from that quarter.

From there he moved to the door. Fishing into his own pouch-belt, he produced a tiny, simple lock. It looked like a local native handicraft, but was far stronger and more subtle than any lock on this world. He began to install it on the door.

"Spock and I are going to make one last sweep of our immediate area," Kirk was explaining to the exhausted Char Delminnen, "to make certain Kumara and your brother aren't close at hand. You may as well get some rest in the meantime." He nodded toward the door. "The lock Mr. Spock is installing is coded to respond only to our three voices."

"I'd like to go with you, Captain, but . . . I *am* tired. All right, I'll wait for you here. Wake me when you return. Then I can keep a watch while you and Mr. Spock take some rest."

"Sounds good, Ms. Delminnen. We'll try not to be too long." He reached out to pat her reassuringly on the shoulder—and froze as she leaned forward, up . . . and kissed him.

"Ready, Captain?" a blank-faced Spock asked from the half-open doorway.

Kirk gazed back at her uncertainly, finding her expression more unreadable than that of any other woman he'd ever seen. Whether there was affection, or curiosity, or something utterly incomprehensible in her stare he couldn't say.

"Coming, Mr. Spock."

The incident wasn't mentioned, and Spock gave every indication of having consigned it to the part of his mind reserved for filing inexplicable human actions. Kirk knew Spock had forgotten nothing, but he was grateful for his first officer's efforts to give the appearance of having done so.

Gradually it slipped from his mind too as they moved about the shops and homes and stalls, questioning the natives with increasing ease and the assurance that, while they were undeniably strangers, no one suspected how strange they actually were.

The questioning process became an exercise in consistent futility. No matter how detailed, how graphic, they made their descriptions of Kumara and Van Delminnen, they were greeted with the same negative response.

"No, noble lords, I have seen no one fitting such a description . . ." "Pardon, noble sirs, never have we heard tell of men with eyes such as you claim . . ." "No, I have not heard of them, or set sight of them myself . . ." "I have not . . ." "No . . ." "Not I . . ." "Never . . ."

By the time they returned to the inn, Kirk was too tired to care if Kumara was in this section of the town, or still at the opposite end, or back on the *Klathas*.

"I'd feel a lot better," he told Spock as they started up the stone stairway, "if I knew Kumara's intentions. That's more important than his location."

A scream sounded from upstairs. It was slightly muffled, but still audible enough for both men to know instantly it did not come from a native throat.

"I believe we are about to obtain a partial answer to both questions, Captain."

The transporter could have gotten them upstairs faster—but not much faster. Kirk had a hand out, reaching for the door handle, when it opened from within. He found himself face to face with a short, stocky native. This individual, whose countenance screamed "thug," had one arm wrapped tightly around a weakly struggling Char Delminnen.

They stared at each other in momentary paralysis. The native saw Spock standing behind Kirk, computed the odds, and let go of Delminnen. Turning, he made a run for the open window as fast as his bandy, muscular legs could carry him.

Kirk brushed past the dazed Delminnen and tackled the native just before he could reach the rope dangling outside the window. Both men crashed to the floor, and Kirk discovered that he was grappling with a python. Gravity-stressed muscles shoved him onto his back, and he saw the glint of light on metal as the native raised the knife.

A hand came down on the native's shoulder, fingers moved quickly and skillfully, and the native collapsed. Panting heavily from the exertion under the strong gravity, Kirk slid out from under the unconscious form and climbed to his feet. Another figure drew him over to the far bed.

Char Delminnen was sitting there, shivering noticeably

but otherwise apparently in control of herself. Kirk moved to touch her, hesitated, and drew back.

"He came in through the window?"

She nodded weakly.

"The rope is suspended from the roof, Captain," Spock reported. Holding on to the sill with one hand, he was leaning out over the street and peering upward. Now he came back inside and closed the window behind him. "I apologize, Ms. Delminnen. I was negligent in my analysis of this room's defensive potential. At the time it did not occur to me that one could as easily come down to this room as up to it. Curious oversight."

"Forget it, Spock," ordered Kirk. "I didn't think of it either. We're not used to acting like cat-burglars."

" 'Cat-burglars,' Captain? The reference—"

"Has nothing to do with stealing cats," Kirk hastened to explain. That brought a hesitant grin from Char Delminnen. She stopped shaking and gestured.

"I think my visitor is coming around, Captain."

Indeed, the native was emitting bubbling sounds indicative of rising consciousness. Spock helped him to his feet and steadied the man's staggers with one hand on his shoulder and the other holding an arm tightly behind his back.

The native looked fearfully from Char Delminnen to Kirk. He tried to break free . . . but only once. Then his gaze dropped to the wooden floor, and he muttered sullenly, "What will you do to me . . . noble lords." The last was uttered in a fashion clearly indicating that their nobility was in considerable question.

"Nothing . . . if you answer a few questions," Kirk told him honestly. "Who sent you to kidnap the woman?"

The native remained silent. Spock moved his fingers on the man's shoulder in a certain way, and the man winced.

"Was it a tall man," Kirk continued evenly, "with very small pupils and dry-looking skin? Who moved quickly and with sharp gestures?"

The native's face twisted bizarrely as Spock applied further pressure. Finally: "Yes, yes . . . now let me go, sirs!" As Spock's hand relaxed, so did the native's expression. "I'll tell you what you wish."

The first officer let go and took a couple of quick steps

back, remaining between the native and the now closed window. Sighing in a very humanlike fashion, the native rubbed his neck and shook his freed arm to get the blood (or whatever served for bodily fluid here) moving again.

"Where did you meet this man?" Kirk continued.

"At the Inn of the Six Rains. He offered me three hundred *pahds* if I would bring him a woman he described to me." The native indicated the attentive Delminnen. "That woman."

"Was he alone?"

"No." The native looked thoughtful. "There were two other lords with him. One was very much like the first, but the third was different. He was smaller and quiet . . . in fact, he said nothing while I was present."

"Under orders from Kumara, no doubt, Captain," commented Spock.

"This other lord," Char Delminnen broke in, "who did not speak. Did he look well to you?"

The native eyed her curiously. "As well as the others . . . though I confess I paid little notice to him. It was the largest of the three lords I was concerned with."

"The one who offered you the money," Kirk declared pointedly. "This lord—he told you where to find the woman?"

"No."

Kirk relaxed considerably at that. That meant Kumara was probably not waiting for them downstairs, or rigging the stairway or preparing similar deviltry nearby.

"I found her myself, from the information the lord gave to me . . . gave to all of us."

"All of you?" Spock echoed. "There are more than one?"

"Aye. There were many present to hear the lord's offer."

"Why are you telling us this?"

The native made an indecipherable gesture. "Why should I help some other *cajjy* get rich?"

"It sounds like the sort of thing Kumara would do," mused Kirk sardonically. "Find himself a nice, peaceful room in a comfortable inn near his beam-down point, and then hire half the small-time cutthroats in town to do his dirty work for him, so he doesn't have to risk his own precious skin. Kumara's an atypical Klingon, Spock, but he's still a Klingon."

"I had not intended to dispute that, Captain," the first officer essayed easily. "I do wish to point out a significant new fact, however."

"What? What new fact, Spock?"

"Captain, we now have a distinct advantage. Kumara is ignorant as to our whereabouts, but we now know where he is based."

They exchanged glances. While they do so, the native showed that his body was more alert than his expression. He darted around a not-quite-fast-enough Spock, dove for the rope through the closed window, and missed.

All three rushed to the window. No crowd gathered below to inspect the body. On the contrary, there was a distinct absence of curiosity on the part of the populace.

"One native dead . . . one too many." Kirk looked over at his friend and second-in-command. "I think it's time we paid a visit to the Inn of the Six Rains, Mr. Spock."

"I agree, Captain."

They turned to leave. Char Delminnen was waiting by the door. She eyed Kirk expectantly.

"I can't leave you here and risk having another of Kumara's hired thugs finding you. Do you think you're up to coming with us, or should we hunt for another inn and wait a while longer?"

By way of answering she showed the stiletto, which her attacker had given her no opportunity to use, then slipped it back inside her blouse.

"Let's find my brother, Captain Kirk."

This time, she gave *his* shoulder a reassuring squeeze.

For a worried moment, Kirk was concerned that they might get no closer to the Inn of the Six Rains than the front door of their own inn. The dour manager was waiting for them by his enclosed moat of a desk, with two towering locals. The newcomers wore identical clothing. Kirk didn't think it was because they were relatives; he had been on enough worlds to recognize a uniform when he saw one.

"Captain," Spock whispered as the innkeeper gestured to them, "we could use the rope outside our room, ascend to the roof . . ."

"Easy, Spock. Surely other residents heard the scream. They can testify in our favor."

"There is trouble, my lords," the innkeeper explained sorrowfully.

"I can explain," Kirk began, addressing himself to the two giants instead of the speaker. "We had no intention of killing—"

The giant on the left interrupted. "Our concern is not with your intentions, or the question of killings, noble lord. But it is evident you are strangers here." He indicated the innkeeper, who looked embarrassed. "There is the matter of a shattered window."

It took a minute for the giant's words to penetrate. Once they had, Kirk settled the matter quickly. Spock chided him later for risking his cover by sinfully overpaying, but Kirk paid his first officer little heed. He was too glad to be free of local justice.

One thing was certain: They had encountered an ideal world on which to engage in Kumara's contest.

Local in-town transportation was nonexistent, they discovered the next day, but they had no difficulty in locating the Inn of the Six Rains once they had crossed the town's center. It seemed that everyone knew everything about the town, a consequence of having to walk everywhere.

The inn itself was nearly a duplicate of the one they had left, even to the fortresslike innkeeper's desk and the dining area opposite it. It had the same raised walkway in between, leading this time to a single stairway at its end. They did have the advantage of two things their old inn did not: booths and a noisy crowd.

Kirk found the atmosphere much more saloonlike than that of their own abode. Drinking was going on in earnest around them, and the air was filled with short, intriguing native laughter, shouting, and pungent smoke.

The innkeeper had assured the gentlemen that the three they searched for were indeed domiciled there. No, they were away at present. Perhaps they would return soon, to greet their friends from the country. In the meantime, why not sit and have good drink and pass tall stories around?

Kirk glanced across the busy tables at the innkeeper's station. He had watched the native carefully when they'd inquired after Kumara. Neither he nor Spock could detect any uncertainty at their questions, any sign of nervousness. The native had acted open instead of devious, and there was little they could do to test him further without arousing suspicions that seemed not to exist.

The three of them sat deep in a high-backed booth, playing at drinking thick wooden mugs of native brew while they carefully scrutinized the swinging doorway.

"Do you really think they'll return here, Captain Kirk?" Char Delminnen wondered uncertainly. Kirk touched the frothy mug to his lips and let a little slide down his throat. It was heady stuff, thick and spicy.

"They've no reason not to. That unfortunate native whose abduction we spoiled indicated that all of Kumara's hirelings are working alone. In fact, he exhibited a downright distaste for working with anyone else. So there's no way for Kumara to know that we've discovered his hiding place."

"That is a certainty, Captain," said Spock with conviction, gesturing toward the entrance.

Three figures came through the swinging doors leading into the inn from the street. Kirk had to blink, so thorough was the Klingon facial makeup. Nevertheless, he could recognize Kumara in the lead, followed by a disgusted-looking Van Delminnen, with another Klingon bringing up the rear of the little party.

Kirk had visions of watching them head straight up to their room, waiting until the Klingons were asleep, then stealing quietly upstairs to knock out any local guards and make off with Delminnen. This fantasy lasted until Char Delminnen jumped up and let out a joyful "Van—it's me, Van!"

About the only thing Kirk could salvage now was the memory of the startled surprise that appeared on Kumara's face.

"Come on, Spock!" Drawing their swords, they rushed toward Kumara.

Kirk engaged the Klingon commander, while Spock took on his assistant. It had been some time since he had worked with a saber, but certain things, once learned, are never forgotten. Not by the mind, and not by the body.

So while Kumara pressed him desperately hard at first, Kirk found himself gaining strength and confidence with each successful parry, each near cut. Char and Van Delminnen were clasping each other happily, chatting away as though neither one's fate and perhaps life was hanging in the balance.

The destruction engendered by the battle, which the other patrons were watching with stoic silence, was enough to bring a pleading, agonized innkeeper out from behind his desk.

"My lords . . . Please, I beg you, my lords! Take your quarrels out in the street. Have pity on me, pity my house, my lords!"

Otherwise occupied, the four combatants utterly ignored him.

Finally the innkeeper turned and whispered something to a solemn little boy, who nodded in comprehension and rushed out. That left the florid proprietor standing before his disintegrating dining area, watching the battle, tight-lipped and silent.

"How—did you find us—Jim?" Kumara wondered, his wrist twisting and turning steadily, precisely.

Kirk caught an overhead blow on the flat of his blade, causing it to slide off harmlessly to his left, and countered with a cut of his own to the waist. He spaced his reply carefully between breaths.

"You should—hire a better class—of assassin, Kumara. The one who—found us—was willing to talk. Money never inspires—much in the way—of loyalty. Pity for you."

"A pity—for you, Jim," countered the Klingon commander, his own sword making half circles in the air. "For now, much—as I dislike the thought—I am compelled—to kill you."

He turned the blade and lunged with the point, forcing Kirk backward.

Spock was pressing his opponent much more seriously. That engagement had begun with the other attacking furiously, wildly, drunk with self-confidence. Spock had blocked, retreated, parried every cut and thrust.

Gradually confidence gave way to rage, while Spock continued methodically to defend himself, content to let his opponent wear himself out—which was precisely what was happening. Now it was the *Enterprise*'s first officer who was pressing the attack, with equal precision, never giving his increasingly desperate counterpart a chance to rest.

An especially hard blow from his saber sent his assailant reeling. Panic showed in the Klingon's face. He backed, parrying wildly. Spock followed close—then suddenly his feet were gone from under him. He had slipped in a pool of stagnant drink, and abruptly found himself flat on his back.

Smiling triumphantly, his opponent jumped forward, his sword swinging high over his shoulder, ready to chop down heavily and slice flesh from bone.

Spock flipped his saber in his hand, caught it by the flat of the blade, and threw. The talkative armorer's claims had not been understated, and that possibly saved Spock's life.

The saber struck bone, but instead of snapping, it slid off. Its momentum carried it on through, its point coming out the back of the Klingon's shirt. A surprised, puzzled expression came over his face. His arm came down, and the sword flew from his hand. Spock was able to dodge—but not completely. The blade struck his forehead at an angle.

A hand came up, and then, blood welling from the wound, Spock fell back unconscious.

The Klingon officer's gaze turned slowly, slowly downward. It settled on the hurtful thing which penetrated him from front to back. Then his eyes closed, and he toppled onto a deserted table.

All the while, the crowd watched silently.

Kirk didn't see what had happened to Spock. He had no time. Kumara lunged again, forcing the captain back a little farther, and then made a peculiar thrust with his sword that no human could have duplicated. His blade came under Kirk's at the pommel, shoved and twisted—and Kirk's saber flew halfway across the room.

Grinning, Kumara lunged again, as Kirk grabbed a chair and swept it up before him desperately. The Klingon commander's sword pierced the wood and snapped cleanly in half as Kirk continued his swing with the chair.

Cursing, Kumara pulled and threw his knife, which Kirk caught on the chair's backswing. The captain threw the chair at Kumara, drew his own dirk, and followed the projectile. Kumara's hand came up frantically to catch Kirk's wrist, and then the two men were tumbling over and over each other through the sticky, food-filled gaps between the tables.

Both arms swung out and around to strike one unyielding

chair leg. Kirk's wrist suddenly became numb, and the knife flew five meters. The combatants continued to roll about, arms and legs thrashing violently.

None of the onlookers attempted to interfere. They continued to watch dispassionately as the two strangers were reduced to swinging weakly at each other, each barely able to fend off the attacks of the other.

"Con—cede." Kumara gasped in pain, his head bobbing loose on his neck as though springs and not ligaments kept it joined to his head.

Kirk shook his head slowly, lacking the strength for a verbal reply—and even that action nearly caused him to collapse.

Several giants entered the room, ducking their heads to pass through the entrance. The largest looked at the room, his gaze traveling slowly from left to right to take in the two Delminnens, now also watching the battle on the floor, the two barely erect combatants weaving in its center, the dead one on the floor, and the injured one lying nearby.

He shook his head slowly from side to side, and the gesture was echoed by many in the silent crowd.

XI

A hand moved lazily, drawing delicate designs in the dust. Kumara considered what he had wrought, then obliterated it with a wave of his palm. His sole real complaint about the cell was that there was nothing to lean against save the chill stone walls.

Otherwise, it was the absence of certain devices which made it far more pleasurable a place to idle than its Klingon counterpart. He forced himself to sit away from the wall as he looked across the straw-and-dirt floor at his companions.

Kirk gazed back quietly. Several hours ago he and Kumara had tried their best to kill each other. Now they sat unbelligerently in the same room, in the same fix, and wished devoutly that their captors would put off doing anything until the contest's time limit had elapsed, at which time their respective transporters would pull them back to the safety of the two cruisers.

If not, Kirk mused, Scotty was liable to beam several corpses aboard the *Enterprise*. One area which the sociologists had not researched was Gypsian penology.

His eyes left Kumara and traveled around the windowless cell. Spock was busy rewinding the bandage around his forehead. The Delminnens sat off in a corner by themselves, still engrossed in each other and no doubt cursing Kirk, Kumara, and all the others who'd meddled in their lives.

"I must compliment you, Mr. Spock," Kumara said into the low drone formed by the Delminnens. "I happened to observe you at the moment when you dispatched Lieutenant Kritt. That was an admirable bit of quick thinking and reaction, which Kritt ought to have anticipated." The commander's mouth twisted into an unreadable expression. "Kritt always was an over-confident fool."

"It was," Spock replied, his voice absolutely flat, "the only logical thing left to do. I had hoped merely to disarm him, not to kill."

"I might have supposed you would say something like that," Kumara declared. Spock did not reply, so the commander turned his gaze heavenward.

"Ah, Gods, what a way for a Klingon officer to die. Here I sit, helpless among my enemies—me, the commander of one of the most powerful instruments in the galaxy. Doomed I am to die via some no doubt unimaginative method concocted by a council of superstitious barbarians."

"Quite a performance, Kumara," Kirk commented when the commander's plaint had ended, "but you always did make a specialty of substituting show for substance. I'm surprised at your resignation. If we can stall things for another day and a half, or if our captors remain inactive, our transporters will pluck us safe and free. And remember, it was your idea that we descend without modern weapons."

"Advanced weaponry could have stimulated latent cowardice," Kumara shot back.

Kirk started to move toward the Klingon, but Spock reached out to restrain him. "Easy, Captain, there is nothing to be gained by fighting now. The opportunity to escape may eventually present itself . . . though I am not optimistic." He looked up. "This cell is well designed with an eye toward preventing any such occurrence." His gaze dropped to Kumara. "Even if it was constructed by mere superstitious barbarians, who are advanced enough to confiscate our communicators."

The Klingon commander had no comment.

"Suppose we did escape?" Kirk turned to look over at Char Delminnen, as did Kumara. "Wouldn't you two have to begin again with Van and me?" There was bitterness in her voice.

Surprisingly, it was Kumara who replied. "Young female, if allowing you and your sibling to depart peacefully homeward would do anything to alleviate our present difficulties, I would be the first to see you safely on your way. Unfortunately, I fear that circumstances have long since been in control of all our destinies, so that, while possibly accurate, your accusations will never be put to the test. I suspect that we are all to be tried together—if the concept of a trial exists on this orphaned world."

"Whatever they have planned for us can't be any worse than Klingon justice," commented Kirk with a vicious smile.

Now it was an angry Kumara's turn to start forward.

Spock forestalled further hostilities by assuming a pose of attention and announcing, "Not now, gentlemen. Several people are approaching."

All five hurried to scramble to their feet. A small party of armed men appeared outside their cell. Among them Kirk recognized the jailer, who had brought them food and water, and the leader of the group of giants that had brought them here from the Inn of the Six Rains.

The jailer worked on the crude (but efficient) lock while the rest of the party warily eyed those on the other side of the cementwork.

"You are to be given the privilege of pleading your case before the Justice Council. Come along . . . and mind your words and manner. The Council is not to be trifled with."

Guarded beyond any chance of making a run, they were convoyed up stairs, down corridors, and around bends. The room they finally arrived in was modest in size and decor. At one end was a high bench with a single high podium at its center. This was backed by five empty seats. Auroral blaze lit the room, shafting down through a high-domed glass ceiling.

Several tiered benches formed concentric semicircles at the opposite end of the room, and scattered, somewhat bored natives occupied these. They seemed to perk up a little when the captives entered, though.

Kirk and the others were conducted to a long padded bench which faced the higher bench and podium at the near end of the room. Their guards directed them to sit, then moved to join other guards at the two doors.

A single short, elderly native clad in dress of the utmost simplicity appeared. The grating, off-key tune he played was as weird and unnerving as the trumpetlike instrument he performed it on. At this signal, a hidden door opened behind the podium and five natives—two men and three women—

appeared. They assumed the five seats before the captives. Kirk noted with interest that they were also clad in plain dress, including the old man who took the podium seat. There was nothing to distinguish their office, nothing to differentiate them from the poorest beggar in the streets. Cleanliness, perhaps, but then, even the beggars Kirk had seen in the marketplace had been fairly clean.

They were all solemn and stern-faced, however. "Self-righteous-looking bunch, aren't they?" Kirk found himself whispering to a frozen Kumara.

The Klingon commander let out a derisive snort. "Trial indeed! I will sell you my chance of being found innocent for two *pahds* and a good killing joke."

Spock tapped Kirk on the arm and gestured to the far door at a fat, smug-looking native. "There's the local who called for official help."

Kirk studied the man, who smiled back at him strangely.

"Looks content, doesn't he?" Kirk commented finally, though he was still uncertain of the other's expression. What was behind that peculiar grin? He chalked it up to the simple fact that the innkeeper was by the door while he, Spock, and the others were relative parsecs from that freedom.

Kirk turned his attention back to the judges, for such they had to be. They had all assumed their seats and proceeded to lapse into various postures of indifference. All were incredibly old. One, Kirk noted, was nearly asleep already. Another was deeply engrossed in inspecting her fingernails.

Only the occupant of the podium chair appeared reasonably alert. A portly, grave-visaged native, he took three handfuls of sand from a box on his left and ceremoniously transfered them to a box on his right, all while steadily muttering some whispered alien incantation.

The trial got under way when this formidable-looking individual followed the sand ritual by leaning forward and glaring down at them.

"Well?" he said gruffly.

"Well what?" countered Spock evenly. Kirk eyed his first officer uncertainly.

"How do you plead?" asked the judge irritably.

"I would like to know what we are expected to plead for,"

Spock continued. "To do that, we must know what we are accused of."

The judge looked further irritated. "Oh, very well, if you must." He peered down at something hidden from below. "You are all accused of disturbing the peace, letting blood on a forbidden day, destruction of private property, contributing to unnatural death, obfuscation of a legitimate business . . ."

While the list grew, Kumara leaned over and whispered worriedly to Kirk, "Did we do all that, Jim?"

"If he says so," Kirk murmured back, "I guess we did."

". . . and being a public nuisance," the venerable praetor concluded eventually. He looked back down at them and coughed. "Have you anything to say in your own defense?"

That said, he leaned back, crossed his hands in front of him, and appeared to lapse into sleep.

There was a pause from below . . . and then Kumara was on his feet, gesticulating wildly for attention. "I can explain it all, Your Greatness!" Kirk stared at the commander open-mouthed.

"It is all so simple," Kumara said, talking very fast. "My companion and I were preparing to enter our lodging when, without cause or warning, these two ruffians beside me assaulted us." He took on a grieving tone. "Attacked us and murdered my best friend!"

The paralysis finally left Kirk, and he was practically inside Kumara's shirtfront. "Now just a *minute*!"

"Your pardon, sir," said Spock. The judge cocked an eye at the first officer, then looked back at Kirk and Kumara, who were ready to start in on each other again.

"You two sit down and behave yourselves. You, sir," he said to Spock, "may speak."

Kirk and Kumara resumed their seats as Spock rose. "This man and his companion had taken by force another man"—he indicated Van Delminnen—"whom we were trying to rescue, in order to return him to his sister, whom you see seated next to him. As the abductors were unwilling to return him peacefully, we were compelled to resort to force."

"That's a lie!" shouted Kumara, leaping to his feet again. "If *they* had merely turned the woman over to *us*, none of this would have happened."

"Is this true, sir?" the judge asked Spock.

"Your Greatness, it may be that the single death of the man I killed in self-defense could have been avoided, but in the long run many—"

"But it *could* have been avoided?" the judge persisted. "In fact, the entire fight could have been avoided?"

"Strictly from a logical point of view, yes," Spock, admitted looking rather unhappy, "but one must consider the long view, and when one does that it is immediately apparent that—"

"That's very interesting, thank you," the judge said, cutting the first officer off.

Kumara looked as though he had won a victory of sorts. "Besides, it is well known that all Vulcans are congenital liars," the commander added.

Kirk looked at his enemy in shock. "Kumara! Do you realize what you're saying?"

The judge looked interested. "And what, pray tell, is a Vulcan?"

Kumara pointed, his anger and frustration having driven him past all rationality now. "*That* is a Vulcan, your greatness! An alien in your midst, an interloper, a monster with a computer for a mind and a machine's sense of ethics! An insipid, unimaginative, soulless automation who—"

Spock bore the steady stream of insults and imprecations stolidly. The judge, looking bored, finally cut Kumara off in mid-insult.

"Your claim that you are innocent will be taken under advisement," he told him tiredly. He looked at Spock. "Do you, whatever or whoever you are, acknowledge the truth of any part of this person's claims?"

"Of course not," Spock said, looking straight at Kumara. The Klingon commander threw up his hands and sat down hard on the bench.

"Thank you, sirs." The judge yawned. "That . . . that will do. I will now consult with my colleagues." He slid down from his chair and began poking and prodding the other ancients to wakefulness. Once active, all five retired behind the podium. Kirk could hear the tantalizing buzz of their conversation rise and fall, always just outside the range of decipherability.

"You fool!" Kumara whispered angrily at Spock. "Couldn't you see what I was attempting to do? With even one of us free, he might be able to hire help to rescue those reimprisoned!"

Spock's eyebrows rose alarmingly, though his voice remained unchanged. "And you said that *Vulcans* were congenital liars."

Kumara had a properly sarcastic retort prepared, but the reappearance of the five judges forestalled it. He turned as anxiously as the others while the ancients resumed their seats. All seemed almost awake now, as though it were necessary to bestir themselves at least for pronouncement of sentence.

"I see that your bickering has ceased," the high judge observed, with evident satisfaction. "That is well, as we have deliberated and reached a decision." He yawned again.

"Before you make your decision known, Your Greatness, I would like the answers to several questions. You can hardly deny them if you are prepared to execute or imprison us." Spock waited resolutely for a reply.

The high judge considered, and finally grumbled, "Oh, if you must. But make them interesting, lest we lose interest quickly."

"I believe you will find them interesting enough," Spock declared. He began to pace back and forth beneath the high bench, asking his questions as he walked. Kirk and Kumara watched him with equal curiosity.

"Why is it," the *Enterprise*'s first officer wondered, "that, despite the large number of resting places, and a perpetual daylight that would seem to preclude any regular resting time, we have never seen a single one of you even appear drowsy? Why have we not seen a single live animal, despite an abundance of fresh-killed meat in the marketplace?

"Why the total absence of even simple vehicles, and the lack of interest in our battle to the death at the inn? Such a crowd would seem to be the type most interested in such conflicts, yet they uttered hardly a sound throughout the fighting.

"Then there is the very existence of this world, which defies so many natural laws. Despite this, we find ourselves confronted with a civilization and race that, excepting trivial differences, could be a duplicate of an earlier terrestrial or

Klingon culture. That implies a coincidence of evolution under radically different conditions—a coincidence we have until now had no choice but to accept."

"Spock, what are you getting at?" Kirk asked.

His first officer turned to him, the conviction in his voice growing with each succeeding sentence. "Have the events of the past weeks not struck you as rushed, Captain? Do you accept the existence of the world you see around you here, regardless of the fact that our entire body of scientific knowledge declares it a flagrant impossibility?"

"Your first officer is mad, Captain Kirk," declared Kumara, watching Spock warily. "He denies the evidence of his own senses."

"Senses can be fooled," Spock went on, turning to the Klingon commander, "but a rational mind cannot. It has taken until now for the weight of successive incongruities to point out the greater one. I am beginning to believe my mind, not my eyes." He turned back to Kirk.

"Do you accept the existence of this world as you see it, Captain? Because I do not."

Kirk felt the hard wood of the bench beneath him, looked around and saw the eyes of judges, guards, innkeeper, and spectators on him, breathed deeply of the air, studied the iridescent sky through the glass dome, and replied, "Have I a choice, Mr. Spock?"

Spock sighed heavily. "Think, Captain. We have in the past few weeks encountered two near duplicates of Terran ecology and humanoid civilization. In both cases the natives could, with very slight alterations, pass for human, Vulcan, or Klingon with relative ease. Both the world of Arret, in the negative universe, and this wandering planet support such civilizations in heretofore unsuspected astronomical environments. A mere coincidence? It boggles the mind."

Spock turned to face the judges, and Kirk noted with surprise that all five were now wide awake, more attentive than they had appeared at any earlier time.

"Whatever the explanation, you must confess, Your Greatness, whoever you are, that these coincidences leave a great deal unexplained."

"I would say that is putting it mildly, Mr. Spock."

All eyes turned to the source of that voice. Kirk's thoughts turned upside down, as his whole universe had during the course of Spock's speech.

"Karla Five!"

The woman walking toward them from the near door was none other than their pied piper into the negative universe bridged by the Beta Niobe Nova.

"I don't," Kirk muttered plaintively, "understand."

"Nor do I, Captain, but I have suspected. The very unlikeliness of Arret and this world suggested a possible tie, though I am still ignorant as to what it might be."

"Never mind, Mr. Spock," Karla Five said reassuringly, "it was your willingness to voice what your mind suspected which has decided the trial in your favor. You were beginning to disappoint us." She turned to the judge's bench.

"I believe the time has come to end the masquerade, colleagues." She waved her right arm slowly, expansively.

The courtroom vanished. So did the town. Kirk, Spock, and Kumara found themselves standing alone on a rolling, grassy plain which ran unbroken to every horizon.

Well, not exactly alone . . .

Kirk squinted and held his hands in front of his face to shield himself. Where the judges had sat moments before were now suspended five meter-wide globes of radiant energy, each glowing like a miniature sun. Another globe occupied the position held a moment before by Karla Five.

Perhaps the biggest surprise was the presence of the last two globes, which drifted and swirled about each other in the places occupied only seconds ago by Van and Char Delminnen.

Kirk felt sanity slipping away, like water down a drain, and screamed inside himself for something solid, something real, to hold on to. It was provided by his own mind, which could find no room for panic amid all the curiosity.

"Who . . . what are you?"

The energy thing that had been Karla Five expounded in a deep non-voice. "We are the Wanderers Who Play," the not-words elucidated. "We are Those Who Meddle. We are the ones who long ago—so long ago that your terminology is not great enough to encompass it—deserted our final corporeal bodies for the configurations of pure energy which you now see."

"You said you play," Kirk said, eyes tightly slitted against the wonderful glare. "What do you play at?"

"Existence," the second judge murmured.

"To what purpose?" This typical expression of practicality came, naturally, from Spock.

"Amusement and edification," explained the judge of judges. "At regular intervals we conduct a tour of various galaxies which remain of interest to us. This we do to record the progress and development of the local space-traversing dominants. In this case, yourselves, gentlemen. Our attention is magnified when several dominant forms expand far enough to come into conflict with one another.

"For reasons of convenience, and a certain amount of what you would term nostalgia, we have utilized this world as the vehicle for transporting us through space. It is our original home world. We are attached to it. And, while it serves no real purpose but one, that is sufficient to trouble taking it with us."

"That single purpose is information storage, gentlemen," continued the light that had been Karla Five. "We need a fair-sized solid for that. Our world serves us admirably. We have, of course, no need for the warmth and light which our exceptional atmosphere, as Mr. Spock calls it, provides.

"However, we still enjoy the presence of living things around us. We have the time and patience necessary to luxuriate in the contemplative thought patterns of growing plants."

"You have been undergoing a test," the judge of judges told them, "a test which is now concluded."

"The humanoid civilization?" Kirk asked, gesturing at the open expanse of prairie around them. "The city, its people . . . it was a laboratory experiment, in which we were guinea pigs?"

"Restrain your bitterness, Captain Kirk," said Karla Five. "We mean you neither ill nor good. Allow us this harmless academic pleasantry."

"Lieutenant Kritt didn't find it very harmless," Kumara muttered. Karla Five's reply was filled with reproof.

"That was of your own choice and doing, Commander Kumara. We did not interfere. We only studied. When you and Captain Kirk persisted in your futile battle at the inn instead of attempting to work out a peaceful settlement of your differences, we were most disappointed. Most."

"Terribly sorry," Kumara countered sarcastically. "The experimental animals offer their apologies. Perhaps you didn't bait the maze sufficiently to produce the reactions you wanted."

"Speaking of differences and bait and mazes," Kirk said, "what of that negative universe?"

"It did not exist, not in the form you believed you saw it in," Karla Five told him. "Even we cannot accomplish a passage into something which does not exist. It was created as the first part of your test, from a play theory one of us had generated."

"Mine," said the fifth judge, with a touch of pride. "It was rather a good theory. Pity it does not exist."

"Even if it did," Karla Five went on, "a less likely method of interdimensional travel than diving into a raging nova would be difficult to imagine.

"You accept too readily the evidence of your senses instead of your mind, Captain Kirk, Commander Kumara—even you, Mr. Spock. Think again on the people of Arret—would a race which appeared with all the knowledge it would ever have be able to exist, once its devolution was a known fact? No, it would go mad with the knowledge. Would an Arretian child be born in a grave, as a senile adult form, only to die within a living mother? For that matter, by what process would a new Arretian come into existence?

"I am surprised at you all for not seeing through that first fabrication. But then it was necessary to bring you together, to see if you would react more sensibly than you did apart. As you know, you have not."

Kirk looked over at Kumara, and found the commander staring back at him. "Negative universe—you too, Kumara?"

The commander nodded slowly. "A mere two *tri-aines* ago. We did not think we would survive. The negative world which aided us was a near duplicate of Klingon. In fact, its name was—"

"Nognilk," put in Spock.

"The very same," admitted the tired commander. "The inconsistencies . . . Why did we not sense them before!"

"And the Delminnens?" Kirk asked.

Somehow the judge of judges managed to convey the impression of indicating the two globes which swirled and darted about each other.

"These two Wanderers were given the task of playing at being human, at being the humans Delminnen. The message from your Starfleet base, Captain Kirk—and your Imperial Sector headquarters, Commander Kumara—was an artifice of ours, designed to bring you hastily to the system designed. We followed your foolishly primitive attempts to unite the human couple through violence with considerable sadness.

"In the end, it seemed that total destruction of one vessel or the other must result. Hence our appearance here at the crucial moment, to prevent that. It was we, Commander Kumara, who planted the suggestion of a contest in your mind."

Kumara looked shaken.

Spock broke in: "But the Delminnens are real people."

"So they are, Mr. Spock," admitted Karla Five. "They continue their hermitage on the far side of their moon from where you set down, quite unaware that anything out of the ordinary has taken place. Incidentally, they are as harmless as your records indicated. Should you return to their system, you will find planets Eight and Nine orbiting their sun unchanged—their 'destruction' merely being another of our engineered illusions."

"World-maker or not," Kumara whispered to Kirk, "I'd hit it if I could be sure of contacting something."

"We must leave you now, gentlemen," Karla Five continued. "There are many among us who have profited from your actions of the past seconds—seconds only to us, of course, weeks to you. We are sorry at the laggard pace of your development."

"What do you intend to do with us?" Kirk asked hesitantly.

"You will all be returned to your respective ships and permitted to return home. But carry with you this warning, which we make most regretfully.

"If your races have not made substantial improvement over your present degree of maturity, or rather lack of it, by the time of our next visit to this portion of this galaxy, we will be compelled to regard you as degenerates incapable of proper development. Consequently, you will be eliminated from the cycle of advance.

"Good-bye, Commander Kumara." Karla Five glowed bluely, and the Klingon commander was gone.

"Back to his vessel, and McCoy to yours," the globe explained. "And now—"

"Wait!" Kirk shouted. "Why do you care? Why this concern with our development, this need for elaborate interference?"

There was a pause; then: "We strive constantly to upgrade the maturity of those races we encounter, Captain Kirk, in the faint hope that one day one or more of them will reach our own level. It is very lonely to exist at the apex of creation, for an apex is surrounded always only by emptiness."

"How much longer do we have . . . before you return again?" the captain asked hurriedly.

"Not long, I fear," confessed the judge of judges. "No more than another twelve of your millennia. Now go . . ."

And they were gone.

Sulu was studying standard readouts from the world below. He turned to inform Uhura of one especially interesting discovery—and nearly fell from his chair as the captain rematerialized in his. Uhura had started to turn at Sulu's call, only to pause and gasp as the science station was once again occupied by its usual tenant.

Although he stood between the two materializations, Dr. McCoy was too pleased to see both men return alive to be shocked. That would come later.

"Jim . . . Spock! How did I . . . How—what happened down there?"

Kirk felt the comforting solidness of the command chair. That, at least, was real . . . wasn't it? At least it was as real as the mystifying globe sitting alone in the viewscreen. Amazing how one could overlook the obvious when confronted by the impossible.

"Mr. Sulu?"

"Yes, sir?"

"What is the mass of the world below us?"

Sulu looked puzzled, while at Kirk's right McCoy was

barely able to hold himself in check. "The mass, Captain? But we already measured—"

"Compute it again, Lieutenant."

Sulu proceeded to carry out the puzzling order, bent closer over his instrumentation, and finally looked back in total confusion.

"I don't understand it, sir. There's a new reading, but it's impossible."

"What is it?"

"According to the latest readings, the mass of Gypsy is only point six four that of Earth. But the gravity reading remains constant. That's impossible."

"Not this time, Mr. Sulu. The gravity is correct, and no doubt artificially enhanced. While the mass—"

"—is undoubtedly correct," Spock finished for him, "for a mobile filing cabinet of such size."

McCoy looked askance from one to the other. "Jim, what is all this . . . this talk of filing cabinets and artificial gravity? How did you get back here, anyway?"

"Twelve thousand years," Kirk murmured, not hearing.

"What . . . what's that?"

"Captain," Arex reported, "the *Klathas* is picking up speed. She's moving out of the area on impulse power."

Kirk moved to the intercom. "Engineering . . . This is the captain speaking. Scotty, are you there?"

"Aye, Captain."

"Do we have enough power to get under way?"

"Aye, but barely. I think we can manage warp-two, but not much more."

"It'll do. Thank you, Scotty." He clicked off, then turned back to face the helm once more. "Mr. Sulu, set course for Babel. I have a story that's going to interest Commodore April. It seems he and Sarah owe their unexpected rejuvenation to a dream . . . unless that's an illusion too."

"I think not, Captain," declared Spock thoughtfully. "It was the Aprils who pulled us through the first part of the Wanderers' test. Clearly they were impressed. The Aprils' new life strikes me as a realistic reward for . . . for a maze well run."

"Excuse me, sir," Sulu wondered, "but we have superior speed now. Aren't we going after the Klingons?"

"No, Mr. Sulu . . . and they are no longer concerned with us. Kumara has too much else to think about now."

"In heaven's name, Jim," an exasperated McCoy blurted out, "what happened? Why are we suddenly running from the *Klathas* . . . and it from us? And by the way, where's Char Delminnen?"

"Twelve thousand years," Kirk whispered again. Then, louder: "Home is where the heart is, Bones—if the mind concurs. Rest easy that the Delminnens are perfectly safe."

McCoy turned in frustration to Spock, who was busy as usual at his library computer console. "Spock, you tell me. What's Jim mumbling about? What does he mean?"

"What he means, Doctor, is that we had all best learn to be good little boys and girls or we're liable to get spanked."

McCoy, now unable even to voice his questions, gawked at the first officer. Spock turned casually to Kirk. "There is one more thing which worries me, Captain."

"What's that, Mr. Spock?"

"The negative universe of Arret was an illusion. The world of Gypsy was an illusion. Both were part of a test originated by the Wanderers. Yet we have only their word for their own existence . . . the word of illusion creators. What concerns me, Captain, is . . . might not the Wanderers be only part of some greater illusion, some greater test?

"For that matter, how much of our universe is real—and how much an illusion, created by forces unimaginable merely to test us?"

"Mr. Spock," murmured Uhura, "that almost sounds religious."

Spock started to reply, hesitated, and finally said, "It may be interpreted variously, Lieutenant Uhura, but recent experiences tend to make one pause before disregarding anything. What do you think, Captain?"

Kirk looked at the viewscreen, which showed the globe of Gypsy receding into a vast, star-speckled blackness. "I think, Mr. Spock, that we'd better make the best we can of this universe—it's the only illusion we've got, and it's not a bad one."

He leaned back in the command chair and prepared to record the final log entry to the strange episode, then paused, reflective.

Was all life lived only in an illusion, or was his reality someone else's fantasy? Finally, he shrugged and activated the log. The entry he was about to make, detailing the journey to Arret and the subsequent encounter with the Wanderers, would be real enough to him, would form a real record from which someone else would have to make the final judgments. He smiled.

Anyone who read those log entries couldn't possibly dismiss them as illusion . . .

STAR TREK
LOG EIGHT

For REECE and CONNIE WOOLFOLK
For BEATRICE MURPHY
They don't say much about it, but their kind
of people built this country.

STAR TREK LOG EIGHT

Log of the Starship *Enterprise*
Stardates 5537.1–5537.2 Inclusive

James T. Kirk, Capt., USSC, FC, ret.
Commanding

transcribed by
Alan Dean Foster

At the Galactic Historical Archives
on S. Monicus I
stardated 6111.3

For the Curator: JLR

THE EYE OF THE BEHOLDER

(Adapted from a script by David P. Harmon)

I

"Captain's log, stardate 5537.1. The *Enterprise* is embarked, for a change, on a routine follow-up mission—to search for a survey ship overdue for report-in in the vicinity of Epsilon Scorpii, last known to be investigating the system of a G4 sun designated Lactra on Federation starcharts."

He clicked off and studied the nearing globe and the yellowish, slightly hot sun beyond. The world and its star were no different from hundreds he'd examined personally or on tape. Yet past experience had shown that the innocuous-appearing worlds were often the ones full of surprises—planet-sized paranoia-inducing *piñatas*.

The continuing silence of the survey crew the *Enterprise* was here to locate *could* be due to some easily explainable equipment failure or minor human error. Could be.

But Kirk was a veteran starship captain, and he always wore two uniforms on such missions: Starfleet regulation pull-ons and an intense, personal wariness.

At the moment there was nothing to hint that Lactra VII was anything other than the recently discovered, inoffensive world it appeared to be. Only the small, obviously artificial shape growing slowly and silently larger on the main screen suggested otherwise.

The vessel was a long-range limited scout, of a minor class designed for extensive exploration of possible colonial worlds. It carried a small crew of first-contact xenologists and no frills, moving at high speed on an unvarying course from starbase to eventual destination. Its large quantity of complex instrumentation was announced by the bristling array of antennae, external sensor pickups, and other intricate detection equipment which almost obliterated the small hull.

Kirk noted with satisfaction that the scout looked undamaged. That probably ruled out any messy natural disasters such as meteorite collision and, more important, interference from some inimical spacegoing race. "Disarm phasers, Mr. Sulu," he instructed the helmsman.

"Phasers disarmed, sir."

The captain leaned toward the chair pickup and activated the log again. "Captain's log, supplemental. We have encountered and visually observed the missing survey ship. It continues to maintain communications silence." Glancing backward, he noted Lieutenant Uhura's confirming nod. All attempts to elicit some response from the craft had failed, though she continued trying.

"There is no evidence of violent damage or sentient attack. Mr. Spock will lead a security team in boarding the ship. End entry." Shutting off the recorder once again, he addressed another grid: "Transporter Room?"

"Chief Kyle here, Captain. Boarding party standing by."

"All right, Chief, send them aboard." He glanced backward. "Lieutenant Uhura, pick up visual and aural transmission as soon as transportation is complete."

"Standing ready, sir."

There was a tense pause, and then the view forward changed to an internal view of the scout. Kirk could see armed security personnel moving about as someone's visual scanner played around the ship's interior.

"Boarding party has integrated, Captain," a voice announced clearly . . . Spock's. "Our sensors were correct. Ship appears pressurized normally, temperature likewise."

The view shifted jumpily. Spock was walking through the cabin. "We are dispersing throughout the vessel, Captain."

"Any sign of life?" Kirk asked anxiously.

"Negative. There is ample evidence of previous tenancy, though. It looks as if the crew fully expected to return. There is nothing to indicate they were surprised, or removed forcibly from the ship. Personal effects are lying neatly about. There is no indication that the crew intended to leave their ship for an extended period."

"Very well, Mr. Spock. Continue your exploration."

Several hours sufficed to show that the only living things

left on board the survey ship were laboratory animals. Automatic feeders kept them healthy in the absence of the crew.

Spock did make one important discovery, however.

"Captain, Dr. McCoy," he began as they watched expectantly from around the small table in the Briefing Room, "we found this tape lying in the ship's library, next to the playback slot. There is a duplicate in the ship's banks, but this copy was deliberately placed in a prominent position, obviously to attract the attention of anyone entering the library."

He picked up the small cassette and slid it into a slot set in the table, then depressed the play switch. Attention was focused now on the three-sided viewer which popped up in the table's center.

The tape showed a tense, worried officer in the uniform of Federation Sciences. He was staring into the pickup.

"It is now thirty-two minutes since our last contact with the three members of our crew who beamed down to the planetary surface," the man declaimed. "Each member of that crew was instructed to report in at ten-minute intervals.

"As this deadline has long since passed, and subsequent to our repeated failure to contact any member of the landing party, I have decided to take the following action. As senior officer aboard I, Lieutenant Commander Louis Markel, take full responsibility for this action and any consequences thereof." He coughed awkwardly, then continued on:

"All three remaining members of the survey team, myself included, will beam down in an attempt to discover the whereabouts of our comrades and, if necessary, to effect a rescue. If for any reason we should fail to return I, Lieutenant Commander Louis Markel, do hereby accept and acknowledge that—"

It was too much for Kirk. He jabbed the cancel switch and both picture and audio died. McCoy looked at him questioningly and saw that the captain was struggling to suppress a rising fury.

"What's the trouble, Jim?" he inquired quietly.

Kirk glared at him, the angry words tumbling over one another. "Blatant disregard of standard emergency procedure . . . utter suppression of survey orders! I tell you, Bones, there's no excuse for—"

"Apparently the lieutenant commander felt the need was

pretty desperate, Jim," McCoy interrupted softly. "His friends had vanished, and he decided going after them was more important than anything else."

Kirk calmed down slightly, but McCoy could see the anger still simmering. "It doesn't matter, Bones. Letting personal feelings get in the way of Starfleet regs . . ." He sighed. "Since when were human beings otherwise?"

"True, Captain," commented Spock.

"Regulations specifically state, Bones, that in a situation like this at least two members of the crew—the minimum necessary to operate a ship this size—must remain aboard. In the event that contact with the other four team members is lost, they are to return to the nearest starbase beam region and file a full report. I don't care if the team commander is a full admiral. Regulations must be followed. They were created for a reason. Any sign of danger to Federation civilization . . ."

"But, Jim, there was no sign of danger," McCoy pointed out.

"That does not alter the fact, Doctor, that the survey ship's commander made what is essentially a personal decision," Spock observed.

Now it was McCoy's turn to explode. "Spock, you Vulcans are the most unimaginative, unbending . . . !"

"Easy, easy Bones," soothed Kirk. "You're starting to sound like me." He waited until McCoy had calmed himself, then continued briskly. "None of this is helping the situation any. Nor is it helping Commander Markel and his people—assuming they're still down there and in a position to make use of our help. Barring positive evidence to the contrary, we have to assume that they are."

"Sorry, Jim. Spock just has a way of getting to me sometimes." McCoy grinned. "It's an inborn talent, I guess."

Spock replied amiably, "Some humans are rather more easily gotten to than others, Doctor."

"Mr. Spock," Kirk continued, "what can we expect to find on Lactra Seven?"

"We have little information on the world below us," the first officer began thoughtfully. "What we do have is the result of the drone's preliminary report, coupled with information drawn from the survey ship's library. We may assume this basic information is fairly accurate. Our own sections are working to confirm this now.

"Lactra Seven is a Class-M world. Gravity is approximately Earth-normal, the atmosphere a reasonable analog of Earth-Vulcan. Very little additional useful information is on file. By useful I mean material which could aid in the locating and rescuing of the missing crew. What we do have is available in the printouts before you."

Kirk picked up the slim bundle of sheets and leafed through them. "According to the survey ship's log, Commander Markel and the other remaining members of his crew beamed down six weeks ago."

"Five weeks, three days, two hours, to be precise, Captain," Spock corrected.

"Careless of me, Mr. Spock." He finished scanning the printouts, then let the sheets drop. "No indication of planetary life forms."

"And in particular, of intelligent or large, dangerous ones—that is true, Captain," Spock admitted. "Life sensors are experiencing some difficulty in penetrating a distortion layer in the Lactran atmosphere.

"Given the composition of that atmosphere, the surface temperature, and the presence of large bodies of free water, I would suspect Lactra Seven harbors a considerable amount of life. But without additional data I cannot speculate on the form such life has taken." His brows drew together.

"Despite the distortion layer, the survey ship was specially equipped for obtaining just such information. Their records were surprisingly deficient in this area, one of primary concern to any survey team. Apparently they had no sooner entered into Lactran orbit when this emergency overwhelmed them. Mr. Arex is overseeing a full, detailed sensor scan, which should reveal the relevant information," he finished.

"Eventually," Kirk added. "Anything like a comprehensive scan will take too long to complete, Mr. Spock. Minutes might make the difference between life and death for Commander Markel and his people—if they're still alive. I want a landing party to beam down to the last recorded coordinates in the survey ship's tapes. If they've had the sense to remain in that immediate area we might be able to find them quickly."

"Don't you think that's taking an extreme risk, Jim?" put in McCoy. "If the first three were lost—and remember, they never beamed up any hint that something was wrong, no warning or anything—then we might run into the same silencing trouble."

"True, Bones. But if they experienced some kind of mechanical problem, the risk might be in leaving them stranded while we take endless readings. It might involve that distorting atmospheric layer. For example, maybe it affected their communicators. That would explain why the first crew was unable to contact the ship, and why the second crew failed to activate the transporter to bring them back.

"They could be starving down there, sitting on their acquired information and waiting for someone to haul them out. We have to find out. They could have survived for six weeks. They might not be able to survive six and a half."

"Still a risk," McCoy objected.

Kirk's reply was matter-of-fact. "That's why we're here, Bones." He rose from his seat. "We'll travel light, gentlemen. Phasers, tricorders, communicators—and you'll take a full medical kit, Doctor."

It took only minutes to gather the necessary paraphernalia; then the three officers met in the Transporter Room. Scott was waiting for them. He would handle the beam-down personally.

"Any new information from Sciences, Mr. Scott?" Kirk inquired as they exited from the elevator lift and crossed to the alcove.

"A little, sir," the chief engineer reported. "Mr. Arex says that the distortion layer has been penetrated sufficiently for sensors to reveal a large variety of life forms on the surface. There are substantial concentrations in the area scheduled for your landing, Captain."

McCoy voiced the thought uppermost in their minds. "Any indication of intelligent life?"

"No, Doctor, none." Experienced hands moved over the controls, adjusting settings, checking energy levels. Playing with a man's molecules was a dangerous business.

"No large clusters of life forms in urban patterns, and no hints of city outlines. No rural patterns indicative of large-scale agriculture."

Kirk nodded. "You've set in the coordinates taken from the survey ship's transporter tape? That's where we want to be put down, Scotty."

"Beggin' your pardon, sir," he countered hesitantly, "but if I beam you down in the same place, you could run into the same trouble . . . and end up the same way. Quiet."

"We'll be expecting exactly that, Scotty," Kirk explained. "At the first sign of anything we can't handle, we'll beam back up. Proceed with transporting."

Scott shook his head, ever the pessimist, and mumbled under his breath. That didn't affect the precision with which he engaged the transporter controls. Triple levers rose, and the three officers dissolved into elsewhere.

Kirk experienced the momentary blackout, the disorientation, and the usual twinge of nausea. Then he materialized in an oven.

A blast of humid, hot air struck him like a sockful of hot mud. That first unexpected blast seemed hotter than it actually was. But while conditions at the set-down point were far from arctic, they were bearable.

After checking his footing he turned and took in their surroundings. They were standing on the bank of a steaming lake—Kirk assumed it was a lake; but it could as easily have been an ocean—he couldn't see land across it. Hot springs gurgled all around them, filling the air with feathery streamers of pure steam.

The thermal activity around them was as intense as in the Waimangu valley on Earth—noisy and nervous. But the ground underfoot was firm and gave every indication of having been so for some time. So Kirk discarded his first thought—that the survey crews might have set down on some unstable area, despite the safeguards inherent in transporter sensors.

"Everyone all right?"

Spock nodded, then McCoy.

"Ten meters either way, though," the doctor pointed out, "and we'd have been boiled alive."

Spock already had his science tricorder out and was taking preliminary environmental readings. He frowned. "Unusual that such a lake, of such extent, could exist under the planetary conditions prevalent at this latitude. Most unusual."

"Speaking of unusual, Spock . . . ," Kirk interjected. He was pointing at the surface of the lake directly before them.

A shape was rising from the steaming water. One could read the writhing steam into fantastical forms, but this rapidly growing outline was composed of something considerably more solid than water vapor.

It had a saucer-shaped body, limbs of still unseen design but obvious power, and a short, snakelike neck. A vision of quite adequate ugliness bobbed atop that swaying extension.

Spock nonchalantly turned toward it and readjusted his tricorder to take a biologically rather than geologically oriented reading. He studied the results with undivided attention as they appeared in the tiny readouts.

"Most intriguing," he finally commented.

"I'm not sure 'intriguing' is the word I'd choose," Kirk said, taking a step backward. "That creature may be able to navigate on land as well as in the water." Certainly the apparition showed no sign of slackening its pace.

"I know it can," an excited McCoy decided nervously, "and I don't need a tricorder to tell me so."

In truth, the alien being appeared to be accelerating as it neared them. Beneath heavily lidded eyes, black pupils stared at them with the single-minded blankness of the primitive carnivore. The interlocking fangs which protruded sicklelike from both jaws parted slightly, revealing an uninviting dark gullet.

"Phasers on stun," Kirk ordered sharply. "Stand ready."

Each man pulled out one of the compact weapons, adjusted the tiny wheel on top, and dropped to one knee. Spock held his phaser in one hand and the still-operating tricorder in the other. Both were aimed with precision.

The monster reached the shoreline, and any question of its ability to navigate a nonaquatic environment was answered as it humped enthusiastically toward them.

"Fire!"

Three bursts traversed the space between the men and the huge monster. The creature halted its seallike advance, faltering. The long neck lowered and swung dazedly from side to side.

A second round stopped the monster as if it had frozen. It

sat on the shore, momentarily paralyzed. The nightmarish skull dipped until it scraped the sand.

Then, amazingly, it seemed to shake off the effects of the double phaser blast. Its appetite gave way to a blind desire to escape, however. Turning with surprising agility, it rushed back into the lake and vanished beneath the steaming surface.

"Not a very friendly environment," Kirk observed idly, kicking at the warm earth. "I think the survey crew would have come to a similar conclusion." He turned. "They'd probably try for a friendlier area inland. Let's move."

Picking their way cautiously between pools of bubbling clear water and thick, candylike mud, they started away from the water's edge. Once, Kirk knelt to probe the ground with a finger, and pulled it away speedily. The soil here was painfully hot just beneath the surface, but it was stable.

"What do you think, Mr. Spock?" he asked, referring to their first encounter with a representative of Lactran life.

"An interesting and no doubt dangerous animal, Captain," the first officer replied easily, "but not particularly so, and clearly not invulnerable. Certainly not to the kind of weaponry a survey crew has available as standard equipment.

"Nor is it the sort of beast one would expect to catch experienced personnel off-guard. Such teams regularly expect far more lethal attacks. For it to have surprised and rapidly killed not one but two such teams—no, Captain, I think it extremely unlikely."

"Exactly my opinion, Spock." They topped a modest rise and started down the other side. "In such a situation—"

He cut off in mid-sentence, staring in surprise at the land before them.

No steam rose there. There wasn't a hint of a boiling pool or steaming mud pit. The panorama before them was flat, hot—and dry. Only a few isolated outcroppings of weathered rock broke the gravel-and-sand plain. Here and there an occasional patch of defiant green stood out like a flag. The change was startling.

"Desert," muttered McCoy. "Not a very welcome sight either, gentlemen."

Kirk frowned as he pulled out his communicator. "We're

on a hill here. Let's see if we can pick up anything on the emergency ground bands." He flipped open the communicator and made the requisite adjustments, then addressed it slowly and distinctly.

"This is Captain James Kirk of the U.S.S. *Enterprise*, commanding a Federation rescue party, calling the crew of the survey scout ship *Ariel*. Come in please, come in."

A faint whisper of wind on tired rock, nothing more.

"Try again, Jim," McCoy prompted.

"Captain James Kirk of the Federation cruiser *Enterprise* calling Lieutenant Commander Markel or any members of the Federation survey ship *Ariel*. Are you receiving me? Please acknowledge."

Still silence. Resignedly, he made a slight, standard readjustment on the receiver dial—and was rewarded with a surprise. A slow, steady beep began to sound.

McCoy was startled. "Be damned . . . they're answering!"

The beep continued for several seconds before stopping suddenly. But not before Kirk, who had been frantically adjusting further controls, registered an expression of satisfaction.

"You got a fix on it, Jim."

The captain nodded. "Barely. The signal didn't last very long, and I don't like the way it cut off like that, in the middle of a series." He turned slightly to their left and pointed. "Over that way."

Picking their way down the slight slope, they started off in the indicated direction. "Likely they're close by, staying near the touchdown point like they're supposed to," Kirk murmured tautly. He squinted at the sky. "We'll try this until the heat begins to tell, then have Scotty beam us up for a rest. We can set down and continue on after a break."

"Don't you think it's strange we didn't get a voice reply to your call, Jim?" wondered a puzzled McCoy.

Kirk shrugged. "Could be any number of reasons we didn't. Mechanical trouble with the communicators, as we originally postulated, Bones."

"Never mind counting them, Spock," broke in McCoy dryly, seeing the first officer about to comment. They continued on across the sand in silence, searching for indications of human passage. There were none—no footprints, no trail of shredded tunic, no lost instruments or survival equipment. Nothing but harsh sky, sand, gravel, and heat that stayed just the human side of oppressive.

Nothing moved on that brown-and-yellow landscape. There was no soothing wind to ruffle the compact, squat green growths which leaned possessively to any hint of shade or depression in the ground.

Kirk spent no time studying them. A single casual glance was enough to show there was nothing remarkable about the largest, nothing distinctive about the smallest. It was the fate of six humans that absorbed his thoughts now, not new outposts of alien ecology.

Eventually they reached the other side of the gentle basin they had been crossing and mounted the symmetrical curve of a large dune. Their descent on its opposite side was as fast and awkward as the climb had been slow and controlled. They reached the sandy base and found themselves confronted by another basin, which terminated in a twin of the dune they had just crossed.

"At least it's not thermal springs and hot mud," McCoy observed.

There was a sound like frying fat, and a sheet of flame interdicted their progress. It missed Kirk, who was in the forefront of the little party, by a few saving meters. He scrambled backward.

Slightly to one side of their intended route the gritty yellow-and-brown soil erupted. Sand streamed from crevices and cracks, and a nightmarish skull fringed with spines, its skin decorated like a Gothic cathedral, burst from the ground and turned warty jaws toward them.

"Left . . . run!" Spock yelled, barely in time.

The rippling mouth opened and belched a second stream of fire. It scorched the sand where they had been standing only seconds before.

Stumbling backward even as they pulled their phasers, they found themselves backed against the steep inward side of the dune. All three weapons fired, aimed to strike the monster in that cavernous mouth. The monster paused, then swung ponderous jaws to face them again.

"The lining inside the mouth of a creature that can spit

fire," Spock lectured hurriedly, "would seem to be composed of organic material highly resistant to—"

Without knowing what prompted the thought, Kirk yelled, "Aim for the underside of the neck!"

Once more three beams of intense energy crossed the space between the men and their assailant. All three struck the creature in the area between the lower jaw and forelegs.

Once again the effort seemed futile. Instead of trying to incinerate them this time, the monster lunged forward, jaws agape. It was slow, however, and clumsy. The little group scattered. The primitive machinery of its mind turning slowly, the monster singled out one victim—Kirk. It turned toward him, then rose suddenly on thick hind legs.

Broad spadelike claws on its forelegs reached inward, clawing confusedly at its throat. Then it toppled like a leathery gray iceberg to lie unmoving in the yellow sands.

The impact of the monster's fall had thrown Spock to his knees. Now he glanced around in concern as he slowly got to his feet.

"Captain?"

"Here, Spock," came the reply from nearby. "Are you all right?"

"I am undamaged."

Kirk joined him, brushing the sand from his tunic. "Where's Dr. McCoy?" He looked around, suddenly conscious of the fact that the doctor was nowhere to be seen. "Bones . . . Bones!"

A distant, faintly desperate reply sounded. "I'm . . . *mmpggh!*"

Kirk and Spock turned, looking for the source of that brief cry. There was no sign of Dr. McCoy. Then it sounded again, muffled to the point of unintelligibility.

Worriedly, Kirk glanced to his left, then gestured. "I'm not sure. I think the sound came from back there."

They moved slowly down the length of the unconscious creature's massive body. Spock was the first to notice the two spinelike forms protruding from beneath the thick tail.

"Hang on, Bones," Kirk shouted, "we'll get you out!" The officers moved alongside the two projections, which proceeded to twitch insistently. They shoved, but to no avail. "Again, Spock!"

A second effort, both men straining and heaving, failed to move that limp, incredibly solid bulk. And the shifting sand provided poor footing.

"It would seem," a panting Spock ventured, "that another solution is called for, Captain. We cannot lift the tail. Therefore, we must move the doctor."

Kirk eyed him uncertainly, then nodded in understanding. They dropped to their knees and began digging sand with the speed and efficiency of a pair of small mechanical shovels. The thrashing of the doctor's legs added desperation to their efforts, growing more and more frantic with each passing second.

Finally a lower torso and then a pair of arms became visible. Pulling and additional digging brought the rest of the ship's chief physician into the open once more.

McCoy drew his knees against his chest and locked his arms around them, taking long breaths and digging sand from his eyes, nose, and ears.

Spock and Kirk waited and watched worriedly, until McCoy acknowledged the concern in their eyes. "I'm okay, thanks, but the air was just about gone under there." He glanced back at the sloping pit now leading under the tail. "The flesh was slightly humped above me. I had a small air pocket. Smelly, but I wouldn't have traded it for a bottle of the Federation's finest perfume."

"You're sure you're not hurt?" Kirk pressed.

"No . . . just surprised. I didn't even see the tail falling. It isn't every day a dinosaur falls on you." He sneezed and rubbed his sand-scoured nostrils. "If the ground hereabouts had been hard, I'd be just a smear now. But the sand was deep enough, and soft enough, and I was hit just right for the impact to bury me instead of smash me. I lost a little wind, that's all."

Kirk helped McCoy to his feet, then brushed sand from his hands as he turned his gaze beyond the motionless tail. "How much additional desert do you think we'll have to cross, Mr. Spock?"

The first officer checked his tricorder and pointed in the direction the terse signal had come from. "I have no way of judging for certain, Captain, but, extrapolating from temperature and atmospheric readings, at least several additional kilometers. It could be hundreds."

"No," Kirk objected. "The signal wasn't that strong. But we'd better pick up our pace, regardless. There's no cover here, either from the sun, or from any of the other hungry locals. I'd like to make a bit more progress along the signal track before Scotty beams us aboard for a rest period."

They resumed their march across the sands, detouring around the still-stunned mountain which had almost trapped McCoy. But as soon as they resumed walking, Spock lapsed into an introspective silence which Kirk recognized immediately. Something was troubling the first officer. If Spock had something on his mind, something not yet sorted out, he would inform them about it in his own good time.

His own good time came several dozen meters farther into the dry basin. "You know, Captain," he suddenly murmured, "it was unusual the way I seemed to know, rather than guess, that our phasers would be ineffectual while aimed down the carnivore's throat. The creature itself . . . did it not seem familiar to you?"

Kirk thought a moment, and found, to his surprise, that he didn't have to search his memory for very long. The familiarity of the monster had bothered him all along, but it took Spock's query to crystallize it.

"Of course . . . I've seen soloids of something just like it on Canopus Three. That's impossible, though. Canopus is many too many parsecs from here." He squinted into the unyielding sunlight.

"True, this desert is very similar to those found on Canopus Three." His voice faded. "Very similar. In fact, those isolated growths, the color of the petrographic outcrops—they're all remarkably alike."

"Are you suggesting, Captain, that a similar environment presupposes identical evolution?"

"My shoes," McCoy broke in, with undisguised distaste, "are full of sand."

Spock's concentration was broken. "Doctor, your lack of scientific interest is a constant astonishment to me."

"I'll be glad to discuss that with you, Spock, the next time you drop into Sick Bay for some medication, or a checkup."

"No need to become belligerent, Doctor. That was merely a simple observation."

"Spock, your simple observations," McCoy rasped as they trudged toward the top of the next dune, "tend to get on my . . ."

He stopped in mid-sentence, mid-thought, to gape at the scene before them. And he was not alone. Spock and Kirk had also come to a momentary mental halt.

Spread out at the base of the dune was a wall of green so lush and colorful in comparison to the dull plain they had just crossed that it was almost painful to look at.

Clusters of thorn-laden trees and broad, thick bushes interwove with taller emergents and exotically contoured growths drooping with strange fruits. Practically at their feet a stream emerged, vanishing in a sharp curve back into the thriving jungle.

There were distant hints of moss and fern forest, of swamp and tropical lowland. They could almost feel the humidity, smell the rankness of rotting vegetation.

For all that, it looked a lot friendlier than the country they had just traversed. "Food and water—anyone would have a better chance of surviving in there than on that frying pan we just crossed" was McCoy's opinion.

Spock wasn't as sure. Turning slowly, he studied the terrain behind them. His gaze lifted to the far dune. Beyond it, he knew, lay a violently active thermal region bordering a vast, steaming lake.

Again he directed his attention to the riotous landscape before them, listened thoughtfully to the soft susurration of small living things picking their cautious way through the undergrowth.

"Does it not strike you as peculiar, Captain, that two—possibly three—radically different ecologies exist literally side by side? Steaming, unstable shoreline, backed by a thin line of desert, and now another extreme change of climate and living things."

"I've seen stranger sights in my travels, Mr. Spock. What are you driving at?"

"Nothing yet, Captain. Simply another observation." His voice trailed off as he glared at the rain forest beneath the dune, taking this perversion of natural law as a personal affront.

Kirk flipped open his communicator again. "I don't plan to do much walking through *that*—not without extra equipment." He directed his words to the tiny pickup.

"Landing party to *Enterprise*." There was a brief pause, rife with static and interference. But the special tight-beam broadcast Scott employed penetrated the mysterious distortion layer in the atmosphere. Kirk heard the chief engineer's reply clearly.

"*Enterprise*, Scott here."

"Any new information, Scotty? We're a little puzzled by what we've found down here."

"We've got plenty of confusing readings here, too, Captain," Scott confessed. "There appears to be a large concentration of life forms slightly less than a hundred kilometers north-northeast of your present position. How large we can't tell—this blasted distortion effect jumbles every sensor reading we get. I'm informed that it *could* be a city . . . or just a central gathering place for migratory animals. I said our readings were inconclusive.

"That's all so far. Lieutenant Arex is supervising information resolution. He hopes to have a more specific analysis of the data within an hour."

"Very good, Scotty." He muttered to himself, "Northeast." Then, louder, "That's the direction of the signal we received, Mr. Scott."

"I could transport you to the region of life-form concentration, Captain."

"Negative to that, Scotty. We don't know that the missing crew is part of that concentration. They could be anywhere in between, and we can't risk skipping over them. We'll have to do this kilometer by kilometer. Let us know the moment Mr. Arex comes up with a determination of that reading, though. We'll continue in the plotted direction for a while longer. Kirk out."

"Aye, Captain. Engineering out."

Kirk put the communicator away as they carefully picked their way down the dune. They paused at the edge of the jungle, fascinated by the way the rich flora appeared to spring with supernal suddenness from the periphery of bone-dry desert.

"I don't like it, Jim," McCoy finally ventured. "Too many unlikelihoods here. Why only the one short signal? You can argue all you want, but to me that implies something other than mechanical failure."

"I'm not ruling out anything, Bones," Kirk replied slowly. "Their inability to respond further could be due to something we can't imagine. It does prove that at least one member of the survey team is still alive, though. Alive and alert enough to be monitoring an unexpected query."

"Apparently alive, Captain," Spock amended. "The signal could have been sent by other than human hands."

"There's no profit in pessimism, Mr. Spock. For the moment I choose to believe they are alive."

They reached the edge of the stream. McCoy glanced at it briefly before kneeling to satisfy the thirst that had built up in him during the desert crossing.

His hands had barely broken the surface of the water when Spock put a restraining hand on his shoulder. The doctor looked up, puzzled, to see Spock staring at the pool.

"Allow me to test the water first, Dr. McCoy."

McCoy eyed the first officer dubiously, then turned his gaze downward again and stirred the water with a finger. He shrugged. "Go ahead, Spock, but I've analyzed enough water to know a drinkable stream when I see one. You know that, too."

"Nevertheless," Spock insisted. The readjusted tricorder was played over the surface of the rippling brook. Spock concluded the brief survey and studied the subsequent readouts, sending semaphore signals with his eyebrows.

"Well?" an irritated McCoy finally pressed.

"As you surmised, Doctor, the water is certainly drinkable."

McCoy looked satisfied, if still irritated, and bent again to drink.

"However, that is not what prompted my uncertainty," Spock concluded. McCoy looked up at him. "Captain, this water is *too* pure."

McCoy grimaced and scooped up a double handful. He

downed it, sipped a second and third, concluding by wiping his parched face with wet hands.

"It tastes just fine to me, Spock."

"Despite that, it is too pure, Doctor," Spock insisted emphatically. "Consider what that means."

Kirk chose his words carefully. "Then what you're saying, Spock, is that it's too good to be true?"

"I would say that evaluation is decidedly understated, Captain." Spock studied the silent wall of green as if it might disgorge a hostile alien horde at any moment.

"Water of this purity flowing freely through thick vegetation growing on loose, loamy soil is not only unnatural, it is positively illogical. As illogical"—and he made a sweeping gesture with one arm—"as the proximity of such a rain forest as this to the desert we just crossed." He knelt and scooped up a handful of dirt.

"Note the composition and consistency of the ground we are standing on now." He sifted it through his fingers. "Fine sand and well-worn gravel of feldspar, quartz, and mica." He stood and dropped the dirt. "It barely supports a few stunted shrubs."

He took two steps forward. "Suddenly, I am in a region of climactic floral development, standing on soil"—and he kicked at the thick soil—"of self-evident fecundity."

"I'm not sure I follow you, Spock," the captain commented.

His first officer gestured all around. "Don't you see it, Captain, Dr. McCoy? It's the abruptness. There is no blending of jungle into desert, desert into jungle, or desert into thermal lowland. The borders between widely divergent ecologies are as sharp as if they had been drawn with a knife."

"Which means what?" wondered McCoy.

Spock drew himself up, then spoke slowly. "It is my theory that what we have seen and encountered since we've landed has been carefully manufactured and not naturally evolved. Environmental manipulation on a large scale has taken place here."

"Terraforming," McCoy muttered. "Or Vulcanforming, or whatever . . . I see. A process which implies the presence of highly intelligent life forms." Suddenly he found himself staring at the green ramparts with nervous expectancy.

Kirk rubbed at his dry chin. "Reasonable as far as it goes, Mr. Spock. But Terraforming usually follows a consistent pattern." He kicked at the ground, sending yellow sand to stain the dark earth of the forest. "On the strength of your own observations, this hardly seems consistent."

"It does appear to be almost random choice, Captain. Unless, of course, the randomness *is* the pattern."

McCoy sighed resignedly. "Spock, don't you ever say anything straight out?"

Spock turned a blank stare on him. "I thought I just did, Doctor."

"Gentlemen, please," Kirk pleaded, "not now. We have work to do."

A short march parallel to the lush greenery brought them to a path that charged in lazy curves deep into the forest. It might have been worn by the passage of many jungle dwellers . . . or it might have been cut. It was another piece of a puzzle that seemed to be growing more and more complex.

The jungle itself bore one similarity to the desert region they'd crossed—its familiarity. Like the Canopus III desert analog, this jungle possessed an almost recognizable pattern which Kirk struggled to place in his mental catalog of well-known alien environments. But identification of the forest world in question remained just beyond his thoughts.

Kirk studied the fibrous exterior of the large tree ferns they were now passing between. Those striking purple-and-puce convolutions were familiar from a well-studied text. To find the environment of one planet reproduced here was startling enough. To find two in such close proximity to each other held profound implications.

"Spock," he began easily, "what do you think of—"

A violent warning cough sounded in front of them. It was followed by a hoarse roar. One, two, three forms and more appeared on the open trail ahead. The powerful spotted bodies showed bristling dark fur and deep-set, angry eyes.

The pack of doglike creatures remained frozen, obviously startled by the appearance of the three figures. They sported huge curved claws more suited to some clumsy digging creature like a sloth, and long thin fangs. Insectoid antennae projected from the thick ridges of thrusting bone above the eyes.

Those eyes narrowed now, with all the expectancy of an archaeologist coming upon the bust of an emperor instead of yet another pottery shard. Visual evidence of unfriendly intentions seeped from thick-lipped muzzles. The pack began to edge toward the intruders.

With corresponding caution and patience the three men started retreating.

"There was a cave in that cliff face we just passed," Kirk whispered. "It didn't look too deep—but it's bound to be better than standing here in the open. If we can make it . . ."

They picked up their pace slightly, still facing the approaching pack. But, whether through impatience, hunger, or divination of Kirk's intentions, the pack leaders abruptly charged.

"You two, run for it!" Kirk shouted, pulling his phaser and dropping to one knee. "I'll hold them off. They can outflank us all here."

"May I suggest, Captain, that three phasers—"

"Get moving, Mr. Spock!" The first officer hesitated, then turned and ran with McCoy for the cave. His phaser still set to stun, Kirk fired at the nearest of the loathsome apparitions. It yelped once before folding up on the ground.

That was the signal for the rest of the pack to split up. Sinister rustlings and cracklings began to sound on both sides. Kirk fired again, dropping one lean shape that showed against the green on his right. He couldn't hope to get them all—they would come too often from too many directions.

He saw movement out of the corner of an eye and whirled to find Spock and McCoy racing back toward him.

"I thought I told you two to set up your defense in the cave!" he said angrily.

Spock's phaser beam shot past him to knock the legs out from under one of the creatures that had crawled to within jumping distance of the captain. The animal quivered and was still.

"There is a small problem," he explained smoothly.

"A large problem," corrected McCoy, turning to point back the way they had come and simultaneously firing at a low shape.

With Spock and the doctor covering, Kirk was able to divert his attention long enough to peer back down the path through the jungle. From here the cave entrance was barely visible, a dark shadow beneath the looming, fern-studded cliff.

Something was coming out of that cave.

It slid sinuously along the soft soil, emerging from the recesses of the cave like a worm from an apple. It was massive, reptilian, and two-headed. Further description called for extreme adjectives Kirk had no time to dwell on.

"Stay together—and keep backing up toward it," he ordered tightly.

"Jim . . . !" McCoy started to protest.

"No time to argue, Bones—do it!"

McCoy looked anxious but took up a position alongside the captain. Spock was already firing from his other side. As the pack started to emerge from the forest, the officers kept retreating toward the cave—and toward the horror that was coming out to meet them . . .

11

It reached the point where McCoy decided he would rather turn his phaser on himself. "Jim . . . we can't keep . . ."

He didn't even have time to argue any more, so tight had the pack closed in. Not only that, but it turned out that the resistance of the doglike creatures to the phaser beams was considerable. The beams knocked them out, but those first stunned were back on their feet again and once more closing in for the kill.

"When I yell," Kirk ordered, "cut your phasers and dive for that thick copse over there."

McCoy looked in the indicated direction, but saw only a large clump of high grass too thin to keep out a determined mouse, much less a mass of bloodthirsty beasts.

And Spock nodded, apparently concurring in this madness!

The pack was nearly on them now. It had become so bad that McCoy almost beamed Kirk in taking one of the monsters before it could sink scimitarlike fangs into the captain's right shoulder.

At that point, Kirk shouted, *"Now!"* and plunged headfirst toward the high brush. Spock sprayed the pack with a last sustained burst of phaser fire and joined him. Both were a step behind McCoy.

The pack leaders sprang ahead. That concerted action drew the undivided attention of the oncoming leviathan. Its foremost segments expanded. The driving head opened to seize the nearest pack member in one set of jaws.

The quasi-canine screamed, twisted, snapping uselessly at the armored skull. Its fellows, their memories extending only to the immediate prey, forgot their smaller quarry to attack the flanks of the snake-thing.

Two sets of long fangs cut and stabbed at the iridescent yellow and green body. Pained, the Janus-snake twitched convulsively, pure muscle sending the two attackers flying into oblivion among the surrounding trees.

Less-bloodied eyes watched from the safety of the neutral grass.

"Stay low and slow," Kirk urged his companions, "and let's edge around behind this."

Nothing challenged them, and they reached the head of the path, the point where the pack had emerged, without incident. They kept to the bordering brush for another thousand meters, though, despite the fact that the pack's attention was occupied elsewhere. Like all creatures of limited intelligence, the dog-beasts' span of attention was brief and easily diverted. There was no point in drawing unnecessary attention to their retreat.

Behind them, the monster reptile snapped and coiled about the harrying pack . . . a colossus assailed by hornets.

"I begin to understand the difficulties even an experienced survey team might encounter here." Spock breathed evenly as they jogged down the path, now well away from the bloody clearing.

"I don't see how anyone could survive on the surface of this world for six weeks, cut off from a base ship and outside support," puffed McCoy.

Kirk observed sharply, "Don't prejudge them, Bones— we're still alive, aren't we?"

"That's true, Captain," Spock observed, slowing, his gaze focused on something high up and ahead of them. "However, it is arguable if this can be called surviving." He gestured at the cause of his comment.

"I wonder if hunting is merely bad hereabouts, or if we constitute some sort of edible novelty to the local fauna."

Through the gap in the trees ahead, Kirk could see three narrow-bodied winged horrors heading straight at them in a long, gliding dive. They shared some of the characteristics of both the pack and the two-headed snake-thing. They had reptilian snouts and scaly wings, but the lithe bodies were coated with fur, and they didn't have the cold eyes of the unblinking reptile.

"Keep your phasers on stun, but be prepared to shift to a stronger beam if necessary," ordered Kirk—rather tiredly, McCoy thought.

McCoy was right. Kirk had had about enough of this world's unrelenting attacks. In light of the steady assault, the Federation edicts forbidding the avoidable destruction of alien life were beginning to grate a bit.

Once more the three officers assumed firing position, once again triple poles of light crossed open air. And the winged dragon-shapes continued their confident dive right toward them.

"Useless!" yelped McCoy, his fingers moving to adjust the setting on his weapon.

"Steady, Bones," urged Kirk. "These are just like the dargoneers on Maraville—the stun charge will get to them eventually."

"Before they get to us?" McCoy murmured, his finger moving back from the setting wheel. He held down the trigger of his phaser, as the flying reptiles continued to come nearer and nearer.

Then a most peculiar thing happened.

The dargoneers jerked up in midair, their heads snapping up and back and their wings abruptly beating unsteadily at the air. Ignoring the continued beaming, they seemed to get control of themselves one by one, turned, and flew off in separate directions.

With nothing left to beam, McCoy clicked off his phaser. Lower jaw hanging open, he stared at the spot in the sky where the seemingly unstoppable aerial meat-eaters had come up short.

"Now that," he observed bemusedly, "is more than passing strange."

"An invisible force field, Doctor," Spock observed. "The knife I was talking about before." He turned to look at Kirk. "I think if we attempt to return the way we've come, Captain, we will find similar fields separating the three environments we have thus far encountered. They were absent when we landed but have apparently been restored."

"Plausible enough, Spock," replied a worried Kirk. "But why shut down such fields in the first place?"

"I cannot imagine, Captain. To find out, I believe we must locate those who have created the fields in question, as well as transformed this section of the planet into a multitude of adjoining alien environments."

"That implies—" Kirk began, but something cut off his breath. He had the sensation of being lifted clear off the ground, experienced that peculiar sense of helplessness one has when one's feet no longer have contact with anything solid. It was a common enough experience in free-fall space, but highly disconcerting on solid ground.

He felt something like a metal band fastened around his waist. When he looked down he saw a gray, wide coil tight around his middle. It didn't look like metal. He put both hands against it and shoved.

It didn't feel like metal, either.

Then he turned and looked behind him and saw what had picked him up as neatly as an elephant plucks a lone peanut. He was in the grasp of the tail end—he supposed it could as easily be the front end—of a creature some six or seven meters in length. It was built low to the ground and had no visible external features. No eyes, mouth, head, arms, or legs—nothing save this single flexible tail or tentacle.

It looked very much like a common garden slug, yet it wasn't ugly. The aura of intelligence, of purposeful, controlled power that Kirk sensed, removed any twinge of xenophobia he might have felt at the mere sight of it.

The creature started to move off down a partially concealed path. Kirk tried to observe its method of locomotion and found he couldn't see beneath its slightly horny, skirtlike lower edge. Whether on legs, cilia, horny plates, or something unimaginable, the creature moved smoothly across sometimes uneven terrain.

At the moment Kirk was more interested in the front end of the creature, for he had to assume it was traveling head-first. That end showed a single tubular mouth that seemed to study him at length before turning back ahead. Although unable to slip free, he discovered he could turn his upper body easily enough. Looking back, he saw McCoy and Spock following, each similarly pinioned in the grip of one of the dull-hued creatures.

The limb that held him terminated in several smaller divisions, which were in turn separated into still smaller wiggling filaments. The flexibility of those digits was promptly demonstrated when he tried to reach his phaser. One curled around it and plucked it from his waist.

He managed to pull his communicator clear, but that surprisingly delicate organ circled another part of itself around the compact instrument and tugged it firmly from his hand. The action was irresistible without being crudely violent. Whatever had control of him, then, was interested in keeping him intact and reasonably healthy.

That knowledge, along with the fact that no attempt was made to draw him closer to that strange tubed mouth, enabled Kirk to relax ever so slightly.

As soon as the path opened into a cleared, well-kept trail, the three slugs accelerated astonishingly. Their lower limbs might be hidden, but they were amazingly efficient. And despite the speed, the tail-tentacle held Kirk firmly enough so that the ride was not as bumpy as he had feared.

"Would . . . would you say this is an intelligent life form, Mr. Spock?" he called long minutes later, his initial evaluation of their captors complete.

"It is difficult to say for certain at this time, Captain," Spock called from behind. "Thus far their only action that could be construed as intelligently formulated was the removal of our phasers and communicators. That could be an acquired or taught action, however. They may be more than advanced domestic animals."

As Kirk considered this, he noticed the squarish shape still slung over the first officer's shoulder. "Intelligent or not, they forgot something, Spock. Can you get at your tricorder?"

"I think so, Captain." One arm was pinned firmly to his side, but he still managed to work the other around enough to fumble at the compact instrument's controls. It was hard to adjust the sensors with only one hand. If he could retain control long enough to take even a few preliminary readings, it might tell them a great deal about—

Two protrusions of the multilimbed tail plucked the tricorder neatly from his shoulder.

"I believe I have an answer, Captain, to the basic question. If these are merely trained animals, their attention span and selectivity are extraordinary. Consequently, even if they are not the masters of this world, I think it reasonable to say they can be considered intelligent on their own."

"Personally I could do with a few more answers than that," a discouraged, aching McCoy called from the back of the strange column. "We've been traveling like this for what feels like hours. Where are they taking us?"

"As near as I can tell, Bones, we're moving northeast, in the approximate direction of that life-form concentration Mr. Scott reported on." His expression turned wry. "It would be a help if he had clarified just what that concentration is, and could let us know. We'd have some idea of what we're heading into."

"I think it more likely, Captain, that we will be able to identify it for Mr. Scott." He gestured with his free hand. "Look ahead."

Kirk turned his attention forward again. They were just coming to the crest of a hill, and he had a glimpse of something distant and pale through the green mesh.

Then they were over the steep slope and traveling down on the opposite side, their peculiar captors never slackening the pace.

The city spread out before them, marching in neat ranks of low, blocklike buildings to the distant horizon. It was an urban complex laid out close to the ground, rather than high and skyward as many of the great Federation centers were. The only interruptions in the field of gently rounded structures were provided by glistening bodies of water, pools, and streams—and by an alien-conceived yet still attractive landscaping. It was not a place Kirk would have liked to live in, but that didn't prevent him from admiring its unmistakable, utilitarian beauty.

"Quite a metropolis," he finally murmured. Spock concurred fully.

"If these are the builders and not servants, they are capable of admirable feats of construction."

"I'm thrilled you two can admire the local talent," McCoy

commented sardonically, "but I still have this sick feeling that we're about to become someone's lunch."

Spock looked indifferently confident. "For a creature of this size, Doctor, you would hardly be more than an appetizer."

"Now there's a comforting thought!" McCoy snorted. "Not only am I going to be eaten, but even my passing'll rate hardly a burp."

"We're slowing down," Kirk noticed.

They had come up against the base of yet another hill. Since it was no steeper than the one they had just crossed, Kirk wondered at the stop. Then he noticed that the creature holding Spock had moved to the hill-face and was doing something to a section of the ground.

His guess was confirmed as the reason for their halt became obvious. There was a muted hum from somewhere ahead as the hillside, complete with vegetation and rocky outcroppings, began to slide upward into a concealed recess.

Behind it a large, well-lit cavern appeared, dominated by a huge, silvery cylindrical form which threw back the morning sun in a way only highly machined metal can.

They started forward again. When they neared the cylinder, Kirk thought it was suspended freely in midair. As they moved closer, though, he could see dust motes floating in the air around the base of the metal construct. It was riding on a cushion of air—or something more advanced and less identifiable.

They entered the cylinder through an oval opening in its side. Kirk wondered if their captors also traveled on a cushion of air. That would explain the lack of visible limbs. Come to think of it, this cylinder bore some resemblance to the Lactrans' own bodies.

It grew dark as the humming hillside behind them slid back into place, but only for a moment. Some hidden device compensated, and the interior light grew correspondingly brighter. Kirk tried to identify the source of illumination, but without success. The interior of the cylinder showed nothing like a window, fluorescent panel, concealed tube light, or anything else recognizable as a light source. There was only the smooth metal, his companions, and their three enigmatic, silent captors.

"They're undoubtedly taking us to that city," he ventured aloud, as the faintest hint of motion jarred the craft. "If we could manage to communicate with some of their leaders . . ."

"They don't seem very interested in communication with us," McCoy noted curtly, staring down at the dull gray back of his alien. "That's assuming they're capable of interspecies communication at all."

"I'd tend to think like that, too, Bones," agreed Kirk, "except every now and then I seem to feel something knocking about the inside of my mind, something that won't stay still long enough for me to fix on it. Like daydreaming. When we reach the city—"

He broke off as the oval portal drew aside with unexpected speed. Their hosts slid through the opening, still showing no strain from their bipedal burdens. At no time, Kirk marveled, had they let their load down to rest.

"We're . . . we're already here?" wondered McCoy, staring in all directions. Spock's amazement was still directed at their means of transportation.

"Remarkable. I experienced none of the sensations of traveling at high speed, yet we have obviously been carried at tremendous velocity. I would very much like a look at the mechanisms involved."

Kirk wasn't listening. His gaze was reserved for the big chamber in which they now found themselves. The vaulted room appeared to be divided into doorless compartments dominated by intricate yet massive machinery. Occasionally, complex structures of metal overhead bathed them in intermittent washes of multicolored light.

A short . . . walk, crawl? He couldn't say, but by some means they entered one such side compartment. The powerful tail-hands dipped, and Kirk, Spock, and McCoy found themselves deposited gently on the ground with as much care as they had been picked up.

That was the one comforting aspect of this entire episode so far. Throughout the entire journey and despite their apparent indifference, the slug-creatures had taken pains to avoid even bruising any of their captives. Nor had they made anything resembling an overtly hostile gesture.

"Any ideas, Doctor?"

"Only one, Jim," replied McCoy, studying their uninspiring, pale-walled alcove, "and it's not very appealing. I'd guess they're doing exactly what we would do in a similar set of circumstances."

"Which is?"

"Well," he continued, as Spock knelt to examine the half-metal, half-porcelain surface they stood on, "if we encountered an alien creature we'd never seen before on a Federation world, one which science records made no mention of, the first thing we'd do is make sure it was free of harmful bacteria, germs, and other assorted little surprises.

"I wouldn't be surprised if those colored beams we passed through had something to do with insuring our hosts' health. That accomplished, we'd next proceed to see if our visitor were intelligent."

"Congratulations, Doctor," Spock said, looking up from his study of the floor. "All most logical assumptions."

"I told you you should drop by the medical lab sometime."

"A more important question, gentlemen," Kirk interrupted, "is whether or not there's a way out of here." He pointed. "As you can see, we've been left alone."

Indeed, there was no sign of their captors. The vast floor of the chamber was deserted.

"Gone off to report our appearance, maybe," Kirk suggested. He started toward the exit and was brought up short by a half-anticipated barrier. The sensation was akin to that of running into a giant sponge.

Reaching out, he slowly tested the apparently normal air before them. It wasn't hard and unyielding as some such barriers were. Instead, he could push into it; but resistance grew stronger and stronger until further progress grew impossible. At that point, exerting additional strength merely caused his probing fingers to slide off in various directions, as though he were pressing on slippery glass.

"Force field, all right," Kirk murmured. "It seems harmless enough. In fact, if it's designed to do anything, it's to keep those inside undamaged if they try to escape. Absorbs impact rather than resisting it bluntly."

"The bars of a cage are just as harmless," McCoy observed pointedly, "unless you're viewing them from the inside. And we are definitely on the inside." He moved up to the force field. "Let's see if this field is impervious to everything." He cupped his hands and shouted.

"Hey, listen, let us out of here . . . we're as curious about you as you are about us, blast it!"

Something tickled his head.

"A wasteful use of energy, Doctor," Spock commented. "I believe they can hear us quite well without your shouting." He eyed them closely. "I received definite hints of thought projections. I understand that humans are not as sensitive, but did either of you experience anything just now?"

Both Kirk and McCoy nodded.

Spock looked satisfied. "I thought I had detected similar impressions earlier, but could not be certain. I am now. Clearly, they are purely telepathic."

Kirk looked puzzled. "We've encountered telepathic races before, Mr. Spock, and had no trouble communicating with them. Why can't we get a grip on any of the local transmissions? I have the feeling I can almost see an image forming in my mind, but it never becomes stronger than 'almost.' "

"Analysis of the impressions I have received thus far, Captain, would appear to indicate that their thoughts move at a rate far beyond our comprehension. We can only grasp at a fleeting image here and there. That fleeting image we barely sense probably represents many complex thoughts elaborated on at length."

"Surely we can communicate with them somehow," Kirk muttered, "even if only through bits and pieces of information."

"I do not know, Captain," a discouraged Spock mused. "The sheer rapidity of their cogitation, the incredible transport system which brought us here, certain aspects of the instrumentation we have already been exposed to—that could be as advanced compared to Federation civilization as we are to a colony of ants. There also remains the possibility that they could communicate with us and are simply not interested."

"Don't they think we've anything to say?" growled McCoy. "If that's so, they're sadly mistaken. I've got plenty to say to them. Their methods of greeting visitors . . ." His voice trailed off.

"Wait a minute . . . what were they doing out among those other creatures? We never did figure out all those environments."

"You will recall, Doctor," reminded Spock, "that we recognized at least two species from vastly different worlds and ecologies, and we landed in yet another ecology altogether. Remember how we felt that the environments we were passing through appeared not only unrelated to one another but to this world?

"A civilization this advanced might enjoy transforming part of their own planet to"—he hesitated over his choice of terms—"more conveniently provide for their specimens."

"Are you trying to say that we beamed down into some kind of local zoo?"

"That is precisely my theory, Doctor."

"Maybe they'll be kind enough to explain," said Kirk, turning to face the alcove barrier. "They're coming back."

None of them could tell whether the three Lactrans approaching them now were the same three that had brought them there. They inched smoothly across the chamber floor, moving easily via a still unseen, unknown method of transportation, concealed beneath rippling skirts of gray flesh.

Stopping just outside the alcove, the three aliens regarded those within in contemplative silence.

"Examining us," Kirk whispered idly.

"Well, I'm sick of it!" McCoy snorted. He moved up to the force field and gestured emphatically at their captors. "Look, we're as smart as you—maybe a little smarter in some areas—and we don't take kindly to being locked up. I think it's about time you—"

One of the colored beams from above abruptly winked off as the nearest of the three Lactrans reached in with its manipulative tail member to neatly lift the startled doctor from between his companions.

III

"Wait a minute," McCoy yelled. "Do you—"

His world suddenly turned upside down, and he caught his breath. The slug was turning him slowly in its grip and he found himself facing the floor.

"Hey!" Not caring one bit for the position he found himself in, McCoy struggled violently, beating with both arms at the encircling coil of rubbery flesh. The Lactran took no notice of either the doctor's physical or verbal barrage and continued to examine him as unaffectedly as McCoy would an experimental animal in his lab.

"We've got to communicate with them!" Kirk said tightly.

"By all means, communicate," McCoy mumbled, in no mood for diplomacy. His resistance had faded to an occasional weak blow directed at the clasping coil. "Tell it I'm getting dizzy."

"Try, Spock," urged Kirk. "If we concentrate on the same thought, try to pool our effort . . . Try to think *at* it, tell it to release McCoy and put him—"

They never got the opportunity to try. Kirk's voice and concurrent thoughts were interrupted as the other two Lactrans reached into the alcove, one lifting Kirk and the other Spock. They started toward the far end of the vast chamber.

A large section of the far wall appeared to be constructed of the same silvery material as the transportation cylinder. They paused before it and waited while it slid upward. That action Kirk was prepared for.

What he was not prepared for was the sight on the other side.

He had expected to enter another chamber. Now he blinked

as he found himself out in open air and bright sunlight once again, moving rapidly forward.

He glanced down. They were traveling on a moving road or sidewalk of some kind. At the moment it was devoid of any other travelers.

Immense buildings slid past on either side of the roadway. All were constructed of simple gently curved squares and rectangles. There wasn't a single straight line to be seen. Perhaps the Lactrans attached no importance to architecture on merely *efficient* principles.

Kirk realized that the buildings were constructed with the same simpleness and lack of external ornamentation as their hosts.

Despite the oversized proportions of the structures they moved through and the smoothness of the moving roadway, Kirk estimated they had traveled a respectable distance when they finally emerged from the intensively developed area into a vast open plain.

The abruptness of the shift was startling. One minute they were passing through the depths of the monstrous city and the next found themselves in open country.

At least, it *looked* like open country.

Their speed increased. Kirk saw that the broad countryside was actually compartmentalized, divided into sometimes radically varying ecologies. For kilometers it seemed they passed nothing but arboreal creatures—some of the fliers were recognizable, some less so, and a few that utilized exotic methods to defy gravity teased Kirk's curiosity in passing.

Moving beyond, they entered a region of broad fields dotted with trees and flowering shrubs. One such section of grassland proved to be inhabited by a small herd of unicorns, as neat and appealing as if they had just stepped from the pages of an illustrated fairy tale.

"So much for mythology," McCoy commented sadly, as they passed a horned stallion nuzzling its mate.

"Using a nonspecies standard of appreciation, I confess I find them strangely attractive" was Spock's only comment.

"Something even more intriguing coming up, gentlemen," Kirk called to them.

They turned their attention forward, to where the moving

roadway executed a sharp turn. At the end of the bend was a new habitat at once more familiar and at the same time more alien than anything they had yet encountered. Three small cottages, as perfect as if they had just been transported whole from Earth to Vulcan, were grouped neatly to the right of the roadway. Kirk took in the carefully planned details as their speed slowed.

Each house had its own swimming pool, handball court, and other accouterments. The emphasis, he noted, was on providing plenty of opportunity and equipment for physical exercise. Each complex was set in a well-landscaped garden.

Having thoroughly studied the arrangement, the officers were not at all surprised when they stopped next to it. They found themselves deposited on the grass nearest the roadway.

A gentle nudge from one of those incredibly versatile and powerful tails urged Kirk forward. As he couldn't very well resist, he accepted the prod and took a few steps onto the lawn.

"Better to do what they want—for now, anyway," he murmured to the others. "We'll figure this out, given time." He turned, as did Spock and McCoy.

The three Lactrans rested there, just off the roadway, conveying the unmistakable impression of watching without eyes. Kirk, receiving the vague feeling that he was expected to do something, walked directly toward them, slowly. A couple of steps were sufficient to bring him up against the expected resilience of the invisible field.

"Our cage has been resurrected again, Bones." No reply. He turned. "Bones?"

McCoy was absorbed in a detailed examination of the ground, but he glanced up at Kirk's second query. There was a hint of genuine surprise in his tone.

"This is real grass, Jim. Real Earth-type common grass. Real soil, too. Though I wouldn't bet on how deep it goes."

"Exactly," agreed Spock from nearby, where he was engaged in cursory study of a rosebush. "This area has been laboriously prepared for human types."

"How's that again, Spock?" McCoy prompted, struggling to classify what looked like an Earth-type weed.

"We are now apparently exhibits in this zoo."

"Zoo? Exhibits?" McCoy straightened, botany temporarily forgotten. "Well, I'm no exhibit."

"Keeper-animal relationships have always been fluid, Bones," observed Kirk, "even on Earth. We have one category for ourselves and one for most other animals. But then there are the primates and the cetaceans. Intelligent behavior is often a question of artificially applied standards. Maybe the dolphins consider us part of *their* zoo. On this world I think we ought to be flattered if they've put us into the latter category. In any case, they've taken the precaution of putting us behind bars."

"Perhaps we can find out something from our fellow specimens," Spock observed. "I do not believe they could erect this elaborate habitat for us in such an incredibly brief period, despite their technology. They are not gods."

"Fellow specimens?" McCoy echoed in confusion. Then he looked in the direction Spock indicated.

A uniformed man and woman were coming toward them from the farthest of the cottages, walking quickly, the excitement plain on their faces.

"Hello!" the man called as they drew close. "I'm Lieutenant Commander Louis Markel. This is our primary biologist, Lieutenant Randy Bryce. We're darned happy to see you, whoever you are."

"James Kirk, captain of the U.S.S. *Enterprise*. My first officer, Mr. Spock, and chief physician, Dr. McCoy."

"Pleasure beyond words, Captain," Bryce said, her voice high, almost birdlike. "We received your communicator call and acknowledged as best we could."

"Which wasn't as thorough as it should have been," admonished McCoy, taking in their surroundings with a wave of one arm. "Why didn't you warn us, at least to say you'd encountered intelligent life?"

Bryce looked at once resentful and dejected. "We didn't have time to warn you." She sighed. "Every now and then they'll let us have this or that piece of equipment to play with. We can use it, under their special supervision, of course. Our hosts may look clumsy, but they can move with astonishing speed when they want to.

"We're kept under constant mental supervision. There may not be any of them in sight, but you can't escape the feeling of being studied. Everything they give us is operational . . . except our phasers, of course. We never know which bit of equipment they'll give us next, or when they'll take it back. When we think we can conceal our true intentions from them, by thinking nonsense thoughts for a while, we work on ways to produce an effective weapon using cannibalized components from scientific equipment—tricorders and so on.

"We were just lucky enough to have a communicator when your call came in, and we decided to answer immediately. We didn't know if you'd be able to receive us again, or how long they'd let us keep the communicator."

"The reason we replied with a directional distress signal instead of with an elaborate warning," Markel put in, "was because we felt a nonverbal communication had a better chance of being ignored." He shook his head. "These creatures are far too perceptive for that. They knew what we were thinking, despite our best efforts to mask our thoughts. Or perhaps our unconcealable excitement worried them, or made them nervous. Anyhow, the communicator was taken away immediately and deactivated."

"You mentioned, Commander, that they provide you with certain items of scientific equipment from time to time," Spock said. "I could certainly use my tricorder."

Markel shook his head and smiled apologetically. "Not a chance, sir. They're kept on a special exhibit table beyond the force wall. We get awfully nervous when a new bunch of patrons or scientists or whatever our visitors are show up and start playing with them. We don't know if we're ever going to see them again in one piece."

Kirk had scanned the cottages earlier from their position by the roadway. Now he lowered his tone as he spoke to Markel.

"There were six of you on the survey roster."

Bryce swallowed and stared at the unattainable blue sky to their left. "We didn't beam down in time to save the others." Kirk eyed her questioningly, and she shook her head in response to his unasked question.

"No, we don't think the Lactrans had anything to do with it. They've been too solicitous of our own welfare." She looked up at him. "You've encountered some of the other inhabitants of this zoo?"

Kirk nodded slowly.

"Well, the only reason we're alive and here to talk to you now is because the Lactrans got to us before some of their exhibits did." She shrugged helplessly. "The others weren't as lucky."

"Or unlucky," Markel corrected philosophically, "if you consider our chances of getting out of this place."

"Don't be so pessimistic, Commander," Kirk urged. "Eventually, my people may locate us. Considering the technology we've seen so far, I'm not sure a forcible attempt at rescue would be a wise idea. I'm *hoping* we can find another way out before Engineer Scott becomes impatient with our continued silence."

Markel's expression eloquently indicated how he felt about that possibility.

"There should be one other member of your group, then," commented Spock.

"Oh, Lieutenant Randolph's in the end house," Bryce told them. "She's running a high fever, and we can't seem to bring it down. The Lactrans don't take any notice of our entreaties—shouted, written, or otherwise. I suspect they don't consider her illness severe enough. And while we're well-supplied with food, they give us nothing in the way of medical supplies."

"I'll check her out," McCoy said reassuringly. "It would be ironic if our captors didn't help because they were afraid of wrongly treating a valuable specimen." He looked grim. "Or maybe they're afraid you might try suicide. A quick dose of some medicine could kill you before they could interfere. Has anyone . . . ?"

Bryce looked back at him steadily. "I'd be a liar if I said the thought hadn't crossed my mind."

McCoy nodded, his expression carefully neutral. "Maybe I can at least diagnose what's wrong with her, but I can't do anything else. Not without my medical kit."

Kirk spoke to Markel as Lieutenant Bryce led McCoy toward the house the three survivors had moved into. "What have you learned about the Lactrans, Commander? You've had a lot more time to study them than we have. All we've been able to determine is that they run this zoo, are telepathic, and possess a very high level of technology. How high we've no way of estimating."

Markel looked disappointed. "I'm afraid we haven't learned much we can add to that, sir. It's difficult to study another culture from behind bars. Particularly when you're being studied yourself. We're not fond of the switch. Also, we were captured and brought here at night.

"But we did see enough to know that this zoo"—and he made encompassing motions with both hands—"is so enormous as to be unbelievable. The only boundaries we saw before we were brought to this place were manufactured ones. There's plenty to hint that the majority of the city is built underground."

Spock made a Vulcan sound indicative of surprise.

"That implies a metropolis of truly gargantuan extent, Commander Markel. On what do you base such an assumption?"

"On what we saw before we were brought here, and on the fact that despite these creatures being obviously diurnal, there were many days when we traveled through the city without seeing a single one besides our hosts."

"And I don't see any now," admitted Kirk, looking around. "That means that if we could slip clear of this force field, we'd have a certain amount of freedom and a good chance of regaining our communicators and phasers. That's a considerable 'if,' however. Have you made any attempts to escape?"

Markel made a muffled sound. "Oh sure." He scooped up a handful of pebbles and spoke as he chucked them into the air. They traveled only a short distance before coming up against the force field and dropping vertically to the ground. "A dozen different ways, a few of them bordering on the insane.

"For example, we tried using one of our communicators, when they allowed us one, to cause a disruption in the field. You can imagine how well we did with that one. We tried the inevitable tunnel." He half smiled, but there was bitterness in it. "I suppose we ought to have guessed that wouldn't work when they permitted us to continue. We couldn't very well hide the work.

"The force wall extends as far below the surface as you're willing to dig. Then we all tried going on a hunger strike. All that brought about was a steady change in our meals. There was nothing to indicate that the Lactrans regarded it as anything like a voluntary protest by intelligent beings. We decided to give it up before we actually starved to death." He threw the final pebble, hard. "Nothing worked. I think we were getting a little crazy when we received your broadcast."

"Have you tried to communicate?" wondered Spock.

"Naturally, sir. Constantly, endlessly. We've tried talking to them, writing, thinking at them, rearranging the landscaping—everything. As far as we can tell, the only response we've been able to generate with our combined efforts is an occasional peculiar quivering movement on the front part of their bodies. I'm afraid I'm not much on quiver semantics."

"They seem motionless enough now," Kirk informed them, nodding toward the roadway. "It looks like we've got company again, gentlemen."

They turned to face the near section of field wall. Two Lactrans were approaching with that by now familiar eerie smoothness. They settled themselves opposite the captives and succeeded in conveying the impression of lavishing their undivided eyeless attention on the tiny group of bipeds.

It produced, Kirk decided, a very cold feeling.

Since the Lactrans appeared content to rest and watch, Kirk and the others decided to use the opportunity to study their captors in turn. They strolled over and stood at the edge of the force field.

"They built this sealed environment for us shortly after we were captured," Markel murmured. "Fairly sprang up around us. That was one of the first solid indications we had that they were telepathic." He stared at the nearest alien, striving to penetrate whatever shield blocked the mind contained within that sluglike mass of protoplasm. "None of us was thinking consciously of anything like this layout," the commander continued, "when we were deposited here. Our thoughts were about as far from comfortable cottages and swimming pools as possible."

"That would appear to indicate that they are capable of

reaching into one's mind and withdrawing imagery from memory,'' Spock suggested. Markel nodded agreement.

"I'd think that would also convince them of our intelligence," Kirk mused. "Still, we haven't even defined our own parameters of intelligence. We've no way of imagining what the standards are in Lactran." He glanced at his first officer.

"You mentioned correctly, Spock, that where mental reception is concerned, you as a Vulcan are more sensitive than the rest of us. That goes for thought projection as well. Try. You may have more luck than Commander Markel and the others."

"I will attempt it, Captain, but I am not optimistic."

Standing still and silent, Spock closed his eyes and drifted rapidly into a trancelike state. Kirk and Markel continually shifted their attention from Spock to the two Lactrans near the field.

Without apparent cause, the front ends of both aliens lifted slightly and twisted, puttylike, toward each other. Whether this action was the result of Spock's efforts was something only the first officer himself could answer.

Spock kept up the effort for several long minutes, then slumped, visibly exhausted by the strain.

"There are the same glimmerings of something supernally intelligent, Captain," he reported slowly. "Far different from anything I've ever encountered before. But again, the rapidity with which they process their thoughts defeats me. I cannot break through on their level. It does not help that they seem to be absorbed in conversation with each other. A two-way effort is required."

"I see. And if one directed its thoughts at you, then it wouldn't matter because it could detect our intelligence on its own." He looked disgusted. "I hate cyclic problems." He brightened.

"Perhaps we'll have more success with a technique I'm sure Commander Markel has tried. A combination of Vulcan thought projection and something graphic. Try writing something, Spock, and concentrating at the same time. Navigational computation, perhaps."

Spock nodded. He broke a suitable dead branch from a nearby tree, then located a patch of ground where the grass cover was nearly nonexistent. The formula he scratched in the bare earth was complex enough to indicate mental powers beyond simple random doodling, yet basic enough to be readily recognizable to any creature with a working knowledge of elementary chemistry. At the same time his eyes glazed over, indicating he was striving to project his thoughts at the watching Lactrans.

This time Kirk noticed a slight shaking, a rippling of the gray mantle that lined the front fringe of both aliens. This was accompanied by coordinated, extensive movements of the tail-tentacle.

"You seem to be getting a response," Kirk murmured with repressed excitement.

Spock stirred, his discomfort apparent even through his muddled voice. "I have . . . have the vague impression that . . . they are laughing at me."

That implied a general conception of what Spock was writing and at the same time contempt—it didn't make sense. It didn't add up.

It was frustrating and infuriating.

"But basic mathematics," Kirk almost shouted, "has been a universal language among every intelligent race the Federation has encountered."

The first officer blinked and left his state of concentration. "That may be the problem, Captain. Our formulations may be too basic, though this equation is far from simple. It is possible that they are so far ahead of us mathematically that my attempt was comparable to a child's futile struggle to make words with letter blocks. Many creatures can scratch out imitative lines analogous to mathematical equations. Talent in mimicry does not imply the power of creative thought."

"Try something else," Kirk ordered irritably.

"Yes, Captain."

Once more the trance of projection, again a new formula etched into the dirt. Kirk anxiously studied the Lactrans for the signs of recognition due their captive's intelligence. That they were paying attention to Spock seemed clear.

There were definite reactions. The quivering increased and spread to other parts of the aliens' bodies. But, wish as he would, Kirk saw no indication of anything like shocked amazement, no sign of an attempt to contact him. Nor was there anything pressing at his mind.

This line of attack was useless. There was no point in tiring his first officer needlessly. "It's no use, Spock, you may as well relax."

Spock tossed the stick away and rubbed with both hands at his forehead and temple, like a runner massaging his thighs after a steeplechase.

"At least we know they are capable of humor," he observed.

Markel was not amused. "We haven't seen anything funny about this so far, Mr. Spock."

Spock replied imperturbably, "Animals in a zoo rarely do."

Kirk broke the rising tension between the two by turning away from the Lactrans and starting toward the occupied cottage.

"Let's join the others. Right now I feel the need for a bit more human company, and a bit less alien." He wasn't sure whether the unbroken, eyeless stares of the Lactrans were making him angry or uneasy, or both.

Letting either emotion overwhelm continued study of their predicament would not bring them closer to a solution, he reminded himself as they entered the house.

The interior was frightening in its cheeriness. Frightening because the creatures that had constructed the wooden chairs, printed the bright wallpaper, were anything but human. Frightening because those paper and chair designs had been drawn unbidden from the minds of unknowing human beings.

A tall, middle-aged woman was lying on the couch beneath the front window. Her expression and pose, even in that naturally relaxed position, hinted at far more than normal exhaustion. Sweat stood out on her forehead like quicksilver on a plastic sheet.

Lieutenant Bryce stood nearby as Dr. McCoy continued his methodical, patient examination—limb by limb, joint by joint, pressing, feeling, laying on hands because of the absence of instruments of metal and plastic and ceramic. While less accurate, however, those hands were equally sensitive.

Bryce turned at their approach, offering a wan smile.

"Captain Kirk, Mr. Spock." She gestured at the prone form. "Lieutenant Nancy Randolph, our cartographer and navigator."

Randolph managed a grin and limp handshakes all around, but even that slight effort clearly exhausted her. Kirk waited until McCoy had concluded his extensive examination, then drew him off toward the rear of the room.

"How is she, and what's the matter with her?"

"She's not well, Jim. As to what's affected her, it's almost impossible to make anything like an accurate diagnosis without proper instrumentation." He took a deep breath.

"If I had to guess, though, I'd say she's picked up some kind of malarial-type infection from an insect bite. I can't tell for certain, of course, much less prescribe any kind of corrective treatment beyond applying cold compresses in hopes of keeping the fever from rising. Bryce has been doing that anyway." He grunted. "If she's not improving, at least she's not getting any worse. But her body can fight the infection only so long. I've got to have my medikit, Jim! Guesses make lousy medication."

Kirk nodded, then turned to walk back to the large front window. The better to enable them to see out? he wondered—or to allow visitors to see in? Angrily, he shrugged the thought away.

The pair of Lactrans had not moved from their resting place. They stayed there, squatting and staring at the house, only occasionally turning front ends to face each other. Kirk knew they were conversing as surely as if they had been shouting in Federation English.

"We haven't seen another Lactran since we arrived except these two," he declared. "Is this standard procedure, Commander Markel? Do these two have a function—are they scientists, or what?"

"It's our joint opinion that they're guards, sir," Markel told him. "Or keepers—the terminology depends on your mood of the moment. Sometimes there are three instead of two, but always at least a couple hovering around somewhere, except when large groups of them appear. They're probably there to see we don't damage ourselves, or each other."

McCoy grunted again. "Very thoughtful of them. I suppose we should feel flattered."

"You mentioned regular meals," Kirk went on. "Do they feed you or supply game so you can fend for yourselves?"

Markel shook his head. "They bring us a large case of various edibles once a week. The stuff is funny-looking, but it tastes okay. I think they synthesized our emergency rations." He smiled at a sudden thought. "If I'd known, we would have beamed down with steak and seafood instead of concentrates."

"How do they get it to you?"

"I'm not certain. We've never been able to tell if they shut the force wall down completely or just at the point where the food is sent in."

"The point?" Kirk perked up. "They always bring it to the same place?"

"Always," Bryce admitted, nodding. "Near the display case."

"Display case . . . what display case?"

"Behind this house," she continued. "Commander Markel mentioned the table our equipment was kept on. It's set up there, outside the force wall. They have all our toys in there, our digging stones and pointed sticks. That's only appropriate, isn't it?" She turned a worried, tired gaze down to the feverish navigator. "It's all part of the main exhibit—us."

"Phasers, communicators, medical supplies, tricorders, and packs—everything we brought down with us," Markel finished.

"That means my medikit should be there, too," McCoy surmised. "We've got to get it back somehow."

"Possibly we can persuade them to give it to us, Captain," Spock suggested. "It is certain that they are aware of the potential of each device. That is shown by their refusal to return the phasers at any time."

"But the medical equipment wouldn't be harmful," McCoy noted. Spock shook his head, once.

"We have already commented on the possibility of voluntary injury to a despondent captive," the first officer commented, ignoring the sensibilities around him in favor of cold reason. "That explains their reluctance to turn such material over to their captives."

"Even at the expense of losing one of those valuable specimens," McCoy snarled, staring helplessly at the recumbent figure of Lieutenant Randolph. His arms were held stiffly at his sides, the hands curled tightly into fists.

"A strong emotional projection, Doctor."

"What of it?" a belligerent McCoy objected.

"Possibly nothing, but continue with it. Reinforce it, concentrate on it to the exclusion of all else."

McCoy started to say something, hesitated, then nodded as understanding of Spock's intention dawned on him. He let the rage and frustration flow freely over him, dwelt masochistically on the image of a twisted, emaciated Randolph writhing on the couch in her death throes. His face contorted and wrinkled, and he fairly vibrated with the tension. McCoy was almost a parody of concentration.

Parody or not, it seemed to have some effect. Spock was staring out the front window as McCoy concentrated. As he watched, one of the two Lactrans abruptly turned and scurried off out of view.

"One of the aliens has just left his companion, Captain," he reported.

"Keep it up, Bones."

"I'm . . . trying, Jim . . ." McCoy's face was a portrait of exaggerated yet honest concern.

"A little bit longer. Give them a chance and we'll see what happens . . ."

They waited. Markel suddenly broke the silence. He was staring out one of the back windows and called excitedly to the others.

"Back here, Captain!"

His concentration broken by the interruption, McCoy turned and left the house through the back door, along with Spock, Markel, and Bryce. They were just in time to see the Lactran who had left, or possibly another one, withdrawing its multiple-ended tail from the force-field boundary. At a corresponding point inside was a pile of exotic but nourishing-looking fruit and vegetables.

"Food—different food, and it's not feeding time," a puzzled Markel observed.

"I think I understand," began Kirk. "They must have sensed Dr. McCoy's projection of want, of need, and interpreted it as a desire for food. The strength of the projection might explain the new offerings. Possibly they feel we require a different diet than you, at least at the beginning of our captivity." He considered the pile of edibles carefully.

"That means that their telepathic sense is less than perfect, or they would have given us the medical supplies. I'm sorry they didn't, but at the same time it would be foolish to say I'm not glad to see a hint or two of imperfection on our captors' part."

"It's nice to have confirmation of that fact, Jim," agreed McCoy tiredly, "but I could have told you that already. And while you might think me a reactionary anthropomorphist, I can also assure you that they're not pretty." He wiped perspiration from his brow. The steady concentration had exhausted him, though in a fashion different from the way such strains affected Spock.

Logic ordered no rest, however, as Spock suggested, "I believe we should all concentrate on the need for Dr. McCoy's medikit, emphasizing our intention to use it only to help preserve one of our members."

Markel shrugged. "Worth a try."

All five of them went silent, some with eyes closed, others staring hard at the slowly retreating Lactran, each using the method which seemed most effective to him.

The subject of this concentration responded with satisfying suddenness. It turned to regard them quietly, then sidled over to the oddly curved display table.

Waivering over the metal, the tail hesitated over several objects before picking up . . . the captain's phaser! For a wild moment Kirk thought that one of their weapons might be returned to them. Similar thoughts occurred to several of the others.

Either because of their thoughts or because of the Lactran's own knowledge, the bulky alien immediately put the weapon down. Kirk cursed himself for giving in so childishly to the offensive image his mind must have conjured up. He resumed concentrating twice as hard on McCoy's medikit.

The Lactran's next choice was more assured. It picked up the necessary container. Handling it as delicately as if it were the prize glass sculpture of a master, it moved toward them and set the kit on the lawn behind the house.

Kirk watched the entire procedure intensely, but there was nothing to indicate any button depressed or lever moved to deactivate that section of the force field.

Still, someone somewhere must have done exactly that. He couldn't believe that the Lactrans possessed the physiological ability to walk through their own restraining field with impunity.

He mused on the problem while the others made a run for the precious medikit, lest the alien change its mind and return to snatch it from them.

"No telling when they'll decide we've had it long enough," Markel explained as they ran toward it. "We've been permitted to keep other equipment anywhere from a few hours to a week."

As McCoy anxiously examined the kit and the others crowded around him, Kirk walked on past to study the section of force wall the Lactran had inserted it through.

"It's all here—no damage and nothing altered," declared McCoy finally. "They haven't removed any of the emergency ampules, either."

"Unfortunately, nothing's changed here, either," Kirk replied. "The field's back on." He stared outward, looking longingly at the table laden with phasers and other equipment, their own as well as that brought by the survey team.

"So near and yet so far," he murmured sadly.

Behind him, McCoy was heading for the house. "Have to see to my patient," he muttered in satisfaction. Doctor, patient, and medical supplies—the tripartite components of his Aesculapian universe were once more complete.

Kirk watched them walk toward the house. He bestowed a final, concentrated thought on the retreating Lactran, pleading desperately for a simple, harmless toy—his communicator.

The Lactran ignored him completely.

IV

Meanwhile others were striving to pierce the isolation which had swallowed up the captain, first officer, and chief physician of the *Enterprise*.

"Are you raising anything yet?" an anxious Scott inquired of Lieutenant M'ress. He stood near the communications console and stared at the squiggles and lines which appeared on various readouts, in the hope that one of them might spell out an answer in plain English.

No explanation was forthcoming from those dispassionate, uncaring instruments, plain or otherwise.

"Not a thing, sirr," M'ress replied. She had answered the same query from Scott with the same information every five minutes since she had taken over for Lieutenant Uhura.

Scott responded with the same order. "Keep at it. They're down there somewhere."

Furiously, he turned over the same old possibilities in his mind. It was highly unlikely that all three officers had experienced a simultaneous breakdown of their communicators, regardless of what might have happened to those carried down by the survey crew.

That left three possibilities.

One, they were unable to use their communicators, for what reason Scott couldn't imagine. Two, their communicators had been rendered inoperative by outside forces. Three . . .

He refused to consider Three. As long as he denied the possibility, it could never come about.

Scottish reasoning can be notoriously perverse, and this was one instance in which Scott utilized its roundabout methodology to the fullest. Spock could say that Scott thought in pretzels all he wanted to . . . as long as the absurd first officer was all right.

As long, the *Enterprise*'s chief engineer thought furiously, as he was all right . . .

The little knot of humans left McCoy to his doctoring, aware that their presence could only hinder his ministrations. Lieutenant Bryce lingered the longest, but eventually she, too, left the couch and its tired occupant to join the others in gazing out the front window.

Both guards stood, or sat, where one had been moments before. They regarded the inhabitants of the house with identical but featureless stares. The inhabitants stared back with somewhat more animation.

"Let's sum things up, Commander," Kirk started firmly. "Based on everything that's happened to you since you've been trapped on this world, what's your evaluation of the situation?"

Markel considered for a moment and ticked off his observations on the fingers of one hand. "The Lactrans treat us quite well. They want us alive and healthy and are willing to go to some inconvenience to insure that we remain so . . . though they do make occasional mistakes—underestimating the severity of Lieutenant Randolph's condition, for example. Most importantly, they want to keep us right where we are."

"A natural reaction for the curators of a zoo," Spock observed drily.

"We've managed to keep from going crazy," continued Markel, "only just. Part of the time we make studious analyses of our guards, trying to discern differences between them . . . with little result. The rest of the time we occupy by plotting absurd escape schemes and executing them, and by making observations of this world not connected with our captors. For example, we've worked out a calendar according to the movements of the Lactran sun and moon. It's a close duplicate of our own, which helps us a little. Oh, and every nine days we draw quite a crowd."

"Undoubtedly the local equivalent of a periodic rest time," commented Spock.

Markel was silent for a while as attention was divided

between the guards and the couch, where McCoy made steady, assured motions with his hands and paraphernalia. Then he turned a concerned, unwinking gaze on Kirk.

"Sir, do you think there's any chance of getting out?" It wasn't the sort of statement the leader of a survey crew ought to make, but then, Markel didn't feel much like a leader at the moment. He felt like a laboratory rat crouched at the far corner of its cage, regarding a monstrous hand moving inexorably toward it.

"As long as they keep us alive, there's a chance," Kirk replied, properly encouraging. His private thoughts went unvoiced. "Sometimes the strongest force fields can be negated by the simplest procedures. Tonight we'll try to find a frequency commonality using Dr. McCoy's instrumentation, slightly rearranged, of course."

"I'd say there was no commonality, Captain."

"Not very encouraging, Mr. Spock."

"I am not one for fanciful dreams, sir, as you well know," the first officer replied evenly.

"I never met a Vulcan who was." Markel did not look across at Spock.

"I hope," the target of that barb said carefully, "that was meant to connote the value of being a Vulcan."

"I'm sure it was," Kirk said hastily.

Spock was well in control of himself, but Kirk saw that the survey commander was being pushed by Spock's constant coolness. Spock could only be Spock, however, and he continued relentlessly. His mind could not make room for childishly optimistic speculation where no grounds for such existed.

"I think we should face our situation realistically, Captain. We are specimens in a zoo. We have been taken captive by an alien race of unusual technological accomplishments and unpredictable psychology. To them, we are caged for life. These facts, coupled with the Lactrans' undeniable demonstrations of superior intelligence, do not add up to a very convincing set of factors for eventual escape. And, while not very encouraging, Captain, that is my reasoned assessment of our present situation."

"Thank you, Mr. Spock," Kirk replied. "And mine is, let's sleep on it."

* * *

Randolph was a new person the following morning, thanks to McCoy's skilled treatment. New, but not her old self, not yet. Her system would need plenty of time and rest to return to normal strength. So she remained on the couch under doctor's orders as the other five officers left the house.

Kirk was the first one out, and he pulled up short, staring around in surprise. The others followed and displayed varied expressions of equal amazement.

"We seem," Spock observed mildly, "to be drawing quite a crowd."

Indeed, where only the presence of two guards had marred the broad horizon the previous day, there now milled a thickly packed throng of Lactrans. The only visible differences between individuals were slight variations in color and somewhat greater ones in size.

"This is that ninth day I mentioned," Markel informed Kirk, unnecessarily.

"I'll be hanged if I'm going to do tricks for them," grumbled McCoy.

"We can move about as we wish, Doctor," agreed Spock, "but we cannot evade their mental vision. I suggest we attempt to ignore them and make ourselves comfortable."

They moved around to the side of the house, Lieutenant Bryce going inside briefly to inform Randolph of what was going on. The recreational section outside boasted a number of comfortable chairs, and it was into these that the members of the trapped group settled themselves.

Bryce returned, indicating the pool and surrounding equipment. "As you can see, they've given us extensive facilities for enjoying ourselves—and for making sure we stay healthy." She snapped out the words. "A very comfortable wheel, only the rats aren't in the mood to climb in and run in place.

"They feed us," she continued as she relaxed into a freeform of orange plastic, "and apparently think this is all we want. To run, eat, sleep, and"—she paused only slightly—"play."

"Exactly what we would expect from the animals we have in our own zoos," Spock commented. His tone was almost approving. Almost.

"Well, I am not an animal," McCoy muttered disconsolately.

"Scientifically speaking, we all are," Kirk reminded him, then turned to each in sequence. "Instead of learning about us, a subject we're pretty familiar with, why don't we follow Commander Markel's suggestion and try to learn something about them."

Markel looked resigned. "I don't see what more there is we can learn, Captain, unless we can either penetrate their minds or convince them of our intelligence."

"Known fact: They are purely telepathic," Kirk began, restating the obvious. "Mr. Spock is, like all Vulcans, peripherally so, but as yet has not been able to make successful contact with them."

"Their intelligence is so different that I can find no common basis for an exchange of information, let alone for complicated visualizations," Spock added.

"Exactly what did you learn yesterday?" Markel wondered.

"That the thoughts and expressions of adults are incomprehensible to a six-year-old infant," the first officer declaimed, "and that the infant's babblings are regarded with equal incomprehension by adults." He did not have to place his companions into one of the two categories.

"I think we're missing something, Spock," the doctor said.

The first officer turned an interested gaze on McCoy. "What do you mean?"

"Well, we're assuming this extraordinary, impenetrable intelligence level is uniform throughout the population. In any civilization there are the gifted, the norm, and the slow." He nodded once toward the smoothly shifting crowd. "Maybe there are less highly developed minds out there today. It's only natural to expect the keepers to be reasonably advanced. That's not necessarily so of those who come to gawk. Try them. At least we'll have the general public's impression of us, if we're lucky."

"A fine suggestion, Doctor." Spock turned his stare outward, concentrating without exerting the maximum effort of the previous day.

"It is only a vague generalization," he finally murmured

softly. "I could be completely wrong, but we appear to frighten some of them—at least the smaller ones. Probably juveniles. The others have mixed feelings: Some are indifferent, some curious, a few find us rather ugly." He blinked. "It is a sign of their advanced civilization that none projected any hint of antagonism toward us."

"Okay, the feelings are mutual," McCoy commented without rancor. Changing the subject abruptly, he asked Kirk, "What about those on board, Jim?"

"Scotty's patient, Bones, when he has to be. Left to his own feelings, he'd probably have beamed down yesterday to see what happened. But he's under orders. He'll exhaust every ounce of patience, try everything to regain contact with us without taking offensive action. But eventually, he's going to get worried enough to take action.

"As I said before, the *Enterprise* might not come out on top in a fight with our silent hosts. No, Scotty will hold off. He'll need some proof we're in danger before sending down an armed force—and we're probably safer here than on board the ship, thanks to the concern of the Lactrans."

"We have to do *something*, then," McCoy exploded, "besides rest on our fundaments and juggle the odds of a Federation–Lactran battle . . . with us in the middle."

"I have a suggestion, Captain, when the doctor is finished."

McCoy threw Spock a sour look and mumbled, "I'm finished, Spock, what's your grand solution?"

"Not solution . . . suggestion," Spock corrected efficiently, completely missing McCoy's sarcasm. "Evidently they can pick up our thought patterns if we all concentrate on the same thing. *If* they care to go to the trouble."

"This is the main problem. Believing that we are animals, it is therefore not worth their effort to descend to our level. Who cares what the vermin think?"

"Yes, yes," Kirk agreed rapidly, "we've already proven that by getting them to give us the medical kit. Where do we go from here?"

"I see no reason not to try an idea that has worked once a second time." The others eyed Spock expectantly. "One of us must pretend to be seriously ill. Even more important, the rest of us must *believe* in the falsified illness, so that our true intentions are masked from the Lactrans. The lie must be close to the truth, for us to have a chance. Our captors are perceptive and react quickly. We have to concentrate strongly on the thought that a communicator is vital to the patient's recovery.

"Naturally, we need not specify in our minds exactly *why* a communicator is required, but it is a thought all of us should be able to hold to." He paused, then went on easily, "Surely a return to the *Enterprise* would be one method of seeing to the health of an ill individual."

"Sounds possible, Spock," Kirk finally concurred. "Let's try it. And, visual stimulus being an aid to concentration, let's move back behind the house so that we can look at the communicators while we're concentrating on one."

There were far fewer Lactrans clustered at the rear of the cottage than they had encountered out front. That was only natural, Spock pointed out, since the best view in any zoo was in front of the cage. Possibly their novelty was wearing off, because no rush of Lactrans appeared to gaze at them from the new vantage point.

Only a small number were clustered by the display table. As they neared the field wall, Kirk saw that one of the smaller aliens was busily engaged in examining the equipment laid out on the table. The larger ones rested nearby, apparently deep in telepathic conversation.

"Okay, who's our candidate for convincing convulsions?" McCoy wondered aloud.

"I'll do it," Kirk said immediately. "I'm sick of this place and sick of our situation, so I won't have to exaggerate too much. The rest of you concentrate like hell on the nearest communicator."

"Maybe we'll get lucky," Markel observed, his attention focused on the display table. "That's a little one pretty much alone with the instruments. If Mr. Spock's right, it could be a youngster."

"Spock wasn't sure, Commander," Kirk reminded him. "It might merely be a small adult. Or maybe the adults are the smaller of the species." Markel looked disappointed.

"Try to think about Captain Kirk's visible manifestations of illness," Spock advised the others, "instead of considering his actual condition. We must strive to project an aura of intense worry and concern, to the exclusion of all other thoughts."

"And remember, we have to be quick," Kirk admonished. "As soon as I get my hands on a communicator, I'll try to get enough information through to whoever answers so that they'll know we require an immediate beam-aboard." He settled himself close to the field wall.

"Ready now . . ."

Kirk became a dervish, spinning, whirling, hopping about, clutching at his head, and finally bending over with both hands pressed to his stomach. He rolled on the ground, bugging his eyes and choking, generally presenting the appearance of a being whose health was somewhat less than ideal.

The others moved to form a half circle around him, leaving the section between Kirk and the force field unblocked. They stared down at the body in spasms, their faces reflecting the agony they forced themselves to feel.

The effect upon the small Lactran studying their equipment was immediate. It turned its front end toward the enclosure and gave that eerie impression of ogling without optics. Moments came and went, while Kirk struggled to maintain the illusion of impending death and Spock wondered if they were wasting their time.

The versatile tail drifted over the exhibit table, finally settling on some of the survey team's emergency medical supplies. Turning sideways, the Lactran extended its tail and deposited the sealed containers inside the field, close to Kirk's thrashing legs.

"It has the idea," Spock murmured, his eyes never straying from Kirk's writhing form. "We must concentrate harder on the necessary remedy. The communicator . . . it is the only thing that will save the captain. The only thing . . . he'll die horribly without it, remember. That's all you can think about, the captain dying . . . unless . . . he gets . . . the communicator . . ."

Several minutes of truly inspired gesticulating on Kirk's part coupled with his companions' shunning of the proffered medical supplies, prompted the Lactran to reach farther into the field cage to nudge the containers closer to the pitiful, suffering specimen.

When this further offering was also ignored, the slug turned back to the exhibits. This time it picked up one of the communicators, the compact device looking even tinier in the grip of that massive gray limb.

But the ruse was only partly successful. Either the Lactran suspected the depth of their need for this particular instrument, or else it was unsure of itself, but, whatever the reason, it decided to keep a close eye on its utilization. So instead of handing over the communicator, it entered the enclosure with it.

Like an elastic crane the tail swooped around and down, to offer the instrument to Kirk. Apparently the Lactrans held to the "heal thyself" principle. Well, Kirk was more than willing to abide by it. He raised a quivering, feeble hand and grasped it, bringing the instrument down toward his mouth. As soon as he had it opened and activated, he underwent a remarkable transition. In fact, his symptoms of advanced disease vanished as though they had never existed.

"*Enterprise, Enterprise*, this is the captain. Beam us aboard immediately, all of—"

The communicator was torn from his grip before he could finish. Had he not let go, the Lactran would have taken his arm along with the instrument.

Whether it was the physical or mental commotion, or both, something finally caused the two large Lactrans standing nearest the exhibit table to cease their inaudible conversation and whirl. They started toward the force field.

A familiar flickering in the air had commenced behind the force wall, a colorful shimmering that Kirk gaped at in horror. The transporter effect was not engulfing himself, Spock, or any of the other anxious captives.

The smaller Lactran brightened once and was gone.

Scott fought the transporter controls, having reacted instantly to Kirk's shipwide call. He had focused on the area surrounding the exact position of the communicator, as pinpointed by the *Enterprise*'s communications computer.

Readouts indicated he had locked onto a substantial mass—presumably the captain and the rest of the landing party, including any survivors from the *Ariel*.

He stared expectantly at the alcove, where something was beginning to take shape.

"Captain," he began, "for a minute we thought sure . . ." He stared, swallowed. "What in cosmos . . . ?"

Instead of the captain, Mr. Spock, or anyone else, a two-and-a-half-meter-long monstrosity was coalescing in the chamber. It looked like a cross between a cucumber and a squid, combining the least desirable features of both.

Its front end—or was it the back?—moped around rapidly, until it was pointed at Scott. The engineer's hackles rose as he felt as if something unclean were picking at his mind. At the same time the long tail whipped around, secondary limbs contracting.

Scott ducked down behind the console. The tentacle probed. As it did so the *Enterprise's* chief engineer made like a foot soldier and scuttled fast for the door.

A first palm thrust sent the metal partition sliding shut behind him. A second activated the wall intercom.

"Scott here . . . Security, full team to the Main Transporter Room, on the double! We've—" Metal groaned behind him.

The door had begun to buckle inward. It was still bending when three security guards skidded around the corridor corner, phasers held at the ready.

"I beamed up something out of a bad hangover," Scott yelled at them. "The captain sent an emergency message, and instead of him we got—"

The door gave in with a musical *spannggg,* and Scott's half-coherent explanation went no further.

"Watch it!" he yelled, stumbling backward.

The door slammed down against the deck. Scott thought of yelling for phasers to be set on stun, but changed his mind when he remembered through the confusion of the moment that security phasers were never preset to deliver a lethal charge.

Nor was it necessary to give an order to fire. Faced with an eight-foot-long slug emerging from behind a crumpled door and a wildly gesturing officer, they decided unanimously to try nonverbal means of persuasion on the apparent cause of the trouble.

Three phasers fired, three beams struck the Lactran. Its skin seemed to ripple slightly . . . and that was all. But the creature stopped, though both Scott and the security personnel had a feeling it wasn't because of the phaser attack.

Scott began retreating down the corridor to organize a larger capture party, but immediately came to a jerking halt as though an invisible cable around his head had snapped taut. Both hands went to his suddenly throbbing skull, where tiny gnomes had set up a small warp-engine and were running it at overdrive.

All three guards, being closer to the intense mental blast, had been knocked to the floor. Sliding along the deck like a heavy metal ingot on oil, the invader sprinted forward, swept up Scott with its tail, and raced down the corridor.

Behind, the guards struggled to find their phasers, their composure, and the tops of their skulls . . .

V

Far, far below, the situation was no less tense, if somewhat less hectic.

"Captain, I believe that for the first time they are making an effort to transmit a comprehensible thought pattern toward us," Spock told them. "Our speculation as to the relationship between age and size appears to have been correct. They are worried about their child, the one caught in the transporter beam.

"These, I gather, are the parents of the missing one. Despite the lack of external sexual characteristics, the standard male-female partnership is in existence here."

"Never mind the biological details, Mr. Spock," a tense Kirk ordered, eyeing the two silent Lactrans warily. "While they're worried about their offspring, I'm more concerned about what it might do to the *Enterprise*. Even an adolescent probably possesses considerable mental as well as physical powers."

"What in Carrel's scalpel went wrong, though?" a bemused McCoy wondered.

"I'm not sure, Bones. Obviously Scotty received our call for help, a call that was sorely lacking in details. That thing snatched the communicator before I could give him any details. As soon as the alien took the communicator from me, well, it was still activated when it was grabbed away. Scotty centered on it, of course."

Spock was swaying slightly, drifting deeper into trance. "They seem to think you made the child disappear," he murmured, "since you were the one who operated the device. Their reaction . . . their reaction . . ."

"Go on, Spock."

"They are surprised, and concerned. The concern is for their missing offspring. They are surprised because we had not been classed as either an intelligent or a dangerous species. And they are somewhat shocked to discover that we may be both."

"We can't stand here," McCoy said nervously, "we've got to do something . . . or they will."

Kirk tried to calm the jittery McCoy. In fact, everyone appeared increasingly nervous. That could only make the Lactrans worry more about their child.

"Calm down . . . all of you. Let's not give our captors cause for concern. The best thing we can do is—"

He doubled over and fell to the ground, twisting in pain—and this time he wasn't acting.

"Jim!" McCoy was at his side, feeling helpless. "What is it?"

"My head! Inside . . . my head." The words came out with an effort. "I think . . . the baby. What happened to the baby?"

There was an odd, hollow tone in those last words, as if something unhuman was trying to operate a human voice mechanism.

"Fight it, Captain," Spock urged, "fight it as hard as you can. Don't try to listen, don't try to let them use you." He turned to McCoy.

"They think so fast, their patterns of cogitation are so complicated, that their own thoughts are too complex for a human brain to assimilate." He watched as Kirk rolled to his knees, tried to keep his balance, and failed.

"If he gives up, even for a moment," Spock explained with deathly precision, "he may go mad. The Lactran thought processes will overload his neural capacity."

M'ress uttered a sound halfway between a screech and a feline yowl as the Lactran, still holding Scott firmly in its grasp, charged out of the turbolift onto the bridge. Arex rose from his position at the navigation console, but despite the shock and consternation, no one moved to abandon his post, no one ran for an exit.

And that was the last thing Scott wanted, since the presence of others seemed to make his captor nervous. The chief engineer had been treated to one of the slug-thing's mental assaults and had no desire to endure another.

"Everyone clear out," he ordered, seeing that no one was going to budge without being told to do so. "Don't antagonize it."

"Antagonize what?" M'ress asked quietly, bearing Scott's admonition in mind. "What *is* that thing?"

"I don't know . . . yet. But it hasn't injured anyone badly . . . yet. And I have the impression it doesn't want to. It could have sent pieces of me all over the ship by now but hasn't taken that option." The Lactran headed toward the center of the bridge. As it began to move, the bridge personnel started to edge around toward the turbolift doors.

"All rright, what do you want us to do, sirr?" M'ress queried, standing by the open doors.

"Just leave quietly, lassie. Report to Lieutenant Seelens, tell her to set up security teams on all transporters. I don't expect any more visitors, but I want to be ready to greet them in case I'm wrong."

"Yes, sirr," she acknowledged. "But what arre you going to do, sirr?"

Scott let out a resigned sigh. "What do you think, Lieutenant? Whatever it wants me to."

M'ress filed into the lift behind Arex, turned, and started to say something. The closing doors cut her off soundlessly.

He was alone on the bridge with the alien invader.

The front end of the creature waved back and forth, like an elephant sensing the air. It slid forward and placed Scott in the command chair—gently and right-side up, the chief noted with thanks—and then turned its featureless front to stare at him.

"Now look," Scott began, "supposin' you and I talk this over?"

No response from the slug.

"You can talk, can't you?"

Silence, and that continuing eyeless gaze.

"If you can't talk, how do you communicate?" He tried Federation sign language. "Well, what can you do?"

The creature turned and began examining the control consoles nearby, beginning with navigation and working its way around to Spock's library-computer station. The tail end touched several switches, and the multiple screens at the station lit and began pouring forth a torrent of information. Scott couldn't even identify the sections the creature was studying, much less follow its progress.

"Listen, you've got to be careful here," he explained patiently. "This is the control room of a—hey!"

The tail had reached out and lifted him again, then replaced him in the chair. If this was the alien's method of indicating one should be silent, it failed to impress Scott. The chief was growing increasingly nervous as the alien continued to touch this or that control.

"Now, look," he began as the Lactran switched off the library and moved around to face the helm and navigation consoles, "just keep your grubby little whatever-it-is off things you don't under . . . *no, don't touch that*!"

Too late. The multitipped tail was moving across the consoles with blurring speed, far too fast for Scott to follow. It touched switches, pushed buttons and levers, activated telltales, and checked readouts, while its front end slowly weaved back and forth from one console to the other.

"Listen," Scott howled desperately, "if you keep that up, you'll send us runnin' off to the back of wherever!"

His attention was diverted by the already altered picture on the main viewscreen. It was anything but reassuring. It showed a rapidly shrinking green and white globe, Lactra VII, become a pinhead circle instead of a screen-filling orb.

Seconds later the warp-drive was engaged. An enraged, horrified Scott could only stare and hurl Highland imprecations at the gray hippo before him. His horror sprang from the knowledge that any idiot could activate the *Enterprise*'s warp-drive engines; but the matter of navigation, of determining where those engines were taking the ship, was a chore for experience and expertise.

And he had the sick feeling that the voiceless mass in front of him had neither.

The two Lactrans abruptly turned from the enclosure to converse with each other. Simultaneously, Kirk's body relaxed. His face was pale and his tunic drenched with perspiration. As the others watched anxiously, he rolled over, sat up, and let out a long *whoosh* of exhaustion.

"Have they stopped, Jim?" McCoy finally asked, when he felt Kirk had recovered enough to answer. The captain looked like a man who had just come out of an eighteen-hour sleep. "How are you?"

"They've left off . . . for now," Kirk told them. "I think I'm okay, Bones. But I'm tired . . . so tired."

"Understandable," McCoy agreed. "Spock, what do you think of . . . Spock?" McCoy turned, to see Spock staring as if frozen at the pair of concerned Lactrans. He was startled to see three more of the full-sized aliens sidling up to the first two. It seemed the alarm had been raised.

At least, he thought grimly, they had succeeded in getting their captors to notice them.

Spock left his trance and glanced down at Kirk. "I am not certain, Captain, but I believe they have concluded that they cannot break into your mind on an individual or even a dualistic basis. They are surprised."

"Good!" McCoy exclaimed. "Maybe they won't try it again."

Spock turned a somber gaze on him. "On the contrary, Doctor, they are now readying the mental strength of five of their number in a more powerful attempt."

A wild, faintly desperate tone underlined Kirk's reaction. "I can't hold out against that many. It's not possible. I don't know why they stopped the last time. You've no idea, Bones, what it's like." He turned an anxious stare on the gathering of Lactrans.

"I don't know if I'll come out of another attack like that last one, let alone one of more than twice the strength."

"Every one of us must help the captain," Spock instructed. "Concentrate on him, try to become one with him, a part of his mind and thoughts. Perhaps we can create some kind of screen, or at least—"

But Kirk was already on the ground again, spinning in pain and screaming for something to leave him alone.

"It's tearing—!"

Their concern was too great for those surrounding him to erect anything like an effective mental screen, if such a thing were even possible. Kirk rolled about for several minutes until his body quit. He lay still, only a quivering of arms and legs and an occasional jerk of his head indicating that his spread-eagled form was still fighting back.

His continued resistance was as obvious as the fact that he was slowly weakening. More minutes passed. Kirk rolled onto his face, limp as a rag doll now, his form twitching from time to time as if touched by a live cable.

A number of wholly alien feelings were approaching eruption inside the *Enterprise*'s first officer when a familiar and unexpected glow appeared in the air inside the force screen, as if someone were shining a colored light on a rippling sheet of clear silk.

Two figures began to emerge. "The Lactrans are coming into the enclosure," Markel began, "but why in this fashion if—"

He broke off as the shifting hues solidified. One of the two figures was Lactran, all right. But the other . . .

It was a surprise to see the small Lactran reappear, but it was a positive shock to see Chief Engineer Scott held firmly in its tail-grip.

The surprise and shock worked equally on the five Lactrans outside the field. Their concentration was shattered by the appearance of the small one, and the results were immediately apparent as Kirk finally ceased his helpless spasms.

The adolescent put Scott down gently. As soon as the chief had moved off a bit, two of the larger Lactrans—not even Spock could tell if they were the original two—reached in and drew the smaller one outside the boundary of the force screen. Rather roughly, McCoy thought, as he turned his attention back to the still supine Kirk.

The others were already gathered around him. He turned onto his back, and McCoy saw his eyes were glazed. Slowly, he tried to sit up, but nearly collapsed. McCoy bent to help.

"No, I'm all right, I'm okay," he muttered thickly. But he did not reject the support of McCoy's shoulder after he had struggled to his feet. His eyes were clearing rapidly.

"Whew! I feel like my brain's been pulled through a wringer." He looked around at the assemblage of worried faces. "You've no idea what it's like, Scotty." He blinked. "Scotty? What are you doing here?"

The chief jerked his head to indicate the activity behind them. "My alien acquaintance brought me."

Spock looked incredulous, though his words were as evenly modulated as ever. "You succeeded in making contact with it?"

"Not exactly." The object of sudden startled attention grinned. "It made contact with me. I gather it was a tremendous effort for the poor child to slow down to my level."

"You were right, Mr. Spock. Our attempts at communication were properly directed, only at the wrong members of this society."

"What did you learn?" Kirk asked.

The chief engineer considered the question carefully. "Some of it doesn't translate verra easily into human terms," he explained slowly. "But I did succeed in grasping a few definite concepts.

"For one, our small friend is the emotional and physical Lactran equivalent of a human six-year-old. Mentally, however, it is considerably superior to any of us. The first thing it did on appearin' on board was pick the nearest mind for useful information. *Mine!* Then it went on and absorbed all the knowledge in the ship's library computer, science center, and general storage facility. Bein' a curious laddie—or lassie—it decided to play around with its new toys. That included operating the ship's helm. Sent us tearin' right out of orbit."

Kirk, who saw the *Enterprise* gallivanting all over known space at the mercy of a playful alien infant, swallowed hard. "How did you convince it to come back?"

Scott turned introspective. "I think it was my concern for the rest of the crew that persuaded it. That, and the fact that I never showed any hatred toward it." He shrugged. "I suppose any child can tell instinctively when a threat is present and when it's not. And there was my willingness, the willingness of another, uh, child, to chat with it."

"Infant-to-infant communication," Spock observed, showing no resentment at being likewise classified. "My congratulations, Mr. Scott."

"Anyhow," the chief continued, "I managed to convince it that I wasn't anybody's pet, and that we're no mere grubbers in the dirt. And that it would be a sight better for all concerned if it would bring the ship back into orbit around its own home world. From there, it wasn't too hard to convince it to reenter the transporter so we could return home. By that time the youngster was pretty sure I meant it no harm. What finally reassured it was my readiness to come along too. I think they can sense friendliness in another's thoughts as readily as they can much more complicated concepts. If we could only—"

Spock cut him off softly. "A moment, please, Mr. Scott." The *Enterprise*'s first officer shook his head irritably, like a man trying to throw off the first assault of an advancing migraine. "I believe . . . they are trying to contact us directly. I can . . . make out . . . something. It is very difficult. The adults . . . so concise, so fast in their mental formulations . . .

"They are . . . trying now . . . to slow down for us. Communication involves the insertion of many transitional concepts they have long since discarded as superfluous. The . . . child . . . has explained to them. Adults are attempting to rephrase their normal thoughts into . . . baby talk." The evident irritation and minor pain gradually faded, while his attitude of attentive listening remained unchanged.

"There . . . it's better now. The child has learned much from us, particularly from Mr. Scott. It has also acquired an enormous volume of information about us, and is relaying this to its parents . . . though I can recognize only glimpses and snatches of what it is relating. It is like trying to follow every ripple in a fast-flowing stream." A pause; then: "It has concluded, Captain. Already it has told its parents all about the Federation and the many aspects of its composition, including all the races it comprises."

"Already," gulped McCoy, wondering not merely at a youthful mind capable of delivering a torrent of material so rapidly, but also at those more mature minds able to absorb and assimilate it.

At the moment, however, there were other concerns tempering Kirk's admiration of the Lactrans' mental calisthenics.

"All that information ought to include enough facts about ourselves to convince them we're not common animals. How do they look at us now, Mr. Spock?"

"It would appear that they have indeed revised their initial opinions of us," Spock replied, swaying slightly as he struggled to codify the Lactrans' rapid flow of thoughts. "Apparently we are now classed as simplistic life forms in the process of evolving rapidly into a higher order."

"Vulcans included?" McCoy couldn't resist the opportunity.

Spock's intense concentration didn't keep him from sounding slightly annoyed. "Yes, Vulcans included." He frowned as the Lactrans continued to relay information.

"They are confused now."

"That's a hopeful sign," Kirk murmured. "I was beginning to wonder if they were infallible."

"It would seem not, Captain. Several of them are arguing that on closer inspection we may prove in certain unexpected ways to be equal or even superior to them. I cannot follow all of the discussion, but much of it involves the efficacy of instinct as opposed to pure thought."

"No need to ask which of those we're supposed to represent!" McCoy snorted. "I don't know if they're flattering us or insulting us."

"It is purely a zoological question to them, Doctor," Spock explained. "The question of value judgment does not enter into it."

"I can see why they're using you as their go-between," McCoy murmured, but so softly that no one else could hear. Aloud, he observed, "So they think that as far as we're concerned, equality is just around the corner?"

Spock nodded absently, as usual taking no notice of the doctor's sarcasm.

"At the moment I'm more interested in getting back on the *Enterprise* than in reaching their mental level," Kirk declared pointedly. To McCoy's professional gaze the captain appeared and sounded fully recovered from the withering Lactran mind probe which had almost rendered him comatose.

Kirk had no time to consider the speed of his recovery. It had occurred to him that, despite the Lactrans' apparent reconsideration of their human captives, they might find other reasons for not releasing them.

"How do we manage that return—or do we?"

Another pause followed while Spock listened to intense Lactran babytalk and strove to comprehend. If such delays were merely irritating to Kirk, to Markel and Bryce they seemed interminable.

"It appears that we do," the first officer finally informed them. Bryce began to smile. "Under one condition." The smile died aborning.

"While we are still classified as beneath Lactrans on the scale of evolution, they do concede that we do not belong in their zoo. We grade high in certain abilities and low in others. This apparent contradiction continues to puzzle them."

"That's hardly surprising," observed McCoy. "The contradictions within ourselves have been confusing mankind since the beginning of its history."

"What's this condition they're talking about?" Kirk asked, somehow sensing that it involved more than the Lactran equivalent of a handshake. Their captors had some purpose in mind.

He would never have guessed it in a hundred years.

But the Lactrans refused to be hurried.

"Their abstract imagery . . . so difficult to interpret." Again a frown of intense concentration contorted the first officer's face. "They do not feel that those who maintain zoos belong in them."

"I wouldn't have put it that way," Markel commented, fairly shaking with impatience. "How do we get out of theirs, then?"

Spock blinked, turned to the Lactrans, and said, "Like this." He walked toward the display table, past where the invisible wall had been, and over to the table itself. There was no hum, whine, or revealing flash to announce the abrupt termination of the restraining force field. One moment it was present, and the next it simply was not.

Still pondering the mysterious condition under which the Lactrans would agree to release them, Kirk followed his first officer's lead. McCoy, Scott, and Markel followed him. Lieutenant Bryce hesitated, then turned and started back toward the house to rouse the still weak Randolph.

As the former captives left the enclosure, the front ends of all five Lactrans turned in unison to follow them with almost mechanical precision—attentively, Kirk thought. While he could not be sure, he was willing to bet that their captors were prepared to prevent any sudden "instinctive" surprises—such as a rapid attempt to beam back up to the ship.

Eyeless stares followed the movements of the humans as they picked up activated phasers, tricorders, and other equipment. Kirk did not miss the expression on Markel's face as the leader of the survey team lovingly fondled the familiar instruments he had longed for these past weeks. There was much more to the way he checked out the devices, replacing many on his belt and survey suit, than simple pleasure at regaining denied possessions. They no longer had the significance given them by captivity, but regaining them held a symbolic significance far greater. Markel found a freedom in handling Federation devices manufactured by Federation machinery and hands, instead of falsely familiar constructs manufactured by an alien keeper.

The survey commander had ample time to indulge himself in the inspection of his lost equipment, because it took some time for Lieutenant Randolph, aided by Bryce, to join them. When she finally appeared, McCoy hurried forward to examine her, moving his hands toward his medikit. She shook off the incipient attention.

"Please Doctor, no drugs. I want to savor every second of our departure from this place. I promise not to collapse until it's into a Federation bed." McCoy hesitated, then smiled and nodded understandingly.

Kirk tried to appear interested in the remaining survey instruments, but his attention was actually focused on the Lactrans, who appeared to be observing the byplay between McCoy and Randolph. The captain's hand shifted imperceptibly toward the communicator, which once more rested in its familiar place at his side.

The movement was not as imperceptible as he thought, however, because as his fingers touched the smooth edge of the device, the front end of one of the watching adults turned toward him. The fingers slid on past and above the communicator to scratch easily at his belly. He sighed reluctantly. So much for trying to beam clear from under the mental gaze of *these* jailers.

"Very well, Mr. Spock, let's have the details of this condition. I give my word we'll abide by whatever they have in mind." Easy enough to do, he mused sardonically, without a hope of otherwise departing. For a brief moment, he thought he sensed an alien mental laugh.

Spock strained again, beginning to show some signs of fatigue. The process of acting as translator was starting to wear on him.

"It is still difficult, Captain. Their thought processes are so incredibly fast. It is becoming slightly easier, though. We are learning from each other as we continue to communicate. Somehow, I gain the impression that the condition in some way involves this 'zoo'—not quite the proper term, but it must serve."

"If they think we're going to volunteer some substitute exhibits," McCoy began heatedly.

"No, no, Doctor . . . it does not involve the continued presence of humans, Vulcans, or any other Federation-member race."

McCoy calmed down, satisfied.

"It is more complex than that."

"How so, Mr. Spock?" Kirk pressed curiously. The first officer had turned to face the largest of the adult Lactrans.

"I am told by the Old One that their collection is not complete. It will probably never be complete, since the desire for expansion and acquisition has faded on Lactra. There are temporal referents that I do not understand. The Old One explains gently that this does not matter. Apparently, one especially desired creature is overdue for collection. It is this that they wish us to help rectify."

"One creature?" McCoy echoed uncertainly. "You mean, they want our help in capturing some unknown specimen?"

"Essentially, that is correct, Doctor. It seems that there is one creature they have known about for hundreds of our years yet have not been able to capture because"—the young Lactran moved jerkily, and Spock turned to gaze blankly in its direction—"because they have given up the knowledge of how to construct artificial devices—ships like the *Enterprise*—capable of ranging deep space. They have been content in past centuries to range for specimens close to their own system, and to use the years for refining their mind control. The emphasis in Lactran society has shifted during this period from the practical to the purely aesthetic.

"Yet they still retain knowledge of this one special creature, and wish to obtain a live example of it. It is for this that they request our aid."

Kirk considered gratefully the courtesy of the Lactrans. That they could as easily take control of the *Enterprise* as request the voluntary help of its crew was something he did not doubt. But for some reason it was important to them that such help be given freely.

McCoy walked close. He whispered cautioningly, "I wouldn't be too ready to accept their claim that they've 'forgotten' how to build deep-space ships, Jim."

"If it's an evasion, Bones, there's not much we can do about it. We can either believe them or call them liars. I don't think it would be wise to do the latter. They obviously have their reasons for wanting the use of the *Enterprise* . . . and us."

"Then consider this," the doctor persisted. "If the Lactrans, with all their amply demonstrated abilities, their mental powers, and considerable technology, have been unable to capture this boojum so far, what makes them think we can do any better?"

"Good point, Bones," Kirk agreed willingly. "Transportation we can provide, and we have had some experience handling live alien specimens—everything from tribbles to wauls. But interstellar big-game hunters we're not." He looked back at his first officer, and his voice rose.

"Explain to them, Spock, that we agree. We're willing to aid in any way we can, in return for our eventual safe departure from Lactra. How should we begin? Do they have any idea where to start looking for this prize creature? We certainly have no experience of it, or the Lactran youngster would have discovered some reference to it during its *very* thorough examination of our library."

"On the contrary, Captain," explained a listening Spock, "they say we have looked upon the jawanda without seeing it—'jawanda' is the nearest pronunciation-conceptualization they can provide. The actual name is quite unpronounceable.

"Locating one of the creatures is not the difficulty. It is the method of capture, which requires apparatus of a very special type which the Lactrans do not have access to. Nor do we, I am told. Such apparatus is beyond our technology."

"Then how in blazes do they expect us to bring one of

these indescribable whatsises back?" McCoy wanted to know.

Spock explained slowly. "To do this we must travel with them to a world known as Boqu. When the Lactrans traveled the Long Crawling past far-distant worlds many *ghids* ago, they chanced on this planet of the Boqus. These people had developed a method of controlling the jawanda. It is the Lactrans' hope that they have not lost that knowledge."

"Hope?" asked Kirk. "Don't they know for sure?"

"No, Captain. There has been no contact between Lactra and Boqu for several *minaghids*."

"*Mina*—how long is that?" McCoy queried, trying to make some sense out of all this talk of jawandas and *ghids* and such.

"It is not precisely—"

"Translatable," the doctor finished for him. "I know, I know."

"But it is a considerable time," Spock concluded.

Kirk thought rapidly, gazing idly at the display table. If the Boqus had lost the required knowledge, the *Enterprise* would simply return its passengers to Lactra. Boqu might not even be inhabited any longer. Or, despite the Lactrans' encyclopedic store of information, their story could turn out to be a myth accepted as truth.

Nonetheless, it would be even better if he could talk the Lactrans out of the idea. He was very much aware of the compound behind them, its falsely attractive little houses and grounds waiting ominously to rewelcome the recent tenants. The Lactrans could force them back into that landscaped cage as easily as let them leave. He would have to be careful.

"Explain that we would do our utmost to help, Mr. Spock, but that the *Enterprise* has no facilities for the housing and the care of unknown zoological specimens. Even if we managed to capture one of these jawanda creatures, it could die for lack of proper care on the way back to Lactra."

Another of those nerve-tingling silences ensued while he awaited Spock's version of the alien's reply. It was unexpected.

"Their initial reaction—I cannot be positive, of course, Captain, but it seems to be one of mirth. Now the explanation-reply is coming through. They assure us that it will not even be necessary to utilize the *Enterprise* to transport the jawanda. The capture method itself, by its very nature as well as the nature of the jawanda, handles all problems of transportation and care."

Well, it had been worth a try, Kirk reflected. "It all sounds reasonable," he replied guardedly. "How do we go about finding this mysterious Boqu? I've never heard mention of such a world. And, assuming we *can* locate it, how do we contact the local population and go about explaining what we need?"

"They are not surprised at our ignorance," Spock countered. "Boqu is not an easy world to locate, nor one we would stumble upon in the course of normal exploration. As to finding the planet, as well as to the problems of contacting the Boqus and making the request, they have a simple solution.

"Two of them are going to come with us."

VI

This time it was Kirk's eyebrows which rose in surprise. "I see," he muttered. The thought of having a couple of Lactran superminds on board the *Enterprise*, minds which could at any time take control of the ship, was not a comforting one.

Not that he had any choice, if he did not want to experience the cold comforts of the force cage again. He battled with himself, uncomfortably aware that his answer was awaited.

What was he so worried about, after all? Now that the aliens had been apprised of the actual intelligence of their former captives, now that they were actively seeking their cooperation, what reason to suspect treachery? He could not think of one. Naturally, that set him immediately to try to conjure half a dozen threatening possibilities.

While the captain was debating himself, Spock cocked his head slightly to one side, like a man striving to make sure of something just overheard.

"It appears," the first officer announced finally, "that we may be host to three rather than two Lactrans. The pair which have been selected to come with us are the parents of the young Lactran who was accidentally beamed aboard ship. The youngster is presently arguing vociferously with his parents, insisting that he be allowed to accompany the expedition."

"Doesn't make much difference, I suppose," murmured McCoy. "Two Lactrans or three."

"Our feelings have nothing to do with it, Doctor," Spock informed him. "It is the elder Lactrans' concern which opposes the youth's desire to participate." A pause; then: "They are trying to explain to their offspring that this undertaking is potentially too dangerous to permit it to come along."

McCoy stopped his nervous pacing and glanced up sharply. "Hey, if this is too dangerous for a Lactran youngster, who's already shown he's capable of taking over the ship, I'm not sure I want to—"

Kirk cut him off. "We have little choice, Bones—remember?" His attention was drawn to Scott. Strangely, the chief engineer was grinning. "You find the situation amusing, Scotty?"

"What? Well, part of it, Captain, yes. I canna follow the chatter of the adults, like Mr. Spock, but I have a bit of a rapport with the youngster. He overheard what Dr. McCoy just said. Now he's tellin' his parents that if they don't allow him to come along, then *we* might consider the trip too dangerous for *us*. So they have to take him along to convince us."

Kirk found himself smiling in response. "Not only precocious, but a budding diplomat. How is his argument going over, Mr. Spock?"

The first officer replied slowly. "Very well, it would seem, Captain. The adults acknowledge the validity of the youth's claims, which is more important to them than our possible refusal. They could force us to do their bidding"—Kirk shuddered in remembrance of the mental assault he'd so recently endured—"but feel that for two already stated reasons this would not be right: because we are not animals, and because the success of the undertaking requires full and enthusiastic cooperation on both sides."

"We've already consented to cooperate, Mr. Spock," Kirk replied readily, "though I can't vouch for our enthusiasm. All right, we'll aid them in capturing a single jawanda, whatever it is, and in returning it and them to Lactra. That will discharge our obligation to them." He did not bother to ask what assurance the Lactrans would give that they would adhere to their end of the bargain. He could not very well force them into anything. The men of the Federation were entering into a possibly dangerous situation on faith, a course acceptable only because of the absence of alternatives.

But he was curious. "What kind of guarantee do they want

to insure that we'll follow through on our part of the agreement?"

Spock frowned as though Kirk had said something betraying ignorance of the obvious. "They see the honesty of your response in your mind, Captain. No further assurance is necessary. They are appalled that such a thing could be considered."

Kirk grunted; he was satisfied. "So much for intangibles. Getting down to basics"—he studied the huge bulk of the adult Lactrans—"we come to the matter of accommodations."

"They say you have no reason to worry, Captain," the first officer declared. "While their society may appear complex, it is actually as simple as their needs. From what their offspring has told them of the *Enterprise*, they feel they will be quite comfortable in an empty cargo hold. They see no reason why our food synthesizers cannot produce nourishment acceptable to their systems. Other than this, they anticipate nothing in the way of special requirements even if the trip should prove one of extended duration."

"That's a relief," Kirk answered feelingly, leaving aside for the moment the troubling question of what constituted a journey of "extended duration" for a Lactran.

Just how far away *was* this Boqu?

McCoy had sidled over close to him. "Just had a worrisome thought, Jim."

"Only one?" Kirk managed the first real smile in days. "What is it now?"

"We're supposed to be carrying out a straightforward rescue mission. Before too much more time passes, Starfleet Headquarters is liable to get nervous about the absence of reports. What do we tell them if they manage to contact us?" He nodded once, significantly, toward the silent Lactrans.

Kirk shrugged. "They'll assume we're still searching for Lieutenant Commander Markel and his ship. If anyone inquires beyond that . . ." He paused thoughtfully. "We needn't go into details. Sometimes a starship captain has to make treaties with newly met races without the aid of formal diplomacy, has to create procedure in order to respond to exigencies not covered in the manuals. Our agreement to cooperate with the Lactrans has the status of a temporary treaty."

"Under what classification?" McCoy inquired relentlessly.

"Expediency." The captain's smile vanished as Kirk considered exactly what they might be getting themselves into. "Maybe it would be better to tell the truth and, if anyone asks, say we've gone a-hunting. I wish we knew for what."

"The Lactrans are prepared, Captain," Spock informed him. "They have given in to their young, and it will accompany them. If all is in readiness, they are anxious to depart."

Kirk wasn't anxious, but saw no excuse for further delay. He spoke to Scott. "Tell Chief Kyle to beam us back aboard, making allowance for three regular-size guests and three large ones." He gestured toward the Lactrans.

The chief engineer already had his communicator out and open. "All right, Captain."

"And have the chief use the transporter nearest Shuttle Bay for our Lactran visitors. The corridors are larger there and will make it easier for them to move around, if they so desire."

Scott nodded assent and relayed the instructions to the ship. The Lactrans appeared thoroughly absorbed as several of the humans vanished. Then they themselves were gone, accompanied by Kirk and Spock.

Once back on board the *Enterprise*, Kirk's first concern was to make certain the Lactrans were comfortably ensconced in their temporary quarters. Despite the sterility of the surroundings in the empty cargo hold, they professed to be quite satisfied with the amenities.

Leaving Spock to tend to any immediate alien requests, Kirk made his way quickly to Sick Bay. McCoy and Nurse Chapel were already well along in their detailed examination of the three surviving explorers.

"Markel and Bryce are in excellent shape, Jim," the doctor told him, "as would befit valuable exhibits."

"And Lieutenant Randolph?"

"She'll be all right eventually, but she needs about a month of doing nothing." McCoy grinned. "Sometimes that's the hardest prescription to assign. She's an active type, physically and mentally, and it's going to be difficult to keep her confined in a bed." The smile faded, to be replaced by a look of concern. "Confined she'll be, though. Her system is badly weakened."

"It may be improved when the official report reaches Starfleet, Bones. Endurance under conditions of stress is often grounds for promotion. At least you won't have to worry about the jawanda—assuming we can find and capture such a creature. The Lactrans are convinced it won't require any kind of attention. Spock is still trying to draw the details of the animal out of them, but the conceptualizations, as he keeps putting it, are confusing. Also, some of our preconceptions about jawandas appear to amuse our guests no end."

"I'm glad they think it's funny," McCoy observed wryly, indicating that he saw very little humor in the situation. His gaze, revealingly, was on the bedridden Randolph. "I haven't exactly warmed up to our elephantine guests."

"Think friendly thoughts, Bones," Kirk advised him strongly, reminding him of the Lactrans' mental abilities.

Satisfied that the three survivors were okay, Kirk headed for the bridge. Jawanda, jawanda . . . the name meant nothing to him. He could not even vaguely relate it to any creature he had ever heard of. Well, the Lactrans would have to clarify the nature of their quarry soon enough. There was no real need to worry so long as it wasn't going to be transported on board the ship.

It didn't occur to Kirk to consider the possibility that perhaps, for certain reasons, it could not be.

Spock and McCoy were waiting for him when he returned to the bridge. Their presence was expected; that of their new companion was not.

"I was about to order the installation of a special intercom unit for the use of the adult Lactrans in the converted hold, Captain," explained the first officer, "so that they would be in constant communication with us. They informed me that this was not only unnecessary, but a waste of equipment." He gestured at the long gray mass near the science station, the front end of which was presently exploring Spock's instrumentation.

"Their offspring will remain on the bridge. As it is always in telepathic contact with its parents, it can convey their impressions to us and a description of what takes place on the bridge to them instantaneously, without the need for, as they put it, awkward mechanical contrivances. He fits into the turbolifts, while the adults do not."

"Thank the adults for their consideration, Mr. Spock," Kirk told him. While he was not thrilled by the prospect of having a superintelligent child underfoot for the duration of the journey, he could not deny the logic behind its presence.

While it might be unnecessary, there was something else he ought to do. Moving to the command chair, Kirk activated the interdeck communications network and addressed the pickup:

"Attention, all personnel. This is the captain speaking. We are about to embark on an expedition of indeterminate length to perform a service for our newfound friends, the Lactrans, inhabitants of the planet about which we are orbiting. Concurrent with this, we will have as our guests three representatives of that race. Several of you have already noticed their arrival on board. The Lactrans are natural telepaths and . . . curious. The actions of an alien life form, or its shape, should not prove offensive to any of you or you wouldn't be part of this crew.

"Two adult Lactrans are presently installed in temporary quarters in cargo hold Fourteen-B. A third, an adolescent of the species, is at present with me on the bridge, but it has been given the run of the ship." He forbore adding that there was no way he could restrict the youthful alien's activities. It was only good diplomacy to grant gracious assent to the inevitable.

"Bear in mind that this is the young, however intelligent, of a species. It may be inclined to act in sometimes inexplicable fashion. Rest assured that, however misdirected, such actions are in no way hostile. I stress this so that no one will react in a manner in any way other than friendly toward our guests." So that, he finished silently, our guests don't get peeved and decide to take over the ship.

Ending the transmission, he rose again and spoke to the helm: "Stand by to get underway, Mr. Sulu."

"Standing by, sir," the helmsman acknowledged.

"Spock, Bones—let's go greet our passengers and find out the details of this expedition."

* * *

The two adult Lactrans were lolling about the cargo hold, apparently somnolent. Spock assured Kirk and McCoy that, despite the appearance of inactivity, the minds of both adults were as active and alert as ever. As he sat down, Kirk felt a tingling probe at the back of his skull and knew the correctness of the first officer's announcement.

He had expected the young Lactran to accompany them for this formal explanatory session, but the youngster had chosen to remain on the bridge, in the company of Engineer Scott. Several members of the crew had already remarked that the young alien followed Scott around like a dog attending its master.

"Before you enjoy that analogy," the chief engineer had responded, "keep in mind that in this case the 'dog' is twenty times smarter than the 'master.' "

Glancing approvingly around the hold, Kirk saw that Scotty's technicians had installed some recreational simulacrum machinery. Despite their insistence that nothing in the way of material comfort was required, he thought he sensed the Lactrans' approval at the way in which the "simplistic" machinery projected three-dimensional reproductions of the Lactran surface on the bare metal walls.

"They are indeed pleased, Captain," Spock informed him, unnervingly confirming his unspoken supposition, "though more by our concern for their comfort than by the actual projections themselves."

Kirk shifted in his chair. "If everyone's comfortable, then perhaps they can give us a course?"

"Naturally, Captain." Spock paused a moment, then replied, sooner than Kirk had expected, "They apparently have already done so."

There was a buzz from the cargo-hold intercom, and Kirk rose to answer it. "Kirk here."

"Captain"—it was Sulu's voice: excited, confused, and just a bit awed—"something just jumped inside my head. It was—"

"A series of coordinates," Kirk finished for him, turning to study the impassive Lactrans respectfully.

"Yes, sir—but how did you know?"

"Never mind that, Mr. Sulu. Were the coordinates precise?"

"Very, Captain."

"That's our new course, then. Lay them in. All ahead warp-factor four."

"Yes, sir," the helmsman replied, his tone slightly dazed. "Bridge out."

Kirk walked back to the chair and resumed his seat slowly. "Mr. Spock?"

"The adults relayed the information to their offspring, Captain, the moment they sensed the request in your mind. The youth, in turn, planted them clearly in the thoughts of Lieutenant Sulu."

"Wonderful communications system," observed McCoy, a mite sourly, feeling even more left out of things than usual.

"I presume the terminus of those coordinates is Boqu?" Kirk commented, expecting a casual assent. It wasn't quite forthcoming.

"The Lactrans hope so, Captain," Spock told him. It took barely a second for the import of that reply to sink in.

"Hope?" a startled Kirk blurted quickly. "What do they mean, 'hope'? I understood that they knew exactly where this world lies!"

Spock was shaking his head slowly, his eyes half glazed. "They do and yet they do not, Captain. It was such a long time ago that the last Lactran ship went out to Boqu. The records involved are quite old. The coordinates should lead us directly to Boqu, but the Lactrans cannot say this for certain. For various reasons its position in the plenum is not easy to plot."

"What," Kirk went on, taking a long, slow breath, "if Boqu doesn't exist where these ancient coordinates insist it's supposed to?"

This time Spock's reply was longer in coming. "If that is the case, the Lactrans say, we will have to begin a search for its present location."

Kirk started to object, then caught himself. It was impossible to tell what the aliens might consider an unfriendly gesture. Pointing out to them that the *Enterprise* could not spend an infinite number of years looking for a world that might be only an old rumor might so be interpreted. Which led him uncomfortably back to the possibility of the *Enterprise*'s operating under Lactran control, without his cooperation.

He saw the *Enterprise* spiraling farther and farther out from an empty point in space, stopping only to take on fresh supplies at support bases, to pick up new dilithium crystals and power elements. He watched their Lactran hosts insist on a continuation of the search, the ship's crew growing older and older in pursuit of a mythical planet . . . How long did Lactrans live, anyway? He suspected that it was well beyond the normal human or even Vulcan life span.

It would be best to shunt that unpleasant scenario aside and hope that the Lactrans' ancient records were as remarkable as their mental powers.

"Now that we know where we're going," he declared to Spock, and thus to the pair of watching aliens, "perhaps we can have some more information on what exactly it is we're going for? Can they describe one of these jawandas for us?"

Spock, attentive, recited slowly, as though from the pages of an old, old book: "A jawanda is a large, asexual creature of unusual appearance with interesting coloring." He blinked and looked across at the other two officers. "That's all."

McCoy grimaced. "That's not very informative, Spock. Couldn't they be a little more descriptive?"

"The Lactrans wish they could, Doctor," the first officer explained. "They indicate that much information is contained in records long since become dust. It is yet another reason why they have been so anxious to secure a specimen for their collection."

Kirk's fingers drummed softly on one arm of the chair. "You said it was a large creature, Mr. Spock. Do the Lactrans know how large?"

Spock assumed an expression of indifference. "It varies considerably from specimen to specimen, it seems. Again, the old records are distressingly poor in detail."

"If information is so scanty," an impatient McCoy muttered, "how do they expect to identify a jawanda? They're not even sure what it looks like." The Lactrans appeared for the first time to confer between themselves.

"They say this does not matter, Doctor," announced Spock languidly, with only a slight frown.

McCoy threw up his hands in a gesture of frustration. "Now how can anyone go hunting for something when they aren't sure of its appearance? Of all the—"

"The Lactrans go on to say, Doctor, that there is even a chance the jawanda looks like nothing."

"I've had it, Jim! Sounds to me like we're on a wild-goose chase—and we're not even sure what the wild goose looks like."

Kirk rose from his chair. "It looks like there's only one way we're going to find out, Bones, and that's to go to Boqu. The answer to the Lactrans' riddle is supposed to lie there. We'll find out the same time they do . . . if we get to the world all right."

"If there *is* a Boqu," grumbled McCoy, rising to join him in leaving the hold.

Silent, the adult Lactrans watched them go.

The following day Kirk entered the bridge determined to locate the world in question. It could be incredibly obscure, but there was still a good chance it circled a sun listed in the star catalog, even if it was itself as yet unsurveyed.

Already he knew it lay a respectable distance from the Federation periphery. A simple comparison of the coordinates with the many maps locked in his memory had told him that no explored systems were situated in their present path. Even so, the actual figures provided a greater surprise than he'd anticipated. Sitting in the command chair, he studied the printout on the main viewscreen.

"Deeper, Mr. Sulu," he said, and the helmsman replaced the chart with the star configuration lying behind it, and then replaced it again. And again. And yet again. Their present course showed as a glowing red line from one end of each three-dimensional chart to the next without intersecting a single system, without passing near even a postulated solar body.

Finally Kirk was prompted to ask, "Mr. Sulu, are you certain of those coordinates?"

The helmsman looked back over his shoulder and nodded readily. "Absolutely, sir. They appeared in my mind like fluorescent block letters, and remained there until I had them memorized in spite of myself." He shook his head admiringly. "Our visitors convey their information in a manner I envy."

"I see." Kirk studied the uninformative chart projection a moment longer. "Double-check it anyway, please." He turned toward the science station. "Mr. Spock?"

The first officer went into a momentary trance, regarding the gray mass nearby. Seconds later, Sulu also appeared to drift into a brief dreamlike state before looking back to Kirk.

"No question, sir . . . we're on the course they've indicated."

"Thank you, Mr. Sulu. That's all."

Leaning back, the captain considered their present path. A divergence of even a fraction of a degree in one of several directions would have led them to at least three systems, all unexplored but logged. Their actual course, however, was taking them out of the galaxy at approximately a right angle to the galactic ecliptic. No wonder the charts were rapidly growing devoid of stellar phenomena.

"Deeper, Mr. Sulu," he ordered again. The chart was replaced by another, almost blank, save for a few isolated, lonely suns and several drifting nebulae. Beyond was nothing. Absolutely nothing.

"Mr. Spock," he began, looking toward the science station and studiously ignoring the Lactran offspring, "have the Lactrans recheck their memories. Maybe there are several possible locations given in their old records for this planet."

Spock listened to something no one else could hear. Eventually he replied, "They have been monitoring your conversation through their offspring, Captain. They assure me that the coordinates transferred to Mr. Sulu are the only ones given by the ancients for the world known as Boqu."

"Are they aware," Kirk continued gently, "that if we continue on our present course, the first sun we encounter will be an unknown star in M33, the Triangulum Spiral, roughly two point three five *million* light-years away?" He added drily, "If this is the location of Boqu, we won't get there for quite a while."

"While regarding this as a doubtful possibility, Captain, they refuse to discount it," Spock replied. "They are considering it with some interest."

"Not as much as I am," Kirk responded rapidly. "Long

before we could reach that system, everyone and everything on board, including the warp-drive engines, would be long dead—the Lactrans included."

"They are aware of this, Captain," Spock continued, listening hard. "They theorize that Boqu must lie somewhat nearer."

"Somewhat?" McCoy muttered nervously.

"There is something else, Captain," the first officer added. "They are wondering if the Boqus will still retain the knowledge and means necessary for capturing a jawanda. They also recall information indicating that the Boqus are a traditionally private folk, and wonder if they might not also have forgotten their former association with the Lactrans. If this is so, there is always the possibility of a hostile greeting."

"Charming," Kirk noted dully. "Any other small details like that last one that they might have neglected to tell us?"

"No, Captain," Spock insisted evenly. "Not at the moment."

Days lengthened into weeks, with no sign of a possible destination. The *Enterprise* was still running at warp-four, two factors below her maximum safe cruising speed. Instead of nearing some unexpected system on the fringe of the galaxy, they drew farther away from all signs of activity and motion. The last star marking the boundary of the home galaxy lay far astern. Kirk had watched it fade from the rear scanners, a dying beacon, and could not shrug off a sense of awesome isolation.

More days passed, and Kirk found himself brooding in the command chair for long hours, staring at the viewscreen. Long-range scanners focused rearward showed a falsely dense-seeming arc of brightness behind them: the spiral arm of the galaxy they were crawling away from. Somewhere back there lay the Federation, and life in all its swarming multitudes.

Ahead lay a darkness so vast and empty that he felt like a child tiptoeing into a colossal cavern—the incomprehensible abyss of intergalactic space.

And still the Lactrans insisted stonily that they were on course for Boqu. Kirk's sense of desperation reached the point at which he was considering forcing a confrontation with the starship's imperturbable passengers, even risking a takeover, when a cry came from the helm:

"Captain, I've got something on the fore sensors!"

"Position, Mr. Sulu?" Kirk inquired, trying to keep the excitement from his voice.

"Dead on course, sir." A pause; then the uncertain information, "It appears to be a star, sir, but not much of a star."

"Confirmed, Captain." Kirk's attention moved to the science station and to Spock, who was staring intently into his gooseneck viewer. "It is a star, with from six to eight companion planets and two belts of asteroidal debris. A K0 dwarf, I think, and probably fairly old. Surface temperature low, even for a weak star of its type."

"Anything out here can be classed as a freak, Mr. Spock," Kirk commented interestedly. "Planets it may have, but I don't see how a habitable world could circle a sun that weak. It would have to lie awfully close in, and there would have to be a host of factors compensating for—" he broke off at a loud *humphing* sound from near the science station.

The young Lactran was giving every indication of heightened interest as its front end regarded the screen, which now showed a distant point of white-orange light. Obviously, it was communicating with its parents and with Spock.

"According to all indications," the first officer announced, "that is the Boquian system."

Kirk wanted to believe, but "I don't understand, Mr. Spock. A habitable world out here, circling a sun like this one, and completely isolated from the rest of the galaxy! It staggers the imagination. It's impossible." There was a buzz, and Spock paused long enough to acknowledge a report from belowdecks.

"Not according to the astronomy section, Captain. They cannot wait until we enter the system and they can begin close-in observation."

"You said there were six to eight planets, Mr. Spock," Kirk went on, wishing he could be as unrestrainedly happy as the astronomers. "Which one is Boqu?"

"The old records are barely adequate for identification, Captain. However, I am assured that we will know it when the adults, through the mind of their offspring, sight it."

"Very well. Mr. Sulu, begin survey with the outermost world and take us in one planet at a time."

"Aye, Captain," the helmsman acknowledged.

They moved into the system, passing and rejecting several large dead worlds. Planets five through three proved to be gas giants. The second out from the chill star looked no more promising.

"Boqu," Spock declared firmly, staring fascinatedly at the viewscreen.

"Are you sure, Spock?"

"The Lactrans are, Captain."

Kirk shrugged. "Place us in parking orbit, Mr. Sulu."

"Yes, Captain."

Boqu looked like yet another gas giant, but as they moved nearer the *Enterprise*'s sensors began to produce some surprising information.

Boqu possessed certain similarities to Uranus and Jupiter, but it was not a Jovian-type planet. It did put out more radiation than it received from its cinder of a sun. A certain amount of this radiation was being trapped beneath a dense orange cloud layer, heavy with carbon dioxide.

The resultant greenhouse effect was as natural as it was unexpected, creating a surface warm enough to shelter life, though life that would have to be radically different from that on Earth or Vulcan. There was little water vapor and no evidence of free water on the surface.

Boqu was an enormous world, as large as Neptune, but a true planet and not simply a small inner core covered by a huge atmosphere. Yet its gravity was barely half again as Earth's, indicating an absence of heavy metals and a light core.

Still, it was not what Kirk would call a hospitable world. Life-support belts would provide them with warmth, a breathable atmosphere, and protection from strong radiation, but could do nothing to counter the stronger gravity. They would have to handle the strain of one and a half g's as best they were able.

He thought of the Lactrans. Undoubtedly they could tolerate the gravity, but they had evolved on a world similar to Earth. To travel comfortably on the surface of Boqu they would need life-support belts too. Constructing life-support belts for the Lactrans would fall to Mr. Scott's ever inventive staff, but the problem might prove troublesome even to those resourceful minds. Not all the Lactrans' mental prowess would prevail against a poisonous atmosphere. Therefore, the first explorations of Boqu's surface would fall to members of the *Enterprise*'s crew—if there was any reason to explore that surface.

Several days of shifting orbit around the planet served only to justify Kirk's initial pessimism. With every scientific instrument on board trained on the surface, they were unable to discover any sign of life.

Kirk became convinced that if anything had ever inhabited this peculiar world, it had long since become extinct. Spock and the Lactrans were not so readily persuaded.

"There could be any number of reasons for our failure to detect life below, Captain," the first officer argued, following another day of fruitless searching. "For one thing, the enormous quantity and variety of radiation the planet is generating makes it extremely difficult for our sensors to separate signs of intelligent surface communication from natural emissions."

"If there *is* any intelligence down there," sniped McCoy.

Spock continued, ignoring the doctor. "Surface conditions on such a world might have forced the inhabitants into other methods of long-range communication."

"It's not only that," a troubled Kirk admitted. "We have instruments capable of piercing the cloud layer. They detect nothing we recognize as motile life on the surface."

"What *we* recognize as life forms a very narrow band in the spectrum of possibilities, Captain."

"A valid point, Spock, but that still leaves us with the problem of identifying *any* life form below." He gestured at the screen, where dense orange-and-pink clouds completely covered a surface many, many times greater in area than Earth's.

"Presumably we could detect life firsthand, but this world is gigantic. To drop below the atmosphere and explore visually from shuttles would take forever." He brooded silently a moment. "What about the Lactrans? Do they have any suggestions?"

"No, Captain," confessed the first officer. "They can add

nothing . . . except to reaffirm that this system and this world fit all the ancient descriptions of Boqu. Though they are willing to grant, when I press them, the slim possibility that, for all their reputed knowledge and advanced technology, the Boqus may have become extinct."

"Advanced technology on a world devoid of heavy metals—that's something else I find difficult to swallow," Kirk murmured. "I admit the existence of this world because I'm looking at it, but that's all." His gaze turned to the quiet young Lactran. "Tell the youth to convey this to his parents: We'll circle and study for another of our weeks. If by that time we've turned up *no* evidence of intelligent life, they'll consent to return home." His eyes moved to the rim of the planet, to the total blackness of intergalactic space beyond. No friendly stars formed a perceivable backdrop for this world.

"It's cold out here."

A longer-than-usual wait ensued before the Lactrans replied. Clearly, the guests of the *Enterprise* were struggling through some hard debating among themselves.

"They are reluctant to return empty—a conceptualization I cannot translate, Captain—without a specimen. Yet they do not dispute the validity of your statements. They are agreed. We shall search the surface another week and then we may depart."

"With our obligation to them discharged? We'll leave Lactra's orbit unmolested?"

Spock nodded. "There will be nothing more to restrain us."

The light struck them on the fifth day.

VII

Alarms howled and sensors on the bridge and in all the attentive science stations went berserk as the brilliant beam illumined the *Enterprise* from below, pinioning it in a shaft of intense white radiance powerful enough to pierce the thick clouds. It hit without warning, harmlessly.

When it became apparent that the beam was not dangerous, the brief moment of fear and panic was instantly replaced by curiosity. The radiance was not a gesture of belligerence, but rather the cutting cry of someone shouting, "I'm here, I'm here! Look below, and find me!"

The light vanished, then winked on again. This time instruments other than alarms were ready. The light blinked on and off in regular, obviously unnatural sequence. There was no doubt that it originated from an artificial source.

A source, Kirk mused, of tremendous power, to be able to penetrate that smothering atmosphere and still light up the exterior of the *Enterprise*. The on/off pattern continued for several minutes before halting—permanently, it developed.

"A signal, certainly," Kirk observed, voicing everyone's conclusion aloud. "But why did they break off? Why not continue to guide us down?"

"Perhaps they are incapable of maintaining that strength for very long, Captain" was Spock's comment. "Merely to pierce the cloud layer with such force once is a remarkable feat. To repeat it several times is almost beyond comprehension. Clearly there is intelligence of singular ability still active on the surface below."

Kirk looked to the helm. "Mr. Sulu, did you obtain a fix on the source of the beam?"

The helmsman studied his instrumentation a moment longer before replying. "Yes, Captain—as clear as I was able without actually having direct line of sight to the surface. I'm assuming it traveled outward in a straight line, though it could have been bent or otherwise distorted by some layer in the atmosphere."

"I think not, Lieutenant," countered Spock. "Any beam of sufficient intensity to penetrate that cloud layer and still retain its power of illumination at this distance, apparently undiminished, would likely not be affected by any cloud formation nearer its source."

"We have a destination, then," Kirk noted, rising from the command chair. "Mr. Spock, Dr. McCoy, you'll accompany me to the surface." He nodded at the young Lactran. "Together with our youthful friend, if his parents are agreeable."

Spock's eyebrows arose, and even the Lactran adolescent looked surprised. Kirk felt unaccountably pleased at having been able to startle the seemingly unshakable aliens.

"But how, Jim?" McCoy asked. "Scott's technicians are still working on the problem of life-support belts for Lactrans and—"

"We'll descend in the shuttlecrawler, Bones. It's spacious enough to hold four of us and our young guest, if not either of his much larger parents."

"They are concerned, Captain, but see no reason to object. It is important that they be represented in some fashion. They agree to let the young one go, even though it must remain in the crawler."

Kirk had no idea which gesticulations were indicative of pleasure among Lactrans, but it seemed certain that the youngster was performing some of them now.

He turned to communications. "Security, Lieutenant Uhura. I'll want Lieutenant Meyers to pilot the shuttlecrawler."

"Very well, Captain." Uhura moved to contact the crewman.

With the young Lactran aboard, the shuttlecrawler was loaded close to maximum. So much so that there was no room for the large, well-armed security team Kirk would have liked to take along—he hadn't forgotten the Lactrans' claim that the Boqus might seek to enforce their privacy.

Instead, he had to count on the Lactrans' familiarity and former association with the race which now might still survive on the hidden surface.

The shuttlecrawler's descent to the coordinates plotted by Sulu and others was memorable, a welcome change from the convenience but monotony of the transporter. They soared down through an atmosphere structured like a cotton candy parfait.

Its outermost layers were thick, rich orange and gray and pink. These colors gave way gradually to bright red-orange, then kilometers of raging maroon, then to a wholly unexpected layer of brilliant blue-green, which merged in its turn into a lavish red.

Eventually they emerged into a relatively clear layer above the surface and were able to look up at the sky as the Boqus saw it. Overhead rolled a thick collage of mauve cumulus, while hundreds of kilometers off to the south-southeast the threatening hemispheres of argent nimbus seemed to bubble and collapse like shiny balloons in a bucket of blood.

Kirk forgot their mission momentarily as he, Spock, and McCoy stared raptly at the silver storm. Sequential flashes of many-fingered lightning bolts deluged the surface with millions of volts.

Rising to meet the shuttlecrawler was a dimly visible landscape of orange and brown. The ground was pock-marked with deep pores filled with liquid ammonia. Kirk would do no swimming on this world. Lieutenant Meyers remained professionally oblivious to this beauty as he skillfully guided the craft down through unexpected blasts of hurricane-force wind.

Vegetation became identifiable as Lieutenant Meyers dropped them still lower. It was predominantly yellow and orange, with isolated patches of sparkling white. Kirk thought he saw a multiple-limbed growth half as big as the *Enterprise* reflecting the light like a diamond and hinting of a composition other than cellulose.

Meyers spiraled in around the point plotted by Sulu. It was near the end of their approach that McCoy exclaimed in surprise and pointed forward.

Ahead lay a valley. One end was dominated by the glassy

surface of a large lake of as yet unknown composition. The other was filled with an enormous fanlike artificial construction mounted on struts sufficient to make a millipede jealous. In the foreground was a city.

"Meyers?" Kirk inquired simply.

"Yes, sir. According to my coordinates, that should be the source of the light beam." Visual reconnaissance accomplished, he banked the awkward shuttlecrawler in the direction of the fan end of the valley. They began passing over the city, and the expectations suddenly raised so high vanished. Even the young Lactran appeared to droop.

Because it was dead. Dead as the hollow sockets of an old, bleached skull. Not that it was crumbling and broken like a hundred similar urban mausoleums Kirk had seen before. In fact, it looked remarkably well preserved. But nothing moved in its streets; no vehicles stirred between structures or above them. The silence below them was of the dead, or, at least, of the dying.

They flew on for a surprising distance over abandoned edifices, past towering spires and the gaping defunct domes resembling antique jewelry from which a patient thief had pried all the gems. As the city continued to unroll beneath them, Kirk began to sense its true size, and that of the fanlike structure they were nearing.

Almost as if in response to their filling spirits, a faint sign of life caught their attention, as well as that of the sensors.

From the far end of the valley, defining their destination, the light beam began to rise, this time but a feeble imitation, a shadow in light of the cloud-piercing shaft which had bathed the *Enterprise* in unexpected radiance. It barely rose above the valley, straining for an intensity apparently no longer attainable.

Once, twice, it flickered, the second time almost reaching to the lowest layer of orange clouds before dying.

But those on board the shuttlecrawler, who had begun to give up hope, it was as encouraging as a neon sign the size of a Starfleet station. Meyers swung the shuttlecrawler lower, cutting speed as rapidly as he dared in the tricky, buffeting winds.

"Ask our friend," Kirk told Spock, "to see if he can sense

any alien thoughts nearby." In contrast to this world, the young Lactran seemed welcomingly familiar.

There was a short pause, at the conclusion of which Spock informed them, "There is nothing, but I am told it does not matter. It is only what was expected. According to the records relevant to Boqu, they were never able to communicate mentally with the inhabitants over any distance. A Lactran, to touch the mind of a Boqus, would have to be in its actual presence."

Kirk refused to be discouraged. "Something caused that beam to be generated, whether the Lactrans can detect the mind behind it or not. Something that wanted to signal the *Enterprise* and a moment ago attempted to signal us."

"It could have been automatic, self-sustaining machinery, Captain," Spock pointed out coolly.

"Always encouraging, that's our Spock," declared McCoy with false gaiety. The shuttlecrawler rocked in a gust of hot orange wind, and he put out a hand to steady himself.

"I wish you would refrain from overutilization of the possessive form, Doctor," the first officer replied. "I was merely pointing out that—"

"Later, you two!" Kirk snapped. "Have a look at that." He pointed out the side port.

They were nearing the metallic fan, as peculiar a conglomeration as Kirk had ever set eyes on. It resembled the work of some careful colossus of a spider. Not that of a web spider, whose miniature marvels of engineering follow magnificently mathematical patterns, rather the simple cobwebs of the less precise arachnid, which throws and tosses its strands of silk with seeming abandon in any convenient corner, creating a less dignified though equally effective trap.

To the immediate right of this enormous arrangement of struts, beams, cables, and things Kirk couldn't name was a long, low building isolated from the nearest part of the city. Like the other structures they'd passed over, this one appeared relatively well maintained.

"Try to set down as close to that building as possible, Meyers," Kirk instructed.

"Yes, sir. I think there's enough clear space alongside."

As they commenced their final drop, Kirk gazed wonderingly at the huge construct. That it was the generator of the light beam he had no doubt. "It's not a mirror, Spock," he commented, "it has exactly the opposite of a smooth surface."

"According to the Lactrans," the first officer explained, "the peculiar light-metal and stone technology of the Boqus originated in a unique mind. The Lactrans do not find it unusual, therefore, that Boquian physics should find unique expression—"

"You can ask them yourself in a minute, Jim," McCoy broke in, settling himself tensely in his seat. "We're setting down."

Meyers made an admirable landing under difficult turbulence conditions. Once down, he engaged the ground engine, and the shuttlecrawler instantly became a vehicle for surface transport. They moved slowly toward the single large building near the fan construct.

Kirk saw that it was several stories high, with a gently curving roof. Totally devoid of windows or similar apertures, it appeared to be constructed of gray rock, though he did not doubt that on closer inspection the material might turn out to be something considerably more sophisticated. A race did not evolve and mature on a world like this, make contact successfully with an advanced people like the Lactrans, retain the technology capable of producing, even briefly, that atmosphere-slicing light beam, while building out of plain rock.

Gradually they neared the barnlike structure and began hunting along its edge for something that might be an entrance. They finally discovered one, facing the immense latticework of metal, which towered above them now like a forest of gigantic trees grown in free-fall and then transported to the planet's surface.

Kirk unstrapped himself and moved to the port, walking with considerable difficulty under the strong gravity. Beyond lay the vast enigmatic building, containing either aid for additional journeying or only a mechanical apologist for a dead civilization.

"I feel like I'm wearing lead boots," McCoy complained, fighting to keep from falling over under the increased gravity.

"At least we don't need armor suits, Bones," pointed out Kirk. "Be grateful for small favors."

"The only small favor I'll be grateful for is an indication we can return home," the doctor replied irritably, though his irritation was directed more at his own clumsiness in the one and a half g's than at the captain.

Like men drugged, Kirk, Spock, McCoy, and Meyers spent several long minutes moving experimentally about the cabin of the shuttlecrawler, trying to acclimate themselves to their increased weight. The young Lactran watched with interest. His strange physical configuration enabled him to move about with relative ease, though there were no signs that might be interpreted as amusement as he regarded the awkward movements of the men. Possibly, Kirk mused, the trip was having a maturing effect upon him.

"It regrets being unable to accompany us, Captain, but will be in constant communication with us through me as we explore the building. It expresses anxiety for our safety."

Kirk made an effort at effortlessness. "Tell it we'll manage," he told Spock. "Life-support belts, gentlemen."

Each man donned one of the thick, self-contained belts which had long ago (excepting special situations) made the restrictive "space suits" of primitive times obsolete. Activation produced lime-yellow auras around them, whereupon they entered the lock of the shuttlecrawler and waited as machinery cycled the air and opened the outside door. Walking carefully but with increasing confidence, they moved down the ramp and found themselves standing on the densely packed, gravelly surface of Boqu.

"Anything from our young friend, Spock?"

"Nothing, Captain. He can sense nothing."

Kirk hadn't expected anything else. "Tell it to keep us informed of any change it can sense . . . and of any suggestions it comes up with as to how to proceed."

"Very well, Captain."

More than anything else, the featureless structure resembled an enormous warehouse, though Kirk doubted that was its actual function. It rose seamlessly above them and blended into the distant curving roof.

Directly before them what looked like several doors were recessed into the wall, scattered seemingly at random at various distances from one another.

"Might as well try the nearest one as any and go on from

there," Kirk announced, his open communicator carrying his words to his companions.

Lightning flashed nearby as they began walking slowly toward the closest door. Spock's attention was still partially diverted by the giant jackstraw arrangement behind them. "A remarkable feat of engineering," he murmured. "The principles behind it imply a metallurgic technology radically different from our own. I wish I knew how it was built, let alone how it generates the radiance it does."

"Maybe the Boqus can tell you," advised McCoy, "if any are left."

They had all reached the wall and stopped before the first recess. The door was of an unmistakably different composition from that of the structure's exterior, and had the look of machined metal. The recess was narrow at the top and quite wide at the base, rather like a pyramid with a domed crown, and rose to a height of two and a half meters.

"Indicative of heavy-gravity physiology," observed Spock easily.

"That's assuming this entrance is designed for the Boqus themselves," argued McCoy. "For all we know, this could be a local livestock barn. Maybe the Boqus were tall and spindly and just raised squatty cattle."

"Unlikely, Doctor," countered a disapproving Spock.

Attempts to open the door which formed the far wall of the niche met with failure. Attempts to open succeeding doors met with successive failures. Not only did none of them show signs of opening, they betrayed no hint of how they might be opened. Inspect as they might, the little party could find nothing resembling a handle, knob, keyhole, depression-response pit, or anything else they would have recognized.

Kirk was about to try a swift kick on the sixth and last door, a gesture which would have been not just futile but dangerous in the heavy gravity, when it slid aside smoothly. Life-belt sensors carried a thick whine to them as powerful machinery shifted the massive door, fighting its inertia.

"Automatics?" Meyers asked rhetorically, regarding the dim interior with a professional's eye.

"Maybe," murmured McCoy, "though despite my first impressions I've got to admit it looks more and more like we're expected. After you, Spock," he said, gesturing.

Once past the door (which, Kirk was gratified to see, showed no inclination to close suddenly behind them), they found themselves in a long trapezoidal hallway. At regular intervals its walls and ceilings were lined with panels phosphorescent with orange light. It bent and wound confusingly, but the distance covered was less than it seemed (the gravity wearing on them again) before they emerged into a vast, brightly lit chamber.

The roof arched overhead, and the surrounding walls were filled with consoles and instrumentation as alien and unrecognizable as the material they were constructed of. Larger panels threw more light here, though it was still of that uniform orange hue. Kirk found the warm tint it lent to the metal furnishings very attractive, though it could never take the place of the familiar light of Earth's sun.

The greatest surprise, however, was not the instrumentation but the decor. On first glance, the chamber appeared to be lavishly landscaped, filled with strange bushes and small clusters of trees. McCoy had moved to feel the petals of a purple leafed growth, and drew back in surprise, apparently at the tactile sensation he received from the bush. For a fearful second Kirk thought the doctor had been stung.

"Are you hurt, Bones?"

"What? No, Jim, it's this thing." He glanced around at the other growths. "It's all of them, probably. The surface is cold . . . and hard. Hard as rock."

Kirk moved to stand alongside him, and regarded the construction. "Interesting . . . is it mineral sculpture, or what?"

Nearby, Spock was studying a taller specimen. "If so, Captain, the imitation is carried to remarkable extremes." He gestured at the base of the tree-thing, where it disappeared into the open earth. "It seems to enter the ground, obviously drawing support from it. I wonder if it may not draw more than that."

"Oh, come on, Spock! It's stone, or something equally inorganic. Obviously it—"

A friendly, oddly prickling thought appeared abruptly in McCoy's mind—in all their minds.

"Nothing is obvious, everything is infinitely indeterminate," the thought explained sharply. "You look intensely, physician, but not well."

Kirk spun and glanced around the chamber. It still appeared deserted. "Where are you," he asked warily, adding almost as an afterthought, "man of Boqu?"

"Closer than you think, Captain Kirk."

One of the "trees" nearby started toward them.

Kirk found himself face to . . . well, to something, with one of the strangest creatures he had ever seen. By comparison, the bulky, limbless Lactrans appeared almost normal.

The being moved on a base two meters across, consisting of hundreds of long dark yellow limbs. Stiff and many-jointed, they rippled with an eerie clacking along the hard floor, like the march of millions of ants on a sheet of paper.

The centilimbs radiated from a thick central post twice as broad as a man's body, roughly circular in form, like an addled fence post. This main part was shaded a deep brown, almost the color of unpolished mahogany, and was veined with exterior vertical ribs of gold.

It rose in three jointed sections to the level of Kirk's nose, then tapered slightly before spreading out into a wide circular plate whose upper surface was plano-convex, like the upper half of the *Enterprise*'s primary hull.

The head, or such Kirk considered it, was a milky opaque crystalline substance resembling rutilated quartz. Black striations ran through it, bunching into dark nodules at various points within.

From the flat underside of the head, set several centimeters in from the fringe, dangled long articulated tentacles of dark yellow. They were similar in shape and form to the hundreds of skittering feet projecting from the Boqus's base. They swayed and moved easily, under obvious control.

It was impossible to tell whether the expedition was facing the creature's front, back, or side, or indeed if such terms meant anything in regard to a Boqus. Equally, there was nothing faintly identifiable as a mouth, nose, eyes, ears, or anything else indicative of a face.

Kirk elected to regard the portion of the being facing him as its front. "I'm—" He cleared his throat, still recovering from the initial surprise of the Boqus's unmasking. "I am Captain James T. Kirk of the U.S.S. *Enterprise*. This is my first officer, Mr. Spock; my chief medical officer, Dr. McCoy; and sec—our vehicle pilot, Lieutenant Meyers."

This produced an agitated jangling of those dangling tentacles, and the creature seemed to draw back. Could he have made a mistake already, Kirk mused?

He had not. "Chief medical officer!" came the excited thought. "Then you have come in response to the prayers of the *animax*!"

"Prayers? Animax?" McCoy echoed in confusion. The Boqus's limbs relaxed, but its thoughts were still in turmoil. "You have not come in response to our need, to end the epidemic?"

Kirk suddenly understood the reason behind the deserted metropolis they had passed over, and felt saddened as McCoy replied, "I'm truly sorry. We know nothing of any local epidemic."

The Boqus appeared to slump, and the opaqueness in its crystal skull increased until the striations within could no longer be seen.

"Why then," it inquired with sudden brisk curiosity, "have you come here? I cannot believe it was by accident."

That Kirk could sympathize with. Boqu was not a world the casual explorer would stumble upon. "We are here at the request of an ancient race acquainted with your people," he explained, "the people of Lactra."

"Lactra, Lactra," the uncertain thought reached them. "I know them not. I am old, visitors, yet this is something well past my forming. Admitted it is that we Boqus are sadly lacking in methods of history and social record. We follow our past not as well as we ought to."

The suspicions brewing in McCoy's mind, temporarily interrupted when the Boqus had revealed himself, now surged back full strength, not to be denied.

"Jim, these bushes and trees around us—the Boqus himself—Spock's hesitation in classifying them was justified. They're not sculptured any more than you or I are sculptured." He rushed on, flushed with excitement. "We've long postulated the possibility of a living organism based on the silicon atom instead of carbon. Boqu . . . Boqu is a whole world based on that substance. A world of living crystal."

"I sense carefully concealed distaste in your mind, physician," came the thought from the creature before them. "Pity us not. It is we who have always been sorry for those we know of you. You poor carbon-based creatures, with your saggy, flexible, unrigid limbs. Your bodies lack discipline and form and true beauty.

"Even so, for all our inherent superior endurance to disease, we are not immune, it seems." The thought seemed to brighten in Kirk's mind, brighten with uncertain hope. "It is true you are a medical scientist, Bones McCoy?"

"I'm a doctor," McCoy replied readily. "My job's to make sick people unsick."

"Concise, yet thorough enough," came the response. "A great epidemic of tragic proportions has ravaged Boqu for many *nevars*. It is conceded among the surviving scientists that a new approach to a solution is required. We have despaired of ever finding one. Yet here you are."

"Now just a minute," began a cautious McCoy, but the Boqus rambled on.

"If you could find a cure for this devastation, you would gain the eternal gratitude of all the people of my world." Many limbs moved, indicating all directions simultaneously. "This is but one of many laboratories scattered about the surface of Boqu, isolated to protect those surviving scientists while they exhaust every means in the search for a solution. I was granted the opportunity of watching for an unlikely savior from afar. It was I who signaled you with the light, and it was you who responded. I solicit your aid."

Everyone, it seemed, needed their help, Kirk thought. McCoy returned to his protest.

"I don't know how to cure a sick rock. I don't know the first thing about silicon biology."

"No one does, Doctor," pointed out Spock, "since until this moment such a thing was not thought to exist."

"However," McCoy added reluctantly, at the overpowering sense of desolation the Boqus projected, "I'm willing to try."

"No more than that could be asked," replied the Boqus ringingly. "I am Hivar the Toq, and will aid you . . ." The thought faded, to be unexpectedly replaced by a mental frown of contrition. "But you are here for another reason, at the request of these beings you call Lactrans. I cannot interfere with prior obligations."

"I don't think it will matter," Kirk informed him. "Matter of fact, the Lactrans are here to ask for *your* help."

"Poor help we can give now, for anything," Hivar the Toq confessed. "Yet I would hear the circumstances."

"The Lactrans," Kirk explained, "have made much of their world over into a great zoo, a collection of diverse life forms the inspection of which provides them with knowledge and pleasure. They wish to add one last creature to this assemblage, one creature they have failed to capture over the centuries. We were told that only your people possess the means to capture such a being, which they call a jawanda."

Hivar considered for a moment, its mind intent on unscrambling this new riddle.

"The creature your friends call the jawanda troubled Boqu for many *multinevars*," it finally informed them. "We have not had the need to control them since then, for they have learned to avoid us. Yet I have some knowledge of the means you speak of."

Kirk glanced to Spock, then McCoy. The Lactrans had been reluctant to divulge details of the jawanda, for reasons unknown. Perhaps true ignorance was the honest one; possibly the evasion was intentional. Regardless, Hivar the Toq apparently knew of the creatures. At the moment they were in mental contact with the young Lactran, but out of immediate danger of Lactran attack. If there was a serious reason for this concealment of facts . . .

Kirk made his decision and asked hastily, "We're still not too sure what a jawanda is. If you could explain . . ."

No mental blast sent him writhing to the floor, but the Boqus didn't respond with an answer, either.

"I will bargain with you, Captain Kirk," Hivar announced, scuttling in small circles, "and with your friends of Lactra." Several crystalline tentacles pointed sharply at McCoy. "If your medical scientist Bones McCoy can discover a cure for the disease which plagues my people, then I will consult with the surviving guardians of the trust of science to see what can be done about the jawanda."

"Listen," McCoy objected, "I said I'd be willing to try. But I've no experience. Making our journey's success contingent upon my solving something which hasn't even been imagined until now just isn't fair."

"Somehow you must do more than try, medical scientist."

Kirk had the impression of a stone back being turned to them.

"Whatever you need will be provided instantly. We can expect no other visitors, for our signals have gone unheeded. Your presence is proof of that, since you are not here in response to them. We can expect no help beyond your own."

"How can you expect me, someone totally ignorant of your body chemistry, your very makeup, to succeed where your own best scientists have failed?" an exasperated McCoy wanted to know.

Hivar the Toq replied almost sullenly. "I do not know myself. I know only that a new approach offers the best remaining chance of a solution. Your very ignorance saves you from the misconceptions and false approaches which have stifled us."

"First time anyone ever complimented me for ignorance," McCoy grumbled. "I've got to forget four thousand years of biology and start from scratch."

"Does that mean you're convinced you can't do it, Bones?" wondered a concerned Kirk.

McCoy shook his head. "No. It means I'd better get started. Let's see . . . I'm going to need Nurse Chapel, and Ensigns M'baww and Prox to help with the beginning research, certain equipment . . . and I'm sure the Lactrans will have suggestions and instruments I'll have to learn about."

Kirk was studying the equipment set in consoles and banks throughout the chamber. "There's plenty to keep the rest of us occupied in the meantime, Bones. I don't think the Boquses will object to answering a few questions."

"We do not, Captain Kirk," Hivar the Toq admitted softly, "so long as there are any of us left to answer."

VIII

With the aid of Hivar and information relayed from various centers of research on Boqu, McCoy made progress which surprised him. It took two weeks to understand what the result of the disease was.

"I know what's happening to the Boqus now, Jim," he explained, "but as to the cause, I've no more idea than they do." He gazed helplessly around the small medical lab which had been set up in the shuttlecrawler, enabling him to work outside the constraints of a life-support belt.

He gestured toward a table laden with slides and instruments. It reminded Kirk of something familiar, yet elusive. His attention was taken by McCoy.

"Something is causing an alteration in the structure of the Boqus' upper parts, changing the chemical composition in such a way that death is inevitable. Imagine the blood in your veins suddenly petrifying and you'll have some idea of what's happening to Hivar and the others.

"I've spent days hunting for a way to attack this thing and, Jim, I don't have the faintest notion of how to begin. This is as alien to my experience as we are to the Boqus."

"I have a suggestion, Doctor McCoy," came a prickling inside their heads.

"Who's that, Spock?" Kirk asked.

"One of the Boquian scientists who has traveled many *nevars* to reach here," the first officer explained. "It has been observing us at work and has considered the situation. Our presence—our very existence—has given it an idea it wishes to propose."

"I'm all . . . whatever it is I'm supposed to listen with," McCoy announced.

"There is no need to tense, Doctor," soothed Spock. "The idea has been communicated to me to relay to you. It is suggested that since your function is the study and treatment of carbon-based forms, you consult with one of the many on board the *Enterprise* who are experts in compounds of silicon."

"Spock," Kirk began, "we've already explained to them that life based on silicon instead of carbon is unknown—was unknown—to us until we came here. We have no one who—"

"Of course!" McCoy blurted unexpectedly. He ignored first Kirk's stare, then his query, as he hurried to the forward intercom. *"Enterprise, Enterprise!"* When no reply was immediately forthcoming, he stared angrily at the console. "Now what's the matter? Don't our maintenance techs realize that delays . . . !"

Spock quietly activated the communications unit for him and stood aside.

This time McCoy's entreaties were rewarded with a flood of static, as the communicator strove to force its way through dense atmosphere and the barrage of internal Boquian radiation.

"*Enterprise*, Lieutenant Uhura speaking. Is that you, Dr. McCoy?"

"Yes, Uhura. I want to speak to Lieutenant K'ang Te." He glanced at Spock as if for confirmation, and the first officer nodded readily.

Kirk searched his memory for one name out of the hundreds on board the *Enterprise*. K'ang Te, lieutenant; Sciences; head of the geology section.

Then he wondered why he hadn't thought of it. It had been a Boqus's turn to find a different approach . . .

With the veteran mineralogist's assistance, McCoy began to make progress—man and woman, physician and geologist, working together in search of a solution. Kirk watched them drive themselves mercilessly and wondered worriedly which they would find first—an answer, or total exhaustion.

It appeared to Kirk to be a dead heat between the two possibilities when McCoy, drawn from the work and the debilitating affect of hard labor under an extra half gravity, staggered onto the bridge a week and a day later.

"Bones, you look terrible!" Kirk exclaimed.

"I know. And I feel wonderful!"

"You—you did it, then? You actually found a solution?"

"K'ang Te and I, yes . . . At least, we think so."

Kirk looked past him. "Where is the lieutenant?"

"In Sick Bay, where I sent her." A hint of a smile graced the doctor's dry lips. "It's easy to prescribe treatment for someone when you're suffering the same symptoms." He sank gratefully into a seat vacated by Spock, too tired to counter the gesture with sarcasm—or too thankful for the small courtesy.

"I am certain the solution is as fascinating as the disease, Doctor," Spock ventured, by way of impelling McCoy to explanation.

"You don't know the tenth of it, Spock. The trouble was with their circulatory system—you ought to see it, Jim! Their blood, if we can call it that, is thicker than machine oil, and flows just fast enough to be called something better than paralyzed. In past centuries certain crucial components within the blood haven't been breaking down as they should have. Call it a buildup of impurities, if you will. The Boqus thought something in their own systems responsible for handling the breakdown of these impurities had failed, and they've been going slowly insane trying to discover it. We found it, but the real problem was finding an antidote." He shook his head slowly. "The Boqus were too close to the problem."

"As so often happens," Spock finished for him. "I am intrigued, Doctor. What kind of remedy did you discover capable of affecting the buildup of unwanted substances in the 'blood' of a silicon-based creature?"

"To begin with, Spock, I had to disregard, throw out, forget, and otherwise ignore everything I knew about serums and standard antidote chemistry. Not only did it seem unlikely I'd be able to find something the Boquian researchers had missed, but I wouldn't have the faintest idea of how to go about inoculating a rock—for all its stiffly formal mobility, I can't help thinking of Hivar and its kind in those terms. Our eventual solution came from medicine by way of physics, born out of mineralogy." He settled himself into a chair, lowering himself gently.

"According to their meteorological records, Boqu is periodically afflicted with long periods of constant storm. We nearly hit one of them on our way down—remember the tremendous lightning display?"

Both Kirk and Spock recalled that casually awesome discharge of energy clearly.

"After more experimentation and search than I care to think about, we discovered that in the case of this last series of storms, the cloud layer over most of inhabited Boqu had become so thick as to block out certain radiations from the system's feeble sun. This was accomplished by having Astrophysics prepare a complete breakdown of the radiation the sun was putting out, and comparing it with readings taken on the surface. From that point, we had to proceed with special caution. One of those screened-out wavelengths might be responsible for breaking down the unwanted substances in the Boqus' blood—but the others might prove lethal if too strong a dose was delivered."

He sighed slowly. "As it turned out, nothing of the sort happened, though that didn't keep all involved from worrying constantly about it. We tried four different radiants on several fatally ill Boqus. Two did nothing, the third made the experimental subject retch remarkably, and the fourth—the fourth had its subject on its, uh, feet in a few hours. Similar radiation treatments ought to have most of Boqu back to normal inside a month. The equipment involved is simple to reproduce. A technical team is on the surface now, helping them set up facilities for duplicating the proper projectors."

"Fascinating, Doctor," commented Spock with admiration. "I would enjoy a more detailed look into such a unique physiology."

McCoy's expression turned solemn. "That shouldn't be too hard a wish to fulfill, Spock. At present Boqu enjoys a surplus of corpses. They'd probably find the dissection of a Vulcan cadaver equally interesting."

"Undoubtedly," agreed the first officer, missing the irony of the doctor's statement completely.

Unexpectedly, McCoy grinned. He leaned his head on his left hand as he reminisced. "I don't think we'll ever see a

Boqus jump. They're not constructed for leaping. But, Jim, when that last patient suddenly showed signs of recovery and we knew we'd found the answer, Hivar and the Boqus medical scientists present came as near to kicking up their heels as their bodies permit."

"How long does the treatment last?" Kirk wanted to know.

McCoy considered. "Only about one of our weeks. So until the intensity of this severe storm cycle begins to lessen, every Boqus will have to spend about fifteen minutes a week under a radiation projector in order for its blood to return to normal—like humans used to do under sun lamps."

Spock looked querulous. " 'Sun lamp,' Captain?"

"An old obsession of people in the Dark Ages, Mr. Spock. Many of them used to spend hours, even days, under the concentrated radiation of an ultraviolet generator, trying to artificially darken their skin."

The first officer's confused expression did not fade. "I see, Captain. But I was under the impression that during that period of human history the humans with light-toned skin discriminated against the darker humans."

"That's right, Spock," Kirk admitted.

Spock's puzzlement deepened. "Then why would the light-skinned humans try to burn their skin dark? This is not logical, Captain."

"Human actions of the Dark Ages rarely were, Spock. As a matter of fact, I seem to recall that certain humans of dark skin used artificial means to try to lighten their skin."

"So the light-skinned humans tried to make their skins dark, and some of the dark-skinned humans tried to make theirs light?"

"You've got it, Spock."

The first officer assumed an air of finality. "I will never understand human beings fully, Captain."

"Don't worry about it, Spock," advised McCoy, for once in complete agreement with him, "you've got plenty of company. Actually, if you bother to consider that . . ." He stopped in mid-sentence, aware that the first officer was no longer listening. Instead, Spock's mind was drawn to something deeper.

"It is the Lactrans, Captain," he finally declared, confirming what the watching Kirk and McCoy had already suspected. "Though growing impatient, they applaud Dr. McCoy's ability and great talent in finding a solution to the Boquian epidemic."

"It's not a question of talent," an embarrassed McCoy muttered, "just persistence."

"I have so informed them," Spock added drily. "They wish to know if we have made inquiries among the Boqus for their help in locating and capturing a jawanda."

"They can ask our hosts themselves shortly." Kirk thumbed a switch on the chair arm, activating the intercom.

"Engineering," a familiar voice acknowledged.

"Scotty, this is the captain. How is that special tech section coming on those big life-support belts for the Lactrans?"

"I was about to call in myself, sir," the chief engineer told him. "They're undergoin' final tests. I think our guests will be pleased with them. No need to use the shuttlecrawler any more. It wasn't too difficult a job—even for us 'primitive types.' Just time-consumin'. They can even take 'em off and put 'em on themselves, with those flexible snouts of theirs."

"Thank you, Scotty. Kirk out." He turned back to the motionless Spock. "You can tell our friends they can describe jawanda-catching requirements to Hivar the Toq in person. Mr. Scott's people have built three specially modified life-support belts for them. They can beam down to the surface with us."

When they beamed down that afternoon, Kirk saw hints of tremendous activity in the direction of the formerly moribund city. On the nearest outskirts, crews of rejuvenated Boqus were at work in incomprehensible machinery, modifying certain structures, demolishing others, building still more.

Obviously, McCoy's antidote was already having extensive effects. Certainly, the captain thought as they made their way cautiously through the heavy gravity of Boqu, Hivar and its colleagues should now be overjoyed enough to provide all the aid the Lactrans desired.

Those three massive aliens were sliding along smoothly behind Kirk, Spock, and McCoy. The captain envied them their ease of locomotion in the Boquian gravity.

At the moment they were deep in conversation among themselves, long front ends bobbing and weaving as they conversed at a speed which to human minds was only a confusing, head-throbbing blur. Enormous lightning flashes arced from thick clouds to ground off to the north.

"What are they so intent on, Mr. Spock?" his curiosity finally prompted him to ask. "The electrical display?"

"No, Captain." Kirk forced his way through thick, clinging mud that wasn't there. "The laboratory structure of Hivar the Toq." Kirk gazed at it, but saw nothing remarkable about the large building save its lack of windows.

"What about it intrigues them so?"

"The acuteness of its construction, Captain. It is all sharp angles and abutments, excepting the roof, whereas Lactran architecture is based on an absence of sharpness. Their buildings and machines, if you recall our stay on Lactra, were all rounded—curves, ovoids, hemispheres and circles. It seems that structure follows form. The Lactrans are as rounded as their constructs, the Boqus as sharp-edged as theirs."

"And what about us?" asked McCoy curiously. Spock paused a moment.

"We are considered acute formations by the Lactrans and curvilinear by the Boqus. It seems we partake of something of both."

"So we're mediators in form as well as in fact," noted Kirk. "It's nice to be consistent."

This time the last door of reflective metal was open, awaiting their arrival. Scott probably could have beamed them directly into the central chamber, but Kirk wanted Hivar to have time to prepare for their arrival—and it might prove useful to discover if the Lactrans could negotiate the building's passageways.

Nothing of the irritability mentioned in the Lactrans' old records was evident in the manner of Hivar the Toq as it greeted them warmly. The Lactrans studied the instrumentation and the layout of the circular laboratory with admiration.

The Boquian scientist had been taking McCoy's radiation treatments, and the change in its appearance was dramatic. The gold ribbing on its central trunk shone as if polished, Kirk observed immediately.

Even more striking was the difference in Hivar's upper region, the part that Kirk had come to think of as a head. Except for a few isolated patches of color, the opaque milkiness which had characterized that hemispheric crystalline structure on their first meeting was gone. Now the dark internal striations and peculiar clumps and nodes of denser material showed clearly, reminding Kirk of ferns and flies frozen in Earth's ancient amber.

It was a measure of this creature's personal strength, Kirk realized suddenly, that in all this time since their initial meeting Hivar had never once indicated that it was too severely stricken with radiation deficiency. Kirk wondered if he could have remained as personally unconcerned if their positions had been reversed—if he had been the one dying of a disease thought incurable and Hivar the possible savior.

"Greetings, Captain Kirk, Mr. Spock, Doctor Bones McCoy." Kirk had the impression the Boqus was glancing behind them, though, try as he might, he could not identify Hivar's organs of sight. "And anxious visitors from our far past." Something scratched at Kirk's mind as the Lactrans and the Boqus exchanged silent mental hellos.

When it continued, he wondered for a nervous moment if something had gone wrong, if the Lactrans had touched some ancient trouble. Spock reassured him.

"According to the youngster, its parents and Hivar are engaged in parallel telepathic conversation of an advanced mode. I can believe that, as I have tried to listen in and have experienced only a mild mental concussion as a result. While the Lactrans must turn their thoughts to baby talk and slow their conceptualizations to a crawl in order for us to comprehend, no such restriction exists between them and the Boqus."

Whether Hivar the Toq sensed Kirk's uneasiness at being so completely left out of what was obviously a critical discussion or was just being polite, Kirk would never know. In any case, he appreciated it with loud thoughts of thanks when the Boqus slowed its own river of conversation enough for the humans to make some sense of it.

"A jawanda you want to capture and take back with you to your home world? A jawanda!"

The Boqus' expression of surprise, coming when they had

expected a more casual acknowledgment, left the humans startled.

"Now listen," McCoy began, "we've been put off about this jawanda long enough. I think it's about time we—"

Hivar the Toq pivoted on centilegs, the gesture of turning away from them more significant than anything else. "I promised you our aid, it is true, but . . . I do not know." It was muttering mentally. "Long ago we had a device for manipulating the jawandas. But this was used only to protect Boqu, to drive the creatures away from our world. Never to capture one!"

"Just a second, Hivar," McCoy interrupted, waving his hands. "Let's back up a minute. You said drive them *away* from *Boqu*?" The doctor eyed Kirk uncertainly, and was rewarded by a cautioning look of equal puzzlement. "Aren't the jawandas native to Boqu? Are you trying to tell us they originate on still another world?"

"None of the other planets of the system appeared capable of supporting even rudimentary life," Spock commented, without committing himself utterly. Perhaps some minor error in their initial hurried observations, some small factor of atmosphere overlooked . . .

"Do not tax yourself, friend Spock," came the answering thought from Hivar the Toq—accompanied, Kirk sensed with surprise, by a twinge of amusement. "It would appear that your friends the Lactrans have been less than informative, Captain Kirk."

Kirk turned his gaze on the always silent aliens. The answer to his unvoiced question came, as usual, from Spock.

"No, Captain, they have told us no untruths, they have not lied to us. They have simply neglected to mention certain details concerning the jawandas."

"I can imagine!" exclaimed McCoy feelingly.

"It is these details which they have not supplied which should be of particular interest to you, Captain," Hivar added helpfully. "I have said that we manipulated the jawandas out of necessity, to keep them clear of our world. This does not mean they come from another. We have never been able to determine the origin of the jawandas—if, indeed, such a term has application in their case. We know only where the jawandas exist . . . out there." Half a dozen reticulate upper tentacles pointed jerkily skyward.

"The jawanda is truly a creature of the universe," Hivar explained to a rapt audience of bipeds. "They live only in intergalactic space, drifting for unknowable eons in the gulf between galaxies. We know very little of their life, save that they are simple yet marvelously efficient energy-mass converters, feeding on the faint radiations extant in the vast Out There."

"If these creatures exist on radiation," Spock inquired, "why remain in the comparative barrens of intergalactic territory? Why do they not come nearer the galaxies themselves, and the suns which produce the radiations on which they feed?"

"Gravity," was the terse explanation. "Should a jawanda come within the influence of a modest sun, it could easily be trapped forever in orbit about it. While there is no reason for assuming that a jawanda could not live, even thrive, in such a confined existence, it seems that they prefer freedom to satiety. It may be a survival instinct or an actual mental preference—we likely shall never know. For whatever reason, they avoid the gravitational density of galaxies and star clusters. Only the isolation and weak pull of our star made them bold enough to come near Boqu."

"Why Boqu, though?" asked McCoy.

"Remember our measurements on approach, Doctor," Spock reminded him. "Boqu puts out more radiation than it absorbs, qualifying it in certain astronomical lexicons as a protostar itself."

"Correct, Mr. Spock," the Boquian scientist concurred. "Jawandas used to frolic freely about our world, successfully defying our sun's poor gravity. Normally, this troubled Boqu not at all. The jawandas' absorption of radiation lost freely to space did not affect us.

"Occasionally, however, it did, according to the old records. No, Dr. McCoy, the question I see framed in your mind is reasonable but not relevant. The jawandas did not screen out any particular radiation from our sun—such as the vital one you isolated as the cause of our epidemic. Instead, they blocked out a majority of radiation, that wavelength included. More important than any disease, this unpredictable screening caused slight but disconcerting shifts in the surface temperature of Boqu, lowering the warmth in the regions affected by substantial amounts."

"I can see where it could be uncomfortable to be enjoying warm weather one minute and having it turn to winter in a few seconds," Kirk admitted readily.

"This situation persisted for thousands of our years," Hivar continued, "until we found a way to drag the jawandas away. While doubtless they are dull, thoughtless creatures, they do seem capable of learning through repetition. They learned long ago not to approach Boqu."

Hivar abruptly went silent, and Kirk and McCoy looked to the attentive Spock. "The Lactrans wonder what has become of the mechanism for manipulating the jawandas and whether it can be adapted to serve their needs. Hivar has replied that it can conceive of no reason why the device should not be so utilized, though it has never been done before. The Boqus wished to drive the jawandas away, not capture them."

"I do not even know if the mechanism still exists, and, if so, whether it remains operative," Hivar broadcast mentally, slowed now so that the intensely curious humans could also listen in. "Should it prove so, you may employ it, though this must be done with care. Certain of the extended components of the mechanism hold a historical attraction for us. We would not wish to see them lost."

"What components?" Kirk wanted to know.

That great crystalline head turned toward him. "Boqu is circled by nine moons, Captain Kirk. For manipulating the jawandas properly it is necessary to make use of six of them."

"Six . . . moons." McCoy gulped, turning to the *Enterprise*'s first officer. "How big did they say one of these creatures is?"

"It has not been stated, Doctor. All references to size have been of an indeterminate nature."

"Big enough to live in intergalactic space, Bones," Kirk commented slowly. "Big enough to pass between sun and planet and cause climatic changes on the surface. Big enough to . . ." His voice trailed off, and he turned to face the Lactrans. "We gave our word to help. That agreement stands." He directed his final statement to Hivar. "Find the device.

Can it be mounted on the *Enterprise*, or does it have to exist in free space?"

"No, Captain Kirk," the Boqus replied, bowing with surprising grace for so nearly inflexible a creature. "The actual console for controlling the confining elements of the mechanism is quite small. It will fit easily on board your vessel. As will I."

"You?" McCoy gaped at the scientist. "You're coming along?" Impressions of a mental nod of assent. "But why? You don't owe the Lactrans anything."

"Your guests, no . . . but you, Doctor McCoy, are owed a great deal. In any case, it is necessary, since only a Boqus could properly operate the mechanism."

The mysterious control console of the capture device turned out to be something of an anticlimax. Kirk had been prepared to have technicians cut out bulkheads and even cabins surrounding the Shuttlecraft Bay in order to provide a space large enough to accommodate a monstrous construction. As it turned out, the actual instrumentation bulked only about three times the size of the *Enterprise*'s navigation console. Hivar had found it in the nearby city housed in a huge old scientific warehouse that looked brand new, a testament to the foresight and talent of Boqu's pioneering engineers.

Hivar activated the ancient machine and spent several days replacing certain components and realigning internal components while Kirk fidgeted nervously on board the *Enterprise*, his sleep troubled by snaggle-toothed apparitions bigger than starships.

When, before long, the renovation was complete, Kirk inspected the incredibly dense machine and ordered the bracing beneath a bulk-cargo transporter reinforced before beaming the device aboard. He was trying to imagine where they could conveniently place the machine—and how—when Spock proposed a solution so simple that Kirk had overlooked it.

"Why trouble to move it anywhere, Captain? Leave it where it is, on the transporter platform. If the Boqus can operate it from here, there's really no reason to shove it around the ship."

"How about communication?" Kirk mused, studying the

distance between the transporter platform and the nearest intercom unit.

His first officer considered. "We will request that the young Lactran remain here with Hivar," he finally suggested. "The youngster will be in constant communication with its parents and with myself, on the bridge, as well as with Hivar."

"Boqus to Lactran to Vulcan," Kirk concluded, adding with firmness, "We'll keep all intercoms activated and open anyway."

When finally beamed aboard with the mechanism, Hivar reactivated it and pronounced itself satisfied with the arrangements. Pressed for a more precise translation than "mechanism" or "device," the Boqus scientist confessed it was unable to name it any better for his human hosts.

"At least that's in keeping with its appearance," Kirk murmured, staring at the object in question. It looked like a large blob of free-form slag composed of half a hundred materials, metallic and otherwise.

He studied the bumps and spikes and wires sticking out of the amorphous mass, trying to rationalize the haphazard appearance of the thing with the knowledge that it was an intricate, complex feat of alien engineering. There was slight consolation in the fact that it looked as absurd to the lumpish Lactrans as it did to him.

Duplicating the outward form of the thing would be no trouble, Kirk thought. Simply take a room full of engineering components and turn a low-power construction phaser on it. Several hours later you would have produced a close approximation of the object now squatting on the cargo-transporter platform.

As Hivar the Toq moved reflecting limbs across the mound's surface, however, it generated lights and hums and whines no half-welded dollop of metal could ever produce.

"The mechanism," the Boqus told them, "contains its own power source, which in turn links it with the much more powerful old engines locked into the crusts of the moons Drasid, Mett One and Mett Two, Lethiq, Lathoq, and Oj." It completed a few final adjustments, turned with a crystalline flourish to face them.

"All is in readiness, Captain Kirk."

An awkward moment of uncertainty followed, before Kirk finally replied, "You'll have to tell us how to begin." He glanced at the young Lactran, who showed no sign of providing instructions or suggestions. "No one else on board has any idea where to start looking for a jawanda."

"I expect your vessel possesses adequate equipment for the transmission of sound waves, since this is the method you use for personal communication," Hivar ventured. "Do you also have the ability to detect other types of electromagnetic radiation?"

"With considerable accuracy," Kirk informed it.

"Then there is no difficulty. Instruct your monitors of the appropriate instrumentation to listen for"—and Hivar provided a figure Spock understood—"which is the range of the jawandas' cry."

"Interesting," the first officer commented. "They communicate among themselves, then?"

"So it is believed by many," the Boqus acknowledged, "yet these sounds may be produced for a variety of reasons having little or nothing to do with communication. Should we continue outward from Boqu, away from the galaxy, we will eventually encounter one." A pause; then: "I see your confusion, Captain Kirk. Given the density of our atmosphere, how is it our knowledge of astronomy is so advanced? Let me say simply that our progress in what you might call radio astronomy and related areas which do not require visual observation has been substantial."

"That wasn't really what was bothering me," responded Kirk. "It was your use of the term 'eventually.' How long is eventually?"

Hivar transmitted a mental shrug. "It could be tomorrow . . . or it might be a hundred years. I would tend toward the former."

"I sincerely hope you're right," declared Kirk with feeling.

Once back on the bridge, Kirk's first concern was that the complex telepathic communications system—which, after all, relied on an adolescent of an alien species—was functioning smoothly.

"Mr. Spock, what's the maximum acceleration Hivar's mechanism can match?"

Again the relaxation into semistupor, which no longer troubled Kirk; then the first officer replied, "Warp-three, Captain. Should we attempt to travel any faster, the six moons which form the bulk of the system will fall behind, soon to be lost to control."

Kirk nodded and glanced at the helm. "All ahead warp-three, Mr. Sulu."

"Ahead warp-three," came the acknowledgment. It was followed by a hesitant question: "On what course, sir?"

Kirk looked expectantly at Spock, who informed him, "Hivar says to use your own judgment, Captain. One course should prove as efficacious as the next, so long as we continue to move outward from our galaxy."

"Um. Mr. Sulu, resume our former course heading, continuing on out from Boqu."

"Aye, Captain," the helmsman replied unquestioningly.

Kirk's gaze went to the main viewscreen. It provided an expansive panorama of obsidian emptiness, speckled fretfully with the pale light of far-off galaxies and star clusters hundreds of thousands and millions of light-years distant.

Given the *Enterprise*'s marvelous instrumentation, of course, it was next to impossible for them to become lost. Even so, one could not be certain of anything this far from familiar starmarks. The idea of becoming lost in this benumbing nothingness, to wander forever on the fringes of the galaxy, was an eventuality he had no wish to cope with. Resolutely, the captain forced it from his mind.

There were other things to think about. Like the actual size of the mysterious jawanda, for example.

"Activate rear scanners, Mr. Arex," he ordered. The depressing view ahead was temporarily replaced by a shrinking Boqu aft. Raging upper-atmospheric disturbances stirred orange-and-maroon clouds like a giant's finger dipped in paint. And there was something else.

Six points of darkness, artificially highlighted by the ship's scanner-computers, were following them at a respectful distance. Six moons, detached from orbit, trailed the *Enterprise* like balls on a string. Kirk assumed that the long line was for convenience of manipulation. Surely the actual use of the moons in jawanda capture involved some more-complex configuration.

The lift doors slid aside, and McCoy strolled onto the bridge. "You'll be happy to know, Jim, that Lieutenant Randolph is fully recovered. I discharged her from Sick Bay an hour ago." His gaze went to the screen. "Our six attendant satellites?" Kirk nodded.

"I hope Hivar knows what it's doing with that archaic hunk of machinery." McCoy gestured at the trailing moons. "Even if they are all smaller than Luna, I'd hate for Hivar to make one of them zig when it should zag. If the *Enterprise* accidentally got caught between them, we'd end up looking about as streamlined as a Lactran."

IX

On the sixth day out from Boqu, Lieutenant Uhura turned from her communications console and informed Kirk, "I am receiving broadcasts in the range indicated by the Boquian scientist, Captain."

"You're certain, Lieutenant?"

"Yes, sir. Pickup is clearly within the frequency specified."

"Mr. Arex, obtain a fix on the broadcast source. As soon as you have it placed, instruct Mr. Sulu on the necessary alteration in our course for planned intercept."

"Very well, sir," the Edoan navigator replied.

Kirk glanced back at Uhura, intending to thank her—and hesitated. The lieutenant was chewing her lower lip, and she looked more than simply thoughtful.

"Something the matter, Uhura?"

"I don't think so, sir. It's just that . . . well, I'm sure I recognize those sounds. I've heard them before."

"That hardly seems likely, Lieutenant," commented Spock.

"I know, Mr. Spock," she admitted, "but I'm still positive I've encountered these particular noises in the past—or at least sounds very similar."

"Amplify and put them on the bridge speakers," Kirk decided.

She spent a moment adjusting the controls; then the bridge was filled with a moderate crackling sound. It alternated occasionally with a regular electronic chirp, which devolved rapidly into a low buzzing. One moment it sounded like random noise, the next almost like a programmed broadcast.

"My apology to Lieutenant Uhura," Spock finally said

into the silence. "I recognize the sounds myself." Kirk was about to add that he also was familiar with such noise when Spock added, "I have communicated our discovery to Hivar, who is anxious to hear it."

"By all means. Uhura, transmit to the Bulk Transporter Room the Boqus is located in." There was a long wait.

"It is the cry of a jawanda," Spock announced, Hivar's own conviction mirrored in the first officer's tone.

Kirk was only confused further. "But that's a familiar sound, Mr. Spock. Large radiotelescopes, even the oldest ones on Earth, have been picking up buzzes and crackles like this one for hundreds of years. Of course," he added softly, "there are many whose origin has remained a mystery."

"Certain of those unsolved origins may now be explained, it seems," Spock went on, showing excitement of an intellectual sort even in his role of communicator. "It appears that in addition to quasars, pulsars, radio nebulae, and other known phenomena which are sources of deep-space radio waves, we must now include the jawanda."

"Proceeding on new course, Captain," Sulu announced, "warp-factor three."

Kirk had a sudden thought. "Mr. Spock, the Boquian mechanism restricts us to a maximum speed of warp-three. Ask Hivar how fast a jawanda can travel."

The reply took longer than usual. "No faster than our present velocity, Captain . . . or so it is believed. There is no way Hivar can say for certain, since its race was always concerned with putting distance between them and the jawanda and not closing it."

Kirk found himself once again trying to adjust to the idea of a creature which could move at a speed exceeding light. It made no sense—but then, the universe was full of things which did not make sense.

"Quarry is traveling at an angle to us, Captain. There is no indication that it has taken notice of our presence. We are proceeding on an intercept course which will bring us to capture range within twenty hours."

But it was a day longer before the extremely long-range visual sensors were able to pick anything up. There was a pause while Sulu adjusted instrumentation—and then they were gifted with their first sight of a jawanda.

It was all at once more magnificent and unexpected than Kirk had anticipated: an enormous rippling rectangular shape. The sensors were observing it from its flat side; otherwise, as with Saturn's rings, there would have been almost nothing to see. Were it not for the fluorescent colors which ran rippling across its featureless surface, even the computer-enhanced visual pickups would have shown nothing. The dancing lights, radiation consumed and transformed, gave outline and dimension to the creature.

"Looks like a big plastic sheet trying to digest an aurora," McCoy offered.

"Details, Mr. Spock? Preliminary measurements?"

Spock was bent over readouts and indicators. "Its method of locomotion is unknown, Captain, though it appears to throw off energy as well as to absorb it. Thickness is apparently constant from one end to the other, with no significant tapering at either end."

"How thick, Mr. Spock?"

"Approximately one millimeter, Captain. Viewed from the side, even at close range, the creature would effectively vanish. By contrast, its length and breadth are considerable."

"You're starting to sound as vague as a Lactran, Spock," grumbled McCoy.

"It is difficult to estimate its surface area, Doctor."

"Why—because some of it appears edge on?"

"No—because there is so much of it, and because the rectangular appearance is only approximate." He looked up from his readouts and gazed straight at Kirk. "I would say that this particular specimen is capable of covering most of the North American continent on Earth . . . though, of course, only to a depth of one millimeter, and that assuming the continent to be uniformly flat. Actual surface area is concomitantly somewhat less."

"That's . . . all right, Spock," Kirk assured his first officer, when he had his voice back. "It's big enough for our needs—and the Lactrans'." He sat staring at the unimaginably huge creature. Electric purples, mauve, metallic green, and azure drifted through its nearly transparent vastness, the discharges ample evidence of continual energy transfer.

"As a collector of stray radiation, it is a wonderfully designed organism," commented an admiring Spock. "It maximizes surface-collection area while minimizing mass. Absorbed radiation is converted into operating substance and at least two kinds of radiant discharge. One is the radio wave we detect, while the other doubtless propels it through the cosmos in some fashion we do not yet fathom. I would give ten years of my life to know how it does this."

"If we can capture it, the Lactrans may give you the chance to find out, Spock."

"Captain!" Kirk looked sharply at Sulu. "It's changing course."

"Spock, ask Hivar if we're within capture distance yet."

Quickly now: "No, Captain. Hivar says we must move considerably closer before the mechanism can be effectively employed."

Sulu spoke again. "Definitely senses us, sir—moving almost directly away from us now."

"Speed, Lieutenant?"

"Warp-three, sir."

Kirk rubbed tiredly at his forehead. "Can it sense a trap?"

"Most certainly it can detect the gravitational fields of the six moons trailing us, Captain," Spock pointed out.

"If that's the case, then we're going to have trouble getting close to any of the beasts." He considered a moment and decided, "Let's continue following for another half day. It may grow tired."

But as he made his way back to his cabin to sleep, he found himself skeptical of outlasting a being which existed comfortably in the space between galaxies . . .

Sure enough, when he returned to the bridge he found the jawanda still traveling with apparent ease at warp-three, directly away from them. They had not closed the distance by a meter.

The simplicity of the dilemma didn't lessen Kirk's frustration. If they accelerated to warp-four, they would overtake the fleeing quarry—but without the means necessary to capture it. And there was something else he was beginning to wonder about, something which intruded on his thoughts to the point where he found it necessary to put the question to their guests, via Spock.

"Is a jawanda dangerous, Mr. Spock?"

"Hivar does not know, Captain, nor do the Lactrans. The

Boquian mechanism was always operated from ground control, never from a ship. Hivar actually has no idea how a jawanda might react to one—particularly one moving free of the protection of a strong gravitational zone."

"I thought our guest considered it impolite to read thoughts," Kirk observed mildly.

"Hivar apologizes, Captain, but replies that the image in your mind was so strong it could not ignore it."

The image the Boqus was referring to involved Kirk's proposal to drop clear of the trailing moons and proceed at a higher speed to overtake the jawanda.

"Once we do that," Kirk concluded, "we'll have to find some way of turning the creature back toward the six satellites."

"Hivar is not certain," Spock relayed slowly, "that this is a good idea. Despite its apparent fragility, a jawanda remains a being of unknown defensive capabilities, but one through which courses a good deal of controlled energy. Hivar desires that its ignorance of such abilities not serve as a pretext for foolhardy action."

"I see. What is the Lactrans' opinion?"

"They are of a similar mind, though equally uncertain."

"Does any of them have any better ideas?"

A hopeful wait, after which Spock declared, "They do not, Captain. Free space is not the element of Boqus or Lactrans. It belongs to the jawanda—and, at present, to us far-ranging primitives. The Lactrans concede that you must make the decision."

"What of Hivar?" Kirk pressed, knowing that without the Boqus's cooperation further pursuit of the jawanda was useless.

"As Hivar can think of no alternative save to disengage and search for a jawanda at a more favorable intercept angle—"

"Which might not happen for that proverbial hundred years," Kirk pointed out sharply.

"—he consents, reluctantly, to follow your designated course of action."

"Tell him to break free of the six moons, then."

"He has already done so, Captain. He adds that—" but Kirk had no time now to listen to the cautions and concerns of Hivar the Toq, or the superior-minded Lactrans. Primitive creature or not, it had been given to him and his fellow savages to successfully bring to a conclusion this unique hunt.

For the first time since they'd left Lactra, he felt in complete command of his ship.

"Mr. Sulu!" he barked. "Mr. Arex! Compute new course to bring us around and in behind the jawanda." Both helmsmen and navigator rushed to comply.

Sulu looked back alertly moments later. "Course computed and laid in, sir."

"All ahead on new heading, warp-factor five," Kirk ordered.

Moving far faster than their quarry now, the *Enterprise* leaped ahead, circling in a great arc around the fleeting creature, the ship's powerful engine enabling it to all but vanish from the jawanda's immediate vicinity.

"Any indication it's detected us, Mr. Spock?" he finally asked when they were moving toward the creature instead of away from it. The *Enterprise*'s science officer studied the information fed back by long-range scanners.

"Apparently it has not changed direction, Captain. Either it is convinced we are still in pursuit, or it believes itself no longer threatened."

Distance shortened rapidly. "Reduce speed to warp-two, Mr. Sulu. Let's see if dropping to a velocity below its capabilities affects it."

"Still no change, Captain," reported Spock seconds later. "Coming directly toward us." A pause; then: "Hivar the Toq expresses some concern."

"Thank Hivar for its concern," replied Kirk, too busy now to worry about diplomatic niceties. "Slow to warp-factor one, Mr. Sulu."

"Slowing, Captain. I have visual contact." A quick adjustment and the jawanda appeared again on the viewscreen forward. Only now the sparkling, rippling shape, a living microthin continent, was charging toward them at warp-three.

"It's beginning to slow, Captain," Sulu reported, a touch of anxiety in his voice. "Still coming toward us, though."

"Phasers on low power, Lieutenant."

"Phasers, sir?" the helmsman inquired uncertainly.

"That's right. We're going to try to turn it back toward the six moons of the Boquian mechanism. Fire as soon as it comes within range." If it comes within range, he added silently.

"Creature is slowing . . . warp-two . . . warp-one . . . range still decreasing . . . it's not going to turn or stop in time, sir."

"Fire, Mr. Sulu." Kirk leaned forward and gripped the arms of the command chair tightly. If they killed it, they'd have to begin another search.

"Firing," came the helmsman's even reply. Two dull blue beams jumped across the shrinking gap toward the onrushing monster, struck the ever-twisting surface . . . to no apparent effect.

"No indication of reaction from the jawanda, Captain," Spock informed him.

"Still coming at us, sir." Sulu looked back at the command chair for instructions.

"Increase phaser power to half strength, Mr. Sulu. Fire."

Once more the two beams, this time shining far more brightly in the darkness, crossed the space between ship and jawanda. It reacted this time, slowing even further—but for some reason Kirk felt that the decrease in velocity had nothing to do with the *Enterprise*'s attack.

It continued to rush toward them.

"Full power, Mr. Sulu!" he ordered hastily. All that could be seen ahead now was the lightninglike display of color rippling through the jawanda's substance as it transformed and dissipated untold energy with the ease of an earthworm digesting dirt.

This time the two beams which touched the creature were intense enough to blind, had not the ship's battle computer automatically compensated for the anticipated brilliance by suitably adjusting the forward scanners.

Those two beams, striking with the full energy of the *Enterprise* behind them, were capable of piercing the thick hull of any vessel in existence, of reducing mountains to rubble and boiling away small seas. They struck the underside (or perhaps the topside) of the jawanda.

Flexible, incredibly tough cells contracted, reacted where

the beams hit. That enormous surface curled like foil in five-hundred-kilometer-wide swirls.

But it did not stop, did not turn aside, and did not slow further.

"We're going to crash, Jim," McCoy murmured fatalistically, his fascinated gaze frozen on the viewscreen.

"All decks, red alert, Lieutenant Uhura. Brace for collision! Mr. Sulu, evasion course, warp-six—emergency gravity compensation!"

Engines operating near idle suddenly gulped great amounts of energy as abrupt demands were made on the ship's warp-drive units. The *Enterprise* shot forward to one side—three-quarters of a second too late.

A thin filament of jawanda, a living peninsula, caught the ship's secondary hull. It was a small extension of the creature—probably only a few hundred kilometers long and wide.

A gentle shudder went through the fabric of the ship. It was felt on the bridge, in the recreation rooms, in Engineering, throughout. One by one the exterior scanners went dim as they were covered by jawanda.

The body of the monster was so thin that at first the scanners could penetrate its substance. This lasted until the jawanda began to fold in on itself, burying the hull in more and more of its body, millimeter piling on millimeter, until the cruiser was completely enveloped in successive folds of jawanda.

"Slow again to warp-factor two, Mr. Sulu." The helmsman complied, but the action had no effect on the jawanda. It continued to turn in on itself, still only millimeters thick, but growing deeper and thicker, like sediment deposited by some strange intergalactic stream. Total darkness soon showed on the screen as the jawanda's density finally grew impenetrable.

"I've seen a spider do the same thing to its prey," McCoy muttered, "wrapping it again and again in folds of silk. When it's finished, it bites through the silk and—"

"Don't arachnemorphize, Doctor," interrupted Spock.

McCoy blinked, his morbid visualizations temporarily shattered. "Don't *what*?"

"Don't ascribe spiderlike characteristics to an alien being."

"Captain?"

Kirk bent quickly to the intercom. "What is it, Scotty?"

"I dinna know for sure, sir. We're puttin' out as much power as usual, but for some reason it's not being utilized properly in the engines."

"Mr. Sulu," Kirk asked tightly, "what's our speed?"

"Warp-two, Captain . . . no, wait a minute." The helmsman studied his instruments in disbelief. "That is, we're supposed to be moving at warp-two—but we're not. In fact, we seem to be slowing!"

"I believe I know what is happening, Captain." Kirk looked over at Spock, could sense Vulcan mind-wheels turning rapidly. "The jawanda is an energy converter, and a remarkably efficient one. We are currently putting out a tremendous amount of radiant energy, compared to what it normally receives in the comparative emptiness of intergalactic space. This energy is highly concentrated, yet available without the threat of an attendant gravitational field. To the jawanda the *Enterprise* must seem a magical apparition of the greatest delicacy.

"Naturally, it wishes to maximize this unexpected new food source. By enveloping us in repeated folds of its absorbtive surface, it is logically attempting to contain all the radiant energy we produce, trying to prevent it from escaping into free space."

"Warp-factor one, Captain," came an excited voice from the speaker at Kirk's elbow. "Dilithium crystals showing stress patterns along interval cleavage planes," the chief engineer added. "If we don't shut down the drive now, sir, we risk losin' any chance of reactivatin' it."

Suddenly the awesome depths of the intergalactic gulf were pressing intimately around Kirk's mind. The very possibility of becoming trapped out here, many light-years away from the outermost fringes of the Milky Way, let alone the Federation, was not pleasant to dwell upon.

"All right, Scotty, if you think it's that vital, shut down the converters. We'll use impulse power to maintain life-support functions only—and hope the jawanda isn't so starved it begins to drain that too."

"Aye, Captain."

Kirk heard him shouting commands to assistants and subordinates. His concern paramount, Scotty even forgot to sign off.

Kirk closed the open link to Engineering himself. A low whine rose in intensity for a brief moment, then faded to silence, the dying wheeze of an electronic zephyr. For an instant the lights on the bridge flickered confusedly before the changeover was complete. They brightened again, as strong as before, dimmer only in Kirk's anxious imagination.

"Any comments on our situation from our alien guests, Mr. Spock?" the captain inquired hopefully.

Spock listened and informed him, "Hivar the Toq had not considered the possibility that the ship's radiation might prove an attraction to the jawanda. Conversely, the Lactrans are delighted."

"Nice to know that the present predicament is pleasing to someone," McCoy murmured sardonically.

"They commend you on your speed in capturing one so easily and in such a subtle fashion, and wonder how soon we can begin the return journey to Lactra."

"That's fine, Spock, except our friends have things a bit mixed up. It's the jawanda who's captured us, not the other way around." Kirk thought several uncomplimentary things about Lactrans, for the moment not caring particularly if his emanations were detected. Still, he mused, their present troubles were not the fault of the Lactrans. Nor of Hivar the Toq, whose knowledge of jawandas had admittedly extended no further than the atmosphere of Boqu.

"It is possible, Captain," Spock added, "that the creature will depart the *Enterprise* of its own accord, now that the main generator of radiation on board has been shut down. I do not think we should wait for this dubious eventuality. Somehow we must make it release the ship, at least long enough to permit us to get safely underway, at a speed sufficient to prevent a recurrence of the present awkward situation."

Awkward! McCoy shouted silently, amazed as ever at the first officer's capacity for understatement.

"It certainly can't worsen our difficulties to make the attempt, Spock," agreed a thoughtful Kirk. He studied the blanked-out scanners for a moment, then decided, "Let's take a firsthand look at what we're dealing with. Bones, you come too."

McCoy glanced at him curiously. " 'Come'? Come where, Jim?"

"Outside, of course. We can't tell very much about the jawanda from in here."

While McCoy gaped at Kirk, Spock wondered easily, "Shall I contact Chief Kyle, Captain?"

Kirk made a negative gesture. "No, Mr. Spock—no transporters. The creature could drain the power from the transporter as fast as it was renewed, though I don't think it would notice such a small output of channeled radiation. But I am concerned that the transporter beam might fail to penetrate the energy-sensitive substance of the creature's body. Remember what Hivar told us about its screening capabilities? Rather than take that indeterminate risk, we'll go out through one of the emergency-access ports—and hope the jawanda doesn't decide to suck the energy from our life-support belts."

Before long the three men found themselves standing within the lock of the emergency port nearest the bridge, on the upper section of the ship's primary hull.

"Activate life-support systems," Kirk ordered. Lime-yellow auras instantly enveloped them all. Kirk saw by McCoy's approving nod that his own system was functioning properly. That slim yellowish halo was all that stood between them and the absolute cold of intergalactic space.

"Cycle the lock, Mr. Spock." The first officer touched the necessary switch, and the exterior door began to slide aside. Kirk felt a slight pull as the wisps of atmosphere missed by the ship's recyclers rushed out through the widening gap.

Looking out, he saw only the expected darkness. Yet there *was* something different about it. There should not have been a total absence of distant light, but there was.

Putting out an aura-shielded hand, he encountered resistance where none was expected. A slick rubbery wall sealed the lock exit, though the slickness was more imagined than felt, since his fingers did not actually make contact with the jawanda's body. Experimentally, he pushed. The dark material gave with surprising flexibility. Kirk had had no idea what to expect—something hard and resistant, perhaps, or soft like dark jelly. Instead, there was only this easily elastic smoothness.

For a moment he wondered if this was actually the body of their continent-sized nemesis. Then he jumped slightly as several small purple coruscations ran in uneven spurts across the living surface before them. The jawanda was sweating fire.

"Wonderful creature," Spock murmured.

"Let's admire it from a distance, Spock," suggested McCoy tersely. "What about trying a phaser on it, Jim?"

"Mr. Spock?" Kirk stepped back from the exit and regarded the dark substance expectantly as Spock removed the small hand phaser from his waist. The first officer set the beam on low power and directed it outward.

Blue light touched the black film blocking the doorway. Where it contacted the surface of the creature the material began to glow. The dark substance turned a light yellow at first. This melted rapidly into orange, then red, and finally into a rich purple. The mild assault was exquisitely beautiful and wholly ineffective.

"Try more power, Spock," Kirk advised. Spock did so, gradually adjusting the phaser until it was on maximum. The intense emissions produced only a slight rippling in the jawanda's body, causing it to retreat outward about half a meter from the edge of the lock.

Of course, this could have been due to sheer enjoyment of the radiation bath as much as to discomfort or injury.

"That's enough, Mr. Spock," Kirk finally declared. The first officer flipped off the phaser and reset it on his waist. Kirk was only slightly disappointed. He hadn't really expected that the tiny phaser would be capable of threatening the enormous organism.

"It absorbs energy like a sponge, Captain," commented Spock.

"What about the ship's main phasers this close to it?" wondered McCoy.

Spock considered, "I think the effect would be essentially the same as before, Doctor: a futile waste of energy. There is so much jawanda to dissipate so little power . . . and it could put a severe strain on our already dangerously weakened power supply."

Kirk studied the blank wall of living material. The purple glow was fading slowly, contentedly. "What about the possibilities of a biological assault, Bones? Some sort of injection?"

McCoy almost laughed. "On a creature the size of North America? As thin as it is, I think it would handle the most massive dose I could give it the same way Spock says it would a blast from our main phasers—by dissipating it throughout its body. That's assuming I could concoct something able to affect its body. There doesn't appear to be anything remotely resembling a central nerve center, or even nerves. They might exist, but even if the creature allowed it, we could vivisect a few dozen kilometers and miss any vital points by a week's march.

"No, thanks, I'm not ready to tackle this. Give me a nice simple problem instead, like solving a Boquian epidemic." He gestured helplessly at the black film blockading the exit. "I'm sorry, Jim, but there's nothing I can do."

"Then that leaves one thing," Kirk said determinedly, "that we haven't tried." After double-checking to insure that the gravity specifics of his life-support system were engaged, he walked forward, put both hands against the dark skin—and shoved hard.

The jawanda's body parted like a torn sheet, and Kirk's hands went right through.

Rather than expressing satisfaction, he sounded abashed. "We overlooked the obvious in favor of the technical. A common mistake of mechanically minded civilizations." Using his hands, he widened the gap. The substance resisted steadily, but continued to give way under the captain's firm pressure.

"Follow me." Stepping carefully through the hole, he walked out onto the surface of the jawanda.

They emerged facing rearward. Instead of the sloping back of the *Enterprise*'s primary hull, flanked by the two torpedo shapes of the warp-drive propulsion units, they saw only a black formlessness. It turned the streamlined cruiser into a dark nebula of constantly shifting outline.

A long tail like the back of a black comet stretched into the distance aft, glowing now and then with vibrant sparks and the random chromatic streaks of internal lightning.

"Wonder what we look like from a distance," McCoy murmured aloud, at once amazed and appalled by the sight.

"The cape of some fantastic giant," Kirk hypothesized, "or the image of legended Azathoth . . . We've become a child's dream, Bones."

"Or its nightmare," McCoy countered.

"It is conceivable," Spock ventured, refusing to be drawn into such useless, illogical speculation, "that by utilizing the manual labor of the entire ship's complement we could physically remove the creature from the hull. However, this would prove futile in the end, since there is no way to prevent it from reestablishing itself once all hands have returned inside."

"I dislike the thought of totally abandoning the ship to automatics, even for a few minutes," Kirk added as they made their way across the black substance. It rippled eerily underfoot wherever an aura-clad boot touched down, like concentric circles fleeing a stone flung into a pond.

Kirk put a foot down with experimental firmness, then raised it quickly. Gently the material reformed itself over the exposed circlet of metal, apparently undamaged. Leaning over, he peered intently at the dark flesh, but could detect nothing resembling a seam or repaired wound.

"Remarkably efficient in all ways," Spock declared, also studying the area where Kirk's foot had pressed down.

"Yes. It seems to—" He broke off, staring rearward.

"What is it, Jim?" a worried McCoy inquired.

"Is it my imagination, Bones, or is the jawanda starting to move?"

McCoy looked around, and even as he watched the activity Kirk thought he had sensed increased visibility. "No, I see it too, Jim."

At the edges the colossal mass seemed to be rippling and fluttering with great violence. A moment later their life-support belts reacted to similar action underfoot, keeping the men firmly attached to the immediate surface beneath them as it too began to move up and down in increasingly higher arcs.

"Captain, I think it best that we reenter the ship, at least until this sudden activity subsides."

"You won't get any argument from me, Spock," admitted

Kirk readily. He was already moving as fast as possible back toward the open hatchway. Despite the knowledge that the life-support systems would hold them tight to the jawanda, he had to fight down an urge to drop flat and hug the surface.

"Why do you think it's reacting like this, Spock?"

"There may be any number of reasons, Captain," the first officer responded, a smooth thrust of body-substance sending him arching meters above Kirk and McCoy. Then Spock had dropped into a low pit and they were looking down at him.

"Possibly it is irritated by our presence, though I think that unlikely. It may be seeking to realign itself to further maximize its energy gathering potential. Or . . ." He paused. "It is possible that, with the ship's warp-drive units deactivated, the reason for its enveloping the *Enterprise*—to be wrapped tightly about a source of intense and now vanished radiation—has disappeared. It may be preparing to leave."

"Then I suggest we hurry," advised McCoy, exercising a bit of understatement himself as he increased his pace.

After another couple of minutes had passed, Kirk slowed his progress across the rolling surface. Frowning, he muttered, "We should have reached the hatchway by now." Turning in a slow circle, he examined the living terrain behind them. All was shifting, hilly blackness. No comforting light showed through.

"As a matter of fact, how are we going to relocate it? The jawanda is so dense now that the light from the lock can't penetrate it."

There was silence, each man wrapped in his own thoughts. Then McCoy said hesitantly, pointing, "I think it was over that way, Jim."

Slowly they retraced what they hoped had been their original steps—slowly so that they wouldn't overrun the lock entrance, and also because the jawanda was now heaving up and down in twenty-meter-high ripples. Only plenty of experience working in low-g environments kept them from becoming violently ill.

After five minutes McCoy had to admit that his guess had been wrong. Kirk and Spock were equally disoriented.

"It is imperative that we do not continue to search blindly

about, Captain," Spock declared, his even, controlled tones a great comfort in the fleshy chaos heaving around them. "I believe we must risk the utilization of transporter energy to have ourselves beamed back into the ship. So long as the jawanda remains attached to the hull, we will never locate the open lock."

"I agree," McCoy added quickly, the distant glow of the Milky Way galaxy bobbing drunkenly behind them. "Even though the creature hasn't threatened us, I don't like the idea of being stuck out here as our life-support charges run down."

"We don't know for certain that the jawanda is harmless, Doctor," Spock observed coolly, not enhancing McCoy's current state of mind.

Kirk nodded his assent to Spock, who removed his communicator from his waist and flipped it open. His words carried to his two companions as he addressed the open speaker grid.

"Spock to Main Transporter Room, Spock to Main Transporter Room." There was a silent pause. The first officer looked across at Kirk. "Acknowledge, Transporter Room." Still no reply. "Nothing, Captain—not even normal background noise."

"Maybe your communicator is malfunctioning, Spock," Kirk suggested. Reaching down, he opened his own instrument. "This is the captain speaking. Transporter Room . . . bridge . . . anyone receiving, please acknowledge." Only the emptiness of space sounded from the tiny grid.

"I should have guessed," Spock broke in, in his own quiet way furious with himself. "Naturally the energy-screening abilities of the jawanda blocks out the weak waves produced by our communicators. There is only—"

Despite superhuman balance, he lurched forward as the surface moved beneath them. Kirk nearly fell backward, and McCoy tumbled flat.

The jawanda, its primary source of radiation now completely cut off, was once again feeling the need to spread its energy-gathering bulk as wide as possible to gather the stray radiation drifting across the intergalactic gulf. The violent contraction which had thrown everyone off balance was caused by the creature's beginning to separate from the *Enterprise*.

Kirk fought to keep from screaming in panic as the starfield wheeled crazily around them. The energy-eater finally straightened out, having unwound itself from the hull.

Looking back, Kirk saw the *Enterprise* behind them. It was shrinking at a terrifying pace at the tail end of a vast dark carpet.

Ahead of them lay nothing but black infinity . . .

X

Kirk rolled over and managed to sit up. "Communicators, Spock. There's nothing to screen them out now." But his first officer was already reaching for the compact instrument, flipping the top open.

"Spock to *Enterprise*, Spock to *Enterprise* . . . Come in, *Enterprise*."

A faint voice barely recognizable as that of the ship's helmsman issued from the speaker, weak with increasing distance and distorted by the crackle of radiant discharge from the jawanda beneath them.

"Mr. Spock . . . what's happened? Our scanners are operating again. The jawanda has broken free and—"

"Transport us back aboard, Mr. Sulu," Spock interrupted urgently. "Immediately."

"What's that, Mr. Spock? I can't . . ." There was a burst of static. ". . . quite hear you." Dimly they heard, "Sensors seem to indicate you are no longer on the ship's hull. What—"

"Activate engines!" Spock ordered crisply. "Follow the jawanda and overtake. We are stranded on the jawanda, repeat, *on the jawanda*. It is moving out of visual range. We are—"

"Never mind, Spock," McCoy advised, an odd tinge in his voice, "they can't hear us any more."

But Spock persisted, his voice never breaking as he continued broadcasting. Rapidly the *Enterprise* became a shapeless dot, then a star . . . and soon was lost to sight as the jawanda sped away at a rate no living creature should have been able to attain.

Three men more isolated than any in the universe sat themselves with unnatural calm on the thin surface of their unbelievable steed and took stock of their situation.

It was not promising.

"We are fairly sure the *Enterprise* is faster than the jawanda," Spock noted, "but it must get underway rapidly in order to be able to track us." Glancing to the side, he saw the vast circle of the home galaxy dominating the darkness like a gigantic pinwheel.

"Even if they temporarily lose contact with us," McCoy pointed out, with more confidence than he felt, "they ought to be able to pick up the energy field surrounding the creature. We located it in empty space once before, by the sound it emits. No reason why Sulu and Uhura shouldn't be able to do it again." He essayed a timorous smile.

"All very true, Doctor," an almost but not quite shaky Vulcan voice agreed, "unless the ship's instrumentation locks onto *another* of the creatures. If that happens and the ship follows a different jawanda for even a short while, we could be carried far beyond easy sensor range."

"Thanks, Spock," McCoy muttered morosely. "I can always depend on you to cheer me up." Absently he ran a hand over the smooth obsidian film beneath them. Glowing phosphorescence trailed his hand, like the night wake produced by a boat traveling one of Earth's oceans. "I've been marooned on several worlds and a few moons before, but never on a living creature."

"We've discovered a flying carpet that would astound humanity's ancient story-tellers," Kirk mused. "I wonder where it's carrying us."

It was amazing, he reflected, how rapidly he had adjusted to the possibility they might never be found. At least they would die in space, and quickly, when the energy powering their life-support belts gave out or was drained away by the jawanda. His gaze moved again to the lambent spiral of the Milky Way. A more fitting subject for the final sight of a starship captain could not be imagined . . .

As had so often been the case in times past, Captain Kirk's resignation proved premature. Spock had been standing rigid for long moments, almost at attention. When he spoke again, his voice was relaxed.

"There is no need for concern any longer, Captain. The *Enterprise* is tracking us."

McCoy scrambled to his feet, and together he and Kirk stared rearward—or at least in the direction Spock was facing; it was impossible to determine true direction. Kirk strained, could see nothing but distant star clusters and nebulae, not even a moving point which might turn out to be the ship.

"How can you tell, Spock? I can't make out a thing."

"I am in communication with one on board. The connection at this distance is tenuous, but with no other intelligent minds around us—"

"The Lactrans!" McCoy exclaimed.

"Yes, the Lactrans," Spock confirmed. "While they have been unable to assist in the capture of the jawanda, it seems that their presence has produced an unexpected but welcome benefit. The young one is in communication with its parents, who relay instructions through it to Mr. Sulu and Mr. Arex."

Shortly thereafter the most beautiful sight in the universe hove into view: the *Enterprise*. It grew to the size of a small flower and finally loomed huge behind them.

Or perhaps now it was before them, since they seemed to be rushing toward it. Kirk studied the ship as the first fold of jawanda reached outward. Spock's comment mirrored his own thoughts.

"The creature is once more rushing at the *Enterprise*, sensing the nearness of renewed radiation from her engines."

Behind them, a towering black wave was curling overhead, arcing downward like an onyx tsunami. It blotted out the bright glow of the home galaxy, surged ahead and downward. All three men had to fight down an unusual tendency to claustrophobia as the black curtain descended on them. No crushing weight shoved them flat as they hurried toward the nearing hull. The blackness settled with feathery lightness. Each time a new fold of jawanda curled over them, they pushed upward with stiff arms and forced a temporary gap in the creature's body, emerging into the starlight again and again.

Finally the jawanda stopped wrapping itself about the ship. They found themselves standing once more on a black-coated hull, unable to recognize a single feature through the amorphous structure of the creature.

"We're right back where we started," McCoy observed, sighing heavily. "I can't say I'm disappointed."

"On the contrary, Doctor, we are not back where we started," objected Spock. "I am still in contact with the Lactrans." Turning slowly, he faced toward the front of the ship and pointed. "That way."

Following the first officer's lead, they walked over to an area which looked no different from any other, or from the one they'd just left. Spock gestured slightly ahead and down. "We're here, Captain."

Kneeling uncertainly, Kirk reached out and shoved with both hands. Once again the multiple folds of jawanda parted—but this time a gleam appeared in the opening thus produced. It was the most welcome sight Kirk had seen in a long time.

Widening the gap with his hands and with McCoy's help, they were soon able to slip back into the comforting closeness of the emergency lock. Undamaged, the jawanda reformed behind them, shutting out the universe once more.

Spock activated the lock and it cycled shut behind them. Atmosphere was automatically pumped into the chamber as soon as the airtight telltale went on, and the all-clear sounded a second later. Gratefully, Kirk deactivated his life-support belt, as did Spock and McCoy. The doctor opened the inner door.

A large, cylindrical mass the color of lead filled the corridor beyond. Kirk still could not tell when the young Lactran was standing or sitting—or if those terms had any referent to Lactrans. He had the impression that the youthful alien was regarding them attentively.

"It apologizes, Captain," Spock announced.

"Apologizes?" Kirk wondered if the surprise was as clear in his mind as it was in his voice. "Its parents just saved our lives." He returned the creature's eyeless stare. "We are more grateful than we can—"

"Nevertheless, it persists in its apologetic attitude, Captain. The sudden disengagement of the jawanda which carried us away from the ship caught it and its parents by surprise."

"They weren't the only ones," Kirk countered feelingly.

"They are sorry for the delay incurred in directing the ship to us, and hope that our simple minds have not suffered any damage as a result of this negligence."

"Tell them our primitive cognitive apparatus is functioning normally," Kirk replied with a grin. "If they hadn't acted when they did, we wouldn't be functioning at all."

Making a strange weaving motion with its multiple-digited front end, the Lactran adolescent turned and scuttled off down the corridor.

"It begs to be excused, Captain. It wishes to visit its parents. The strain involved in reaching across such a distance has weakened them. We must return to the hunt, they insist—with the foreknowledge that this time they may not be able to help us."

"From now on we're going to stay inside the ship," declared McCoy. "You can tell them that, Spock." He turned to Kirk. "What now, Jim?" he asked as he set his life-support belt in its proper rack, making sure the recharge light was on.

"Back to the Bridge, Bones. From there . . . I don't know. Any ideas?"

Neither McCoy nor Spock had come up with the hoped-for miracle solution by the time the turbolift deposited them on the bridge. Kirk acknowledged the warm yet restrained welcomes of the crew as Spock moved to his science station. McCoy relaxed nearby.

"I have a small theory, Captain," Spock announced, sitting down in his chair.

"Pursue it, Mr. Spock." The first officer's theories often turned out to be more solidly grounded than many supposed facts. Spock bent to the library-computer console with a will.

Glancing at the main viewscreen, Kirk was rewarded with the expected picture of dull blackness occasionally enlivened by scratchy streaks of maroon-and-emerald lightning.

"Status, Mr. Sulu?"

This time it was not necessary for the helmsman to check his instrumentation. "The jawanda has once more enveloped the *Enterprise*, Captain. As soon as we learned that you were safely back aboard, Mr. Scott deactivated the drive again."

Sulu gazed uncertainly back at him. "What do we try now, sir?"

"I don't know, Lieutenant." Kirk considered. "For our purposes the creature reacts favorably to physical pressure, but I can't have hundreds of people out on the hull shoving and pushing. Energy weapons are useless against it—in fact, they probably strengthen it. A photon torpedo might have some effect, but we can't very well explode one against the creature when its body is only millimeters from the ship. Besides, we want to capture it whole, not chop it to pieces. The devil of it is, we have the jawanda right where we want it. Only we can't use the warp-drive engines to carry it and ourselves back to Lactra."

"A moment, Captain," Spock requested, as Kirk was trying to think of a way to utilize the jawanda's docility under physical pressure. The first officer was bent over the main readout from the library-computer console.

"I am concluding certain calculations. There." He looked up, staring for a moment into nothingness, before turning to Kirk and informing him, "The Lactrans also believe the idea is feasible, though dangerous. They refuse to support or to reject the proposal."

"What proposal?" Kirk wondered guardedly.

"To impel the jawanda to release us by providing too much of what it wants. In a word, we shall appeal to its sense of gluttony."

"I'm not sure I understand what you're driving at, Spock."

"Consider, Captain. When we collided with the creature we were moving, according to final readout, at warp-four, coming up to warp-six, which we never fully attained. If we suddenly fed a sustained burst of emergency power to the engines, the equivalent of warp-factor seven or eight, it is possible that the surfeit of energy—of food—would dangerously strain the creature's absorptive capacities.

"It would have two choices: to burst from overconsumption or abandon its hold on the *Enterprise*. If the former happens, we will at least be free to search for another jawanda, with our knowledge of its abilities and habits enlarged. If the latter, we may be able to engage the Boquian mechanism before the engorged creature can escape."

"It sounds good," admitted McCoy hopefully. "Why are the Lactrans leery of trying it?"

"Their reasons are twofold, Doctor. Should the jawanda *not* be overloaded by the surge of energy, we run the risk as stated by Engineer Scott of losing our warp-drive capability altogether. This would leave us with only impulse power on which to recross a considerable amount of space." His gaze momentarily checked a figure displayed on one of the science station's several screens.

"On impulse power it would take us approximately three hundred and sixty-five standard years to reach the outskirts of our galaxy, with the Federation a good deal farther away. That is assuming the engine components last that long."

"Let's hope we don't have to try it," Kirk said. "What about our guests' other concern?"

"It has already been mentioned, Captain," Spock declared. "They worry about damage to the specimen."

Kirk forebore formulating his first thoughts. It wouldn't do to insult someone who had just saved your life.

"Any other proposals, Spock?" he asked, hoping for an alternative that carried less of an air of finality.

"I am afraid not, Captain. This course of action seems to offer our best hope of breaking clear."

Kirk sighed and activated the armchair pickup. "Engineering?"

"Scott here. What is it, Captain?"

"Scotty, this creature drinks radiant energy. Since we can't pull away from it, we're going to have to try to convince it to let us go—by generating a cosmic bellyache. Somehow we've got to overfeed it. I'm going to want maximum emergency power from the converters for as long as you can provide it."

"Aye, Captain," the chief engineer assented reluctantly. "I dinna know how long we can maintain it, the way that monster drains our production."

"We want it to drain us, Scotty—until it's sick of it. Keep the converters functioning for as long as you can. This *has* to work."

"I understand, Captain," Scott replied solemnly. "Engineerin' out."

Kirk clicked off and looked forward. "Mr. Arex?" The

Edoan navigator acknowledged, his bony-ridged skull turning three soulful eyes on the captain.

"Yes, sir?"

"If we do succeed in breaking free of the creature, we're going to want to come back for it . . . monumental pain in the stern that it's been. We're liable to break completely free at warp-seven or warp-eight, so you'll have to try to retain a position fix on it."

"I'll manage, Captain."

"I know you will, Mr. Arex." He studied first the living dark matter covering the scanner, then the viewscreen, while searching for a flaw in Spock's reasoning and finding none. How many times, he mused, had he found himself betting his existence and that of his crew on a cut of the deck by Fate. *His* record for turning up aces was unblemished . . . so far. It was time again to try to extend the streak: "Mr. Sulu, all ahead warp-factor seven, emergency power."

"Engaged, Captain," came the response from the helm.

A steady whine began to sound, more felt than audible. It rose to a pitch just shy of setting everyone's teeth on edge, then held steady. Instead of the normal rush of lights across the screen, they continued to see only blackness. A minute passed, two, three . . . Angry jagged bolts of crimson and gold began to race bizarrely through that living film. Four minutes, five . . .

"It doesn't seem to be having any effect, Captain," Spock reported calmly, his gaze locked to the gooseneck viewer. "The jawanda is still wrapped completely around us."

"Increase to maximum emergency overdrive, Mr. Sulu," Kirk said. "Warp-factor eight."

Sulu hesitated the briefest instant, started to look backward, then murmured a tight "Yes, sir" instead.

The whine became a painful drone like the keening of a single gigantic bee. Kirk felt a faint throb through the metal structure of the command chair as the ship's fabric sought to remain intact under the enormous energies generated by her engines.

Six minutes, seven, eight . . . a voice shouting from the intercom, barely recognizable, "Captain, we canna hold this much longer! Converters are beginnin' to fail."

"Warp-factor seven, sir," Sulu suddenly announced. "Warp-factor six, five . . ."

Kirk snapped at the intercom, "Scotty, maintain full emergency power! Never mind protecting the converters now, we need everything you can—"

"That's what we're givin', Captain," the chief engineer countered. "I'm tryin' to tell you—the energy's not bein' translated into thrust. That thing's sucking up everything we can generate and searching for more."

"Warp-factor four," Sulu declared worriedly. The bone-grating whine of emergency overdrive had long since faded, along with its comforting throb of power.

"We must make a final decision immediately, Captain," exclaimed an anxious Spock, "or the converters will permanently collapse."

Kirk's gaze was fixed on the viewscreen, fascinated by the now continual display of lightning so brilliant the battle compensators were hard pressed to sop the intensity to below pain threshold. Every hue of the rainbow was present in those unending discharges as the jawanda fought to dissipate surplus energy. Kirk wished he could be floating free in space nearby. The trailing cometlike portion of the jawanda must present a spectacular sight. Indeed, an unsuspecting observer who chanced to pass through the immediate spatial vicinity would see jawanda and *Enterprise* as a colossal oblate opal, lit with internal fire.

Kirk was about to order an end to the seemingly futile effort when the colors vanished, revealing the far plainer but much more welcome isolated lights of distant galaxies pinwheeling through the gulf.

"We're clear!" McCoy yelped joyously.

"Disengagement confirmed, Doctor," concurred Spock, considerably less exuberantly. "It worked . . . barely."

"The creature is falling rapidly off screen astern, sir," Arex announced, in a tone almost as relaxed as Spock's.

"Warp-factor five," Sulu declared, "factor six and increasing."

"Reduce speed to warp-four, Mr. Sulu!" Kirk ordered quickly. "Don't lose our quarry, Mr. Arex."

"Not to worry, Captain," the navigator assured him, examining his own sensor readouts. "It is now by far the most obvious object in the heavens, due to the amount of energy it continues to radiate."

"Plot a return curve to bring us directly back at the creature, Mr. Arex. We can't waste time and allow it to regain its flexibility in converting energy." He voiced a quick question to the arm pickup: "Scotty—how are the engines?"

"Recoverin' rapidly, Captain," the chief engineer reported, the strain of the last minutes evident in his voice, "but it was a near thing. I wouldn't like to chance it again."

"We're going to do our best not to, Scotty," the Captain assured him, before clicking off. His stare moved repeatedly from helm to viewscreen. "What about the jawanda, Mr. Arex? Is it trying to escape?"

"It does not appear to be succeeding, if such is its intention, sir," the Edoan announced carefully. "It is moving away from us, but very slowly, and in an erratic manner."

"Bloated," McCoy decided firmly. "The overload was too much for its converters to handle. I'd venture to say that its whole system has been affected."

"The Lactrans," Spock put in, gazing momentarily at the wall before him, "hope there is no permanent damage."

"We do too," admitted Kirk, "so long as the alternative doesn't turn out to be rapid recovery."

"It is continuing to move away, Captain," Arex said softly, "but more slowly now."

"Sensors indicate it is discharging energy at an incredible rate, Captain," declared Spock. "It may be regaining some of its ability."

"I wonder—Spock, do you think it's capable of anger?"

"I don't know, Captain. But the instinct to defend oneself is basic to many very primitive organisms." He eyed Kirk expectantly. "You have something in mind?"

"Somehow, Spock, we have to distract it long enough for Hivar to engage the capture mechanism. If the creature doesn't actually conceive of us as a threat, it should at least regard the ship as a challenge. By now it should be dazed and disoriented—its present movements indicate that. I can only see one way to draw it within range of the Boquian device—and that's to tempt it into chasing us."

"Jim!" McCoy exclaimed, startled. "If it manages to envelop us again . . ."

"I know it's a risk, Bones, but we've got full motive power back. We'll have to cut it close, but if it gets too close we can outspurt it at the last moment." *I hope,* he added silently.

Spock helped him make up his mind. "I agree it should be tried, Captain."

"What do the Lactrans think?"

Spock listened silently. "They are agreeable to anything which has as its final purpose the capture of a jawanda."

"Good. Mr. Sulu, slow our speed gradually. I want it to look like we're having trouble of our own."

"Slowing, Captain," the helmsman responded. "Should I notify Engineering?"

Kirk considered and half smiled as he replied, "Better not, Lieutenant. I can guess Chief Scott's picturesque opinion of this idea." He became all seriousness again as a pulsing spot appeared on the viewscreen, an object the size of his thumbnail, a seething pool of color.

Fat and sassy, he thought. Probably thickened its waistline by an enormous amount—maybe even another whole millimeter. If the monster had the instincts of an amoeba, it should be spoiling to defend itself against anything that smacked of an attack—particularly an attack by a source of food. Still, the jawanda's ability to relieve itself of excess energy remained an unknown, unmeasurable factor. As important as the time factor was, they would have to proceed with caution.

"Speed of target, Mr. Arex?"

"Still moving away from us, Captain, approximately warp-factor one point two two."

"Spock, we're counting on its reacting like any other living organism, but we still have no idea how advanced it really is. Any chance it could be intelligent?" *That,* he thought, *might complicate events considerably.*

"I doubt it, Captain," the first officer declared, glancing up from his instrumentation. "Its instincts should be quite primitive. It gives every indication of existing only to perform three basal functions: eating, excreting, and reproducing."

"I agree. It better . . . I'm tired of surprises, especially potentially lethal ones. Is Hivar the Toq ready?"

Spock paused. "The Boqus is standing by its equipment, Captain. All elements of the mechanism are in readiness."

"Position?"

"Still too far away." Not that Kirk had expected any other reply—they would have to draw the dazed jawanda into the trap.

"Captain!" Kirk looked back to Arex. "The creature is turning. It has reversed its direction and is now moving toward us."

"Mr. Sulu, you are aware of the position of the Boquian mechanism?" Kirk inquired hurriedly. The helmsman nodded confirmation. "Change course then, to take us through its center. Continue to slow speed toward warp-factor one."

"Coming about, sir . . . slowing."

Long minutes passed, while the jawanda, its thin body still blazing with all the fury of a translucent reactor, expanded on the screen with startling speed. The reason was evident: The *Enterprise* had to change course in a wide curve, while the jawanda had simply folded in on itself, in effect going instantly into reverse.

"It's closing on us, sir," Sulu announced. "Coming on at warp-factor one point . . . warp-two." He threw a hasty glance over his right shoulder. "Should I increase our own speed?"

"Steady as she goes, Mr. Sulu," responded Kirk calmly, his eyes never leaving the viewscreen.

A shorter pause, then, "Still gaining rapidly on us, sir."

How beautiful it was, Kirk had to admit to himself. Rippling, convulsing in smooth arcs of its body, the jawanda enlarged to fill the rear scanners, emitting energy in glowing discharges hundreds of kilometers long. What other inhabitant of the universe, however high, however low, sweated such magnificence?

"Captain," Sulu began worriedly.

"It's all right, Mr. Sulu. Attention to your station." He flicked a look sideways. "Mr. Spock?"

"Another minute yet, Captain."

Kirk considered. The jawanda was almost within contact distance of the ship's warp-drive units. If he accelerated, he chanced discouraging the creature. Or, worse, making it wary. Was it still angry or hungry enough to continue following them, even if he speeded up? Or would it—

"We are within the cage, Captain," Spock announced

sharply. "Hivar has activated the mechanism." The first officer watched with interest through the images funneled to him from the Lactrans as Hivar the Toq drew strange sounds and lights from the free-form shape of the Boquian console with smooth movements of many-jointed crystalline limbs.

"Quarry is slowing, sir," reported Sulu. "Showing indications of uncertainty in its pursuit."

"It senses the collapsing gravity wells," Kirk murmured. Was the jawanda capable in its energy-engorged state of breaking clear of the cage?

"Slow to warp-one, Mr. Sulu."

"Reducing speed . . . It's beginning to change course, sir."

"Definitely suspicious now," muttered McCoy, staring raptly at the screen. They were about to play out the last act of the drama begun seemingly so long ago, back on the surface of Lactra.

"Full course change," Arex announced, "and it is accelerating."

"Bring us about on a pursuit course, Mr. Sulu . . . but slowly. Let's see if it can break free."

The *Enterprise* commenced another wide curve, which would bring it around behind the jawanda again—if Kirk chose to give the order to increase ship velocity, for the energy-eater was now fleeing in the opposite direction.

Kirk knew that if it broke free of the Boquian mechanism they would never be able to approach within capture range again.

"It's slowing, sir," Sulu declared positively. "Slowing . . . It's stopped!"

On the heels of the helmsman's announcement, Spock informed them, "Hivar pronounces itself satisfied as to the mechanism's performance. All six moons have been properly aligned, and the jawanda is trapped by their gravity."

"For how long?" McCoy whispered, gesturing at the screen. "Look."

Twisting and writhing like confetti in a tornado, the jawanda was rushing in tight circles around the inside of its invisible cage. Incredible bursts of pure energy bristled on its surface as it hunted frenetically for a hole in the trap.

Accelerating breathtakingly to warp-three it probed violently at the weakest points of the cage, between the moons. But no matter which way it darted, it could not escape the attraction of at least four of the controlled satellites. The octahedral prison proved secure.

"That's a lot of energy it's throwing off," Kirk noted. "Mr. Sulu, activate our defensive screens." The helmsman touched several switches—not a minute too soon, it turned out, as something powerful shook the bridge. There was a pause and then a second enormous purple bolt of energy crossed the space between ship and jawanda.

"It may not be intelligent," Kirk observed, stilling the slight shaking in his hands, "but it's not blind and helpless, either." He knew the power of the *Enterprise*'s defensive screens, but it was one thing to consider them from the standpoint of abstract statistics and another to do so while looking down the throat of an energy charge as big around as one of the ship's warp-drive units.

As Kirk ordered the cruiser to back off as far as possible, the madly convulsing jawanda continued to throw harmless if awesome bolts at them.

Spock observed dispassionately, "We already know that the creature is able to transmute great quantities of energy, Captain. It is not surprising that so efficient a converter should be capable of utilizing its ability to discharge excess energy for defensive purposes."

They remained in position while the attacks from the jawanda decreased steadily in intensity.

"Damage report, Lieutenant Uhura?"

"All negative, Captain," she replied. "All decks and stations report no injuries and no damage, although Engineering reports that the first several charges put considerable stress on the defensive screens. Since then, however, they report all attacks shunted aside with ease."

Kirk's attention went once again to the screen. Save for throwing an isolated spark toward the *Enterprise*, the jawanda had apparently given up its assault. Its movements, also, were much subdued. There was no more violent spinning about and contorting. Now it drifted in one place, its black surface rippling slowly like the stomach of an exhausted, overweight man drawing in painful breaths after a long run.

Bright bursts of light continued to show within its great body, but they came in fitful spurts now instead of the regular patterning previously observed.

"We've tired it out, I think," Kirk commented. "Is the Boqus ready to move, Mr. Spock?"

The first officer nodded. "Hivar indicates that the ancient components are performing well. Given a modest amount of power to feed to the control console, it foresees no difficulty in sustaining the cage indefinitely. The Lactrans," he added unnecessarily, "are overjoyed at our success."

"We're not in orbit around Lactra yet," Kirk pointed out. "I'll accept congratulations later. What about the possibility of our prisoner absorbing fresh strength from the radiation we'll encounter once we reenter the denser region of our galaxy?"

"All the energy it could assimilate from passing stars cannot possibly match the quantity it has already sapped and discharged from the warp-drive engines, Captain," the first officer insisted, after performing several calculations on the ship's computer. "We have already handled its best assault without damage."

"That's all I wanted to know. Mr. Arex?"

"Captain?"

"Plot a course to Lactra, presumably retracing our original tack via Boqu. Mr. Sulu, ahead warp-factor three."

Their acknowledgments sounded simultaneously, and soon the *Enterprise* was again Lactra-bound. Kirk's attention was still focused on their giant captive. He hoped Hivar the Toq was concentrating as intensely on his mechanism. They couldn't dare allow the jawanda even a small chance to escape.

But the octahedral cage formed by the six moons kept the energy-eater locked between them, dragging it smoothly along as they sped back toward the galaxy—although Kirk would have employed a term weaker than "sped," since at warp-three, they seemed to crawl along. But they were restricted to the maximum speed of which the old engines in the moons were capable.

During the following days Kirk had ample time to inspect that remarkable Boquian relic, its peculiar power leads, and the strange broadcast antennas temporarily installed on the epidermis of the *Enterprise*—antennas which somehow carried Hivar's instructions through the shapeless console to the six satellites caging the jawanda.

"Remarkable piece of instrumentation," Spock commented, bending to study the back of the console. It looked no different from the front.

"Prompted by a remarkable need," thought Hivar.

"How was it built?" inquired Kirk, wondering if it would last the duration of the journey back to Lactra.

"I do not know . . . I was able to learn only how to operate it." Hivar's concern mirrored Kirk's own. "The sooner we deposit the creature in orbit around your other guests' home world, the better I will feel, as it will signal the beginning of my return to Boqu."

The intercom buzzed for attention, and Kirk moved to acknowledge the call. "Bulk Transporter Room Three. This is the captain speaking."

"Lieutenant Uhura here, sir." There was an underlying hint of anxiety in that dulcet tone which made Kirk pay closer attention.

"Trouble, Lieutenant?"

"It's not certain, sir. According to Mr. Sulu, the creature is generating an unusual amount of energy. I've confirmed its output with my own instruments."

"You mean it's throwing energy bolts at us again?"

"No, sir." Kirk relaxed considerably, even though they'd already successfully fended off one such attack. "The discharge is in the form of radio waves."

"We already know that the jawanda is capable of producing those, Uhura," Kirk reminded her. "I presume you've detected something out of the ordinary about its present output or you wouldn't have called it to my attention."

"I think so, sir," she said slowly. "The emissions are in short, intense bursts of a type previously unrecorded. I have no idea what significance this holds, if any. But it's such an extreme departure from everything the creature has generated so far that I thought you'd wish to be notified."

"Rightly so, Lieutenant. I've no more idea than you what the meaning of this new activity is." He glanced back toward the attentive Spock.

"Nor have I, Captain," he admitted.

"Keep monitoring the output, Lieutenant," Kirk ordered her, "and begin taping." He flipped off the intercom and looked at the curious Boqus. "You'll have to continue the explanation of the mechanism's history later, Hivar. It's probably nothing, but . . ."

"But what, Captain Kirk?" came the thought, strong and heady.

"It's probably nothing." Kirk decided he was worrying unnecessarily over a harmless new phenomenon, when he had plenty of known dangers to plague himself with. A few moments of study should suffice; then he could dismiss the development from his mind. But those few moments were not to be ignored. Their knowledge of jawandas still bordered on the nonexistent.

On returning to the bridge, Kirk's first instructions were for Uhura to play back some of the noise the jawanda had already produced. As it turned out, recordings weren't required.

"It hasn't let up, sir," the communications officer informed him. "It continues to repeat the same pattern, identically modulated as the initial outburst. Here, I'll put what it's currently broadcasting onto the speakers." Her hands adjusted controls.

An ear-splitting shriek drenched the bridge in bone-grating waves of sound. Kirk's hands went instinctively to his head. That soul-rending howl was piercing his skull over and over. The impression was worse than the actuality, since it was barely a couple of seconds before Uhura could reduce the volume to a bearable level.

"I'm sorry, sir," she apologized contritely. "I thought I'd reduced the level considerably." She eyed an isolated readout angrily. "Here's the trouble—the creature has intensified its output tremendously since I first contacted you." She shook her head in awed amazement. "The amount of energy it's putting out is just incredible, sir."

"I see. Mr. Spock, your opinion?"

Spock concluded his preliminary sensor study of the new emissions and looked up thoughtfully. "Perhaps it is merely another form of energy release, Captain, an instinctive reaction to the unusual situation in which it presently finds itself, akin in spirit if not function to the defensive charges it attacked us with before.

"At first I suspected that the noise might merely be the normal energy discharge of the creature, its intensity the result of all the radiation it had absorbed from the *Enterprise*. Now that I have heard it, I begin to doubt this explanation. My uncertainties are compounded by Lieutenant Uhura's insistence that these discharges are of a type previously not detected." She nodded ready confirmation. "Beyond the normal excretion of surplus energy, I cannot begin to imagine what function these violent pulsations have— Wait . . . wait . . ."

A clumsy gray shape squeezed out of the turbolift onto the bridge. The young Lactran was already in close communication with Spock.

"The youth is relaying concern from Hivar the Toq," the first officer explained thickly. "The Boqus wishes to hear the sound for itself."

Kirk, picturing the eyeless, earless Boquian scientist, wondered if it "heard" in the same fashion as humans, or if the sound waves were absorbed uniformly across its sensitive crystalline surface. The latter was quite likely. The sound conductivity of crystals was known on Earth as far back as the Dark Ages.

"Pipe the broadcast through to the transporter chamber the Boqus is located in, Lieutenant," Kirk directed Uhura.

Her hands again adjusted controls. "Transporter Room locked into circuit, sir," she replied.

Something about the sound must have been familiar to the Boqus, because Spock's relayed response followed immediately on Uhura's announcement.

"Hivar recognizes the sound, Captain. There are recordings of identical vibrations on Boqu, and although they are extremely ancient Hivar insists the duplication here is unmistakable."

"Duplication of what?"

"A jawanda distress call."

That caused Kirk to pause, all right! There was only one possible corollary, but he asked the question anyway. "Distress call? To—others of its own kind?"

Spock turned to face him, though his gaze remained focused on a point halfway between the command chair and the science station. "Exactly, Captain."

Rapidly Kirk performed some crude calculations in his head, then relaxed slightly. Even if his estimations were a little off, there was still no reason to panic. "We could do without visits from our captive's cousins, Spock, but, judging from its initial attack, and taking into account that we'll be prepared this time, our screens ought to be able to handle energy charges from a modest swarm of jawandas. Particularly from jawandas who haven't been sucking up energy from our engines. No, I don't see much reason for concern. We're already traveling at warp-three. Even if the calls are picked up, even if a few of the creatures have an intercept angle on us prior to our reentering the galactic field, they'll have only their natural store of energy to draw upon." He started to rise, intending to return to the transporter room to conclude the examination of the Boqus's console.

"Hivar the Toq begs to differ with you, Captain," countered Spock. "Hivar urges that in the event another of the creatures is contacted, we release our captive and accelerate away as rapidly as possible."

A thoroughly stunned Kirk settled slowly back into his chair. "But . . . why? For what reason? My evaluation—"

"The Lactrans are arguing strongly against such a possible course of action," the first officer continued. "Hivar sidesteps. It insists that such an eventuality is unlikely, but that it must be considered."

"I still don't see why." Kirk frowned.

"The Boqus is embarrassed, Captain. It has withheld information, in the manner of the Lactrans, but claims that in this case it was only to"—the first officer strained, trying to translate alien concepts—"spare us needless worry. Hivar now feels that the worry is needful. The Lactrans could not know, but Hivar explains that if the old records are correct, we have captured an immature jawanda."

McCoy spoke for the first time since Kirk and Spock had returned to the bridge. He had remained unusually silent, standing by the engineering station and listening to the strange moans of their captive. But this latest information moved him to comment.

"You mean that monster is a baby?"

"Equivalent terminology has not existed in reference to jawandas, Doctor, but in the present situation Hivar feels it is appropriate."

"Then how big," McCoy wanted to know—or did he, he wondered—"does an *adult* jawanda grow?"

"No one knows," Spock murmured. There was silence on the bridge.

XI

"Hivar is struggling to recall long-dormant, little-used knowledge, Captain," Spock finally said into the lingering silence. "The estimate of our captive's immaturity is based on such information. The largest jawanda the Boqus were ever forced to drive away was . . . a moment . . ."

The pause was too much for an impatient McCoy, who soon pressed, "Was what, Spock?"

"Please, Doctor," the first officer cautioned calmly. "I am attempting with Hivar's aid to convert ancient Boquian measurements to Federation equivalents." A longer pause; then he announced firmly, "The largest specimen recorded by the ancients was approximately two hundred ten thousand by fifty-two thousand kilometers. That is only an approximation, remember."

Kirk tried to envision a living creature with a surface area five times that of the Earth and gave up. "That's only the largest the Boqus *know* of. I suppose . . ." He hesitated, and the question came out in a whisper. "The possibility exists that there could be larger ones?"

"As a matter of fact," Spock agreed, readily confirming Kirk's worst imaginings, "the planet-bound Boqus theorized from specimens they observed and far-distant radiation they recorded that exceptionally mature jawandas could grow considerably larger."

"How big," the captain queried masochistically, "is 'considerably'?" He was still trying to adjust to the information that the continent-sized energy-eater trailing them was but a midget of its kind.

"Hivar suggests without humor that you use your imagination, Captain. Theoretically, there *is* no upper limit. There are no physiological restraints on a jawanda's growth, and nothing is known of their age. Hivar goes on to say that there is no reason to suppose that, barring a collision with a star, a jawanda could not grow to the size of a sun. Though he reminds us that this is only theory."

"How encouraging," muttered a dazed McCoy.

"Never mind, Spock," declared Kirk suddenly. "I have no desire to tangle with anything even half the size of that old recorded supergiant, whether the Boquian mechanism can shove it around or not. But it will take something that size, which can demonstrate its power, to make us abandon this catch. Because I'm not sure which would be worse—fighting off such an antagonist or starting this hunt all over again, from the beginning." He looked forward.

"Mr. Arex, maintain maximum resolution on all long-range scanners."

"Yes, sir," the navigator replied tersely.

"Lieutenant Uhura, I want you to engage your own long-range detectors and initiate a full-spectrum sweep in the region immediately astern, with regular adjustments to scan every second of sky."

"Monitoring wave sweep, sir," she declared several minutes later.

Kirk's thoughts then turned inward, brooding on ominous possibilities as he studied the viewscreen. Five thousand kilometers of thin organism rippled slowly aft. Listening to the steady, powerful bursts of energy which still sounded over the muted speakers, he considered the history of man's efforts to turn amplified ears to the stars. Little had any of those ancient scientists realized, when they'd fought to make sense of the strange pops and crackles and hums, that among that stellar babble might be the cry of a troubled child.

"It will not be long at our present speed, Captain," announced Spock encouragingly, "before we enter the first fringe star-clusters along our return path into the Milky Way. According to the information imparted by the Boqus, this should be enough to discourage any pursuit."

"How can it be so sure?" wondered McCoy. "The risk of permanent imprisonment, or even death, wouldn't be enough to dissuade a lot of human parents from trying to rescue their offspring."

Spock eyed him reprovingly. "You are anthropomorphizing, Doctor. We cannot ascribe even faintly human or Vulcan motivations to these creatures. They lie outside the boundaries of familiar xenobiology. Besides, it is likely that they reproduce asexually, which renders the parent-child relationship absurd."

McCoy stared at the viewscreen. "I only hope you're right, Spock."

Days passed during which the captured jawanda continued to emit regular cries. It showed no sign of weakening. On the contrary, as they drew near the outer fringe of the galaxy, the outbursts intensified slightly.

Listening closely, Kirk sought to identify something recognizable as a cry for help in those dips and squeaks of electromagnetic radiation. He failed, with a consistency that pleased him. The purely electronic wail enabled him to regard the thing behind the ship as an elemental force of nature instead of a living creature which might possibly possess a glimmer of the thoughts and emotions Spock insisted it did not.

"Captain," Uhura announced slowly, "I think I've got something." Amazing, Kirk mused, how much was contained in that single word, "something."

"It's at the extreme end of my scanners," she went on. "It may be nothing at all, but we're still in intergalactic space, and I thought that—"

"Of course," Kirk cut her off impatiently. "You've isolated it?"

"Yes. It's definitely not a stable intergalactic phenomenon. At first I thought it might be a very small radio nebula—it's definitely generating strong radio pulses. But it wanders about too much. I can't tell yet whether it's moving toward us or not, but . . ." She gazed significantly at Kirk.

"Keep monitoring it, Lieutenant," Kirk instructed her. "Mr. Spock, initiate intensive sensor scan along the coordinates being studied by Lieutenant Uhura. Let me know what you turn up."

"Very good, Captain."

"How much longer before we reach a star with sufficient gravity to hold a jawanda?"

Spock checked library information. "At least another three days at our present speed, Captain, possibly four. Naturally, that time would shrink rapidly at warp-four or warp-five."

Kirk spent a few moments ruminating on their options. "Contact the Boqus, Mr. Spock. Inquire if there's *any* chance, however slight, that the six moons could attain a faster speed."

A short wait, and Spock replied, "Hivar says no, Captain. We might as well abandon the creature now to retain control of the mechanism. The Lactrans are again arguing strenuously. They are willing to jeopardize their lives in order to return the jawanda to Lactra."

"That's noble of them," snorted McCoy, "but what about the rest of us who don't care to stick our necks out so they can add that"—and he gestured toward the screen—"electrified tinfoil to their zoo?"

"Easy, Bones," Kirk advised him, "we're not at that point yet. It may turn out to be just a false alarm."

The alarm was ringing louder the following day. Whatever was generating those powerful pulsations was doing so at a steadily rising rate.

"Estimated distance to the object, Lieutenant Uhura?"

She checked her readouts. "It's still hard to say, sir. The strength of the emissions, and by inference the distance separating us, could vary greatly depending on the size of the creature."

A sinking feeling ran through him. "You're convinced the signals are emanating from another jawanda, then?"

She hesitated. "The differences in the type of pulsations are significant, sir, but the frequencies are identical. Say better than fifty-fifty that it's another."

"An inaccurate observation, Lieutenant," Spock commented mildly. He would never cease to be fascinated by the human tendency to offer approximations in place of absolute figures in matters scientific.

"Let it go now, Jim," urged McCoy. "We'll circle far around and find another specimen for the Lactrans."

"Not yet, Bones. This new arrival—if that's what it turns out to be—may only be curious. Maybe it's not coming in response to the other's cries. We've come too far and worked too hard to give up easily. Remember our obligation to the Lactrans."

"Remember our obligation to the ship."

Kirk threw him a sharp look. "I'm fully aware of that, Bones."

McCoy turned away. "Sorry, Jim . . . Forgot myself for a moment."

"Forget it. We're all operating under stress. The possibility of fighting something that could envelop a few Earths is enough to rattle anyone's thoughts."

What was troubling Kirk was not the chance that another jawanda was the source of the new emissions—that already seemed fairly certain. It was the fact that the mysterious generator was continuing to gain on them—without an intercept angle. It was approaching rapidly from almost dead astern.

That meant that at least some jawandas were capable of moving at speeds above warp-three. Given that, there was no reason to suppose that one of the creatures might not be able to exceed warp-eight—the maximum emergency velocity of the *Enterprise*.

If Spock was right and the jawanda was purely a superefficient energy-converting organism, then it should be as incapable of experiencing the desire for vengeance as it was of feeling parental concern. In that case, it didn't really matter how fast certain jawandas could travel.

On the other hand, if Spock was wrong and the creatures were able to feel higher emotions . . . Kirk refused to consider the possibilities. Long before that he would have to make other decisions.

"It is obvious that we have two choices." Spock pontificated from the science station. "We can retreat at top speed toward the safety of stellar gravity, abandoning our capture in the process, and hope this will be sufficient to discourage any pursuit. Or we can continue as we are and hope that the creature closing on us will become disinterested, give up, or prove unable to hamper our movements."

"Neither of which is an especially appealing alternative," Kirk commented distastefully.

"I concur, Captain. With your permission, therefore, I should like to initiate what is known in human vernacular as a decoy action."

"Decoy?" McCoy echoed. "What are we going to do—have the ship's nonmetallic fabricators make up an artificial jawanda?"

"No, Doctor. I doubt that a visual simulacrum would have any effect. These creatures obviously detect one another by means of their emissions. Sight would be a superfluous sense in the void."

"Go ahead, Mr. Spock," Kirk urged. "Whatever you have in mind can't worsen our situation."

"I hope it can better it, Captain." He faced Communications. "Lieutenant Uhura, have you a precise record of the pattern of the captured jawanda's output?"

"Many, Mr. Spock. Its broadcast has remained consistent, and I've had more than enough time to examine its wave generation in depth."

"How complex is the pattern?" Kirk began to have an inkling of his first officer's plan.

"Not very . . . Oh, I understand. I don't see why our equipment couldn't generate a similar signal, Mr. Spock."

It didn't take long for an emergency engineering and tech crew to ready one of the cruiser's shuttlecraft for a highspeed deep-space run. Lieutenant M'ress supervised the modification of the shuttle's communications equipment, which involved installation of components which would permit the tiny craft to channel far more power than normal into its communications instrumentation.

The hasty alterations completed, the shuttlecraft hangar was cleared and the remotely guided craft launched away at its maximum acceleration. There followed a period of anxious waiting for the shuttle to reach a decent distance from the *Enterprise*. All the while, the source of new radiation drew nearer and nearer.

"Time enough," Spock announced, looking up from his readouts. "Begin broadcasting immediately, Lieutenant Uhura." As she acknowledged, Spock faced the command chair.

"Utilizing the full broadcast power of the *Enterprise*'s communications equipment, Captain, as rebroadcast out into space through the shuttlecraft's modified instruments, we should be able to produce considerably more noise than our captive does. Hopefully, the pursuing jawanda will consider the shuttlecraft's broadcast as the distress call of a second one of its kind. We are hoping that it will opt to aid the louder of the two calls."

Spock's logic, as always, seemed sound. Uhura adjusted her controls, and soon a second jawanda cry for help was filling space, one twice as powerful as the first.

"Captain?"

Kirk looked toward the navigator. "What is it, Mr. Arex?"

"I believe the second creature is changing its course. Indications point to—"

A rhythmic screech drowned him out. Hastily Uhura adjusted her instrumentation once again, and the volume dropped.

"What happened, Lieutenant?"

Uhura studied her gauges and sensor feedbacks. "Apparently our captive has increased the strength of its own radiations, sir. The level is considerably above what we are rebroadcasting through the shuttlecraft."

"Second object shifting direction again, Captain," the soft-spoken Edoan announced. "It is once again following—and it appears to have increased its speed."

Kirk wondered if they could fool their still unknowable pursuer another time, wondered if it felt anger at deception or was simply continuing to follow the strongest signal.

"Increase broadcast power, Lieutenant," Spock directed her.

"I'm sorry, Mr. Spock." Uhura threw him a look of helplessness. "We're broadcasting at maximum strength now. In fact, we can hold this level only another twenty minutes before components begin to melt."

"That won't be necessary, Uhura," Kirk told her. "Maintain power, though. Mr. Sulu, vary the course of the shuttlecraft—random pattern, simulate erratic behavior. Let's see if the second jawanda reacts to that."

"Course still unchanged, sir," Arex reported five minutes later. "Still in pursuit."

Kirk sighed and faced the science station. "It was a good idea, Spock—only it didn't quite work. If we could put more power into our decoy broadcast . . ." He shook his head slowly.

Spock's head tilted at the odd angle Kirk had come to

recognize often these past weeks. "Before abandoning the idea, the Lactrans wish to make an attempt of their own." He looked around. "And they want your approval before they do so . . . Doctor."

"Me?" McCoy was taken aback. "Why mine?"

"Because what they wish to try involves a certain amount of discomfort for every member of the crew."

McCoy turned pensive and finally said, " 'Discomfort' is a mild word. Do they think whatever they have in mind could be dangerous?"

A pause while Spock relayed: "They do not think so, Doctor, but admit that they cannot be sure. It is a new thought of theirs, something never before tried, because the opportunity to do so with minds like ours has not previously existed."

Kirk wasn't sure he liked the sound of that. Still, he had to consider the enigmatic threat closing on them every second.

"Bones?"

McCoy looked askance at Kirk. "This is crazy, Jim. How can I estimate the danger when I have no idea what they're going to try?" He turned to Spock again. "You're sure you've got your 'conceptualizations' straight, Spock? They did say 'discomfort' and not 'disablement'?"

"Quite sure, Doctor."

McCoy shrugged. "Then I suppose I can't object."

"All right, Spock," Kirk said warily, "tell them go ahead." He activated the general intercom and explained to the crew as well as he was able what was about to happen. He clicked off finally. "Tell them also that the second we receive any indication that anyone is being seriously affected, they'll have to stop whatever they're doing."

"They understand and agree, Captain," the first officer informed him instantly.

Silence followed. Kirk sat tensely in his chair, waiting for something to happen. When minutes passed and nothing did, an impatient, nervous McCoy asked, "When are they going to begin, Spock? If they don't hurry up . . ."

"They already have, Doctor. They are proceeding slowly, so as to be certain they do not hurt anyone—including themselves. Don't you feel it?"

"Feel what, Spock? I don't . . ." Something was whispering inside his head. Irritated, he tried to shake it off, but, like a persistent mosquito, it refused to go away. Instead, it intensified slightly, still irritating but not quite painful. The internal humming became a headache, then a throbbing behind his eyes, relentless and unresolved. He started to speak to Spock, but decided not to when he saw that the first officer was sitting rigidly at attention. The more intensively McCoy tried to analyze the sensation, the more the ache increased.

"Captain," Uhura groaned, holding both hands to her temples, "how much longer does this go on? I can't stand it and monitor the sensors as well."

" 'Discomfort' was the right term, Spock," the captain admitted, wincing. "It's not quite as bad as a migraine—but I hope we're not supposed to endure it too much longer. What are they doing?"

Spock's reply came slowly, since he was speaking under the dual stress of translating and this new mental strain. "They say it will grow no worse. As to the activity itself, the proposal occurred to them when it became clear how limited was the broadcast capability of the *Enterprise*. They are surprised that we did not recognize the presence on board of several hundred additional generators of modulated electrical impulses. The mind of every crew member is such a transmitter.

"It is an ability of all Lactrans to serve as a focusing point for such energies, much as a magnifying lens concentrates sunlight. They are presently utilizing the generative capacity of every mind on board to beam a simulacrum of the jawanda's distress call to the same point in space as the shuttlecraft. The combination of the shuttle's own broadcast and this mental projection may be strong enough to—"

Arex, who alone of the bridge complement seemed relatively unaffected by the Lactrans' activities, made both aliens and science officer into seers: "Captain—our pursuers are changing course once again. They are definitely inclining toward the retreating shuttlecraft, by a significant number of degrees."

Kirk's response struggled through the pounding in his brain. "Lieutenant Uhura, what reaction from our captive?"

"No . . . change, sir," she replied, her expression contorted from the effort of interpreting her readouts. "It's maintaining the same level of broadcast intensity. Maybe it's reached its limits."

"Still continuing on a divergent course, sir," Arex reported. "They are definitely headed away from us now and are beginning to fall behind."

"Thank you, Mr. Arex. Continue close sensor scan on—" He broke off, rehearing the navigator's recent words. "A moment ago you said 'pursuers,' Lieutenant. There are more than one?"

"It appears likely, Captain. I am tracking three to four sources sufficiently far apart to preclude any other explanation. I thought at first that the one very large creature might be generating signals from various regions of its body, but it seems now that the distance between sources is too great. All, however, are angling toward the shuttlecraft."

Kirk wondered if the relief was visible in his expression. To have one of the monsters closing on them was frightening enough. Three or four . . . "Mr. Sulu, how long before we reach the gravity well of a strong sun?"

There was no formal "border" to the home galaxy, of course. Distances between suns were so unimaginably vast that the term was more suggestive than descriptive. But, compared to the reach of intergalactic space, the gravityless habitat of the jawanda, the region they were about to enter was rich in stars and jawanda-pinioning gravity.

"Twenty-two minutes ship time, Captain," the helmsman finally responded. Kirk's anxiety lightened a little at that encouraging report.

"Keep a close scan on our decoyed pursuit, Mr. Arex. Let me know the instant they show any sign of changing course again. Mr. Spock, can the Lactrans sustain their broadcast for the requisite time remaining?"

"They reply that they will have to, Captain."

Kirk nodded understandingly, his gaze shifting back to the long-range scanner view now on the main screen. It showed only dark, empty space aft of the imprisoned jawanda. For another twenty minutes it had to stay that way.

They crept along at warp-three, Kirk chafing at the restrictions of the Boquian mechanism which forced them to travel at far below normal cruising speed. As the Lactrans had promised, the throbbing grew no worse, but neither did it decrease.

Glancing around the bridge, he saw that Uhura, Sulu, Arex, and even Spock were beginning to show signs of real strain. He heard his own discomfort reflected in the concern in McCoy's voice. The doctor walked over, massaging his temples with slow circular hand motions.

"Jim, even a headache can produce damage if it's allowed to continue untreated. I can't prescribe treatment for something like this."

Kirk checked the official chronometer set in one arm of his chair. "A few minutes more, Bones. We can survive a few minutes more."

Then they would enter the vicinity of NGC 7332. An unremarkable M3 star, hitherto unvisited by anything more complex than a Federation long-range mapping drone. But the cold orange-red giant was a nearing haven for the *Enterprise*, a ten-million-kilometer-wide beacon whose gravity was now akin to the fire with which primitive man had frightened off pursuit by hulking furry carnivore.

He berated himself for falling into the trap McCoy so often entangled himself in, ascribing familiar characteristics to the unfamiliar—in this case the jawanda. That inexplicably efficient inhabitant of deep space was neither furry nor carnivorous.

A shout came from the normally placid navigator's station.

"What is it, Mr. Arex?" he asked quickly. "Have the signal sources changed course again?"

"No, sir." Something in the Edoan's voice sent a tremor along Kirk's nerves. "I have detected a new source of radio emissions. It is larger . . . than all the others combined."

"Bearing?"

"Directly for us, sir . . . warp . . . warp-*seven*!"

"Time to gravitational tangency, Mr. Sulu?"

"Three minutes twenty seconds remaining, Captain," the helmsman shot back.

"The new source is far off, Captain. We should just slip into the safe zone before it reaches us."

"Recalculate for precision," Kirk ordered, thinking in astonishment that that was one phrase he never had expected to direct to his first officer.

"Inconclusive, Captain," Spock replied immediately. "Distance undeterminable at this time."

"Source accelerating!" Arex gasped in disbelief. "Nearing warp-eight!"

"Less than two minutes to go!" shouted Sulu. "Plotting minimum possible orbital radii to maximize gravity effect."

Still nothing on the rear scanners. Where was the apparition? "Emergency magnification on long-range sensors, Mr. Sulu," he directed the helmsman.

Sulu acknowledged, and once more the retreating emptiness jumped perceptibly—to show only a narrower view of nothingness.

"Sixty seconds, Captain."

"Warp-nine, sir," the Edoan said dazedly. "Moving up to warp-ten."

Whatever was after them was now traveling faster than any Federation vessel in existence. It must be converting energy at an incredible rate.

Equally unbelievably, Kirk suddenly felt better than he had in some time. Then he realized that the throbbing in his skull had vanished.

"The Lactrans are aware that their ruse is not discouraging this new, nearer threat, Captain. They see no reason for continuing their broadcast, especially since one of them is verging on unconsciousness and they feel we may soon require our full abilities."

Kirk had time to feel ashamed. While he'd been suffering along with everyone else during the amplified mental broadcast, he'd neglected to consider what toll it might be taking on the amplifiers—the Lactrans themselves.

"Fifteen seconds, sir." Sulu was counting down. "Eleven, ten, nine . . ."

"NGC 7332 in sight on forward scanners, Captain," announced Spock reassuringly. Sulu continued to count off eternities.

"Four, three, two—"

An explosive shriek of outrage and disappointment erupted from every bridge speaker despite Uhura's desperate attempt to reduce it to bearable intensity. Sparks flared from various seals and seams in the communications console, and a small explosion blew out several gauges, the concussion throwing her from her seat. McCoy was at her side in an instant.

"Entering the strong gravitational pull of NGC 7332, Captain," Spock informed him solemnly.

Kirk didn't hear him. He was still seeing something which had appeared for a brief second on the viewscreen, details of its appearance uncertain because the overloaded scanners had automatically blanked themselves out immediately after contacting it.

For an instant something gargantuan had drifted there, filling the screen with discharges of purple and crimson energy whose diameter exceeded that of half a hundred Earths.

Then the scanners came on again and the sun-shape was gone, frustrated, soaring in angry desperation back to the gravitational void of the abyss . . .

"Status, Mr. Spock?" Kirk asked slowly.

"We still retain control of our captive," the science officer assured him. "It seems to have ceased all broadcasting. Undoubtedly it realizes that it has passed the gravitational point of no return."

Kirk swiveled his chair. "Lieutenant?"

Uhura was back on her feet and studying her damaged station with professional concern. "I'm all right, sir. That last outburst—overwhelming." She smiled at McCoy. "Thanks, Doctor." McCoy nodded and moved away, still keeping an inconspicuous eye on her to make sure she was as stable as she claimed to be.

"Hivar the Toq," Spock continued, "states that the mechanism is undamaged and still operating well. We should have no difficulty in retaining control of the captive all the way back to Lactra. The Lactrans are tending to themselves. They are extremely wearied, and the youngster expresses some concern. Both adults are extremely pleased with us. We did not panic, as lower animals would have, and permit the jawanda to escape."

"I'm glad we came up to their expectations," replied Kirk drily. "Continue on course to Lactra at our present speed, Mr. Sulu."

"Aye, sir . . . with pleasure."

"How's your headache, Bones?"

"Completely gone, Jim. No after effects, either." McCoy looked thoughtful. "It occurs to me that the Lactrans' ability to focus the mental output of many minds into various wavelengths could be a powerful weapon."

Kirk agreed. "True, Bones, but I don't think we have to worry about that. Not only aren't the Lactrans a belligerent race, but they'd hardly bother to involve themselves in the petty private squabbles of such primitive creatures as ourselves." He grinned and looked toward the navigator's station.

"Mr. Arex."

"Yes, Captain?"

"Before we entered the gravity well of NGC 7332, I thought we had a momentary view of our pursuer—certainly not extensive enough a glimpse to tell anything. You were monitoring the long-range sensors aft at the time. Did they succeed in recording sufficient information to give us an idea of its size?"

"They did, sir," the Edoan announced slowly. "Quite incredible. It appears that even the Boqus' estimations of the jawanda's upper growth limits were on the conservative side. Were our last pursuer so inclined, and able to withstand the radiation, it could have enveloped Sol."

"No wonder they exist only in intergalactic space," Kirk whispered after a moment's reflection. "They need the room."

McCoy was trying to adjust to the existence of a living organism that size. He could not, naturally. It was beyond the visualizing ability of the human mind. One could write a one and follow it with nine zeros and call it a billion, but the sum could not really be comprehended.

So it was with their final nemesis, an unimaginable colossus turned at the last possible instant by a star trillions of times greater in mass than itself.

From NGC 7332 the journey back to Lactra was mercifully uneventful. Their captive jawanda, now revealed as a true midget of its kind, occasionally testified to its continued health by emitting outbursts of subdued electronic noise.

But it somehow comprehended its position. It made no

fresh assaults on the *Enterprise* and did not attempt to flee the gravitational bond of the octahedral cage.

At warp-three the trip back to Lactra took much longer than the journey out, and Kirk and the rest of the crew luxuriated in every minute of it. Eventually, though, the jawanda was installed in polar orbit around that strange world, to circle it forever like some huge foil-shaped moon.

Now fully recovered, the two adult Lactrans and their boisterous offspring were transported back to the surface, though not before confessing that the expedition had enriched their knowledge as well as their zoo.

Thus, free of further obligation to the elephantine superminds, Kirk was able with inexpressible relief to give the order to return at warp-six to Boqu.

Everyone experienced a few moments of apprehension as the *Enterprise* once again left the safety of the galactic arm, apprehension engendered by the fear that a vengeful cluster of mature jawandas might be lingering to ambush them.

But, for all their great size and efficiency at converting energy, the jawandas were the most elemental of organisms, from a mental standpoint. If they possessed minds, these seemed not extensive enough to include memories. The return to Boqu was as peaceful as the race to NGC 7332 had been panicky.

Hivar the Toq and the marvelous Boquian mechanism were returned to the planet's surface, which was still undergoing a burst of activity, thanks to the solution to the pandemic discovered by Dr. McCoy's team.

There was even a remote chance, Hivar assured Kirk, that Boqu might one day apply for admission as the Federation's farthest-flung member—an eventuality which could be extremely discomforting to such as the Klingons and Romulans.

There was much more to be learned from the sociable Boqus than from the aloof inhabitants of Lactra. In fact, the entire geology section volunteered en masse to remain on Boqu to study the incredible silicon-based ecology. A reluctant Kirk had to deny their applications, for there was no telling when another Federation ship might reach the distant, isolated world.

Leaving the orange-and-mauve storm clouds of Boqu, they returned again to the comforting light of the home galaxy. It was as they were traversing the final stretches of intergalactic void that Spock looked up from his station, wondering aloud.

"One thing continues to prey on my mind, Captain."

"Not fatally, I hope," McCoy quipped.

Spock continued, ignoring the doctor. "We were astonished at the size of the jawanda we captured, only to subsequently discover that it was but an immature specimen of its kind. This was emphasized by the apparent size of its unsuccessful rescuers, who themselves shrank into smallness by comparison with that somewhat larger—"

" 'Somewhat larger,' " McCoy murmured derisively.

"—last pursuer," the first officer concluded, with an admonishing stare at the *Enterprise*'s chief physician. "It continues to occur to me that that final colossus might have its own masters out in the depths of the abyss."

That conception was sufficiently stupefying to silence even McCoy. Together with Kirk, he stared at the view brought close by the ship's after scanners. It was hundreds of thousands of light-years to the nearest pinpoint of light— the outlying stars of Nubecula Major. True, the size of their last pursuer had been unimaginable . . . but what was more unimaginable than the vastness of the intergalactic gulf?

"I don't know, Mr. Spock," Kirk mused softly. "Until we encountered the jawandas I'd always been accustomed to thinking of living beings in terms of meters, or, rarely, in thousands of meters. The jawandas have changed that to thousands, maybe hundreds of thousands, maybe even millions of kilometers." He gestured toward the viewscreen. "Perhaps someday we'll encounter creatures out there who'll dwarf the greatest jawanda, and then we'll have to grow used to measuring organisms with light-years instead of metrics."

That was a bit extreme for McCoy. "Now think a minute, Jim, about the impossibility of a living being a light-year in length. Just consider . . . consider . . ." His voice trailed off. "On second thought, I'm not going to consider it right now. One lingering headache in the past couple of months is plenty. I think it's time to consider an extended session in the

Rec Room." He left the bridge, the doors of the turbolift closing behind him.

But not before Kirk saw that the doctor's final speculative gaze was focused on the screen and the darkly ominous yet beckoning reaches of the fading intergalactic gulf.

STAR TREK
LOG NINE

**For Charlie Lippincott,
with admiration and friendship**

STAR TREK LOG NINE

Log of the Starship *Enterprise*
Stardates 5537.3–5537.9 Inclusive

James T. Kirk, Capt., USSC, FC, ret.
Commanding

transcribed by
Alan Dean Foster

At the Galactic Historical Archives
on Ursa Major Lacus
stardated 6111.3

For the Curator: JLR

BEM

(Adapted from a script by David Gerrold)

I

"Captain's log, stardate 5537.3."

Kirk directed his voice toward the log recorder as he settled himself more comfortably in the command chair. "The *Enterprise*, having concluded the Lactran affair and having returned officers Markel, Bryce, and Randolph to Starbase Sixteen Survey Headquarters, is proceeding according to directives on standard survey run." As Kirk shut off the recorder, he decided this mission wasn't *quite* standard.

With all ship's operations functioning smoothly, he was able to lean back and relax slightly. The small portable reader screen set into the left-hand chair arm was playing back an ancient history of Starfleet. Presently the screen displayed the half-legendary story of how one Matthew Jeffries first conceived of the Constitution Class vessels, of which the *Enterprise* was but one of many now.

Fascinating as the tale was, wreathed in myth and the uncertain garb of Terran history, Kirk soon found his mind wandering. He had originally intended to pause at Base 16 and add his own personal observations and comments to the report of the rescued survey team. Instead, he had to settle for submitting the appropriate taped report and excerpts from the ship's log. As usual, the completion of one mission meant that half a dozen more awaited the *Enterprise* in the backlog of Starfleet's central computer network. There were never enough ships, never adequate personnel available to handle the continually growing task of taking some of the mystery from newly discovered worlds.

The Federation's tireless drone probes, immune to fatigue, had recently located several previously unknown and closely packed systems of planets and satellites. These potential colony worlds required the kind of in-depth, and thorough, preliminary study only a major-class starship could provide. So the *Enterprise* was immediately dispatched to carry out routine observations.

At least, the journey would be as routine as one could expect with the opening up of several new worlds—each one filled with a googolplex of new problems and dangers and promises. There would be one other small break in routine— one minor alteration in assigned personnel. An extra, official observer had been added to the roster for the duration of the mission. What made him important was not that he was nonhuman, non-Vulcan, and even nonhumanoid, but that he was a representative of a recently contacted intelligent race.

The orders Kirk had received went on to explain that the Federation was going through a very delicate stage in its relations with the government of Commander Ari bn Bem, of the system of Pandro. The Pandronians had requested that a representative of theirs be permitted to observe a Federation crew carrying out precisely the type of mission the *Enterprise* had just been assigned.

Such simple requests could not be refused. According to his orders, both the Klingons and the Romulans had expressed an interest in deepening their ties with the Pandronians. Every opportunity should be taken to convince the Pandronians that their interests would best be served by a close alliance with the Federation, particularly since several Federation worlds existed in a strategic position relative to Pandro. What all that meant was that Pandro held a position of vital concern to several Federation worlds—but the official phrasing of spatial relationships was more, ah, realistic.

Federation DIPS—members of the Diplomatic Psychology Corps—were convinced that the Federation was gaining the upper hand in the battle for Pandronian influence—a battle that had to be augmented by the cooperation and aid of everyone in Starfleet. Captain Kirk was therefore directed to extend to Commander bn Bem all courtesies normally extended to an attached observer, with special regard for the precarious diplomatic situation, keeping in mind the need to . . .

Et cetera, et cetera.

Well, Kirk had it in mind, all right! The matter had been

foremost in his mind since that always underfoot, irritating, and occasionally downright rude Pandronian had come aboard. Unless something happened to change their visitor's attitude, Kirk feared that Federation-Pandronian relations could be severely damaged. He was also afraid that Commander bn Bem might be severely damaged. The list of angry complaints from insulted or challenged or otherwise provoked crew members was approaching critical mass.

He managed to shove the problem from his thoughts as he added a short entry to the log. The view now on the main screen—a handsome world of swirling white clouds and blue ocean—did much to blank out all thoughts of their obstreperous visitor.

"Captain's log, stardate 5537.3. We are taking up orbit around Delta Theta Three, a newly charted Class M planet—the last world on our current mission. The original drone scout reported the possible presence of aboriginal life forms on Delta Theta Three, life forms of undetermined intelligence and accomplishment.

"Upon entering orbit the *Enterprise* will proceed to carry out standard survey procedures and investigation, placing particular emphasis on a detailed study of the local sapient life form."

Kirk clicked off the machine as he rose, heading for the turbolift. The presence of even a marginally intelligent life form would be a most welcome conclusion to this expedition, which had been remarkable only for the mediocrity and unattractiveness of the worlds they had examined thus far.

And then there was the remarkable unattractiveness of the singularly trying Commander bn Bem. The Pandronian was one guest Kirk would be glad to be rid of. As he rode the lift toward the Transporter Room, he broke out in a satisfied smile at the thought of the moment when Commander bn Bem would be officially returned to the Pandronian mission at Starbase 13.

He came upon the rest of the initial landing party in the corridor leading to the Transporter Room—Sulu, and Spock, with Scott accompanying them.

"Anything new on your potential hosts, Captain?" Scott called to him.

"Sensors have located several possible groupings of aborigines, Scotty," Kirk informed them. "The xenologists are sure of one thing—Delta Theta Three isn't another world of superminds like Lactra. The natives here are definitely primitive. Bear in mind, gentlemen, that like all primitive peoples they may tend to spear first and think later. I want everyone to keep in mind that no unnecessary risks are to be taken, no matter how important the information in question." He indicated the compact, cylindrical instruments each man held.

"These monitoring devices have to be hand-planted close to a center of local activity, if we're going to get any long-term data on these people. That accomplished, we'll beam up. Study of flora and fauna, geological features, and the like can be best accomplished by specialized teams afterwards.

"Lieutenant Uhura will be tracking us throughout, and Mr. Kyle will be standing by." Chief Engineer Scott nodded reassuringly. "If there is trouble of any kind, beam up immediately. Don't try to be a hero, and don't place intelligence gathering above your own life." This last comment was directed, as usual, at Spock, who, as usual, took no notice.

As the door sensed their approach, it slid aside, admitting them to the Transporter Room. Entering, they started toward the transporter alcove—and froze. Chief Kyle was present, but not in his accustomed position behind the console. Instead, he stood to one side, uncertainly eyeing the creature who occupied his station. At the entrance of the captain and his companions, Kyle turned and threw Kirk a helpless look.

Kirk nodded once as he turned his attention to the console. The biped who stood behind it, fiddling with every control in reach, was more or less of human size. Resemblance to anything manlike faded rapidly after that. The creature was bulky, blue, and hirsute—all three characteristics amply apparent despite the concealing full-length uniform it wore. The interloper had also noted the entrance of the four officers and turned to bestow the toothy equivalent of a Pandronian grin on an unamused Kirk.

"Ah, Kirk Captain," he rumbled in a voice like a contrabassoon full of marbles, "welcome and greeting. Settings are almost complete."

For the moment Kirk elected to ignore the Pandronian's unauthorized manipulation of the transporter controls. And there was no reason to reprimand Kyle, who had only been following the orders regarding bn Bem. As honorary Federation commander, the visiting Pandronian had free run of the cruiser. The mounting stack of complaints back in Kirk's office attested to the extent to which bn Bem had exercised his privileges.

Ordered to stand aside by a "superior" officer, Kyle had done so. The transporter engineer would have his chance to report on this incident later. At the moment, it was the Pandronian's presence which concerned Kirk most.

"Commander bn Bem, exactly what are you doing here? I thought you would be down in Sciences, studying procedure as information on the world below is gathered."

bn Bem replied readily in the highly contemptuous manner which perfectly complemented his personality. It was almost, Kirk reflected, as if the Pandronian were granting them a gigantic favor by deigning to grace the *Enterprise* with his presence. "This One," bn Bem sneered, "has decided to accompany contact team for observation of Delta Theta surface."

Kirk ignored the tone of the envoy's voice. He had learned these past days to tune it out. Nevertheless, he couldn't keep all trace of irritation from his reply. "Commander bn Bem," he reminded the other with as much control as he could muster, "you were assigned to this ship in an 'attached observer' status. Yet you've spent the past several planetary circumnavigations holed up in your quarters—when you weren't intruding for 'observation' into the private quarters of my crew. You haven't made anything like a detailed study of our survey methods—until now, it seems, when we are about to deal with a world that may very well sport a hostile primitive culture."

bn Bem's answer took the form of a controlled, basso chirp, made softly, but just loud enough for Kirk and the others to hear. "Patience . . . every planet is dangerous to the ignorant." Now speaking in a normal conversational tone, he resumed. "This One has decided that the nexus is now. Must now observe workings of starship and crew. This One is not impressed by outside recommendations for study time. A teacher is not instructed by students."

"You've had ample opportunity to 'observe workings' both

on board and on-surface during our last several planetfalls—at all times in comparative safety. This beam-down is not for the casual observer, especially one as diplomatically sensitive as you know you are. It could be hazardous and—"

"I am prepared," bn Bem countered simply.

Kirk started to say something, turned, then muttered to his first officer. "Mr. Spock, I don't like this at all. Diplomatic relations could be endangered if anything happens to this—this—to Commander bn Bem while he's our guest."

"It is not merely political considerations that dictate our actions, Captain," Spock reminded him. "There is the fact that the Pandronians are also very advanced in certain exotic areas of medicine and biology. There is much we can learn from them—much that Starfleet would rather we learned than the Klingons, say. And remember—orders expressly stated that Commander bn Bem be given anything he requested."

"Within reason," Kirk added. "But I don't think this request to join the landing party is reasonable."

"Starfleet may feel otherwise."

Kirk started to offer further objection, but found Spock's reminder inarguable. He let out a frustrated, heartfelt sigh and turned back to their guest. He'd make one last try.

"Commander bn Bem, this is not going to be a pleasure excursion. I really cannot, in clear conscience, permit you to beam down to this planet with us. You understand my position, I'm sure."

"Understanding it is," bn Bem replied, "but dirty conscience if required. This One is adamant and bystanding to accompany on landing."

Kirk growled back, wondering at the Pandronian's perverse preferences. "This is an odd time to be adamant."

There wasn't much Kirk could do about it, except say no—and that could undo all the courtesy they had so painfully extended to bn Bem thus far. "All right," he finally grumbled, "let's go. There's a world waiting for us." He stomped toward the transporter alcove.

"Scotty, if you'll set—"

bn Bem interrupted him even as the chief engineer was moving to the console. bn Bem was an accomplished interrupter. "Waste not the time. This One has already controls set, Mr. Scotty."

"Mr. Scotty" eyed the Pandronian distrustfully and proceeded to make an elaborate, overthorough inspection of the settings in question. Hard squints and florid gestures notwithstanding, he was finally compelled to look toward the alcove and nod slowly.

"Everythin' appears to be okay, Captain," he announced. "The coordinates are locked in on the preselected touchdown site, and everythin' else looks proper."

bn Bem let out a snort of satisfaction, which no one could fail to hear—least of all Scott—before taking his place in the alcove next to Kirk, Spock, and Sulu. "Time waste," he muttered disgustedly. His human companions resolutely ignored him.

They were joined a moment later by Scott as Kyle assumed the position behind the transporter console. Kirk checked to make certain everyone still held the important automatic monitoring devices, then nodded toward the console.

"Energize, Chief."

The room faded around them. . . .

Delta Theta Three was a name devoid of planetary personality, but the little group was soon to discover the world so designated was well equipped with same.

All at once five roughly cylindrical forms of glowing particles appeared near the shore of a lake and commenced to coalesce.

The lake itself was covered with brown scum and riotous blue growths, shading in color almost to black in places. Equally bloated vegetation thrived in the swampy region draining into the lake. A meandering stream entered the lake to the right of the rapidly solidifying figures, the water drifting with infinite slowness. Black and brown cypresslike trees, long creepers, and twisting vines occupied much of the open space between the larger boles. But despite the luxuriant growth, there was an absence of grass and ground cover, giving the jungle an underlying appearance of desolation.

The few open, meadowed spaces were muddy and unwholesome-looking. In contrast to the somewhat ominous landscape, the cries of innumerable tiny climbers and other hidden creatures sounded merrily from within the thickly overgrown areas.

The five cylinder-shapes became more distinct, added detail and resolution, and turned into the five explorers transported from the *Enterprise*. Something caused a split-second delay in the final transformation of each figure. Scott resolved first, stumbling slightly as he did so on the soft, sloping shoreline. Sulu appeared next to him, stumbling awkwardly enough to fall momentarily to his knees.

bn Bem was next. The Pandronian actually materialized a full meter above the shore, which did not affect him as the slight difference had affected Scott and Sulu. His legs instinctively extended the additional meter to allow him a gentle setdown. Once established on the ground, those elastic limbs retracted to their normal length. No one saw the startling adaptation take place.

Kirk and Spock completed the arrival of the landing party. They rematerialized at a similar distance above the water. Having neither extendable legs, nor wings, the two looked both confused and stunned as they dropped, making a pair of undignified splashes. Fortunately the water was only chest deep.

As the only one of the arrivals with a sound footing on land, bn Bem rushed into the water to aid the struggling Kirk and Spock in regaining their footing. Kirk had already suspected their guest of having a many-layered personality, but a multilayered torso was something no one could have anticipated.

The Pandronians were a *very* new race to Federation biologists. Consequently, neither the captain, nor the rapidly righting Spock—much less Sulu or Scott—took note that under the murky surface Commander bn Bem's lower half detached itself from his upper torso with all the ease and naturalness of a shuttle leaving the *Enterprise*'s hangar.

While the creature's upper half made arm motions to aid the floundering Kirk, the lower half swam busily around behind the captain and proceeded to remove his phaser and communicator. These devices were immediately and efficiently replaced with well-made copies. Then the substitution was carried out on Spock.

Above, bn Bem—half of him, anyway—entended an arm as Kirk regained his balance. "Assistance is offered," he said, with barely concealed distaste.

Kirk and his first officer exchanged glances, then Kirk looked back at their guest. "Thanks just the same, Commander. We'll manage."

bn Bem imitated a human shrug, one of his newly acquired gestures. "As you choose." As he turned to leave the water, his lower half reattached itself to the upper. It was an intact and familiar Pandronian who emerged from the lake.

Kirk and Spock struggled out of the plant-choked stagnant water, both completely unaware that anything untoward had taken place. If they had felt a slight twinge or two, they might have looked more closely at the slight bulges in the Pandronian's sample pouch, dangling loosely from one hip. The pouch looked full, which was odd if one considered they hadn't been here long enough to do much sampling.

Kirk choked back the thousand or so suggestions that sprang immediately to the tip of his tongue and contented himself with saying, "In the future, Commander bn Bem, you will leave the operation of the transporter to Mr. Scott, Mr. Kyle, or one of the regular members of the transporter crew."

"Is response to offer of aid," bn Bem murmured. "Typical." He seemed ready to add a few additional choice observations, but was interrupted himself for a change.

"Captain!"

Kirk looked at the anxious expression on his chief engineer's face. "What's the matter, Scotty?" He shook water from his arms and began stripping the clinging water plants from his tunic, hoping that soggy mess didn't contain anything likely to bite, cut, or otherwise make a nuisance of itself at some future date.

"Maybe nothing, Captain," Scott replied, "but Lieutenant Uhura reports some very unusual activity in our general vicinity."

Wonderful! They had barely touched down, and already they'd gotten drenched to the skin and were now confronted with something else unexpected. He took a couple of steps and hefted the open communicator.

"What kind of activity, Lieutenant?"

Uhura spoke from her position as commander-in-charge, leaning forward toward the con pickup. "Lieutenant Arex has been tracking what appears to be a mobile nonnetwork sensory stasis. It's still very small," she added after looking for confirmation to Arex seated at Navigation, "and it's several thousand kilometers west of your present position."

Kirk frowned. "Say again, Lieutenant?"

Uhura's voice was only slightly distorted, thanks to the ever efficient communicator. "It resembles a ship's sensor field, but there's nothing detectable like a scanning grid or other central point of reference."

Kirk digested this information, his concern mitigated by the distance involved. "You said it was mobile, Lieutenant. How mobile?"

"Lieutenant Arex speaking, sir," came the Edoan navigator's crisp tones. "Brownian movement only—no discernible direction and no hint of a guiding force."

"Most odd," Spock commented from nearby. "The implication is that there is something else on this world beyond aborigines. One would have to suspect something intelligent, yet nothing of the kind was reported in the initial survey." He shook his head. "It hardly seems likely the probes would have missed something we have detected so soon after arrival."

Kirk decided to ignore the implication, for the present. As long as whatever it was presented no immediate threat, they would concentrate on the task at hand. But he could no more stifle his curiosity than could Spock.

"It might be a very low-lying atmospheric anomaly, Mr. Spock. We've encountered other climatic phenomena before which have superficially resembled the activities of something sentient. And keep in mind that a drone probe isn't the most exacting observer. Detailed examination of a world is our business."

"None of which I had forgotten, Captain, and all of which I agree with."

Kirk turned back to the communicator. "Keep monitoring, Lieutenant Uhura. As a precaution only, put the ship on yellow alert. We'll continue the survey and monitor-emplacement mission for now, but notify us immediately if there is any change in the situation. An increase in the intensity of the field, a change of speed or direction, and especially anything that might indicate the field is under the control of intelligence—anything which hints that this might be other than a natural phenomenon. Kirk out."

He closed the communicator, breaking transmission, and handed it back to Scott, then indicated a path through the swampy meadows. "According to the computer plotting, the nearest life-form concentration—presumably the nearest native village—is this way. Let's get on with it."

Footing near the lake ranged "from the oleaginous to the obfuscatory," as Spock pointed out. That remark prompted Scott to redefine it in less precise but more colorful terms.*

The ground they encountered was messy, but not dangerous. There were no quicksands or sandpits. After some hard slogging, they found themselves moving through the forest and meadows with confidence, if not comfort.

"The rain-forest ecology is particularly interesting here," Spock commented absorbedly. "Life on this planet appears to be geologically younger than one would expect, given the age of this star and—"

A familiar voice interrupted, almost on cue. "Now urgent." bn Bem was studying his own tricorder. "Announce: This One is picking up readings which indicate a large group of intelligent-maybes life forms directly ahead."

Kirk held up a hand and called for a halt. "All right. We must take care not to be seen. Part of the prime directive—Hey!"

Commander bn Bem, ignoring all instructions and precautions, took off at high speed toward the hypothesized aborigines.

"Commander bn Bem, come back!" Kirk shouted. He started off after the retreating figure. "Scotty, Sulu—stay here."

"But, Captain—" Scott began.

Kirk cut him off curtly. "Orders, Scotty. Stand by. Come on, Spock." They both broke into a run in pursuit of the galloping Pandronian.

Their bulky guest appeared to be slowing as they crossed a swampy meadow. He vanished into a clump of tightly packed black trunks laced with interweaving vines.

---

*Transcriber's note: Ethnic highland terminology omitted here by curator's directive.

"He won't get far in there," Spock commented with satisfaction.

Kirk's reply was tense. "I hope not—for his own sake, as well as ours."

They headed for the dense thicket. Spock's estimate was reasonable as far as it went, but it did not go far enough to include a Pandronian.

bn Bem came up against a veritable dead end, a place where the small trees grew so close together that no one his size could possibly squeeze through. So the commander split into three parts, each of which was small enough to ooze through any of several openings in the wall of wood. Once successfully past the barrier the tripartite alien promptly reassembled himself and continued blithely on his composite way.

Unfortunately, neither Kirk nor Spock was capable of such bodily diffusion, nor was either aware that their recalcitrant guest was. They came to the same dead end, only in their case the description was fitting and final.

"He's gone," Kirk exclaimed, spinning to search every crevice, each potential hiding place.

But Spock continued to stare in disbelief straight ahead. "He could not have reversed his direction and slipped past us. To escape he had to go through here."

"That's impossible, Spock," Kirk said confidently, turning. "There's no way—" He stopped, moved to a gap in the trees the size of his chest, and stared through. He got only a brief glimpse of a blue bipedal figure disappearing into the distance. But unless this world was inhabited by blue, two-legged aborigines, Kirk had a pretty good idea who it was.

"There he is, all right." He frowned. "I don't know how he got through, but get through he did." Kirk took hold of the smallest trunk bordering the gap, got a good grip with both hands, braced himself, and gave a mighty heave. The tree moved about as much as one of the *Enterprise*'s warp-drive engines would under similar circumstances.

"Come on, Spock, we'll have to go around."

They began to circle the dense grove of saplings and vines, well aware that bn Bem could be far ahead by the time they found a way. Something else was puzzling Kirk.

"That Pandronian's actions just don't make sense. Never

mind for the moment how he got through that tight space. Right now I'd like to know *why* he did it. No sense, none at all."

"His actions might make sense to another Pandronian, Captain," the always pragmatic Spock suggested.

"I suppose so," Kirk confessed. "I've got to admit that one thing I've never found it easy to understand are the motivations of another species."

"Indeed?" exclaimed his first officer, with an inflection that indicated there was something more to his remark.

They detoured until they reached a section of the closely bunched trees which was penetrable. The forest closed in around them, shutting out the meadow and nearly doing likewise to the sun. As it turned out, the intertwined trunks were a disguised blessing, for the surface here was too soft and deep to permit rapid walking. They made much better time through the branches.

"I believe that is the direction, Captain." Spock said finally, when the trees showed signs of thinning. "Or possibly it was more to the left. Or perhaps—"

"We've lost him," Kirk finished succinctly. He was studying the small open area ahead, equally uncertain which way to go, when he heard a low murmur off to their left.

"That way—something over there."

Some frenetic crawling and running brought them to a wide clearing. They were about to move out into the open by jumping a fallen log when each man's hand went to his companion's shoulder and the two dropped down behind it.

They had seen the movement simultaneously.

"It would appear to be a native food-gathering party," Spock ventured, peering at the still-distant, slow-moving forms.

"Yes," agreed Kirk, "and part of the food they've gathered is Commander bn Bem."

At this distance it was difficult to obtain an accurate picture of the aborigines, but they appeared to stand just under an impressive three meters in height. Their skin was bright red; the overall impression was of reptilian, dull-witted, and probably belligerent creatures.

Commander bn Bem stood in their midst, looking decidedly unhappy. For the moment his usual haughtiness and air of self-satisfaction was completely absent.

Equally anxious minds studied the situation from more comfortable and more remote surroundings. Strange information was coming through on the *Enterprise*'s instruments.

"Lieutenant Uhura," Arex finally declared, "I'm picking up mounting activity on the surface. Initial indications point to an expansion of the still unidentified sensory anomaly."

Uhura nodded, glanced backwards. "Lieutenant M'ress, contact the landing party."

"Aye, aye, Lieutenant."

Scott's gaze shifted from the placid surface of the vegatation-choked lake to his communicator as it buzzed urgently.

"Scott here."

"Mr. Scott, where's the captain?"

"He's separated from us. Commander bn Bem ran off into the forest and—"

"Ran off into the forest?" came Uhura's startled echo.

"Yes. I know it's undiplomatic of me, but I say good riddance. However, the captain's not in a position to do so. He's responsible for that hairy— Anyway, he and Mr. Spock took off after our Pandronian charge. They're out in the brush somewhere. Sulu and I were ordered to remain here." He looked into the trees, staring in the direction the two senior officers had taken too many minutes ago.

"That was a while ago, and it doesn't look very friendly down here." He chewed his lower lip. "Have you tried contacting them directly since they disappeared?"

"Yes, we have. Neither the captain nor Mr. Spock acknowledges his communicator. Nor," Uhura added, "do they show up on the scanning grid. We can detect only one energy source, and it hasn't moved. That would be you and Sulu.

"It's their absence on the grid that really worries me, Commander Scott. The silence almost screams that their communicator responders have been disconnected. Also, we're picking up increased sensory activity."

"The large anomaly?"

"Yes. Nothing threatening. At least, it's as unthreatening as something that big and inexplicable can be." Her voice turned firm. "You're certain Mr. Spock went with the captain?"

"Aye, Lieutenant."

Her voice faded slightly as she apparently addressed someone on the bridge. Scott heard the order faintly. "Lieutenant Arex, initiate a detailed sensor scan for the captain and Mr. Spock, using Commander Scott's communicator pack as a center point." She directed her words to the pickup again.

"Landing party, prepare to beam up."

"Lieutenant Uhura," Scott countered, "Sulu and I could track down the captain and Mr. Spock from here."

"I'm sorry, Commander Scott," she replied. "You know standard procedure in a case like this—better than I do, I suspect. We've had no response from the missing men. We can't take additional chances without further information on their whereabouts and/or condition."

"We are talking about the *captain*," Scott fumed.

Uhura's voice rose, strained. "I know that, Commander." There was a pause, and when she spoke again her tone was quieter, though no less strained. "We have to follow orders, and regulations. An unresolved situation of this type on a new world, involving an unknown race of still indeterminate potential—and then there's that anomaly. No . . . stand by to beam up, Mr. Scott."

The chief engineer started to reply again. He outranked Uhura, but she was officially in charge as long as he remained on the surface. Besides, she made sense.

"Standing by," he told her tightly. "And—my apologies, lassie. You're right, of course."

If Uhura responded, he didn't hear it, because a faint fog was beginning to obscure vision and perception. The chief became a cluster of chromatically colored particle-wave energy, as did Sulu. The cluster faded, disappeared.

Nothing moved on the shore of the halcyon lake save a few small beetlelike things and one curious quasi lizard, whose attention had been momentarily focused on the incomprehensible apparitions. They were gone now and the creature's blank gaze turned back to the beetles. They were much more interesting, and comprehensible.

* * *

"We could rush them, Spock," Kirk surmised as he studied the size and number of aborigines surrounding the captive bn Bem, "but someone might get hurt. I'd rather it wasn't any of them, and I darn sure won't let it be one of us. Their weapons may be crude, but they're effective." He thought a moment. "Maybe we can do it the easy way, simply beam him and then ourselves out of here."

"A facile solution, Captain," concurred Spock.

Kirk brought out his communicator, flipped it open. "Kirk to *Enterprise* . . . Kirk to *Enterprise*."

Silence. He looked down at the compact instrument, listened hard. Even the barely audible low hum which indicated proper activation was absent. Carefully Kirk closed the top, then opened it again. "Kirk to *Enterprise*."

No hum, no reply—so he then began staring at the device. His particular personal communicator had been in his possession for some time. Only . . . this wasn't it. A glance over at Spock showed that his first officer was examining his own communicator.

"This isn't my communicator, Spock. I know every scratch and smudge on it, and they're all missing from this one."

"Nor is this one mine, Captain," the first officer replied evenly. "Not only is it not mine, it is not anyone's. These are not Federation communicators but clever forgeries. Very clever forgeries." He hefted his experimentally. "Even the weight is correct, though I venture to say they contain anything but operative electronics."

"But it's not possible," Kirk objected dazedly. "This communicator's been with me since we beamed. . . . What now?"

Spock had his phaser out and tried it experimentally. "Our weapons are also substitutes." For confirmation Kirk attempted to rattle a small sapling with his own phaser. Not so much as a leaf was disturbed.

"So our phasers and communicators have been swapped for phonies, Commander bn Bem has run off and gotten himself taken captive by the local primitives, and we've been separated from Scott and Sulu." It was the captain's turn to hike a rarely raised eyebrow. "Mr. Spock, something mighty funny is going on."

His first officer nodded somberly. "I would put it in less colloquial terms, but that is certainly an accurate appraisal of our present circumstances. It would appear that a course of action other than what we originally planned is advisable, until we can discover what is happening, and why."

"Agreed, Spock—except for one thing." He looked back across the log, keeping his profile low. "Commander bn Bem's difficulty seems genuine. Phasers or not, we have to rescue him. If he should be killed while under Federation protection, not to mention ours . . ." The sentence trailed off unfinished.

"Hold it—they're moving."

Both officers watched as the natives began to move off to the west, picking their way easily through the muddy meadows and swampland. Commander bn Bem hiked along readily, making no attempt to slow his captors' progress or leave a trail for would-be rescuers to follow.

Kirk was suddenly struck by the Pandronian's curiously complaisant attitude. "He doesn't act like someone on the verge of being dissected by alien aborigines."

"There's not a great deal he can do, in his present circumstances," Spock suggested.

"I don't buy that, Spock. He ought to be making it difficult for them—struggling, making noise, anything to delay his removal from here. Especially knowing that we were chasing after him. The motives—"

"—of a Pandronian are unknown to us," finished Spock. "In any case, we are badly outnumbered—not to mention being unarmed. We might return to contact Mr. Scott and Lieutenant Sulu. Hopefully *their* phasers and communicators are in working order."

Kirk shook his head. "Can't risk it, Spock. The group is moving. We might never be able to find them again in time to save bn Bem, not in this swamp. And if Scotty's and Sulu's equipment also turned out to be fakes—no, at least now we have the commander in sight.

"Let's stick with them. As long as we stay under cover, we have a chance to surprise them."

Careful and occasionally treacherous pursuit brought them

unseen to a vantage point slightly above the natives' destination: a small but neatly arranged village. Several large wooden cages, empty now, reposed at its center. The convoy appeared to be in the process of installing Commander bn Bem in one of the cages.

The thatched huts comprising the village looked competent enough. They were in no way spectacular, not even for primitive architecture. Little in the way of drying sheds, baskets, pottery, or other tools and constructions was visible in the small community. There was nothing to indicate to Kirk that these aliens ranked in the forefront of known primitive races. Spock was obviously dwelling on the same thought.

"These aborigines appear to be in a late primitive state, below urban tribal infrastructure but far above mere nomadic hunters and gatherers. Based on what we have seen thus far, one can deduce that they are at least moderately intelligent and possess a basic language and well-developed social structure. I would assume that a well-developed system of morals, taboos, and traditions is present in the appropriate proportions and degrees of advancement."

He paused, considered a moment before adding, "The standard method of dealing with strangers in such societies may include dismemberment, consumption, or various other unfriendly actions we cannot imagine." He directed a nod toward the now tightly imprisoned Commander bn Bem.

"Judging from the way they have treated the commander so far, I believe we can safely discard such hopeful possibilities as the commander's being treated as a god from the sky, or being adopted into the tribe."

"That's too bad," Kirk murmured. "I think he belongs, somehow. But I agree, Spock." Once again he found himself puzzled by the Pandronian's nonchalant attitude. bn Bem stood calmly in the center of the wooden cage, not pacing or testing the bars or imploring his captors.

"You'd think Commander bn Bem would be able to look at these people and see the same things, yet he's given no indication he finds capture and confinement especially objectionable. If anything, he's behaving as if he's half enjoying it." Kirk shrugged, resigned.

"Well, maybe this is the standard Pandronian way of reacting to capture. As you've pointed out, Spock, we know so little about them." He slid down behind the rotting log in front of them.

"In any case, we can't do anything for him before nightfall. I just hope these aborigines' night vision isn't as well developed as their biceps."

The time remaining until dusk wasn't passed in idleness. Studious searching through the underbrush around the little rise they had encamped on turned up several broken but unrotted sections of tree. These would serve as clubs. A few fist-sized stones coupled with some lengths of native creeper and a little dexterous Vulcan handwork produced a set of efficient-looking bolos.

Thus armed, they waited until the sun had vanished behind the trees in the abrupt manner common to all jungles, before proceeding cautiously down the slope toward the village clearing. Civilization here hadn't reached the elevated plane of intertribal warfare, so Kirk and Spock encountered no posted guards as they entered the outskirts of the village.

Once, something like a cross between a cat and a chartreuse sofa crossed their path. It stared at them with startled red eyes, uttered a single soft yelp like a warped tape, and waddled rapidly out of sight. None of the natives were about. Occasional muffled sounds drifted out from various huts.

"Shhh," Kirk whispered.

"Of course," Spock agreed in near-normal conversational tone. Kirk threw him an exasperated look.

Several moons—one globular, two others of irregular cast—lit the village in ghost light. Eight shapes—the two men and their shadows—moved toward the central cage.

bn Bem noticed their approach and had the grace not to cry out. Silently, Kirk and Spock set to work on the lashings of the cage door.

"Kirk Captain—?"

"Shut up," Kirk ordered, scraping fingers on the crude fiber of the bindings. "We're rescuing you."

"You are interfering with observations."

Even Spock was startled. "*This* is how you observe? By being captured?"

"The opportunities for first-member study are best."

"Assuming the studied don't decide to do a little vivisecting of their own," the first officer observed.

bn Bem adopted a pose of contempt. "Is as *logical* a way as any, Spock Commander."

"Maybe so," put in Kirk, "but I don't think Starfleet would approve. You're being rescued, Commander, whether you like it or not. Come on."

The lashings finally undone, Kirk yanked the door aside. For a minute, as bn Bem stood stolidly in the middle of the cage, the captain was afraid the Pandronian was actually going to resist the rescue. But he finally left the confines of the wooden bars, muttering to himself, using some of the logic he professed to have.

They started for the hill, but were confronted by the unexpected appearance of a light. It did not come from any of the orbiting satellites above. It was small, intense, and wavered slightly.

A second light joined it, then another, and still more. Each light lit a semihumanoid reptilian face, staring into the night. The torches formed a circle around the men. In the flickering light the aborigines' skin took on an ominous blood-red hue.

Kirk took a step backward. As he considered running for it, there was a faint blur before him and something went *ka-thunk* at their feet.

Looking down, he saw the quivering length of a rough-hewn but deadly-looking spear. As a nonverbal means of interspecies communication, it was brutally effective.

"Gentlemen," Kirk observed as the circle of torchbearers moved closer, "I think we're trapped."

"Ineluctably," Spock murmured.

None of them got much sleep the rest of that night, due in large part to the steady noise of saplings being felled around the village and to the steady rumble of their own thoughts. Only Commander bn Bem seemed composed as he studied the native activity.

"Why, Kirk Captain," he exclaimed once, "you are not *observing*."

Kirk thought a few choice thoughts and ignored the Pandronian's sneers. A steady stream of most undiplomatic images eventually lulled him to sleep.

II

When the sun rose again, Commander bn Bem was back in his cage. The village was unchanged, except that the commander now had company. Two cages to his left were also occupied. One imprisoned Kirk; the other held his first officer. A single native guard stood close by, the villagers undoubtedly having decided one was required should any more of the evil strangers suddenly appear.

Kirk had spent futile hours in the predawn darkness testing the lianas which held his cage door closed. But while the aborigines were primitive, they were not stupid. The new knots were far too solid and complex for Kirk to unravel.

A small knife would probably have been enough to saw through the woody lashings. But he didn't have a small knife. Instead, he had a phaser which could carbonize the entire village in a couple of minutes. Only *this* phaser was a fake. It wouldn't incinerate a *Starfleet Technical Manual*.

Kirk doubted that the natives, however lethargic they might otherwise appear concerning their captives, would give him time to gnaw through the bindings with his teeth. He wished he had the tech manual now, anyway. At least it would give him something to read.

Instead, he had to be satisfied with standing morosely at the front of the cage, eyeing the massive guard and muttering to himself.

"How's that, Captain?" Spock queried, overhearing a portion of Kirk's ramblings.

"I was wondering how come we always end up like this, Mr. Spock."

"I assume that's a rhetorical question, Captain."

Kirk sighed, pulled his arms free of the supportive crossbar, and stared through the poles at his first officer. "I was just expressing my astonishment at our ability to get into these situations."

"The common complaint of every human since the dawn of time, I believe," Spock commented philosophically. "It's fate, Captain," he murmured.

Kirk looked surprised. "Fate, Mr. Spock?"

"I think that is the correct term," his first officer said, looking curious rather than uncertain.

Apparently stirred by this incomprehensible alien gabble, the guard strode over to Kirk's cage and poked at the captain with his spear. Kirk jumped back.

"Well, I'm not going to rely on fate to get us out of here." He eyed the guard, who stared back unimpressed. Then Kirk turned a significant expression on Spock.

"Why don't you coax him over to your cage and try a quick Vulcan nerve pinch, Mr. Spock?"

Spock eyed the aborigine warily as the enormous biped turned a neolithic gaze on him. "Captain, I'm *only* a Vulcan. There are limits to what even I can do. It is possible that I could surprise this creature. I could also fail. For one thing, I am unfamiliar with its internal physiology and, specifically, its neural network. Should I guess wrong, it might irritate the creature. I do not believe being taken apart by an aroused native would enhance your own chances of escape, while mine would no longer be in question. Logically, therefore . . ." He shrugged.

Kirk turned his attention back to Commander bn Bem, who had been mercifully silent all morning. "I'm afraid this means we're not going to be able to rescue you at this time, Commander."

His sarcasm was lost on the naturally sarcastic bn Bem. "Good intentions, Captain, are not enough. Planet Pandro will be much displeased. Starfleet Federation told us you were best captain in the fleet. Actions to date deny this."

Kirk had finally had enough. To hell with diplomacy. "Commander bn Bem," he yelled, "you are personally responsible for our present situation!

"You deliberately disobeyed orders, orders given for your own good, by running off. Your attitude during this entire mission has been extremely abrasive. And I don't know how you did it," he continued dangerously, "but I'm convinced now that you're the one who switched our phasers and communicators for imitations."

"You place too much dependence, Kirk Captain, on phasers and communicators." If Kirk's accusations had dented the Pandronian's insufferable egotism, he gave no sign of it. "Petty instruments. One should rely more on personal resources instead of artificialities."

"Either one of those 'artificialities' could solve our problems right now," grumbled Kirk.

"Is that all?" bn Bem sneered contemptuously. He reached into the pouch at his waist—and produced both phasers and communicators.

"Our phasers!" Kirk exclaimed excitedly. "Throw one—" His excitement was abruptly tempered by realization of what the magical appearance of their devices meant.

"Commander bn Bem," he began carefully, "if you've had those phasers and communicators all this time, why didn't you use them to escape?"

The Pandronian's attitude was that of a parent patiently lecturing a couple of dull-witted children. "You recall will, Kirk Captain, my say that this is best way to observe. As observation is completed, is now time to leave. This One, though, does not demean self by the use of casual violence to accomplish simple goals."

"Oh." Kirk wasn't sure whether he was more fascinated than furious.

"However," the commander concluded, "you may demean yourselves if you wish."

"If we *wish*? Commander bn Bem, I want those phasers and communicators *now*—and for O'Morion's sake, toss them over carefully. They're pretty rugged, but—"

bn Bem waved him off. "Compliance with request is, but is no need to throw. This One must disassemble."

Kirk stared blankly at the Pandronian, the commander's words echoing meaninglessly in his mind, until bn Bem showed what he meant.

Detaching his lower half, the commander split neatly in two and squeezed out through the gaps in the bars, his top half carrying phasers and communicators easily.

Kirk gawked, fascinated, while Spock murmured, "Remarkable." The Pandronian reassembled and handed each of them their instruments. "Truly remarkable. Commander bn Bem is a colony creature. Or perhaps we should begin calling him Commanders bn Bem."

"Commander," Kirk wondered, leaving aside for the moment the question of whether the Pandronian should be addressed in the singular or plural, "if you could split yourself into separate sections, why didn't you escape on your own earlier?"

He set his phaser on low stun and beamed the guard. The huge native slumped, unconscious, on his supporting spear. A careful readjustment of the setting wheel and Kirk was burning away the lashings on his cage, as Spock did likewise to his.

bn Bem watched their efforts idly and continued in the same lecturing tone. "I explained, was not concluded with observating. Also, would deny you the chance to prove your people's value to planet Pandro by rescuing This One from possibly dangerous situation to same."

"For the last time, Commander bn Bem," Kirk declaimed in exasperation, "this is not a laboratory. Not for testing the locals, not for testing us. This is a new, hostile world. And," he added forcefully, "Mr. Spock and I are not your private experimental animals."

"I did not say that," bn Bem objected mildly.

"But you implied it." The Pandronian did not reply. "I have no choice this time," Kirk went on. "Commander, consider yourself under protective custody. We're going to protect you from any further escapades. Mr. Spock, keep an eye on him while I call in. On *all* of him." He flipped open his communicator.

"Kirk to *Enterprise*, Kirk to *Enterprise* . . ."

From his position at the con, Chief Engineer Montgomery Scott leaned forward toward the communications console and asked for the tenth, or possibly hundredth, time, "Lieutenant Arex, have you located them yet?"

The Edoan looked back over a feathery shoulder. "No, sir. It is a large world, filled with many distracting life forms."

Uhura looked up from the main readout screen at Spock's

science station. "Mr. Scott! That sensory anomaly—it's expanded to cover the whole northern continent."

"Try more to the south of where we set down," Scott suggested to Arex. "It's possible that—" He blinked, spun in the chair to face Uhura. "What's that, Lieutenant?"

"The sensory distortion—it's covered the entire region. We aren't receiving any information from that area."

"That explains why the detectors are so confused," Arex noted with satisfaction. "I thought they were giving awfully peculiar readings."

Scott left the command chair and walked over to check the readouts at the science station. "That does it, Lieutenant," he said finally. "You couldn't locate the Loch Ness monster through that." His face wrinkled in disgust as he examined the distortion-plagued information.

"These figures look like a regurgitated mass of undigested haggis, and they're about as encouragin'." He looked back at the navigation console. "Nonetheless, Mr. Arex, you've got to keep tryin'."

"Yes, sir."

"Kirk to *Enter*—" The captain paused, studied his communicator. "There's some kind of advanced interference on all channels, Mr. Spock." He looked around nervously. "We're going to have to get out of this village on our own—horizontally, for now. I doubt we'll be able to manage that without being seen."

"I'm afraid I agree, Captain," said Spock, turning to study the still-silent huts.

"Remember, keep your phaser on stun. There are no advanced weapons here, no reason to put a native down permanently. Let's get moving."

They started toward the low rise that he and Spock had descended so hopefully the night before. The concentration of thatched houses was thinner there, but to no avail. As soon as they had emerged from the central clearing, they were spotted by the villagers. The shouting and angry natives reacted to this second escape attempt, as Spock declared sadly, "Most unreasonably."

First one, then a couple, and soon the whole tribe was charging down on them, brandishing spears and clubs and howling deafeningly. The native in the lead, a huge, husky fellow, raised his arm and prepared to hurl one of those thick weapons. His companions started to do likewise.

Apparently the community decision had been made that these strangers were not worth keeping alive any longer.

"Fire," Kirk ordered, at the same time depressing the trigger of his phaser and pointing it at the first aborigine.

Something happened.

His finger froze on the button, unable to depress the trigger the necessary millimeters to fire the weapon. His legs locked in place and his arms were held in an unbreakable yet velvety grasp. Even his eyelids were paralyzed. He tried to blink and couldn't.

Fortunately he wasn't staring at the sun, but he could see Spock nearby, held rigidly in a similar pose in the act of firing his own phaser. Commander bn Bem had been likewise deprived of all mobility.

Around them, the spectrum had gone berserk. He could still see clearly. The charging natives had also been frozen in place, spears poised for flight, clubs held ready to strike—but nothing, nothing looked natural.

Normally brown trees now glowed lambent maroon and sported fluorescent pink foliage. The blue sky overhead had turned a deep green, while the earth underfoot shone orange shot with black. And everything had a hazy, befuzzed edge to it.

Then the Voice sounded.

It was firm, faintly feminine, and hinted at immense power held easily in check. The Voice seemed to originate several centimeters behind Kirk's forehead, and it echoed all around the hollow places within, reverberating gently between his ears.

"No," the Voice instructed, "do not attempt to use your weapons." Kirk experimentally tried to comply and found he could raise his thumb from the trigger. The loosening of control was generalized, enabling him to move his extremities now—fingers, toes, eyes, and mouth.

He utilized the latter to announce unnecessarily, "I'm paralyzed, Mr. Spock."

"We are being held in a new, unique type of force field, Captain," the first officer commented thickly.

"Put away your weapons," the Voice continued. "These are My children. Do not attempt to harm them."

Kirk put aside the question of who was about to harm whom in his desire to learn what was at work here. It was certainly no manifestation of the spear-wielders' minds.

"Who are you?" he asked.

"Who are *you*?" came the reply.

Proceed slowly, he warned himself. This is a powerful, unknown quantity with unknowable motivations. Don't anger it, and don't give anything away.

"I'm Captain James Tiberius Kirk of the Federation cruiser *Enterprise*. On my right is my first officer, Mr. Spock, and on his right, Honorary Commander Ari bn Bem of the Pandro system of worlds."

Kirk received the impression that this honest recounting of names and titles satisfied the Voice.

"Why are you here?" it inquired with what sounded like true curiosity. "Why do you disturb this place?"

"It is part of our mission," Kirk tried to explain, striving to make their assignment sound as innocuous as possible. "We are required to classify this planet. We have to take readings, examine the native population, report the state of—"

The Voice interrupted, not angrily, but annoyed. "What gives you the right to intrude here? This planet was not created for your use. My children are not created to be subjects of your tests. Your weapons, bad things, will be nullified."

Kirk watched the phaser he held simply melt away. He experienced no pain, no sensation of heat—only a slight tingle in his palm after the phaser had completely vanished. The tingling faded rapidly.

"I would say 'nullified' was an understatement, Spock."

Natural color returned without warning. Kirk stumbled, his muscles stiff from being held motionless so long.

Seeing the intruders stumble and the peculiar shiny things disappear from their hands, the natives slowed. They lowered their spears and clubs and clustered tightly around their captives.

"There are times, Mr. Spock," Kirk went on, staring in amazement at his now empty hand, "when I think I should have been a librarian."

"There are those who believe the task of librarian would be equally challenging, Captain," Spock responded as the circle of lowered spears grew denser around them. Sharp points touched the midsections of the three captives. "Though it is undoubtedly less dangerous. . . ."

"The disturbance was temporarily localized, Mr. Scott," Uhura reported from the science console. "I have been able to fix it near what appears to be a village of local native life. It's not far from where you originally set down."

"Never mind the disturbance," Scott muttered, eyeing Arex. "Have you found the captain and Mr. Spock yet?"

"I've located emanations which could be the captain's and Commander Spock's," he explained carefully, with the emphasis on the 'could be.' "But the sensory anomaly has so interfered with our instrumentation that it is impossible to make positive identification at this time."

"Which means—" Uhura began, but Scott cut her off.

" 'Could be' is good enough for me, right now, Lieutenant. Ready a security landing squad. We're going down there with questions and phasers." He rose from the con and headed toward the turbolift.

Kirk, Spock, and bn Bem found themselves secured within the three cages only recently vacated. This time they were surrounded by several guards who looked alert and ugly. Kirk did not enjoy the return to familiar surroundings. Their moment of liberty had been short-lived and short-circuited by a mysterious unseen power which saw fit to side with the antisocial locals. And now they didn't even have the possibility of recovering their phasers or communicators. The former had been melted into nothingness, and the latter were confiscated by their captors.

As might be expected, Commander bn Bem did not improve the situation any. "You've mishandled problem again, Kirk Captain," the Pandronian berated him. "This One judges you not an intelligent captain."

Kirk was almost too discouraged by their failed escape and subsequent recapture to respond. "Commander bn Bem, Mr. Spock and I are here in the first place because we thought you were worth rescuing. Don't misunderstand me. It was to preserve good relations between the Federation and planet Pandro, not out of any overwhelming affection for your person."

"Planet Pandro," bn Bem riposted, "is unconcerned as to fate of This One. Planet Pandro will not have dealings with ineffectual and inferior species. You've failed everything you have attempted. You have not rescued This One and you have not been able to handle local primitives."

At the conclusion of this sneering polemic, seeing that the guards were temporarily inattentive, the commander literally came apart at the seams.

His head hopped down off his shoulders, moving on short stumpy legs. His upper torso, headless now, walked on long arms, while both legs, joined at the top, slid easily through the bars of the cage. These parts were followed by the rest of the commander.

The head turned back to call to Kirk and Spock. "This One wishes you—what is the Federation-Sol word—luck? Yes, luck. You will require it."

With a contemptuous salute from one of the arms attached to the upper torso, the components of the commander scuttled separately into the surrounding brush.

"Wait! Unlock us—set us free!" Kirk finally gave up shouting at the unresponsive forest. Meanwhile, the guards noted the sudden disappearance of one of their captives, yet again. Much frantic gabbling and gesticulating ensued, after which most of them started off into the jungle, following the tracks of bn Bem's main legs. Some shook spears and clubs at the two men still imprisoned, made faces promising dire developments on their return.

Kirk sympathized with them.

"So much for interspecies loyalty and Pandronian-Federation friendship," he muttered angrily. "Well, fine! We're going to get no help from our guest, we cannot communicate with these natives, and we can't get through to the ship. What now?"

"Perhaps," Spock mused thoughtfully, "we can regain the attention of the powerful local intelligence and reason with it."

The aborigines had left the communicators unguarded nearby. Spock succeeded in unraveling enough of one vine to make a small lasso. Kirk watched uneasily, expecting some native to happen along at any moment, while Spock patiently cast and recast the line.

Eventually they regained their communicators. But a furtive attempt to contact the ship produced the same results as before—nothing.

Kirk studied the device as if it were capable of producing the miracle they hoped for. "It's worth a try, I suppose." He started to talk, then hesitated. "How do you address something you've never seen and cannot imagine?" He shrugged as Spock regarded him silently.

"Oh, well . . . Kirk to alien intelligence, Kirk to alien intelligence. This is Captain James Kirk calling the controlling intelligence of this world. Answer—respond, please."

He felt something of the fool talking into a communicator directed at thin air. It probably would be as effective to throw his head back and howl at the sky. But using the communicator couldn't hurt.

He continued trying, to continued nonresponse.

"Perhaps an offering of some sort, Captain," suggested Spock.

Kirk eyed his first officer evenly. "Whatever we're dealing with, Mr. Spock, I don't think we can bribe it. Not that we've much to bribe with, but somehow I think it's imperative we be honest with it." He directed his voice to the small pickup and tried again, earnestly.

"Kirk to alien intelligence, Kirk to alien intelligence." He paused, shaking his head. "Good idea, and that's all, Spock."

"Hmmm," the Vulcan murmured. "If we connect our two communicators, we can generate a single high-energy burst, several times the strength a single communicator can put out. That might draw more attention to us." He finished the proposal unwaveringly:

"Doing so will also render both communicators powerless in a very short time."

"Do it," Kirk concurred. "They're useless now anyway, if we can't reach the ship through them."

"The interference could clear later, Captain."

"Yes, but by then our jailers will be back and will take

them away from us again. They'll put them way out of reach. Let's take the gamble, Spock."

"Precisely my thoughts, Captain." He extended both hands and arms through the bars of his cage.

Kirk moved over to the side facing Spock's cage. He made a one, two, three gesture with the hand holding the communicator and let it fly with a soft underhand toss. Spock caught it neatly and bent immediately to the task of mating the two instruments.

Ordinarily he could have accomplished the task in a couple of minutes, but the circumstances were not as conducive to such work as were the labs on board the *Enterprise*. Nevertheless, he managed it.

When they were firmly locked together, he tossed the hybrid back to Kirk, who checked the reintegrated circuitry and nodded approval. He switched it on, felt the warmth immediately as the double-powered device began to build toward overload.

"This is Captain James Tiberius Kirk calling the ruling intelligence of this world. Can you hear me? If so, please acknowledge."

He repeated the call over and over, working against the mounting heat in the joined communicators, steadily adjusting the frequency modulator.

"Kirk to entity, Kirk to entity. This is Captain James Tiberius Kirk calling the—"

The wooden bars of the cage turned violet, the ground became orange shot with black, and he found his fingers frozen on the double communicator.

"I am here," the Voice announced gently.

"We apologize for our intrusion," Kirk explained hurriedly. "We didn't realize the true situation here. If we had, we certainly would not have proceeded as we have. If you will permit us, we will leave immediately in our vessel and not return. Nor will others of our kind come.

"If we do not return, then others of our Federation will surely come and you will be troubled no end. Please understand, this is not a threat. They will come not as destroyers, but rather as curious explorers."

There was a long silence during which Kirk discovered that despite his paralysis he could still sweat.

"This is good," the Voice finally decided. Kirk let out a private shout. "Go, then—go now and do not return."

The paralysis vanished. Kirk stretched in relief. "Just one more thing: There's a third member of our group."

"I detect no third intelligence here," the Voice responded, sounding puzzled.

"He, uh, left this immediate area," Kirk hastened to explain.

The Voice ignored him. "You must go. You must not interfere with the natural activities of My children. I will allow you to contact your ship again, but go *now*."

Kirk didn't hesitate. Rapidly he disconnected the two communicators and checked the power leads. "Still functioning—*whew!*" A second sufficed to reset his own communicator on standard ground-to-ship frequency.

"Kirk to *Enterprise*. Kirk to—"

Response was gratifyingly fast. *"Enterprise,"* an excited voice sounded over the little speaker. "Uhura here. Captain, are you all right?"

"Affirmative. Stand by." He looked across at Spock. "We're not leaving without bn Bem. He's still our responsibility, and I won't abandon him here—no matter how much he deserves it. I can't play personalities in this." He returned his attention to the communicator.

"Lieutenant Uhura, beam down a security squad with tricorders set for Pandronian scan."

"Aye, aye, sir. Mr. Scott has already readied one, with phaser cannon."

"Belay that, Lieutenant!" Kirk ordered frantically. "No heavy weapons—just tricorders. Hop to it. Kirk out." He flipped the communicator shut and stuck it back to his waist.

"Cannon or no, the intelligence will still be most displeased, Captain."

"I'll worry about that when I have to, Mr. Spock," replied Kirk firmly. "Our primary concern now is to recover Commander bn Bem, whatever the opposition." He looked toward the center of the village clearing. "Here they come . . ."

Small rainbow whirlwinds began to form before them. Six crew members appeared, five of them clad in security tunics, the sixth in that of the engineering division.

"Captain, Mr. Spock," Scott exclaimed the moment he had fully rematerialized and had time for a look around, "are you all right?" He pulled his phaser, adjusted it, and began burning through the fastenings on the cage door.

"All right now, Scotty," Kirk replied.

The last fiber gave and Kirk was freed. One of the ensigns had performed a similar service for Spock.

"Spread out, staying within sight of each other at all times. You're all familiar with the *Enterprise*'s guest, Commander Ari bn Bem of Pandro?" There were nods and signs of affirmation, several of them embroidered with personal opinion.

"This is a priority assignment," Kirk warned them sternly. "Personal opinions and feelings have no place here. We may encounter hostile native bipeds. Stun only for self-protection, and then only as a last resort.

"Now, let's spread out and try to locate Commander bn Bem. He's split into three individual parts."

"Beggin' pardon, sir," Scott blurted, voicing the general confusion. "Three parts?"

"Commander bn Bem is some kind of colony creature," Kirk explained. "He can operate as a single large individual, as you've seen him, or as three separated segments—maybe more, we don't know." He grinned tightly. "I guarantee you won't confuse part of him for native life."

The group turned and started off toward the section of forest the Pandronian had run into, spreading out as Kirk had directed and working their way through the beginnings of the thickening undergrowth.

As it developed, they got no further than Spock, Kirk, and bn Bem had the previous night.

Captain's admonition or no, when confronted by the sudden appearance of numerous screaming natives three meters tall, all charging toward them waving spears and clubs, none of the security personnel hesitated. Low-power phaser bursts colored the air and several natives dropped, temporarily paralyzed.

The Voice, despite Spock's fears, did not interfere. The ground remained brown, the leaves green, and their limbs mobile. They continued into the jungle.

It wasn't long before they encountered the main body of

warriors. They were returning to the village with a recaptured (and intact) Commander bn Bem in their midst. He was tied like a tiger, every part of his body secured with vines and lianas.

A few phaser bursts were enough to send the rest of the natives running in terror. They left their weapons and fallen comrades and vanished into the trees, leaving a securely bound bn Bem standing alone behind them. Kirk thought the commander looked rather embarrassed.

"We couldn't help it, sir," Scott declared, running over to join Kirk as the captain moved toward the Pandronian. "The crew had to defend themselves."

"Don't worry about it now, Scotty," Kirk reassured him, anxiously studying the sky and the terrain around them. "Let's get our guest and get out of here before we make any real trouble."

bn Bem's head inclined forward and there was a moroseness, a modesty in his tone Kirk had never heard. "Embarrassment results," he declared softly. "This One is shamed. This One has failed in its judgment."

If that was a plea for sympathy, it was wasted on Kirk. "You have endangered all of us by your actions," he chastised the commander, "and you've forced us to interfere with the natives of a world that deserves prime directive protection—not to mention outright quarantine."

The Pandronian struggled to regain some of his former haughtiness. "This One exists by its own standards," he announced, rather lamely.

"Not on my ship, you don't. Not any more. I'll stand for a lot, Commander, but when the *Enterprise* itself is endangered, diplomacy takes a back seat." He kicked at the dirt and reached for his communicator.

The dirt turned orange and froze in midfall as colorful aberrations swept the landscape and all Kirk's fears were suddenly realized. He fought the paralysis, fought to activate his communicator. If he could just make one shout, relay one order to have them beamed up . . .

But the effort was useless. His finger wouldn't move another millimeter closer to that crucial switch.

There was no fury in the Voice. No spite, no indignation. Kirk had the impression that such petty emotional flavorings were beyond the mind behind the Voice. If it contained any recognizable inflection, it was one of puzzlement.

"You are still here," it announced solemnly. "And you are still interfering." Then it added, without any change in tone, "I am angry."

"We didn't mean to interfere," Kirk explained desperately. "We have our own rules of conduct which forbid intrusion into the affairs of others. We—"

"Then you have not only disobeyed My rules, you have broken your own as well."

"No. We simply could not leave one of our own behind. It is our responsibility to take care of those placed under our protection, just as it's your responsibility to take care of yours.

"We could not leave Commander bn Bem where he could interfere with your"—he hesitated—"children. Would you really want that?" He waited tensely for the response.

"Yes," that rippling voice finally replied, "it is so. You have some wisdom, James Tiberius Kirk. The lost one is found, then?"

"He is found," Kirk admitted. "We will leave."

Another voice sounded—bn Bem's. "This One is greatly distressed. This One has erred. The mission was to judge, and the right of judgment no longer exists. This One must disassemble unity."

"Disassemble?" Kirk started.

"Never again to exist as a cooperation. This unity is defective, insufficient, inadequate, and false. This unit must cease to exist."

Kirk started to protest—certainly a severe reprimand was in order, but as he understood it the Pandronian was contemplating suicide. His personal inclinations were overriden by more powerful concerns. *"No!"*

bn Bem looked around wildly. "What . . . ?"

"Do not destroy yourself."

"But—This One has erred," bn Bem protested. "This One has tried to judge Kirk Captain and Spock Commander, only to be found himself wanting. This One has acted wrongly."

"You may have made a mistake," the Voice declared, without judging the Pandronian's actions in any way, "but if you disassemble you cannot learn from your error. Errors demand recognition. They also demand nonrepetition. If you disassemble, you will not be able to never repeat your mistake."

Spock admired the logic of it while bn Bem argued uncertainly. "And you—you do not demand punishment, for the breaking of your laws?"

Kirk was ready to scream; was bn Bem trying to get them *all* disassembled? He needn't have worried. He was underestimating their observer.

"Punishment?" Now the puzzlement was unmistakable. "What is punishment?"

"Revenge."

"Revenge? Intelligent beings require no revenge. Punishment is necessary only where learning cannot occur without it. You are behind such things as I am above it. My children here are different. That is why you must leave, so as not to corrupt their development with such obscene concepts as punishment and revenge."

The last comment was uttered with an inflection of contempt so strong it made Kirk momentarily dizzy.

"I am humbled," was all bn Bem managed to whisper.

Suddenly Kirk found that his own anger at bn Bem had become a source of embarrassment. "We'll be on our way now, if we may," he asked humbly.

"Yes. Go now . . ."

Natural coloration returned to the jungle and Kirk regained control of his body. For a long moment he studied the landscape, but saw only trees and vines, heard only the sounds of bird-things and shy crawlers. There was the rustle of a breeze. Nothing more.

He took out his communicator, addressed it slowly. "Kirk to *Enterprise*. Beam us up . . ."

bn Bem was with him as the captain resumed his position at the con. "Stand by to break orbit."

Spock was back at the library station, awaiting instructions. "Mr. Spock, classify this planet, Delta Theta Three, as being under strict Federation quarantine from this stardate forward. Said quarantine subject to Starfleet review of the official report of this mission. Under no circumstances is any vessel to approach this world."

"A restriction planet Pandro will also respect," bn Bem declared helpfully.

"I compliment you both on a wise decision, gentlemen," said Spock, working to prepare the necessary documentation.

"It's necessary for them as well as for us, Spock," Kirk explained.

Spock nodded, turned his gaze to the main viewscreen. It displayed a wide-sensor picture of the planet in question, still rotating demurely below them, giving no hint of the extraordinary alien intelligence inhabiting it.

"It is fascinating, Captain. A highly advanced alien entity using this system as a laboratory for guiding another people to racial maturity. Almost a god, you might say."

"Such comparisons are as meaningless as they are farfetched, Mr. Spock. By contrast to the ruling mind of Delta Theta Three, we are all children."

"In This One's case," bn Bem mumbled with becoming humility, "is still an eggling."

Kirk looked gratified. If, despite all the trouble, this expedition had taught the Pandronian a little modesty, then it was worth all they'd been through.

"Take us out of orbit, Mr. Sulu. It's time to—"

Uhura broke in with an exclamation of surprise. "Captain, I'm picking up a transmission from the surface."

"Put it through the bridge speakers, Lieutenant."

Kirk, Spock, and bn Bem recognized that wizened, maternal voice, which rippled and heaved with vast sighs like some midocean wave:

"Go in peace. Go in peace, children. You have learned much, though you have much left to learn. Be proud and—someday, perhaps—return."

That was the tantalizing bequest they bore with them as, at warp four, the *Enterprise* left the system of the sun Delta Theta.

That was a promise worth carrying home. . . .

III

Kirk and Spock remained affected by their contact with the extraordinary intelligence experimenting on Delta Theta Three, only in their case the effects didn't show. The opposite was true of Commander Ari bn Bem.

In contrast to the first part of the voyage, the commander had turned into a model passenger. His demeanor as they traveled downward toward Starfleet Science Station 24 was downright subdued.

Previously his interest in Federation procedures and operations had run from nonexistent to outright disdain. Following the humbling experience on Delta Theta Three, he exhibited a powerful desire to use the limited time remaining to him to learn all he could about the methods of Federation survey, navigation, research, and other exploratory techniques. So furiously did he plunge into his new studies that Kirk feared for his health. The commander refused to slow down, however.

"Have wasted much time already, Kirk Captain," bn Bem told him in response to Kirk's expressions of concern. "This One's ignorance must be assuaged. Cost to body self is negligible in comparison."

bn Bem's prior intransigence manifested itself now and then, but only when the material he wished to absorb wasn't instantly available, or when he chose to dispute a bit of science or procedure. So hard did he question various technicians that they almost wished they were again victims of the Pandronian's contempt instead of his voracious desire to learn.

It had been Kirk's intention to leave the commander at Science Station 24. According to the captain's original orders from Starfleet Command, the commander would remain at the station for a month, intensively researching Federation analytic methodology until a Pandronian ship arrived to take him home.

But Kirk was not to lose bn Bem's company as soon as he thought.

"I have contact with Science Station Twenty-four, Captain," Uhura announced. "They have an urgent message."

"Classified?" Kirk asked discreetly, with a glance at the science station, where bn Bem was engaged in earnest discussion with Spock.

Uhura checked her instrumentation. "It doesn't appear to be, Captain."

"Very well, Lieutenant. Put it on the screen." Kirk swiveled the command chair as Uhura moved to comply. A brief burst of static and the viewscreen produced a portrait.

The face of Lieutenant Commander Kunjolly stared back at him. Long white sideburns looking like puffs of steel wool flared out from skin the hue of dark chocolate. In an age of scientific miracles, the station commander's smooth pate was a glaring anomaly.

"Captain Kirk," the slightly high-pitched voice offered in greeting. "Good to see you again."

"Hello, Monty," a smiling Kirk replied. "Nice to see you, too. I have some good news for you." It would be considered more than good, he reflected, when the no doubt apprehensive station staff learned of their incipient guest's transformation.

"And I have some puzzling news," Kunjolly riposted, "though not for you. But go ahead and tell me yours first."

Kirk looked uncertainly at the screen. "All right." He glanced over at the science station. The conversation between bn Bem and Spock had grown lively.

"Your assigned visitor had an experience at our final survey stop which seems to have modified the inherent irascibility of his kind. I don't know how familiar you are with the Pandronians, but you'll be glad to know that this one's become almost charming."

Kunjolly grinned back at him. "That's very gratifying to learn, Captain." The grin turned to a concerned frown.

"Though I wonder if we'll be enjoying his company for long."

Kirk's puzzlement grew. "What are you talking about, Monty?" Visions of having to play host to even a reformed bn Bem rose in his mind.

The station commander shuffled some papers out of Kirk's view, then looked back into the pickup. "I'm holding a sealed message for your Pandronian VIP, Captain, beamed straight to us from his homeworld of Pandro."

"For me a message?" came a startled query. Apparently bn Bem hadn't been as totally absorbed in his conversation with Spock as Kirk had thought. Now he ambled over to stare at the screen, then down at Kirk.

"What means this, Kirk Captain?"

"I was hoping you could tell me, Commander."

"This One is expecting no sealed messages from home," bn Bem declared openly. "This One is thoroughly puzzled."

"You've no idea what the message is?"

"None more than you, Kirk Captain."

"Oh, and something else, Captain Kirk."

Kirk glanced back up at the screen. "What is it, Monty?"

The station commander looked to his left. "I have additional orders for the *Enterprise* from Starfleet Command. They read as follows:

" 'The *Enterprise* is hereby directed to provide, pursuant to Federation law and naval restrictions, all services requested by Pandronian representative Commander Ari bn Bem subsequent to his receipt of important message to him from his government.' "

"That's all very irregular," Kirk observed, a mite testily. "Why wasn't the message sent directly to us? It could have reached us several days ago."

"The Federation orders came through only this morning, stationtime, Captain Kirk. As for the Pandronian message, there wouldn't have been any point in sending it to you."

"Why not?" Kirk wanted to know.

"It was stated explicitly in English accompanying the Pandronian that delivery of the message was to await complementary orders from Starfleet—the one that came through this morning.

"Besides, it's all in Pandronian code. I wouldn't like to try transcribing it for rebroadcast. No one here has any clue as to the contents of the message."

"Someone at Starfleet must, Captain," Spock put in, "if they acceded so readily to the Pandronian request."

"Not necessarily, Spock," Kirk mused thoughtfully. "The Pandronians might have made a request for unspecified aid. Starfleet wants Pandro as an ally badly enough that they might have promised our help without knowing the specifics of what that help is wanted for."

"That is possible, Captain," Spock conceded.

"Very well. The sooner we dock in, the faster we'll find out what this is all about." He snapped directions to those manning the con. "Mr. Sulu, Mr. Arex, bring us into Station Twenty-four. Gently, if you please." His attention returned to the screen.

"We should be in your office in a little while, Monty. I expect you're as curious to know the nature of that message from Pandro as we are."

"I am, Captain Kirk. However, the orders from Starfleet are all-inclusive, which means that Commander bn Bem need not apprise us of his message's contents."

"I know," Kirk admitted, trying not to let his worry show. "*Enterprise* out."

"Station Twenty-four out," a solemn Kunjolly acknowledged, closing the transmission.

"Well, Commander," Kirk began, facing bn Bem, "still no idea of what's going on?"

"Not ever before have I heard of such a thing, Kirk Captain," the Pandronian replied. He seemed genuinely concerned. Reflecting his nervousness, his head shifted from side to side on his shoulders.

Even though he knew that a Pandronian could separate his body into at least three major sections—each one capable of independent motility—Kirk still found it unnerving to see the commander adjust his structure so casually.

"It must be important, Captain," insisted Spock from his position at the science station. "By requesting such extreme assistance from Starfleet, the Pandronians are jeopardizing their neutrality. That is a great deal to risk merely to speed the commander on his way. Obviously, his presence is desired for some emergency so severe that they cannot wait for one of their own ships to come and pick him up."

"Makes sense, Mr. Spock," the captain agreed. From what he knew of Pandro, which was little, Kirk found the entire situation unlikely. Something had worried the Pandronian government enough for them to modify their fierce independence. That was all to the Federation's good, but not necessarily to that of his ship.

Science Station 24 consisted of a central hub in the shape of a slowly turning disk from which the multiple spokes of connector passageways protruded. Various-shaped modular stations bulged at the terminus of each long pressurized corridor; spheres, cubes, ellipsoids, and combination of these and other forms held laboratories and living quarters, the whole station a hallucinant's vision of an exploded popcorn ball.

Each module housed a different function, from complete laboratories dedicated to the study of zero-g biology to long tubular structures filled with facilities for examining the movement of subatomic particles.

One of the longer spokes ended in a simple large airlock. No other modules were placed near it. Even so, it was a delicate maneuver on Sulu's part to align the *Enterprise* properly with the station docking port. The simple spoke provided none of the navigational aids of a completely self-enclosed Starfleet station dock, but those weren't required here. Only supply ships and occasional ships like the *Enterprise* on special missions stopped at the isolated research stations. Elaborate facilities would have been wasted.

Gravity increased to near normal as the turbolift carried Kirk, Spock, and Commander Ari bn Bem down the long pressurized shaft toward the central station hub. From the central turbolift depot, where cargo and passenger lifts transported supplies and personnel to the many distant lab modules, it was a short walk to the outer offices of the station commandant, Lieutenant Commander Kunjolly. An ensign greeted them and after a short conversation via intercom, directed them to the inner sanctum.

"Good to see you again, Captain Kirk," Kunjolly exclaimed as the three entered. He left his desk to shake Kirk's hand, then repeated the formality with the *Enterprise*'s first officer. "And you, Mr. Spock."

"Dr. Kunjolly," the science officer said by way of return, using a warmer title than the station chief's military one. Spock was anxious to learn the nature of Kunjolly's extraordinary message for bn Bem, and the sooner formalities, however pleasant, were over, the better he would like it.

Spock's concern was echoed by the tall blue form alongside him. "Anxiousness This One expresses to observe message," stammered bn Bem hurriedly.

"I understand," Kunjolly declared. Returning to his seat behind the big desk, he passed a palm over its left side. There was a soft beep, duplicated by a second beep as his hand crossed over the spot once again.

A panel flipped open behind the desk. All three guests watched as the station commandant used an electronic key to open a locked drawer. After removing a tiny metal cube he relocked the drawer and pressed a hidden button. A three-panel viewer common to conference rooms on the *Enterprise* popped up in the center of the desk. Kunjolly inserted the message cube properly and hit still another switch.

Kirk and Spock stared expectantly at the tripartite screen as it lit up, but the flow of information which raced across was disappointingly incomprehensible. Not that either man had anticipated understanding the Pandronian message, but Kirk had half hoped he could make something out of the communication.

The complex cryptography proved totally alien, though, as alien as the Pandronians themselves. While Kirk waited impatiently, Commander bn Bem avidly examined the steady stream of information. Occasionally the Pandronian would produce a low gurgling noise, sounding like a faulty water pipe, but otherwise he remained silent as he studied the message. At the conclusion of the message, bn Bem let out a startling yelp, his eyes rolled over, and he collapsed to the floor.

"Commander bn Bem!" Kirk shouted, rushing to kneel above the motionless form. Kunjolly hurried around from behind his desk, and Spock also bent over the prone Pandronian. The commander's eyes remained shut and his upper torso appeared to be shivering slightly.

Kirk put out a hand toward one shoulder, intending to give the body a gentle shake, and abruptly hesitated.

"Mr. Spock, how much do we know of Pandronian physiology?"

"Practically nothing, Captain."

Kirk's hand drew back.

Kunjolly's hands had tightened into worried fists. "There must have been something powerful in that message. It appears to have induced a fatal shock."

"No matter the cause," Spock noted grimly. "If he dies here, aboard a Federation outpost while under Federation protection, we will be blamed. Not for inducing the shock—that is surely the fault of the message—but for not knowing how to cure its effects. Pandronian-Federation relations will suffer."

Kirk noticed that the shivering continued. "He's not dead—not yet, anyway. Monty, get in touch with your medical personnel. Mr. Spock, contact Dr. McCoy, explain what's happened, and have him rush down here. Perhaps working together we can—"

Spock put up a hand for silence. "Just a moment, Captain, Dr. Kunjolly." The station commandant paused at his desk, one hand ready to activate the intercom there.

Kirk stared in fascination. The body of the unconscious Pandronian was coming apart. First the lower torso slithered away from the commander's stomach. The upper torso, moving on mobile arms, detached itself at the lower part of the neck. Both lower and upper body sections moved independently to take up positions on either side of the limp head.

Tiny cilia extending from the upper part of the hips commenced a feathery caress of the face while the two hands massaged the back of the skull, which raised up slightly on cilia of its own to provide easy access for the arms.

Kirk stared openmouthed at the nightmare scene being played out before them. "The Pandronian form," Spock commented quietly, "appears capable of taking care of itself under circumstances which would leave a human—or Vulcan—relatively helpless."

As if to confirm further the first officer's speculation,

Commander bn Bem's eyes blinked open seconds later. Still moving on neck cilia, the now-alert head adjusted itself on the floor. Rushing about like a family of varmints scurrying to flee an owl, the remaining sections of the commander's body reattached themselves at neck and stomach.

bn Bem placed both hands on the floor and sat up, staring at the stupefied onlookers with a puzzled expression. "This One fainted at import of message, Kirk Captain. Something the matter is?"

"Uh, you fell down without warning. We thought you needed assistance."

bn Bem got to his feet, a touch of his natural aloofness reasserting itself. "Is not to worry. Natural superiority of Pandronian lifeform assures self-care in such matters." He moved to the desk, addressed a still-dazed Kunjolly. The station commandant, Kirk reminded himself, had not seen the startling Pandronian separate-but-equal performance before today.

"Import of message overwhelmed This One temporarily. Must run through again, please."

"What?" muttered Kunjolly, in the voice of a man emerging from a dream.

"Must see again the message." bn Bem gestured at the blank triple screen.

"Yes . . . of course." The station commandant regained his composure and pushed the appropriate button. Once more the coded Pandronian message splashed its cryptic contents across the desk screens.

Spock chose the moment to whisper to Kirk, "A most interesting display, Captain, on the commander's part. Apparently the shock of the message only incapacitated the brain, leaving the rest of the body free to work at restoring consciousness. A useful function for an intelligent being to have. The advantages would apply to a host of diseases—the problems of hangover, for example."

"True," agreed Kirk readily. "I can see where—" He paused, gaped at his first officer. "Now, why would a non-imbibing Vulcan be interested in hangover remedies, Mr. Spock?"

"While not subject to such a primitive malady, Captain, I can still appreciate the luxury of a physiology which keeps the rest of the body from suffering for the transgressions of a poorly functioning brain."

Kirk was about to reply when he was interrupted by a series of shouts and yelps from Commander bn Bem. The Pandronian was twisting his hands about one another in an unfamiliar fashion while shaking his head from side to side. On occasion as the commander gave vent to his emotions his head would lift up slightly on its motile cilia and run back and forth on his shoulders, sometimes turning complete circles. This was an upsetting sight even to one who by now should be inured to the unique abilities of the Pandronian form.

"Oh, woe! Oh, incomprehensibility! Oh, abomination most sublime!" bn Bem turned eyes filled with disbelief on Kirk. "Something that cannot be imagined has happened."

Kirk noted that the screens were blank once again. The message had run its course for the second time. He wondered how much of this naked emoting was for his benefit, in anticipation of a request yet to come.

At least the commander's head had ceased its gyrations and had seen fit to sit in normal head-fashion solidly on bn Bem's shoulders. For this Kirk was thankful. "Is there something we can do to help?" he asked, knowing full well that the Pandronian government had already made that request of Starfleet Command, albeit in a generalized form.

"Is," acknowledged bn Bem tersely. "Must go This One with you to planet Pandro immediately."

"With us?" Kirk exclaimed, his eyebrows suddenly matching Spock's for altitude.

"That explains the orders, Captain," Spock pointed out.

"Yes, to go immediately all of us," the excited Pandronian insisted. "No delay to be brooked." He brushed past Kirk and Spock as he headed for the outside corridor leading toward the central station hub. "Without pause follow now, Kirk Captain. Of the essence is time."

"But we—" Too late; the commander was gone, presumably on his way back to the *Enterprise*.

Kirk took a deep breath, turned back to a dumbfounded Kunjolly.

"I'd like to see those Starfleet orders for myself, Monty."

"Of course, Captain," the station commandant replied

understandingly. Reaching into his desk, he withdrew another cube, replaced the Pandronian message cube with it, and activated the playback.

This time the triple screen bloomed with the face and upper body of a Starfleet admiral. A second human hovered in the background of the recording. Kirk didn't recognize the nonspeaker's face, but the trim uniform of the Federation Diplomatic Corps was unmistakable. Both he and Spock listened as the verbal orders played through. It was quiet in the office for a long moment after the communiqué ceased.

"But surely, Monty," Kirk argued out loud, "rendering services can't mean that Commander bn Bem is permitted to commandeer the *Enterprise* for his own private transportation."

Kunjolly looked thoughtful, then ventured almost apologetically, "What are your next stated orders, Captain?"

"Actually, we don't have any." Kirk told him. "On dropping off Commander bn Bem here we were supposed to"—his voice sank—"await new directives from Starfleet."

"In the absence of additional orders or specifics, the message appears inarguable, Captain," Spock finally mused aloud. "We are to provide whatever services Commander bn Bem requires, while keeping within Federation law. The commander desires to go directly to Pandro, therefore we must take him there.

"I confess I too have mixed feelings about traveling to the world which developed those attitudes the commander espoused prior to our experiences on Delta Theta Three, but naturally we cannot allow personal opinions to interfere with the Starfleet directive."

"Naturally," Kirk concurred. "Though just this once I wish that—" He stopped, frowning. "Spock, we don't know why the commander has to go to Pandro so quickly. Could it violate Federation and Starfleet law if he fails to tell us?"

"Unfortunately," Spock responded, "I am afraid that because our orders were so general in scope, he need not. But considering his altered attitude, I have grounds to believe he will."

"Good-bye, Monty," Kirk said quickly. "It looks as if

you'll have to wait a while longer to entertain a Pandronian representative."

"From what I've heard and seen, Captain," the station commandant replied, "I don't think the delay will upset too many of my associates."

After rushing for the turbolift depot, Kirk and Spock had to wait around for an empty capsule. In his haste to return to the *Enterprise*, a frantic Commander bn Bem had taken the last one by himself.

"I hope," Kirk noted with wry amusement, "he has the decency to wait for us to return before leaving. I wouldn't put it past him to try to order the *Enterprise* about on his own!"

IV

The Pandronian commander didn't go quite that far, but his impatience was unmistakable to Kirk when he walked onto the ship's bridge.

"Is in greatest hurry to depart, Kirk Captain," bn Bem rattled off at top speed, accompanied by much waving of hands and rolling of eyes. At least the eyes remained in place in his head, Kirk mused gratefully. "Is of the urgency utmost to proceed to Pandro at maximum velocity."

"Just try to take it easy, Commander," Kirk advised the apoplectic Pandronian as both he and Spock resumed their stations. "We'll get you there as fast as is practicable."

"Not to delay," bn Bem advised him, his voice assuming a warning tone. "Is best for all to remember the delicate nature of present negotiations between planet Pandro and Federation, not to mention Pandro and Klingon Empire."

"Don't threaten me, Commander," Kirk told him quietly. "I have my orders, which instruct me to take you home if that is your wish. I'll carry those orders out." His voice rose ever so slightly: "But threats from you or anyone else won't slow me or speed me in doing so."

"Slow you or speed you in doing what, Jim?" another voice inquired.

Kirk glanced over a shoulder, saw that McCoy had entered the bridge. "In going to Pandro, Bones."

McCoy's body, unlike Commander bn Bem's, was incapable of separating into three independent parts. The expression of the good doctor's face as he heard Kirk's announcement, however, seemed to suggest that he felt ready to give it a try. His gaze traveled incredulously from Kirk to the phlegmatic bn Bem, then back to Kirk again.

"Pandro! I thought we were going to leave this—going to leave Commander bn Bem here at the station, then proceed on new orders."

"Those *are* our new orders, Bones, as interpreted by Mr. Spock and myself. We are to render unto bn Bem whatever bn Bem requires. Right now he requires that we get him to Pandro pronto."

"But why, Jim? Why us? Why not a Pandronian vessel?"

"Yes, why the unusual haste, Commander?" asked Spock from the science station.

"Insensitive beings!" bn Bem raged, a touch of his former personality reasserting itself. "Unfeeling ones! Explanations to demand while sacrilege occurs!"

Still fuming at the incomprehensible insult caused by Spock's simple question, the commander stalked off the bridge.

McCoy stared after the fuming alien until the turbolift doors had closed behind him, then glanced sardonically back to Kirk. "Well, now that everything's been made clear . . ."

"Do not be too harsh on our guest, Doctor," advised an ever considerate Spock. "From what we now know of his psychology I have to guess that his fury is motivated not by hostility but by some real atrocity which has taken place on his homeworld. I believe that if we do not press him for information now, he will inform us of the cause of his anguish before we arrive at Pandro."

For a long while it didn't look as if the first officer's prediction would come to pass. Commander bn Bem remained secluded in his cabin, having his meals sent in and refusing to have anything whatsoever to do with anyone. All invitations to emerge were met with a stony silence, broken occasionally by gruff mutters in Pandronian which sounded vaguely like cursing.

All that changed of necessity when the *Enterprise* eventually entered orbit around Pandro and the transporter room was prepared to beam them down. Or so Kirk thought as he, Spock, and McCoy stood waiting in the chamber for the commander to appear.

"Surely, Jim," a still disbelieving McCoy murmured, "we're not going to beam down to a world possibly populated by arrogant megalomaniacs without having the slightest idea of what we're letting ourselves in for?"

"Don't worry, Bones. We're going to stay right here until I get some kind of explanation out of bn Bem."

"If you recall the wording of our orders from Starfleet, Captain . . ." Spock put in by way of gentle reminder.

"I recall the wording perfectly, Spock. We are to render service to Commander bn Bem as he requires."

When it became clear that the captain had nothing to add, Spock pressed on. "Would you still refuse him beam-down then, Captain, if he continues to refuse information?"

Kirk smiled knowingly. "Of course not, Spock. As you just noted, I couldn't do that without violating our orders. But I'm betting that bn Bem, this close to home, won't want to chance that."

Several minutes passed in idle speculation among the officers as to the cause of the Pandronian commander's extraordinary summons home. No one had produced a likely explanation by the time the subject of their conversation arrived.

Spock and McCoy followed Kirk into the Transportation Chamber, while Commander bn Bem exercised his newly won knowledge by moving to the transporter console where he instructed Chief Scott on beam-down coordinates. Scott had to admit to himself that the Pandronian had done his homework: the coordinates were precise and neatly translated from Pandronian navigational terms.

The commander moved rapidly then to take up a position alongside the three waiting officers. Kirk nodded toward the console.

"Stand by to energize, Mr. Scott."

"Standin' by, sir," replied the chief engineer.

Kirk waited a couple of seconds for effect before he turned to stare hard at the Pandronian. "All right, Commander bn Bem. We've brought you this far unquestioningly, but we're not beaming down until I find out what we're likely to encounter. What was that message you received all about?"

"At once to beam down!" the commander retorted angrily. "At once to waste no more time. Is for you to remember orders that—"

Kirk was shaking his head slowly. "Sorry, *that* won't work

any more, Commander. Our orders directed us to render you whatever service you required in accordance with Federation law and regulations. For us to beam down ignorant of surface conditions which might prove hazardous to Federation personnel—ourselves—would be in violation of those laws." bn Bem said nothing, but continued to stare belligerently at Kirk.

"Well," Kirk finally prompted the Pandronian, "which'll it be? Do we get some information, or do we sit here until I can get clarification from Starfleet headquarters? And unless Pandronian bureaucracy is astonishingly more efficient than its Federation counterparts, you know how much time *that* will take."

Commander bn Bem's gaze turned toward the deck and he was obviously struggling to control himself. "Is time for This One to have patience," he mumbled. "Is better to be pleasant with misunderstanders."

Eventually he looked up and explained tersely, "You will comprehend full meaning not, but has been *stolen* the Tam Paupa." His enunciation of "stolen" conveyed a sense of intense disgust and disbelief, evident to every listener on the bridge despite their differences in species.

"The Tam Paupa?" Kirk repeated, wrestling with the supple but guttural pronunciation. "I'm afraid we don't know what that is, Commander bn Bem."

The Pandronian looked exasperated. "Did I say not you would not understand? This One endeavors to elucidate.

"Has been worn well Tam Paupa by every ruler of United Planet Pandro for"—he hesitated briefly—"for twelve thousand of your years. To understand importance of Tam Paupa you must realize, hard though it be, Kirk Captain, that on rare occasions we Pandronians can be slightly testy, and argumentative even."

"Oh, we couldn't possibly think of you that way," McCoy chirped in sarcastically, "but if you say it's true, I suppose we'll have to believe you—hard though it be."

"Take it easy, Bones," Kirk whispered to the doctor, but McCoy's sarcasm was apparently lost on the worried Pandronian.

"Is the wearing of Tam Paupa," bn Bem continued, "which gives elected premier of Pandro the ability to govern fairly and without animosity toward others. Is talent recognized and honored by all Pandronians. Wearer of Tam Paupa never accused of injustices or favoritisms. This has preserved our civilization, Kirk Captain, has permitted Pandro to reach present heights. To imagine government without Tam Paupa not possible.

"An example This One gives. Sixteen hundred of your years ago, was stolen from premier, Tam Paupa. Chaos and civil wars resulting took three hundred years to recover from. That this again should happen is unthinkable." He looked simultaneously revolted and downcast. "Yet happen it has."

"I think I understand, Commander," Kirk responded sympathetically as bn Bem turned away to hide his emotions.

Kirk whispered to the nearby Spock and McCoy, "This Tam Paupa is some sort of crown or other device that somehow enhances the decision-making ability of the elected Pandronian leader while assuring the general populace of his continued impartiality. I'd like to have a look at the mechanism."

"So would I, Captain," Spock agreed readily. "Such a device, if it truly does what the commander says it does, could benefit others beside the Pandronians."

"And now it's been stolen," added McCoy. "Last time it caused three centuries of civil war." He whistled softly. "No wonder the Pandronians are panicked."

"It would appear, Captain," the first officer went on, "that we have been presented a chance to solidify the Federation's position vis-à-vis formal interstellar relations."

"You mean do more than just transport the commander home, as our orders indicate?" Kirk said. Spock nodded slowly and Kirk considered uncertainly. "I don't know, Spock. We know so little about Pandro. What little we do know seems to point to a highly developed society fighting to survive on a primitive world."

"No more time to waste on murmurings idle," a pleading bn Bem interrupted them. "Now to rush-hurry-quick with transporting."

Devoid of any reason to stall further, Kirk gave his assent. The three officers resumed their positions prior to transporting as Kirk faced the console.

"You can energize, Mr. Scott."

"Aye, Captain," the chief engineer acknowledged from

behind the console. "I dinna know where these coordinates will set you down. I hope the commander knows what he's doin'."

Kirk recalled the last time they'd set down on a world after bn Bem had programmed the transporter. He uncomfortably remembered rematerializing several meters above open water. But he said nothing, mentally seconding Scotty's wish.

His first impression was that he had materialized at the point of a gun. That was his thought as he stared at the tubular-shaped, lethal-looking instrument a grim-faced and very blue Pandronian was pointing directly at his chest. Glancing around, he saw that the little group was surrounded by similarly armed, equally determined Pandronians.

"What's this all about, bn Bem?" McCoy asked, fighting to keep his anger in check.

"An explanation would certainly seem to be in order, Commander," Spock added more calmly. But he didn't take his eyes off the Pandronian covering him.

"A precaution only, gentlemen," the commander assured them. He spoke to the guards in his own language. Abruptly the weapons went vertical and the intimidating circle turned into an escort of honor.

"This way, please," bn Bem indicated. Kirk, Spock, and McCoy followed the commander at a rapid pace down a high-ceilinged, triangular-shaped corridor, their former captors flanking them on either side.

"I still do not understand," Spock persisted.

"Is sad to admit, Spock Commander," bn Bem proceeded to explain, "but are somewhat paranoid we Pandronians where other races are concerned. As was This One until enlightening experience on Delta Theta Three."

Privately Kirk felt that describing Pandronians as "somewhat paranoid" severely understated their state of mind, but it would have been undiplomatic to argue the point.

They turned several bends in the corridor as Spock wondered aloud, "How did the guards know where we were going to materialize, Commander? You had no contact with the surface prior to our beaming down."

"Oh, is standard landing coordinates for all un-Pandronian visitors," bn Bem told them. "Detectors in chamber sense utilization of various transporter fields and so are alerted the guards."

That satisfied the first officer. It also inspired Kirk to reflect on the fact that the Pandronians were an advanced people whose friendship was well worth cultivating even if their personalities could be somewhat disagreeable.

It also caused him to wonder how the Tam Paupa could have been stolen, since the Pandronians were clearly very security-minded.

A final bend in the corridor and they came up against a closed and guarded door. Commander bn Bem spoke to the two neatly uniformed guards standing before it, and the little party was admitted instantly.

The room they entered was roughly circular in shape. A broad window across the floor showed that they were at least thirty meters above the surface of Pandro. A view of the disjointed Pandronian architecture of the capital city of Tendrazin was visible through the transparent acrylic. Green trees and fuzzy growths of all kinds brightened the cityscape, as would be expected on a world which was primarily savanna and jungle.

The chamber itself was domed, the roof blending into walls of blue, green, and yellow tile. Light filled the room, courtesy of the vast oval skylight above. Where the skylight met the walls, the glass or plastic was composed of multihued mosaics depicting scenes from Pandronian history.

From various points above, globular lamps hung by long thin tubes to provide additional illumination. Scroll cases and sealed cabinets of a wood like oiled cherry lined the walls, alternating with closed doors.

A large half-moon desk of darker wood rested on a raised dais at the far end of the impressive chamber, backed by the sweeping window. Several rows of curved, thickly padded benches formed concentric arcs before it, the seats adjusted to accommodate the Pandronian physique.

"This is the innermost *Pthad*," bn Bem explained with a touch of pride in his voice, "the seat of our government. Here meet the integrals of the high council to determine policy for all Pandro."

McCoy's attention was focused not on the sumptuous appointments or the view of the city beyond, but on something sandwiched between two nearby cabinets.

"What's that?"

bn Bem glanced in the direction indicated by the doctor. "Is one of the premier's favorite pets."

McCoy strolled over to the large rectangular cage. It was formed of narrow slats of some bright gray metal. Its floor was covered with what appeared to be a mixture of natural growth and dry wood shavings.

Resting in the center of the cage floor lay an animal. It had a plump round body covered with bristly brown fur about a centimeter in length. Seven pair of legs protruded from seven clearly defined segments. A double tail tipped one end while a tiny ball of a head indicated the other. A single eye glared from its center, with nostrils set to either side and a mouth both above and below the eye.

At the moment, the apparition was munching sedately on some leaves or green paper—Kirk couldn't decide which. It peered up at the onlookers, its single blue eye blinking placidly.

"Not a very cuddly-looking pet," McCoy commented with distaste.

"The *diccob* is amusing, though," countered bn Bem, "and responsive. Watch."

Clapping his hands twice, the commander let out a low-pitched whistle. Immediately the *diccob* eyed him—and went all to pieces. Literally.

Eight sections, including the head, fell away from each other and performed a little scurrying dance, weaving about themselves. As if on cue, they unexpectedly came together. Only now the *diccob* stood erect, a bipedal form. Two segments served as legs, three as a body above, with a pair for arms topped by the head. The twin tail had also divided itself, and each tail formed a gripping tentacle at the terminus of each arm.

Apparently as content in this new shape as in its former one, the *diccob* returned to its eating. Kirk wondered at the marvels of adaptive internal physiology which permitted such rapid dissolution and reforming without any evident harm or loss of efficiency to the animal.

"Amusing, is not?" bn Bem inquired.

" 'Fascinating' would be a better term," a thoroughly engrossed Spock suggested. "Is it capable of assuming more than two forms?"

"Watch," was all the commander said. Under his hand and voice directions, the *diccob* executed several more collapses and reassemblies, concluding with a fully circular shape which rolled spiritedly around the cage like an animated wheel, the cyclopean head tucked safely on the interior of the wheel.

"Some *diccobs*," bn Bem explained to his mesmerized audience, "only one or two new combinations can manage. Premier's *diccob* can do twenty nearly. Is prizewinner."

"I can imagine," McCoy said. "My stomach does flip-flops just watching it."

"Is the *diccob* the most flexible form of Pandronian life?" Spock inquired curiously, "or are there other native types equally adjustable?"

"Difficult to answer that question is," bn Bem began, his tone oddly thoughtful. "To understand, first you must know that on Pandro is—"

The commander's reply was interrupted by a soft chime. Everyone turned toward the direction of the sound.

One of the numerous doors on the other side of the room opened inward and two Pandronians entered the chamber. One appeared to be slightly younger than Commander bn Bem, while the other, judging from his movements and coloring, was of an advanced age. Touches of yellow had crept into his natural blue skin, and he walked toward them with the deliberate caution of the incipient infirm.

Commander bn Bem bowed before him as Kirk, Spock, and McCoy did their awkward best to imitate the gesture.

"I present the Supreme Integral of all Pandro," bn Bem announced grandiosely as he returned to an upright position, "Premier Kau afdel Kaun. This Other One I know not," he concluded in referring to the premier's companion.

"Greetings to you, bn Bem Commander. To you greetings also, Federation representatives, and thanks be for your returning the commander home," the premier said in a shaky voice. "For you back to be is good, Commander, though sorry This One is that your visit and study of Federation must interrupted so shockingly and suddenly be."

Despite his aged body, the premier spoke in English for the benefit of his alien guests, Kirk noted admiringly. There was no condescension in his voice, and neither was there the arrogance the captain had come to associate with Pandro: a result, Kirk decided, of the premier's long association with the missing Tam Paupa.

He began gesturing to the younger Pandronian at his side. "Be known to Lud eb Riss, Commander and visitors. Of the atrocity on us visited he will tell you. This One tires." On unsteady legs the premier mounted the dais and slumped into the chair behind the curved desk.

"At the wall here," the younger Pandronian indicated, leading them to a blank space near the dais. Depressing a segmented tile caused a large map to descend. It was filled with Pandronian glyphs which none of the Federation officers could read, but a two-dimensional map was difficult to misinterpret no matter what its origin. Kirk felt certain he could identify large cities, mountains, an ocean, and other features.

"Was stolen the Tam Paupa," eb Riss told them, "several"—and he uttered a term in Pandronian which was evidently untranslatable—"ago. Thus far to it recover all efforts failed have."

With a hand he indicated a large symbol in the approximate center of the map. "We know it is not in Tendrazin or in any of other cities secondary nearby. Still scoured are other major cities of Pandro being. Search and seizing of known elements criminal nothing has produced. All are outraged by theft of Tam Paupa too."

"That's surprising," McCoy commented. "Why should the theft of the Tam Paupa bother them?"

"History has shown that crime flourishes best under stable governments, Doctor."

"Even on Vulcan?"

"Such sociological aberrations, Doctor, are more typical of less advanced societies such as—"

"Spock, Bones," Kirk muttered a warning. Both men returned their attention to eb Riss as if nothing had been said.

The Pandronian's hand moved to encircle a huge shaded area near Tendrazin, which grew to encompass a considerable section of the map west of the capital city.

"Has never been fully explored this region," eb Riss explained for their benefit. "Development halted here at Tendrazin. In this vast area we suspected the *ibillters* who have defiled Pandro have the Tam Paupa taken." eb Riss turned to stare at them, but his gaze was concentrated principally on bn Bem.

"Is thought that none there can survive, yet investigators believe perpetrators of blasphemy there have fled. Explained can be, since *ibillters* probably insane are."

"To the *varbox* fled?" an appalled bn Bem gasped. "Mad are they for surely."

"Why surely?" Kirk wanted to know. "What is this *varbox*?"

"A region filled with wild integrals and integrators, so dense and swampish to enter there is to court death in fashions unimaginable and certain."

"One thing I still don't understand," Kirk continued. "How can your capital city be built so close to a dangerous, unexplored wilderness?"

"Much of Pandro unexplored is, Outworlder," eb Riss snorted with typical Pandronian contempt. "You comprehend not."

"We admit we know very little of Pandro," Spock confessed. "We would like to know more. When formal association between Pandro and the Federation takes place, we—"

"*If* takes place," eb Riss snapped brusquely. "I explain simple for you. Are surrounded most of our cities by largely untraveled jungle wilderness. Is due to nature of Pandronian biology. Is no such thing as Pandronian science of biology."

McCoy almost smiled. "Now, simple or not, that's impossible."

"Listen clear, McCoy Doctor," bn Bem advised him. "Are constantly changing, Pandronian life-forms. Most shapes unstable and ever altering, like *diccob* without training. A few integrators like ourselves"—he indicated his own body and its three independent sections—"discovered long ago that to stay in permanent association was benefit to all parts. Others have likewise evolved.

"But for rest of much of Pandro life, existence is struggling continual to find satisfying combination of sections. So is ever changing much of Pandro zoology, and some plant life as well. How can one classify species which exist a few days only?"

"I see," Spock murmured. "Pandro's ecology is unstable. I assume, Commander, that such steady mutations are limited to the higher forms of life?"

"They'd have to be, Spock," McCoy pointed out.

"Is true," bn Bem confirmed, "or otherwise ever altering diseases, bacteriums and virus forms, would all Pandro life have wiped out long ago. But forms microscopic constant are. Permanent integrators like self can build resistance to others."

"Is why," eb Riss put in, "all Pandronian cities and towns with history have old fortress walls around them, built by ancestors to hold out dangerously changing jungle lifes."

"What I still don't understand," muttered McCoy, "is why anyone would want to steal your Tam Paupa. If even the criminal elements have an investment in keeping it where it belongs, who does that leave as a potential thief?"

"Would only we know that ourselves, outworlder," came the sad voice of Premier afdel Kaun from behind the great desk. "Unheard of is this thing." He winced and both hands went to the sides of his head. "Is certain one thing only: Unless Tam Paupa soon recovered is, This One will lose ability to make sound objective decisions."

The supreme ruler of Pandro assumed a woeful expression. "Is certain. Can feel already This One divisiveness and personal opinions entering mind. At same time slips away slow and steady the intelligence needed to govern Pandro. Is terrible helpless this feeling."

"We must Tam Paupa recover, Kirk Captain," an anxious bn Bem added. "Or Pandro society sinks again into mindless raging against self." The commander drew himself up. "Have done what of you was asked, Kirk Captain, in bringing This One home. To you and your government goes thanks of planet Pandro."

Spock leaned over and whispered to Kirk, "Remember, Captain, our opportunity to gain a decisive march on the Klingons by ingratiating ourselves forever in the minds of the Pandronians."

"I haven't forgotten, Mr. Spock," the captain replied. He faced the raised deck and directed his words to the premier.

"Perhaps a new approach, or the benefit of outside thought processes, would be of some help to you, sir."

"Yourselves explain," afdel Kaun implored.

"Well," Kirk continued, "from what we've learned so far, we know that Pandronian science is far advanced in certain fields. Yet the Federation is more advanced in others. We're not afraid of the *varbox*."

"Bravery of ignorance," snorted eb Riss, but Kirk ignored him and pressed on.

"We have certain weapons in our possession, unknown on Pandro, which would be of much help in making one's way through the jungle you fear so strongly."

"Is true," bn Bem confirmed.

"Enough intelligence I retain to know that to accept your offer of aid is wiseness," the premier said solemnly. "How soon can you join expedition into *varbox*?"

"Inside an hour," Kirk replied quickly. "We'd like to return to our ship briefly to outfit ourselves properly for the journey, and also to obtain heavier weaponry. We'll need something more than hand phasers if the inhabitants of this jungle are as intimidating as you make them sound."

"Danger lies in not knowing what one may confront, Kirk Captain," bn Bem told him. "Time we will save if you beam back down into *zintar* yards."

"Whatever you say, Commander," Kirk replied, not bothering to inquire as to what a *zintar* yard might be. They would know soon enough. He flipped open his communicator as Spock noted a new set of coordinates.

"Kirk to *Enterprise*."

"*Enterprise*—Scott here, Captain."

"Beam us up, Mr. Scott, and stand by the transporter. We'll be coming back down shortly."

"Aye, Captain." A pause, then, "Back down, Captain?"

"That's right, Scotty. It looks like we're going to see more of Pandro than we originally thought. . . ."

V

After drawing jungle fatigues, appropriate survival equipment, and type-two mounts for their hand phasers, the three officers beamed down to the surface of Pandro once again.

A *zintar* yard turned out to be an enormous stable, although Kirk was reminded more of a repair yard for large shuttlecraft. Rank on rank of the huge, barnlike metal sheds were arranged alongside one another before a broad sward of green growth, cut short like grass.

Each long metal cell contained a sinuous reptilian creature which was a near analog of the ancient, idealized Terran Chinese dragon. But these were covered with gray, brown, and green fur.

"Like my own people," bn Bem informed them, "has found the *zintar* a combination of integrals advantageous to maintain. Advantageous to us as well." The commander introduced them to a tall, swarthy-looking Pandronian who sported short whiskers and managed to look like the Pandronian equivalent of a pirate.

"This is ab Af, who will our *zintar* in charge of be." ab Af made a curt gesture indicative more of a being interested in minding his own business than of standard Pandronian arrogance.

"eb Riss and six others will arrive to join soon," bn Bem continued. "They a third *zintar* will ride, while a second supplies carry. *Zintar* is only creature by us tamed which not afraid of forest. Better than machine. *Zintar* runs off other Pandronian life and will not break down. Very little there is that a *zintar* is afraid of."

"I can believe that," Kirk agreed, staring up at the weaving, bobbing dragon-head of the forty-meter-long creature.

It yawned elaborately, displaying thin, needle-like teeth in front and flat grinders behind. Four spikes or stiff whiskers—Kirk couldn't decide which—dangled from the front corners of upper and lower jaws.

bn Bem directed them to step aside as ab Af urged the monster out of its stable. The handler utilized verbal commands and prods from a small charged metal tube.

Kirk noticed the wide saddles set between protruding vertebrae on the creature's back even as bn Bem asked, "If all are ready, Kirk Captain?"

McCoy ran a hand through his hair as he examined the attenuated apparition. "I don't know if all are," was his comment, "but as long as I'm not expected to feed one of these oversized horned toads, I guess I'll give it a try."

"Good is, McCoy Doctor," bn Bem complimented him. He barked something in Pandronian to ab Af. The handler stood to one side of the swaying skull, touched the *zintar* between the front legs, and shouted a command.

Docile as a dog, the six-legged colossus appeared to collapse in on itself. Its short, stumpy legs never moved, but the central body slumped to the ground between them, like a ship being lowered between six hydraulic lifts. Its stomach scraped the dirt.

"Intriguing arrangement of ligaments and muscles," was Spock's observation at this unexpected physiological maneuver. "Both appear to be extraordinarily flexible." Using the thick fur for handholds, the first officer mounted one of the Pandronian saddles notched into the animal's backbone and seated himself as best he could. Kirk and McCoy followed, the captain envying the ease with which eb Riss and his six armed followers mounted their *zintar* nearby.

Once everyone was properly seated—Kirk felt "aboard" would be a better term to describe mounting a creature this size—ab Af uttered another command. Kirk felt himself rising, a sensation not unlike that produced in one of the *Enterprise*'s turbolifts, as the *zintar* raised its body between its legs again.

Then they were on their way, moving at a surprisingly rapid pace through the wide streets of Tendrazin. McCoy had started in surprise when the *zintar* began to move. The movements beneath him were unique. It was a peculiar—but not necessarily uncomfortable—sensation, he reflected. Had he ever ridden a large camel, the motion would have been somewhat more familiar to him.

Before Kirk had gotten his fill of the fascinating architecture around them—a curious and exciting mixture of archaic and ultramodern—they had passed through a very old, heavily guarded gate in the ancient city wall and were traveling steadily across a broad open plain.

"Many of our crops," bn Bem lectured them from his position just behind ab Af, "are grown within old city walls, to protect the cultivators from incursions by wild Pandronian lifes. Space here and around most cities are clear kept for reason the same, Kirk Captain."

"We are obviously headed on some predetermined course," Spock commented from two places behind Kirk. "Why this way? I thought you said you didn't have any idea where the thieves had fled, except into the very large area you called the *varbox*."

"Are going that way now," bn Bem replied. "Have tried all sources in cities. Was one noncity theory which implicated *varbox*, but could not get Pandronians to try until you your weapons aid offered." His voice turned conspiratorial.

"Several citizens of Tendrazin home returning from fraternal meeting one night reported encountering large group of nervous-seeming Pandronians leaving city by gate now behind us. Suspicious Ones were on *coryats* mounted. One citizen asked destination and Nervous One replied his group to Cashua going. Cashua a medium-sized city several hundred *laggets* to northeast of Tendrazin."

"What's so suspicious about people going from one city to another?" McCoy wanted to know.

"Not where—when," bn Bem told him. "No One travels at night near forests on Pandro if not in armored vehicles. "Also, *coryats* good forest walkers, if protected well.

"Only recently this report checked in detail," the commander continued. "Was found that time necessary to travel between Tendrazin and Cashua, even allowing for reasonable delays, should have shown travelers there within four *daams*. No party on *coryats*, or of similar number to that reported by citizens, ever seen arriving at Cashua or other nearby cities. Party not sighted by aerial surveyests.

"So ground from Tendrazin outward hunted for clues. Many tracks of vehicles and animals near city, but few near forest. Found prints of *coryats* entering forest. Entering forest *there*," and he pointed ahead of them, to a slight break in the marching ranks of green and brown.

"Is old hunter trail, one of many," he went on. "No other trail show signs of *coryat* passage. May not be significant. Many Pandronians enter jungle on own, some for reasons legal not. Few return after long stay. Maybe these not wish to return.

"Is lucky dry season this is. If they did enter forest here, *coryat* tracks will remain."

In a short while the *zintars* slowed, approaching the first fringe of jungle. A small group of soldiers was waiting to greet them. eb Riss's *zintar* did the body-slumping trick and eb Riss dismounted to confer with one of the soldiers, apparently an officer. There was a short, animated discussion during which both Pandronians studied something on the ground out of Kirk's vision. He could imagine what the subject of their conversation was: the *coryat* tracks, which these troops had doubtlessly been placed here to protect against destruction—intentional or otherwise.

eb Riss confirmed Kirk's suspicions when he passed by them on the way back to his own *zintar*. "Tracks remain still," he called up to them. "Party of six to twelve entered the *varbox* here. Is more than first guessed. Too large surely it is for a larking group."

"True that is," agreed bn Bem, while Kirk and the others wondered at the purpose of a larking party. "On our way to hurry."

eb Riss gestured confirmation and trotted back to scramble monkeylike up the leg of his *zintar*. The expedition plunged into the forest.

Immediately the usefulness of the *zintar* in such terrain manifested itself. Not only did the creature's size intimidate and frighten off potential attackers, but its bulk shouldered aside or smashed over much vegetation, some of which was dense enough to impede the progress of any ground vehicle. The *Enterprise*'s heavy groundcraft could have done as well, but not nearly at such a pace.

Kirk mentioned his opinion as he continued to study the

uneven, swampy ground below, which was thickly overgrown with alien roots and climbers. And this was supposed to be a trail!

"I can see why the Pandronians prefer organic to mechanical transportation, Spock."

"Indeed, Captain," the first officer agreed, eyeing a particularly wicked-looking cluster of thorny vines which the *zintar* simply strode through without apparent ill effects. "Even a powerful landcraft would sacrifice mobility for movement here. And there is also the matter of logistics. It is evident that the *zintars* can live well off the land."

They were many hours into the jungle when the head tracker shouted back to them from his position on eb Riss's mount. Handlers halted their *zintars* while the Pandronian scrambled down one postlike leg and examined the ground. He gestured and babbled until several other troopers dismounted and followed him into the dense underbrush to one side of the forest path. The greenery swallowed them up quickly.

bn Bem and eb Riss started to show signs of nervousness when the tracking party failed to call out or return some minutes later. The two officers were about to order the *zintars* into off-trail pursuit in search of their vanished comrades when the little group reappeared.

The head tracker looked disheveled and tired, but the excitement was evident in his face. He walked to stand below eb Riss, began talking rapidly and with many gestures.

"The tracker says," bn Bem translated for them as the discussion progressed, "that a small but definite animal path within lies. Is evidence also of *coryats* passing. Age of tracks," and now the commander was hard pressed to restrain his own enthusiasm, "is proper to correspond with time suspicious party was noted leaving Tendrazin. Is further confirmation to clinch in tracker's hand."

Kirk leaned as far to his right as he dared, squinting. The slim tracker was waving what looked from this distance to be a torn bit of black fabric. At bn Bem's request, the incriminating cloth was passed up to him. A brief inspection and then he was conferring with eb Riss in Pandronian while Kirk, Spock, and McCoy waited tensely for information.

eb Riss's *zintar* handler shouted and tapped his mount on

its shoulder with the charged tube. One by one the three great creatures turned like seagoing ships to bull their way into the growths on their right. After a short walk the dense brush thinned somewhat, enough for Kirk and the others to see that they were truly traveling down a cleared and marked trail. It wasn't as broad or well used as the hunter's path they had entered the forest by, but a path it was.

bn Bem turned in his saddle, passed the bit of black material back to Kirk. His face looked grim. "Is first possible explanation to part of puzzlings, Kirk Captain. Now things become clear a little maybe."

"It's just a rag to me," Kirk told him, turning to pass it back to Spock. "Where's the significance for you?"

"A popular color on Pandro black is not, Captain. May again mean nothing. Is little to be gained by to conclusions hopping, but still . . ."

"But still—" Kirk prompted.

"Is on Pandro," the commander explained, "a small society of"—he paused for a second, hunting for a proper translation—"best I can come is physiological anarchists. They believe that holding integration to form perpetuating species is against natural orders. Would have all Pandro lifes, including This One, return to separate integrators and recombine as do wild forms. Mad Ones believe better integration than present developers of Pandronian civilization will eventually result.

"Very young and stupid most of them are. But they believe strongly in their madness, Kirk Captain. Have been troublesome in few incidents past, but not really dangerous. Is conceivable they could react violent enough against Pandronian heritages to perform heinous deed like theft of Tam Paupa. If any Pandronians could, would be them for sure.

"Part of their belief is to wear heavy black clothing, as if to hide the shame of their integration from universe."

"I take it the Tam Paupa was always well guarded," Spock said.

"Well guarded truly, Spock Commander," concurred bn Bem.

"I am puzzled, then," the first officer confessed, "as to how a small coterie of mildly annoying revolutionaries could suddenly jump from being youthfully irksome to executing a deed as elaborate as the Tam Paupa's theft."

"Agree wholesomely—no, wholeheartedly," bn Bem replied after a moment's consideration. "Is most strangeness. Would indeed not give group credit for such talents." He performed the Pandronian equivalent of a shrug.

"May be more than anarchist types after all. Into place pieces beginning to assemble. Still is missing important integers."

Kirk, Spock, and McCoy could only agree.

An urgent beep sounded in the Main Transporter Room on board the *Enterprise*. Transporter Chief Kyle stared blankly at it for a moment, then moved quickly to the console intercom when the beep was repeated.

"Transporter Room to bridge, Engineer Kyle speaking."

"Chief Scott here. What is it, Mr. Kyle?"

The engineer waited until a third beep confirmed the previous message and reported, "Sir, I'm receiving a direct nonverbal emergency signal from the surface on personal communicator frequency. There seems to be," and he hurriedly checked two readouts, "sufficient strength to indicate that the signal is being generated simultaneously by two—no, by three communicators."

A short pause, then, "It must be the captain, Mr. Spock, and Dr. McCoy, though I canna imagine why they're usin' nonverbal signalin'. They can tell us soon. Home in on them and stand by to beam 'em up, Mr. Kyle. We'll find out what happened soon enough."

On the bridge Scott turned to face Communications. "Lieutenant Uhura?"

"Mr. Scott?" the communications officer replied.

"See if you can raise any of the landin' party and get an explanation of what the trouble is."

"Yes, sir." Uhura turned back to her instruments and rapidly manipulated controls. She glanced back concernedly seconds later.

"No response, sir."

"Verra well." He directed his words to the command chair pickup again. "Beam 'em up quickly, Mr. Kyle."

"Aye, aye, Mr. Scott."

"Rematerialize slow as you safely can. I'm coming down." He rose from the chair. "Lieutenant Uhura, you're in command until I return with the captain."

"Very well, sir." As a precaution, she buzzed for Lieutenant M'ress to come on duty, on the unlikely chance that she would have to vacate Communications and take up position at the command station. Safety procedures were good to keep up, even if certain key personnel lost a little sleep in the process.

Moving at maximum speed, Scott entered the Transporter Room even as Kyle was bringing up the crucial levers.

"They're coming in now, Chief," the engineer indicated, sparing the approaching officer the briefest of glances.

"Carry on, Mr. Kyle."

Three forms slowly solidified, began to assume definite outlines in the transporter alcove. The last flickers of transporter energy were dying away as Scott charged reflexly for the alarm switch.

The paralysis beam projected by one of the forms standing in the alcove caught the chief engineer just above the knees. With a desperate twist and lunge, Scott was just able to fall forward enough to slap a hand down on the red control.

Klaxons commenced sounding all over the *Enterprise*. On the bridge, Uhura declared a general alert, then activated the command chair intercom.

"Transporter Room—Chief Scott, Mr. Kyle, what's happening down there?"

Kyle fought to reply even as he was dodging immobilizing beams from behind the shielding bulk of the console. Scott fought to pull himself out of the line of fire using only his hands.

"I don't know!" the transporter engineer shouted toward the intercom pickup. "Chief Scott's been hurt." The three things in the alcove were rushing toward him, firing as they came. "Three boarders, bipedal, type un—"

Transmission from the Transporter Room ceased abruptly.

"Engineer Kyle—report," Uhura yelled into the intercom. "Report!" The intercom gave back a steady slight hiss—and faint sounds as of something not human moving about the chamber. She turned, spoke decisively to where a now wide-awake M'ress sat ready at the controls.

"Lieutenant, contact all security stations. Seal off the entire deck around the Main Transporter Room and have security personnel close in."

"Yes, sirr," M'ress acknowledged without thinking. "What arre they to look forr?"

"Three invaders, bipedal in form. Beyond that, your guess is as good as mine. Whatever they are, they've injured both Chief Scott and Mr. Kyle. Warn Nurse Chapel to stand by for casualties and to alert backup medical personnel."

Uhura turned to face the helm as M'ress relayed her orders through the ship. "Mr. Arex, maintain orbit and begin attempts to contact the landing party. Mr. Sulu?"

"Yes, Lieutenant?"

"Take over security operations. You will personally assume charge of the rescue of Chief Scott and Mr. Kyle."

Sulu was out of his chair and heading for the turbolift. Uhura watched him leave, wishing she could go in his place. But she had been left in command, and personal reasons were no reasons for altering orders—especially in an emergency situation. But, she thought furiously, if the three who had beamed up weren't the captain, Mr. Spock, and Dr. McCoy, then who were they? More important, why weren't the *Enterprise* crew members responding from Pandro?

In the Transporter Room below, Scott rolled over onto his back and pushed himself to a sitting position against a wall. Kyle, he saw, had been completely paralyzed by the strange weapon which had so far only affected the chief engineer from the waist down. Around him the general alert continued to sound, but it didn't appear to panic or otherwise affect the three figures standing over Kyle and conferring among themselves.

Each was clad in a long black robe. Black hoods covered their heads. At the same time as Scott recognized their chatter as Pandronian they flipped their hoods back and began to disrobe. They were Pandronians, all right.

Somewhat to the chief's surprise, Commander Ari bn Bem wasn't in the group. He was glad of that. Had bn Bem been one of the belligerent boarders, it would have meant that the captain and the others were in serious trouble below. They still might be, but the wild-eyed, disorganized appearance of these three gave Scott some hope that at least the Pandronian government wasn't involved.

But if that was the case, how had the creatures managed to board the *Enterprise* so neatly?

All were sullen and grim-faced. One pointed at Scott, then jabbered at his companions. A second replied curtly and they bent to examine Engineer Kyle.

Scott ground his teeth in frustration and anger as they roughly turned the body over. With relief Scott saw that Kyle's eyes were open and functioning, even if the rest of his body was frozen into immobility.

Further discussion in the alien tongue and suddenly the three Pandronians became nine. Each split into its three component parts while Scott gaped. He knew of the Pandronian ability from the report of what had transpired on Delta Theta Three, but this was the first time he had actually seen the process in action—not to mention in triplicate.

Each section grasped a sidearm in various hands, toes, or cilia, and the three heads, three torsos, and three lower bodies ambled out the Transporter Room door. As it shut behind them, Scott moved, fighting to drag himself toward the intercom.

He had no idea what the Pandronians were up to other than that it was inimical to the good health of the ship and its crew. And, he realized with a start, he had reported three of them. Without knowing that the invaders were Pandronians, Uhura and everyone else would be hunting for only three shapes, leaving six sections to stroll freely about the ship.

Hopefully they would be detected as sections of mature Pandronians, but Scott had no intention of leaving true identification to others. Despite the fact that the paralysis seemed to grow worse the more he moved, he continued hunching and pulling himself across the deck. The tingling numbness had reached his waist by the time he reached the console.

Exhausted by the effort, he started to shout. The intercom should still be open, since the Pandronians hadn't bothered to shut it off. If so, the directional pickup should gather and transmit his voice.

But the tingling moved rapidly now, creeping eerily up his arms and chest and into his throat. He couldn't operate his voice. Screaming furiously with his eyes, he slumped to the deck, falling across the legs of the motionless transporter engineer and rolling slightly to one side.

Apparently the paralysis left the higher functions unimpaired, for Scott found he could still see and hear, could still think clearly. Moving his eyes, he saw Kyle staring helplessly back at him. With silent glances the two men managed to communicate a wealth of emotions to each other. Not least was a mutual anger at their inability to warn the rest of the ship as to the nature of their attackers.

A patrol of three security personnel was first to spot the invaders. Phasers set on stun, they exchanged fire with the unrecognized antagonists. Incredibly agile and too small to hit easily, the aliens slipped away.

But now the crew knew what they were up against, for the ensign in charge had recognized the similarity of the sectioned creatures to a former passenger.

"Pandronians!" Uhura exclaimed. "I don't understand." She leaned a little closer to the pickup to make certain she heard correctly. "Was Commander Ari bn Bem, our former visitor, among those firing back at you?"

"It's impossible to say, Lieutenant," came the reply from the security officer. "But from the pictures we were shown of him and from the couple of times I myself met him in corridors, I don't think so. Of course, there's no way to tell, and they were all split up in parts. Nine parts. I guess they could even be in disguise."

"Thank you, Ensign," Uhura acknowledged. "Keep your phasers set on stun. They haven't killed anyone yet. If they do," she added warningly, "appropriate orders will be forthcoming."

She clicked off, turned to Communications. "Lieutenant M'ress, keep trying to contact the landing party."

"I'm doing so, Lieutenant Uhurra, but therre seems to be some kind of interrferrence."

"Natural or artificial?" Uhura demanded to know.

"I don't know yet, Lieutenant. Without detailed inforrmation on Pandrro, it is difficult to say." She turned back to her instruments, leaving Uhura frustrated and unsatisfied, but helpless to do more than wait.

The squad that had originally spotted the invaders turned

down a corridor. Three dim shapes could be seen scuttling around a far bend.

"There they are!" the ensign in charge yelled. "Come on!"

Phasers at the ready, the two men and one woman rushed down the corridor. Each got halfway to the turn the three shapes had vanished behind when they grabbed at midsection or head, tumbling one after another to the deck.

Three sets of arms and chests slipped out of a crevice to inspect the motionless shapes lying on the metal flooring. Two lower torsos with heads set incongruously in their middles came around the corridor bend they had previously turned. The heads jumped off the hips, made room for the middle torsos and arms, which then picked the heads up and set them on their respective shoulders.

Thus reassembled, the three Pandronians started back up the corridor the way the security team had come.

VI

The *zintars* continued to make rapid progress through the forest. Kirk, Spock, and McCoy used the deceptively tranquil ride to marvel at the incredible diversity of life around them. Such abundance of forms was only natural in a world of constantly changing species, where an entire genus might consist of only one creature. And that creature might choose to annihilate itself and its place in any textbook of Pandronian biology by freely dissolving into its multiple components, or integrals.

These endlessly variable animals were in never-ceasing competition to create a form more successful, better able to compete, than the next. The steady flux led to a number of forms bizarre beyond belief, forms which—bn Bem told them—rarely lasted out a day or more before the component integrals realized their own absurdity.

They saw tiny mouse-sized creatures with enormous heads and pincushion mouths full of teeth, impressive but impractical on creatures so small. Massive armored bodies teetered precariously on the lithe limbs of running herbivores. Tall bipedal trunks armed with clawed arms and legs ended in bovine faces filled with flat molars suitable for mashing only the softest of vegetable matter.

"Such extreme mismatches ludicrous are, Kirk Captain," the commander pointed out. "Outlandish shapes continue to join, though, brief as they may last. So fierce is the compulsion new forms to create."

"How many possible combinations are there?" asked a thoroughly engrossed McCoy. "How many varieties of hands and legs, torsos and heads, trunks and so on exist?"

bn Bem looked dolefully back at him. "No one knows,

McCoy Doctor. Have been already cataloged many hundreds of thousands of shapes and millions of integrals. Sometimes cataloged ones vanish and new ones take their place. Is impossible job which never ends."

"I see," an impressed McCoy replied. "How often does a new successful form, like yourself or the *diccob* or *zintar* evolve?"

"Cannot give figure," bn Bem responded, "but is rare occurence. About forty percent Pandronian lifes maintain permanent association and reproduce same form. All can break down, though, if such is natural willing, but this is very rare. Cannot tell what will find next."

The officers were soon to discover the truth of the commander's concluding statement. The group made camp in a partial clearing on a slight rise of ground. Gentle though the rise was, it placed them high enough above the surrounding terrain to provide reasonably dry footing.

Kirk studied their surroundings. Only the different colors and designs of the encircling vegetation, the peculiar alien cries filling the evening air, made this jungle any different from half a hundred others he had visited or read about, including those of Earth itself.

To the south, the Pandronian sun was slowly sinking. It was slightly larger and redder than Sol, a touch hotter as well. The three massive *zintars* were bedded away from the camp, where they made their own clearing by simply walking in tighter and tighter circles until trampled vegetation formed a soft bed underneath. Well trained, they were left by themselves, their handlers secure in the knowledge that nothing known would risk attacking them.

eb Riss and his men unpacked supplies from the third pseudodragon, taking care not to tangle lines in the creature's fur. They produced several oddly shaped, roughly globular tents and some equally odd foot stores, which bn Bem assured Spock he and the others could eat. Had he not partaken with reasonable satisfaction of food on board the *Enterprise*?

The bonfire the troops raised in the middle of the encampment was the only familiar thing around, and McCoy in particular was glad for its cheery crackle and sputter.

"You can always count on the familiarity of a fire," he

pointed out to his companions, "no matter what kind of world you're on."

"That is not necessarily true, Doctor," Spock mused. "Depending both on the nature of the atmosphere in question and the combustible materials employed, a fire could be—"

"Never mind," McCoy advised with a sigh. "Sorry I mentioned it, Spock."

A heavy mist closed in around them as the sun dropped lower in the sky. The nature of the yelps and squeeps from the surrounding jungle changed slightly as the creatures of the day faded into their holes and boles and the inhabitants of dark gradually awoke.

"I can see," Kirk found himself musing conversationally to bn Bem, "how Pandronians could develop a feeling of superiority to other races."

"A conceit to be deplored," the reformed commander responded.

"No, it's true," Kirk insisted. "You're not to be blamed, I think, for such an attitude. You live on a world of constant change. Coping with such change is an incredible racial feat. You have reason to have developed considerable pride."

"Is so," bn Bem was unable to refrain from concurring.

Their conversation was shattered by a violent yet muffled howl from the depths of the forest.

"What was that?" McCoy blurted.

"Is no telling, McCoy Doctor," bn Bem reminded him, eyeing the surrounding trees appraisingly. "Is as your saying, as good as mine is your guess."

"Generally," Spock ventured, striving to see through the opaque wall of emerald, "those creatures which make the loudest noises do so because they have no fear of calling attention to themselves. That roar was particularly uninhibited."

As if to back up Spock's evaluation, the howl sounded again, louder, closer.

"I believe," the first officer said slowly, "it would be advisable to concoct some kind of defense. Whatever is producing that roar seems to be moving toward us."

"Is not necessarily true," bn Bem argued. "Strange vocal organs of Pandronian lifes can—"

Something not quite the size of a shuttlecraft rose like a

purple moon in the almost dark, towering out of the underbrush. It bellowed thunderously, took a step toward the camp—and stopped. It had encountered a pair of huge trees too close together for it to pass between. It hammered with massive limbs at the trees, shrieking its outrage.

Fortunately, Kirk thought as he retreated toward the bonfire in the center of the camp, the components which had combined to compose this creature had not included more than the absolute minimum of brains.

The creature snarled and howled at the tiny running shapes so close before it while continuing to try to force its way between the two trees. It could have backed off, taken several ponderous steps to either side on its five pairs of scaly legs, and charged the camp unimpeded. Thankfully, it obstinately continued battering at the stolid trees.

Kirk watched as the Pandronians struggled to set up a large complex device. It consisted of several shiny, featureless metal boxes arranged in seemingly random order. A long, rather childish-looking muzzle projected from one end of the collage and various controls from the other.

By now the thought had penetrated the attacking abomination's peanut mind that to go around might be more efficient than trying to go through. Backing up like a lumbering earth mover going into reverse, the creature moved to one side of the right-hand tree and started forward again.

Only its slowness allowed Kirk and his companions a measure of confidence. Kirk felt he could easily outrun the thing, but would prefer not to have to try. Spock was regarding the still-frantic Pandronians, and he concluded aloud, "It seems our friends were not expecting an assault of this size. I suggest, Captain, that to preserve the camp and supplies we disregard the egos of our hosts and restrain it ourselves."

McCoy already had his phaser out and was holding it aimed on the unbelievably slow carnivore. It showed a mouth lined with short saw-edged teeth. The cavity was wide and deep enough for a man to walk around in without stooping. Four eyes set in a neat row near the crest of the skull peered down at them dumbly, crimson in the glow of the campfire.

Nonetheless, McCoy wasn't impressed. "How can any meat-eater that slow expect to catch any prey? It's got to be an unstable form."

"True, Bones," Kirk acknowledged, "but if we don't stop it, it's going to make a mess of the camp."

"Maybe if we rubbed its tummy it would calm down a little," the doctor suggested.

Spock looked uncertain at the suggestion. "An interesting notion, Doctor. How do you propose we convince the creature to turn onto its back?"

"Don't look at me, Spock," McCoy responded innocently. "I just make up the prescription. I don't make the patient take it."

"I think something more convincing is in order, Bones," Kirk decided as the creature neared the first of the tents. "On command, fire."

Three beams brightened a small portion of the night. They struck the creature, one hitting the side of the skull near the neck, the other two touching higher up near the waving dorsal spines.

Letting out a hideous yowl, the monster halted. Two front feet rose off the ground, and the nightmare head jerked convulsively to one side. The creature shook off the effects, took another half tread forward.

"Again, *fire!*" Kirk ordered.

Once more the phaser beams struck; once again the effects were only temporary.

"Aim for the head," Kirk ordered, frowning at their inability to injure or even to turn the monster.

"Captain, we don't even know if that's where its integral brain is located," declared Spock, who shouted to make himself heard above the creature's snuffling and yowling.

"Why don't you ask it?" McCoy suggested as he tried to focus on one of the four pupils high above.

Spock frowned. "The creature does not appear capable of communication at the higher levels, Doctor." He fired and ducked backward as the head, making a sound like two steel plates crashing together, snapped in his direction.

But by now the Pandronians had assembled themselves behind their funny-looking little wheel device. All at once there was a soft thud from the muzzle and something erupted from its circular tip.

Several hundred tiny needles struck the creature, distributed across its body. The creature took another step forward, the head almost within range of a quickly retreating Kirk, and then it stopped. All four eyes blinked sequentially; a second time. A high mewling sound began to issue from the beast, incongruously pitiful in so threatening a shape.

Then it started coming apart like a child's toy. Various segments—legs, tail parts, and pieces of skull—dropped off, each running madly in different directions, until the entire apparition had scattered itself into the jungle.

"That's quite a device," McCoy commented, impressed. He walked over to study the machine. It no longer looked funny. "What does it do?"

"Is difficult, McCoy Doctor," the Pandronian commander explained, "to kill a creature whose individual integrals retain life independent. Would have to kill each integral separately.

"This," and he indicated the weapon, "fires tiny syringes, each of which a chemical contains which makes mutual association abhorrent to creature's integrals. Is very effective." He gestured at the forest wall.

"Attacking carnivore integration suddenly found its components incompatible with one another. All broke free and fled themselves. Will not for a long time recombine because of lasting effects of the drug."

"I offer apologies," a new voice said. Kirk turned, saw a distraught eb Riss approaching them. "We did not an assault by so large a meat-eater expect, Kirk Captain. Was oversight in camp preparations on my part. Sorrowful I am."

"Forget it," advised Kirk.

"To produce a carnivore so large," eb Riss continued, "requires an unusually large number of integrators. The *fasir*," and he indicated the device that had fired the hypodermic darts, "is not ordinarily prepared so large a dose to deliver. And the first time we certain had to be dose was large enough to disassemble creature, or half of it might have continued attack we could not stop in time."

"An interesting method of fighting an unusual and unpredictable opponent," observed Spock with appreciation. "It would be interesting to consider if such a drug could be effectively employed against non-Pandronian life-forms. The fighting ability of another person, for example, would be severely impaired if his arms and legs could be induced to run in different directions. And if the parts could later be made to recombine, then a battle might be won without any permanent harm being done. There remains the question of psychological harm, however. If one were to literally lose one's head, for example . . ."

Mercifully, Kirk thought, McCoy said nothing.

"Is strange, though," bn Bem commented as he studied the forest, "to find so large a carnivore here. Far though we be, is still close for one so large to Tendrazin."

McCoy gestured at the jungle. "Do you think maybe it has a mate out there?"

Both bn Bem and eb Riss favored the doctor with a confused expression. "A mate? Ah!" bn Bem exclaimed, showing understanding. "Is evident you have no knowledge of Pandronian reproduction methods. Can become very complicated with multiple integrated beings. When we have year or two together will This One be pleased to explain Pandronian reproductive systems."

"Thanks," McCoy responded drily. "We'll pass on it for now."

"Any word on the whereabouts of the Pandronian boarders, Lieutenant?" Uhura inquired of M'ress.

"Nothing," came the prompt reply. Abruptly the communications officer placed a hand over the receiver in one fuzz-fringed ear. "Just a moment. Casualty rreport coming in."

Uhura's fingers tightened on the arms of the command chair.

"One securrity patrol incapacitated—thrree total."

"How bad?" came the unwanted but unavoidable next question.

"They appearr to be subject to some forrm of muscularr parralysis. It is selective in that it does not affect the involuntarry musculaturre, perrmitting vital functions to continue." Something on the board above the console beeped for attention, and M'ress rushed to acknowledge.

"Anotherr rreporrt, frrom Sick Bay this time. Trransporrterr Chief Kyle and Lieutenant Commanderr Scott have been similarrly affected. Commanderr Scott has been only parrtially affected, it appearrs. He is waiting to talk to you now."

"Put him through," she snapped. "Mr. Scott?"

"I'm okay, Lieutenant Uhura."

"We know its Pandronians. What happened?"

"They came through as I was enterin' the Transporter Room. Surprise was total. They used some kind of weapon that puts your whole body to sleep—everything but your insides. I dinna know what they're up to, but there is one thing I do want to know—verra badly, lass."

"I'm thinking the same thing, Mr. Scott." She could almost hear him nod his agreement.

"Aye . . . How did they know what frequency to simulate to convince us it was the captain and the others who wanted to be beamed back aboard?" There was a pause, then the chief engineer continued in a more speculative tone.

"The only thing I can think of is that they've taken the captain, Mr. Spock, and Dr. McCoy prisoner and learned or knew in advance how to broadcast the emergency signal."

A lighter but no less serious voice sounded over the communicator. "Now, you just lie down, Mr. Scott, and no more *but*'s, *if*'s, or *maybe*'s about it."

"Who's that?" Uhura inquired.

"Nurse Chapel here, Lieutenant," came the reply. "The paralysis shows no signs of worsening or spreading in any way which would threaten life functions. But I've four and a half cases in here, counting Mr. Scott as partly recovered. None of the others show any indication of similar recovery yet. I don't want to put any strain on anyone's system." She added, obviously for Scott's benefit, "No matter how well they're feeling."

"I agree absolutely," Uhura declared. "Let me know when anyone's condition changes—for better or worse."

"Will do, Lieutenant."

"Bridge out." Uhura turned back to stare thoughtfully at the communications station. Her gaze did not fall on the busy M'ress, who was striving to coordinate the flow of security reports from around the ship, but went past her.

How *had* the Pandronians known what signal to duplicate? And how had they managed to do it? Was Scott right? Had the captain and the others been captured? Or was there another, as yet unforseeable explanation?

An excited yelp came from Communications, a cross between a growl and a shout.

"Take it easy, Lieutenant M'ress," Uhura advised. "What is it?"

"I have contact with the landing parrty, Lieutenant!" she replied gleefully. "It's weak, but coming thrrough."

Uhura was hard pressed to keep her own enthusiasm in check. "Put them through."

There was a beep, followed by a burst of white noise. Exotic sounds drifted over the bridge speakers, but Uhura didn't relax even when she heard a familiar, if distorted and slightly puzzled, voice.

"Kirk here," the badly garbled acknowledgment came. "What's the trouble, Mr. Scott?"

"Mr. Scott has been injured, Captain," she said quickly. "This is Lieutenant Uhura, acting in command."

"Scotty hurt?" came the cry of disbelief. "What's going on up there, Lieutenant? Report in full."

"We've been boarded, Captain. By Pandronians—three of them." She hesitated, then asked, "Are you sure you're speaking freely? If you can't, try to give me some sort of sign."

There was a long pause and everyone on the bridge could hear Kirk discussing the incredible situation with someone else. A new voice sounded.

"Spock here. We are perfectly all right, Lieutenant, and able to converse as freely as if we were at our stations. What is this about the ship's being boarded by Pandronians? Such a thing should not be possible. The Pandronians don't possess the requisite technology."

"I'm sorry, Mr. Spock, but I want to make sure you're okay. What are you doing now, and where are you?"

Mildly incredulous, the ship's first officer replied with forced calm, "We are at present aiding local authorities in an attempt to recover something called a Tam Paupa, which is vital to the maintenance of stable, friendly government on Pandro. That is not important at this time.

"What is important, Lieutenant, is how Pandronians, and

hostile ones at that, succeeded in gaining access to the *Enterprise*."

"We don't know for certain," Uhura tried to tell them. "Somehow they managed to simulate the precise frequency of your hand communicators, in addition to duplicating the emergency beam-aboard signal in triplicate. Mr. Scott and Mr. Kyle naturally assumed *you* were broadcasting those signals and so locked in on them and beamed the villains aboard.

"Instead of you, three Pandronians appeared. They used some kind of paralysis weapon to stun the chief, Mr. Kyle, and at least one entire security patrol. Nurse Chapel says it doesn't appear to be fatal, but all five people affected are still immobile. Mr. Scott can talk, but that seems to be about all."

"What steps have you taken, Lieutenant?" Kirk demanded to know.

"All security forces have been mobilized and are now hunting the Pandronians, Captain," she reported. "The ship is on full alert, and all personnel are aware of the Pandronians' presence."

"What do they hope to achieve?" Kirk wondered aloud, static badly crippling the transmission.

"Excuse me, Captain," Spock broke in, "but it seems clear that the Pandronians who boarded the *Enterprise* are in some way connected with those responsible for the theft of the Tam Paupa. Yet I do not understand how they could know we are aiding the government—or how they are performing technical feats supposedly beyond their capacity."

"I want answers, Mr. Spock, not more questions. Stand by, Uhura."

"Standing by, sir," she replied. There followed a period of intense discussion on the surface below, none of which came over the speakers understandably.

Arex used the interruption to address the command chair. "Lieutenant Uhura?"

"What is it, Mr. Arex?"

The navigator looked thoroughly confused. "It is only that in routine observation of the surface below us, I have recently detected something which may be of interest."

"What is it?"

The Edoan manipulated instrumentation. A topographic

photomap of a large section of Pandro was projected by the main viewscreen forward. A cross-hair sight appeared, was adjusted to line up on the map's northeast quadrant. Several concentric circles of lightly shaded blue were superimposed over the region, the colors intensifying near the cross hairs.

"There seems to be an unexpectedly high level of controlled radiation active in this region," the navigator explained. "It is far more intense and sophisticated than anything else operating on Pandro, more concentrated even than anything in the capital city itself. It may be that it is a secret Pandronian installation."

"Just a second, Lieutenant Arex. M'ress, switch the lieutenant's intercom into the ship-to-ground broadcast." The Caitian communications officer executed the command, and Arex repeated the information for the benefit of those on the ground.

"Most interesting, Mr. Arex," came Spock's reply after the navigator had finished relaying his discovery. "Could you compare the center of radiant generation with our present position? Dr. McCoy will also activate his communicator to provide you with our most powerful detectable signal."

Several anxious moments followed during which M'ress pinpointed the source of the communicator broadcast. She then relayed the coordinates to Arex, who compared them with the location of the cross hairs on the photomap, then gave the information to Spock.

"*Most* interesting," the first officer replied in response, without bothering to indicate why it was so intriguing. "Thank you, Lieutenant."

"Uhura?" Kirk's voice sounded again. "Maintain red alert until the Pandronians are taken—alive, if possible. We believe they may have something to do with a tiny but dangerous rebel faction that opposes the constituted Pandronian government. But we don't know how they're doing what they're doing, or why.

"You can regard them as dangerous fanatics liable to try anything, no matter how insane. If they belong to the same group, they've already committed the ultimate act of outrage against their people. Consider humans in a similar position and treat these boarders likewise. But no killing if it can be avoided."

"We'll watch ourselves, Captain," Uhura assured him firmly. "Make sure you watch yourselves."

"Advice received and noted, Lieutenant. Contact us when something has been resolved—if you're able. The radiation Mr. Arex detected is undoubtedly responsible for our difficulties in communication. Kirk out."

"*Enterprise* out," Uhura countered.

Kirk put his communicator away, turned his attention to his first officer. Spock was making sketches on a small pad. "Tendrazin is here, Captain," he explained, indicating a small circle. "Our present position is approximately here, according to Mr. Arex's information."

Kirk called Commander bn Bem over and showed him Spock's sketch, explaining what the symbols meant.

"Yes, correct is," the Pandronian agreed, indicating the distances and relationships of Tendrazin and their current location.

"We are traveling in this line," Spock continued, using stylus and pad to elaborate. "The source of the unusual radiation, as detected by instruments on our ship, Commander, lies about here." He tapped an X mark slightly north and west of their present position. "Almost in a direct line with our present course away from Tendrazin. Does the Pandronian government or any private Pandronian concern operate an installation in that area which might produce such radiants?"

"In the *varbox*?" bn Bem stammered unbelievingly. "I have from home away been, but not so long as that. But to make certain is always good idea." He called out in Pandronian.

eb Riss joined them, giving Spock's crude map sketch a quick, curious glance. "Have in this region," and bn Bem pointed to the radiation source, explaining its meaning, "any government post been emplaced since my leaving?"

eb Riss's reaction was no less incredulous than the commander's. If anything, Kirk felt, it was more intense. "In that area lies nothing—nothing," he told them assuredly. "Is most intense and unwholesomest swampland. In such territories exist the most dangerous life-forms in the constant state of battle and recombination. No sane Pandronian would there go, and total Mad One would live not to reach it."

"Our readings wouldn't be off so drastically," Kirk informed him. "There is unquestionably a great deal of activity of a sophisticated nature going on there."

"Natural sources, maybe?" ventured eb Riss.

Kirk shook his head slowly. "Absolutely not. The quality and kind of radiation stamp it as artificial in source. If it was natural, Lieutenant Arex wouldn't have bothered to mention it to us unless it was dangerous."

"Is all very hard to believe," eb Riss muttered. "Certain is This One no representative of Pandro government there has been. No private group could build installation there, not even stealers of Tam Paupa. Must be mistaken your ship's detectors."

"Unlikely," Spock said sharply. "Nor is Lieutenant Arex the type to make such a report without triple-checking his readings."

"Are you so sure the rebels couldn't have a hideout in that area?" McCoy pressed bn Bem.

"Are mad and evil the blasphemers, McCoy Doctor," the commander admitted, "but suicidal are not. Remember, ourselves would not be here now if not with aid of your advanced energy weapons. Life-forms here and certainly there would overwhelm These Ones, even with *fasir* to defend us. Mad Ones have no such helping." He looked to eb Riss for confirmation.

"To knowledge of This One, *no* Pandronian has ever entered great swamps—or at least, entered and come out again to tell of it." eb Riss indicated agreement.

"And still," Kirk murmured thoughtfully, "Arex insists there's something in there. Something throwing off a lot of controlled energy. Something that's been interfering with our communications to the *Enterprise*." He eyed bn Bem firmly.

"Whatever it is, it's not very far off our present path. It'll be interesting to see if your tracker leads us toward that area. Don't you think that would be a mite suspicious, if these *coryat* tracks curve toward the radiation source?"

"All may come to be, Kirk Captain," eb Riss admitted, "but if does, tracks will there end. Not best tracker on Pandro can follow prints in swamplands."

"They won't have to," Spock explained to the pessimistic Pandronian. He flourished the map sketch. "The *Enterprise* has located the source of radiation. If we turn toward it, we need only continue on through the swamp in its direction. If required, we can recheck our position at any time by contacting the ship. Provided," he added cautioningly, "communications interference grows no worse."

"Very well so," eb Riss said, dropping his objections. "If holds true, we must proceed toward *suspected* radiation source." Evidently the Pandronian officer still refused to believe that any Pandronians could have constructed something in the inimical swamplands. "But only if *coryat* tracks lead there and no place else."

"I disagree," bn Bem said firmly. Kirk and the others looked at the commander in surprise. "I enough have seen of Federation science facilities to know that what *Enterprise* officers say is truth." He gestured with a furry arm into the jungle ahead.

"Could be circling track designed to throw off any pursuings. Could follow we *coryat* tracks for many *fluvets* and find nothing save more *coryat* tracks. *Enterprise* findings to me significant are. I think we to radiation source should proceed, no matter where go *coryat* prints."

"I concur not, Commander," objected eb Riss strongly. When bn Bem merely stared back, the other Pandronian made a hand movement indicative of resignation. "But is outranked This One. It as you say will be."

"*Slateen,*" bn Bem announced in Pandronian. "Is settled, then. We toward there turn," and he pointed to the *X* on Spock's map.

eb Riss headed back to ready his own troops and to mount the lead *zintar*. As McCoy walked toward his own patiently waiting dragon he jerked a thumb toward the forest, toward the two huge trees their assailant of the previous night had tried to break through.

"Apparently," he told bn Bem, "we're heading into an especially bad area. Does that mean we're likely to encounter any more visitors like last night's?"

"Is not likely, McCoy Doctor," the commander informed him.

McCoy was surprised, but relieved. bn Bem added, "Creature that attacked us last night would not be able to compete with dangerous animals in swamplands."

"Oh," was all McCoy said, trying to conjure up an image of something that could take the monster of the forest apart integral by integral.

"Surely the thought of confronting larger primitive carnivores does not intimidate you, Doctor," Spock declared. "You have faced far more dangerous creatures on other worlds, which could not stand up to a type-two phaser."

"It's not that, Spock," the doctor explained. "It's just that the Pandronians don't even know what might be festering and growing out there. How can they, when potential antagonists break up and form new combinations every couple of days? I can take the thought of coming up against all kinds of different killers, but the idea of facing something never before in existence until it stands up and screams in your ear, and doing that maybe a couple of times a day, is a bit overpowering."

"It does reduce one's ability to prepare for defense," the first officer had to admit. "Still, that only adds to the interest of the occasion. Imagine being able to remain in one place for a while and watch evolution take place around you."

"Thanks just the same, Spock," McCoy replied. "Me, I think I'd prefer a little more biological stability." And he shivered slightly in a cool morning breeze as the howls, hoots, and shrieks of creatures which had only just come into being sounded the arrival of a new day.

VII

The low-intensity blast of a phaser set on stun exploded on the wall behind one of the three Pandronians. That was followed immediately by a distant cry of "There they are! Notify all other units."

The Pandronian that the bolt had just missed shouted to his companions. Together they increased their pace as they ran down the corridor.

In addition to hearing the faint call with their own auditory organs, the boarders had also detected it far more clearly over the pocket communicators each of them carried. Although those communicators differed substantially from Federation issue, they still received the on-board broadcasts of the *Enterprise* with shocking electronic competence.

Their very presence was something no one—not Scott, not Uhura, nor anyone else striving to locate the three intruders—could have suspected. So even as instructions to various security units and the rest of the crew were being sent through the ship, the Pandronians who were the subject of all the conversation were overhearing every word.

At that very moment the interlopers were listening to instructions passed to a large security team close ahead, directing them to block off the corridor. While the three had managed to evade the group which had nearly caught up with them, they knew that couldn't last much longer. More and more security teams were concentrating in this area, sealing off every possible escape route.

Or so they thought.

Realizing the importance of the narrowing cluster of pursuers, the Pandronians did a curious thing. They stopped. The tallest of the three fumbled with his backpack and removed a small box. A tiny screen was set on top of it with controls below.

Once activated, the screen began to display a rapidly shifting series of schematics and diagrams. Not everyone could have recognized them, but an engineer would have known what they were instantly. They displayed, in excellent detail, the inner construction of a Federation heavy cruiser.

The operator touched a switch, freezing one diagram on the screen. All three Pandronians examined it. This was followed by a brief, intense discussion after which they hurried on down the corridor once more.

Very soon they came to a small subcorridor. Instead of rushing past, they turned down it. The subcorridor was a dead one, according to the diagram, but the Pandronians were not looking for an appropriate place to be captured or commit suicide.

Stopping near the end of the subcorridor, one of them opened a carefully marked door on the right. It opened into a cramped room, two walls of which were lined with controls. The largely automatic devices were not what interested the Pandronians, however.

By standing on a companion's shoulders, the tallest of the three was just able to reach the protective screen in the roof. The lock-down seals at each of the screen's four corners opened easily. According to the diagram they had just studied on the tiny display screen, this shield opened into a ventilation tube. Said tube executed several tight twists and turns before running down the section of the ship they desired to traverse.

Once the shield screen had been opened, the third Pandronian closed the door behind them and then climbed up onto his two companions and pulled himself into the tube above. Reaching down, he helped the first one, then the other into the shaft.

Turning in the cramped quarters, the last Pandronian to crawl in reached down to reseal the lock-downs from inside, using a small hand tool from his own pack to reach through the fine mesh to the locks on the outside.

Very soon thereafter, six armed security personnel turned down that same dead-end corridor in the course of scouring ever possible avenue of escape. They moved to its end. With five phasers covering him, the ensign in charge tried the door on the left. All instruments inside the little room appeared undisturbed and registering normally.

Then he turned to the door on the right. The room beyond was likewise deserted. "No sign of them." He turned to leave.

"Just a minute, sir," one of the crew said. "Shouldn't we check out that overhead vent?"

The ensign retraced his steps, leaned back to stare up at the uninformative grill overhead. "Could they have slipped in there?" He wondered aloud. "It doesn't seem likely, but we'd better make certain." He pulled out his communicator. "Engineering?"

"Engineering. Lieutenant Markham here," came the crisp reply.

"This is Security Ensign Namura. We're hunting the Pandronian boarders, and just now I'm standing in ventilation operations cubicle"—he peered around at the open door—"twenty-six. There's a sealed ventilation shaft overhead. Could a man crawl through it?"

"Just a second, Ensign." There was a pause as the engineering officer ran the schematics for that region of the ship through his own viewscreen.

"Got it now. Several men or man-sized creatures might get up in there, but the shaft goes straight up for about four meters. Then it does a number of sharp doglegs to connect with other ventilation tubes before running into a main shaft. No way a man could get through those turns, not even a contortionist."

Namura moved, stared up into the dark tube above. "Hang on, Lieutenant." Removing a small device from his waist, the ensign activated it, sending a powerful if narrow beam of illumination upward. It lit the entire four vertical meters of shaft, which were manifestly empty.

"They're not up there. Thank you, sir," the ensign said, replacing the light at his hip and speaking again into his communicator. "Security team twelve out."

Shutting off his communicator, he directed his words to the other five. "They're not in here. Let's try the next service corridor down." Relaxing slightly, the group turned and trotted out of the subcorridor.

Contact by the average member of the crew with Pandronians or things Pandronian had been infrequent and rare. So it was unfortunately only natural that in his anxiety to run down three man-sized intruders, Namura had overlooked the basic nature of Pandronians, had not considered their physiological versatility. Far above and beyond the security team, in the very bowels of the *Enterprise*'s ventilation system, nine segments of three whole Pandronians made their rapid way around twists and turns which no man-sized creature could have negotiated.

An hour passed and a worried Uhura faced Communications. "Still no contact with the invaders, Lieutenant? It's been much too long."

"No, Lieutenant Uhurra," M'ress replied. If anything, she looked more haggard than her superior. Ears and whiskers drooped with exhaustion, her energy drained by the effort of coordinating dozens upon dozens of uninformative security reports from all over the ship, compounded by the tension which still gripped everyone on the bridge.

"Therre hasn't been a sighting of the Pandronians in some time—only false rreporrts. One securrity team thought they had the boarrders trrapped nearr the Main Trransporrter Rroom, but they managed to slip past all purrsuerrs. I don't know what—"

Alarms suddenly began sounding at Communications, the command chair, and at several other stations around the bridge.

"Now what!" Uhura shouted.

Below, in another section of the cruiser, a badly dazed technician dragged himself to the nearest intercom. Acrid smoke swirled all around him, and the mists were lit by flashes of exploding circuitry and instrumentation shorting out. Phaser bolts and other energy beams passed through the choking air above and around him.

"Hello, hello!" he coughed into the pickup grid. "Bridge . . . emergency—"

"Bridge speaking; Lieutenant Uhura here. Who is this?"

"Technician Third Class Camus," the voice replied, shaky and barely discernible through the sounds of destruction around it. Something blew up close by and he was thrown slightly to one side. But one arm remained locked around the console containing the intercom. Bleeding from a gash across the forehead, he blinked blood from his eyes and coughed again.

"Camus—*Camus*!" Uhura yelled over the intercom. "What's your station? Where are you?"

"I'm . . . on . . . secondary bridge," he managed to gasp out. "We've been attacked. Only myself . . . two others on duty here. Standard maintenance compliment for . . . area. Aliens attacked us . . . slipped in before we knew what was happening. Must be . . . the Pandronians." He blinked again.

"Can't see . . . too well. Smoke. We didn't expect anything. Thought . . . they were several decks above us."

"So did we," replied Uhura grimly. She glanced away, back toward Communications. "M'ress, notify all security teams that the Pandronians are attacking the secondary bridge." She turned her attention hastily back to the intercom.

"What happened, Mr. Camus?"

"Explosive charges . . . not phasers. Shaped demolition, from what I can see." The smoke burned his eyes, and tears mixed with the blood from the gash above his eyes.

"Damage report?" Uhura queried.

"Helm's . . . okay. So's most everything else, except for minor damage. But communications are completely gone. We were lucky . . . I think."

"Report noted, Mr. Camus," Uhura told him. "This is important," she said slowly as something banged violently over the speaker. "Was the destruction achieved randomly or did they go for communications intentionally?"

"Don't know . . . Lieutenant," the technician reported, trying to see around him. "Happened too fast to tell anything."

"Understood. Listen, if they're still there, try to tie them down with your phasers," Uhura ordered him. "Security teams are on their way to you."

"Will do, Lieutenant," the technician acknowledged, just before something touched him in the middle of his back and he slumped to the deck unconscious.

Uhura looked again at M'ress. "Direct all security teams in that area to block off all turbolifts and stairwells, seal all corridors near the secondary bridge. Maybe we can pin them down there. Also notify Sick Bay to send a medical team over—they've obviously experienced casualties." Her expression was not pleasant. "If any of those techs die, every phaser on this ship goes off stun."

There was a low murmur of agreement from the rest of the solemn bridge personnel. "Verry well, Lieutenant," the communications officer acknowledged.

"I also want extra security sent to Engineering at warp-drive control and at all approaches to the main bridge."

"Yes, Lieutenant."

Uhura voiced her thoughts aloud. "If they *were* trying for communications, or anything else on the secondary bridge, then their intentions are obvious. They're trying to cripple one or more ship functions. If that's the case, then I think they'll try for Engineering or the bridge next."

She leaned back in the command chair, resting a fist against one cheek and trying to make sense of what was going on. Several minutes passed and she noticed that the navigator had his eyes focused on her.

"Well, what are you looking at, Arex?" she snapped.

"I am as worried as you are, Lieutenant Uhura," the Edoan replied in his soft singsong voice.

"Staring at each other isn't going to help the situation any." The Edoan looked away, but remained deep in thought.

"I just can't help wondering why Pandronians, even the rebel Pandronians the captain mentioned, are trying so desperately to damage the *Enterprise*. They must know that three of them can't do any serious destruction, can't carry out anything we won't eventually repair." She shook her head slowly, wishing the solution were as simple as operating ship's communications . . . communications.

Apparently the same thought occurred to Arex. "If it is our communications they are trying to destroy," he theorized, "and not the ship itself, it seems to me there can be only one reason behind this. They are attempting to prevent us from keeping in touch with the landing party. Yet for them to want to do so must mean this rebellious faction knows the captain, Mr. Spock, and Dr. McCoy are, as they mentioned, aiding government forces. If that is the case—"

"If that's the case," an excited Uhura finished for him,

"since only the Pandronian government knows we're helping them, that means that government is home to at least one traitor. The captain needs to be told."

"I believe the Pandronian government should also be notified," the always empathetic Edoan added.

"Lieutenant M'ress," Uhura began, "call the authorities in the Pandronian capital—anyone you can make contact with. Tell them it's vital for both their security and ours that we speak immediately to someone high up in the government. Then get in touch with the captain."

"Aye, aye," the tired Caitian replied. She turned back to her control console and prepared to carry out the orders.

She was interrupted by a loud thumping from somewhere across the bridge. Like everyone else, she paused, listening. Now the strange noise was the only sound on the bridge. It didn't remain stationary, but instead seemed to move from place to place. Abruptly, the noise ceased.

It was dead quiet for a minute, and then a loud bang sounded from overhead. "They're in the repair access space above us!" Uhura shouted.

"M'ress, emergency alert! Get a security team in here on the double. We've got to—"

Carrrumphh!

A powerful concussion shook the bridge. Smoke and haze filled the air, and nearly everyone was thrown to the deck. A hole had been blown in the roof, just to the right of the science station. Recovering well, everyone dove for cover in anticipation of the coming assault. Three sections of Pandronian dropped through the ragged gap, hurriedly assembled themselves into a complete assailant. Sections of a second came close behind, the three integrals joining together like midget acrobats.

As the second alien came together, the turbolift doors to the bridge slid aside to reveal four battle-ready security personnel, phasers drawn and aimed outward.

Everything happened very quickly after that. Huddled behind the command chair, struggling for every breath, Uhura was able to absorb only isolated glimpses of the subsequent fight.

One Pandronian fired a burst at her from an unfamiliar weapon, which glanced harmlessly off the arm of the protective chair. The alien whirled quickly to fire at the turbolift. This second shot caught one of the charging security techs in the shoulder and sent her spinning to the deck.

Her companion slipped clear of the confines of the lift car and fired. The stun beam struck the first Pandronian in the midsection. As the alien collapsed, he came apart again. Ignoring the immobile midsection lying still on the deck, the head hopped onto the lower torso. One leg reached down, regained the weapon still held in a stiff hand, and prehensile toes commenced operating the gun as if nothing had happened.

The second, by now completely reformed Pandronian ignored the battle and raised a device whose muzzle was wider than its handgrip was long. He aimed it to Uhura's left and fired. The awkward-looking instrument emitted a dull *pop* which was barely audible over the noise and confusion swirling around the turbolift.

Luckily, M'ress had seen the alien point the weapon and had rolled aside. She escaped injury when the short, stubby missile landed in the middle of her console. For a microsecond the flare from Communications was too bright to look at directly. As it vanished, Uhura could see puffs of white smoke covering the console and surrounding instrumentation.

The Pandronian reloaded his weapon for a second shot. But by this time security personnel were pouring onto the bridge via walkways as well as the turbolift, faster than the three Pandronians could shoot them down.

Short and furious, the gun battle ended before the second Pandronian could unload his second missile. It ended with all three aliens—or rather, all nine independently mobile sections of same—paralyzed and motionless on the floor.

When the last operative Pandronian integral, a furiously resisting head, had been stunned, Uhura, shaken, stood up from behind the command chair. One after another, the rest of the bridge complement rose or crawled out from their respective hiding places.

Only the security personnel who had resisted the attackers had been hit. Everyone else appeared healthy and able to resume his post. Security teams continued to pour onto the bridge, followed closely by medical teams responding to the emergency calls issued by the first to reach the bridge. It had grown incredibly crowded beneath the gap the attackers had blasted in the ceiling.

Uhura and Arex moved to examine the nine motionless shapes scattered across the deck. "Which one belongs to which one?" a bewildered security officer wondered.

"No telling," muttered Uhura. "Take the whole collection down. They can sort themselves out when they regain consciousness. When that happens, I've a few questions I want answers to—and I'll have them, or these three will be disassembled into a lot more than nine pieces!"

Under the close guard of a dozen security personnel, supervisory medical technicians loaded the various sections of dismembered aliens onto stretchers and carted them down to the security area of Sick Bay.

Once the bridge was clear of Security and Pandronians, Uhura used a pocket communicator to contact Engineering and request a repair team. Then she moved to stand before the shambles that had been the communications station.

M'ress met her there, trying to peer into the wreckage, yet careful to jerk clear whenever something within the whitehot mass would flare threateningly.

"I don't know what was in that missile," she confessed to Uhura, "but whateverr it was prroduced an enorrmous amount of heat. They couldn't have chosen a betterr way to make a thorrough mess of things."

It didn't take an expert to see what M'ress meant. Instead of being blown apart, the communications station had been melted, fused into a half-solid wall of metal and plastic slag. Where they could have replaced the damaged or destroyed areas resulting from an explosion, now the entire section of wall would have to be cut clear out to the depths of the heat damage and the console would have to be literally rebuilt.

When Scott heard what had happened, there was no holding him in Sick Bay, despite Chapel's admonitions. Having recovered the use of all but his legs below the knee the *Enterprise*'s chief engineer was on the bridge minutes later. He propped himself up on the mobile medical platform and directed the engineering team which had already commenced repairs. His steady swearing was directed at those who had dared violate his beloved equipment in so horrid a fashion.

It wasn't long before the subjects of Scotty's ire began to recover from the effects of security phasers. Uhura sat in the sealed security area and watched the activity within the Sick Bay cell as the Pandronians reassembled themselves.

"The lower portions recovered first, the head last," Chapel was explaining to her. "I expect that's only reasonable, since the heads contain the greatest concentration of nerves and would be most strongly affected by a phaser set on stun."

However, when Uhura began questioning them via a hand translator, the Pandronians might as well have remained unconscious, for all the loquaciousness they displayed.

"Why did you board the *Enterprise*?" she inquired for the twentieth time. All three sat quietly at the rear of the cell, ignoring the energy barrier and those beyond it while they stared with single-minded intensity at the back wall.

"Why did you destroy our communications facilities?"

Silence of a peculiarly alien kind.

"Was it to prevent our communicating with our landing party on Pandro? If so, how did you know about it?"

Perhaps, she thought, a question which should strike closer to home.

"Are you," she began deliberately, "connected to the rebel groups of Pandronians operating on Pandro? If that's true, why interfere with us? We have no desire to interfere in Pandronian domestic squabbles."

That was an outright lie, since the captain, Mr. Spock, and Dr. McCoy were openly aiding the present planetary government, but it produced the same response from the quiescent three, which was no response.

Uhura made a sound of disgust, turned to Chapel. "You're certain the paralysis has completely worn off?"

"From everything I can tell, they're fully functional. Any paralysis of the vocal apparatus is voluntary, Lieutenant."

"Fully functional, huh?" Uhura muttered sardonically. "Let's see some functioning, then." She raised her voice, all but screamed herself hoarse. "At least identify yourselves! Or are you going to insist you're not even Pandronians!"

Unexpectedly, the middle alien turned to face her. "We are the representatives of the True Order," he said contentedly.

Uhura was not impressed. "I seriously doubt that, whoever you are and whatever that's supposed to mean. But it's nice to know that you're capable of speech."

The Pandronian assumed a lofty pose. "Can talk to lower forms when mood occurs."

"Goody. Maybe you'd condescend to chat with this representative of a lower order about a few things. Once more: Why did you sneak aboard our ship?"

Dead silence. Uhura sighed.

"All right, if you don't want to talk about what you're doing here and why you've brutally assaulted those who mean you no harm, maybe you're willing to answer questions about yourselves." She began pacing back and forth in front of the energy barrier.

"What is this True Order you mentioned?"

"The Society of Right Integration," the Pandronian replied, as if talking to a child. "Only the True Order to restoring the natural order of lifes on Pandro is dedicated. Dedicated to bringing end to desecrating civilization now existing. Dedicated to eliminating vile government which perpetrates unnaturalness. To cleansing running sore of—"

"Take it easy," Uhura broke in. "You're giving me a running headache. What's this natural order you're so hot about restoring?"

Shifting his position slightly, the Pandronian gazed upward. "In beginning all lifes on planet Pandro had freedom of integration complete. Could integrate one life-form with any other to achieve integrated shape pleasurable for moment or lifetimes. Had even primitive Pandronian intelligences like This One great flexibility of form. Often primitive rites including dividing and recombining to gain new insights into existences." The alien's voice turned from reverent to remorseful.

"Then did bastard civilization now grown huge begin to take hold. To become rigid, unfluid, frozen was Pandronian intelligences. Recombinations among intelligent Pandronians were," and his words became coated with distaste, "law forbidden. Realized only a few true believers, first of True Order, that this was horrible wrongness! Themselves dedicated to restoring naturalness of Pandronian lifes!"

His head dropped and turned resolutely from her. Further

questions elicited only silence. Having delivered their sermon, the captives apparently had nothing more to say.

Uhura had listened stolidly to every word of the diatribe. Now, when it became clear they would learn nothing more from the three, she turned and spoke bitterly to Chapel.

"A bunch of religious fanatics. Wonderful! So somehow we've gotten ourselves mixed up in some kind of theological, philosophical rebellion against Pandronian society. A normal group of revolutionaries I'd know how to deal with, but these," and she gestured back at the silent Pandronians, "are of an impossible type anywhere in the galaxy. You can't talk reason and logic and common sense to them. Whatever such types are rebelling against is never worse than what they represent."

"I wonder," a concerned Chapel murmured, "if the captain and the others realize how fanatical their opposition is?"

"I don't know," Uhura muttered. "I hope so, because according to Chief Scott's preliminary estimation of the damage to ship's communication's facilities, we're certainly not going to be telling them about it for a while. Even energy-supplemented hand communicators would be hard pressed to reach the surface, assuming we could cannibalize enough components for them. And that kind of signal wouldn't get two centimeters through the radiation distortion now blanketing that region of the planet.

"I only hope the captain and Mr. Spock aren't as easily surprised as we were. . . ."

Once the strange roll-and-jolt novelty of riding the *zintar* had worn off, Kirk relaxed enough to enjoy their journey. One thing the ride never became was boring. Not with the incredible diversity of life that swarmed around them.

Kirk was able to study the constantly changing vista as the three *zintars* parted greenery and snarling animals alike, living ships plowing through waves of brown and green. In places he felt as if he recognized certain plants and, more infrequently, familiar animals that they had encountered before. As bn Bem had indicated earlier, these were the members of Pandronian nature which had found success and harmony in a particular combination of integrals. So much so that they reproduced as a continuing species.

These conservative representatives of Pandronian life were seemingly far outnumbered by the biologically unfulfilled. One could never predict what might hop, leap, run, or fly from behind the next tree, or scurry across a brief flare of open space ahead.

The excitement was intensified because the Pandronians were as new to many of these unstable shapes as Kirk. The thrill of never-ending discovery was intoxicating. In fact, he mused, that was the best way to describe the state of life on Pandro, where nature was on a perpetual drunk.

For the first time he had leisure to speculate on a host of related, equally fascinating possibilities. How, for example, did the Pandronians insure the stability of their domesticated animals? Imagine a farmer going out in the morning to milk the local version of a cow, only to find himself facing a barn full of bears.

Or what about mutating crops which could be nourishment incarnate when the sun went down and deadly poisonous on its rising? Even the stable forms of Pandronian life, like bn Bem and his ilk, were capable under proper stimulus of disassociating.

He didn't think, exciting as it was, that he'd care to be a Pandronian. Not when you could wake up one morning and find your head had gone for a walk.

Another full day and night of crashing through the undergrowth brought them to the end of the tracks. Dismounting from the lead *zintar*, the chief tracker confirmed that the *coryat* trail swung neither left nor right of the muddy, murky shoreline straight ahead, but instead vanished at the water's edge.

Perhaps coincidentally, the tracker also located evidence of considerable recent activity at that location on the shore, as of numerous creatures milling about in the soft soil where the tracks disappeared.

ab Af spoke to the *zintar* he was riding and the long furry form executed its elevator movement so that its riders could dismount easily.

McCoy was the first to approach the scum-laden edge of the water. "Not very appealing country," he commented, eyeing the unwholesome muck with professional distaste.

"An understatement, Doctor." McCoy turned, saw Spock

standing just behind him and likewise surveying the terrain. "It is no wonder that the Pandronians have not ventured into it, or that eb Riss doubted Lieutenant Arex's information."

What lay before them was neither water nor mud, but something which partook of both qualities. Where it didn't eddy ponderously up against solid ground, the thick brownish sludge bubbled softly under the impetus of noisome subterranean gases. Delicate gray-green fungus floated over much of the shoreline shallows. It drifted and clung viscously to the boles of massive multirooted trees. Vines and creepers and things which might as easily have been animal instead of vegetable hung draped haphazardly from intertwined branches, forming a cellulose web above the waterways between the trees.

Noting the absence of screeches and screams, McCoy commented, "It's unusually quiet here, compared to the territory we've crossed." He walked back, questioned bn Bem. "Is it quieter here than in the forest because the swamps aren't as fertile?"

"No, McCoy Doctor," the commander assured him. "Swamp lifes strive noise not to make. Unhealthy to call attention to Oneself in swamplands." Kirk joined them, and bn Bem turned his attention to the captain.

"According to tracker ours and instruments yours, Kirk Captain, our quarry in there somewhere has gone." He made a broad gesture to encompass as much of the morass as possible. "Is still hard to believe any Pandronian would into swamplands flee, but seems so. To follow we must a raft build." He started to turn and walk away, but paused at a thought and looked back.

"Is *certain* your people found radiation source that way?" He pointed straight ahead into the depths of the stinking riot of growth.

Spock held out a confident arm, matching the direction of the commander's own. "Directly along this line, Commander."

"So it be, then," bn Bem agreed reluctantly. He faced eb Riss, "Set all to raft constructing. Must push and pull our way through. *Zintars* and handlers here will remain to await our return."

"What return?" eb Riss snorted resignedly. "In there to

go is new death for all. Is madness to do, especially," and he glared haughtily at Kirk and Spock, "on word of outworlders."

"Forget you that *coryat* tracks lead here and signs of many creatures waiting disturb this place," bn Bem countered firmly. "Is advisable to go to source of strange radiation."

"Is not my objection to that," eb Riss corrected him. "Is getting to there from here my worry."

"On that I'm with you, Lud," McCoy commented, still studying the hostile nonground ahead of them. "Can't we just transport up to the ship and have Mr. Scott beam us down at the coordinates given for the radiation source, Jim?"

Kirk smiled apologetically. "You know that wouldn't be very good strategy, Bones. Remember the attitude of guards toward us when we first beamed down here with the commander? And they were expecting us. No, in this case slow but sure does the trick—I hope." He pulled out his communicator, flipped it open.

"But I don't think we'll have to fool with a raft." He glanced reassuringly at the curious bn Bem and eb Riss. "I'll order some strong folding boats sent down from ship's stores.

"Kirk to *Enterprise*." The normal brief pause between signal and reply came and passed. Frowning slightly, he tried again. "Kirk to *Enterprise* . . . come in, *Enterprise*." An arboreal creature squawked piercingly from somewhere behind them.

"Mr. Spock?" Kirk said, eyeing his first officer significantly. Spock activated his own communicator, repeated the call, and was rewarded with equal silence.

"Nothing, Captain. Nor is it radiation interference, this time. There is no indication that the ship is receiving our signals." He glanced over at bn Bem, who was watching anxiously.

"It would appear, Commander, that the rebel faction which we are tracking and which placed several of their number on board the *Enterprise* has managed to somehow interrupt ship-to-ground communications. Of course, we cannot yet be absolutely certain it is the same group, but evidence strongly points to it."

"I wonder if that's all they've managed to interrupt, Spock," McCoy grumbled.

"We've no way of knowing, Bones. And the breakdown could be due to other factors besides obstreperous Pandronians." McCoy could tell from the tone of Kirk's voice how little stock the captain placed in alternate possibilities. "We might as well proceed as sit here."

"To commence construction of the raft now," bn Bem directed eb Riss. The other Pandronian officer acknowledged the order and moved to comply.

Construction of two large rafts of local wood proceeded apace under eb Riss's skillful supervision. Kirk had to admit that the Pandronian, whatever his attitudes toward the Federation officers, knew what he was doing.

They were aided by the extreme mobility of the Pandronian troopers. Their ability to separate into two or three sections enabled each of them to perform functions no human could have duplicated, and with amazing speed.

As the day wore on they were attacked only twice while working on the rafts. According to bn Bem, this was an excellent average, considering their proximity to the teeming swamps. Kirk was thankful he wasn't present here on a day when the local life chose to act belligerently.

The first assault came when something like a large, supple tree trunk slithered out of the sludge nearby and panicked the Pandronians working nearest the shore. The creature sported long, branchlike tentacles. Its mimicry was lethally impressive: It looked exactly like a section of tree.

Under selective phaser fire from Kirk, Spock, and McCoy, the branches broke away, scampering in all directions on tiny legs to retreat back into the swamp and along the water's edge. Despite repeated phaser bursts, however, the main body of the tree snake remained where it had emerged from the muck, exhibiting no inclination to retreat.

Close inspection revealed the reason for this obstinacy. The thing didn't retreat because it couldn't. The trunk that looked like a tree was just that—an old warped log which the many small creatures that resembled branches had adopted as a central body.

"A poor choice of association," Spock commented. "Surely the branch animals could not hope to blend successfully with a vegetable."

"True is, Spock Commander," bn Bem agreed. "Is defensive integration for little long eaters. Other predators would be by size of this 'body' frightened off. Tomorrow will branch lifes be maybe spines on back of big carnivore, or maybe decorative striping along belly of big plant grazer."

The second attack on the raft builders was more insidious and dangerous than that of the almost pathetic branch imitators.

Kirk had gone for a stroll along the swamp edge, moving just deep enough into the forest to frustrate anything lurking below the sludge's surface. To snatch him from between these intertwining trees would require a Pandronian killer with more flexibility and brains than any Kirk has seen thus far.

He was taking care to remain within sight of the construction site when he heard the low thumping. It sounded something like a muffled shout.

Drawing his phaser, he moved cautiously forward, toward the source of the sound. In a partial clearing he discovered a rolling, jerking shape making frantic, nearly comprehensible noises. It was submerged under a blanket of olive-green puffballs. Two long ropes of interconnected puffballs were dragging the smothered form toward the ominous waterline nearby.

Kirk recognized that gesticulating, helpless shape immediately, was shouting back over a shoulder even as he ran forward.

"Spock—bn Bem—this way, hurry!"

Breaking into the clearing, he set his phaser for maximum stun and raised it toward the two living green ropes. At the same time he was assaulted by a horde of other fuzzy spheres. Not one was larger around than his fist. All were faceless, featureless. Other than the unbroken mantle of green fuzz, all that showed were three sets of tiny, jointed legs ending in a single short hooked claw.

Kirk experienced a moment of panic as the creatures swarmed around and onto him, began attaching themselves to his legs and feet. There was no pain, no biting sensation from unseen jaws. The puffballs neither stuck nor clawed nor punctured his skin, but merely grabbed tight and held on.

A similar multitude had blanketed McCoy to the point where only the doctor's hands, lower legs, and face remained visible. He was using all his strength to keep the fuzzy spheres clear of his mouth, nose, and eyes, so that he could still see and breathe. Every time he opened his mouth to call for help, one of the puffballs rolled over it, and he had to fight to clear the orifice. Meanwhile, the two long lines of interlocked balls, like knotted green hemp, continued to drag the doctor ever closer to the shore.

Kirk's phaser, carefully aimed, cleared some of them off his own arms and McCoy's body, but even as dozens fell stunned, other newcomers swarmed out of the underbrush to take their place. In seconds, however, Spock, bn Bem, and several Pandronian soldiers had joined him. With the addition of Spock's phaser, they were able to keep the fuzzy reinforcements at bay.

bn Bem and the soldiers were rushing toward the trapped McCoy. Each Pandronian brandished a long prod ending in a hypodermic tip. Working smoothly and efficiently, they began poking each individual bristle ball with the needles. Kirk learned later what he was too busy then to guess—each poke injected a puffball with a minute quantity of the same drug that the *fasir*'s syringe darts carried.

bn Bem and his companions began at the spot where the twin chains of green were holding on to McCoy. As soon as one ball fell away, another rushed in to take its place and continue the seemingly inexorable march toward the swamp.

But with Kirk and Spock now holding all reinforcements at the edge of the forest clearing, re-formation of the two green chains took longer and longer. Finally the chain was permanently broken and the Pandronians were able to begin picking individual puffballs off McCoy. When that was concluded, they chased the remaining spheres into the depths of the forest.

"You okay, Bones?" Kirk asked solicitously as he hurried over to the doctor. McCoy was sitting up, slightly groggy, and brushing at his clothing where the tiny creatures had clung.

"I guess so, Jim. They didn't break the skin or anything."

"How did it happen, Doctor?" asked Spock.

McCoy considered a moment before replying. "I was bending to get a closer look at something that looked like an overgrown aboveground truffle over"—he abruptly began searching around, finally pointing toward a tree deeper in the forest—"over there. Then it felt like someone had dumped a hundred-kilo bale of hay on me.

"Next thing I knew I was rolling over on the ground while those little monstrosities poured over me." He kicked at a couple of the immobile, now innocent-looking green balls.

"They were all over me in an instant. And they won't be pulled off." As Kirk helped him to his feet McCoy queried the commander, "What are they, anyhow?" His face contorted irritably and he resumed rubbing at his clothes. "They may not bite, but they sure itch like the devil."

"*Vigroon,*" bn Ben replied, nudging several of the olive globes with a blue foot. "A successful life-form we well know. Even near Tendrazin we have them, but they are not dangerous generally, since occur not nearly in such impressive numbers.

"By selves are harmless eaters of insect forms and other small things. But in integration they act concerted—as you have had opportunity to observe, McCoy Doctor."

"Saints preserve me from such opportunities," McCoy mumbled, trying to scratch a place on his back he couldn't reach.

"Are found near water only, when in dangerous numbers," bn Bem went on helpfully. Kneeling, he pushed six legs and fur aside on one of the immobile *vigroon*, to reveal a tiny circular mouth lined with minute teeth.

"Single, even fair number of *vigroon* could not kill any animal of size. Jaws too small and weak, teeth too tiny. But in large number integration can associative *vigroon* smother large prey or drown it. Last named what they try to do to you, McCoy Doctor.

"Many *vigroon* jump on prey creature to keep it from fleeing. Others link up to pull into water, where held under until drowned. Can then devour nonresisting corpse at their leisure. You would a great feast have been for them, McCoy Doctor."

"Thanks, but I don't feel complimented," McCoy muttered in response to the commander's evaluation.

"You sure you're not hurt, Bones?"

"I'm fine, Jim. Even the itching's beginning to fade—thank goodness."

Kirk turned to his first officer. "Mr. Spock, try to raise the *Enterprise* again."

"Very well, Captain." Activating his communicator, Spock attempted to contact the ship, with the same results as before.

"Still no response whatsoever, sir."

Kirk sighed, sat down on a rock, and ran both hands through his hair. "Things happen awfully fast with Pandronians. I still haven't figured out how those rebels managed to board the ship, not to mention knock out our communications. Pandronian technology just isn't supposed to be that advanced."

"We admit to knowing little about Pandro, Captain. It is conceivable that our preliminary fleet reports understated their achievements in certain areas by several factors. Given what has taken place so far, it would seem more than merely conceivable—unless another explanation can be found."

Kirk glanced up hopefully. "Have you any alternative in mind, Mr. Spock?"

The first officer managed to appear discouraged. "I regret, Captain, that I do not."

VIII

From the moment the two rafts were launched into the murky water Kirk could sense nervousness in the Pandronian troops. As they poled and paddled their way clear of the shore, the nervousness increased—and there was nothing more unnerving than watching a Pandronian with the jitters, their heads shifting position on their shoulders with startling unpredictability.

Kirk could sympathize. There was no telling what might lurk just beneath the surface of a swamp on any world, and on Pandro that was true a thousand times over. But as they traveled farther and deeper into the seemingly endless morass of sweating trees and dark waters and nothing monstrous arose to sweep the rafts out from beneath them, the Pandronians gained confidence. Oddly, though, the more relaxed and assured the regular troops became, the more concerned and uncertain grew Commander Ari bn Bem.

Kirk was finally moved to ask what was the matter. "Why the nervous face, Commander? We've had no trouble so far—less than we had when we were 'safely' on shore building the rafts." He peered into the dank mists ahead. "I don't see any sign of trouble, either."

"Is precisely what worries This One, Kirk Captain," bn Bem told him softly. "Should we have been assailed by unwholesome lifes several times by now. Not only has that happened not, but is little sign of any kinds of lifes, antagonistic or otherwise.

"In fact, the deeper into *varbox* we go, the scarcer becomes all life-forms. Is strange. Is worrisome. Is most unsettling."

"Is it possible," Spock ventured, "that the rebellious

Pandronians, who presumably have retreated through here on many occasions, could have committed so much destruction and taken so much life that the surviving inhabitants of this region have fled to other sections of the swamp?"

"Would take army of Pandronians all equipped with *fasirs* to clear even tiny portion of *varbox*," the commander countered, "and then would suffer heavy casualties in process. Would not think Mad Ones had such power or abilities at their command. If so, would believe they would have caused Pandro government much more trouble than they have before now. Find possibility unworkable, Spock Commander," he concluded firmly.

"Can you offer an alternate explanation for the comparative tranquillity of our passage, then?" the first officer wanted to know.

bn Bem openly admitted he could not. He repeated his feelings again: "Worries me."

Lud eb Riss, who was in command of the second raft poling alongside them, didn't share the commander's paranoia. "I see not why it should," he exclaimed almost happily. "Lucky can These Ones count themselves. Personal opinion This One is that if we not another meat-eater see again, will be more than pleased. Not to look gift *zintar* in the masticatory orifice."

They made excellent, unimpeded progress through the *varbox* all that day. When it grew too dark to travel accurately, they camped on the rafts for the night, mooring them to each other and to four great trees. The thick boles formed a rough square, and their nets of vines and creepers provided a psychologically pleasing barrier overhead.

Soft hootings and muted howls colored the night, but none of them came close enough to trouble the sleepers or the Pandronian troops on guard duty. Except for the humidity, the following morning was almost pleasant.

"When do we reach this place by your ship's supposedly infallible instruments located, Kirk Captain?" an irritable eb Riss wanted to know when the morning had passed.

Kirk turned to his first officer. "Well, Mr. Spock?"

Spock frowned slightly, his attention shifting from the view forward to the figure-covered sketch he held in one hand.

"We should have reached it already, Captain. I confess to being somewhat discouraged, but we may still—"

A loud Pandronian shout caused him to break off and, along with everyone else, look ahead. The second raft was moving a little in advance of the other, and a sharp-eyed trooper standing precariously on the foremost log was chattering excitedly in Pandronian. bn Bem and eb Riss were both straining to see something no one else had.

Kirk, Spock, and McCoy did likewise, and the reason for the lookout's enthusiasm became evident seconds later. They were once more nearing solid land. It rose in a smooth, firm bank from the sludge's edge. Despite the thick cover of growth, there was no concealing it. The ground looked as solid as that they had left the long Pandronian day before.

"I thought you once mentioned, Commander," Spock murmured, "that the width and length of this swampland was far greater than this."

"So This One did," bn Bem replied positively. "And so it is." He gestured at the muddy beach they were approaching. "Cannot possibly be other side of *varbox*. Can only one thing be: an island in *varbox* middle."

"But you cannot be certain?" the first officer persisted.

bn Bem turned to face him. "Cannot, since no Pandronian has ever penetrated into *varbox* this far—and returned to tell about it. But can be ninety-eight percent positive is *not* other side of *varbox*. Island must be. Could be many others."

"We can count at some future date," Kirk interrupted them. "Right now I'm interested in finding out what's on this particular one."

"Is seconding feelings, Kirk Captain," said bn Bem fervently, his hand fondling the dark sidearm strapped to his hip.

Both rafts grounded on the muck of the narrow beach. Amid much grunting and struggling by Pandronians and Federation officers alike, the waterlogged rafts were pulled far enough up onto the mud-cum-earth to insure their not drifting away. Probably they needn't have bothered with the effort, since the current here was nearly nonexistent.

No one, however, wanted to chance being marooned in the center of the dismal region without an immediate means of retreat. If the island turned out to be small, there might not be enough suitable lumber present to duplicate the rafts.

But as they moved cautiously inland it became slowly apparent that the island they trod was one of respectable size, despite the difficulties of seeing vary far to either side because of the dense ground cover. Had it not been for bn Bem's and eb Riss's assurance that they could not possibly have traversed the entire swamp, Kirk would have felt certain they had landed on its opposite shore.

Gradually the trees gave way to brush and thick bushes, the jungle turning reluctantly into less dense savanna. It appeared they might even be entering an open area, like a grassy plain. The low, easily ascendable hill looming ahead of them was almost barren of growth. Only a few scraggly bushes poked forlorn stems above the waving pseudograss.

"We ought to be able to get a good look at the rest of the island from up there," Kirk surmised, indicating the low summit. "This can't be a very high island. Not if the *varbox* maintains its similarity to Terran swamplands."

Starting forward, he pushed aside several bare branches and took a step upward.

The hill moved.

Jumping clear, Kirk joined the rest of the party in retreating back toward the jungle. Disturbed, the hill continued to quiver and rise heavenward.

"Nightmare!" bn Bem shouted in Pandronian. But Kirk felt he could translate the commander's exclamation without resorting to instruments.

At full extension the apparition was at least ten meters tall, equally wide. As to how long it actually was they had no way of telling, because they couldn't see around the thing.

A minimum of twelve heads glared down at them. Each head was different from the next, no two alike, boasting various numbers of eyes and nostrils and ears. Each mouth save one (which showed a round sucker at its end) displayed varying but impressive stores of cutlery.

Each head bobbed and twisted at the end of a different neck. Some were long and snakelike, others short and heavily armored. Still others were jointed like a long finger. Several of the 'growths' Kirk had noted on the creature's side and top moved independently, along with limbs of all shapes and sizes scattered seemingly at random along both sides of the horrible mass.

Grossest abomination of all was the huge body itself, a bloated ellipsoid whose skin alternated from feathers to scales to a smooth, pebbled epidermis not unlike the surface of certain starships. The skin was squared in places, round in others, concave in still more.

It looked as if something had taken a cargoload of creatures and thrown them into a vast kettle, then pounded and boiled the entire collection together and somehow reanimated the ghastly concoction. As the thing moved, the most awful cacophony of whistles, tweets, howls, and bellows issued from the various mouths. Round eyes big as a man glared down from one skull, flanked by slitted pupils in a second. One great burning red crescent shone in the midst of a third.

Somehow the beast moved, on a assortment of limbs as diverse as the rest of it. Short, thick pseudopods alternated with stubby, thick-nailed feet and long-clawed running limbs. It humped rather than walked toward them.

Still retreating into the jungle, the Pandronians fought to assemble their *fasir*. With phasers set on maximum, Kirk, Spock, and McCoy blasted away at the oncoming behemoth. It was like trying to stop a three-dimensional phalanx instead of a single creature.

Various sections and integrals would drop away—injured or killed—but the undisciplined collage would retain its shape and purpose. One, two, three heads were sliced away by the powerful handguns. The remaining nine continued to dart and probe for prey as if nothing had happened.

The Pandronians had almost assembled the dart-thrower when a high whining sounded. Every Pandronian, from the lowest-ranking soldier up to bn Bem, abruptly fell to the ground. They lay there, moaning and holding their heads.

Completely unaffected, a dumbfounded trio of Federation officers stood nearby, uncertain whether to aid their fallen allies or to continue firing at the lumbering mountain in front of them.

Events decided for them. As the first whine sounded, the creature's dreadful roars and yowls turned into a pitiable assortment of mewings and meeps and cries of pain. It turned like a great machine and began flopping off gruesomely toward the south, smashing down vegetation as it went until it had passed from sight.

Once the beast had vanished, the sound stopped.

When no explanation for this fortunate but inexplicable occurrence presented itself, Kirk turned his attention to something hopefully more understandable.

"What happened to the Pandronians, Bones?"

McCoy looked up at him. He was bending over one of the soldiers. "Beats me, Jim. The sound that drove off that grotesque impossibility also hit them pretty hard. Don't ask me why, or what produced it."

The soldier's normal healthy blue color had faded drastically. Every other Pandronian had similarly paled, though now their normal hue began to return.

"Inside my head, suddenly something," a panting bn Bem told them. "Painful, but more shock than anything else, This One thinks. Could tolerate if had to, but would rather not."

"From the look on your face, I can understand why," a sympathetic McCoy agreed. "What felled you drove off the monster as well. I suppose we should be grateful for that, but somehow I'm not so sure. At best this was a pretty indiscriminate kind of rescue."

"I do not think that term is entirely appropriate, under the circumstances," a voice objected. Everyone turned to its source.

Standing in a slight gap in the undergrowth leading toward the center of the island stood a semicircle of Pandronians. Kirk experienced no elation at the sight of their black robes and hoods. They wanted their suspicions about the Pandronian rebels confirmed, but not under these conditions.

More important even than the presence of Pandronian rebels here deep in the *varbox* were the modern hand weapons they held trained on the government party. They differed noticeably in their sophistication from anything Kirk had seen on Pandro so far. He almost recognized them—no, he *did* recognize them.

The source of the weapons—and probably the explanation for a great many other as yet unexplained occurrences—was to be found in the middle of the Pandronians: one, two . . . three Klingons.

Holstering his own sidearm, the one in the middle walked forward, stopped an arm's length from Kirk. "Captain James Kirk, I presume? I am Captain Kor of the Imperial Science Division. You and your companions—he gestured to include the dazed Pandronians as well as Spock and McCoy—"are my prisoners."

"What's the meaning of your presence here, Kor?" Kirk snapped, unintimidated. "What are you up to on this world?"

"You will probably find out in due course, Captain," Kor assured him. "Until then, I require your sidearm, please?" He held out a hand for the gun in Kirk's fist.

Kirk studied the surrounding group, all armed with Klingon weapons, and then reluctantly handed over his phaser. Spock and McCoy followed.

Black-clad Pandronians immediately ran toward them, disarming their counterparts and confiscating anything resembling a weapon, including the partially assembled *fasir*.

Under close guard, the helpless group started into the island's interior.

"Actually," Kor said imperiously, "you should all thank me for saving your lives. Had I not ordered the controller activated, the creature would likely have exterminated you by now."

"Not true," protested bn Bem with dignity. "*Fasir* would have induced deintegration in monster."

"Perhaps," Kor admitted, showing white teeth in a wide grin. "Primitive though they are, your local weapons are effective, in their fashion. And the creature was, after all, only one of our more modest experiments."

"Experiments?" echoed a curious Spock.

"First and Science Officer Spock," Kirk said tightly, "and this is our ship's chief physician, Dr. McCoy."

Kor did not acknowledge the introductions. After all, the officers were prisoners. "Experiments," he conceded, "yes. Experiments which it has been your misfortune and our inconvenience for you to have stumbled upon, Captain Kirk. Why could you not simply have returned to your ship and taken your troublemaking selves elsewhere?"

"I don't know about the misfortune part," Kirk replied, glaring as a black-clad Pandronian prodded him with the muzzle of a weapon, "but you can bet on the inconvenience.

The presence of armed Klingons on a world of high sentience like Pandro, without the knowledge and consent of the Pandronian government, is strictly forbidden by all Federation-Klingon treaties. Your presence here constitutes a violation of the most serious order, Captain Kor."

"No doubt certain parties would consider it so," the Klingon captain replied, "if it were ever to come to their attention." His grin turned predatory. "But that will not happen. And besides," he added, affecting an attitude of mock outrage, "we are *not* here without the Pandronians' permission."

"I beg to differ," said Spock. "No one in the government mentioned anything to us about the presence of a Klingon mission on Pandro. They surely would have."

"Can be of that certain," bn Bem finished.

"That depends on who you chose to recognize as the official government, Mr. Spock," Kor pointed out pleasantly. "We happen to feel that these representatives of a free society are the legitimate representatives of the Pandronian people." He indicated the black-clad figures escorting them. "Not the illegitimate government which has its seat in the city of Tendrazin."

"Government has support of overwhelming majority of Pandronian people," an angry bn Bem protested.

"A question of figures—mere quibbling," countered Kor, obviously enjoying himself.

"How do you have the gall to call these rebels a legitimate government?" Kirk demanded to know.

"They are for free disassociation and reassociation of all Pandronian life," the Klingon explained.

bn Bem could no longer contain himself. "Means destruction of civilization!" he shouted. "Would These Mad Ones destroy all civilization on planet Pandro by having intelligent Pandronians return to unordered integrals!"

"Anarchy," Spock concurred, "would be the undeniable result." He quieted when one of the Klingons gestured warningly with his gun.

Kirk suddenly looked thoughtful. "A lot of things are becoming clear now. How the rebels managed to simulate our communicator signals and get themselves beamed aboard the *Enterprise*, for example. And if they were responsible for the breakdown of communications between the ship and ourselves, how they knew where to go and what to destroy. Klingons were helping them every step of the way." He glared at Kor.

"I would be unduly modest if I denied aiding these brave Pandronian patriots," the captain confessed. "When you do not return to your ship, Captain Kirk, your death will be attributed to the malignant Pandronian swamp life—which will in fact be the truth." Kirk didn't like the sound of that one bit.

"It is hoped," Kor continued, "that the *Enterprise* will accept that information, along with your bodies, and leave Pandro orbit."

"You don't know Scotty," Kirk warned him.

"Scotty?" The Klingon looked puzzled.

"My current officer-in-charge. He's not the kind to gracefully accept three corpses without a more detailed explanation of how they came to be that way."

"Our explanation will be sufficient, Captain," Kor assured him. "We will concoct something so reasonable, so logical, that even the most skeptical mind will accept it. The story will have the advantage that none of you three or any of these misguided Pandronians," and he indicated bn Bem and the soldiers, "will be in a position to refute it."

"If you want us dead," Spock asked, obviously confused, "why didn't you allow that creature to kill us when it had the chance?"

"A couple of good reasons," Kor replied readily. "First, the possibility did exist that the Pandronians' *fasir* might have caused the creature to permanently disassociate. We do not like our expensive experiments ruined, not even the small ones."

"Small one," McCoy muttered.

"It was still a viable subject for further experimentation," the Klingon continued, "and therefore valuable to us. More important, we could not have permitted the destruction of our most valuable Pandronian operative."

Kirk stumbled, saw that bn Bem was too shocked even for that. "Valuable operative? Are you saying . . . ?"

"It would appear," Spock said, looking around carefully, "that our good friend Lub eb Riss has gone elsewhere."

bn Bem uttered a long string of Pandronian curses.

"The good eb Riss," Kor informed them, "is already ahead of us, on his way to our headquarters building. He has kept with him a small, supremely efficient Imperial communicator. With this we have easily been kept apprised of your progress." The Klingon shook his head sadly.

"You should have followed his advice to turn back instead of entering the *varbox*. He did his best to dissuade you, but you fools wouldn't listen. It would have spared me some awkwardness, not to mention what it would have spared you." He sniffed.

"However, you are here. So now you must be disposed of, and in a manner to satisfy your Mr. Scotty and everyone else on the *Enterprise*, Captain Kirk."

Another several dozen meters and the brush vanished entirely, revealing a cluster of fairly large prefabricated structures of Klingon style. Despite the speed with which they had clearly been put together, the buildings conveyed an impression of solidity. Multiple antennae bristled above one structure. Kirk also took note of what appeared to be a barracks for Klingon regulars and a series of interconnected science labs.

Ample use of local vegetation had been made, and the buildings gave every indication of being well camouflaged from the air. Off to the left, across a grassy open space, light danced and flared, indicating the presence of extremely powerful energy barriers—the partial source, at least, of the radiation that had so engaged the attention and curiosity of Lieutenant Arex.

"What do you keep on the other side of those fields?" Spock inquired, nodding in their direction.

"Our important experimental subjects, of course," Kor responded. "You will have an opportunity to see them at close range before too long—under unfavorable circumstances, I fear." He looked toward the swirling, shifting barrier. "At the moment they are all down toward the far end of the island. They prefer to stay as far away from the controller as possible."

"You mentioned this controller before," McCoy reminded him.

"Yes. It is the device which produced the frequency that

drove your attacker away," Kor explained, "and incidentally stunned your Pandronian friends. Our true-thinking Pandronians," and he again pointed to the silent rebels around them, "are provided by us with special devices that fit over the head and cancel out the frequency. We have located one, you see, which causes considerable discomfort to all Pandronian life-forms."

"Monsters you are," bn Bem growled. "Will never the Klingon Empire now bring Pandro under its influence. Ourselves will align with the Federation."

bn Bem's declaration constituted a Pyrrhic victory at best, Kirk knew, since it was growing more and more unlikely the commander would be able to return to Tendrazin to convey his recommendations to the government. Kor's threats were hardly idle. Given the severity of the treaty violation represented by this installation's presence on Pandro, he couldn't chance releasing any of them alive. That had been self-evident from the moment Kirk had identified him as a Klingon, back near the jungle's edge.

"But what's your purpose behind all this?" he asked, indicating the extensive illegal station. "Why are you risking so much to carry out a few experiments? Or are you going to let these rebels use your frequency modulator to attack Tendrazin?"

"Certainly not," Kor insisted. "That would be dangerous to us, as well as unnecessary. For one thing, our rebel friends don't really have the expertise required to operate such advanced equipment as the controller. For another, its widespread use could be easily detected by any off-world observer. The Pandronians themselves would know immediately that the device was not developed on Pandro, and could notify any number of nosy busybodies."

"The Organians, for example?" suggested McCoy.

"There are certain parties," Kor admitted, "that might frown on such aid to one group of dissidents on an independent world. And there *is* that awkward treaty you mentioned, Captain Kirk. No, the controller is not a subtle weapon. And strong-willed Pandronians could resist it enough to fight back. Our friends are still few in number."

"Is clear now," a slightly subdued bn Bem observed. "They seek the collapse of our society for their own ends."

"Everything suddenly makes sense," Spock agreed. "The rebels destroy the present Pandronian government and take over, thus instigating a massive wave of disassociation among the planet's sole intelligent species. The Klingons, who are waiting on the sidelines, promptly step in, declare themselves selfless benefactors, and commence restoring Klingon order amid the chaos they themselves have helped to bring about." He reached for his translator, eyed Kor expectantly. But the confident Klingon captain offered no objection to Spock's use of the instrument.

Turning to the nearest black form, the first officer more or less repeated what he had just said, concluded by saying, "I am surprised you Pandronian rebels, whatever your personal beliefs, do not realize this."

"We assurances have," the Pandronian replied, "that once present unnatural government of Pandro is broken, Klingons will leave us in free disassociation. We only need permit them to establish base or two and count planet Pandro among their worlds of influence."

"If they go back on their promise to you," Spock argued, "you'll have no effective government with which to oppose them."

The Pandronian made his equivalent of a shrug. "Is disassociation and return to natural order that important is most. All else incidental is."

Spock gave up. "Rousseauian philosophy carried to a dangerous extreme, Captain."

"Mad," was bn Bem's evaluation. "All are mad."

"You will be properly dealt with soon enough, Captain Kirk," Kor told him. "But there is no great hurry, and as you have expressed an interest in our experiments here, and as to how we intend to aid our rebel associates, I see no reason why you should not go to your extinction well educated." He drew out a small control device.

"This remote is locked into the large controller inside the installation. It is convenient to be able to work out in the open, especially since our more successful experiments could never fit inside. Let's see"—he gazed down the wall of energy on their left—"I think the nearest cell will be most appropriate. The barrier also splits into individual cells for different experiments, you see."

He adjusted controls on the small box. Again the whine they had heard earlier sounded, but it was not as intense this time.

"It is now a bad headache like," bn Bem complained, wincing noticeably.

"It will get worse," Kor told him without a trace of compassion. "The various broadcast units are already operating full strength at the other end of the island, thus driving the creature toward us instead of away."

McCoy was staring intently through the energy barrier. "I don't see anything."

"Patience, Dr. McCoy," Kor advised him. "It is a large island, and the objects of our experiments must have room to move about freely."

They continued to wait in expectant silence. Except for a few intermittent flashes of fire across its fabric, the energy barrier was perfectly transparent. Most of the time there seemed to be nothing there at all, but Kirk knew that if he walked forward he would eventually encounter an invisible wall capable of stopping much more than a lone man.

As promised, the whining grew stronger, until bn Bem and the other Pandronian soldiers were once again writhing in pain. Captain Kor coldly ignored them and turned a deaf ear to McCoy's entreaties.

"Ah, it approaches. One of our noblest products to date, Captain Kirk."

"Something is certainly coming toward us, Captain." Spock announced, staring off into the distance.

Totally awed, they all gazed openmouthed as the living mountain moved toward the barrier. It dwarfed the monstrosity which had attacked them on landing at the island, made it appear a newborn puppy by comparison. Nearer it came, nearer, until it seemed it couldn't be any larger. And yet there was more of it behind.

Kirk forced himself not to flinch as the colossus halted on the other side of the barrier barely five meters away.

"We are quite safe," Kor told them. "There is a double barrier, one inside the other, in case by some unlikely mischance one should fail. Each is quite able to restrain such creatures. We take no chances with our experiments, you see."

Gazing up and up at the gargantuan thing, Kirk could understand why. It was hard to believe the mountain was alive. It was easily a hundred meters high and at least twice that in length. Comparing it again to the monster that had attacked them earlier found that smaller beast a model of symmetry compared to this thing. At least it had faintly resembled an organized creature. This sported head and necks in no special place or order. Only the legs appeared even vaguely arranged according to natural law. From time to time new eyes or ears or mouth orifices would appear along the rolling, quivering flanks, while other organs would vanish within. The creatures apparently existed in a continual state of re-integration and disassembly.

"An impressive mass," Kor observed rhetorically. "It weighs many thousands of qons." There was an evil pride in his voice as he enumerated the virtues of his crime against nature.

"This is the most mobile one of its size we have been able to produce, although the barrier restrains some much larger but not nearly so agile."

"How," McCoy wondered, staring up at the burbling mountain, "did you succeed in getting so many small integrals to combine into such a monstrosity? Even Pandronian nature operates according to some laws."

"It is a forced, artificially induced association, of course," Kor explained. "The integration is accomplished by employing a combination of controller frequencies and a hormone we have synthesized. The hormone is essentially the antithesis of that used by the Pandronians in their weapons, such as the *fasir*. That drug forces Pandronian life-forms to disassociate, while our chemical impels them irresistibly to associate, to combine into larger, ever larger forms."

"It's still impossible," McCoy insisted. "How could something that big feed itself?"

"To begin with," Kor told him, "it is basically carnivorous. You can tell that from the preponderance of teeth and claws. Such a mass would ravage this entire swampland quickly enough, would eat its way across an entire planet in short order. We synthesize enough raw protein to keep our experiments like this one satiated. Of course, when we eventually succeed in developing a creature with high mobility, it will support itself when necessary."

"I would still know your purpose behind this," Spock said quietly.

"Oh, come now, Mr. Spock. I expect better of a Federation science officer. The universe is full of weapons. Not all need to be inorganic. A creature of this size," he went on as the experiment in question began to pound with awesome but silent futility against the inner force screen, "could assault a position defended even by phaser cannon. Because when one small portion of itself is destroyed, the rest continues on, thanks to its individual integrals.

"One would need to concentrate an enormous amount of firepower on it to reduce it to sizes susceptible to hand-weapon fire. By that time the creature would already have overwhelmed any field position, no matter how well emplaced and defended. The controller would see to that."

"Impractical," Kirk snapped. "Transporting several such monsters to a world in combat would be an impossible problem in logistics."

"Not at all," Kor countered. "We simply use the Pandronians own disassociation drug—in a diluted formula—thus causing the creature to disassemble into manageable sizes. These will then be transported like any breakdown weapon to the world in question and there reassembled on the battlefield through the use of the integrator hormone and the controller.

"Naturally," the Klingon captain added after a moment's pause, "not everything is perfected as yet. The problem of high mobility, for example. But do not worry—perfection is not far off. When that comes, Pandro will be turned into an organic arsenal for the Empire!"

IX

"What," Spock inquired as they were being led toward the nearest building, "do your Pandronian allies think of your plans?"

Kor showed no hesitation in replying. "The brave Pandronians who have chosen our assistance to aid them in their struggle against the regressive autocrats of Tendrazin care nothing for what we might wish to do in the swamplands, provided we permit free association and disassociation among intelligent beings on Pandro. They know that the results of our experiments will be utilized on other worlds, not here."

Kirk tried to imagine the colossus thundering against the impenetrable barrier before them let loose on a mechanized battlefield, or dropped into the center of a large city whose inhabitants might elect to resist Klingon rule—and he shuddered.

"The reb—patriots," Kor continued, "have granted us full permission to make use of all the Pandronian lower life we require for our experiments."

"You're not going to use the frequency modulator, you're not going to unleash your abominations on this world, and yet you say you're going to help the rebels topple the government without using Imperial weaponry. I'd like to know how," Kirk wondered.

"The Pandronian government will fall of its own accord, rotten as it is," Kor announced solemnly.

"You mean, unhelpful to Klingon as it is, don't you?" said McCoy angrily.

"Actually," the Klingon captain added in less pontifical

tones, "it will collapse because we aided the rebels in one slight sortie."

"The theft of the Tam Paupa—so that's how this motley assortment of fanatics managed to pull that off."

"You malign our patriots," commented a disapproving Kor. "Nevertheless, it is here. Would you like to see it?"

"The Tam Paupa . . . it here is?" a reverent bn Bem whispered, his head ringing.

"Would I lie to you?" grinned Kor.

"Would a Klingon—" McCoy began, but he was restrained by Spock. Why he couldn't have his say he didn't know, since they were going to be killed anyway; but Spock always had good reasons for employing physical restraint. The comment died aborning.

"Inside, please," Kor commanded them. They entered the building.

bn Bem expressed relief. "They have turned off the controller, This One thinks."

"I still can't believe you haven't used heavy weapons on Pandro, in contravention of still another treaty point," Kirk essayed. "How do you keep the dangerous swamp life clear of your pathway through the *varbox*, not to mention off this island?"

"That's no problem, Captain Kirk. Consider the modest experiment you encountered just inland. We let a few that size roam more or less freely about the perimeter of the island, and run some back and forth through the swamp path we've chosen with the use of controller remotes like this one." He tapped the control box at his waist.

"Most Pandronian life gladly makes haste to other regions. Those that do not help by reducing somewhat our need to produce synthesized protein." He smiled wolfishly.

"By the way, Mr. Spock, I know that you've had your communicator on open broadcast since we captured you." The first officer stiffened slightly. "It is of no consequence. Your unit could not penetrate the radiant screening around this installation. Even if it could, our operatives on board the *Enterprise* have evidently accomplished their task of disrupting your ship's communications equipment.

"By the time they have ship-to-surface capability restored, you will not be around to signal for beam-up. But your communicators will, so that you can be beamed back aboard—what's left of you, that is. I might point out that the modern weaponry which so concerns you, Captain Kirk, still has not been used on Pandro—but only on the *Enterprise*."

He pushed through a door leading into a busy lobby. Variously uniformed Klingons mixed freely with black-clad Pandronians. "Before too long the absence of the Tam Paupa will begin to make itself felt in government cities. Soon word of its absence will breach government security and spread to the general populace.

"Panic will ensue. The government will be in complete disarray. The Pandronians' natural bellicosity will come to the fore and *cusim*—no more planetary government."

The group halted at the end of the lobby, where Commander bn Bem and the other Pandronian soldiers were separated from Kirk, Spock, and McCoy.

"If not meet again, Kirk Captain," bn Bem murmured softly, "was for This One good to have known you. For you sentiments same, Spock Commander, McCoy Doctor."

The Pandronians were led away, while the *Enterprise* officers were taken down a nearby narrow corridor. At its end was a door flanked by a pair of arrow-straight Klingon guards. Kor used an electronic key attuned to the electron levels of the lock alloy to open the door. They entered, saw a small, dimly lit room. The room itself was almost empty and as warm as the outside. Some stands holding a smattering of scientific equipment were placed around the chamber. Cases and cabinetry lined one wall. At the far end was a bench supporting a medium-sized glass case.

"In there, gentlemen," Kor advised them as he pointed toward the case, "lies the Pandronian Tam Paupa. If local records are accurate, and we have no reason to believe they lie, the most frantic search the Pandronians could mount would not locate another for at least two hundred of their years. Their government and civilization should collapse inside forty."

"I can see why it's so difficult to locate," McCoy commented, squinting. "I can't see it even now."

"The inferiority of the human form," smirked Kor.

"That may be," Spock conceded, drawing a vicious glare

from McCoy, "but it does not apply to me, and I see nothing inside that case save some shredded vegetable matter."

Kor's smirk gave way slowly to confusion as he also stared at the case. "It should be in plain view," he muttered. "Watch them closely," he directed the guards as he walked rapidly toward the bench. He looked down into the case.

"Odd." Taking a metal probe, he reached inside and stirred the bark shavings which apparently served to cushion the Tam Paupa. His stirrings grew frantic.

"Something the matter, Kor?" Kirk wondered pleasantly. But the Klingon captain's eyes had widened and he showed no sign of having heard.

"Guard—chamber guards!" Both tall Klingons who flanked the doorway stuck their heads into the chamber.

"Has anyone had access to this chamber since," and he hurriedly checked his personal chronometer, "eight *fluas* ago?"

Looking puzzled, the guard replied in Klingon, "No, Honored Captain. But we assumed duty only six *fluas* ago."

"Get back to your post!" Kor screamed. Rushing to one of the cabinets lining the left-hand wall, he thumbed an intercom switch, then spoke in Klingon, which all three officers understood reasonably well.

"Security Central . . . this is Captain Kor speaking. Who was on duty in the secure chamber as of seven [fluas] back?" A pause, then, "And for the period before that?" Another pause, followed by a violent command: "Get all of them up here immediately! I don't care if they are on rest period!" Kor's voice dropped menacingly. "Would you like your head separated from its shoulders like a Pandronian? You'll find reattaching it not so simple."

They waited while Kor glared furiously from empty case to intercom and kicked at another cabinet as if it were personally responsible for his troubles. Abruptly his attention returned as someone reported at the other end of the intercom.

"Yes—what is your name and rank? This is Captain Kor, that's who, you lower-grade moron! And stop trembling—it garbles your words. Now, think carefully if you are capable of such: Who had access to the secure chamber where the alien Tam Paupa thing was being kept? Only him? You are certain? Very well . . . No, you are not to be disciplined. Return to your activity previous. It matters nothing now."

He clicked off, stared blankly at the floor.

"Well?" Kirk prompted, unable to keep silent. Kor did not look up immediately.

"I had wondered why eb Riss had not come along to enjoy this victory," the Klingon murmured with barely controlled fury. "It is now clear he was planning one of his own."

"Such loyalty does a Klingon inspire among its minions," McCoy whispered, soft enough so that Kor didn't hear. In any case, the captain had other matters on his mind as he activated the intercom once again.

"Stables? Yes, I suspected. Who could have guessed? Prepare the others for emergency run. Yes, immediately." A quick flip transferred him to a different department. "Security Central—this is Captain Kor. I want a full squad of our Pandronian allies and an Imperial platoon at the stables—yes, fully armed. I don't care what Headquarters will say if we have to use energy weapons—the Tam Paupa's been stolen. Yes, by Lud eb Riss, our"—he paused, then concluded, his voice dripping venom—"most trusted contact in the Pandronian government." He flipped off the intercom, faced a curious but not displeased triumvirate of Federation officers.

"The traitor has taken a *coryat*, which is capable of negotiating the swamps. There is only one way he could run, and that is through the pathway cleared by our experimental creatures. But we will catch him and I will bring him back with me—alive, to know the exquisite refinements of Klingon justice."

Still under guard, they were led from the empty room. In passing, Kor gave an order to one of the chamber guards. "Get onto the intercom. I want all the captured Pandronians brought to the front entryway, even if interrogation has begun. I have no time to go to them in the holding pens."

"It shall be done, Honored One," the guard responded.

Moments later they were back at the entrance to the headquarters building, where they were soon joined by a troop of tired, worried-looking Pandronian soldiers led by Ari bn Bem. Pandronian rebels kept them packed tightly together.

Kor went straight to bn Bem. "I must know what Lub eb

Riss is likely to do; therefore I must know what sort of person you consider him to be."

The commander looked uncertain, but replied offhandedly, "He is a traitor to his race; what more is there to know of him?"

"He has restolen the Tam Paupa," Kor explained, "and is even now riding for Tendrazin. What is he likely to do there?"

At this information a strange sort of verbal bubbling poured in increasing waves from bn Bem's mouth. Since the common soldiers could not understand Klingon, he translated Kor's announcement for them. Immediately they began to mimic his bubbling noises, some bubbling so hard they could barely keep their feet. Their heads and middle sections shifted on their bodies as if they were coming apart. Kirk recognized it from previous experience with bn Bem as the Pandronian equivalent of laughter.

Captain Kor was not amused. He drew a small sidearm from his waist. It was clearly not Pandronian in origin and differed also from the hand weapons held by the Pandronian rebels. It very much looked like a poorly disguised, standard-naval-issue Imperial energy weapon.

Kor pointed it at bn Bem's head. "I will burn you integral by integral where you stand if such a disrespectful outburst occurs again. Tell *that* to your subordinates."

bn Bem dutifully translated and the laughter died down. Despite the threat, the commander couldn't prevent himself from declaring, with some satisfaction, "So have the traitors betrayed been. Is for justice too perverted, but is pleasing still."

"You should choose your coconspirators with greater care, Captain," Spock suggested, noticing the Klingon's finger tightening on the trigger of his weapon. Kor, properly distracted, stared back at Spock. "We are now presented with an additional question of interest: To be precise, who here was using whom?"

"Shut up, you," Kor ordered him warningly. Forgetting that he was about to kill bn Bem, he directed another question at the Pandronian. "What can we expect eb Riss to try to do with the Tam Paupa?"

"To return it was clearly never of his intention," bn Bem

surmised. "By now should high council be incapable of acting with a Tam Paupa-less premier. eb Riss intelligent is always, but now appears That One more intelligent than any believed. Also cunning, also calculating.

"This One would guess Tendrazin That One will enter surreptitiously. Will move freely, as is his rank, in government central. With aid of Tam Paupa, eb Riss will have own abilities enhanced. This One believes he could himself have anointed premier."

"The shortsighted imbecile," Kor rumbled. "Doesn't he realize we can have him removed the same way we removed the Tam Paupa from that doddering old fool who is the present head of government?"

"That may not be as easy as it was the first time," Spock felt compelled to point out, moved by the logic of it. "The present premier and his supporters had no idea there were Klingons scheming on his world, whereas eb Riss knows precisely where you're located and what you're up to. He used you all along."

"To make himself supreme ruler of Pandro," Kirk continued when Spock had finished. "If his plan succeeds and he makes himself premier, and if this brain-boosting Tam Paupa is all its cracked up to be, then I don't see how you can give him much trouble. This rebellion you're supporting will fail and you'll have to renegotiate your position on Pandro—this time bidding against the Federation. I know eb Riss's type—he'll be interested in joining up with the side that offers *him* the most, not the one that promises the best for Pandro."

"There'll be no such trouble if we catch him first," Kor reminded them sharply. His weapon came around to point at Kirk. "In any event, you three will not be around to witness the eventual outcome. I see no reason for putting off your demise any longer.

"You will be fed to one of the experiments. I could burn you here, but I dislike waste and inefficiency. Your partially consumed bodies will be rescued and at least one communicator activated. We will lower our screens long enough for your ship to locate your communicator signal and beam up your remains. They will accept the evidence of the marks on your corpses, and there will be none to dispute this." He gestured meaningfully with the weapon. "Outside, please."

Devoid of expression, the three men and the Pandronians were marched toward the exit. The guards at the wide doorway moved aside smartly and the transparent panels slid apart to let them pass.

Kirk had barely taken a step outside when a tremendous explosion slammed him hard to the ground. As he was trying to recover from the initial shock of the concussion, a second explosion occurred. Glass and metal fragments whistled over his head, followed instantly by a series of nonstop, slightly smaller eruptions.

"Spock, Bones—run for the rafts!"

They were on their feet then, nearly falling several times as continuous blasts shook the earth all around them, though the actual explosions came from behind. Kirk looked around, almost falling again, and saw bn Bem and the rest of the Pandronian soldiers following. In the confusion which had thrown everyone to the ground the well-trained Pandronian troops had reacted more professionally than the Klingon-led rebels. They had overpowered their guards at the cost of several casualties.

Now only Captain Kor and two Klingon guards remained outside, for the initial explosion had collapsed the entryway into the main building. Seeing that he was outmanned and now outgunned, Kor had time to visit a look of helpless rage on Kirk. It turned to panic when another eruption ripped the air behind them.

"The power station!" Kirk could hear him yell desperately. "Get to the backups quickly or everything is lost!"

An ear-splitting moaning sounded from behind and to the right as they ran. Kirk saw that a second abomination had come up alongside the first. Even as he watched, both horrors suddenly slipped five meters closer to the Klingon installation.

"What the hell's going on?!" McCoy shouted. His answer came from the scurrying blue bi-ped now running on his left.

"Told all This One that Lud eb Riss's cunning was great," bn Bem told him breathlessly as they raced into the jungle again. "Expected the traitor some pursuit from Klingons.

Would guess he left charges to create confusion and panic among them."

"I heard Kor yell something about a power station," Kirk told the others, gasping for breath as they hurried along. The rafts should be close now.

"That would cause panic indeed, Captain," Spock concurred with enviable ease as he strode along nearby. "It means that the double-force barrier the Klingons have erected will come down, and that the central frequency-modulator installation will also be inoperative. It follows that the results of the Klingon biological experiments will soon be free of all restraints."

"Talk about Frankenstein unbound," McCoy panted.

"Frankenstein unbound? What is that?" Commander bn Bem wanted to know.

"I'll explain later," McCoy replied, "but basically it's a Terran catch phrase meaning you'd better run like mad!"

Trees rose all around them now. Kirk stole a last glimpse backward. Energy bolts were beginning to rise from the smoking rubble that had been the Klingon station. Kirk couldn't see what they were firing at.

But he had a brief sight of one target as they reached the rafts. It raised three legs and four tentacles, each as big around as a shuttlecraft, and brought them down on the exterior of the main building they had been so briefly imprisoned in.

It was not an educated assault, but it was effective. The structure simply disappeared beneath thousands of kilograms of sheer mass. Screams began to sound above the noise of battle.

Every so often a Klingon energy beam would strike one of the several colossuses now assaulting the installation and burn a hole in it. A section or two of the creature would fall away, blackened and burning, without slowing its former body in the least.

"The Klingons are becoming victims of their own experiment," he noted aloud. "Poetic Justice."

"The justice will be more than poetic, Captain," Spock reminded him, "if eb Riss also had the foresight to destroy our rafts as he retreated."

But when they broke through the last thick brush above

the narrow beach and tumbled gratefully to the water's edge, the two unsightly craft were exactly where they had been left, grounded on the gentle slope. To Kirk they were as beautiful as a Federation destroyer.

"It may be, Captain, that eb Riss was unable to move the heavy craft by himself, or he may not have wished to delay himself by doing so," Spock theorized, even as he was lending his own muscle to that of four Pandronians as they fought to slide one raft into the swamp sludge.

"Or he could have expected us to be trapped in the explosions," McCoy countered. "Captain Kor couldn't have chosen a better time to feed us to his pets."

Both rafts slid buoyantly into the murk. No group of professional oarsmen could have moved those two clumsy constructions faster through the water than did the three men and squadron of bedraggled Pandronian troops.

"Look!" McCoy shouted, pointing behind them. They had already put some distance between themselves and the island.

Kirk turned, saw an enormous elephantine neck stretched perhaps a hundred and fifty meters into the sky. It towered far above the tallest of the island trees.

Six mouths formed the terminus, each filled with teeth the size of concrete pillars. Two of the jaws were crunching sections of metal wall, while another was devouring a thick cylindrical shape, munching on the hard formed metal as though it were a cracker.

An eye-searing flash ensued, followed by a rolling explosion. The momentary flare lit the swamp around them and threw everyone on the rafts into eerie shadow.

"That was a fuel tank, chemical type," Kirk finally declared assuredly as he looked back.

The huge waving neck was swaying wildly about. All six mouths and the gargoylish head they had been mounted in were gone, as was about twenty meters of upper neck. But the blackened, charred stump continued to flail about without ceasing.

"The danger now imminent is," bn Bem brooded as he regarded the now distant horror. "All will proceed to act as would any meat-eater. All must now obtain own enormous masses of food to survive."

"*Varboxites* will flee in all directions from them," the commander explained. "Creatures' senses will direct massive forms to largest mass in region which flees not."

"What would that be?" Spock asked, already more than suspecting the answer. bn Bem gazed at each of them in turn before replying.

"In Tendrazin city, is naturally."

"I wonder if eb Riss foresaw that also," Kirk muttered. "Can they get through the swamp?"

"Are you kidding, Jim?" McCoy looked back toward the island, which was now long since out of sight. "It would take nothing short of a thermonuclear demolition charge or a ship's phaser banks to slow any one of those babies."

"Mr. Spock?" Kirk inquired. Spock already had his communicator out, but shook his head after several tries.

"The interference shield generated by the Klingons has vanished, Captain, but there is still no indication we are being received by the *Enterprise*."

That meant that the damage inflicted by the Pandronian boarders still hadn't been repaired, Kirk reflected. They were on their own, then.

"Is hard to believe eb Riss would plan so well and not see results of destroying Klingon aliens' control machines," bn Bem was musing. "Must That One have some plan for turning creatures from Tendrazin."

"You still don't seem to grasp the magnitude of what eb Riss has done, Commander," Kirk advised him. "Turning on his own people, then turning on those who helped him—I wouldn't put it past him to sit idly by while the Klingons' monsters ravage the whole city. Then he could make himself supreme ruler of Pandro without worry of any interference whatsoever—not with the seat of government obliterated."

"This One cannot believe such crime even of such as eb Riss," a horrified bn Bem replied. And then he appeared to wilt slightly. "Still, has he participated in theft of Tam Paupa twice. Loyalty must remain only to self. Can This One sorrowfully put nothing past him. It may be that eb Riss is madder even than the rebels he once helped."

A shout sounded from the other raft. bn Bem looked attentive as he exchanged words with a particularly bedraggled Pandronian soldier. Then Kirk recognized the other speaker.

It was the head tracker, the Pandronian who had led them to the edge of the swamp.

At the moment, he was gesturing at a passing tree. "Broken small branches and missing leaves," bn Bem informed the curious men. "All signs of a *coryat* taking sustenance while on the run.

"Could be another creature have been made, but tracker thinks sure a *coryat*. Is good sign that eb Riss traveling same direction."

"Any chance of our overtaking him?" Kirk asked.

bn Bem looked sad. "*Coryat* built for speed, can outrun *zintar*. And travels much faster than raft."

There was one more surprise waiting for them when the rafts grounded on the mainland the following day. The *zintars* were arranged in a circle, their three handlers camped behind the protective bulks and armed with dart sidearms.

bn Bem conversed with their own handler, ab Af, and learned that eb Riss had indeed been by this way. He had tried to surprise the group, but the handlers detected him too soon and he passed them by, presumably on his way to Tendrazin.

"eb Riss decided not to challenge three handlers and trained *zintars*," bn Bem concluded.

"Why should he risk himself?" McCoy declared. "He got what he really wanted—the Tam Paupa. The Klingons won't give him any trouble; they'll be lucky if any of them get off that island alive. And he knows no one can beat him to the capital."

"Can but try," bn Bem countered grimly. "We ride, gentlemen."

The situation was explained to the *zintar* handlers as the great tame animals were being mounted. Soon they were traveling at a startling pace back toward Tendrazin.

Somewhere within that huge old city, man and Pandronian alike knew, Pandro's greatest traitor in its civilized history had by now secreted himself.

X

Halfway back to the city Kirk nearly fell from his saddle in his haste to acknowledge the suddenly beeping communicator at his waist. The steady jounce of a *zintar* at the gallop nearly caused him to drop it under thundering feet—but he held on.

"Mine is also signaling, Captain," Spock reported.

"And mine, Jim!" added an excited McCoy.

Kirk took a deep breath, flipped the cover back, and spoke hesitantly into the pickup. "This is the captain speaking."

"Lieutenant Uhura still acting in command, sir. Mr. Scott remains partially incapacitated by the Pandronian low-grade stun beam. The effects have almost worn off, though. Nurse Chapel is confident there will be no permanent aftereffects."

"And the Pandronian boarders?" Kirk wondered.

"They succeeded in completely disabling our communications, Captain," she informed them as Kirk ducked a low-hanging vine. "Somehow they knew exactly where to go and how to get there. I don't understand. I thought the Pandronians weren't that advanced."

"They've had plenty of the wrong kind of help, Lieutenant," Kirk told her. "There are Klingons operating on Pandro—or, there were."

"Klingons!" A moment's silence, then, "But I thought the Pandronians hadn't decided—"

"They haven't, Lieutenant. This installation was present without either the approval or knowledge of the duly constituted Pandronian government. I'll explain later. For now, suffice to say that the Klingons had some typical Klingon ideas about exploiting the peculiar Pandronian ecology for their own uses. But we don't have to worry about them any more," he finished grimly. "Though you might keep a sharp watch for Klingon warships. Their base here had to be supplied periodically from outside."

"The ecology they played with is now running wild. According to Commander bn Bem, natural instinct will probably lead the animals involved to move toward the largest stable concentration of life on this part of the planet, which would be the Pandronian capital city. Now, what about other damage and casualties?"

"Several other paralyzed security personnel are also showing signs of recovery, Captain," Uhura reported crisply. "Ship damage appears to have been limited to our communications facilities. Under Mr. Scott's supervision, though, we have managed to rig a ship-to-surface link sufficient to get in touch with you—though Mr. Scott insists he can't guarantee how long it will last. Do you want us to beam you up, Captain?"

Kirk was considering a reply when Uhura broke in again. "Captain, Mr. Sulu has sensor contact with another vessel."

A long, tense pause while they waited helplessly for further information.

"What's happening up there, Uhura?" Kirk finally called, unable to stand the silence.

"I was awaiting identification, Captain," came the reply. "Klingon cruiser escorting a cargo ship. We can't beam them and they're not beaming us."

"Probably surprised to see you," Kirk ventured. "Their captain's undoubtedly wondering at the lack of response from the surface, not to mention the presence of the *Enterprise*. I suspect he'll remain silent in orbit, hoping we'll leave—which we will, eventually. But keep a close watch on them, and report any indication of impending hostilities, Lieutenant."

This was all he needed—a Klingon cruiser confronting the *Enterprise* at this crucial moment. He had to decide—did they beam up to join the ship, or remain to try to help the Pandronians?

The Klingons were obviously here to supply their ruined base. When a party from the cruiser finally beamed down into the wreckage, Kirk was willing to bet the cruiser captain would head for home with a report, rather than chance a pitched battle with a Federation ship for no particular reason. But he couldn't be certain—not until the Klingon left orbit.

But while it remained, the *Enterprise* couldn't use its ship's weaponry to halt the attack on Tendrazin. That would put her in an untenable tactical position which would be like waving a red flag in front of the Klingon cruiser. No, they would have to try something else to halt the lumbering assault on the city, at least until the standoff above was broken somehow.

"What do you think, Spock, Bones? Should we beam up?"

Spock shook his head once, quickly, and McCoy grumbled without looking at Kirk, "The least we can do is try to fix the mess the Klingons have made of Pandro."

"Stand by in the Transporter Room, Lieutenant," Kirk announced into his communicator, "but we're not ready to beam up just yet. We've got something we have to do here first. We'll keep you advised."

Ahead, Commander Ari bn Bem executed the Pandronian equivalent of a smile.

"What about the Pandronians who boarded the ship?" Kirk asked.

"We're holding them in the security section of Sick Bay, Captain," came the reply from above. "No matter how small they can subdivide, I don't think they can slip through a force screen. They refuse to discuss their mission, but they admit to being part of some kind of fanatical Pandronian society."

"Fanatical doesn't half say it, Lieutenant," Kirk told her. "Keep them locked up, and whatever you do, don't let one of them get behind anybody."

"No chance of that now, sir," she assured him. "I only wish we'd known their true capabilities when they first beamed aboard."

"This seems to be the day to learn all about Pandronian capabilities," was Kirk's response. "The Klingons learned the hard way. Kirk out."

"*Enterprise* out."

Once they entered the government stables, bn Bem was first off a *zintar*. He waited impatiently for Kirk and the others to dismount.

"We must hurry to the government chambers and convey our information to the premier and the council. Action must in effect be put to wrest the Tam Paupa from the traitor eb Riss."

Alternately walking and running, they followed the commander through the winding corridors of the government building. A queried courier told them that the premier was presently meeting in session with the full high council of both Tendrazin city and planet Pandro.

"Are all in private meeting chamber," the dazed courier called as the commander and his three aliens rushed by her.

bn Bem led them upward. Eventually they confronted a high portal guarded by four armed Pandronians in purple and puce uniforms.

The officer in charge barred their way. "No one to be admitted is," he said resolutely. "High Council and premier in special meeting are."

"I am a high commander myself and envoy extraordinary to United Federation of Planets," bn Bem announced with dignity. "Has This One information vital to safety of city Tendrazin and all planet Pandro."

"Nevertheless," the officer replied, "This One's orders say clearly that we are to—"

"This One claims extraordinary over ordinary," bn Bem shot back, "on all integrals mine and rank of high commander."

"Overranked and absolved is This One," the guard admitted, executing a half bow. "Be it on your association, I admit you." He moved aside, directing the other guards to do likewise.

The door was shoved inward and bn Bem strode importantly into the chamber with the Federation contingent close behind.

Most of the room was taken up by a huge table in the form of an eight-pointed star. High-ranking Pandronians of varying age and venerability were seated at seven of the points. At the star-point farthest from the doorway sat the premier, who abruptly rose and stared at them in shock.

"You," the new premier of Pandro exclaimed, the Tam Paupa positioned securely on his head, "how did you escape from—?"

Lud eb Riss suddenly grew aware he was on the verge of saying too much. Slowly he assumed his seat again and left the startled gaping to the rest of the representatives in the chamber. Those exhalted Pandronians were no less stunned than the new arrivals. bn Bem's hastily composed speech and declaration of emergency was totally forgotten.

"Lud eb Riss," he was finally able to stammer, "This One under arrest declares you as traitor to all Pandro intelligences!" Turning, the commander called back through the still-open door. "Officer of the guard." The officer who had first prevented them from entering came into the chamber, followed by two of his subordinates.

bn Bem pointed across the table. "Arrest Lud eb Riss, the usurper."

"Remain at your posts," eb Riss countered in a new, strangely commanding tone.

"Note the altered voice, Captain," Spock whispered to Kirk. "One of the benefits of wearing the Tam Paupa, apparently. It magnifies more than the decision-making ability of whoever wears it. eb Riss is clearly more than he was. It is no wonder the Pandronians have placed such faith in whoever the Tam Paupa was on."

The officer of the guard hesitated, took a step backward. eb Riss appeared satisfied and to be gaining confidence with every moment.

"What have you done, eb Riss," Kirk demanded to know, "with the real premier, Kau afdel Kaun?"

It wasn't eb Riss but one of the councilors seated at the table who supplied an answer. "Have you heard not? Old afdel Kaun died from the effort of trying to handle the affairs of his office without the aid of the Tam Paupa. The strain was for him too much. The final dissolution his body met these two days past." He gestured toward the far corner of the table.

"Is now Lud eb Riss, wearer of Tam Paupa, premier designate of planet Pandro, to be confirmed this day itself."

"But you can't make him your new premier!" an outraged McCoy insisted. "He's the one who's responsible for the theft of the Tam Paupa in the first place."

Expressions and reactions differed markedly from human ones, but there was no mistaking the shock that McCoy's startling accusation caused at the table. Slowly, the attention of every councillor shifted to the premier's chair.

eb Riss appeared only momentarily shaken by the direct charge, but with the assistance of the Tam Paupa he quickly recovered his confidence—as would be demanded of any planetary leader in such a situation. Kirk had already realized they were not arguing against a single Pandronian, but a Pandronian plus one.

"This a monstrous lie is," eb Riss declaimed with certitude. "Has This One only just risked life and integration to return and warn of danger to city of Tendrazin from beasts created by alien enemy Klingons?"

It had to be the Tam Paupa's assistance again, Kirk realized in frustration, which had induced in eb Riss the brilliant ploy of both denying McCoy's charge and stealing their chance to warn the council of the impending threat at the same time.

"Lies, lies, more and greater lies!" a near-violent bn Bem objected, waving his arms so hard that his middle torso occasionally hopped clear off his hips. "Not only a usurper and blasphemer is eb Riss, but was he himself who cooperated with Klingon aliens and them enabled to produce their monsters on Pandro."

"See how at moment of most crucial need for confidence and stability they dissension and disruption attempt to sow," boomed eb Riss with sly power. "Commander bn Bem has by his stay with Federation aliens been corrupted. Must he for his own good be imprisoned.

"As for alien life-forms, they no better than Klingons are. Only different in shapes and colors. They too wish use of Pandro for their own unknowable ends. Must they be executed immediately, to prevent false panicking of Tendrazin population with their wild, detrimental stories."

"This One—This One knows not what to do, which ones to believe," stuttered Dav pn Hon, the most experienced and respected of all the high councillors. "Wears eb Riss the true Tam Paupa, which knowledge and forthrightness guarantees. Says eb Riss one thing." His gaze swung speculatively to the angry group of aliens fronted by the honorable Commander bn Bem.

"Produces Commander Ari bn Bem outworld aliens for

confirmation of most grave charges. Says bn Bem one thing." He performed a Pandronian gesture indicative of utter uncertainty. "Who is This One, who is council to believe?"

Murmurs of agreement and similar confusion were heard around the polished table.

eb Riss addressed the wavering silence. "Believe in which person you must," he told them, "but whatever you believe, cannot you deny the true Tam Paupa." When this didn't produce an outburst of acclaim, eb Riss played his trump card.

"Anyways, is any present who can offer means of stopping creatures both sides say soon will Tendrazin be attacking?"

More worried mutterings from the assembled councillors. Now their attention shifted from one another to the four figures standing before the doorway.

bn Bem turned to the Federation officers. "Well, Kirk Captain," he asked hopefully, "can you help us?"

"I don't know," Kirk admitted. "Just a moment." Activating his communicator, he turned away from the curious assembly and whispered into the pickup. "Kirk to *Enterprise*."

"*Enterprise*," came the reply, toned to softness by Kirk's adjustment of the volume. "Uhura here, Captain."

"Is the you-know-what still you-know-where, Lieutenant?"

"It hasn't changed position, Captain," Uhura responded, matching Kirk's deliberate lack of specifics with some fast thinking of her own. There was a definite reason behind it. If eb Riss knew there was a Klingon cruiser standing off the planet, the situation could become twice as difficult as it already was.

"Thanks, Lieutenant, Kirk out."

"What about one of your dart-throwing mechanisms such as the *fasir*?" Spock inquired. "Would they not be effective against the Klingon creatures?"

"Perhaps, Spock Commander," bn Bem admitted. "But is not weapons a problem. Is hard for us to produce the dissolution drug. Is not nearly enough in supplies of Tendrazin, not in many cities, to stop creatures so big. Was not ever expected by us to have to fight such impossible accretions of integrals."

"You see," exclaimed eb Riss, taking quick advantage of his opponent's indecision, "they are against their own lies helpless, as well as against assault which soon will come against us. Whereas This One," he reminded them grandiosely, "who wears Tam Paupa is only one who can Tendrazin save. Only This One.

"But will This One save city," he warned them, meeting the eyes of every individual council member in turn, "only if am confirmed immediately and irrevocably by high council as new premier of planet Pandro." And he grinned a Pandronian grin, not at the thoughtful councillors but across the broad table at the anguished face of Commander Ari bn Bem.

"Must do something to stop the traitor, Kirk Captain," the commander pleaded. "Is nothing you can do?"

"Circumstances prevent us from using ship's weapons, Commander," Kirk told him sadly. "As for anything we could beam down, I just don't know. I don't have authorization to use heavy weapons on Pandro's surface, and I don't want to duplicate a Klingon treaty violation by doing so. Besides, I'm not sure a phaser cannon could stop those creatures, and transmitting enough ship's power to be effective would put a strain on the *Enterprise*'s systems which might prove fatal if certain other parties elect to make trouble. I just don't know." He turned to his first officer.

"I am truly sorry, Captain, but it appears we must make a choice whether or not to use modern energy weapons, whether to risk weakening the *Enterprise* or saving Tendrazin."

"What about duplicating the frequency used by the Klingons in their controller?" Kirk wanted to know.

Spock quashed that possibility instantly. "Highly unlikely, Captain. We would have to achieve in a few hours what Klingon scientists clearly took a considerable period to accomplish. We have no idea what the frequency in question was. To locate it requires more time than we have, by a substantial margin.

"Of course, we could have an extraordinary stroke of good luck and hit upon the precise frequency right off, but I consider that a possibility too distant to be worth considering. We must come up with a different methodology."

Kirk looked over at McCoy, who was apparently deep in thought. "You working on an idea, Bones?"

"I was just thinking, Jim. The Pandronians, according to Commander bn Bem, might be able to handle this attack with their own weapons. All they need is a sufficient supply of the dissolution drug. Well, I've been producing drugs in large quantity all my life. I don't see why the *Enterprise*'s organic synthesizers couldn't turn out all the drug the Pandronians need.

"Even so," he added cautiously, "I'm not sure massive doses of the Pandronian drug will be enough to reduce to harmlessness what's coming this way. The commander's right when he says it will take one helluva lot of the stuff poured into those hulks. They might still be big and strong enough by the time they reach the city to cause a lot of damage."

"Is true," bn Bem agreed woefully. "Even best efforts with drug could not reduce last two creatures we saw while leaving *varbox*."

"There's got to be a way to make it work," Kirk insisted, trying to will a solution into being. "There's *got* to be!"

"For yourselves see," eb Riss cried in triumph, "admit the aliens their helplessness to save city. Cannot they preserve you. Only can This One. For This One wears the Tam Paupa!"

"It just doesn't look possible, Jim," McCoy insisted. "Whichever way the Pandronians turn they're faced with a dog-eat-dog situation."

"Bones, if we risk transmitting ship's power and you-know-who decides to attack, then we . . . we . . ."

He paused. Enlightenment dawned on his face.

Spock's eyebrows went up slightly. "Whatever your immediate thought, Captain, I do not see how Terran canines can be involved in our present situation in any way."

"It's not that, Spock, it's—" Kirk started to explain, but the same thought apparently struck McCoy.

"It just might work, Jim."

The first officers eyebrows advanced to his hairline. "Terran canines *are* involved? Captain, I don't understand what—"

"It's just an expression, Spock," Kirk told him offhandedly, his attention on McCoy. "You're sure you can synthesize the dissolution drug the Pandronians use, Bones?"

"Unless its a much more complex protein chain than I suspect, I don't see any reason why not."

"And in sufficient quantities?"

McCoy nodded. "As much as is needed."

"Captain, may I point out again the size and flexibility of the creatures the Klingons produced."

"I'm not thinking of destroying them before they reach the city, Mr. Spock. It seems clear we haven't that capability. What I *am* thinking of is moving them to the point of least resistance."

"If you are thinking, Captain," the first officer declared, "of changing the path of these creatures the way we did the dranzer stampede on Ribal Two, I don't believe it will work. The situation here is not analogous. We are dealing with only a few colossal creatures instead of millions of smaller ones.

"Furthermore, there is no species link between our attackers as there was on Ribal. Each one is different from the next, and there exists nothing like a chosen leader."

"I'm not talking about trying to run them in a circle like we did on Ribal, Spock. Obviously, if what Captain Kor told us about their protein requirements is true, nothing could possibly turn them from the nearest large, stable source of meat, which is Tendrazin.

"But if we can mount enough dart launchers on either side of their approach path and keep a steady quantity of the drug raining into them, we should at least be able to force the two creatures on the flanks to move away from the source of irritation. In other words, they'll continue to advance, but packed closer and closer together. Then if we can shove them tight enough, the combination of pressure, threat, and the presence of so much protein so close should unnerve them enough to start attacking *each other*."

"I wish I had your confidence, Jim," McCoy told him, "but I must admit your idea has a chance."

Kirk looked for confirmation from his science chief. "Well, Mr. Spock?"

"On the surface it seems plausible, Captain," Spock admitted. "Yet," and he was straining to gather in a fleeting thought, "something about the very concept troubles me, and I cannot say precisely why."

"Have you any better suggestions?" Kirk asked hopefully.

"No, Captain, I do not. And my worry in not grounded in fact. The idea *seems* reasonable."

"A fool's plan," snorted the transmogrified eb Riss. "Can never work. Only This One can save you all. Must make your decision now."

"Just a minute!" Kirk shouted as several council members seemed about to speak. "You don't have to make your final decision yet. eb Riss is a traitor of hardly believable proportions."

"So you say," injected a solemn Dav pn Hon.

"But what if we're telling the truth?" Kirk argued anxiously. "Give our idea a chance. If we fail, and eb Riss is truly as omnipotent now as he'd like you to believe, then he can still save you."

Trapped by his own vanity, eb Riss was forced not to refute Kirk's appraisal of his self-proclaimed abilities.

"Dr. McCoy, Mr. Spock, and I think we can force these monsters to turn on themselves," Kirk went on determinedly. "If we fail in this, you can always turn to whatever miracle eb Riss has planned. But you must give us this chance! Afterwards, when the threat to Tendrazin has been eliminated, you can consider the question of who should be your next premier without having to do so under pressure. Isn't that worth striving for?"

Rumbles of uncertainty from the assembled councillors, ending in grudging assent.

"And as long as we're on the subject of saving Tendrazin," Kirk shot across at eb Riss, "I'd like to know just what your plan for saving the city is, anyway."

eb Riss sat up straight in his seat and folded his arms. On his head the Tam Paupa, a metallic green circle surrounded by decorative projections and sparkling cabochons, shone bright in the light from overhead.

"Surely, Kirk Captain, you cannot think This One will reveal idea for use until is confirmed as premier? This One will wait as need be until high council comes to realization of truth."

"Yeah," snapped McCoy, "even if that turns out to be too late to save Tendrazin."

eb Riss made a Pandronian shrug. "Has This One presented offer to council."

"Look," McCoy muttered, "why doesn't someone just walk up to him and yank that holy crown whatsis off his rotten head?"

"Is against all Pandronian law and histories," Dav pn Hon informed them. "Would any to take Tam Paupa from who is wearing it, That One would be as guilty as whoever first stole it."

"And never mind that the one who stole it is now wearing it," a frustrated Kirk muttered. "Try to get around *that* one." He glared at eb Riss. "Your treachery is worse than a Klingon's, eb Riss. I believe you'd sacrifice the entire capital city to further your own personal ambition. Human history has had its share of types like you."

"This One not threatened by alien comparisons," eb Riss declared with dignity. "This One has passed point where personal wishes matter. Must do what must do, and means this insisting on my terms. Tendrazin not in This One's hands now." He eyed Kirk challengingly. "In your hands, Kirk Captain."

"Have we no choice," another councillor lamented. He faced Kirk. "If you fail, Kirk Captain, we must turn to eb Riss, traitor though maybe he be, in hope of salvation. This is our way."

"I understand, sir," Kirk replied soberly. He activated his communicator. "Kirk to *Enterprise* . . . Transporter Room."

"Transporter Room on standby—Ensign M'degu on station, sir."

"We're ready to beam aboard, Ensign. We—" He paused as a hand came down on his shoulder.

bn Bem looked hard at him. "This One would go with you, Kirk Captain." The commander was fighting to control his emotions. "To be of assistance to McCoy Doctor." He indicated his own waist band and its pouches. "Have in sidearm and weapon case several doses of dissolution drug. Will need to duplicate." He looked to his left.

"Is sufficient, McCoy Doctor?" he inquired, flipping open the case to show the half dozen darts within.

McCoy glanced at them, nodded. "Is sufficient, bn Bem Commander." He smiled broadly. Like Kirk's and Spock's, McCoy's opinion of the commander had come a long way since the latter had first set foot on the *Enterprise*.

"Besides," bn Bem added, glaring back across the table, "if remain here knowing what This One knows, may do something fatal to self and other party. Would be dangerous to leave This One behind. Might violently disassemble eb Riss, even though fight could end with Tam Paupa damaged."

"I see your point," Kirk said knowingly. His voice directed to the communicator again. "Ensign, there will be four in the beam-up party. Mr. Spock, Dr. McCoy, myself, and Commander bn Bem. We're localized," he added as all four moved close together, "so don't worry about catching someone else. The transporter is holding the commander's pattern."

"I have it, sir," the transporter operator reported. "Stand by."

As the high council watched silently, the four figures were engulfed in a storm of dissolution no Pandronian life-form could match. Then they were gone, leaving the councillors to stare at one another—and with mixed emotions at the calm, assured form of the mentally inspired Lud eb Riss.

Once back on board ship, McCoy wasted no time, but set to work immediately with several of the ship's chemists and Spock's assistance to synthesize the dissolution drug contained in bn Bem's dart-syringes. As expected—and hoped—the drug turned out to be a comparatively simple organic construction, which the *Enterprise*'s organic fabricator had no trouble reproducing.

With production underway, Kirk was able to devote some time to considering the Klingon threat. Actually, it was a threat only on the basis of past incidents, for the cruiser sat close by its companion cargo vessel and offered no contact. That was fine with Kirk. Now if the Klingons would only cooperate by staying put and letting their minds puzzle over what had happened to their secret ground installation, he might just have enough time to work everything out.

It was while he was dividing his thoughts between the enemy cruiser on the main viewscreen and the timetable Spock had worked out for the approach of the creatures to Tendrazin that bn Bem approached him, leaning over the command chair with an apologetic expression on his blue face. "Your pardon for disturbing thoughts, Kirk Captain."

"That's all right, Commander. I wasn't having any brainstorms anyway. What can I do for you?"

bn Bem, for the first time since Kirk had known him, seemed to be having difficulty finding the right words. Finally, he murmured, "Is Pandronian problem but seems insoluble by methods Pandronian."

"If you're still worried about what we'll do if the drugs fail to act as planned—" Kirk started to say, but the commander waved him off.

"Is not that. If McCoy Doctor can produce enough dissolution drug and if your plan succeeds, will still remain matter of traitor eb Riss having possession of Tam Paupa. He will not give it up voluntarily."

Kirk didn't understand. "But once we've disposed of the threat to Tendrazin created by the Klingons' experiments, then can't the council deal with eb Riss without fear?"

"You still not comprehend fully importance of Tam Paupa, Kirk Captain," bn Bem tried to explain. "Remind you that no Pandronian can take Tam Paupa by force from whoever wears it. Also, consider that Pandronian who wears Tam Paupa is best suited for making decisions on all Pandro."

"Are you saying," Kirk muttered in disbelief, "that in spite of what we've told them about what eb Riss has done, the high council could still possibly confirm him as premier?"

"This One really knows not," bn Bem confessed worriedly. "Never in memory has such a series of circumstances followed. So high councillors face unique situation.

"Is merely advising you that your help may further be required before certainty of planet Pandro's alliance with your Federation is. As you said, eb Riss if he survives will for himself strongest bargain drive."

"I guess we've been underestimating the spiritual importance of this Tam Paupa all along," Kirk mused, "while concerning ourselves only with its biological effects."

"There may be a way, Captain, to part the Tam Paupa from eb Riss." Kirk looked across to where Spock was regarding bn Bem thoughtfully.

"According to the commander," Kirk reminded his science officer, "Pandronian law forbids the removal by force of the Tam Paupa from whoever wears it."

"Is so," confirmed a forlorn bn Bem. "Removal and exchange must be voluntary."

"I realize that, Commander," Spock replied. "It is merely an idea I have, not a concrete proposal. Give it a little more time."

XI

Four days later McCoy and his research team had not only cracked the organic code of the Pandronian dissolution drug and successfully reproduced it, but they were now drawing it from the ship's organic fabricator in hundred-liter batches.

Each fresh tank of the drug, after being tested for dissolution toxicity, was beamed down to the surface of Pandro. There, under the disdainfully aloof gaze of eb Riss, Commander bn Bem was overseeing the distribution of the liquid. Tendrazin's government armories were turning out hypodermic darts at a furious rate. After being suitably charged with the drug from the *Enterprise*, these thousands upon thousands of loaded syringes were placed in the concealed *fasirs* and other dart-firing weapons that had been placed on both sides of the approach to the city.

Facing the distant *varbox* and much closer forest, a broad cultivated plain and cleared area separated the former from the outer, ancient city wall. On either side of the plain facing the approach path to the city, the Pandronians had labored mightily to create two earthen dikes nearly twenty meters high. These formed a wide *V*-shape leading to the city gates, the point of the *V* actually being somewhere inside the city.

Everyone was preparing for the coming attack on the assumption that no quantity of the drug could cause the creatures to turn back. Naturally, the modest walls of the city would never stop a charge from even the smallest of the Klingons' experiments. But they would serve to channel the oncoming behemoths a little faster into smaller and smaller quarters. They were also excellent sites on which to mount the Pandronian dart-throwers.

When word was passed to the *Enterprise* via the communicator given to bn Bem that the onrushing monstrosities were about to break clear of the forest, Kirk, Spock, and McCoy beamed down to join the city's defenders.

Sensing the nearness of a really substantial quantity of raw protein, the creatures had apparently increased their speed. Kirk had hoped they would have several more days to produce even more of the dissolution drug, but the increased speed wasn't the real reason for the upsetting of the defenders' timetable.

"We have had scouts out monitoring the approach the past three days, Kirk Captain," bn Bem told them as they walked toward an unknown destination. "It appears the creatures do not sleep. Yet all integrals do sleep."

"I believe I can see how that is managed," Spock essayed. "The beasts are so enormous that while a portion of the integrals comprising each one engages in rest, there are enough remaining which perform similar functions to keep the body going at all times."

They had entered a semimodern Pandronian building near the outskirts of the city and been whisked by elevator to the top.

"Should from here have good view, Kirk Captain," bn Bem assured them as they walked out onto the roof of the structure. The commander's assessment turned out to be accurate.

From a position forty meters above the ground and close to the city wall, Kirk could see all the way to the distant forest. Tendrazin lay spread out behind and on both sides, a modern capital city which had retained the charm of its ancestry. One of the attractive, well-kept relics was the old city wall, which was presently lined with dart-armed Pandronian soldiers who would form the last line of defense against the onslaught of an ecology gone mad. Beyond them, only cultivated fields of stabilized associative plants moved in the slight, warm breeze of morning.

Farther off lay the cleared area that separated Tendrazin from the forest proper. Stretching off to either side were the two low earthen walls which the Pandronians had so painfully erected, working in round-the-clock shifts.

"What if the creatures, dumb as they are, choose to turn?" Kirk wondered at a sudden thought. "Suppose they decide to attack the gunners mounted on the walls instead of continuing on toward the city?"

"If Captain Kor's description of their appetites was accurate, Jim, I don't think that's likely." McCoy seemed confident. "They haven't the brains, I don't think, to guess where the irritation will be coming from, and the few soldiers on the ramparts don't represent a thousandth of the potential meal in Tendrazin. No, they'll keep advancing on the city, all right."

"Has already small-scale evacuation been started," one of the assembled councillors told Kirk. "From far side of Tendrazin. Is younglings and elderly only, as precaution. Always precaution. Should your idea not work and that of the wearer of Tam Paupa," and he indicated eb Riss, who was staring interestedly across the plain, toward the forest, "not work, hope we to still save most of population, even if city destroyed is."

"I hope that's what it remains," Kirk told him, "just a precaution."

"A rider comes!" someone called out. Everyone rushed to the edge of the bordered roof. A single *coryat* was rushing toward the city from the forest fringe, both legs of the tall running animal swallowing up the intervening distance with long, loping strides. A moment later the rider himself, panting for breath but otherwise composed, had joined them on the rooftop.

"Are near to emerging from forest," he gasped. "Have all impossible ones increased their speed as they near the city."

"They detect food in ample amounts," McCoy commented, finding the prospect of anyone here ending up in some Klingon experiment's belly discouraging.

"Is noted," Dav pn Hon told the rider. "Have you and all riders done well." The rider, dismissed, took his leave. pn Hon turned to face Kirk.

"Are all gunners ready. Have been given your instructions to fire on nearest creatures and continue fire as long as are able, Kirk Captain. Should last long, thanks to ample supplies of drug produced by McCoy Doctor."

"Not me," objected an embarrassed McCoy. "I had

plenty of help in analyzing the drug, and the ship's organic fabrication engineers did the real work."

"Even now is too late, yet still you to these aliens listen," came a stinging accusal from eb Riss. "For chance last to save Tendrazin, throw outworlders and bn Bem into prison and to me alone listen."

As the point of no return approached, several of the councillors appeared to waver slightly. They looked to pn Hon as their spokesman. He turned to face bn Bem, said quietly, "What you say first will we try, as have promised."

eb Riss snorted and turned away from them all. If he held any concern for his own hide he didn't show it. Or, Kirk mused, he might have been trembling inside, only to be calmed by the soothing actions of the Tam Paupa.

"Here they come," McCoy announced.

Trees were smashed aside, large bushes and ferns crushed to pulp under their weight, as out of the forest barrier came a collection of six to twelve of the most bizarre living creatures anywhere in the galaxy. Hopping, stumbling, rolling, they lumbered forward, differing from one another only in size and shape.

All were undisciplined assemblages of the most impossible arrangements of teeth, nostrils, eyes, legs, and other body parts. Kirk had to correct his initial appraisal: They differed from one another in one more respect, besides size and shape.

There was the question of which was most hideous.

The largest of them was hunched forward slightly to right of center. It was so enormous Kirk couldn't see it all, at least not well enough to estimate its true dimensions. One of the councillors, in spite of having been told what to expect, cried aloud. Another found the sight so repulsive he covered his eyes and turned away.

bn Bem was peering into a pair of Pandronian magnifiers. Moving them from left to right, he was surveying the *fasir* positions.

"Our gunners firing steady now are," he informed them. "As yet no change visible on creatures' progress, Kirk Captain."

"Give the drug and the gunners time," McCoy urged. "Its going to take every drop of dissolution drug to have any kind of effect on those leviathans."

Confirming the doctor's words, the monstrosities continued their advance on the city. They were into the cropland now, and the councillor representing Tendrazin and its surrounding lands moaned steadily at the destruction.

Flopping and crawling, somehow moving their stupendous bulks over the ground, they ignored the steady hail of dart-syringes as they progressed. Behind them lay long dark streaks—gouges in the land dug by sheer mass.

At this range the rain of darts formed two clouds of silvery mist on the flanks of the advance. "Still no observable effect," bn Bem reported. Then a hint of excitement entered his voice. "No, wait. On the right is something happening."

Kirk had noted it, too, without the need of magnifiers. So had Spock and McCoy.

It was a little thing, an almost imperceptible shift in one creature's actions—but at least it was a beginning. The monster on the far left, nearest the embankment and guns on that side, had appeared to flinch, its whole hundred-meter-high body arcing to the inside.

Moving inward, it scraped hard against the abomination next to it. Several jaws and grasping limbs on each creature snapped and dug at each other, but the two creatures continued to move forward, though now jammed tight together.

"It's working!" McCoy exclaimed. "The one on the inside was forced inward by the darts, Jim. The drug cost it too much of itself." And he pointed to the affected sections of the creature, which lay like large limp rags in a retreating line back toward the forest.

"It's working," Kirk agreed tightly, "so far."

"There—on the side other!" one of the councillors shouted. Everyone's gaze swerved to the other side of the broad open plain. Sure enough, the beast nearest the irritating weapons there had swung inward, shoving the next creature in to one side, where it pushed up against still another monster.

Sounds of rising fury began to become audible from the approaching armada of integrals, but they continued to come on.

"They're still not fighting, Jim," McCoy complained. "They're jammed almost on top of one another, but they're not fighting among themselves."

"It still has time to work, Bones," Kirk responded. "It has to work."

Pandronian soldiers at the forest end of the dirt ramparts who had now been passed by the marching monstrosities were struggling to move their mobile weapons down the line. As a result, the barrage of darts grew more intense the closer the creatures came to the city. By now they were near enough so that the men and the Pandronians on the rooftop could discern individual features on each animal.

Never in his wildest nightmares as a child had Kirk envisioned anything so ghastly as any one of the oncoming gargantuas. Tendrazin was being assaulted by creatures a dying addict could not have imagined in his most frenzied moments.

Now they were packed so close to one another by the dissolution drug that there was no room left for the creatures inside to move any direction but straight ahead. Any brains contained by the monsters were lost in the task of simply running the huge collection of integrals.

Kirk watched in absolute fascination as the rain of darts continued to strike the outside of the two creatures nearest the narrowing battlements. As each dart injected its tiny portion of drug, a small portion of creature would slough away, to run, hop, scramble back toward the forest, all will to integrate lost. Those on the flanks had lost considerable mass by now, but the remaining majority of creatures in between were only weakly affected.

"Something's got to happen soon," McCoy said nervously. "There's hardly enough room for them to move without stepping on each other."

At first it seemed as if McCoy was wrong, that the abominations would continue their inexorable side-by-side march on the city. But soon a great tintinnabulation arose among the heaving mass of integrated flesh, a cacophony produced by the simultaneous activating of ten thousand mouths.

Coming to a slow, ponderous halt, one creature turned furiously on its neighbor, and it in turn on the next, and it on yet another, so that soon jaws and limbs were engaged in a frightful battle the likes of which no world had ever seen.

"That's done it!" McCoy exulted. "They're attacking one another. They're going to . . . to . . ." His voice faded, crushed by the enormity of what was taking place out on the innocent plain.

"Oh, my God," Kirk murmured.

Indeed, the results of the Klingon experiment had begun to turn on one another—but not in the way Kirk had predicted, and in a fashion none had foreseen.

No more limbs were torn, no flesh ripped from a fellow mountain of integrals, no teeth dug great sores in the body pressing so claustrophobically upon it.

"They're not fighting any more," Kirk whispered in disbelief. "They're integrating with *each other*."

Panic had fallen like a wave on the high council. "Sound full evacuation!" one was yelling repeatedly. "All to retreat! Is lost Tendrazin . . . Is lost Pandro . . . !"

Gunners continued desperately to pour their unceasing hail of darts on the flanks of the attackers, which were attackers no longer. In their place the ultimate horror had been created, forced for survival to close integral ranks instead of fighting among itself. Under the constant prodding of the dissolution drug, the lumbering horrors had blended, joined to form one single, awesome, pulsating mountain of flesh. It towered above the highest structures of central Tendrazin and cast a long, threatening shadow over the plain and city wall behind which Kirk and the others stood.

So enormous was it that it blocked out the sun. Thousands of jaws bellowed and snapped along its front and sides, thousands more eyes of all shapes, sizes, and colors rolled madly in all directions. With a heave that shook the ground, the Pandronian mountain threw itself forward in a half hop, half fall. The action was repeated again, covering more distance this time.

With energy born of desperation the gunners on the enbankments flanking the quivering hulk poured more and more of the dissolution drug into its clifflike sides. Integrals continued to fall and tumble from the creature's sides, looking like pebbles bouncing down a canyon wall.

"It's not going to work, Jim," a frantic McCoy declared. "We've failed."

"It's my fault, Bones," a disconsolate Kirk replied. "I didn't imagine this possibility."

"Do not blame yourself, Captain." Spock viewed the catastrophe with typical detachment. "Neither did I, though something was bothering me about the concept from the first. Who would dream that the attackers would combine to create one invulnerable beast instead of fighting one another, as would be expected of carnivores in such a situation."

"There's still one last chance, Spock."

The first officer noticed the wild gleam in Kirk's eye. "Captain, I must object. We cannot transmit ship's power. To so weaken the *Enterprise* while it lies in range of a potentially belligerent enemy vessel—"

"I know, Spock, I know!" Kirk's voice was agonized as he fought to make the decision, while the oncoming colossus rolled steadily nearer.

The Pandronians could not wait for Kirk to make up his mind. All had rushed as one to stand before eb Riss, who glared down at them, apparently indifferent to approaching annihilation. They took turns pleading with the wearer of the Tam Paupa to save them, as Pandronians had done for thousands of years in moments of crisis.

eb Riss finally deigned to speak. "Is This One confirmed as premier?"

"Yes—yes!" several voices acknowledged hastily.

"Too easy," eb Riss objected. "It must by the Oath of dn Mida be so sworn."

The members of the high council began to recite in Pandronian a long, involved, unchallengable oath. When concluded, it would irrevocably install the traitor eb Riss as supreme head of the planetary government—no matter what anyone might decide subsequently. Having been sworn in by the oath, eb Riss could not be removed from office.

It looked, Kirk thought, as if the master Pandronian manipulator was about to gain everything he had planned from the very beginning. eb Riss had made use of Kirk and his companions, of the Klingons, and of his own people to achieve absolute power.

And there didn't appear to be any way to stop him.

"Hold your oath a moment. Councillors of Pandro!" Spock's cry was loud and strident enough to startle the councillors to silence.

eb Riss eyed Spock warningly. "Listen not to this alien outworlder. Finish the oath!"

Spock turned, pointed toward the field. "Closely to look at what happening is, gentlemen," he insisted in halting Pandronian.

In spite of themselves, in spite of the anxiety of the moment, all of the council members gave in to the urge to see what this strange alien was so insistent about.

"It—it's stopped," McCoy stammered in amazement.

Similar wondrous mutterings rose from the group of high councillors, for truly, the ontumbling mountain had come to a halt.

"The organism has reached a critical organic mass," Spock explained to the mermerized onlookers. "The demands of an impossible body have overridden the arguments of its nervous systems. Organic demands insist that it can proceed no further without massive ingestions of food. And food it will have."

All gaped as thousands of mouths tore at the flesh nearest to their respective maws, shredding limbs and scales, necks and motile limbs in a frenzy of hunger.

"It's devouring itself," Kirk said for all of them.

"One section no longer can communicate with another," the first officer went on. "Internal communication has collapsed under the all-consuming need for sustenance.

"It has become big enough to go mad."

Steadily one section of the monster vanished into another, all internal direction submerged in the orgy of mindless feeding. Soon the irrigated croplands just outside the old city wall were awash in a sea of Pandronian animal blood. Claws and fangs continued to rip away at helpless body parts.

The rejuvenated Pandronian gunners had no time to cheer. They were too busy, continuing to pour an unending flood of drug-laden darts into undamaged integrals. Now the individual sections of the creature commenced to fall away in clumps instead of single components. The retreat of disassociated integrals back toward the forest grew from a steady stream into a stampede.

Between its own depredations and the effects of the massive infusion of drug, the ultimate monster dissolved like a steak in an acid bath.

"Will they ever recombine?" Kirk mused.

"I think not, Captain," ventured Spock. "The effects of

the dissolution drug are long-lasting. In any event, it was only the Klingon hormones and frequency controller that induced the component integrals to combine into such huge, unnatural associations. That hormone is now being broken down by the dissolution chemicals. Those integrals which are not drugged will likely experience no desire, retain no drive, to form anything other than natural integrations again."

By now the monster had shrunk to half its initial size. Dead sections, paralyzed or wounded integrals began to pile up around its pulsing base like so much living talus. At the rate dissolution was proceeding, the creature would shortly be reduced to manageable proportions. It already appeared to Kirk that the number of wounded or dying integrals exceeded the healthy ones still constituting the living body.

"We give thanks to you for aid," Commander bn Bem told Kirk gratefully, "for having Tendrazin saved from greater evil than could be imagined." Turning, he addressed the silent council members.

"Have done the outworlders of the Federation what they said could be done, what This One said they could do. Have we now another task before us of equal importance." His gaze went past them. "To choose new premier of planet Pandro."

Somehow a shaken eb Riss managed to retain a modicum of composure, although his previous arrogant confidence had vanished. If it weren't for the Tam Paupa he wore, Kirk suspected, eb Riss would long since have been running for the nearest exit.

"Still This One wears the Tam Paupa," he boomed shakily. "Are among you any who would oldest Pandronian law violate to take it from me?"

Not one of the by-now-angry councillors took a step forward, nor did bn Bem.

"What are we to do, Kirk Captain?" he wondered, bemoaning the seeming standoff. "Cannot anyone take Tam Paupa from wearer without incurring wrath of all Pandronians past. Cannot we confirm nonperson eb Riss as premier, but cannot we have premier without Tam Paupa."

"I still don't see why the situation doesn't warrant an exception to the law," Kirk objected. "For this one time, can't you try and—Spock?" He broke off, staring at his first officer, who was standing utterly motionless, looking into nothingness. "Spock, are you all right?"

McCoy had noticed Spock enter his present state from the beginning, and he cautioned Kirk, "Easy, Jim—Vulcan mind trance."

Already Kirk had noticed the familiarity of Spock's peculiar vacant expression. The Vulcan body swayed ever so slightly, but remained otherwise rigid. Kirk followed the direction of that blank-gaze of concentration and discovered it was focused directly on Lud eb Riss.

Gradually that Pandronian's air of determined defiance faded, to be replaced quickly by first a look of uncertainty and then one of alarm. On his head the Tam Paupa seemed to quiver, just a hair.

"No," eb Riss stammered, stepping back away from Spock. "Stop now, Outworlder!"

But Spock's attitude did not change one iota, and the Tam Paupa's quivering increased. Kirk, McCoy, and the other Pandronians were united in their dumbfounded feeling—but for different reasons.

Kirk had no idea what Spock was up to, but he knew better than to try to question or interfere while his friend and second in command was locked in that trance.

The oscillation of the Tam Paupa continued to increase, until a fully panicked eb Riss was forced to put his hands to his head to try to steady it. Both hands came away as if the Pandronian had immersed them in fire.

Something else seemed to go out of the traitor. He stumbled backward blindly, crashed into the restraining wall lining the top of the building, and slumped to a sitting position. He wore the look of a badly beaten boxer.

At that point, when Kirk began to feel he was gaining some understanding of what was going on, something happened which dropped his lower jaw a full centimeter.

Rising on a ring of glistening cilia, the Tam Paupa lifted itself into the air. Microscopically fine filaments withdrew bloodlessly from a circle around eb Riss's scalp. As he stared in disbelief, Kirk could just barely make out a line of tiny eyes, much like those of a spider, running around the front rim of the brilliantly colored circle.

What had given the appearance of metal now revealed itself as organic, having the same sheen as a shiny-scaled Terran lizard. Gemlike bulges in front now declared themselves to be eyes, which stayed glazed over while the Tam Paupa was being worn.

While eb Riss lay like one paralyzed, the Tam Paupa slowly crawled off his head, down his face, and away from his body.

"I'll be an imploded star," Kirk exclaimed, "the blasted thing's alive!"

bn Bem spared a moment to turn a curious look on Kirk. "Of course is alive the Tam Paupa. You mean you knew this not?"

"We thought," murmured McCoy, "it was some kind of crown."

"Is crown truly. Is crown alive," the commander hastened to explain. "Why you think we not make new Tam Paupa when this one first stolen?"

"We thought this one had some particular cultural or spiritual significance," Kirk reasoned.

"Has that," admitted bn Bem, "but is much more why. Tam Paupa is maybe rarest integral on Pandro. One found only every two to five hundred our years. Is why this one missed so badly. Immature Tam Paupa types live plentiful, but useless to us. Have no ability to integrate with Pandronian mind, to aid in decision-making."

"It's an intelligent creature, then?" a skeptical McCoy wondered.

"Not intelligence as we say," the commander continued. "Is most specialized integral—perhaps most specialized on all planet Pandro." He frowned a Pandronian frown.

"But This One not understand why it left eb Riss. eb Riss not dead."

"What happens when the Pandronian wearing—no, I guess I should say associating—with the Tam Paupa does die?" McCoy inquired. "Surely Pandronians don't live six hundred years or so."

"No. When that happens, council or similar group of potential premiers is assembled. At moment of decision Tam Paupa leaves now useless body of former integration and chooses new one to associate with. That One becomes new ruler of Pandro.

"Is most fair and efficient method of choosing new Pandro leader. Tam Paupa always selects best mind present to associate self with. Is also why Pandro never have any fat premiers," the commander added as an afterthought. "Tam Paupa draws sustenance as uneating integral from its Pandronian host-partner."

"Sort of like a mental tapeworm," McCoy observed fascinatedly.

"But still remains question, why Tam Paupa leave eb Riss traitor? Is That One not dead," and he gestured at the dazed but still very much alive eb Riss.

"I think maybe I can answer that," Kirk said slowly. "When he enters a Vulcan mind trance, Mr. Spock is capable of mental communication to a certain degree. What he's doing to, or with, the Tam Paupa I can't imagine, but he's obviously doing *something*.

"I wonder how long Spock's known that the Tam Paupa was a living creature and not a hunk of metal, Bones."

"No telling, Jim," the doctor replied. "Could have been from the beginning, or he might have discovered it just now. We never discussed it among ourselves, so if he did know, he probably saw no reason to bring the subject up. Besides, you know Spock when he really gets interested in something."

"I know, Bones. Sometimes he forgets that the rest of us might not see things as clearly as he does," Kirk noted. "And speaking of seeing things clearly . . ." He pointed downward.

After a long pause next to eb Riss's motionless body, the Tam Paupa had apparently concluded its scrutiny of the assembled prospective candidates. It began to move again on its hundreds of tiny cilia—directly toward Spock.

"We've got to wake him up, Jim," McCoy exclaimed, alarmed at the direction events were taking. "He may not be aware of what's happening." Indeed, the *Enterprise*'s first officer was still staring off into space, and not down at the shining circle approaching his feet.

"Bones, I don't know. Maybe—" Kirk moved to intercept the creature, bending and reaching down with a hand.

A strong blue arm grabbed his shoulder, pulled him back. "No, Kirk Captain," bn Bem warned him. "Not to touch the Tam Paupa. Recall that creature which can live six hundred Pandronian years in unstable jungles of Pandro has defenses other than mental. Recall recent actions of traitor eb Riss."

Kirk thought back a moment. When eb Riss had sought to prevent the Tam Paupa from leaving him, he had reached up with his hands—and promptly yanked them away, in evident pain. Now Kirk scrutinized those limp hands and saw that they were burned almost beyond recognition.

"When so wishes, can Tam Paupa secrete extremely caustic substance for protection," bn Bem went on to explain. "Protects self also from disassociation, even while wearer sleeps."

"Then how the devil," McCoy wondered, "did the rebels manage to remove it from old afden Kaun?"

"That answer's obvious, Bones, if you stop a minute and think."

"Sure—the Klingons have methods of handling anything, like we do, no matter how corrosive. They must have supplied the rebels who committed the actual theft with everything they needed." His attention was directed downward.

"Right now I'm more concerned with what that impressive little symbiote has on its mind," the doctor finished, voicing professional concern.

"We can't stop it, Bones," a tight-voiced Kirk reminded him, "and it would be highly dangerous to try beaming Spock up while he's still in trance state. He must have known what he was chancing when he began this. Let's hope he has some control over what's happening now."

The first officer of the *Enterprise* showed no signs of retreat or awakening, however, as the Tam Paupa continued its deliberate approach. Although Kirk knew it was a benign creature, he couldn't help comparing the scene to a large spider stalking its prey.

Reaching Spock's feet, the front end of the Tam Paupa touched his left boot. Kirk stiffened, started to reach for the hand phaser at his hip—no matter the consequences to Pandro if he vaporized the creature. More important were the consequences to Spock.

But his hand paused when the creature did. It remained there for long minutes, and Kirk wondered if it could detect his implied threat to kill. Abruptly, it backed away, hesitated again, and this time started straight for Commander Ari bn Bem.

With a mixture of excitement and horrid fascination, Kirk and McCoy stared as the creature touched bn Bem's foot, crawled up the back of his right leg, crossed his chest, went up the back of his neck, and settled itself like a bird scrunching down in its nest on the commander's head.

bn Bem's eyes had closed and remained closed when the Tam Paupa first touched him. Now they opened, and a different bn Bem looked out on the world. It was the look of a wiser Pandronian, one more compassionate and understanding, devoid of the omnipresent arrogance of Pandro.

"Is done," he told the councillors in a deep voice. "Has chosen the Tam Paupa." One by one he locked eyes with the assembled high council members. One by one they wordlessly confirmed him as premier. No oaths or formalities were required, not now.

"Have we been without a leader too long," declaimed High Councillor Dav pn Hon. "Commander former Ari bn Bem, are you now legitimate Premier Ari afbn Bem, ruler of planet Pandro. Done this moment by choice of high council and the true Tam Paupa."

"Is good this resolved well," afbn Bem agreed, without a hint of smugness or personal satisfaction in his voice at the Tam Paupa's choice. He turned now, to face the approving gazes of Kirk and McCoy—and of Spock, whose trance had broken the moment the Tam Paupa had settled itself on the commander's head.

"All thanks is to you, Kirk Captain, McCoy Doctor, Spock Commander. Is once again government of Pandro stabilized."

But while Kirk heard every word the commander said, his attention was focused irresistibly on the Pandronian's forehead. Somewhere in a circular line there, he knew, thin silky filaments had been sunk through the skin into afbn Bem's head, probably into the brain itself.

Hard as he peered, he could see no hint of the connection, so fine were the filaments involved. His gaze moved slightly higher, to note that once more the multiple eyes had glazed over. Again they resembled so many jewels set in a motionless crown.

The Tam Paupa, content in its new partner, was at peace. So apparently, was Ari afbn Bem, and so was the government of Pandro.

"To you, Spock Commander," the new premier was saying, "must go highest of all thanks."

"It was the only way," a diffident science officer replied modestly. He was rubbing his temples. The strain of holding the mind trance was always somewhat wearying.

"What way, Spock?" asked McCoy. "How did you do it?"

"Naturally it was clear the Tam Paupa could not be forcibly taken from eb Riss," Spock went on to explain. "Not only would the Tam Paupa resist with its own particular defenses, but the shock of tearing loose the filaments would have killed it, as well as eb Riss. Only with advanced medical technology could it be done. That's what the Klingons obviously employed in removing it from afdel Kaun, but we had no time to engage in even modest surgery." McCoy nodded in agreement.

"I had gradually grown aware that the Tam Paupa was a living organism complete unto itself, and found myself drawn to study of its extraordinary circular brain."

"Circular brain?" Kirk muttered.

"Yes, Captain. Functions of both spinal cord and brain are combined in one organ which runs the entire circumference of the body.

"Only recently did I feel I might be able to contact that unique mind. We did not actually engage in mental speech or telepathy of any kind. It was more in the nature of exchanging whole concepts all at once.

"I concentrated on communicating one thing to it: that Lud eb Riss was an unsuitable host. The Tam Paupa was uncertain. I tried to show it that while eb Riss's mind might be organically sound, its decision-making process was aberrant and diseased. To illustrate this, I used examples of eb Riss's recent behavior in an attempt to convince the Tam Paupa that such a mind was not a healthy associative partner because it could at any moment turn upon itself.

"In other words, I tried to show that by logical standards—

and the Tam Paupa is a very logical organism, Captain—eb Riss was insane. In the end, the creature agreed with me and left eb Riss for a more suitable partner." He indicated afbn Bem, who was standing nearby, listening with interest.

"Yet it started for you first, Spock," Kirk pointed out.

Spock looked mildly discomfited for a minute. "I had only conceived of persuading the creature to abandon eb Riss, Captain. I did not consider that once having done this it might settle upon me as the most reasonable new host. Had the creature persisted in its first decision I do not know what might have happened.

"Nor could I break the mental link I had so firmly established between it and myself. Had it completed a full integration with my mind, assuming it could do so with a non-Pandronian life-form, I suspect I would have ended up resigning my commission and remaining here for the rest of my natural life as ruler of Pandro."

"*Spock!*" McCoy looked aghast.

"I had no choice in the matter, Doctor," the first officer insisted, turning to face him. "The Tam Paupa's power is concentrated foremost on its own needs. I could *not* break that mental bridge. For so small a creature its mental strength is quite incredible.

"Fortunately, it decided at the last minute, perhaps partially as a result of reading the reluctance in my mind, that my resistance to the prospect of ruling Pandro was so strong that it eliminated me as a suitable host. A more receptive mind was required, hopefully one which would actually welcome the prospect of ruling the planet. It chose, as we have seen, Commander bn Bem."

"Don't tell me the Tam Paupa has a compulsion to rule, Spock," McCoy commented in disbelief.

"No, Doctor, it is not that at all. But if you wished to maximize your opportunities for a good life, what better person to associate with than the supreme ruler of the dominant race of the world you live on? It is the Tam Paupa's way of optimizing its survival quotient."

"Argue we not with the Tam Paupa's choice," declared the elderly pn Hon. "Is known well to us premier afbn Bem's integrity and abilities. Still," and he looked puzzled, "are many present with longer experience and, intending no impoliteness, greater administrative talents. Why, then, Ari bn Bem chosen?"

"I can hazard a guess," Spock told him.

Kirk nodded. "Go ahead and hazard, Mr. Spock."

"Remember our experience on Delta Theta Three, Captain. Commander bn Bem was exposed to the influence of the planetary mother-mind. As we subsequently observed, his attitude was altered significantly for the better by that chastising encounter.

"Perceptive a creature as the Tam Paupa is, I have no doubt that it detected this shift in normal Pandronian state of mind, which none of the other councillors present have had the benefit of."

"What about him?" McCoy demanded to know, compelled by professional concern to pay more attention than he desired to the only suffering member of the group.

"eb Riss?" a councillor said, noting the direction of McCoy's gaze. "We do not believe in killing, though never was it so warranted."

"We will not kill him outright," bn Bem explained, "but will he be given maximum punishment under Pandronian law. He will a massive dose of the dissolution formula be given, so that his integrals no longer one another will be able to stand. As all such criminals deserve, he will to wander the streets and fields of Pandro be condemned—in pieces, never again to exist as a fully-functioning Pandronian."

McCoy shivered. "I don't think I'd care to spend the rest of my life not knowing where my arms and legs and body were. No, I'd far rather be killed."

"Is not quite same sensation for Pandronian, McCoy Doctor," afbn Bem told him. "But will insure eb Riss harms no one ever again."

Under order from one of the councillors, guards were called and Lud eb Riss was led away to his fate.

"Owe we you all an immeasurable debt, Kirk Captain," the new premier declared when eb Riss had been removed. "Not only This One personally, but all planet Pandro. Is little enough, but can This One assure you that high council will soon approve application for associative member status in United Federation of Planets."

"That ought to make the Klingons happy," chuckled McCoy.

"Depart in harmony and full integration," afbn Bem told them. "To return as soon as are permitted, Kirk Captain. Will then see some changes made in Pandro and Pandronian attitudes, of which I was once worst example."

"I'm sure you'll make a fine premier, Commander," replied a gratified Kirk, "With the Tam Paupa to help you." He activated his communicator. "Kirk to *Enterprise*."

"*Enterprise*—Scott here—finally."

"Scotty!" exclaimed a surprised but pleased Kirk. "You're all right again."

"Aye, Captain," the chief engineer replied, obviously in high spirits. "The paralysis was temporary, as Nurse Chapel decided it would be. I'm fully recovered."

"And the other crew members who were affected?" McCoy inquired over his own communicator.

"They're all comin' along fine, Dr. McCoy. Chapel says they should all be up and about in a couple of days."

"All good news, Scotty," responded Kirk, "and just as good down here. You can beam the three of us up. We're finished. Pandro is going to join the Federation and our friend Commander bn Bem has just been made premier."

"bn Bem?" Scott muttered uncertainly, unaware as he was of the commander's complete transformation. "Captain, are you certain . . . ?"

"He's changed quite a bit since he first stepped on board the *Enterprise*, Scotty, and he's the first to admit that it's been for the better. Also, the Klingons have experienced a severe case of diplomatic foot-in-mouth disease."

"That doesn't send me into fits of depression, Captain."

"I didn't think it would, Scotty. Whenever you're ready."

"Aye, Captain. Stand by."

The entire Pandronian high council snapped to attention. Led by their new premier, every member performed an intricate Pandronian salute as Kirk, McCoy, and Spock dissolved in pillars of fire and vanished from the surface of Pandro.

As soon as he was sure transportation was proceeding normally, Scott left the conclusion of the operation to his assistant and rushed toward the alcove. He was moving to shake Kirk's hand almost before final recomposition was completed.

"Good to see you back on your feet, Scotty," was Kirk's first observation as he stepped down from the alcove.

"There don't seem to be any aftereffects, either, Captain," his chief engineer informed him. "I'd be willin' to bet that the Klingon's Pandronian allies were so unstable and unpredictable that they couldn't be trusted with really dangerous weapons."

"I'd come to the same conclusion, Scotty, even allowing for the demolition equipment they brought on board. They're still in custody?"

"Aye, Captain."

"You can direct Security to bring them here and beam them down to the surface. Use our last coordinates. I think they'll find a suitable reception waiting for them."

"With pleasure," Scott replied. "A more sour and fanatical bunch I've never encountered. It's a good thing Uhura was the one who interviewed them. I dinna think I would have been quite so gentle."

Kirk nodded, turned to his companions. "Mr. Spock, Bones, we'd better be getting up to the bridge."

"If you don't mind, Jim," McCoy murmured, "I'd just as soon check on those injured security people first."

"Of course, Bones. I forgot." McCoy smiled slightly, left quickly for Sick Bay.

Although still on full alert because of the presence of the Klingon cruiser nearby, it was an understandably happy bridge crew that noted Kirk and Spock's reappearance. There were no shouts of joy, no demonstrations. But nothing in the regulations forbade personnel under alert status from smiling, and everyone seemed to straighten slightly.

"Any change in the Klingons' position, Mr. Sulu?"

"None, Captain," the helmsman replied. "They're still just sitting there."

"Our communications are functioning again, Captain," Uhura put in. "Should I try to contact them now?"

Kirk considered, then smiled a little himself. "No, Lieutenant. Never mind. They know we know they're here. They're probably waiting and hoping that *we* don't start anything, or just go away. We'll oblige them. Any sign of transporter activity since they arrived, Mr. Sulu?"

"No, sir."

Kirk appeared satisfied. "Naturally not. They're afraid we'd detect it and want to know what they were up to on a neutral world. They must be frantic with worry, since they haven't been able to raise their secret installation. I don't think they're going to like what they find.

"Mr. Arex, lay in a course for Starbase Sixteen. Much as I'd like to be around when the Klingons discover what's happened on Pandro, I'd prefer to avoid unnecessary hostilities. And the Klingons are going to be feeling particularly hostile."

Navigator and helmsman moved to execute the order. As they were preparing to do so, Kirk noticed that his first officer seemed in an especially thoughtful mood.

"What is it, Spock?" Abruptly he had a thought of his own. "Don't tell me you regret leaving Pandro?"

"It is not that, Captain. Naturally I had no desire to remain and rule the planet. But there was something else the Tam Paupa offered which I cannot get out of my mind." He looked speculatively across at Kirk.

"It insisted in its own way of communicating that it could instruct me how to fully disassociate in the fashion of the Pandronians. The possibility of being able to separate my body into several independent sections was so intriguing that I confess for a brief moment I was sorely tempted."

"I'm glad you didn't accept, Spock," Kirk told him honestly, appalled at the picture his mind conjured up of three Spock sections running haphazardly about the ship. "I like you the way you are. In one piece."

"That was my eventual feeling also, Captain. Besides, while the Tam Paupa was positive it could teach me to disassociate, it was not quite so certain it could show me the way to reintegrate again. The only thing I want following me through the universe is my shadow. Not," he added strongly, "my arms or legs. I'd rather be a whole Vulcan than a parade."

"Amen to that," Kirk concurred. Then his mood turned somber as the viewscreen replaced the receding planet Pandro with a spacious view of stars and nebulae.

"You know, the Klingons with their experimental creatures weren't behaving much differently than children do with building blocks. Their toy just got out of hand at the end." He stared at the vast panorama on the screen, which formed a very tiny portion indeed of one infinitesimally small corner of the universe.

"In a way we're all like Captain Kor and his people—children playing with building blocks that we don't always understand. We have to be careful and keep the castles we build out of them down to sizes we can manage, or one day they're all liable to come tumbling down on us. . . .

STAR TREK®
LOG TEN

STAR TREK LOG TEN

Log of the Starship *Enterprise*

Stardates 5538.6–5539.2 Inclusive

James T. Kirk, Capt., USSC, FC, ret.,

Commanding

transcribed by
Alan Dean Foster

At the Galactic Historical Archives
Ursa Major Lacus
stardated 6111.3

For the Curator: JLR

SLAVER WEAPON

(Adapted from a script by Larry Niven)

1

Stardate 5538.6. Transmission/private-personal. Code to officer annual allotment #C-5539, personnel budget U.S.S. *Enterprise,* on patrol in sector (censored) to: Mr./Mrs. Alhamisi Uhura, rural route 5, Kitui province, Kenya state, Africa, Earth 100643.
Begin transmission:

Dear Mom and Dad:

Not much new from out here, since the scenery doesn't change too quickly. By the time this letter reaches you, Dad, the harvest should be in. I hope the corn has done well, because I understand that hog prices are fairly high and are expected to go higher, so you and Mom ought to be able to do very good business this year.

How is everyone else back home? I am fine, thanks, and so is everyone else on board. We are enjoying a little routine, quiet patrolling for a change. Quite a relief after all the trouble we had with the Pandronians. I'm sure you read about that business in the local news. While I'm not at liberty to discuss details, take my word for it that there's more to that story than you've heard. We almost lost Mr. Spock to a (details deleted, ship compucensor).

Dr. McCoy has promised to send brother David some interesting information on the multiple-community Pandronian life systems (at least, anything which Star Fleet doesn't censor). It's purely biological material and should be passable for communication. David could get a paper or two out of it, I think. Dr. McCoy will send it to David's office at Makere University Hospital in Kampala instead of to the house there, so it can be transmitted as official business.

I'm still enjoying my work tremendously and am doing what I really always wanted to do—help to push back the frontiers of knowledge just a little bit. I've never been sorry for going into Star Fleet or for having specialized in communications.

Do you realize, Mom, that when I'm on duty on the bridge I'm the only one who knows what's going on all over the ship? That's because I'm constantly monitoring interlevel and interdepartmental communications as well as deep-space transmissions. What other career could offer me anything to compare in excitement with what I'm doing right now?

Well, got to go now. This letter will use up all my personal communication's allowance for the next month, so you won't be hearing from me again before then.

Your loving daughter,

Uhura signed the message, punched it into the ship's computer for deep-space transmission, and drifted off into a daydream. She remembered killing the lion.

It was the day after her sixteenth birthday. The midsummer East African sun turned the soil to dust. Motionless regiments of hybrid corn grew higher than a man, hiding any glimpse of the towers of now-distant Kitui or the parched veldt ahead.

Uhura sat pouting beside her father as he guided the car over the lightly traveled roadway. She held the elaborately decorated spear indifferently, though she was careful not to let the sharp point scratch the transparent bubble-dome of the car. There was a certain boy she could have been picnicking with, and she would have far rather been there than here.

"I still don't see why I have to kill a lion, Dad."

Her father looked over at her, smiled through his neatly trimmed beard. "It is traditional. Once upon a time the tradition applied only to manchildren. But"—and his grin grew wider—"you women changed that a couple of hundred years ago. So now the ritual applies to you as well."

"*I* didn't change it." She folded her arms, looked exquisitely bored. The air-conditioning was crawly on her body. The short skirt she wore provided little warmth.

"Besides, it's cold in here. Can't I put my shorts and halter back on?"

"Tradition should be upheld, Uhura. Sometimes that's all one has to remind one of the past. Tradition says that to prove you have become a woman, you must kill a lion with a single spear, by yourself. Since you must do this in the manner of your ancestors, that means you must do it wearing their archaic attire also."

She fingered the heavy metal and bead necklaces which hung awkwardly from her neck. "Can I at least take these off? How could anyone fight while wearing five kilos of jewelry?"

Her father tried to soothe her. "Come now, it's not that bad. This will all be over with soon enough. You will do well, too. Your grandfather has foretold it in the bones."

"Chicken bones don't indicate the future." The lithe young girl snorted derisively. "They only indicate the former presence of an unlucky chicken."

"Your grandfather has more respect for ancient lore than most of his contemporaries, and certainly more than you children today! One day you'll admire him for it. Besides, he does no worse with his bones than the computer does when it comes to forecasting long-range weather."

"*He* loads the tapes," she said, but unconvincingly. Grandfather Uchawi was a lovable but peculiar old man.

Her father turned his attention back to the road. "Besides, you've always been a straight-A student in physical education. I trust in that even more than in your grandfather's bones."

Humming silently, the electric vheicle turned off the main roadway and moved down a much narrower path. Traffic here was infrequent. They had emerged from the yellow-green ocean of corn and were traveling over undulating, grassy plains: cattle country. Shining like milk quartz in the noonday sun, the benign crown of white-capped Kilimanjaro gazed down on them. Soon they would leave private land and cross force barriers into the Serengeti.

Uhura regarded her spear again, wishing the ceremonial feathers tied just below the blade were sewn to one of her summer dresses. Matching feathers were tied behind her, to the base of the oval shield and to the second spear she was permitted. This extra spear was a concession to the times. Since the ancient skills were so rarely practiced, she would be permitted two chances instead of the traditional one. Both weapons, however, looked much too fragile to challenge the tawny king of the veldt.

Her father reached the Serengeti force barrier and turned down a road paralleling it, until they reached a game-park gate. The path beyond was not paved. None of the paths in the vast parkland were.

He exchanged greetings with the automatic gate. It confirmed their names and appointment time and admitted them. For another hour they drove on, passing through rugged brushland. The area looked no different from pictures Uhura had seen of this country as it had been a thousand years ago.

Eventually the land cruiser slowed to a halt, settled gently to the ground. Her father slipped out, helping her with the bulky shield and second spear. Slinging one spear across her back, Uhura, by then resigned to her fate, hefted the shield in her left hand, the other spear in her right, and faced the high thornbrush across the way.

"How will I find the lion?"

"Don't worry, my daughter. The lion will find you. Be ready at all times, don't panic, and remember what you were taught in school."

With that he bestowed a brief, affectionate kiss on her forehead and returned to the land cruiser. She watched it rise, turn, and disappear down the path they'd come.

She stood alone, listening to the warbling of secretive birds.

Her nose itched, and she rubbed it with the hand holding the spear. Clear of the land cruiser's air-conditioning, she was no longer cold. If anything, she was rapidly becoming hot standing in the sun. Then she began to understand the appropriateness of her dress—or rather the lack of it.

With the disappearance of the vehicle, more birds sang freely in the surrounding trees and brush. Sounds of larger creatures moving about reached her. Monkeys, most likely. The sun was beginning to bother her, but she remembered what her lore instructor had told her, and hesitated before retreating into the shade. If there were lions about, the shade was a likely place for them to be resting.

Something brushed a bush on her right. She turned to stare at it, saw only branches. It was probably another monkey. If so, then this would be a safe place to escape from the sun. No monkey would move close to the ground in the vicinity of a lion. But it wouldn't take much to make sure. Finding a suitable rock nearby, she cleared it of ants, aimed it, and threw it into the rustling copse.

Something that sounded like a demolished building crumpling to the earth shook her ears. Though she had heard that thunder on many tapes, the real thing still paralyzed her. A shape the size of a small land cruiser erupted from the brush, an umber nimbus framing a vast mouth full of flashing white fangs.

In place of coherent thought, months of practice at school took over. Instantly Uhura dropped to her right knee. The shield stood braced against her left foreleg as she wrapped both hands tightly around the shaft of the spear, left hand over right as she ground the spear-butt sharply into the dirt.

The lion leaped.

A terrific concussion traveled along her arms and shoulders as the lion came down on the blade of the spear.

A killing strike first time was as much a combination of luck as skill. Uhura had been lucky. She wouldn't need to use the second spear. The point of the first had missed the ribs, slid between them to pierce the heart.

Even so, her posture was not quite perfect and the lion's trailing leg caught her, knocked her over backward, and sent the shield tumbling. But as she rolled to her feet and fumbled for the second spear she saw that the great cat was already lying still on its side. Her first spear protruded brokenly from its chest.

So fast had the attack come that she had the remainder of her allotted hour free. She was sitting in the shade enjoying her sparse lunch when her father finally arrived to pick her up. He emerged from the land cruiser as it settled to the earth. Curious, he inspected the motionless form of the lion, then came over to greet her. Pride glistened in his eyes and she felt a little embarrassed.

"You did very well, child."

"Thanks," she replied. "I'm glad it's over, though." She checked her wrist chronometer. "If we hurry I might still make the end of the picnic."

"That boy again?" He smiled. "All right, we'll hurry."

She pointed to the corpse as they walked toward the vehicle. "I hope I didn't break anything. It hit pretty hard on the spearpoint."

"Don't worry." Her father put an arm around her and playfully tugged the traditional Masai braids that hung from her head. "The operative motors, the generator, and the controlling elements are well protected in the head and legs. I've seen the insides and they're beautifully put together. Made to take a lot of punishment, too. See? The hour's up and they're starting it up again."

Sure enough, the lion rose as they watched. It used one paw to pull the spear free. There was no blood. Just a few shreds of torn plastic. The simulacrum walked over, politely handed Uhura her spear, and loped easily back into the brush.

"What happens, Dad, if somebody misses a kill with both spears?"

"In that case, sugar, the lion comes over, pats you on the head, and goes back into the forest to wait for the next tester like yourself. If you fail, you get to try again in six months."

He regarded the veldt silently for a moment, then added, "In the old days, if you missed with your spears, you never got a second chance."

Another land cruiser had pulled up alongside theirs. Two sixteen-year-old boys jumped out, accompanied by an older man and woman.

"We'd better leave. We're running into someone else's testing hour, and the simulacrum won't begin its stalk until both cars have left."

Uhura trotted alongside her father as they returned to their land cruiser. Both boys eyed her curiously but said nothing. The one nearest her was pretty good-looking, but their minds were elsewhere and she couldn't say anything to them anyhow. That was against the rules.

As she climbed back into the chilled cab of the land cruiser and reached gratefully for her everyday clothes, it struck her that according to modern tribal tradition she was now a fully adult woman. Probably she was supposed to feel different—excited or something. All she felt was relief that the ordeal was over.

The ritual hadn't been as boring as she had expected, however. The simulacrum of the lion had been *very* real, much more so than the ones she had practiced against in school. But her primary emotion was impatience to return to town.

As the land cruiser hummed smoothly toward the park gate, she wondered for an instant what it must have been like hundreds of years ago, when Masai youths had to go out on their own and confront real lions, not a composite of fluids and metals and circuitry. Ones with real teeth, which could cut through a shoulder in a single snap or crush a skull like an eggshell. She shuddered a little, and this time it wasn't an effect of the air-conditioning.

She had often gazed on the wild lions hunting out in the Serengeti. What made her queasy wasn't the thought of being eaten by one, but the concept of slaughtering one of the magnificent creatures simply to prove a point about aging which she found upsetting. Thank goodness she didn't live in such superstitious times, although her grandfather would have chided her for such disrespect.

II

Something beeped in her ear. Uhura woke with a start and activated the incoming call.

"Message from Starfleet headquarters, relayed, priority coded, Captain."

Kirk turned in the command chair to face her. "Restricted access, Lieutenant Uhura?"

She checked the signal code. "It doesn't say here, sir."

"Put it on the main screen then, Lieutenant."

Uhura complied, and a portrait took shape on the main viewscreen forward. The uniform beneath was not that of a military man but of a United Federation of Planets diplomat. Spock's brows lifted slightly in puzzlement. It was highly unusual for diplomatic information to come directly to them without being shuttled through Starfleet channels. Then the scene enlarged slightly to reveal a commodore sitting alongside. Spock relaxed. The situation had changed from unusual to simply curious.

"Captain Kirk," said the man in the diplomatic attire, "I am Joseph Laiguer, personal envoy and ambassador plenipotentiary to the systems of Briamos. I suggest a moment to familiarize yourself with the basic details of Briamos as supplied to all Starfleet vessels."

"Well, Mr. Spock?" Kirk glanced across at his science officer, who replied softly.

"A fairly recent Federation contact, Captain, on the fringe of explored territory. There are three closely aligned solar systems containing five inhabited worlds comprising the government of Briamos. The Briamosites are technologically advanced and possess their own modest space fleet. They are humanoid, though they average a third of a meter taller than human or Vulcan norm and are reputed to be a polite but suspicious people."

"That matches what I can recall about them. Thank you, Spock."

"You have now had time to discuss Briamos with your officers," the ambassador continued as if no pause in their conversation had taken place. "You may already have asked yourself why I am contacting you directly; also why I am calling from Starfleet headquarters if I am ambassador to these worlds. The answer to both is that I was called back for consultation, unfortunately."

"Why unfortunately?" Kirk asked.

"Because," the ambassador said, leaning forward intently, "it seems that the Briamosites abruptly decided the other day to hold a conference on their homeworld during which they will decide whether or not they will enter into a preliminary alliance—social, cultural, and military—with either the Federation . . . or the Klingon Empire."

What had thus far been a fairly ordinary communication was one no longer. Although no one on the bridge neglected his assignment duties, everyone delegated a portion of his attention to the figure speaking from the viewscreen.

"Observers and representatives of both the Federation and Klingon Empire have been invited to participate in the conference and to present their respective positions regarding the Briamosites' intentions."

"And you can't be there," said Kirk, filling in blanks. "Why not?"

"Among other things," the ambassador explained, "the Briamosites are noted for their impatience." He named a date. "As you can see, it would be impossible for me to reach Briamos from Starfleet headquarters anywhere near the time set for the opening of the conference."

"Are the Briamosites so impatient they wouldn't delay the start of such an important conference until you could arrive?" Impatience was one thing, Kirk thought, but this bordered on downright rudeness.

The ambassador was slowly shaking his head. "It is important to them, Captain Kirk. According to the Briamosite way of thinking, we will be the ones guilty of an insult if we do not arrive in time for the beginning of their conference. Therefore," and he rustled some papers before him officiously, "since the *Enterprise* is patrolling in the Federation sector nearest to Briamos, you are directed to proceed there, Captain, empowered to act as ambassador-at-large for the Federation with all due powers and rights in my absence and to act for and in the name of the United Federation of Planets." He dropped the papers, regarded the viewscreen pickup solemnly.

Kirk shifted uneasily in his chair. He would far rather have been informed he could expect to deal with a rapacious alien life form than with the intricacies of diplomacy.

As the ambassador concluded his talk, Spock turned and began speaking softly to his computer pickup. There were important preparations to be made, and he was commencing such activities already.

"That's all I have to say." The ambassador looked to his right. As he did so, the view widened to include the officer sitting next to him. "But Commodore Musashi has a few comments to add, I believe."

Kirk had never met the diminutive commodore now gazing out at him, but he knew of him by reputation: an old-line officer famed for directness and the brilliance of his tactical solutions to logistical problems. With the Romulans on one side and the Klingons on the other, plus assorted bellicose organizations in between, the United Federation of Planets had special need of men with Musashi's particular analytical talents. So, while the older officer would no doubt have preferred a ship command to a desk job, the requirements of the Federation kept him tied to Starfleet headquarters.

Kirk could sympathize with what he had heard. Only loyalty kept Musashi active. In Musashi's position, having to battle figures and charts and petty bureaucratic interference, Kirk probably would have resigned. The fact that the commodore remained to serve the Fleet despite personal feelings only made Kirk pay particular attention to what the man was about to say.

"I cannot overemphasize the importance of this assignment to you, Captain Kirk," the commodore began earnestly. "You must keep in mind at all times that these Briamosites are not only not just your average cluster of primitive aborigines, but are one of the most advanced races we have contacted in a hundred years." Spock turned his attention from various science readouts to pay attention as the commodore paused for effect, then continued.

"Starfleet intelligence has estimated that the five worlds of Briamos have a combined population of well over seven billion. In terms of natural resources these five worlds and the uninhabited satellite worlds of their three systems are quite wealthy. Here at Starfleet the impression of the Briamosites themselves is one of a competent, highly industrious people. It goes without saying that they would be a welcome addition even on a limited-alliance basis to the United Federation."

Musashi leaned back in his seat, sighed deeply. "Unfortunately, they could also become a powerful ally of the Klingons. From what we know of their natural temperament, which borders on brusqueness at times, they could blend in as well with the Klingons as with us.

"Should the Briamosites decide to link themselves with the Klingon Empire and should that relationship be cemented in the future, it would do much more than simply gain the Klingons a powerful friend. Because of their position on the flank of the Empire, the Briamosites could be counted on by the Klingons to anchor that portion of their empire and protect it from attack. Doing so would free their ships immediately to create considerably more mischief elsewhere."

"The term 'mischief' is imprecise, but I have no doubt as to the commodore's true meaning." Spock glanced over at Kirk as he spoke.

"I don't think anyone would, Mr. Spock," Kirk agreed.

Once again the pickup concentrated on the ambassador. "There you have the situation, Captain Kirk. We of the Federation Diplomatic Corps wish you luck and know you'll carry out your assignment to the credit of us all. I wish only that I could be there in person to assist you, but space and time preclude it." He paused, obviously trying to think if he'd forgotten anything.

"Again, keep in mind always the Briamosites' natural impatience. We've already contacted them and informed them that our representative—meaning you—will arrive in time for the conference. What else could we say?" He shrugged slightly. "They replied in their gruffly polite fashion that our representatives would be most welcome—indeed, would be anxiously awaited—but that the conference date is set and will proceed whether or not the *Enterprise* arrives on time." Another pause, and when he resumed it was in a low, almost warning tone.

"I need hardly tell you, Captain, that the absence of the Federation representative at the conference would be tantamount to an expression of disinterest on our part, if not an outright insult. Nothing could be better calculated to drive the Briamosites into the orbit of the Klingon Empire than for the *Enterprise* to arrive after the conference is scheduled to begin."

Kirk bridled at being so openly chided, but held his silence.

"You will proceed to Briamos by way of Starbase Twenty-Five. There you will receive additional briefings and more detailed information on what you can expect upon arriving at Briamos. You should have ample time to attend all the scheduled briefings and still reach Briamos well before the conference begins." The ambassador thought for a moment, glanced briefly over at the commodore, then said almost absently to the pickup at his end, "That's all, then, Captain Kirk. We of the Diplomatic Corps are with you in spirit if not in the flesh."

The picture faded. As it did so, Kirk thought he detected the barest hint of a reassuring grin on Commodore Musashi's face. It was a smile that said, Don't-mind-the-ambassador-he's-upset-because-he-can't-be-there-for-his-moment-of-glory-so-just-ignore-him-and-do-your-job.

"End transmission, Captain," Uhura announced formally as the last vestiges of image faded from the screen.

Kirk considered all he had just seen and heard, then swiveled to regard his first officer. "Well, Mr. Spock, I'd just as soon *not* engage in any professional word fighting, but we don't seem to have any choice. We're prisoners of our spatial position. At least we'll get to meet the Briamosites. They sound like an interesting people. I only wish we didn't have to be civil to a bunch of Klingons at the same time."

"I also have been intrigued by the little I have heard of Briamos and its inhabitants, Captain," replied Spock. "I am looking forward to the starbase sessions we will be attending."

Kirk nodded in reply, turned to face the helm. "Mr. Sulu, set a course for Starbase Twenty-Five."

"Yes, sir," Sulu responded, turning to his console.

"Standard cruising speed, Mr. Sulu." Kirk hesitated, then asked, "By the way, do we have coordinates for Briamos? In the event we run into trouble, we might have to bypass the starbase and proceed directly to Briamos."

Sulu made a rapid check of the navigation computer. "Coordinates for Briamos were entered last input session, sir. If we have to, we can get there from here."

Kirk relaxed a little at that information.

"Anticipating difficulties, sir?" Lieutenant Arex inquired from his position at the navigation station.

"Lieutenant, given the importance of this conference to both the Federation and Klingon, I'd be surprised if we *didn't* run into a little interference."

"Yes, sir," the Edoan acknowledged in his quiet way. "Dense of me not to see that, sir."

"Excuse me, Captain."

Kirk frowned slightly, glanced over a shoulder toward communications.

"What is it, Lieutenant Uhura?"

"Sir, I have"—she sounded a bit uncertain, which was unusual in itself—"another priority message coming in."

It was Spock who voiced the most obvious objection. "Are you certain it's not a ghost of the first message, Lieutenant?"

Uhura was rapidly checking several readouts. "No

sir, absolutely not. I haven't quite traced the place of origin, but it's definitely not coming from Starfleet coordinates."

There was silence on the bridge while Uhura fought with abstract math. As usual, she won. "The signal is very weak, Captain." Again delicate hands moved in an attempt to coax the incoming message to greater clarity. "Odd." She was staring at a single readout now. "According to my instrumentation the signal is emanating from a system known as Gruyakin."

"Mr. Spock?" But Kirk needn't have urged his first officer, who was already reading the requisite information from the science computer screen.

"The Gruyakin system consists of twelve planets circling a K-6 star, Captain," he reported. "Two of the dozen worlds are reported to be marginally habitable, but there are no settlements of any kind. The only item of interest stems from reports of a vanished civilization on one of the two inhabitable worlds."

"Then who," Kirk wondered aloud, "is broadcasting a message strong enough to reach this far?"

"I don't know, sir, but I have an acceptable signal now."

"Let's see it then, Lieutenant." Kirk turned his attention once again to the main screen.

Despite Uhura's best efforts and some heroic image enhancing by the communication computers, the picture that appeared there was fuzzy and distorted. But amid the interference everyone could make out a tired and none-too-clean, middle-aged human woman. They could also discern a few details, including prematurely gray hair, deep-set blue eyes, and an expression awash with worry and grave concern.

"Does anybody . . ." she said, obviously in the middle of repeating a by-now-old message. Abruptly she noticed an unseen control on her left and looked into her own pickup out onto the bridge of the *Enterprise*. Kirk wondered if her view of him was as weak as his own was of her.

"Sorry if we've startled you," he said, "but you were broadcasting on a priority Starfleet frequency."

"I know what we're doing!" she replied, a mite testily. Then it was her turn to apologize as she ran a hand over her forehead to brush aside several trailing hairs. "Excuse me, whoever you are. We've all been under a lot of pressure here. We still are.

"My name is Shannon Masid. I'm in charge of this expedition to Gruyakin Six." She used a thumb to gesture sharply over one coverall-clad shoulder.

"One of the two inhabitable worlds in the Gruyakin system, Captain," Spock whispered to him.

Despite the poor quality of the transmission, Kirk could just make out the curving wall of a transparent dome behind the woman and a very little bit of the landscape beyond. A few hardy, thin plants showed against the dome, as tired and beaten as the topography they grew upon. A lake so dull and black it might have been the source of the Styx lay in the distance.

"What expedition is that?" Kirk wanted to know. "According to our information there are no outposts in the Gruyakin system."

"Not so fast, sir. Who might you be?"

Kirk was a little peeved at what sounded almost like an accusation. This was evident in his reply, which was a touch sharper than he meant it to be. "I'm Captain James T. Kirk, commanding the U.S.S. *Enterprise*, en route to Starbase Twenty-Five."

"*Enterprise* . . . Starbase Twenty-Five." The woman appeared relieved, then said importantly, "Captain, I'm afraid I'm going to have to ask you to alter your course."

"Alter our—?" Kirk was speechless.

"I am sure Ms. Masid has a reason, sir," Spock said gently.

"I'm sure she does, Mr. Spock," Kirk replied firmly, "and I'm sure it's valid—to her." He directed his voice to the command-chair pickup.

"Ms. Masid, the *Enterprise* is on a mission of vital importance to the Federation. I can't imagine any circumstances under which we could alter our course. If you're in some difficulty, please explain its nature and we'll see that relief is sent to you promptly. But I'm afraid we cannot—"

"How do I know you're who and what you say you are?"

For a second Kirk's outrage threatened to overpower his reason. Then he considered the suspicion and fear in the woman's tone. His exasperation gave way to curiosity. This Masid did not look or sound like a fool. Then it came to him, something he had noticed as soon as she'd appeared on the screen but had only placed just now.

She wasn't just frightened. She was terrified. That had not been immediately obvious because she was fighting to keep her emotions under control.

"How do I know," she continued anxiously, "that you're not in some kind of disguise, that your appearance isn't meant to fool us?"

"Mr. Spock, play the visual pickup around the bridge," Kirk directed.

Spock did so, and the woman's darting eyes on the screen showed that she was following everything intently.

"Satisfied?" Kirk asked when the pickup had completed a circuit of the bridge.

"Almost. If this is a ruse, it's an elaborate one. Just one question," she went on rapidly. "Who won the Federation tridimensional hockey championship three years ago in the double-overtime final game, and who was named most valuable player?"

"Really, Ms. Masid!"

"I'm dead serious, Captain," she replied. "That information isn't likely to be in an enemy's computer banks."

"Her seriousness appears genuine, Captain." Spock was convinced of the woman's sincerity. "If you'll wait a moment I'll check the computer files in the recreation section and—"

Sulu interrupted him as he prepared to recover the necessary information.

"That's not necessary, Mr. Spock." The helmsman put himself on the pickup. "The Eridani Gryfalcons," he said. "Most valuable player was center-forward-up Shawn Ge-Yrmis."

"Thank you, whoever you are. That's right." The

woman on the screen smiled gratefully. Sulu glanced at the science station, and Spock nodded approvingly in return.

"That's as conclusive a test as I can think of," the figure on the screen declared. She folded her hands on the battered worktable before her. "I've got to accept that you're who you say you are.

"Our expedition isn't large or permanent enough to qualify for outpost status," she explained. "That's why we're not listed in your computer. I'm in charge of Federation Archeological Expedition Four-Six-Two, investigating the remnants of a dead civilization on Gruyakin's sixth planet."

"That matches the information we have, Captain," Spock declared.

"The civilization of this world," and she gestured again at the desolate, unimpressive landscape barely visible through the dome behind her, "was not particularly important, nor does it seem to us to have been especially impressive. Nevertheless, it was a civilization and all such are deemed worthy of study and investigation."

"I'm familiar with the motives of the Federation Science League," Kirk commented drily. "You still haven't explained your reason for utilizing a priority distress frequency."

"We've found something here which *is* impressive, Captain. It's the reason for our signal, for my unfriendly attitude, and for my caution in dealing with you. We couldn't risk having an unfriendly power learn what we've unearthed here. Captain, we've found a sealed Slaver stasis box."

Silence on the bridge.

Kirk turned to his first officer. "Mr. Spock, what are the odds of finding a Slaver stasis box on . . ." He stopped, waved diffidently. "No, never mind. All that matters is that such a box exists."

"We've been broadcasting our priority call ever since we found the box, Captain." The reasons for the archeologist's tenseness became clear. "Going on two weeks now. We haven't much of a transmitter here. Your ship is the first that's passed within hailing distance." She smiled slightly again. "This isn't a heavily funded expedition. As I said, Gruyakin's not thought to be very important.

"You see now, Captain Kirk, why you must change course. As far from developed Federation worlds as we are, I've been frightened that some unfriendly power or unprincipled group of humans might stumble on our discovery. A sealed Slaver stasis box, of course, is beyond price."

"I understand now, Ms. Masid." Kirk regarded her sympathetically. "You were right to be so cautious. The temptation would be enormous even for an honest man. We'll be there as soon as possible and we'll relieve you of that box."

"Thank you." She was so obviously happy that it was embarrassing. "I can handle responsibility, but this is a bit too much for me, Captain. We'll be anxiously awaiting your arrival here."

"Your pardon, Captain," Spock began urgently, but Kirk hushed him.

"I'll be glad to see the damn thing gone," Shannon Masid was saying. "So we can all get back to some simple, uncomplicated excavating. We'll have our beacon set to provide you with beam-down or landing coordinates. Gruyakin Six out . . ."

"Captain, you cannot afford to miss the orientation sessions at Starbase Twenty-Five and still expect to make credible and accurate ambassadorial decisions." Spock regarded the captain expectantly. The hoped-for suggestion was not long in coming.

"No, I can't, Mr. Spock. But *you* can."

"That was my thought as well, Captain."

Kirk completed a mental outline. "You, Lieutenant Uhura, and Lieutanant Sulu will travel via shuttlecraft to Gruyakin Six and take custody of the stasis box. While you are doing that, I'll be undergoing briefing sessions on Briamos at Starbase Twenty-Five. We'll depart from Briamos upon completion of those sessions or immediately on your arrival from Gruyakin, whichever falls nearest to the time set for the beginning of the conference." He paused thoughtfully, added, "I'd rather have you undergo those same sessions, Mr.

Spock, but I'm confident that as long as one of us attends them, he can fill in the other on Briamosite protocol and such with the aid of tapes."

"I believe I can cope with the material sufficiently, prior to our arrival at Briamos, Captain."

Kirk smiled imperceptibly. "I'm sure you can, Spock." The smile vanished. "I wouldn't consider sending you three," and he gazed in turn at each of the three designated officers, "prior to so vital a conference if an unopened stasis box wasn't of nearly equal importance."

"Captain?"

"Yes, Spock?"

"Rather than have Lieutenant Commander Scott substitute in my place, Captain, and have someone take over in turn for him, I request permission to have Lieutenant Vedama of Sciences handle my duties in my temporary absence. I'll have little time to brief him, but he's a highly competent officer who deserves the opportunity to gain some experience in a command position. He has served as chief science officer on smaller Starfleet vessels. For him to take over for me on short notice, even for a week or so, will be excellent training."

Kirk nodded approvingly. It was like Spock to have the interests of a younger officer in mind even as he was about to embark on a serious mission of his own.

"I haven't heard anyone speak ill of the officer you mention, Mr. Spock. Request approved. You'll detail the lieutenant personally before you depart."

"Of course, Captain."

Rising from the command chair, Kirk met with the three department officers near the turbolift doors. "You'll leave as soon as possible. If you reach Gruyakin and have even a suspicion that another vessel might be in your spatial vicinity, get in touch with us immediately."

"What could you do in such a situation, Captain?" Spock wanted to know. "You still cannot deviate from your appointment with the briefers at Starbase Twenty-Five."

"One crisis at a time, Mr. Spock." He went on more seriously. "I really don't know. Much would depend on our exact position relative to Gruyakin and the base, and the position of the other ship, its markings, and so on. The difficulty stems from the fact that the contents of a Slaver box might be worth more than an alliance with Briamos, or they might be worthless. Let's hope no such problems arise. Just pick up the box and get out of the Gruyakin system as fast as you're able."

All three officers acknowledged the captain's orders, then hurried to their cabins. Only the minimum of personal effects would be taken. A shuttlecraft had very little spare room. But they wouldn't be gone very long and nothing beyond the basics was required.

Not long after leaving the bridge, they were clustered in the shuttlecraft bay. Engineer Scott was waiting to greet them, having just finished a personal checkout of the little shuttlecraft *Copernicus*.

"Have a nice trip, Mr. Spock, Sulu, Uhura," he said. "Bring back lots of pictures."

"From what I've seen of Gruyakin Six, Mr. Scott," Spock replied perfectly deadpan, "visual mementos would not be of much interest. However, I'm certain you'll find what we're going after of considerably more interest."

"And what might that be? I was only told to make the shuttle ready for a fast flight."

"Everything's been happening all at once, Mr. Scott," Sulu explained. "An archeological expedition on Gruyakin Six has found a Slaver stasis box."

"A Slaver—" Scott let out a long whistle, looked impressed. "No wonder the captain's in such a hurry. Why isna the ship goin'?"

"The *Enterprise* must reach Starbase Twenty-Five by a certain date, Mr. Scott." Spock was making his own, inevitable fast inspection of the shuttle. "Sending out a shuttle to Gruyakin is the only way everything can be properly accomplished in the time remaining to us. The sooner the stasis box is aboard the *Enterprise*, the better it will be for the Federation."

"Aye, Mr. Spock. Here to Gruyakin to Starbase Twenty-Five. I dinna think I'd care to be makin' that trip myself."

"I share your concern, but we have, as I've explained, no choice."

Scott gestured at the shuttle. "Well, there's no need to worry about the *Copernicus*. I've triple-checked everything myself and you've got long-range supplies bulging every storage locker. If you have to stay out longer than you plan, you're equipped for it."

"I hope not." Uhura looked anxious. "I'm curious to see what these controversial Briamosites are like. I've never heard of Starfleet speaking so highly of a new civilization or potential new ally. They must be something special."

"They can hardly be more special than a sealed stasis box," said Sulu fervently. "I've heard about them all my life, read about them on tapes, seen pictures of them, but I never expected to see one in person."

"In appearance," Spock commented as they entered the shuttle, "a stasis box is not particularly impressive. The knowledge of what lies inside more than makes up for any abstract esthetic deficiencies, however." He turned in the doorway, looked back out into the shuttle bay.

"Good-bye, Mr. Scott. We'll be seeing you again very soon."

Scott waited until the shuttle door had sealed itself, murmured a heartfelt, "Amen to that, Mr. Spock." Then he jogged to the near wall and punched an intercom switch.

"Attention, attention! Chief Engineer Scott speaking. All personnel are directed to clear the shuttlecraft bay. Clear the shuttle bay for launch." He thumbed another switch, was rewarded by the clamor of the bay alarm, then hit the communications nub once more.

"Bridge . . . Shuttle bay."

"Kirk here. That you, Scotty?"

"Aye, Captain. Clearing the bay. I'll be out myself in a second."

"Thanks, Scotty. We'll take it from here. Bridge out." He turned to the communications station, now manned by Lieutenant M'ress. "Communications check, *Copernicus*, Lieutenant."

"Checking, sirr," The Caitian officer purred back at him as she studied her console. "Channel open."

Kirk spoke into his chair pickup. "Mr. Spock, this is the captain speaking."

"Communications check good, Captain," came the clear reply. "All shuttle systems check out normal. Ready for departure."

"Stand by." Kirk turned to face the slight, nut-brown little man seated at the science station. "Open the shuttle-bay doors, Lieutenant, Vedama."

"Opening shuttle-bay doors, sir." The science officer's voice was almost as gentle as Lieutenant Arex's, but clipped at the end of heavily consonanted words. Vedama's ancestors had fought for a subsistence existence outside a bloated city on Earth named Bombay. Now the great-great-grandson of those struggling peasants commanded more knowledge at his fingertips than had all his ancestors combined.

At the stern of the *Enterprise* vast metal panels slid ponderously aside. There was no one in the chamber, now open to space, to see the few wisps of unreclaimed atmosphere puff out into emptiness. Several lights flashed on and then off, were matched by smaller telltales on the ship's bridge.

"Shuttlecraft away, Captain," Vedama reported.

"Close bay doors."

"Closing doors, sir."

Kirk turned his attention to the main viewscreen. "Lieutenant M'ress, give me shuttle channel and the view from aft scanners." M'ress nudged certain controls and a picture of the *Copernicus*, floating behind the *Enterprise*, appeared on the screen.

"Mr. Spock?"

"All shuttle systems continue to function normally, Captain," came the instant reply. "Preparing course to Gruyakin."

"Mr. Spock," Kirk continued more softly, "I meant what I said earlier. If you encounter another ship in the Gruyakin system, notify me immediately. Don't try to save time by coping with an intruder yourselves. You're not equipped for it."

"I understand, Captain. Hopefully we will see nothing but subsolar shuttles at our destination. We will rendezvous with the *Enterprise* at Starbase Twenty-Five at the appropriate time. *Copernicus* out."

"*Enterprise* . . . out." Reluctantly, convinced he had forgotten something, Kirk switched off.

After a while he considered beaming the shuttle again, but he had really nothing more to add. Spock was not the reckless type, but— Then it struck him what was actually bothering him. He wanted to be on board the *Copernicus*, racing to Gruyakin. Not on his way to sit like a schoolboy again before a set of repetitive lectures.

There were no such things as adults, he mused idly. Only older children . . .

III

From the time it left the *Enterprise*, the *Copernicus* was traveling at maximum shuttle speed. Spock intended to retrieve the Slaver stasis box as fast as possible, both to insure its safety and to make sure that they would reach Starbase Twenty-Five in time for them to sit in on the last of the Briamos briefings. Consequently, it wasn't too long before they had entered the Gruyakin system and taken up orbit around its sixth planet.

That world was no more impressive from orbit than it had been when seen on the main screen of the *Enterprise*. It was clearly a tired, worn globe, an old world with no high mountain ranges and only shallow oceans. Yet at one time in the distant past it had been home to a hopeful civilization. Perhaps the people of Gruyakin had also yearned to reach the stars, only to fall back in failure. Galactic archeology had long ago proven one thing: Those races who reached the stars expanded, advanced, and grew. Those who did not often fell to squabbling among themselves over petty tribal differences, only to disappear long before their natural time.

The same thing might have happened to Vulcan. It had come very near to happening on Earth.

Yet down there among the dead cities and forgotten memories lay one of the most valuable single objects in the galaxy, a Slaver stasis box. How and why it had come to be in this unimportant place was a question the archeological expedition might answer in the future. For now, it was important to place that box and its as-yet-unknown contents under more protection than a group of scientists and researchers could offer.

"I've located their beacon, Mr. Spock." Uhura glanced up from the *Copernicus*'s modest console.

"Homing in," reported Sulu, as he angled the shuttlecraft in the direction provided by the beacon.

Uhura made adjustments to another section of the console, then announced with satisfaction: "Audio contact."

"Identify yourselves," a strident voice demanded in the small cabin of the shuttle. "Our main phaser batteries are trained on you! Identify yourselves."

Sulu chuckled, but Spock spoke normally into the pickup. "You can drop the subterfuge, Gruyakin Six. This is the shuttlecraft *Copernicus* from the U.S.S. *Enterprise*, here to pick up . . . cargo. Commander Spock speaking. Is that you, Director Masid?"

An audible sigh reached them over the speaker. "Yes, it is, Commander. Excuse our bluff. It's not much, but it's the best we could think of." A pause, then: "We're mighty glad you're here. The *Enterprise* isn't with you?"

"No. This is the only way we could satisfy two vital commitments within a limited time."

"What difference does it make?" Uhura looked askance at Sulu, who shrugged.

"You have our beacon?" the director asked.

"Yes. With your permission, we will land immediately."

"The sooner the better. Gruyakin out."

Spock thought to ask a question, but decided not to call back. They would be down on the surface soon enough and he could ask it in person. He was feeling some of the same concern as Uhura. There was something going on down on the blighted surface of this world...

It wasn't often Sulu had the chance to pilot a shuttlecraft, much less to make a planetary landing. The transporter was a far simpler and faster device. But one couldn't have told this from the smoothness of their touchdown, which was a silent, safe tribute to the lieutenant's training and natural ability.

He brought the shuttle to a halt alongside the dark lake they had first observed during the initial transmission from Gruyakin to the *Enterprise*. Black volcanic sand along the narrow beach extended out indefinitely into the water and explained the lake's grim coloration. Ruined buildings, testaments to a forgotten alien architecture, lined the far shore of the lake.

Immediately to their left and slightly farther from the shoreline shone the familiar bubbles of pressurized domes. In the bleak setting they provided a comforting, if spartan, reminder of civilization. The expedition's quarters were far from luxurious. Love of science and the quest for knowledge could often enable people to endure hardships no sensible person would otherwise willingly submit to.

"Peculiar," commented Spock as he regarded the horizon near the domes. "They knew we were coming right down. I'd think there'd be someone here to meet us."

Sulu frowned as he studied the terrain. "Not a pretty world." He checked instruments, gazed at readouts. "Atmosphere is breathable, which is to be expected, but thin. Altitude equivalent of roughly three thousand meters on Earth. That might explain why no one's running to greet us." He peered closer at an isolated dial. "Judging from the content of certain trace gases, I don't think this world's going to smell very good, either."

Uhura squinted and then raised a hand to point. "Here they come. There's a vehicle of some kind."

A small, oval-bodied crawler was speeding toward them from the general region of the domes.

"Driver's a little reckless," Uhura observed disapprovingly.

Covering the intervening ground at high speed, the vehicle whined to a stop before the shuttle as Sulu let down the ramp. The atmosphere which now filled the shuttle had a faint flavor of overripe vegetation tinged with sulfur. Sulu tried not to look pained as they moved to meet their greeters.

Spock recognized the woman getting out of the far side of the crawler as expedition director Masid. Two men followed her toward the shuttle.

"They appear worried," he said speculatively. "I'd have thought they would be relieved by our arrival. I'm anxious to learn why they're not."

Uhura's nose twisted as they started down the ramp. "Phew! I think I'd wear a life-support belt here, even if the air is considered fit for breathing."

"An injudicious waste of energy, Lieutenant," Spock chided her as they walked toward the approaching threesome. His own nostrils twitched as a particularly noxious odor brushed them. He had to confess privately that Uhura's idea was not without merit.

Masid noted his insignia, went straight up to him and extended a hand. "Commander Spock." Her grip was surprisingly firm.

"Director Masid." He took in the expressions of the two men who were accompanying her. All three humans wore expressions akin to those who had recently placed large bets on a sure thing, only to learn that it wasn't so sure and that they had three minutes to withdraw their bets.

More significantly, the taller of the two men had a recent phaser burn scarring the left side of his neck.

"You've had trouble," Spock said. It was not exactly a question.

The director was panting heavily, fighting for air and not because of Gruyakin Six's thinner atmosphere. It was clear she had been running hard. "It's the box," she said reluctantly. "It's been stolen."

"Stolen!" Sulu couldn't believe it. "Didn't you have it under guard? Something that valuable—"

"Please, Mr. . . . ?"

"Lieutenant Sulu," he replied.

"Lieutenant," she explained wearily, "try to understand my situation here. This is purely a scientific expedition. I'd thought that I could believe the psychological profiles in our records. Those profiles were accurate save for one man. Even given the possibility that one of my people might conceivably be tempted by the wealth the box could represent, I thought that our isolation here, with no way for anyone to get off-planet until the relief ship arrives, would prevent any criminal action toward the stasis box. Well, I was wrong. The psychologists were wrong."

"You had best fill us in on exactly what has taken place," Spock suggested gently.

"The man's name is Jaiao," she began tiredly. "One of our excavators. Just because he's not as bright as some of our scientists was no reason to suspect him of harboring dishonest thoughts. Jaiao's difficulty is not unique. He simply feels he's not as wealthy as he would like to be." Her face twisted into a sardonic grin. "That's the problem."

"He stole the box by himself, then?" inquired Spock. "He is acting alone?"

"As far as we can tell." Masid gestured toward the distant domes. "Leastwise, no one's rushed to help him so far."

The criminal bent of certain humans never ceased to perplex Spock, and the present situation appeared founded on less logic than most such incidents.

Masid shook her head. "Be stunned if I know what came over him." Again she gestured at the domes, taking care to indicate the bulge farthest from their right. "He's locked himself in a storage dome."

"Have you tried to reason with him?"

She eyed the first officer strangely. "For some five minutes, until it became clear the devil himself couldn't talk him out of his foolishness. We also tried exhausting the air in the dome, but he has a life-support belt and plenty of power packs for it, so *that* didn't work."

"What can he do against you, to keep you from simply rushing him?" Sulu asked.

"He has a weapon in there, a model 6BB displacer.

That's one of the portable tools we use for excavating the ruins. It's clumsy compared to a hand phaser, but in the hands of someone like Jaiao, who knows how to use it, it makes a pretty nasty weapon, as Charlie here can tell you."

The man with the ugly burn mark on his neck nodded. "He's not fooling with that thing. He didn't miss me by much—and I don't think he was trying to miss me at all."

"If you tried exhausting the air in his dome, he'd just cut his way out into thinner but still livable atmosphere," Sulu pointed out. "You must have *some* weapons, or at least other displacers and people who know how to run them. How many of you are there here at the station?"

"I know what you're thinking, Lieutenant." Masid nodded. "It won't work. I didn't mean to imply that Jaiao is stupid. He's not, he's just not as brilliant as some of our higher-ranking professionals here. But he knew what he was doing before he took the box, had his strategy pretty well planned out. He went straight for the storage dome, with its ample supply of water, power, and food.

"If we rush him," she finished somberly, "he's threatened to use the displacer to try and open the stasis box."

"If we could be certain there was nothing in the box for its mechanism to protect . . ."

"Oh, it's sealed all right, Commander," she told him.

"Isn't there some way we can neutralize the field without him knowing about it, Mr. Spock?" The helmsman looked hopefully at his superior.

"I fear not, Mr. Sulu. An unopened, sealed box maintains its stasis field by means we still do not understand. Inside that field, time stands still, perfectly preserving whatever its original owners wished to put inside.

"There are methods of safely opening a stasis box. It has been done a number of times. But if the opening is not carried out with the utmost care and proper instrumentation, the results can be disastrous. I personally know of one stasis box that was opened hastily and improperly. It contained a variety of disruptor bomb. It may also have contained many other things, but we will never know of them. When the box was tampered with in that sloppy fashion, the bomb went off.

"I have heard of other means, equally lethal, which the Slavers employed to assure the security of their boxes. This person's threat to open this one in a hasty, crude fashion is a very real threat to anyone nearby."

"Sorry. I apologize, Director Masid." Sulu looked contrite. "I should have guessed you had reasons for not having made a direct attack on him already."

She smiled back at him. "We're researchers here, not members of the military. We don't know how to proceed or what to do next. We do have one shuttlecraft, located far on the other side of the domes, for emergency use. Our main relief ship isn't due for another three months. There are several inhabited systems within the range of our own shuttle."

"I can imagine what he is demanding," said Spock knowledgeably.

She nodded, once. "Free access to the shuttle and a guarantee of noninterference until he reaches it. He won't get that from *me*. We'd sooner have him break the box seal and destroy the whole base rather than let him slip away to maybe sell the box to someone with belligerent intentions." There were murmurs of agreement from the two men flanking her.

"Of course," Spock pointed out, "the box may not contain anything that might be of use to such people. Neither weapon nor weapon-adaptable device."

"But we can't take that chance . . . of course." Masid eyed Spock approvingly. "We think alike, Commander."

"I will accept that to a certain point," Spock agreed cautiously. "I still believe our best attempt to, ah, defuse the situation is to reason with the man."

"It's hard to reason with someone who has most of his sense in his back, Commander," declared Masid firmly. "Maybe you can do better than we have, but I doubt it." She eyed him with suspicion.

"We must at least give the appearance of negotiating in good faith." Spock looked thoughtful as he glanced toward the domes. "I want to see what the physical situation is, before deciding how to proceed. In order to do that we must convince him to talk with us."

"All right," agreed the director. "The fact that you're Federation military might have some effect on him. I'm afraid he's convinced himself that he's gone too far to back out now."

"I don't think so," Uhura disagreed. "So far he's guilty of nothing worse than simple theft."

"And assault with intent to kill." That came from the unforgiving-sounding man on Masid's left, the one with the burn from the displacer.

"Perhaps he will talk to *you*." Masid appeared ready to half persuade herself that something might be done before someone was killed. "Just remember that Jaiao has visions of endless wealth running through his head and he figures this is his one chance in life to get it."

"All I require is that you tell him who we are and aid us in getting to talk with him." Spock started toward the car. "The sooner we begin, the better it will be. We are on a tight schedule ourselves."

The cargo compartment of the battered little land vehicle was spacious enough to hold them all without crowding, if not in comfort. Once inside, Masid piloted the vehicle over a circuitous course across the surprisingly rugged terrain. Lava had flowed here in the recent past and there were cracks and rills to be avoided.

On the way they passed other members of the expedition. All of them worked hard at being interested in their assigned duties, but they glanced furtively and often in the direction of the car and the new arrivals within. Sulu noticed several of the anxious faces. He couldn't blame them. If the undoubtedly nervous man in the storage dome tried to force open the stasis box, everyone nearby might instantly vanish from existence.

The lock leading into the domes was simple in design and fragile in execution, and heavy-duty seals weren't necessary. The lock was present for convenience only, to permit the expedition to maintain the slight comfort of normal atmosphere within its living quarters. On dour Gruyakin, even the slightest luxury was worth a little extra expense, the helmsman mused.

Inside, they followed a corridor to where a man and woman were crouching behind a tripod-mounted device of metal and plastic. Spock recognized it as a displacer of a type similar to the one Director Masid had already indicated was in the hands of the thief. Such a device was designed to move modest quantities of earth and stone with fair precision. His own small hand phaser contained more destructive power. The displacer could still neatly remove a man's head from his body, however.

As they approached, the woman rose, eyed the three officers speculatively, and addressed the expedition head. "He's still holed up in there, Director. He's been very quiet."

"Asleep?" Spock queried.

She looked up at him. "No. We heard some crates being opened. He's using the time to build up his easily accessible supplies, I think."

"We thought of that too, Commander," Masid said regretfully. "I told you Jaiao had this planned out. He says he's set up an alarm system to warn him if anyone gets within three meters of him. That's not much warning, but I don't want to risk the lives of any of my people finding out how fast his reaction time is. Anyhow, we can't tell when he's sleeping and when he's not. He blew out the visual monitors in the dome's roof, and he stays out of sight."

"Sounds like he's ready to settle down for a long stay," observed Sulu as he moved forward.

Masid took a couple of quick steps, cut him off. "Take it a little slower here, please, Lieutenant. Jaiao's shown a tendency to be a bit trigger-happy." She gestured upward and they saw the dark streaks on the tough dome material where blasts from the displacer had struck.

Keeping close to the near wall, they moved cautiously toward the storage dome. They reached a place where the corridor opened into a two-story-high single large chamber. In places, it was stacked almost to that curved ceiling with tubes, cylinders, and crates of all sizes and colors.

Sulu was in the lead and cautiously peeked around

the last bend in the corridor. "I can't see him," he whispered back to the others.

"A little to the left of room center," Masid advised him. "He's built himself a nice little barricade with a couple of big gas tanks in front."

Sulu shifted his gaze slightly, located the bulky metal cylinders. "Still can't see him . . . He's well hidden, all right." The helmsman kept an eye on the disconcerting arrangement of containers. One of the brightly colored shapes moved slightly. "I see him now. He's staying down low, Mr. Spock. I don't think we could get a phaser on him clean."

"What about reflective surfaces, Mr. Sulu?"

The helmsman stared long at the makeshift fortress in the center of the room. "No good, sir. Everything that's piled close to him is plastic, ceramic, or some other dulled material. Nothing polished enough to risk bouncing a beam off."

"I didn't think of that." Masid looked impressed. "But don't attribute it to Jaiao's intelligence. I don't think he's *that* smart. We just don't have much stored in metal or glass cases, that's all."

Spock started forward. "Let me have a look, Mr. Sulu."

The lieutenant hugged the wall as he edged back into the corridor, trading places with the first officer. Spock peered around the corner, immediately located the thief's makeshift ramparts.

"What is his last name, please?" he asked.

"Beguin," Masid told him.

Spock nodded, turned, and leaned as far into the room as he dared.

"Jaiao Beguin," he called sharply. No answer. He tried again. *"Jaiao Beguin!"*

A rustling sound reached them from the jumble of crates and cylinders, though no face appeared among them. "You know what I want! I'm getting impatient!" The voice was high-pitched, angry.

Sulu leaned over, whispered to Uhura. "Not even Mr. Spock's going to be able to reason with this one. The director's right: He's a little crazy."

Ignoring the byplay behind him, the first officer of

STAR TREK LOG TEN   35

the *Enterprise* concentrated on analyzing the reply to his call, dissecting every nuance, building a temporary psychological profile of the speaker out of a couple of short, terse statements.

"This is Commander Spock of the Federation cruiser *Enterprise*. I am in command of a landing party from that ship. We are here to recover the Slaver stasis box, which is valuable property belonging to the Federation government and all its peoples.

"At this very moment, heavy phasers are trained on you both from my position and from outside this dome. You cannot escape. We can kill you if we have to, instantly, before you can damage the box—and the box and its contents will not be affected.

"Thus far you can only be charged with simple theft and assault. If you turn over the box and surrender, it will go much easier on you."

The reply to Spock's carefully worded combination of promise and threat was a peal of barking, none-too-stable laughter that bordered on the hysterical. "I don't believe you!" it declared imperiously. "If you could kill me and not damage the box you would have done so already, without giving me any warning. Who do you think you're fooling with?"

Spock could have answered the man's question, but it would do no good to antagonize him further. Besides, Spock hadn't expected the man to give in readily.

"Didn't you hear our shuttle land?" he called.

"Yeah, I heard it," Beguin admitted, his voice a bit softer and more speculative now. "You could have a cannon trained on my forehead for all I care. I've got the box right in front of me, between my legs. It's sitting on the workplate of a compacter. You know what that means?"

Masid looked startled, and whispered to Sulu and Uhura. "Our compacter is a device for crushing rocks and other material for detailed analysis of their constituent parts. It's got an idle control. If it's running and he trips the trigger for fast release, it'll throw about a thousand kilos of pressure onto the stasis box!"

Sulu looked worried. "Is that enough to crack the box, Mr. Spock?"

"It is possible," the first officer finally replied after considering the problem thoroughly, "depending on the strength of the field inside the box and how much of it shields the box material itself. I would prefer not to risk it."

The nervous, taunting voice of the thief interrupted them. "Go ahead and shoot, why don't you, Mr. Spock of the *Enterprise*? Why don't you shoot? You might kill me before the auto-release I've set on the compacter can trigger it . . . but I don't think so. In any case, I'm betting my life that you're not willing to take that gamble. I'm going to bet that you're not going to risk the lives of all the people in this station, including your own."

"You are quite correct," Spock shouted back at him, "but neither can you escape with the box. It is a stalemated situation you cannot win."

"I don't see why not." Bravado mixed with assurance in the man's voice. "I've planned this pretty careful. You can't do anything to me without having me throw the compacter pressure onto the box. And while you sit and make up your minds I can get along nice, thanks."

"What about sleep?" Spock countered. "All the food and water in the world won't help you when you need rest, nor will your imaginary warning device if we rush you from several sides simultaneously."

"I figure with the stimulants I've found," Beguin responded, "I can stay awake operating efficiently for another forty hours or so. But you're right, Commander Spock. You could make trouble for me if I fell asleep. So this is what we're going to do: If I don't hear something positive about my request for the shuttle in forty hours, and I find myself falling asleep, I'll just have to assume you've all outsmarted me. That'll mean all my work's been for nothing, won't it? I'll be very discouraged and depressed. I think," he concluded, his voice rising slightly, "that in that event I'll just let the compacter go on the box anyway, to see what happens."

Spock and the others ignored the laughter drifting

out of the room. "We now know how much time we have left to work in."

"What happens if the forty hours are up and we haven't figured out how to pry him loose from that box?" Uhura stared straight at Spock.

"We will deal with that eventuality in thirty-nine hours, Lieutenant," Spock informed her crisply.

"He's got it all planned out, all right," she observed. "He's smarter than I thought."

"There is a difference, Lieutenant, between true intelligence and animal cunning. The latter is the virtue our opponent possesses and it is that we must cope with."

"Whatever, it's *working* for him," she argued.

"True enough." Spock turned his gaze to the attentive director. "Are there any other entrances or exits to this storage dome?"

"No, none," Masid informed them.

Spock nodded knowingly. "Given the care with which this theft has been carried out thus far, I would not be surprised if that is yet another reason why he retreated here. Did you consider cutting another entrance?"

"We did," she confessed. "I decided there's no way we could do it without Beguin hearing or seeing us, or both, and the last thing I wanted to do was panic him."

"Quite right." Spock eyed his companions. "I have a thought . . . but I would prefer an idea with a better chance of success than I postulate for my own."

"What about inducing some kind of odorless, colorless gas into the dome's ventilation system?" Uhura proposed. "If it was seeped in gradually, it might knock him out before he knows what's happening."

"I would almost consider that, Lieutenant," Spock admitted, "save for one drawback. If he is staying as close to the compacter and the box as he insists he is, then I would be surprised if he is not keeping a hand close by the compacter trigger at all times. The danger of knocking him out without anyone else around is that his hand or body might fall on the compacter trigger." He glanced briefly back into the chamber.

"Somehow we must get someone close to him, so

that he cannot possibly throw the compacter switch in a last futile, defiant gesture." He paused. "I see one possibility. There is a very large container just to the left and rear of his likely resting place." He glanced backward. "What does it contain, Director Masid?"

She crawled forward, peered around the corner. "I see the one you mean, Commander, but I don't know what's inside. I can't keep track of everything that comes in in the way of supplies. Just a minute."

She retreated, climbed to her feet, and disappeared down the corridor. Several minutes passed before she returned with a tall man in tow, the one with the scar on his neck.

"Charlie's our quartermaster. It's his bailiwick that Beguin appropriated. That's how he got that burn." She gestured to him and they both managed to glance into the room. "The big crate on Beguin's left, Charlie ... what's in it?"

"Give me a second." The man leaned farther into the room, squinted at the container in question. Just as he ducked back into the corridor, a faint but lethal bolt from the displacer scored the floor where he had been a moment before.

"That's just to let you know that I'm still watching!" a loud voice warned them. "Lucky for you I'm not asleep, or the whole place would go up!"

Leaning back against the corridor wall, Sulu eyed the smoking trench in the floor respectfully.

"I do not think we can reason further with him," Spock announced.

"I knew that in the first place." Uhura sniffed at the odor of burnt duraplastic.

"Nevertheless, it had to be tried. One is always hopeful—"

Charlie cut him off. "I remember now. I wanted to be sure. The crate holds bulk food rations, Commander. Should be mostly small containers of raw proteins, natural sealed meats and stuff."

"Nothing that would make much noise if it fell within the crate?" Spock asked.

"No ... I wouldn't think so."

Masid's gaze narrowed. "What are you planning, Commander?"

Spock gestured just behind them, at the couple manning the makeshift weapon. "You have other displacers besides that one?"

"Sure," she said quickly. "They're all out at the various sites we're working but—"

"How long to bring two of your best ones in and set them up near here?"

She still didn't quite believe what Spock was indirectly proposing. "Within an hour, I guess. But I thought we already ruled out any attempt at cutting through—"

"Not to cut," Spock corrected her, "to *dig*. We will position the displacers precisely and tunnel beneath the dome. The tunnel will come up under the box very slowly and quietly. We'll make a little natural background noise, but the ground will muffle the sound of the displacer, which I understand is a relatively silent instrument when operated at low power."

"That's so," Masid admitted.

"Whoever goes through the tunnel can cut through the bottom of the container manually. A phaser set on low power should slice through the plastic container material quickly and with little noise. Then he can pass the contents of the container back through the tunnel. Simultaneously we will engage Mr. Beguin in conversation."

Masid gave him a very querulous look.

"I had not expected enthusiasm," Spock confessed. "It is far from an ideal plan. I am not pleased with it myself. But in the absence of any alternative . . ."

No one said anything for a long moment. Then the director nodded to Spock. "All right, Commander. This sort of work is more your job than mine. I don't like it, but we'll try anything."

The displacers were brought in. After careful calculating, they were set in place and turned on. Their efficient operators had muffled the already-quiet devices with insulating material and they dug in near silence. Nor was there any noticeable vibration.

Nonetheless, to be absolutely certain Beguin didn't grow suspicious—and to try to wear him down a little mentally—Masid and the three officers from the *Enterprise* took turns arguing, threatening and appealing to the barricaded thief. Helpfully, he argued back, seeming to enjoy their futile attempts to cajole him out of his hideaway. Occasionally he would fire a blast from his displacer in their direction, apparently for no other reason than because it kept him amused.

Spock had no illusions about what would happen when the drugs started to lose their effectiveness and Beguin found himself growing drowsy. His maniacal humor would fade concurrent with his alertness.

At the moment, the first officer was watching the dirt and rock emerge in buckets from the rapidly lengthening tunnel. It would take longer this way, but a conveyer would be dangerously noisy.

Uhura studied a small diagram, drew some lines on it, and compared them with calculations scribbled in the diagram's margin. "They should be in position any minute now, Mr. Spock."

"Yes. I'll want both you and Mr. Sulu to cover the area as best you can with your phasers. Don't fire unless you're certain he's clear of the stasis box and the compacter. Don't worry about hitting me. I'll try to get him away from the compacter trigger, and then—"

"Excuse me, sir." Sulu took the liberty of interrupting his superior. "I think I ought to be the one to go."

"This was my idea, Lieutenant, and I'll be the one to take the necessary risks, since I'll be the one responsible for this attempt's success or failure."

"Exactly, sir," pressed Sulu urgently, "and that's the very reason I should be the one to go."

"Explain yourself, Lieutenant."

"Mr. Spock, you can hold this man's attention better than any of us. That's the really critical part of the operation: not charging him from behind but distracting him from the front. If we can do that effectively, then anyone can jump him."

"He's right, Mr. Spock," Uhura agreed.

The first officer considered the objection only briefly. "I do not like the proposal but I cannot counter your arguments. Very well, Lieutenant Sulu. You will be the one to attack from inside the crate. Take special care with your phaser setting when you get ready to cut through the container bottom. It is imperative Mr. Beguin not hear you. As time passes without our meeting his demands, he grows progressively more unstable."

"Don't worry, sir," Sulu assured him. "I've seen what his displacer can do. I don't want it pointed in my face when I come out of there..."

IV

The displacers finished their work quickly. After a final conference with his companions and a wish of "Good luck" from Uhura, Sulu found himself crawling on hands and knees through the smooth passageway. Half-fused earth slid by under his palms.

Small lights had been placed at regular intervals in the tunnel by the excavators, so he had no trouble seeing his path. Nor did he have to be told when he was nearing his destination, since the tunnel floor and ceiling turned sharply upward. The excavators had used their displacers to cut long notches in the floor there. Otherwise the intermittently slick surface would have offered poor purchase for ascending.

Aware that he was under the storage dome now and that the highly excitable Beguin was somewhere above and just to his right, Sulu continued with greater caution. He passed the last emplaced light, which threw just enough illumination for him to make out a dark mass ahead: the bottom of the crate.

Edging close to it, he removed his pre-set phaser and trained it on the dark, thick material. Silently, the low-power beam cut through the dull-surfaced substance. Sulu had to move slightly, hugging the wall of the tunnel, to avoid drops of liquid, hot plastic dripping out of the steadily widening hole.

When he had enlarged the gap enough for a man to fit through, he turned off the phaser and replaced it at his waist. All was silent above, save for distant voices. Spock and the others were doing their part, arguing with Beguin and keeping his attention focused elsewhere.

Carefully, Sulu edged upward, began the dangerous task of removing the smaller packages from within the crate. Working fast and efficiently, he soon emptied the crate of a substantial portion of its contents, sliding them down into the tunnel. Then, a short pull—and he was on his knees inside.

For the last time he rehearsed his next moves in his mind. First, he rechecked his position. Beguin ought to be off to his right, through that wall of his crate container, there. Sulu shifted more containers, giving himself a clear path to the crate wall in the opposite direction from Beguin's position. Then he activated his phaser again.

Gently Sulu applied the soft, short beam to one of the crate walls, near the top. Once more the preformed material softened, ran down into the crate. Fortunately, the plastic melted without an odor, as Spock and Masid had assured him it would. He reminded himself that there was no reason for Beguin to go for a stroll and every reason for him not to, but he still worried that the thief might somehow notice what was going on behind him.

As the hole appeared and widened and lengthened, the distant voices became clearly audible. Spock was arguing with Beguin, using all the semantic forces at his command, trying to convince him to surrender the box. Chances of that were slim, but the critical thing was to keep the thief occupied long enough for Sulu to slip clear and make a good run at the compacter and its half-hysterical guardian.

With a top line cut through, Sulu started curving the phaser beam down along one side. That done, he switched to the opposite side, still straining for the sound of footsteps outside the crate. As the opening enlarged, he found he could follow the details of the conversation taking place behind him. Spock's steady, calm words alternated with the irregular, high-pitched retorts of Beguin.

Then the phaser began cutting across, parallel to the bottom of the container. Sulu slid his fingers slowly into the nearest vertical crack, gripped firmly. It wouldn't do to have the thick slab of plastic tumble outward to the dome floor. A final snick and the opening was complete. Steadying the cut section with his right hand, the helmsman switched off his phaser and set it down. Then both hands gripped the cutout and pushed. It slid neatly outward and he laid it quietly on the dome.

If his position had been properly gauged, Beguin should be on the exact opposite side of the crate from him. A cautious glance showed only stacks of cylinders and containers ahead.

After a minute had passed without a displacer beam abruptly roasting his container, Sulu crawled out and readjusted his phaser. A first glance around the tall black square revealed additional piles of material, containers of all sizes and shapes scattered about. There was a hint of motion and he drew back, still watching.

A head and gesturing arm appeared. "Why don't you quit trying to talk me out of here?" Beguin shouted warningly. "I'm not giving up the box."

"You are not leaving Gruyakin with the box in your possession," Spock's distant voice countered immediately.

Beguin was beginning to sound tired. "You already know what happens then. If I don't get what I want in"—there was a brief pause—"in twenty-one hours, I open the box with the compacter and we all die."

"Not necessarily," Spock objected. "We do not know for certain that this box contains a disrupter bomb or other destructive device. In that case, *you* will be the only one to die."

"Maybe you're right," Beguin conceded readily. "I've heard that some of the stasis boxes that were found were undefended. But it doesn't matter, because you can't take that chance, can you?" Beguin concluded with an unholy chuckle.

Everything indicated that the thief's attention was concentrated solely on the one entrance to the storage dome and that he suspected nothing. Sulu began his approach, working his way patiently across the floor using scattered crates and containers for cover. If anything he was being over-cautious. He would have been difficult to spot even if Beguin had been looking for him.

Very soon he was crouched directly behind the small wall of piled crates and cylinders Beguin had shifted for his own protection. Starting immediately he would have to be extra careful. He wouldn't have any cover inside the circle of containers.

He considered his options once again. At such close quarters, it would be difficult to miss Beguin with a phaser burst. But there was still the chance the thief's limp body could fall across the compacter trigger, so phaser fire remained a last resort. Somehow he had to find a better way to get the man away from the compacter controls.

At first he had been glad of the jumble of cylinders and crates. They had made his approach to this point fairly easy. But they no longer served a useful function. He hoped to find a gap in the container barricade that he could rush through, but as he inspected the piled boxes he could find no such break in the wall. Certainly he couldn't start pulling crates away. Beguin wouldn't be so distracted by Spock that he would fail to notice someone pulling his ramparts down behind him.

There *had* to be an opening somewhere in the barricade. Moving on hands and knees and keeping as close to the floor as possible, Sulu started off to his left. He had circled almost the entire barricade and was dangerously close to Beguin himself before deciding that this half of the wall was impenetrable. The ongoing dialogue between Spock and the thief formed a surreal accompaniment to his explorations.

Returning, Sulu repeated his search to the right of his original position, with similar results.

One place, where the wall was rather low, was the best he could find. As long as Beguin remained distracted, there was a chance Sulu could scale the wall there and reach the compacter before the thief could trigger it. Once he cleared Beguin from the controls, the commotion would bring Spock, Uhura, and the others running.

Returning to his chosen spot, Sulu leaned against the crates and started edging to a standing position, positioning his right leg for the jump he would have to make. The conversation had faded, but he would wait until the arguments resumed before making the leap.

Sulu's head meanwhile slowly came up and for the first time he glanced into the center of the circle of containers—straight into the startled eyes of the thief! Beguin was gobbling provisions from an opened storage crate. Both men were paralyzed for the briefest of seconds.

Then Beguin whirled, made a dive at the compacter. Desperately Sulu made a jump for him, but even the adrenaline suddenly surging through his body didn't provide him with enough lift to clear the barrier completely. His right foot caught on an upthrust cylinder and sent him sprawling to the floor in a clatter of dislodged crates.

"Wait," Sulu shouted frantically. "*Don't!*"

Beguin, his eyes wild, and perhaps temporarily not sane, was at the compacter. He threw himself onto the trigger. Voices yelled in the distance as Spock and the others, having heard Sulu's shout, began charging the barricade.

They could not outpace the compacter. With a whirr the sides of the device engaged, slammed into the stasis box. A peculiar bone-tingling screech resulted, like a thin metal point dragging across a piece of slate. The sound increased until Sulu's teeth hurt. One edge of the stasis box appeared to crumple slightly inward. Fascinated, Sulu could only stare at what might prove to be the cause of his imminent annihilation.

He had no place to run to, of course. Instinctively he threw an arm across his face to protect his eyes. But if a disruptor bomb were presently being engaged within the box, his arm would make no difference.

Out of the corner of an eye Sulu saw something rise from the surfaces of the box. He was certain the lid hadn't opened and no crack appeared in the smooth metal sides. There was no explosion, no sudden disintegration of matter within the storage dome. Instead, there was a short, soundless, actinic flash that temporarily blinded the helmsman.

The sound of running feet and anxious voices reached the barricade, people swarming over it. Someone bent over Sulu, helped him to his feet.

"Are you all right, Lieutenant?"

"Sulu! What happened?"

He blinked, and tiny suns faded as rods and cones adjusted to the normal light. Spock and Uhura were supporting him, one at each arm.

"I'm okay." He blinked again, rubbed at his eyes with both hands. "What did happen?" Then he was staring apologetically at Spock. "I'm sorry, sir. I couldn't stop him from throwing the trigger. He was standing right next to me when I looked inside for him."

Spock didn't appear angry. On the contrary, his reply was more curious than reproving. "It appears not to matter, Mr. Sulu." The helmsman noticed that the first officer was no longer looking at him, but instead was staring at something else nearby. "This stasis box is defended, but not by a disruptor bomb. It acts only upon those in its immediate vicinity who try improperly to open it. Look."

Sulu finally did so, turning to stare in the same direction as his superior. The stasis box, to all outward appearances unaffected, still rested in the paralyzed jaws of the compacter. One of the scientists was standing next to the device, which had been turned off, cautiously inspecting the tightly held box.

Jaiao Beguin stood nearby, a surprised expression on his face. He appeared to be completely encased in a softly glowing, silvery material like chrome paint.

"What happened to *him*?" Sulu asked, gaping at the statuelike figure of the thief.

"It would seem," Spock theorized, "that anyone who attempts to open this particular stasis box is promptly enveloped in a stasis box of his own."

"It's not a fatal method of defense, then," said Sulu, unable to keep from staring in fascination at the frozen silvery figure of the unfortunate Beguin.

"Not technically, no," Spock agreed. "Our thief will remain conveniently frozen in time, as would anything encased by a stasis field, until such a time as a stasis-field disruptor can be used to release him safely. It will be quite a useful method of restraining him until a Federation expedition can arrive here with a disruptor and release him from his own field." He added firmly, "At that point he will be transferred to a less exotic but equally confining place of imprisonment."

"If that's all the box does, Mr. Spock, why can't we try and open it ourselves? The worst that could happen would be that the opening device or its operator would also be encased in another stasis field." Uhura eyed the box excitedly.

"Not necessarily, Lieutenant," Spock hastened to correct her. "We do not know by what method the box's defense system decides on who is trying to open it improperly. This time it encased only the immediate operator of the opening device. We cannot assume that if we attempt the same thing the box will not decide to encase the entire station. We have no idea of its limits."

Uhura looked downcast. "We'll have to wait to see what's inside it, then."

Spock nodded. "At least until we rejoin the ship, Lieutenant. I am certain Engineer Scott can construct an adequate stasis-field disruptor." He walked over to the compacter, exchanged a few words with the scientist inspecting it. The woman threw a small switch and the sides of the compacter moved away from the box. Spock picked it up. It rested inert and innocent in his arms. He turned to his two companions.

"First, we must get to Starbase Twenty-Five and rendezvous with the ship. The captain and I allowed ample time for us to reach here, pick up the box, and make rendezvous, so I do not think our unexpected delay will be of any consequence. We still have plenty of time to reach the base before the *Enterprise* is required to depart for Briamos. Nevertheless, I wish to get there as quickly as possible."

Uhura concurred. "I've got to admit I'll feel a lot more comfortable back on board myself."

"And *I'll* feel comfortable," Sulu added fervently, "only when that"—he pointed at the quiescent cube resting in Spock's grasp—"is safely on board the *Enterprise* . . ."

"I want to thank you, Commander," Director Masid was saying as the three officers prepared to board their shuttlecraft, "for relieving us of responsibility for that," and she indicated the stasis box. "Its potential for causing trouble is too explosive for us, even if its defensive mechanism isn't."

"There is no need to thank us, Director Masid," Spock replied from his position atop the boarding ramp. "We were fortunate, and that is no substitute for being skilled. We were all lucky that the box contained something besides a disruptor bomb to defend itself with. Good-bye for now, and good luck with your digging."

"Thanks to you," she murmured as the shuttlecraft thundered into the dark sky, "I think I may be able to enjoy it for a change." She turned to the car waiting to take her back to her office in the administration dome.

It's amazing, she reflected, how a reprieve from expected death can make formerly ordinary work seem fresh and exciting . . .

V

"Captain? Captain Kirrk!"

Kirk swung the command chair and looked toward the communication station. "What is it, Lieutenant M'ress?"

The Caitian communications officer who had taken over for the absent Lieutenant Uhura had one paw pressed to the left side of her head. She was slightly bent over in her seat and it looked to Kirk as if she was wincing.

"What's the matter, Lieutenant? Are you in pain?" He was immediately concerned.

"No, not exactly, sirr. I . . . I'm not surre what's wrong, but something . . . is. I feel very peculiarr all of a sudden. Dizzy. It's almost familiarr, like something I've felt beforre, but . . . I can't place it." She rose unsteadily in her chair. "I'm afrraid I have to ask to be excused frrom duty, sirr."

"You don't have to ask and there's no need to apologize, Lieutenant. I only hope it's nothing more than a bad headache."

"It . . . doesn't feel like a headache, sirr."

"Report to Sick Bay immediately," Kirk ordered her. "Lieutenant Talliflores will take over for you."

"Yes, sirr." M'ress made a few adjustments to the controls on her console, her hands moving with unaccustomed awkwardness over the familiar instrumentation.

At that point Kirk was out of the chair and striding over to her. "Never mind contacting your relief," he said, worried. "I'll do that myself. Just get to Sick Bay. Think you can make it by yourself?"

"I believe so, sirr."

Despite her assurance, Kirk helped the lieutenant to the turbolift. He left her with a reassuring smile, which turned instantly to an expression of troubled concern when the doors closed behind her.

Back in the command chair, he activated the intercom. M'ress's relief was on recreation time now and probably wouldn't be in his cabin. He set for shipwide general broadcast.

"Lieutenant Talliflores, Lieutenant Talliflores. Report to the bridge immediately."

That task concluded, he leaned back and mused over M'ress's sudden ailment. Why it should trouble him so, he couldn't say. It was only natural that occasionally one of his bridge crew should take sick, despite their usual exemplary healthiness. Perhaps it was because M'ress was always so vibrant and alive. Try as he could, this was the first time he could recall the communications officer falling ill.

And yet . . . hadn't she indicated that her symptoms were akin to something she had suffered before?

He was still mulling over the incident when Lieutenant Talliflores arrived, worried and out of breath.

"I'm sorry, sir, if I—"

"Never mind. There's no problem." Thus assured, the swarthy officer relaxed. "I'm going to have to ask you to take over the remainder of Lieutenant M'ress's shift. You can do double duty until she returns, Talliflores. Your recreation time will be accredited accordingly."

"Yes, sir." Talliflores moved to take up station at communications. In the middle of his standard checkout of the instrumentation, it occurred to him to ask why he was taking M'ress's normal position. "If I may inquire, sir, is anything wrong? Lieutenant M'ress and I went sliding only yesterday. I didn't notice anything wrong with her."

"She complained of not feeling well, and of being dizzy." Kirk offered the officer reassurance he couldn't feel himself. "Probably just a headache. It didn't seem serious, Lieutenant. I expect her back before her shift is up."

"That's good to hear, sir." Talliflores looked relieved. He was a close friend of both M'ress and Uhura. That was only natural since they shared the same station, performed identical duties on different shifts.

But after several hours had passed without the reappearance of M'ress, Kirk felt compelled to check on her condition. He thumbed the intercom.

"Sick Bay, this is the captain speaking."

"Sick Bay, Nurse Chapel speaking."

"How is Lieutenant M'ress, Chapel?"

There was a brief pause before McCoy's assistant replied. "Fine, as far as I know, Captain. Why?"

Now it was Kirk's turn to hesitate. Something was wrong here. "What do you mean, 'As far as I know'?" he finally replied. "What was wrong with her? Or hasn't Bones made a diagnosis yet?"

"Diagnosis, sir? As far as I know Dr. McCoy hasn't seen Lieutenant M'ress except in the officers' mess or maybe in the recreation section." Chapel's tone turned abruptly from one of puzzlement to concern. "Why, is something wrong with her? If there is, this is the first I've heard of it."

Lieutenant Arex glanced back from his place at the navigation-helm. His quizzical stare was matched by that of lieutenant Vedama, who looked over from the science station.

"Chapel," Kirk finally asked, "didn't Lieutenant M'ress report for treatment of a mild cerebral disorder?" He checked his command-chair chronometer. She ought to have been in Sick Bay for several hours by now."

"Just one moment, sir. I haven't been here long. Let me check today's records." There was a pause while Kirk fidgeted impatiently at the delay.

"No, sir," Chapel eventually informed him. "I see no record of Lieutenant M'ress checking in for observation or any other reason. I believe I— Just a moment, sir."

A new voice sounded over the intercom. "Jim, what's this about Lieutenant M'ress?"

"Bones, M'ress left the bridge over three hours ago. She was complaining of dizziness and other unidentifiable difficulties. She was having difficulty operating her equipment, but she insisted she could make it down to Sick Bay on her own." He took a deep breath. "Apparently she couldn't."

"It doesn't look that way, Jim. I just came on duty myself. I haven't seen her and if Chapel says the records don't show her checking in, well, then she didn't check in."

"That's bad. Hang on a minute, Bones." Kirk turned to communications. "Lieutenant Talliflores, give me security in the officer's section, Deck Five." Talliflores did so.

"Security Deck Five, Ensign Atete speaking."

"Ensign, this is the captain. Lieutenant M'ress is missing. Check her cabin. You have permission to break the lock seal if necessary, to enter."

"Yes, sir," the ensign responded alertly. "A moment."

There was a wait, first while the lieutenant checked to make certain it was indeed Kirk who was speaking to him, and then a longer one while he performed the necessary check.

"No, sir," he finally reported back, "the lieutenant is not in her cabin."

"She may be ill," Kirk told him. "It's possible she fell behind something."

"I made a thorough check, sir. She's nowhere in her quarters."

"Thank you, Atete. Bridge out."

Kirk switched back to his chair communicator, where Sick Bay was waiting on hold. "Bones, she's not in her quarters."

"You said she complained of dizziness and that she had trouble with her instruments, Jim," McCoy repeated carefully. "Did she seem to be in pain?"

"I couldn't tell, but if she was she didn't complain about it," was the captain's reply. "She just said she was feeling peculiar, and that she thought it was familiar. I'd say she was as much confused as sick."

"It doesn't sound like a headache, Jim. I could be wrong. I hope I *am* wrong. I'll check our Caitian references. The important thing is to find her. If she's lying unconscious in a corridor somewhere . . . Let's hope she's just sitting somewhere in a daze."

"I'm going to find out, Bones. Stand by at your end." He faced communications. "Lieutenant Talliflores, give me shipwide broadcast."

"Aye, sir." Talliflores adjusted controls, then signaled to Kirk, who directed his voice to the command-chair pickup.

"Attention, all personnel. Lieutenant M'ress of communications was scheduled to report to Sick Bay some time ago. She did not do so. The lieutenant was suffering from dizziness and possibly more severe disorder as well. Lieutenant, if you hear this and can respond, please go immediately to the nearest communicator and check in with either the bridge or Sick Bay. If you are unable to respond verbally, try to make yourself visible.

"While not neglecting your assigned duties, all personnel are requested to keep an eye out for lieutenant

M'ress and to notify Sick Bay as to her location and condition upon seeing her."

He switched off general broadcast, spoke to Sick Bay again. "Unless she's hidden herself somewhere, Bones, that should find her for us quickly."

"I hope so, Jim," the *Enterprise*'s chief physician replied slowly. "It doesn't sound serious . . . yet. But it sure sounds peculiar. Sick Bay out."

"Funny," Kirk mused after McCoy had clicked off, "that's exactly how M'ress described it . . ."

In a quiet section of the small forest that formed part of the *Enterprise*'s recreational area on Deck Eight, a strolling off-duty food technician paused to listen to the Captain's urgent message even as he was curiously eyeing an indistinct form crouching behind a large shrub in front of him, slightly off the main pathway.

As soon as the message ended, he walked toward the bush. "Hey, you there!" The form didn't move out into the open. The technician continued walking toward the bush.

"Say, aren't you Lieutenant M'ress?" he inquired when he got near enough to make out the individual's outline. "Didn't you hear the captain?" Still the figure gave no sign of moving. "You're supposed to report in immediately." Uncertainty gave way to sudden concern. "They said you were supposed to report to Sick Bay. Are you all right, Lieutenant? Can I help?"

He reached out a hand toward the figure. "I said, do you need any—"

Rising in one motion, the figure spun violently on the startled crewman. Wide, glaring cat eyes blazed at him, nostrils flared widely, and the slim figure was puffed to more than normal size. It was not the appearance the technician expected from a ranking officer.

Slowly he took a step backward, away from the heavily breathing figure. "Now take it easy, just slow down a moment, ma'am. If you've got some kind of sickness or something . . . I don't think I'd better—"

The technician whirled, turned to run. His mouth opened as he framed a call for help. As it developed, he managed neither a shout nor retreat. Lieutenant M'ress fairly exploded off the grass. As she landed on the man's back her hands went around his neck and both squirming, struggling shapes fell hard to the ground.

VI

Like a dull white copepod swimming in some unimaginably vast ocean's black depths, the shuttlecraft *Copernicus* raced for Starbase Twenty-Five and its rendezvous with the *Enterprise*. Within the shuttle's control room the Slaver stasis box, fifty centimeters on each side but considerably larger in import, gleamed metallically in the center of the single rest table.

Spock was pacing back and forth near the table while Sulu manned the tiny craft's controls. Uhura stood near him, staring out the fore port at the slowly changing panorama spread out ahead of them.

They were back on schedule, which meant they had plenty of time to reach the Starbase before the *Enterprise* was required to leave for Briamos. But that was small comfort to Spock. He was regretting every hour of the learning sessions Kirk must be attending on Briamos and its inhabitants, sorry for every detail he was not present to absorb firsthand.

In addition, he was as anxious as Uhura and Sulu to learn what the enigmatic stasis box contained. Only on board the *Enterprise* could he and Engineer Scott assemble a proper stasis disruptor for safely opening the ancient container.

Bored with the view forward, Uhura turned to the less spectacular but more intriguing object resting on the table. She gazed speculatively at the box. With ample time to do nothing but reflect on what it might contain, she had managed to conjure any number of incredible wonders—though they were wonders no larger than fifty centimeters on a side.

Inside that unimpressive cube of metal time had

stood still for perhaps a billion years. Certainly whatever relics lay so magnificently preserved had to be valuable, as the contents of stasis boxes usually were. And maybe dangerous as well, as they often were. She no longer had any doubts about the value of whatever lay inside. The box's unique method of protecting itself all but stated that something inside was well worth defending from the casually curious.

Spock was making notations in his pocket recorder when he noticed Uhura's stare. "Speculation is no less intriguing for usually being inaccurate, Lieutenant."

"I *was* wondering what might be inside, Mr. Spock. I know a little about the Slaver Empire, but not enough to make an accurate guess."

"You have a great deal of company, Lieutenant," the first officer assured her. "Our entire store of information concerning the empire of the Slavers is sketchy at best. We know that they were masters of all the intelligent life in this part of the galaxy a billion years ago. That is a long time for anything in the way of reliable information to have survived. It's hardly surprising that so little has."

"Masters of the galaxy until a billion years ago . . ." Uhura murmured wonderingly. "Until one race finally mounted a successful revolt. It must have been a time of chaos." Her gaze went from Spock back to the stasis box. "Are these the only sources of information we have about their empire?"

Spock turned away, eyed the blaze of stars forward. "The only factual ones. Even rumors die in that length of time. But we have learned a little."

Uhura turned to listen, moved forward again. In doing so, she missed the sudden appearance of a slightly blue glow that materialized around the box. Its teardrop shape was silent. The tip of the azure halo pointed forward.

"The Slavers," Spock declared, ignorant of the mysterious aura which had enveloped the box behind him, "and all their subjects were exterminated in the war that followed that eons-old revolt. Intelligent life had to evolve all over again in this part of the galaxy." He fell silent, thoughtful. "So far," he eventually added, "the stasis boxes are the only remnants we've been able to find of those many lost and doubtless great civilizations."

He frowned, noticed Uhura staring as if mesmerized behind him. "Something wrong, Lieutenant."

By way of answer, she pointed. "Why is it glowing like that? It wasn't doing that before."

Spock whirled and saw for the first time the unmistakable aura which had encapsulated the box. Moving to his right, he noted its shape, let his gaze travel naturally from the point of the teardrop shape back out the front port. Ahead and drifting slowly to starboard was an impressively radiating spiral, a stellar object sufficiently spectacular that it had to be on the charts. He thought he recognized it.

His attention turned back to the no-longer-inert stasis box. The point of the teardrop, he was convinced, was not stable but instead was shifting slowly. Not unexpectedly, it was changing to a starboard direction.

"Mr. Sulu, what is our current position?"

Sulu executed a fast check of his instruments and glanced back over a shoulder as he spoke. "Passing Beta Lyrae, sir. One hundred and forty-two degrees northeast of the galactic plane." At this point he noticed the glowing blue cloud enveloping the box. "Where did that come from?"

The point of the blue aura was still moving steadily to starboard, tracking the changing position of Beta Lyrae as efficiently as any instrument.

"We do not know where it comes from or how the box produces it, Mr. Sulu, but it is not a unique phenomenon. I have heard of such a thing happening before. Most unexpected and most fortuitous."

"Fortuitous? I don't understand." The helmsman looked understandably confused.

"The motion of the blue aura surrounding our box," Spock explained, "would indicate that there is another stasis box orbiting Beta Lyrae."

Uhura was equally new to the phenomenon described by Spock. "Another one!"

Spock appeared baffled, almost hesitant to answer.

"It is, as I said, unexpected. Your surprise is well justified, Lieutenant Uhura. It seems most illogical for a stasis box to remain in this vicinity, undiscovered, for so long. Beta Lyrae is one of the most impressive sights and one of the rarest in the explored galaxy. Every ship that passes by would likely slow to observe and enjoy its spectacle at leisure.

"Still, the only known stasis-box detector is another stasis box. Detection is, obviously, by means of that blue aura. Perhaps none of the many vessels passing Beta Lyrae possessed a stasis box. But given the number of observers, both casual and scientific, who must have spent a good deal of time in this vicinity, I confess to being puzzled that a stasis box's peculiar characteristics have remained undiscovered for so long."

He broke off to take another look at the glowing box. By now the point of the teardrop had shifted around to a position facing forty-five degrees aft of the shuttle. Rapidly, he considered the time and date, made some hasty calculations. As important as it was for all three of them to attend the Briamosite briefings at Starbase 25, this was something that they could not ignore. While their presence at the pre-conference briefings was desirable, it was not critical.

"Mr. Sulu . . ." he began, reaching an inevitable decision once all the relevant facts had been considered.

Sulu glanced back at him hopefully. "Yes, sir?" That was all he said. No suggestions were offered, no arguments presented. They weren't necessary. Spock could tell by the expressions on their faces how the two other officers felt. Not that they influenced his decision. His new orders were based solely, as always, on logic.

"Bring us about," he directed the helmsman, fulfilling the latter's hopes. "We will investigate the Beta Lyrae system and attempt to locate the source of the activity affecting our own stasis box."

Sulu couldn't repress a pleased smile. "Aye, aye, sir."

Coming around in a tight arc, the *Copernicus* slowed and plunged deep into the double-star system of Beta Lyrae.

Under Spock's direction, made after a careful study of the shifting stasis box aura, Sulu brought the little ship close in. The closeup view of the unusual binary was as awesome and beautiful as anything in the galaxy. Their viewport was filled with the nebulous yellow giant star, which was the most obvious feature of the system. It was somewhat flattened by the force of gravity and rotation. A line of fiery red hydrogen joined it to its smaller companion, a brilliant dwarf star that shone like a sapphire cabochon. A whirlpool of thin crimson like a streamer of fringed crepe spread out from the blue star in an expanding spiral. The hydrogen faded from pigeon-blood red to dull maroon to a smoky blackness. Even the blackness announced its presence by blotting out the stars lying behind it.

"It's a beautiful universe," Uhura murmured as she drank in the overpowering sight, "and a varied one."

"The beauty's in the variety," Sulu added, equally entranced.

Spock was talking less poetically into his recorder and did not comment so blatantly on Beta Lyrae's attraction, though he admired it as well. Besides its obvious chromatic effects, there was an inherent attractiveness in the order and balance of gravitational and other forces, in the precision of the system's mathematics. Nor was that view exclusively Vulcan. Many human scientists would have found the physical construction of the binary more impressive than its mere visual appearance.

At the moment he was explaining their course into his recorder. "Stasis boxes and their contents are the only remnant of a species powerful enough to have ruled, once, an entire section of our galaxy," he dictated. "Their effect on our sciences has been incalculable. In one box was found the flying belt which was the key to the artificial gravity field presently employed on starships.

"Hence my decision to forgo the briefings preparatory to the conference on Briamos in favor of pursuing a positive lead to another such box in the Beta Lyrae system." He clicked off, put the recorder aside. They were moving near to the object that the *Copernicus*'s compact but efficient instrumentation had long since located.

It was a frozen, almost airless world, a dull white globe too far out to receive appreciable warmth from either of the twin suns. It was as ordinary and unimpressive as the binary was stupendous. In any case, they were not searching for life or a world to colonize but, instead, for another of the Slavers' valuable bequests, the box which was simultaneously inheritance and tombstone.

"Beginning final approach," Sulu announced mechanically, "preparatory to orbital insertion."

Soon they were circling the equator of the chill planet. Measurements indicated that in comparison to the surface rotating beneath them, Earth's most inhospitable tundra was a vision of Elysium and its South Pole a veritable paradise.

"Now, Mr. Sulu."

The helmsman didn't have to look behind him. He knew that the point of the teardrop aura must be stabbing straight down through the mess table.

"Commence landing approach," Spock continued formally. "Try to take us down in as tight a descending spiral as you can, Lieutenant."

"I'll do my best, sir," Sulu assured him, his attention riveted on his readouts and controls.

"That will minimize our searching," Spock informed them, "if we can keep the point of the aura perfectly perpendicular with the surface below us. The second stasis box should be directly under us when we land, or at the very least within walking distance." He moved to stand by the front port.

"If the box is out in the open, visual identification before we touch down is vital. We must take care in that event not to set down on top of the box. In addition to the inconvenience, the box mechanism might interpret our touchdown as an attempt at opening it improperly. We could conceivably find ourselves in the position of our boxed thief back on Gruyakin Six."

"Don't worry, sir," Sulu replied tersely. "I have no intention of standing around for the next billion years, no matter how healthy or well-preserved a stasis field keeps me."

They dropped through the thin, almost nonexistent atmosphere. Sulu brought the shuttle to a smooth stop on a jumbled, frozen plain. Spock assured him they had *not* set down on the box itself. At the last moment the point of the teardrop had shifted slightly to port, indicating that they would land clear of it.

Faint wisps of as-yet-unidentified gases drifted overhead, the only indication that anything lay between the roof of the shuttlecraft and the killing emptiness of interstellar space.

Spock walked back to the stasis box as the helmsman cut the engines. He studied it intently. "What would *you* say, Lieutenant Uhura?"

She bent over, stared beneath the table where the point of the blue aura penetrated. "It's certainly not pointing straight down. I'd say it's inclined slightly in . . . that direction." She rose and pointed.

"I agree." Spock moved forward and stared hard out the port in the direction the aura point indicated. "Yet . . . I see no sign of another box, at least not nearby. It is there, however. This is not surprising, in view of the unevenness of the terrain. Life-support belts."

They moved to the single large storage locker, slipped the belts around their waists. Spock checked Uhura and Sulu's belt operation with a compact device taken from the locker. Then Sulu checked Spock and Uhura; and then it was Uhura's turn. Thus double-checked and assured that all systems were functioning properly, the three officers entered the *Copernicus*'s airlock, each encased in a lime-yellow aura no denser than the mysterious blue one surrounding the stasis box they had taken with them.

Sulu and Uhura each had their phasers out and ready—a standard precaution. They had had little time for pre-inspection of this world and experience had shown that a planet which seemed devoid of life could often provide as many unpleasant surprises as a far more fertile and hospitable globe. Spock was carrying the stasis box, flanked on the right by Uhura and by Sulu on the left. The blue aura now pointed straight ahead. The lock cycled, and a brief puff of unreclaimed air escaped into the alienness beyond.

The three exited into a frozen hell. They saw no hint of any life, malignant or otherwise. Not a plant, not an insect, only an icy plain bordered by rippling, jagged hills and distant mountains of ice-bound stone that had likely never felt the weak warmth of the distant binary. It was difficult for any world orbiting a twin sun to support life, due to the often erratic nature of its planetary orbit. The frozen emptiness of Beta Lyrae I appeared to be no exception.

As they walked across the ice-covered ground the glow from the stasis box in Spock's arms intensified, turned almost azure. In contrast, the lime-yellow halos projected by their life-support belts remained constant. As always, Uhura reflected on how feebly inadequate these seemed, to be the only thing holding back the monstrous cold and airlessness pressing tight around them.

In many ways the stark, dead landscape they were crossing was more forbidding than empty space. The interstellar void was merely sterile, while the corpse of a world on which life could exist, given a few changes in atmosphere and location, was almost palpably threatening.

Uhura was not afraid to give voice to her feelings. Besides, it was reassuring to hear another voice in that desolation, even if Spock and Sulu were right next to her. "I never did like these barren little worlds. They always make me feel as if I'm walking on one huge grave."

"We're not tourists here, Lieutenant," Spock commented firmly. "Kindly keep your mind on the business at hand."

Uhura bristled at the harshness of the reprimand. However, Spock's intention had not been to reprimand her but only to take her mind off the depressing landscape surrounding them, which he succeeded efficiently in doing.

"Mr. Spock?" Sulu stepped lightly over a miniature crevasse. "If it takes one stasis box to find another stasis box, how did they find the very first one?"

"I would like to say that its presence was deduced, Lieutenant Sulu. I would like to relate that it was discovered after a great deal of study based on material carefully assimilated by a number of highly competent researchers utilizing the most modern technology. However," he continued drily, "that is not what happened.

"The first Slaver stasis box was discovered the same way as so many truly unique phenomena are—by accident." He turned slightly to his left, following the compass point of the blue aura toward a low rise topped with freshly cracked ice.

They mounted the rise. Spock halted, retraced his steps several meters, moved a little to his right. At that point the apex of the blue glow jabbed straight down. All that lay visible below their feet was hard-packed frozen gas and water vapor. Sulu pushed at the surface with a life-support, aura-shielded boot.

"The other box appears to be almost under us, or at least very close by," Spock announced. "If I recall correctly what is known about the inter-stasis box relationship, then judging from the hue and sharpness of the field this one is projecting," and he motioned with the stasis box in his hands, "I would guess that the other lies perhaps thirty meters below us. Considering," and he indicated the surrounding tortured topography, "the evidence of violent tectonic disturbances in this region, that is hardly surprising. We should be grateful the box is buried no deeper than it is."

Sulu was adjusting his phaser setting as he spoke. "In that case it shouldn't be too long before we can dig it out, especially if this is mostly ice beneath us." He finished setting the phaser, pointed it downward. "In this low pressure the ice should boil away as soon as our phasers melt it, and on this low a setting"—he indicated his own weapon—"we don't run any risk of damaging the box. We ought to be able to—"

He stumbled as the ground heaved. A violent explosion burst the surface behind them, sending ice fragments flying. Stunned, they turned as soon as they could recover their balance. Uhura remembered what

Spock had said about severe earth disturbances in this region.

But the explosion had been too localized for a quake, too modest for a volcano, and it was immediately apparent that the cause was artificial in nature. A concealed tunnel or cave had appeared in the ice. A half-dozen space-suited figures flew toward them from the opening, propulsive backpacks powering them toward the three shocked officers.

Sulu caught a glimpse of who wore those suits and knew instantly he would have preferred a volcano.

Each suited figure was a little over two and a half meters long. Their pressure suits were armored to withstand both phaser charges and solid-core weaponry. The bubble helmets topping the suits were fully transparent. The suits themselves could have been designed to accommodate human beings, save for their unusual size and the long, twisting segmented sections which extended from the base of the spine. They indicated tailed creatures.

Only one known race fitted those particular proportions.

"Kzinti!" Uhura, crouching and raising her phaser simultaneously, let go a blast. The energy charge glanced harmlessly off the armored suit of the nearest alien.

Another of the Kzinti fired at Sulu. There was a flare of darker light against his life-support aura.

The aliens had surrounded them. One landed just behind the helmsman, tried to lock massive arms around him. Sulu slipped partially clear, wrestling desperately with his much larger opponent.

Behind the helmet a startlingly feline face stared angrily down at him. The alien tried to pin Sulu's arms while keeping a grip on its phaser, a standard-issue Federation weapon which looked grotesquely tiny in an armored, four-digited paw that could easily have enclosed both of Sulu's hands. Bright pink ears that resembled the amputated wings of some tiny flying creature fluttered on the alien's head as it battled in frustration to secure a binding grip on its smaller but agile opponent.

Despite Sulu's agility, this was a fight which could have only one outcome, since the three Federation officers were both outsized and outnumbered by their alien attackers.

Two other Kzinti landed behind Sulu, and he was unable to avoid them all. They soon had him pinned between them.

Just before one phaser blast partially penetrated her life-support aura and knocked her unconscious to the chill surface, Uhura was certain she glimpsed Spock standing calmly nearby, watching the fight. He still held the stasis box in both hands, instead of a working phaser.

As she fell, she saw him handing the invaluable stasis box to one of the huge Kzinti. Her mind refused to accept the evidence of her eyes. The impossible thought that Spock could be a coward or worse occurred to her as the alien environment her life-support aura held at bay seemed to close in tight around and blot all thinking and speculation from her mind.

Sulu had been phaser-stunned when he refused an order to stop struggling. Now the Kzinti muttered among themselves, their attention shifting constantly from the stasis box to the two crumpled humans. They kept a watchful eye or two on Spock. The Vulcan made no move to resist when one of them asked gruffly over his helmet frequency for the phaser the officer still wore at his waist. Spock handed it over as docilely as he had the stasis box.

Once their last possible opponent had been rendered helpless, the aliens relaxed a little. Spock took the opportunity to study the motionless forms of his companions. Both Sulu and Uhura seemed to be breathing regularly. Their lime-yellow auras remained intact and strong, indicating that the belt mechanisms hadn't been damaged. That meant they were in no immediate danger. Their life-support belts would sense the change in their metabolisms and adjust accordingly, just as they would if the two officers had fallen asleep instead of having been stunned into unconsciousness.

Spock's thoughts were mixed but steady as always when, by gesturing, the Kzinti indicated he should move toward the tunnel they had appeared from so unexpectedly. Other Kzinti hefted the unconscious forms of Uhura and Sulu, while one more picked up the coveted stasis box. There was a good deal of recognizable chortling over the prize, which indicated the presence of something far more elaborate than a casual trap.

A short march down a phaser-cut tunnel brought the party to an open airlock. One Kzinti gave Spock an ungentle shove into the open chamber. The first officer made no protest, offered not even a hint of displeasure at the rough treatment.

It took three cycles for every member of the group to be transferred into the fresh air of the Kzinti ship. The design of the lock and numerous other aspects of construction immediately indicated to Spock that they were boarding a vessel, and not a totally unfamiliar one at that. But then, most of Kzinti technology was derivative of Federation or Klingon engineering.

Further marching through the powerfully scented air brought the party to what appeared to be a crew ready room. In keeping with the requirements of Kzinti physiology, the room was huge by Federation standards. An oddly shaped table large enough for several Kzinti to sit comfortably around dominated the center of the room. Lockers and instrument panels lined one entire wall. Again, nothing was remarkable about the instrumentation. Much of it looked familiar, although altered in some cases to accommodate the size of the Kzinti hand.

Gently, almost reverently, a Kzinti put the stasis box onto the massive central table. The rest of the group gathered around and began an animated discussion of their booty.

Spock watched them silently, occasionally glancing sideways at Uhura and Sulu to make certain their condition didn't suddenly take a change for the worse. In his own mind he had already taken full responsibility for the catastrophe. But that was unfair, as any outside observer would have insisted.

True, he had pointed out the unusual circumstance of another undiscovered stasis box lying within an oft-visited system like Beta Lyrae. He should have exercised greater caution in their search for the second box, should have seen the clues to the Kzinti presence even though they were concealed beyond the detecting ability of any mortal.

Kirk would have been the first to point out that Spock had no choice but to pursue the possible existence of the second box, and that he could not possibly have foreseen or guessed at the presence of the waiting Kzinti. But Spock was ever more critical of his actions than anyone else could be.

But an event detrimental to the interests of the Federation had occurred as a result of his decisions. He was guilty and condemned—unless the error could somehow, unlikely as that seemed, still be rectified before permanent damage was done. The Kzinti possessed the stasis box he and the others had traveled so fast and far to pick up. Its contents now became doubly important. Not only would they not be used to benefit the peoples of the Federation, but in the hands of the belligerent Kzinti they could be employed to bring only harm.

How much harm depended on the exact nature of those contents.

Spock was anxious to see inside. He had a perverse desire to know exactly how much damage his actions had caused the people of the Federation and the Federation itself.

A human experiencing the same thoughts might have screamed and damned himself, begging for his captors to shoot him in punishment for his mistake. Spock merely stood quietly. He faced the theft of the box as calmly as he had its acquisition. An observer would not be able to tell from his demeanor that the Kzinti had even arrived. Only his mind was operating much faster than before, and that was not visible.

Moans came from nearby. Sulu and Uhura were beginning to stir, recovering from the stun effects of the phasers. As soon as they were able to stand by themselves, a pair of Kzinti moved to assist them roughly in rising all the way. They escorted both groggy officers over to Spock and left them standing next to the first officer.

Spock had already noted the surface on which he had been directed to stand, and on which Sulu and Uhura now swayed unsteadily. Roughly five square meters of a thick metal mesh, it resembled a carpet woven of steel instead of fiber. He had recognized it as soon as they'd entered the large room. It was a police web, one identical to those used by Federation authorities for restraining prisoners without damaging them. The webs were portable and much simpler to maintain than an energy- or solid-barrier cubicle. When not needed, the jail "cell" could simply be rolled up and tucked away in a locker somewhere.

His observation was immediately confirmed. A Kzin nearby touched a wall control. Spock instantly felt himself paralyzed from the shoulders down. The force field generated by the mesh held him as firmly as any visibly bonds. The field was strong enough to retard perspiration in a prisoner, but given the cool climate of the ready room and the fact that their incarceration was likely to be brief, he didn't expect that would be a problem. As a bonus, the field kept the still unsteady Uhura and Sulu from falling over.

It took an effort, but Spock managed to turn his head enough to see his companions. They were beginning to regain full control of their nervous systems, including their minds. When they came around completely there would be questions, and Spock prepared himself for some awkward ones.

Uhura blinked, tried to take a step toward him, and found she was unable to move so much as a toe. Her head also came around slowly. "Mr. Spock . . . where are we?"

"Inside a Kzinti spacecraft, Lieutenant. Of what size and capability I have been unable to determine."

"Just a minute." Sulu was taking in their surroundings, eyeing the cluster of arguing Kzinti around the table. "Something doesn't make sense here— Wait, I remember now. Kzinti aren't supposed to have hand phasers, let alone space armor. Where did they get those weapons?" He gestured at the nearest Kzin and the pair of phasers slung at its hips.

"I don't know, Mr. Sulu, but you are quite right about their possession of weapons." Spock recited, "The Treaty of Sirius does not permit them any weapons capabilities at all, beyond the operation of a few police vessels. Obviously, the treaty has been broken."

The Kzinti left the room, still growling and grunting among themselves.

"This severe violation must be reported," Spock went on, "as soon as we reach Starbase Twenty-Five."

Sulu's expression was more eloquent than words, as if to say, *You mean, if we reach Starbase Twenty-Five.* But he didn't say that. Instead, his attention shifted to the grated surface they were standing on.

"Police web. We won't be able to do anything unless we can turn it off somehow."

They were left alone to discuss their plight for some time, before equipment-laden Kzinti re-entered the room. Under the direction of one Kzin with engineer's markings they deposited the equipment around the central table.

Devoid of their pressure suits they looked a lot like plump orange cats, save for their fanlike ears and the furless, pink, ratlike tail that twitched and moved restlessly behind each of them. Each was of considerable bulk, and an unmistakable, if feral, gleam of intelligence shone behind every pair of blazing yellow eyes.

As they chattered among themselves and moved equipment and instrumentation about, Spock concentrated on noting differences between individuals. For the most part these were slight. One Kzin had a bright patch of white on its nose. Another's fur was colored to form a pair of dark stripes over both eyes. These minor differences made the startling appearance of the last Kzin to enter the room all the more striking. In contrast to the healthy, robust girth of its companions, the newcomer was thin—downright scrawny. Instead of twitching restlessly about, its tail drooped to drag listlessly on the deck, and the pink batlike ears curled flat against the head as though soaked by a month's rain.

Along all of one flank, the dense orange fur was twisted and matted beyond combing, as if the Kzin slept exclusively on the same side and never moved. The fur resembled the gnarled hair of a dog, repeatedly washed and dried, who broke the cycle by rolling in mud. Nor was the expression of the newcomer normal. Instead of the other Kzinti's usual fierce or proud demeanor, this one wore a look of perpetual disillusionment.

Uhura decided that the scrawny arrival was either dreadfully unhappy or haunted by some as-yet-unknown affliction. "What are they up to now, Mr. Spock?" She gestured with her head at the compact but complex machine that was being erected alongside the central table. "What's that?"

"I cannot be positive." Spock had to raise his voice to make himself audible over the increasing yowls and grumblings of the orange-colored assembly. "But from the haste and excitement with which they are supervising the construction of the device, I would guess that despite differences in design and crudeness of engineering, it is a stasis-field nullifier."

"They're going to try to open the box, then, and there's nothing we can do to stop them." Sulu was simultaneously angry and downcast.

"It is the logical thing to do—and you needn't whisper, Lieutenant. At the moment they seem to have absolutely no interest in us. So we can talk normally, without much fear of being abused, although a certain amount of caution in what we discuss would be advisable."

He gestured with his head toward the far side of the room. "You see the lean, bedraggled Kzin, the last one to enter the chamber?"

"You mean the one back there in the corner?" Uhura asked.

"Yes. He is a reader of minds, a telepath."

"I thought I'd heard something about that." Uhura looked satisfied. "I remember reading that all Kzinti telepaths were unhappy neurotics who'd just as soon not have their special talents." She nodded ruefully. "That one sure fits the description. What a miserable-looking creature." At her last words, the telepath cringed. That also was typical of his condition. A normal Kzin so slighted would be on top of Uhura by now, frothing at the mouth.

Spock warned them again. "There is no sure way to guard our thoughts from him. Orally we can say what we wish, but mentally we must be constantly on guard." He paused a moment, thoughtful, then added, "Lieutenant Sulu, the telepath is not likely to concentrate much on Lieutenant Uhura or myself. For different reasons, she and I are considered by the Kzinti to be inferior beings.

"It will be helpful to keep in mind that the Kzinti are meat-eaters. If you sense that ugly one probing your thoughts, there are better things to concentrate on besides visions of resistance or hate. I believe it would be more effective if you were to concentrate at such moments on enjoying a raw vegetable. The thought of eating anything not-meat is repulsive in the extreme to a Kzin. Even the most perceptive among them cannot think rationally if afflicted with overpowering nausea, and I expect that to hold true for telepaths as well."

"Yes, sir. I'll concentrate on wallowing in salad." Sulu looked pleased at the thought. "Maybe I can goad them into revealing something of their intentions, besides opening the stasis box, of course."

"There is one other things we should all keep in mind." Spock fought his own neck muscles in order to turn his head to look at the *Enterprise*'s chief communications officer. "Lieutenant Uhura, what I am about to say may be critical, and it will be difficult to comply with. While we are in the presence of the Kzinti, do not say anything, do not suggest anything, do not do anything inventive. You must strive to look harmless, ignorant, virtually inanimate."

"Any special reason, sir?"

"Are you forgetting that Kzinti females are no more than dumb animals?" Spock tried to tell whether or not the scraggly Kzin telepath was concentrating on him, then decided that if anything he was still wholly absorbed with monitoring his fellows and possibly also Sulu.

"In an emergency," he reminded Uhura, "the Kzinti may forget that a human female is an intelligent creature, capable of original thought and activities beyond the merely instinctive ones of eating and sleeping."

"Thanks," snapped Uhura. "Thanks a lot, *sir*."

Spock was patient. The lieutenant's gut reaction was only to be expected. "Lieutenant Uhura, I value your intelligence highly. So does Lieutenant Sulu, and everyone else on board the *Enterprise*. But we may be able to seize an opportunity to escape if the Kzinti believe you have none. This is not a time for emotional reactions. Let the Kzinti react emotionally, as they are inclined to do. Our chances lie in calculation and reason ... and in being ready."

Uhura replied much more softly this time. "Yes sir ... You're right, of course." She smiled a dangerous little smile. "Don't worry. I'll do my damnedest to convince our captors that I'm nothing more than an automaton."

VII

Kirk moved continually between the command chair, the science station, and the helm-navigation console. Under the guise of inspecting readouts and information, he was really disguising his nervousness. Having places to walk to concealed the fact that he was in a mood to pace the floor.

Another distraction was the *last* thing he needed. He should have been able to concentrate all his attention on the upcoming conference, save for wondering how Spock, Sulu, and Uhura were progressing in their expedition to pick up the Slaver stasis box. Now he had a fresh, utterly unexpected problem on his hands. There was still no word on the whereabouts of Lieutenant M'ress, and the Caitian communications officer hadn't reported herself in to Sick Bay.

He didn't know it, but his troubles were about to be complicated a dozenfold.

"Captain?"

Kirk slid heavily into the command chair, swung to face communications. "Yes, what is it?"

Lieutenant Talliflores looked confused and unhappy. "I have two reports just in, sir."

Kirk perked up a little. "They've found Lieutenant M'ress?"

"No, sir. One report is from Engineering. Commander Scott says that one of his warp-drive techs, an ensign M'viore, has disappeared." Talliflores checked his recorder readout. "The other report *is* from Security, but it has nothing to do with Lieutenant M'ress. One of their own ensigns engaged in the search, name of R'leez, has vanished and does not acknowledge her orders."

"Both Caitians," a concerned Kirk declared after a brief pause. "That makes three of them: M'ress, and now this R'leez and M'viore." Swiveling in the chair, he looked to the science station.

"Mr. Vedama, I don't believe we have any other Caitians in the crew, but would you check, please?"

"Aye, sir," Vedama responded in his soft, lilting voice. It took only a few seconds to run the check through the computer. "You're right, sir. Those three are the only representatives of the planet Cait listed in the personnel records."

"Obviously we're dealing with a Caitian racial malady, then," Kirk announced. "But what? Some kind of disease, maybe, but how could they all be affected so fast? None was near the others when they were stricken. How could a disease be communicated so quickly throughout the ship? Unless Caitians are subject to periodic attacks of madness. But I've never heard of anything like that affecting them."

"Neither have I, sir," his acting science chief added.

"Excuse me, sir." It was Talliflores again.

"Now what?"

"A report coming in from Sick Bay, Captain. Dr. McCoy wants to talk to you."

Kirk allowed himself a sigh of relief. "At least Lieutenant M'ress has made it safely to Sick Bay. Maybe Bones has some idea by now of what's causing the Caitians to act this way." He flipped on his chair intercom. "Bones, how is she?"

"How is who, Jim?" McCoy sounded unusually tense and irritated.

Kirk's spirits sank. "Didn't Lieutenant M'ress report in to you yet?"

"No, she hasn't, Jim. And now I desperately wish she would, because I have reason to believe she isn't going to."

"You sound awfully positive, Bones. What makes you so sure?"

"Jim, I've got a food technician here, an Ensign Sanchez. He insists that he found Lieutenant M'ress crouching under a bush in the recreation forest area. She didn't respond when he called out to her, so he walked over to see if he could help. He heard your broadcast and thought she might've been too sick to respond."

"Go on, Bones," urged Kirk tensely.

"Not only wasn't she too ill to respond, Jim, but when he approached her she attacked him."

Kirk felt dazed. He conjured up an image of the communications officer in his mind: calm, efficient, usually in complete control of herself . . . It didn't fit.

But neither did her not reporting to Sick Bay.

"Bones, is he certain it was M'ress?"

"Just a second, Jim. You can ask him yourself."

A shaky voice replaced that of Dr. McCoy. "Sir, Ensign Sanchez here. Yes, sir, I'm positive it was Lieutenant M'ress."

Even as he listened, Kirk found it hard to believe. He was even willing to go as far as to ascribe the incident to a delusion on the ensign's part, except that M'ress *was* missing. While Sanchez sounded upset, he was perfectly coherent. There was no reason to discount his description of the encounter.

But Kirk was still incredulous. He had to be certain M'ress's actions were the result of some aberration on her part. "You say she attacked you, Ensign? I've known Lieutenant M'ress ever since she was assigned to the *Enterprise*. She's a competent, responsible officer, hardly the type given to irrational acts and especially to an act of violence against another crew member. You're positive you did nothing to provoke her?"

"Provoke her, sir?" In spite of his condition, the ensign managed to sound suitably outraged. "Sir, all I did was repeat to her what she must have heard herself, that you'd directed her to report to Sick Bay. The moment I made a move to touch her she gave me this crazy look. I started to back off, intending to call for medical help, and that's when she jumped me. I swear, sir, all I did was offer to help her, and when she made it clear she didn't want any help, try to get away."

"I can verify Ensign Sanchez's story, Jim," said McCoy, cutting in. "He has a substantial number of pretty deep scratches. Even well-trimmed Caitian claws can inflict rugged damage if they're used in anger. They're much thicker than human fingernails."

"Captain." It was Sanchez again. He sounded almost defiant. "I'm sorry to have to say this about a superior officer, but I don't think the lieutenant is quite sane. She didn't respond to any of the things I said, either before I approached her or while we were fighting."

"Did she say anything at all, Ensign?" By now Kirk had reluctantly accepted Sanchez's story. The scratches detailed by McCoy were the final convincer.

"Only in Caitian, sir, a lot of yowling and screeching it seemed like to me. I don't know the language, but she *sounded* as angry as she was acting. Frankly, sir, from the look in her eyes I thought she was ready to kill me." Sanchez paused a moment, added emphatically, "It was raw emotion I saw in her face, sir. The kind of expression you expect on the face of a crazy animal, not a superior officer. That's only my impression, of course, and I couldn't get too analytical about things. I was too busy trying to keep from being cut up."

"I understand, Sanchez." The ensign could be forgiven, Kirk felt, for exaggerating his impressions in the hysteria of the moment. Kirk was about ready to give vent to some emotions of his own.

"Bones, you can finish treating the ensign and release him. Sanchez, just one last question for you."

"Yes, sir," said the ensign.

"You told me that you thought Lieutenant M'ress was ready to kill you. Why didn't she? Did you fight her off? I presume neither of you was armed."

"No, sir. At least, if she had a weapon, she didn't show it. But me, fight her off? On the contrary, sir. I'm about her size, maybe a little bigger, but it was like tangling with a small tornado. No, sir, I didn't fight her off. It was pretty funny, now that I think back on it. She just kind of stopped all at once, gave me this real peculiar look . . ."

"What kind of look, ensign?" This was McCoy speaking.

"It's hard to describe, sir. Like she was sorry for what she'd done and yet she'd do it again in a minute. Then she took off and disappeared into the landscaping."

"Do you think she's still down in the recreation area?" Kirk thought to ask.

"I couldn't say, sir." Sanchez sounded exhausted. "I didn't hang around to look for her. All I could think of was getting out of there with the rest of my skin intact."

"All right, Ensign. Thank you. Bridge out."

"Sick Bay out," McCoy responded.

Kirk turned to his science officer. "Lieutenant Vedama, what do you make of all this? First, Lieutenant M'ress disappears and then two Caitian ensigns, and now I learn that one of my most trusted officers is running around silently attacking other members of the crew."

"Sir," Vedama announced apologetically, "I'm no expert on the Caitians."

"My second in command of communications goes berserk, without any visible reason, and no one knows anything!" Kirk sounded understandably peeved. "Lieutenant Vedama, see what you can find on Caitian social patterns. Dr. McCoy will be researching possible medical causes. Maybe it's not a medical problem."

"Yes, sir." Vedama turned to the science computer, began his searching.

Kirk's attention shifted forward. "Mr. Arex, are we still on course schedule for arrival at Starbase Twenty-Five?"

"Slightly ahead of time, sir," the Edoan navigator replied. "Shall I change our speed?"

"No. We'll resolve this trouble before we arrive. Maintain heading and warp-speed." He glanced back at communications.

"Lieutenant Talliflores, relay a message to Security. Tell them I want search teams on every deck to hunt for Lieutenant M'ress and the two absent ensigns. Inform them that all three Caitians are probably dangerous, prone to violent response if approached, and possibly not responsible for their actions.

"Under no circumstances are any of the three to be assaulted with anything stronger than a phaser set for stun. Emphasize to all teams that the three crew members are likely to be suffering from a noncommunicable racial disease as yet unidentified, and that they haven't turned traitor or anything as ridiculously imaginative as that. When captured, all three are to be taken directly to Sick Bay for treatment."

"Yes, sir." Talliflores operated instruments. "Relaying, sir."

In the absence of further information, Kirk leaned back in the command chair and pondered what had happened so far. In the following silence he had ample time to consider and abandon at least a dozen theories concerning the Caitians' actions, none of which seemed even marginally probable.

His chair intercom buzzed for attention.

"Jim," the voice from the speaker announced, "McCoy here. I've received two more casualties."

"What?" Kirk sat up straight in the chair.

"That's right, two more. From different decks. One thinks he was attacked by Lieutenant M'ress. The other identifies his attacker as Ensign M'viore."

"M'viore, too." Kirk felt dazed. "Bones, what the hell's going on here?"

"I wish I knew, Jim. Caitians are normally a very

controlled people. This is the first incident of its kind that I can recall taking place aboard the *Enterprise* or for that matter any other ship I know of, in which Caitians were involved. It doesn't make any sense."

"I know that already, Bones. What about temporary insanity?"

"Occurring simultaneously in three different personalities? Highly unlikely, Jim. I've been checking their records in the medical computer. All three crew members have a history of perfectly normal health, both mental and physical. Not one of them has ever shown any tendency toward mental instability, let alone all three of them. Sorry, Jim, but it has to be something else."

"Anything we could have brought on board, Bones?" Kirk wondered. "Maybe something that could have contaminated their food, affecting them and no one else?"

"I'll check their diets as best I can, Jim, but it's impossible to know exactly what they've eaten lately, never mind for the past few weeks or months. If it's something they did eat, the responsible substance might have been ingested long ago and is only now manifesting itself. There's only one way to check that out and that's to submit all three of them to a detailed biochemical body analysis, to find out if there *is* a foreign substance affecting their stability."

"To do that, Bones, we have to catch them."

"And that's the immediate problem, Jim. In order to cure them, we've first got to find them."

There were three members in the search party. All had their phasers out and set for stun. Ordinarily that would be enough to give them a quiet confidence, but this situation was different from any in recent memory. Even when the quarry was a member of the ship's crew, at least one had some idea what to expect. This time, no one from the captain on down seemed to have any idea what was happening. All they knew was that they were searching for three Caitian crew members who had possibly gone crazy.

Presently they were combing the recreational forest

on Deck Eight, having started from the section where the missing officer M'ress had last been seen. Other security parties were performing similar searches both on this deck and elsewhere on the ship.

"Hasmid," whispered one of the security men to his friend on his left, "I understand that Caitians are supposed to be able to move unheard and unseen through this kind of terrain. Just because it's located in the middle of a starship doesn't mean they can't function as efficiently as they can on the surface of a planet."

"Quiet, Kasuki!" the other responded sharply. "You're makin' me nervous. And this isn't any kind of terrain. It's only the recreation area."

"Shut up, you two!" snapped the officer in charge of the little group.

They were traveling in a line through a particularly dense clump of vegetation. In spite of their attentiveness, they hardly had time to react when the three Caitians hit them simultaneously.

Kirk's chair intercom yammered for attention again. Kirk jabbed the acknowledge button almost viciously. "Kirk here."

"Jim, McCoy again," came the concerned response. "One of our patrolling security details got beaten up. It looks like our three fugitives have joined together somewhere down on Deck Eight."

"One minute, Bones." Kirk switched over to shipwide frequency. "Attention, all security personnel. All security personnel, this is the captain speaking. Seal off Deck Eight. Shut down all turbolift service to Deck Eight. Personnel on Deck Eight are instructed to continue with normal duties. The three Caitians are apparently now operating together, but they've shown no tendency to perform wanton attacks on individuals, and react violently only if approached.

"If you see any of the three crew members in question, do not attempt to restrain them yourselves. Contact the nearest security team and give details of your sighting." Kirk thought a second, then added, "Use extreme caution when approaching the three Caitians. They have already overpowered one security unit.

Henceforth, all security teams will operate in groups of not less than eight per team."

Kirk switched back to the Sick Bay frequency. "Sorry, Bones, but I had to relay some information to Security right away. Go on."

"Jim, there's something else peculiar about this. None of the three Caitians are especially large or strong. The contrary, if anything. Yet they put a whole security team out of commission, a team of personnel whose business is restraining the unruly. The three are all marked up: bruises, scratches, cuts, the works. Ensign Trancas is one of them."

Kirk knew Trancas, a big, burly wrestler type from a slightly high-gravity world. Hardly the sort one would imagine a trio of sylphlike Caitians could overpower, much less beat up.

"They encountered only the three Caitians?" he asked in disbelief, "and they were unable to subdue them?"

"Subdue them! Jim, you ought to see these three. Trancas was in charge of their group. He told me they never had a chance. They thought they had the three fugitives spotted, and approached them with phasers ready. Trancas says they should have beamed them on sight. Instead, when the Caitians showed no sign of aggressiveness, they tried to move them physically. That's when they were jumped, too fast to use their weapons. We know the Caitians are fast, but this other thing has me confused. Trancas says he tried to wrestle M'ress to the deck and she threw him into a clump of bushes."

"M'ress?" The communications officer had never displayed any unusual strength. "Bones, do the Caitians have some special reserves of energy they can call on at will? Perhaps something we don't know about?"

"I wouldn't think so, Jim. At least, I never heard of any such phenomenon, and the Caitians are a fairly well documented race. They've been members of the Federation long enough for any peculiar abilities to have manifested themselves. I think we're still stuck with our original hypothesis: that something they've eaten has affected their body chemistry. The unusual strength is undoubtedly a byproduct of whatever's affecting them. Whatever they ingested isn't sitting well with them."

"It's not sitting well with me either, Bones. Keep hunting, and let me know the instant you think you might've found the chemical that's causing all the trouble."

"If that's what it is, Jim. Sick Bay out."

"Captain?" Talliflores glanced over from communications. "A new report coming in. From a yeoman Loo. He's certain he spotted Lieutenant M'ress and at least one other Caitian on Deck Six."

"Already? They must have slipped away before we sealed off Deck Eight."

"If anyone could avoid patrols it would be the Caitians, sir." Vedama sounded half apologetic. "With their speed and agility, coupled to a natural talent for self-concealment, they will prove difficult to corner."

"I'm fully aware of the capabilities of Caitian physiology, Mr. Vedama." Kirk's frustration made his reply sound more biting than he intended it to be. "More than I want to be, at the moment." He sighed.

"Mr. Talliflores, redirect security personnel to cover all decks, with particular emphasis on Deck Six."

"Yes, sir." He paused, listening at his headset. "Another report coming in. They didn't slip through unnoticed. They confronted another security patrol under the command of yeoman O'Hyr. They're on their way to Sick Bay now."

Events were becoming more complicated instead of less so, Kirk mused. "All eight of them?"

"All but three, Captain," Talliflores reported. "Yeoman O'Hyr is among them. But Ensigns Suarez, Hilambo, and Chevalier were not injured and are presently in pursuit of the fugitives, having delayed only long enough to report in and check the severity of their companions' injuries."

"So three of them weren't hurt, and the Caitians backed off. Whatever's affecting them hasn't made them omnipotent, then. They haven't suddenly become invincible." He hesitated. "Still, five out of eight put out of commission without so much as capturing one fugitive isn't very encouraging either. But at least no one's been seriously hurt or killed yet."

"True, sir," Arex commented from his position at the navigation-helm. "But they will have phasers now, taken from the assaulted security team."

"Mr. Arex, I'm sure they took phasers from the first trio of security personnel they confronted, and yet they haven't so much as fired to stun anyone. That doesn't make any sense either. If nothing else, the Caitians are acting consistent in their inconsistentness." Kirk stared at the vacant viewscreen, which all too soon would be displaying a picture of Starbase 25.

Probably the base had several Caitians in its complement, which meant that M'ress and her companions had to be captured and treated before anyone from the *Enterprise* could leave the ship. A human might not be affected by whatever had possessed the Caitians, but that didn't rule out the possibility of Kirk or anyone else of another species serving as a carrier. If it *was* some kind of racial malady the Caitians were suffering from, he couldn't risk infecting the Caitians at the starbase. Besides which, the Caitians had to be caught so they could be kept from harming themselves, not to mention other personnel.

"Whatever's affected them hasn't driven them completely crazy, Mr. Arex, or they wouldn't have a thought about employing weapons, not to mention severely injuring anyone else. They've been very careful about that." A new thought occurred to him.

"In fact, their recent movements are a testament to their continued sanity. Have you noticed, Mr. Arex, Mr. Vedama, that the Caitians aren't just traveling in a random pattern to avoid the security teams? They're moving upward through the ship. Why, I can't imagine. But if they persist in their movements, and there's no reason why they shouldn't—at least, none I can hypothesize—then maybe we can make it work to our advantage. The bridge is the one level on the ship where we can isolate them and eliminate any possible chance of escape."

"True but risky, Captain," Vedama pointed out.

Kirk replied tensely. "I have three valuable members of my crew running amok, Lieutenant, and if we can stop them before they severely injure any of their fellows or irrevocably incriminate themselves, I'm going to take a chance or two."

"Captain," Lieutenant Arex noted, "if we permit them to reach the bridge unopposed and they are, as you state, not insane, then surely they will suspect something."

"Not if we're careful not to give them reason to, Lieutenant. All bridge personnel will continue to perform their usual duties, as if nothing is amiss. Mr. Vedama, signal Starbase Twenty-Five and find out what they know about periodic maladies among the Caitians. Give them a detailed breakdown of their aberrant behavior lately, plus personal résumés. See if the medical computer there has any information we might use that's not in our banks. And if there's a Caitian or two serving at the Base, try and contact them directly and explain our problem. Maybe they'll know exactly what's wrong."

"Yes, sir. We are still a considerable distance from the base and there is no deep-space relay between. There will be time between questions and reply," Vedama declared.

"Sick Bay calling bridge," the speaker at Kirk's elbow announced. "McCoy here. The injuries to the five members of the last security team are—"

"Not now, Bones," Kirk interrupted him. "The Caitians are moving upward through the ship. I have a hunch they're going to try and reach the bridge."

"Why would they do that? Surely they have no illusions about taking over the ship!"

"We don't know what they might want, Bones."

"Well if you're fairly sure they're coming there, then I'm coming also. They've already demonstrated they can exercise much more than their usual strength. Several of the injured ensigns are positive they hit at least two of the Caitians with phaser bursts when it seemed they were going to be overpowered. They're convinced that's what drove their attackers off, but they don't understand why the bursts didn't stun them into immobility. All I can guess is that their increased strength may also be coupled to an ability to at least partially withstand a phaser set to stun."

"I'll believe that, Bones, when I fire point-blank at M'ress and don't see her fall on the deck."

"Maybe so, Jim, but I'm going to bring something of my own along. It's more powerful than a phaser stun burst, but no more lethal. Ke'eloveen. It's a general tranquilizer that can be adjusted specifically for several different kinds of mammalian metabolism. It won't take long to concoct a batch gauged specifically for Caitian physiology."

"Sounds promising, Bones. Be glad to have you."

McCoy arrived on the bridge shortly thereafter. He carried a small plastic pistol with a multiple barrel. Walking over to the command chair, he showed it to Kirk, reached into a waist pouch and brought out a handful of tiny transparent darts filled with a thick golden liquid.

"Each dart holds enough ke'eloveen to put out several Caitians, Jim. The pistol can fire four darts together or individually. I hope I have enough time to fire one dart at a time. I can fire a quadruple spread in an emergency, but three darts or more striking the same person would create the danger of overdose reactions."

"I'm hoping—unreasonably—that you won't have to use them, Bones." Kirk found the prospect of facing an attack by three of his crew sobering, where others might have found it ludicrous.

McCoy placed the pistol in a ready position at his waist. "Any indication of where the three are now?"

"No. We haven't had any reports on their whereabouts for some time, Bones. Hopefully a patrol will capture them before they can reach the bridge. If not, we have one advantage: They don't know that we're expecting them here."

"How can you be so sure, Jim? They probably know that you've been receiving reports on their movements. They might assume that you *do* know they're heading here and change their direction accordingly."

"I don't think so, Bones." Kirk leaned forward earnestly. "Everything they've done so far has been with a singlemindedness of purpose."

"So you think there's a method in their madness? That they have some definite goal in mind?" McCoy seemed skeptical. "That doesn't sound like any kind of disease function I ever heard of."

"Bones, they've got to be working toward some end. I admit I don't have much grounds for believing that, but their actions almost hint that they're being controlled by something they're unable to resist, some compulsion they can't fight. I don't think they'll consider that we might be waiting for them, because I don't think that whatever's driving them leaves them much room for that kind of abstract speculation. I just wish I knew what they wanted, and why."

"We'll find out soon enough, Jim." And he added, so softly no one else could hear, "Provided we don't have to kill all three of them." McCoy moved away, leaving Kirk to his own thoughts. He took up a stance near the communications console, checking to make certain the tranquilizer pistol was still in place, ready to be pressed into hurried service.

"Remember," Kirk informed the rest of the bridge personnel, "no one is to make a hostile move or indicate that anything out of the ordinary is taking place unless the Caitians provoke us. If that happens, use your phasers on stun."

A chorus of "ayes" sounded in varying degrees of assurance from around the bridge.

"Anything from Starbase Twenty-Five, Lieutenant Vedama?"

"No, sir. They should have received our communication by now. No doubt they are trying to find something to report to us."

Kirk turned to communications once more. "Talliflores, any new word on the present location of the Caitians?"

"No, sir, nothing. None of the patrolling security teams reports a sighting since the last one identifying them from Deck Six—and no word from any other personnel, although everyone on the ship must be looking out for them."

"They're probably not even halfway to the bridge yet," McCoy commented. "Maybe they changed their minds or their imaginary unknown purpose, and are heading in a different direction."

"Maybe, Bones," Kirk conceded, "but I still—"

The turbolift doors opened abruptly. Everyone on the bridge tensed, then relaxed. It was only a couple of ensigns wearing science department insignia. And also wearing, Kirk noted curiously after starting to turn away, oddly matched blank expressions.

"Bridge—!" he started to shout.

Both technicians fell forward, unconscious. Two Caitians emerged from the lift behind them, moving low and incredibly fast and firing phasers of their own.

"—alert!" Kirk finished, even as he was ducking down in the command chair and reaching for his own sidearm.

The order was hardly necessary, since everyone had heard or seen the two bodies of the technicians falling to the deck in front of the lift. Moving forms and flashing beams of phaser power set for stun filled the bridge. That included the phasers of the Caitians, who still displayed a caution entirely out of keeping with their actions. Several members of the bridge complement were quickly immobilized by the Caitians' surprise attack.

Shielded by the command chair's bulk, Kirk was able to aim a touch better than some of his crew. One blast from his phaser struck Ensign R'leez square in the left side, under her arm. She stumbled—but didn't go down. They had been correct in assuming that whatever was affecting the Caitians had also given their bodies the ability to withstand a low-power phaser burst.

But Kirk couldn't consider increasing the power of any weapons to killing intensity. No one had been killed or seriously hurt by the rampaging Caitians. Of course, if it appeared that it was going to be a choice between hurting one of the Caitians and letting them take over the bridge . . .

Arex was crouched behind the navigation-helm console firing regularly. Holding a paralyzed left forearm tight against his side, Lieutenant Vedama provided a crossfire from the region of the science station.

One of the Caitians, R'leez again, made a rush for the command chair and Kirk. The Captain fired at the charging ensign, then rolled out of the feline's path. But it was immediately clear she wasn't after him or the command chair. She rushed past Kirk, ignoring him as she headed for the helm controls.

Arex caught her with another phaser burst. She staggered but again somehow managed to keep her feet. She was almost on top of the console and its protective, tripedal operator when she unexpectedly collapsed and fell across the helmsman's seat.

Kirk had rolled back behind the command chair, panting. Now he noticed the tiny glint of plastic reflected off the syringe-dart sticking out of the Caitian's back. McCoy had shot her with one of his tranquilizer darts.

Then something knocked him aside, moving at incredible speed. It was Ensign M'viore, the other Caitian who had arrived in the lift.

"Bones! Fire, Bones!"

Why didn't he fire?

M'viore leaped for the controls, and Arex emerged to meet her. The Edoan threw three arms around her, wrestled her off. His additional arm prevented her from dealing with him as easily as she and her companions had dealt with the members of the various security teams. Spitting and clawing while a silent Arex held on desperately, she tumbled to the deck on top of him.

"Bones!" Kirk looked around frantically for the doctor. Then he saw why McCoy hadn't fired at M'viore and why he didn't answer now. McCoy was lying sprawled on the deck, stunned by a burst from one of the Caitians' phasers.

Half crawling, half stumbling, Kirk ran to his side, picked up the half-loaded tranquilizer gun. Arex and M'viore rolled over twice before the Caitian came up on top and raised her claws for a swing at the exhausted navigator's face. Vedama and Talliflores hunted for a clear shot at her.

Kirk turned, aimed the unfamiliar but simple device, and fired. The syringe-dart snicked into M'viore just beneath her upraised right arm. She sat perfectly still for a moment, then rose and glanced at her side uncomprehendingly. For a brief instant the expression on her face was almost normal. Then she crumpled to the deck.

A shaken Arex climbed slowly to his feet. Kirk moved to stand beside him, still holding the dartgun.

"Her reserves of strength were startling, sir," Arex told him, "much in addition to what the reports claimed. It was one thing to listen to them, quite another to experience what they were referring to. I found myself being rapidly overpowered." Long, high whistling sounds—Edoan wheezing—issued from the navigator's mouth.

"I thought she was coming for me," a puzzled Kirk murmured. "She was looking straight at me, and then—something more important seemed to take control of her. She forgot me completely in her rush to get at the helm. R'leez was heading for the helm also."

"That's funny, sir," a puzzled technician replied, from across the bridge, "I thought she was coming after *me*."

"I wonder why the helm as a final destination. Where could they want to go so frantically?"

"We'll find out when they wake up." Arex regarded both limp feline forms thoughtfully.

"I hope so." Kirk glanced around quickly, but the bridge and turbolift were devoid of the one figure he sought. "I wonder where M'ress is?"

The Caitian communications officer was closer than Kirk knew. She was in a dark, dark place. It didn't bother her. She was not subject to claustrophobia, and the faint glow from the pocket light she carried in one hand provided more than enough illumination for her cat eyes to make out her surroundings. It was blissfully quiet where she was working, but she wasn't calm and relaxed. The pounding of her heart and the raging emotions controlling her kept both her hands and mind moving desperately.

Nurse Chapel arrived with other Sick Bay technicians. The two Caitians and the members of the bridge crew who had been paralyzed by their phasers were carried from the room.

One particular casualty concerned Kirk, not because he was more severely injured than any of the others, but because his invaluable advice would be sorely missed. "How soon before Bones will recover?" he inquired as McCoy was carried off the bridge.

"It doesn't look as if he received the full force of a beam, Captain." Chapel considered the question briefly. "Not very long. In fact, he may be the first one to recover since he only absorbed a glancing blow. He'll recover faster if I give him a countering neurodrug, but he'll feel the effects twenty-four hours later."

"I need him most in the next twenty-four hours," Kirk told her. "What would Bones say if he was able?"

"To give him the drug," Chapel replied without hesitation.

"Right. Do so. What about the Caitians? I've got to know what's affected them and what M'ress is likely to do on her own, now that her two companions have been caught."

"I understand, sir. I've been working with Dr. McCoy trying to find out, and we've several members of the ship's organic fabrication staff working with us. If anything unusual got into their food, they'll find it. It's slow going, though, backchecking everything that's been processed in, say, the past several weeks. They've found nothing in the way of a foreign substance so far that might be responsible for the trouble."

"Keep them at it, Chapel. Do the best you can. And contact me the moment Bones is conscious."

She smiled. "He'll do that himself, sir."

When the last motionless crew member had been removed and the medical team was on its way down to Sick Bay, Kirk resumed his station at the command chair. Talliflores, Vedama, and himself were the only ones who had escaped the Caitians' assault.

But that wouldn't do, especially not with M'ress still unconfined.

"Lieutenant Talliflores, contact appropriate sections and have them designate on-duty qualified personnel to replace the technicians who were stunned. We need a maximum complement here, in case of any new surprises. Have backups report immediately."

He turned to Vedama. "I wonder why M'ress didn't join her friends in their attack. A third charge might have successfully reached the helm."

"It is possible, Captain," the science officer theorized, "that M'ress might have disagreed with her companions in their approach. Or she might feel different compulsions, have differing motives, and therefore didn't accompany them. Or," and he looked around with concern, "their seemingly well-planned assault on the bridge might only have been a diversion so M'ress could reach some other part of the ship."

"Possible, Lieutenant. Talliflores, give me shipwide channel again."

The communications officer complied and Kirk once more addressed the command chair pickup. "All personnel, this is the Captain speaking.

"Two of the three renegade Caitians have now been tranquilized and are on their way to Sick Bay to receive treatment. Lieutenant M'ress has not been located and presumably is still moving freely about the ship. It is possible that the recent, nonfatal attack on the bridge which you will shortly be hearing rumors of was an attempt to divert our attention from some other deck. Security teams will continue searching on their own levels and all personnel will continue to remain alert for the lieutenant's presence. Thank you."

"If M'ress has any sense left," Vedama commented, "she'll realize that she can't hope to accomplish whatever bizarre intention she and her companions had."

"Relief personnel are on their way up, Captain," Talliflores announced smoothly.

"Good. Hopefully this will all be over soon." Kirk regarded the command chair chronometer. They still had plenty of time to—

The lights went out.

Everyone spent a nerve-wracking couple of seconds in near-total darkness until the self-contained emergency lights cut in, filling the bridge with an eerie, dim glow that was punctuated only by the brilliant but localized illumination of the instrumentation faces and dials.

"I believe, Captain," said Vedama slowly, "that we now know the whereabouts of Lieutenant M'ress."

"Mr. Talliflores," Kirk said crisply, his eyes darting from dark corner to half-hidden bulkhead, "any communications from elsewhere on the ship as to her possible presence?"

"Checking, sir." Talliflores turned to his console. A peculiar expression came over his deeply tanned face. He rapidly adjusted several controls, but these actions served only to deepen his uncertainty.

Eventually he turned back to the command chair. His tone was grim. "Sir, all on-board communications are dead. I can't reach any part of the ship, and if there are incoming calls I'm not picking them up."

"Lieutenant Vedama, try through the science section. See if you can raise anyone," Kirk ordered.

Vedama likewise operated one switch after another before turning sorrowfully to face Kirk. "Sir, not only can't I contact any *one*, I can't contact any *thing*. All links with the main computer have been blocked off."

"So now we know exactly where M'ress is." Kirk found himself slowly inspecting the surrounding walls and the ceiling. "She's got to be in the service crawlway encircling the bridge." He couldn't, despite the seriousness of the situation, keep a touch of admiration from his voice.

"While M'viore and R'leez were attacking the bridge, she was busy cutting controls and connections. We were intentionally kept too busy to use any of the bridge instrumentation, or even to consider that the attack might be diversionary."

His most important remaining question was directed to the only other officer in the room. "Mr. Arex, we've lost communications and computer access. I hope that's all we've lost."

"I follow your meaning, Captain," the Edoan navigator acknowledged. "I am glad to report that we are still on course and maintaining speed. The engineering conduits, which are the most heavily sealed of all bridge–ship linkages, are too strong for her to break."

"Or maybe she doesn't want to break into them," Kirk commented thoughtfully. "If the Caitians' purpose is to take over the ship, they'll want it in operating condition." He leaned forward in the chair, added sharply, "None of this means we can't get reinforcements in here. Lieutenant Vedama, try the turbolift."

The science officer nodded, left his station, and moved to the lift. He touched the controls. The doors did not swing aside.

"Nothing, sir. Not even an acknowledgment light on the panel."

"I retract my statement on reinforcements. Apparently Lieutenant M'ress isn't dazed enough not to think things through." He smiled ruefully. "It's always pleasing to see an officer demonstrate such competence. I only wish it were under different circumstances."

"There's still the way she got here, Captain," Vedama pointed out as he moved back to his station. "Up through the service passageways."

Kirk shook his head. "You can bet that when she entered the serviceway around the bridge, Lieutenant, she took care to block off the approach behind her. The Caitians have demonstrated too much thoroughness so far, to forget something so obvious.

"However, the moment someone tries to contact the bridge—if they haven't already—and finds out that its sealed off, they'll guess what's happened and act accordingly. Even if M'ress has used a phaser to melt and seal the door to the serviceway, it won't take long for someone else to get a torch from engineering and cut through.

"And that means," he finished, hefting the tranquilizer gun tightly in one hand, "that if she still expects to accomplish whatever crazy end she has in mind, she'll have to act very soon."

But they waited in silence. There was no sound nor

sign of movement from any of the several serviceway hatches lining the interior wall of the bridge.

"Biding her time," Kirk muttered softly, "waiting for some special moment. I wish I knew what was driving her and the other Caitians to do this."

A nervous Talliflores suddenly voiced an unspoken concern. "Sir, what about our life-support systems? Couldn't she take over by interrupting our air supply?"

Kirk replied just a smidgen more confidently than he felt. "I've already thought of that, Lieutenant. She could cut our atmosphere, but I don't know if she could restore it for her own use. But M'ress is no engineer. I don't think she could modulate the air supply just enough to knock us out, and I don't believe she'd chance killing us. That would be counter to all their actions thus far. No, I think she'll try and take the bridge without doing anything so drastic."

"I admit they haven't killed anyone so far, sir," Talliflores conceded, "but if M'ress is pressed for time and feels someone breaking in behind her, into the serviceway— I just wish I knew why they're doing this!"

"Easy, Lieutenant," Kirk urged, trying to relax the officer. "If we knew that, I think we'd have the answers to all our questions."

"If you're right, sir," Talliflores mused, "why wait here for her to attack us? She's had the element of surprise with her ever since this business began."

"How do you propose to take it away from her?" Kirk could see along the lieutenant's intended path and didn't like the option it presented. At the same time, Talliflores was quite correct. Kirk didn't see how he could object to it.

The communications officer indicated a nearby service hatch. "She could be anywhere around or above us, sir. There are several entrances onto the bridge from the serviceway. She could be right here next to communications, or waiting by that one." He pointed to the hatch beneath the main viewscreen. "But she can't be behind all of them at once.

"If one of us could get through a hatch, armed with a phaser and in close quarters, he could probably hold her off despite her speed and added strength. Even an agile Caitian needs room to maneuver. One of us could keep her busy while another cut through the sealed downway to go for help. We might even surprise her enough to overpower her before she could react."

"You saw what little effect phasers had on ensigns M'viore and R'leez, Lieutenant. Each of them took two or three bursts and still didn't go down."

"I know that, sir," Talliflores argued, "but it did slow them down. If one of us used a phaser and another was ready nearby with the tranquilizers—"

Kirk was emphatic. "Absolutely not, Lieutenant. Your idea has merit, but . . . no. Keeping the tranquilizers ready right here is one of our two remaining methods to insure that the bridge is protected."

"The other?" inquired the lieutenant.

Kirk hesitated, finally voiced the one thing he'd been fighting to avoid. "In that case, we'll have to set phasers to kill."

VIII

All the Kzinti save one were engaged in setting up the stasis-field nullifier or in supervising its construction. The single exception sat in the far corner of the ready room looking miserable and unhappy as always. But that didn't prevent it from regularly scrutinizing the Federation prisoners. Sulu knew that it was concentrating only indifferently with its rheumy, sensitive eyes. The dangerous attention it was lavishing on them sprang from another organ. The telepath ignored the excitement in the room. It spoke not to its fellows, simply sat and watched and listened with its mind, hoping for unconscious betrayal of useful information from one of the captives.

One of the largest Kzinti spoke a few harsh final words to one of the others, then turned to walk over and study the prisoners. Spock had already singled him out as a leader among the collection of yowling aliens, as much for his bearing and manner as for anything he had said. The gaze the Kzin lavished on the immobile captives was more baleful than that of the other Kzinti. His entire manner hinted at impatience and a natural belligerence he did not even try to suppress.

That was fine with Spock. He preferred a direct confrontation to the subtle spying of the telepathic weakling hunched in the background.

Eyes darting rapidly from one to the next, the big Kzin examined them each in turn. Directing his words to Sulu, he spoke. His standard English was comprehensible enough, though pushed out in a rough, raspy voice, as if the Kzin were speaking with a mouthful of pebbles. The implied threat and harshness of his tone needed no clarification.

"I am Chuft-Captain. You will identify yourselves."

So much for diplomatic courtesy, Spock mused. Well, realistically they could expect nothing better.

Taking his cue from what the first officer had said before, Sulu spoke up as if it were natural for him to be in command. "Lieutenant Sulu of the Federation starship *Enterprise*." He gestured with his head toward his companions. "This is officer Spock."

Chuft-Captain appeared to find nothing unusual in Sulu's failure to identify Uhura. He regarded her once, only long enough to assure himself that she was female, and then dismissed her presence as if she did not exist.

Spock, however, was evidently deserving of somewhat more attention. "You are a Vulcan," declared the Kzin, contempt dripping from every word. "I feel no pressing need to converse with an eater of roots and leaves."

One eyebrow rose slightly, but Spock didn't reply to the taunt. If Chuft-Captain was trying to assure himself of Spock's placidity, the first officer wasn't going to do anything to counter that impression.

Apparently satisfied, the Kzin commander turned back to Sulu. "Humans are at least omnivorous," he growled with the air of one making a major concession. "You are prisoners aboard the privateer *Traitor's Claw*, a stolen police vessel."

Sulu had a questioning response ready, but having

delivered himself of this information, Chuft-Captain showed no inclination to pursue the conversation. Instead, he turned away from the captives.

His subordinates had almost finished the basic assembly of the nullifier and were beginning to place ancillary instrumentation into the complex framework. As the odd-shaped device took shape, the various members of the Kzin crew displayed increasing excitement.

One Kzin took no part in the construction of the stasis-field nullifier. His attention was reserved solely for the stasis box itself. It rested on the far end of the huge central table. Even with the former owners of the box secured within the police-web field, the guard showed no sign of relaxing his vigilance.

If the Kzin commander was reluctant to converse, then it was up to Sulu to persuade him. "Stealing must be a habit with you. The police vessel . . . *two* stasis boxes . . ." The helmsman managed to sound impressively contemptuous himself.

Chuft-Captain spun to face him. Since contempt and insult was a normal component of Kzinti communication, Sulu's manner had no effect on him at all.

"Both boxes are the rightful property of Kzin. One we found was empty. We will soon see about the one your trespassing archeologists found. Yes, we knew of those on Gruyakin—and of the box. We intercepted one of their broadcasts, you see." He looked proud. "We did not know of the box until they contacted your ship.

"Rather than assault the entire installation—an attack which would no doubt have been successful but difficult to conceal—we waited for the box to be transported off the planet. Little could we hope that only one man and two others would be sent to recover it. With that known, we hastily arranged this trap. Your disappearance," he added matter-of-factly, "will be much simpler to disguise. As for the second box," and he gestured at the glowing cube on the table, "it is rightfully the property of Kzin."

"What's all this garbage about trespassing and Kzin property?" Sulu sounded outraged. "Gruyakin is an open system."

"A system long claimed by Kzin," snapped an imperious Chuft-Captain.

"The Kzinti make it a habit to claim half the planets in the galaxy," sniffed Sulu. "It's one thing to stake a claim, another to prove rightful ownership. Saying Gruyakin belongs to Kzin is not the same thing as owning it."

"Both boxes are the property of Kzin!" Chuft-Captain's idea of rational debate apparently consisted of stating that which he believed over and over again, as if his claim would gain validity through force of repetition.

"The stasis box we found some time ago was empty," he explained, "but it served well as bait to draw you here. Now we await the inheritance rightfully ours." He gestured at the box, evidently enjoying himself. "The Slavers possessed weapons that could devastate a civilization. If the gods are with us, there will be one such weapon in that box."

Automatically Sulu's eyes traveled to the glowing container they had recovered with so much difficulty. The box itself was harmless as long as one took care—unlike the unfortunate Jaiao Beguin, back on Gruyakin—not to try to open it incorrectly. Sulu fervently wished that the Kzinti stasis nullifier wouldn't work properly. It would be a pleasure to watch the box's defensive system promptly envelop every member of the Kzinti crew in a silvery stasis field of their own.

Across the room, the Kzinti telepath frowned. Let him. Sulu grinned viciously. They had nothing else to threaten him with.

However, judging from the expertise with which the Kzinti technicians were assembling their own nullifier, Sulu's hope was wishful thinking at best. Again he could only glance at the box and pray that its contents proved as innocuous as its exterior.

Sulu had already assumed an aggressive, angry pose. Might as well maintain it. He continued to lace his comments with contempt. "The Kzinti fought four wars with humankind and lost them all," he declared. "The last one was two hundred years ago. It seems that you haven't learned a thing since."

That touched a nerve. A violent howl rattled the interior of the ship. It was as brief as it was extreme. Aware that he had been provoked beyond control, Chuft-Captain quickly bit off the roar, though it took him several moments longer to regain his composure.

When he finally, dangerously responded, his comments were phrased almost carelessly. "Guard your speech, man. None of my crew has ever tasted human meat as did our ancestors. We would welcome the opportunity."

Belligerence had its place. So did common sense. Realizing he had pushed Chuft-Captain too far, Sulu refrained from responding. The Kzin's threat was not made idly. There was nothing to be gained by advancing the time of their death. While they lived there was always the chance, however faint it seemed at the moment, of recovering or at least destroying the stasis box and its unknown contents. While their present status mitigated against that, they could do even less from inside someone's stewpot.

"Always," Chuft-Captain was saying, "you and your Federation have had superior equipment and technology. We've sought a weapon for a long time which would enable us to defeat you at last."

Sulu jumped on that. "So much for your story about being a privateer. You've just declared that you're really working for the government of Kzin."

One of the other Kzinti, possibly an intermediate officer, looked up from the work proceeding at the table to snarl at Chuft-Captain, who growled back.

"You are presumptuous," he rumbled at Sulu. "All records will show that the *Traitor's Claw* is a stolen police ship. If we are captured, the Highest of Kzin will repudiate us." He smiled, showing sharp white teeth. "No matter what happens, no one except you could possibly prove that this is anything but an illegal privateer crew. And you will not be alive to offer any evidence against us."

A low growling interrupted him. The Kzinti were stepping back from the now-completed nullifier.

Chuft-Captain snarled a reply, started toward the table. He glanced back with a final word for Sulu. "If we succeed and are not captured or intercepted, you will be meat for our tables."

There was an exchange of grumbles and gestures. A couple of the Kzin technicians made some last-minute adjustments to the nullifier. When everyone had stepped clear, the engineer in charge pulled a single switch.

The mood in the room, among captives as well as Kzinti, was one of anticipation mixed with caution. While the stasis nullifier looked efficient and the Kzinti had clearly taken every precaution with its construction and design to insure that it would operate exactly as intended, no one could predict with one hundred percent certainty exactly what a stasis box might do in any situation. For example, it might turn out to be a very intricate Slaver booby trap designed to look like a stasis box.

These fears were overcome by fascination as the nullifier acted on the box. As the nullifying field strengthened, so did the blue aura surrounding the mirror-surfaced cube. Abruptly, the box flared with a light so bright that the Kzinti had to shield their eyes and the prisoners shut theirs tightly.

The powerful flash lasted only an instant, faded as quickly as it had appeared. In its place rested an unremarkable-looking metal box devoid of its original blue halo. Chuft-Captain gestured curtly.

In response, one of the low-ranking Kzinti approached the table. He eyed the box warily. This was a duty he would have preferred to avoid, but under direct order from Chuft-Captain such a thing was unthinkable.

Very carefully, very slowly, he pushed the metal lid up and back. Nothing erupted from the box to shatter its opener or anyone else. No stasis field appeared to freeze the Kzin in time for the next billion years. For all the reaction its opening produced, the box might as well have been made of plastic in the *Enterprise*'s nonorganic fabrication section.

As soon as it was evident that nothing dangerous was going to happen, Chuft-Captain shouldered his crew out of the way in his eagerness to peer into the box. He reached the table, looked into the box ... and stood, staring quietly.

Sulu, Spock, and Uhura all watched closely—the two humans with apprehension, Spock with an intense curiosity.

Chuft-Captain reached into the box and withdrew an object. It was small and pulsed with an inner light of its own. Sulu stared at the form, which was vaguely reptilian in outline and somehow conveyed the impression of considerable size. He blinked. The "size" was a mental suggestion, built into the shape. The glowing object was as small as ever.

A certain amount of awe came into Sulu's voice. "Could that be a solid simuhologram of a Slaver?"

"If so," Spock whispered back to him without taking his eyes off the object as Chuft-Captain set it on the table, "it is the first representation of a Slaver ever discovered. An important historical find."

Again Chuft-Captain reached into the stasis box. This time he drew out a small square of what was unmistakably raw meat. It was wrapped in a peculiar, nonplastic transparent substance. Chuft-Captain examined it, turning it over in his fingers, and spoke to several other Kzinti. They appeared to agree with him as to its identification.

"It looks like fresh meat," Uhura murmured wonderingly. "Over a billion years in that box, and it looks *fresh*. I wonder what it's doing in there."

"It may have been left inside accidentally," theorized Spock. "Or perhaps whoever placed it inside intended to come back shortly and reopen the box, and left itself a fresh snack."

Uhura glanced sharply—as sharply as she could, restrained as she was by the police web—at the *Enterprise*'s first officer, but there was no hint of humor in his expression and had been none in his words.

Chuft-Captain set the little cube of meat down next to the solid simuhologram, which might or might not be a portrait of a Slaver. Sulu thought he put the meat aside a little reluctantly. He could understand that the possibility of tasting billion-year-old meat was very tempting to a carnivore. But Chuft-Captain was not so foolish as to consume an alien substance without ample pretesting. That was a pity. If they were lucky, it might have poisoned him.

Across the room, the telepath frowned again.

Anyway, more important revelations were at hand. Suddenly Chuft-Captain bore a look of great excitement. This time his hands fairly swooped down into the box. They emerged like a hawk with a kill in its claws.

What the Kzin commander withdrew resembled nothing organic, however. It consisted of a silver-surfaced bubble some seventeen centimeters in diameter. Attached to it was a heavy pistol grip. In form it was awkwardly made, and though not designed for human or Kzinti hands, it was unmistakable as to purpose and function.

A slot ran down one side of the hand—or claw, or tentacle, or who knew what—grip. Sulu could make out six settings notched along the slot. Beside each setting were markings in an unfamiliar script. A small toggle ran the length of the slot. At present it was at the slot's topmost setting.

Wordlessly, an enthused Chuft-Captain turned the device over and over in his hands. Anticipation spread rapidly among the other Kzinti as they realized what Chuft-Captain might be holding. They growled and snarled with animation, acting like a bunch of schoolchildren at vacation time, sounding like a section of a Federation zoo.

It was a deceptive demonstration. Their unrestrained enthusiasm masked their natural viciousness. Chuft-Captain turned, using the object to threaten the prisoners.

"Nothing like this has ever been found before in a stasis box. It can only be a weapon. It *must* be a weapon. A Slaver weapon! And we of Kzin are the only ones who have it. Look close at it, human!" He walked up to the police web, shook the device almost under Sulu's nose. "This may mean the end of your flatulent Federation of pacifists and root-eaters!" He turned, walked back to display the device to the rest of the curious group.

"Is he right, Mr. Spock? Could he possibly be right?" Sulu's voice had fallen to a worried whisper.

"I fear it is very possible, Lieutenant," the first officer replied. Then he added a note of caution. "However, I do not as yet see any solid reason to share Chuft-Captain's assurance. Certainly the device *looks* like a weapon. Yet we know so little of Slaver physiology and technology. It may not be a weapon but something else entirely.

"I find little comfort in that, however," he added. "Given the design of the device, even allowing for alien vagaries of technology I must—" He slipped sideways a little, then righted himself.

Sulu and Uhura moved, half stumbling, before recovering their balance. They found they could now move from the waist up. Their arms moved slowly, as long-frozen muscles struggled to obey mental orders.

"They have relaxed the police web," Spock noted aloud. "Preparatory to doing something unpleasant with us, no doubt. Switch on your translators."

The three officers, their hands now free, activated the tiny devices at their waists. Now they could understand the Kzinti without having to rely on the obsidian-edged English of Chuft-Captain.

The Kzin commander was still speaking to several members of his crew. "Have the humans moved to the surface. Be sure they are secured there in the police web. We will utilize them to test the weapon."

"Yes, Chuft-Captain." That response from one of the other Kzinti, another subofficer. He executed an odd sort of salute, then departed. Probably, Sulu thought, to locate a suitable place above for the . . . demonstration.

Several other Kzinti prepared to leave with Chuft-Captain. That worthy paused. For the first time since Sulu had regained consciousness, he saw Chuft-Captain talking to the forgotten member of the crew. Scratching at the scraggly, drooping whiskers on his face, the Kzin telepath gazed up at his commander sadly.

"You have had time to observe the aliens," Chuft-Captain said to him. "Can you read their minds?"

The telepath's voice matched his pitiable appearance. It had none of the power or strength of his brother Kzinti. Its most distinguishing characteristic was a distinct whine.

"I can read the one called Sulu with difficulty, Chuft-Captain. The other human is only a female. Consequently I have not wasted my efforts on her." Chuft-Captain made a grunting sound to indicate he understood. "The third is a pacifistic herbivore." The whine was augmented by pleading. "Surely you would not force me to delve into such a brain!"

"If it is necessary," was the Kzin commander's brutal reply. "I do realize that you need time to recover from each effort at probing." That was as far as Chuft-Captain could go toward expressing concern for a fellow creature. The telepath did not seem very grateful for it.

"Prepare to move them to the surface." At this order from Chuft-Captain, the remaining Kzinti spread out and drew phasers. One Kzin moved to a nearby wall panel and touched a control. The remainder of the police web deactivated.

Several moments passed while the prisoners were permitted to exercise their cramped leg muscles. Under Chuft-Captain's direction they were surrounded by the armed Kzinti and marched back out the way they had entered. Other Kzinti rolled up the police web and carried it behind, along with a portable power unit and set of remote controls.

There was a wait at the lock while the Kzinti donned their suit armor and the prisoners were permitted to reactivate their life-support belts. Then in small groups they passed via the lock to the icy ground outside.

Once more Spock studied the terrain, only now it was with different thoughts than the ones which had run through his mind when they had first arrived on this world of Beta Lyrae. Pressure ridging and earth movements had broken and buckled the ice plain. If they had an opportunity to break free of their captors, they had ample cover to run to.

After setting up the police web, most of the Kzinti returned to the ship. That left only Chuft-Captain, Telepath, and two others. Apparently the Kzinti felt confident of their ability to control their prisoners. And why shouldn't they? There was really only the human Sulu to watch. The root-eater and the female animal could be ignored.

Chuft-Captain responded to a buzz in his helmet. "Yes?"

A raspy voice sounded over the suit intercom from inside the *Traitor's Claw*. "Chuft-Captain, chemistry has finished analyzing the meat that was in the stasis box. The wrapping is composed of an unknown polymer of metal-ceramic. The meat itself is fully protoplasmic and is poisonous to Kzinkind."

That last was disappointing. Chuft-Captain glanced down at the hoped-for Slaver weapon, inspected the silvery bubble shape thoughtfully. "What of the simulacrum?"

The response came this time not from the ship but from one of the suited figures standing next to the commander. "The human Sulu," the telepath said, "believes it to be a three-dimensional representation of an actual Slaver."

Sulu was startled. He had almost forgotten the presence of the telepath. It was the first time the ragged-looking Kzin had actually given proof that it could read their thoughts. The helmsman found it gave him an uncomfortable, dirty feeling, as if someone was rummaging with impunity through his private possessions. All he could do was glare menacingly at the telepath.

"I agree with the human's assessment." Chuft-Captain was recalling the shape of the simuhologram, the impression of size and strength that radiated from it. "It would have made a worthy foe. Secure the prisoners."

Helplessly Sulu, Uhura, and Spock watched as the police web was unrolled, charged, and activated. The test completed, the web was turned off until the three captives were standing on it. Then it was switched on again and all three officers found themselves immobilized once more.

Meanwhile, Chuft-Captain had walked to a nearby rise of ice and rock. He raised the silvery device. It took him several clumsy tries to pull the trigger, since the grip wasn't designed to fit his hand.

Nothing happened.

"Perhaps the small toggle," one of the watching Kzinti suggested.

Chuft-Captain nodded brusquely, moved the toggle in the handle slot down toward the first notch and its untranslatable hieroglyphs. The toggle slid easily and freely, slipped into place as though just lubricated. But as soon as the toggle slipped home, the device started to twist in his hand as if it were something alive. Chuft-Captain made a startled sound halfway between a hiss and a snarl. The other Kzinti and the three captives were equally surprised.

To his credit, Chuft-Captain did not drop the device. The distorting writhing soon stopped. The silvery sphere had vanished. In its place, attached to the same unchanged hand grip, was a small parabolic mirror with a silvery knob located at its focal point. A series of markings with little toggle switches of their own ran across the back of the mirror's surface.

After a brief examination of the device's unexpected new configuration, Chuft-Captain aimed it at the horizon and pulled the trigger set in the hand grip. Again nothing happened. He lowered his aim until he was pointing the mirror at the ground in front of him and held the trigger down. There was no hint of radiation or any sign that the device was doing anything at all.

Snarling in frustration, the Kzinti commander raised the device until the mirror was centered directly on Sulu. Uhura made a shocked sound. Spock didn't say a word.

The helmsman stood quietly, assumed a resigned, outwardly unaffected expression. Chuft-Captain held the trigger down again. There was still no indication that the device was performing any kind of function. Perhaps, Chuft-Captain thought, the device was acting in some fashion not readily visible.

"Telepath," he asked, still holding the trigger down and centering it on Sulu, "am I not affecting him at all? Is the life-support belt interfering?"

Concentrating hysterically, Telepath looked more

than normally miserable. Uhura almost managed to feel sympathy for the poor creature. He had not wished his talent on himself.

"No, Chuft-Captain," Telepath reported, a bit too loudly, a touch too fast. "He hears a faint whine but feels no ill effect. There is a vibration in the material of his metal accoutrements but—"

Telepath winced suddenly as if struck by a solid blow, and reeled backward several steps. When he recovered, he stared wild-eyed and pleadingly at his commander. "Chuft-Captain, he is too alien. He makes me taste yellow root munched between flat teeth. I am made sick, Chuft-Captain. Please!"

"You may stop—for now," the Kzin commander informed him. Grateful beyond words, the telepath turned away and was ill inside his suit. "Be glad you need not read the Vulcan's mind."

Looking closely at the parabolic mirror and the settings on its obverse, Chuft-Captain rumbled musingly to himself and his subordinates, "It may be a communications device of some kind. Or perhaps the vibrations it produces are designed to adversely affect members of a race now extinct. Another setting, perhaps."

With a thick furry finger he shifted the hand grip toggle down to the next setting. This time he didn't jump as the device blurred and curled like a ghost python in his hand. The parabolic mirror metamorphosed into a backward-facing screen arrangement with a small lens facing forward. Several knobs were set around the entire assemblage.

Again Chuft-Captain pointed the front of the device at Sulu and pressed the trigger. Again the helmsman displayed no reaction. But the device did. The screen lit softly to show Sulu standing on the police web.

Chuft-Captain experimented with the knobs on the back of the screen and below it. One touch brought a good, sharp-edged closeup of the stiff-legged human into view. Raising his arm, Chuft-Captain produced a magnified view of the sky above. He lowered the device, stared at it admiringly.

"A good, versatile, portable telescope. They built very well, these Slavers."

"Yet it is of no importance to us," one of the onlooking Kzin crewmen pointed out. "We already have several types of good small telescopes."

Chuft-Captain made a curt gesture of agreement, touched the toggle control once more. Again the device convulsed. When the Kzin commander saw the third configuration, he permitted himself a slight, toothy smile. This one looked much more promising. Set into the handle and trigger grip was a long metallic tube. Several moldings and protrusions blistered the sides of the tube, which ended in a small, thick lens.

Following his previous pattern, Chuft-Captain aimed the end of the tube at Sulu. At the last moment he shifted it slightly to one side before pulling the trigger.

A dense red beam of coherent light emerged from the lens. It contacted the ground just to the right of Sulu's feet and the police web. Ice fragments exploded into the thin air and steam boiled upward where the beam struck. Chuft-Captain released the trigger and the beam disappeared. A modest, still-steaming hole showed in the ice where it had struck.

Sulu had not flinched, despite the proximity of the small explosion. Chuft-Captain fired again, the beam moving closer but still avoiding both the helmsman's boots and the police web. Again Sulu didn't move.

The Kzin commander was moved to admit grudgingly, "I give you credit, human. You are not afraid to die."

"I'm never afraid of the familiar," Sulu replied calmly, nodding at the Slaver device. "That's simply a laser, and not much of one at that. The Federation has had more effective weapons for over a hundred years."

Chuft-Captain permitted himself to look annoyed. Rather angrily he adjusted the toggle to a new setting. Once more the device contorted, as solid in its change as a dream before awakening.

It solidified into a short cylinder. A flared aperture of fair size appeared at its far end. Two flat metal projections extended well downward from the near end of the cylinder. They resembled stirrups so closely that

Uhura couldn't repress a start of recognition. If the downward-pointed surfaces had been attached to a small saddle, the device would have closely resembled the ostrich saddles she had used as a child.

Chuft-Captain found the device's latest manifestation far less intriguing—or familiar. He bemoaned the lack of a gunsight or anything resembling one while realizing that nothing so lethal had adorned any of the device's previous forms. Nothing for it but to try this new setting and get on with the next.

He pulled the trigger.

Instantly he was shooting backward across the ice in a seated, undoubtedly uncomfortable position. Traveling at a respectable velocity he had to exert all his strength simply to hold on to the device.

The other three Kzinti scrambled to clear a path for the errant Chuft-Captain. One bit of flame from the gushing Slaver whatever-it-had-become washed across the slower-moving telepath. He screamed in pain. Completely out of control, Chuft-Captain shot across the police web, straight at the three imprisoned officers. His force was more than adequate to carry him through the comparatively mild restraint field the web generated.

Unable to dodge, Uhura was struck on her side. The impact was sufficient to overcome the withholding force field. It knocked her off the web. Clear of the web, she rolled over, scrambled to her feet, and sprinted for the nearby *Copernicus*.

Meanwhile, one of the two remaining Kzinti noticed the injured telepath. The scorching exhaust of the Slaver device had ruptured the smaller Kzinti's suit. Scooping up the lighter telepath, the Kzin turned and raced frantically for the lighted tunnel leading to the buried ship. Telepath was howling over his suit mike, trailing a fog of freezing atmosphere behind him.

"Telepath's suit has been cut," the remaining Kzin called out to Chuft-Captain.

"Never mind that!" The Kzin commander lay just past the police web. Having finally succeeded in shutting off the runaway device, he was climbing slowly and painfully to his feet. He gestured toward the Federation shuttlecraft. "The female is escaping, fool!"

Puzzled, the remaining Kzin's gaze traveled to the sprinting communications officer. "What of it?"

"Idiot!" Chuft-Captain was trying to find his own phaser. "Human females are intelligent!"

The remaining Kzin fought to assess this piece of incredible information. Though he knew it to be true, it was no less difficult for him to cope with. But he was a Kzin warrior. Time enough to muse later. Act *now*.

Drawing his phaser, he aimed it carefully. Uhura had almost reached the shuttlecraft when the stun burst caught her neatly in the small of the back. Her body arced spasmodically; she took another couple of steps and slumped to the ground.

Replacing the phaser at his waist, the Kzin trudged off to pick up Uhura's recumbent form. Meanwhile the Kzin who had thoughtfully carried the injured telepath into the ship was returning, moving at a fast jog.

"What report, Flyer?" asked Chuft-Captain, showing more concern for the neurotic mind reader in the latter's absence than he had previously.

The Kzin called Flyer responded worriedly. "His suit lost considerable pressure before I could get him into the ship, Chuft-Captain. But he will live."

"Good. We will need him later." Chuft-Captain proffered the new configuration of the Slaver device, handling it gingerly. Flyer examined the complex arrangement of struts and tubes.

"Doubtless a personal rocket motor, some form of one-being transportation device. One could place one's feet on the pedal shapes, there, and balance carefully. With practice, one could obtain great individual mobility."

"In any case, it is certainly not a weapon," concluded Chuft-Captain.

The two argued over the precise function of the new setting as the other Kzin returned with Uhura. They broke off their discussion long enough to guard Spock and Sulu while the other warrior placed the still-unconscious communications officer on the police web. He retreated quickly and the web field was restored. Uhura slumped slightly before the field caught her, held her upright.

"Uhura!" Sulu called as best he could with his head pinned. He turned slowly to look at her. "Lieutenant Uhura!" Her eyelids fluttered, finally opened. She stared across at him, recognition that she had failed dawning rapidly.

"Nice try," Sulu attempted to reassure her.

It did not. "I'm slowing down." She sounded bitter. "I used to run the hundred in record time. How long have I been out? Did I miss anything?"

"Not much," Sulu told her. Unexpectedly, he chuckled. "A lot of good they'll get out of that propulsion setting. I wonder how much fur Chuft-Captain lost off his backside, suit armor or no suit armor!"

"We have been fortunate," Spock said more somberly, "that none of the settings thus far employed have revealed anything superior to known Federation technology."

"Thus far. Look." Uhura tried to point, but found that she couldn't, of course. Her arm was once more held tightly motionless by the police web. Sulu and Spock turned to watch the Kzinti again. It appeared that Chuft-Captain had moved the toggle control, because the Slaver device was writhing in his hands for a fifth time.

The new shape was a total surprise. Not only didn't it resemble a weapon, or something familiar like the parabolic mirror or the laser tube, it didn't resemble anything at all. Spock had to blink to assure himself the device had indeed finished changing, because it looked as if it had frozen in the middle of its new transformation, neither complete nor incomplete but some non-Euclidian nebulosity in between.

The shape should not have been. As he watched, it seemed to alter regularly without moving, to twist and curl in and about itself in a bizarre, topologically impossible fashion. And yet, it possessed the appearance of a solid shape.

"No gun sight," Chuft-Captain murmured softly, revealing a fixation on a single thought. "No evident way to aim it. Still, it must do something." Lifting the device, he pulled the trigger.

Both subordinate Kzinti were staring fixedly at the clump of ice-covered rock Chuft-Captain was aiming at. So none of the three warriors noticed that as soon as their commander pulled the trigger, the yellow glow from the tunnel behind them winked out like a drowned candle.

Uhura nearly fell, then caught herself and stayed motionless. "Mr. Spock, I can move."

"So can I," an excited Sulu whispered, experimentally edging one foot back and forth. "The police web is off."

Spock flexed the fingers of his left hand just enough to make certain he too was no longer trapped. "The fifth setting seems to be some sort of energy absorber. Fascinating. We've had no indication the Slavers possessed anything along such lines."

"Mr. Spock, shouldn't we—?"

Spock cut the helmsman off. "Yes, but in concert. When I give the word, run for the shuttle. Remember to present as irregular a target as possible. You traveled in a straight line, Lieutenant Uhura, and while you cannot outrun a phaser burst there is a chance to avoid one."

"Don't worry," Uhura assured him grimly. She had no intention of being stopped so easily again.

"Ready?" warned Spock. "*Go!*"

Adrenaline substituted for starting blocks as Sulu and Uhura fairly exploded toward the shuttle, twisting, dodging, zigzagging across an imaginary obstacle course. Tired from her previous sprint and still suffering lingering aftereffects of the recent phaser burst she had taken, Uhura fell behind.

Spock wasn't even close. He had chosen a different path toward the shuttle, one involving a slight but critical detour. Before the startled Kzinti could react, the first officer was racing toward them.

By the time their attention shifted from the nonexistent destructive effects of the Slaver device's fifth setting, Spock was on top of Chuft-Captain. The Kzin commander turned a second too late to defend himself.

Spock wasn't fooling with anything as subtle as a Vulcan nerve-pinch. Both legs came up as Spock leaped. His full weight was behind them, multiplied by his velocity, as he slammed both feet into the Kzin commander, high up on the feline's rib cage.

Chuft-Captain doubled over as he began falling backward, let out a loud moan, and dropped the device. Landing on one hand and both feet, Spock grabbed the Slaver artifact before it could bounce twice, and was off and racing for the shuttle.

Sulu looked behind him. Three Kzinti were now firing their phasers, one aiming at Spock, the other two at the more distant humans. A rise of broken rock and ice loomed nearby, just to the helmsman's left. Seeing that he wouldn't be able to make the shuttle, he swerved sideways and took shelter behind the hillock.

Uhura tried to follow him but she was too far behind. A burst from one of the phasers caught her again. She stumbled toward the ground, her last conscious thoughts filled with anger more than disappointment.

Clutching the Slaver device tightly in one hand, Spock continued his erratic, weaving course across the icy surface. Phaser beams repeatedly struck the ground where he had been heading only seconds before. But the first officer was still running hard and fast, and the Kzinti were unable to guess which way he would head next.

Deciding that the Vulcan was too far out of range, Flyer moved to aid Chuft-Captain. The commander was still lying on the ice, doubled-up and clutching at his side.

"Chuft-Captain, what happened?"

"I would rather not discuss it," came the sharp but pain-ridden reply. "Help me into the ship."

Flyer helped his commander to his feet. Chuft-Captain winced, nearly fell as he straightened. Flyer said nothing. It was unthinkable to show sympathy.

They started toward the tunnel leading to their ship. As they walked, it became clear to Flyer that Chuft-Captain had been badly hurt, for he couldn't have walked without help. As the airlock cycled around their suits and Chuft-Captain's painful wheezing sounded in his suit helmet, Flyer was still trying to visualize the unthinkable.

IX

It had been quiet on the bridge for long moments. The emergency lighting remained on, bathing instruments and the four wait-officers in its eerie, subdued glow. Communications with the rest of the ship remained dead, as did computer control. The *Enterprise* was still on course toward Starbase 25, but she was flying blind.

Kirk idly regarded the stun setting on his phaser, resting ominously at his waist. He hefted the tranquilizer pistol firmly. Their phasers would remain set on stun. Lieutenant M'ress and the other captured Caitians were as much a part of his crew, as much personal friends, as anyone else he worked with.

But . . . the ship had to come first. It seemed impossible that the four of them, alerted and expectant, would be unable to overcome a single slim Caitian female. However, everything else that had happened so far had seemed impossible also. With their communications and computer controls out, he couldn't even switch control of the ship to the secondary bridge.

The phaser controls seemed to grow larger in his eyes, the extreme end of the setting beckoning to him hypnotically. But before he would change that, he'd try any alternative. "Lieutenant Talliflores, Lieutenant Arex, if you two would like to try Talliflores's plan, keeping your phasers set on stun and without utilizing the tranquilizer pistol, you have my permission."

"I'd rather have the tranquilizers, sir," responded a doubtful communications officer.

Kirk shook his head emphatically. "Absolutely not."

"We'll try anyway, sir."

"Good luck." Kirk turned to the science station. "Mr. Vedama, if this fails, and Mr. Talliflores and Mr.

Arex fail to return . . . set your phaser to kill." He had trouble finishing the sentence.

"Yes, sir," his science officer said solemnly.

Talliflores palmed his phaser, then left the useless communications console to stand next to a ready Arex. "Since we have no idea where she is, sir, we'll try the hatch closest to the accessway leading to the deck below us."

Moving as quietly as possible, Talliflores and the Edoan navigator edged over the service hatch. Kirk kept the tranquilizer gun trained on the hatch as Arex set about undoing the catches. The resultant opening would be large enough for a good-sized human to fit through. The tripedal Arex would find it a tighter squeeze, but Kirk estimated his navigator should also be able to squeeze through into the serviceway beyond.

"Lieutenant Talliflores," he called abruptly, as the two officers were preparing to release the last catch.

"Sir?" Talliflores was lying flat on the deck, working at the hatch cover.

"You'll move to cut through the sealed doorway to the lower decks, if it is sealed. If not, you'll go for help. Lieutenant Arex will cover you."

"But sir, I'd hoped to . . ." Talliflores began.

Kirk cut him off firmly. "Sorry, Lieutenant. Mr. Arex has already tangled with one of the Caitians and come off considerably better than anyone else." He suppressed a smile. "Mr. Arex has the advantage of being half again as dextrous as a human."

"Very well, sir," Talliflores reluctantly replied.

The last catch was released. Carefully the two officers removed the hatch plate. When neither phaser bolt nor squalling Caitian emerged from the opening, Talliflores leaned forward and peered into the dim crawlway beyond. He glanced once back at Kirk, who nodded—there could be no talk on the bridge now, not with the hatch opened. Talliflores crawled through, vanished into the darkness. After a last glance back at Kirk, Arex followed.

It was as silent as a Klingon consulate on Federation Day. Suddenly someone, probably Talliflores, shouted. Muffled yelling and sounds of a struggle followed.

Vedama took a step toward the hatchway. Kirk ordered him back to the science console.

If Arex and Talliflores couldn't overpower or outmaneuver M'ress in the cramped serviceway, sending in the diminutive Vedama would only result in the loss of another officer. Nor could he enter the fray himself and risk losing the tranquilizer pistol, their only proven means of stopping a berserk Caitian.

The hidden battle continued more quietly. Only an occasional curse, grunt, or peculiar low-pitched feminine yowl punctuated the quiet. Once, Kirk thought he heard Talliflores cry out, but he couldn't be sure it wasn't M'ress.

Then it was silent on the bridge again.

Hesitantly, hopefully, Kirk called out. "Mr. Talliflores, Mr. Arex?"

No response.

Sadly, Kirk turned to face Vedama, gestured significantly at the officer's waist. Vedama drew his phaser, made the agonizingly painful adjustment of the setting ... and sat back to wait.

"Let me take the first shot, Mr. Vedama," Kirk instructed him. "If I miss . . ." He didn't have to finish the directive, and had no desire to.

"Lieutenant M'ress?" He directed his voice to the square black eye of the hatchway. Again, no response. "Lieutenant M'ress, this is the captain. I don't know what you think you're doing, Lieutenant, but whatever you have in mind can't be allowed. Your two companions, M'viore and R'leez, have already been captured and can't help you. You haven't got a chance, Lieutenant."

The black orifice stared back at him mockingly.

He tried a different approach. "Listen, M'ress, I know you're not doing this of your own free will. You've got to realize that yourself. Whatever's compelling you to act this way, I understand. I'm not holding you and the others responsible for your actions. But this has to stop, *now*. You've got to fight whatever's gripping you, M'ress! You've got to break this madness before ... we have to stop you."

"I ..."

It was a faint, barely audible sound, and for a second Kirk felt he had imagined it. But a quick glance showed that Vedama had heard, too. It was more a cry than a challenge, and sounded as if it had been forced out against terrific odds.

"What is it, M'ress?" Kirk called eagerly. "I'm listening. Talk to me, talk and fight it."

"I'm angrrry . . . confused. I . . ." and she mumbled something in broken Caitian which Kirk didn't understand. The Caitian had been mixed with English.

". . . can't . . . stop . . . myself," she moaned, as if fighting with her own voice. "Must . . ."

"Must what, M'ress?" Kirk had to keep her talking. "Tell me what you need and maybe something can be worked out."

"Must . . . go home. Go to Cait."

"Your homeworld? But why?" Kirk had felt sure that when the Caitian's purpose had been revealed, it would clear up the rationale for their bizarre behavior. He was wrong. The knowledge only added one more confusing aspect to the whole incident.

"Can't . . . Must go to Cait-rrrr—" Her voice changed, overtones of anger replacing the desperate striving for understanding. "Must go to Cait *now*, *fast*. Give me contrrol of the ship, Captain. Orr . . . change courrse forr Cait."

Kirk threw Vedama a querulous look, saw that the science officer was equally bemused at the imperious request. "M'ress, we can't possibly go to Cait now. Have you forgotten the Briamos conference? We have to be there on time, to represent the Federation, or the Briamosites will probably align themselves with Klingon. You don't want that to happen, do you, Lieutenant? I know you're not a traitor."

"Must . . . go now to Cait!" It came out a half-order, half-sob. Conflicting desires were tearing M'ress apart.

"You're not being sensible, M'ress," Kirk countered, aware that none of the Caitians had been acting sensibly recently. "It's impossible and you know it. We can't miss the conference. Listen, give yourself up peaceably, right now, and after the conference I give you my word we'll go directly to Cait. You don't even have to give me a reason."

"Captain," Vedama began, "other Starfleet orders—"

"Lieutenant, I have the authority to overrule any subsequent Fleet orders in order to respond to any emergency threatening my ship—barring a Federation-wide danger." He turned back to the open hatchway.

"Did you hear that, Lieutenant?" he asked, raising his voice slightly. "I have the authority to order the *Enterprise* to Cait immediately following the conference's conclusion. I'll put it in the official log, if you want." No response. "Are you willing to bargain, M'ress? Will that satisfy you?"

"Can't . . . help," came the threatening yet pitiable response from somewhere beyond the hatch. "If you will . . . not orrderr us to Cait now, give . . . contrrol to me. Orr . . . I will . . . I *must* . . . take overr yourr brridge."

"You can't do it, M'ress." Kirk sounded more positive than he felt. "I know that you're partially immune, somehow, to phasers set for stun. Lieutenant Vedama's phaser is set to kill. He won't shoot except as a last resort. I'm holding a tranquilizer pistol, M'ress. Dr. McCoy prepared a serum keyed to the Caitian metabolism. That's how we knocked out M'viore and R'leez. The serum will do that to you, too.

"You can't possibly overwhelm two of us from the serviceway and take over the bridge before a security detail finally gets here. They're probably on their way right now, running the turbolift on bypass controls and power, or coming up through the serviceway access below us. They won't have my orders to restrain them, M'ress," he said desperately. "They won't have their phasers set for stun, or wait for me to fire first. Don't you see? You can't possibly win. There's no way you can take over the bridge."

"Tell . . . that to . . . Arrex and . . . Talliflorres," came the half-taunting, half-sorrowful reply.

"Captain?"

"Just a minute, Mr. Vedama. Lieutenant M'ress, let me think about your demand. Give me just a minute."

"Don't want to . . . hurrt anyone," M'ress insisted, sounding as if she meant it. "But *must* go to . . . Cait . . . *now!*"

"What is it, Vedama?" Kirk whispered.

"I've bypassed normal communications and computer network, sir," he murmured tightly. "We have intership communications again. Several sections are calling steadily, trying to contact us. Several sound frantic."

"That's not surprising. If we can just stall her a little longer . . . Give me Security."

"Try your chair pickup, sir."

Kirk directed his voice toward the command chair pickup, his gaze never leaving the gaping hatchway. "Security, this is the bridge."

"Yeoman Dickerson here, Captain. It's good to hear from you. What's going on up there?"

"Lieutenant Talliflores and Lieutenant Arex have been stunned. Mr. Vedama and I are holding off Lieutenant M'ress. She's in the serviceway encircling the bridge. You must try to break through the serviceway door or come up the turbolift. She's cut all bridge power. Under no condition, except as a last resort to preserve the integrity of the ship, is anyone to use a phaser set higher than stun. Is that understood?"

"Yes, sir, but—"

"Is that understood, mister?"

"Yes, sir." The voice sounded disappointed, but the acknowledgment sent a wave of relief over Kirk.

"Then get moving, Yeoman. Bridge out." He glanced quickly back at Vedama. "Who else is calling, Lieutenant?"

"Sick Bay has priority, sir."

"Put them through."

A pause, then an anxious familiar voice sounded over the chair speaker. "Jim, are you all right? Jim?"

"I'm okay, Bones. So far. M'ress has us pinned down here, but I think we have her trapped as well. What's been happening at your end?"

"Jim, we've been doing frantic research on Caitian disorders. That's been part of the problem."

Kirk frowned. "I don't think I understand, Bones."

"We've been looking for a disease, a physical malady, something rare and unusual. It took a while for me to realize that while the Caitians' behavior might be extreme, it might have a perfectly normal cause."

"That sounds contradictory, Bones."

"Jim, I think I know what's causing them to act the way they have. Has it occurred to you that all the seriously injured personnel—security and otherwise—have been men? Or rather, male? And that the women who were part of the eight-person security team that was assaulted were incapacitated but not harmed? Listen to this, Jim."

There came a pause, and then a horrible screeching and yowling sounded over the speaker. It was a frantic, uncontrolled din, and yet somehow it seemed sorrowful rather than ferocious.

"Bones, what the—?"

"That's M'viore and R'leez, Jim," came McCoy's reply. They're both conscious again. I've got them both strapped down so they won't hurt themselves—or anyone else. Needed extra straps to keep them from breaking free. Jim, the level of Caitian-equivalent adrenaline in their blood is unbelievable! But what's most important is their Caitrogen hormone level. Absolutely crazy. Sent my diagnostic indicators right off the graphs.

"I've given them the moderating dosage necessary to bring their hormone levels back to normal . . . the dosage they should have received normally. They should both be sensible in a couple of hours."

"Dosage they should have received?" Kirk thought he saw motion at the hatchway, but decided he was imagining things. The tension had grown worse with the passing minutes. "What are you talking about, Bones?"

"When we couldn't find anything physically wrong with them, I tried to imagine what could induce a Caitian to go insane like they did. Caitians usually control their emotions fairly well. I thought about drugs, the presence of certain stimulants in their food, maybe even accidental self-hypnotism. But the chemists couldn't find anything foreign in their recent menus.

"That's when it occurred to me that maybe they weren't ingesting something they regularly took, instead of having eaten something they shouldn't have. The chemists were put off because their blood tested normal, except for the excessive hormone level. I tied that in with the suddenly realized fact that all the badly injured security personnel had been male, Jim. Couple that with the fact that our three Caitians all happen to be female—"

A definite shadow appeared at the hatchway. Kirk fired reflexively. The syringe-dart struck metal somewhere beyond the blackness and the shadow vanished.

"Neither of the ensigns is coherent enough to give me any help, but their behavior fits what I discovered in the limited Caitian biology references in the medical records. They take biannual doses of a drug called pheraligen, which moderates their body's production of Caitrogen. And that in turn suppresses the otherwise extreme reactions Caitian females used to have at this time of the year."

"This time of year . . ." Kirk finally had the answer to the mystery.

"Apparently," McCoy continued, "the pheraligen is programmed into their diets in innocuous-tasting supplements, Jim. They're so used to receiving it without having to think about it, they didn't realize what was happening to them. Since the regimen is in no way a treatment for a disorder, I didn't know about it. Programming it becomes the responsibility of the science life-support section, not medical."

Vedama had turned pale. "My department, Captain, my department. But I've never had to—"

"And Spock isn't here to check on it. Probably the facts are resting right in his daily work-log: *Caitian female personnel, semiannual pheraligen dose due.* So that's why they've been acting the way they have."

"Right, Jim. All it takes is a standard dose of pheraligen to counter the excessive hormone production and they'll return to normal."

"That's all very well and good for M'viore and

R'leez, Bones, but what am I going to do with M'ress?"

A phaser bolt erupted from the upper right-hand corner of the hatch opening. Aimed with difficulty, it struck several centimeters from Kirk's right foot. Nerves tingling from the nearness of the beam, he abandoned the command chair and limped around behind it. Vedama crouched lower but didn't abandon the science console.

"Bones, M'ress isn't sensible enough to understand what you've been saying, though I think she's trying to. She can't control herself, and I think maybe desperation's making her frustrated enough to kill. She wants to take over the bridge and change course for Cait."

"Not surprising, Jim," came McCoy's voice over the open bridge speakers. "She's only reacting the way primitive Caitian physiology's instructing her to, and there are no Caitian males on board. If there were, none of this trouble would have happened. That's why our security personnel were attacked, and then not killed. Even with their hormone level driving them insensible, they still retained enough knowledge of who they were to stop before committing murder. The injuries to our security teams were inflicted out of frustration, not malice. You've got to get one of those tranquilizer darts in her."

A second phaser burst poured from the hatchway. This time Kirk couldn't be sure the beam was still set to stun.

"She's becoming hysterical, Bones!" Kirk tried to spot the elusive lieutenant, saw only black in the hatchway opening. "She doesn't dare use too powerful a setting, though. If she damages the controls, she won't be able to try turning us toward Cait."

"Captain, if you've no objection . . ."

"What's that? Who's speaking? Scotty, is that you?"

"Aye, Captain. I've got an idea I've been working on since Dr. McCoy found out what was wrong with the two ensigns. With your permission, I'd like to give it a try. I know this business isn't my department, but—"

Kirk ducked as a phaser beam scored the top of the

command chair. "Anything nonlethal, you've got my permission, Scotty. Go ahead with it."

Kirk didn't know how long they could continue to stall M'ress. In between useless exchanges of phaser fire he conjured up every argument he could think of. None of them would have done any good, save for the fact that M'ress retained just enough sanity and sense to respond to them. So she listened and reacted, even if her comments were not particularly sensible.

Of course, Kirk knew he might be deluding himself in thinking that he was keeping her mind busy. She might be waiting for him to grow so involved in his chatter that he would drop his guard and allow her a reasonable charge at the command chair. Eventually, he knew, she would have to come to the inevitable decision that he wasn't going to voluntarily relinquish control of the ship, and that her time was running out.

That moment came sooner than she expected or Kirk had hoped.

A hissing noise reached the bridge. It came from somewhere beyond the open hatchway.

"Captain," M'ress yowled, "call . . . them off. Tell them to . . . stop trrying to cut . . . in."

"I can't," he lied. "They're operating independently of my orders, M'ress."

Her voice rose unsteadily. "I'll use my . . . phaserr on the firrst one who comes thrrough the opening!"

"Lieutenant, you haven't killed anyone yet! Fight what's controlling your mind. We know what your trouble is now!"

Not surprisingly, M'ress refused to listen.

There sounded a sharp *spang* of stressed metal giving way. Any second Kirk expected to hear the slight, deadly hum of M'ress's phaser as she made good her threat on whoever was coming through the opened serviceway.

Instead, he heard a strange yowling from the Caitian unlike anything heard thus far. It was followed by a distinct *phut*, then silence.

A figure started to emerge from the hatchway opening. Kirk raised the tranquilizer pistol, then hesitated.

So did Vedama. The figure that stepped into the dim light of the bridge would have caused them to fire instantly, except for the fact that it was carrying its head beneath one arm!

"Scotty! It worked."

"Aye, Captain." The *Enterprise*'s chief engineer looked relieved. He gestured back toward the hatchway. Sounds of moving feet came from behind it. "Dr. McCoy's inside now. And a whole crew of techs. If the damage M'ress caused isn't too serious, and I dinna think it could be, bridge functions should be"—the regular lights abruptly came back on and Kirk blinked at the bright, familiar illumination—"restored quickly." Scott permitted himself a slight smile of professional pride.

"What about Lieutenant M'ress?"

"Dr. McCoy says she'll be fine, Captain," Scott replied, "as soon as the pheraligen takes effect on her system and she's had a couple of hours' rest." Walking forward, he deposited an object in his right hand on the navigation-helm console. It was a twin to the dart-pistol Kirk still held.

As he approached, Kirk grew conscious of a peculiar, powerful odor emanating from the chief engineer. His nose twitched. Scott noticed it and grinned.

"Strong stuff, Captain. That smell's the only thing that made it work. Dr. McCoy synthesized the appropriate male Caitian pheromones to complement this costume." He indicated the furry, catlike suit he was wearing. I'm not so sure the costume alone would have let me get within shooting range, but the pheromones fooled her—or overpowered her. We only had to distract her for a couple of seconds, long enough for me to get a syringe into her." He gestured at the dart-pistol resting near the helm controls.

Kirk was putting his own weapon down. The crisis was all over, but the tenseness drained slowly from him. "What ever made you think of such a crazy idea, Scotty?"

The engineer looked embarrassed. "From a costume ball I went to, Captain, several years ago. I went dressed as a Fiorellian and a real female Fiorellian mistook me for a male of her species. To complicate matters, *she* was costumed as a human female. So it was doubly disconcertin'."

"I can imagine," agreed Kirk, slowly resuming his position in the command chair.

"Captain?"

Kirk looked over at the science station. "What is it, Mr. Vedama?" When he saw the lieutenant's position, he swiveled fully to face him, frowning. "What's wrong?"

Vedama was standing stiffly before his console, unsmiling. "I hereby present myself for arrest, sir."

"At ease, Lieutenant." Vedama relaxed, but only slightly. "It wasn't your fault. It wasn't anybody's fault, except maybe the Slavers'. They had the poor timing to present us with one of their stasis boxes at a time when Mr. Spock had to be two places at once. I'm sure that by tomorrow or the next day, in routinely checking over his schedule, you would have spotted the instructions to program the pheraligen into the Caitians' diet. It was bad luck and timing that their metabolism chose this particular time to shift into high gear.

"In fact, it's surprising you haven't overlooked more than one thing. You're doing your best, Lieutenant, and so far that's been quite satisfactory. Resume your post."

"Yes, sir." Vedama's salute was crisp.

Scott had slipped out of the suit. "Bloody hot, Captain. I don't understand how the Caitians can stand their own fur."

"They probably wonder, like all naturally furred creatures in the Federation, how we humans can run around almost naked, by their standards."

Kirk stood as several figures emerged from the hatchway. A limp form was passed to one tall medical technician. He handled the comatose M'ress easily. Her eyes were closed tight, arms and legs dangling like pale vines.

"Sick Bay immediately, Ensign," ordered a muffled voice from somewhere behind the hatchway.

"Yes, Doctor," acknowledged the tech, moving toward the turbolift doors.

Kirk was about to tell the ensign that the lift didn't work, when the doors slid aside obediently at the man's request and shut behind him. At the rate they were going, it wouldn't take Scotty's crew long to have the bridge functioning at full efficiency again.

"They'll all be all right, Bones?" he asked the figure emerging from the hatchway.

"I think so, Jim. Except for the mental inconvenience they might suffer for a while."

"How do you mean, Bones?"

McCoy walked over to retrieve first Scott's discarded tranquilizer pistol, then Kirk's. "Consider what they've done, Jim. They've tried to take over the ship. In the process they put a respectable number of their fellow crew members in Sick Bay with assorted scratches and other wounds. Generally they've behaved in a very immature as well as aggressive fashion.

"Of course, they had no control over their actions. Matter of fact, when they come around in a few hours I doubt that any of them, M'ress included, will remember much of what they did. The difficulties will come," he continued after a brief pause, "when their companions tell them what they've been up to.

"That will upset them enough, but it's the reason behind their actions which will trouble them the most. M'ress will stand it better than M'viore and R'leez because she's an officer, but I don't doubt that the two ensigns will take a good deal of kidding about what happened. I think we're going to have to cope with three very embarrassed Caitians."

"But everyone will know," Kirk said, "that they weren't responsible for their actions, that they had no control over the way they were acting."

"Easy to say, Jim, but then *we're* not the ones who have to handle the fact that we lost all composure and intelligence and spent a day acting like, well, like animals."

Kirk turned to the blank viewscreen, thought hard. "I think the Caitians will handle any joking competently, Bones. After all, they can always use the argument that we humans act like animals all the time."

X

Sulu found himself running deeper and deeper into the jumbled landscape, dodging nervously around towering blades of ice, scrambling atop slick-surface boulders to whom the proximity of organic matter was a radical if nonperceived event.

The terrain grew steadily more grotesque in outline, the horizon increasingly tortured. One would have thought two rivers of ice had rushed headlong into one another here, jammed together like massive white wrestlers. Ice and stone pressed and piled over and atop each other to create a chalcedony desert flavored by Bosch. At least the chaotic topography favored Sulu's retreat. No phaser beam stabbed at him from behind. Let the Kzinti follow him if they could—he'd have them ambushing each other.

Sulu turned another ice block half the size of the shuttlecraft, only to see a figure rushing at him. Startled, he tried to back away. Then he recognized the familiar shape and began moving toward it.

"Mr. Spock!" Sulu let out an exhausted but relieved sigh as the first officer neared. "I thought you were one of the Kzinti."

Spock replied simply by holding up the object he carried. "I have the device, Lieutenant."

"Yes, but they've got Uhura. At least, I expect they do. I'm sure I saw her fall before I got out of the open. They've also got subspace radio and have us cut off from the *Copernicus*. If they want to, they can wait for us to starve while they call for help from the nearest Kzinti base."

"No, they cannot," Spock informed him with remarkable self-assurance, "or rather, they will not."

Sulu re-examined the options open to the Kzinti that he had just voiced, and bewilderedly could find no reason why they could not do exactly what he'd claimed. "Why can't they?"

"Because I kicked Chuft-Captain." When Sulu showed no sign of comprehending, the first officer elaborated. "Consider, Mr. Sulu. Chuft-Captain has been attacked by an herbivorous pacifist, an eater of roots and leaves, one who according to Kzinti tradition not only does not fight, but does not resist. Furthermore, I gave the ultimate insult subsequent to my successful attack, by leaving Chuft-Captain alive." Spock moved to the far corner of the monolith, peered cautiously around it.

"Chuft-Captain's honor is at stake, Lieutenant. Before he can seek outside help he must have personal revenge in order to absolve himself."

"Now I understand, sir. That gives us some time, then." Sulu hesitated, eyeing the first officer intently and with admiration. "You did plan it that way?"

"Of course." Spock seemed surprised that Sulu should think of any other possibility.

"Then as long as you stay free, the Kzinti can't or won't do anything until Chuft-Captain's had his chance to regain his reputation." He looked suddenly concerned. "But they could use Lieutenant Uhura as bait to trade for the Slaver device."

The first officer examined the enigmatic construction he held. "That is so, Lieutenant. However, to this point we have not seen it display anything more powerful than devices and instruments Starfleet already has. I would actually go so far as to say that in several cases present Starfleet equipment is superior to some of the device's manifested forms."

"Maybe so." Sulu looked thoughtful. "But I have a feeling, Mr. Spock, that that won't hold true. It doesn't make sense for it to hold true. All those different settings," and he pointed to the toggle gauge, "those different functions. Why so many varied ones and why conceal them behind the initial, inert, bubble shape?" He was studying the device and thinking hard.

"What do *you* think, Mr. Sulu? What could be behind such careful concealment of functions and their multiplicity?"

"I'm not sure, but I can imagine one possibility. Suppose this thing belonged to a spy or espionage agent of some sort? He could carry the bubble shape around openly. Maybe the bubble shape corresponds to some billion-year-old personal ornament or decoration, like a bracelet, for instance. And a spy would be just the one who could make good use of something that looked harmless but could be made to serve as an energy absorber, a telescope, perhaps a communicator of some kind, a personal transport."

"I acknowledge your expertise in the field of weaponry, Mr. Sulu," said Spock readily, "but I do not see how you can determine a possible ownership classification."

"Just look at it, Mr. Spock." Sulu was convinced of his own supposition now. He took the device and held it up to the faint light. Lime-yellow gleamed on its metal surface, reflecting the life-support aura of both officers. "All these settings. I admit we don't know that a common Slaver soldier or even an ordinary citizen couldn't handle them all, but to what end? For a soldier, only the laser is an effective weapon. The other functions aren't necessary for an ordinary warrior's single objective: to kill the enemy. An ordinary Slaver citizen, if there were such a creature, wouldn't require that a multitude of functions be so cleverly disguised. But they *are* disguised.

"For that matter, it wouldn't be necessary for a warrior to have such an elaborately concealed set of functions. If the device produced a shield, well, that would be useful. Possibly the telescope, and certainly the energy absorber. But a communicator, a telescope, and the rocket transport? A soldier might have need of them all, but why put them all into a single device of tremendous technological complexity? No, the thing is too intricate—unless intended for someone who *has* to hide all those functions in a single place."

"Assuming it is a dangerous device intended for use by someone who doesn't wish it to look like that," Spock finally replied, with equal thoughtfulness, "the Slavers would have wanted to keep its secrets a secret. They would never have wanted a potential enemy to know that the device was anything other than a silvery bubble attached to a handle. If so, and if we follow your reasoning through to its logical conclusion, it seems reasonable to assume that the device possesses a self-destruct setting also."

Sulu indicated the toggle switch, which rested at the bottom of its slot. "But we've seen all the phases, all five manifestations of the device."

"Perhaps not." Spock took the device back, turned it over in his hand. "There is the null setting."

"Null setting, sir?"

"The first one, where the toggle was originally set. It is marked with a hieroglyph." One finger traced the strange writing while Sulu looked puzzled. "The device appears to be without function, at this setting. But then why should that setting be present in the first place?" Spock had the look of a mathematics professor on the trail of an errant ingredient in a catastrophe-theory problem. "Why not simply leave the device set at the telescope setting? There is no reason an ordinary person, Slaver or Vulcan or human, could not carry a small telescope about with him. Nor does the first setting correspond to a safety lock of any sort, since Chuft-Captain was able to move the toggle easily to the other five settings."

Sulu shrugged, took the device back, and indifferently nudged the toggle up to the top of its slot. Immediately the device dissolved in his hands, the fifth mode returning once more to the featureless silvery bubble shape.

It certainly looked harmless enough.

"Maybe," Sulu began thoughtfully, "it's the key to some kind of hidden setting, Mr. Spock. Maybe this manifestation is intentionally innocent. If we—" He stopped as a rumble like a distant earthquake sounded.

Beneath them the ground trembled. They turned in the direction of the sound.

Just over the rim of the highest ice block, a shallow cone shape with a flat base was rising steadily spaceward. Boulders and huge chunks of ice fell in a sparkling rain from its flanks. It was the *Traitor's Claw*, the Kzin ship, hatched from its place of concealment.

Narrow projections protruded from the edge of the cone. They looked suspiciously like weapons, weapons which a mere police vessel shouldn't be quipped with. Sulu and Spock hugged the protective overhang of the massive boulder next to them, trying to slip their revealing life-support auras wholly beneath the shielding mass.

Within the observation room of the ship, Chuft-Captain glanced back once to assure himself that the human female remained frozen on the police web. She glared back at him with sufficient animation to tell him that she was alert and fully cognizant of what was taking place around her.

In one massive paw he held a communicator, standard Starfleet issue. He addressed himself to it while staring out the main port, which provided a moving view of the jumbled ice plain beneath the slowly moving ship. Neither of the two escaped prisoners, either the Vulcan or the human Sulu, were visible. That was hardly surprising. They were not fools and must have heard the *Traitor's Claw* lift. By now they should sensibly be well concealed in the crazy-quilt rocks below.

It would do them no good. Being familiar with human and Vulcan psychological orientation, Chuft-Captain knew that the possession of the human female was sufficient to bring the Slaver device once more into his hands.

"This is the *Traitor's Claw* calling Lieutenant Sulu," he said into the communicator. "Chuft-Captain speaks to you. We have the female prisoner. She is in good health, a condition dependent solely on your next actions. Will you bargain with us for the Slaver device or must we take harsh action to convince you?"

There followed a respectable pause during which no response was forthcoming. That did not bother Chuft-Captain. Any warrior would first consider every possible alternative before surrendering. He expected no less of the human.

"If you do not reply," he said into the communicator when a reasonable amount of time had passed without an answer from below, "it will not be pleasant for her."

Uhura might have given Chuft-Captain a reply, but it wouldn't have done her any good. She stood paralyzed on the police web, kept silent, and considered her predicament. It was probably fortunate for her, despite Chuft-Captain's patience, that Telepath was not present to inform him of her hostile thoughts.

The *Traitor's Claw* cruised back and forth over the icefields in a regular spiral pattern, searching the ragged formations below for traces of the escaped prisoners.

"Still no sign of them, Chuft-Captain," Flyer reported from his position at the controls.

Chuft-Captain snarled his acknowledgment, tried to repress a stab of pain and keep it out of his voice as he spoke into the communicator again. "I repeat, Lieutenant Sulu, we have the female human as hostage. You have something that *we* want. We will trade her life for the Slaver device."

Spock and Sulu remained well hidden beneath the overhanging lip of weathered rock. Together they had listened intently to Chuft-Captain's demands. Now Spock stared meaningfully across at his companion.

"Chuft-Captain's offer neglects certain important details, Lieutenant Sulu. Answer him."

Sulu palmed his own communicator, flipped it open, briefly considered his reply before speaking. "This is Sulu. You've taken care of Lieutenant Uhura. What about Mr. Spock and myself? If we're not included we can't consider your offer."

"You must surrender anyway," the Kzin commander's raspy voice said over the tiny speaker grid. "You cannot reach your shuttlecraft. There is no escape for you. But I will give a chance. I offer Mr. Spock single combat."

"Not interested," Sulu said immediately.

Spock only nodded. "Chuft-Captain must fight me. They could beam this entire region on low power, probably kill us without damaging the Slaver device. But he cannot risk letting me die without regaining his personal honor."

Back on board the *Traitor's Claw*, Chuft-Captain's claws contracted reflexively as he clutched tightly at the arm of his seat. Leaning to his left partially concealed the ends of the pale bandages and his uniform hid the the rest. His tail switched lightly above the deck, projecting backward through the slot provided by the Kzin chair.

"Why do you refuse? I am as the Vulcan left me," he informed the communicator, "with two ribs broken. I have not had them set. He may conceivably kill me."

Sulu hesitated, shut off the communicator while he watched his superior. Spock's attention was still on the sky, searching for the patrolling ship, but the helmsman knew that Spock had heard Chuft-Captain's words as clearly as he had. "What about what he says, Mr. Spock? Could you?"

"I kicked him over one heart, but Kzinti ribs have vertical bracing in addition to the horizontal bracing found in humans and Vulcans. His injury would still be severe, but far from crippling." He thought a moment, then added, "I compute the odds of my defeating Chuft-Captain in hand-to-hand combat at sixteen to one against, and that is assuming his injuries are as he claims."

Sulu flipped the communicator on again. "Sorry, offer refused," he said tersely. Putting the deactivated communicator away, he resumed his examination of the Slaver device, puzzling over Spock's suspicion of the innocent silver bubble shape.

Chuft-Captain stared out the fore port, at the endless fields of ice and ragged stone. Eventually, he turned his attention to the figure standing silent and frozen behind him. Uhura glared back at him.

"They think very little of you."

"Wrong." She wished she could scratch her right thigh. "They don't think much of *you*."

That provoked a vicious growl from the Kzin commander. Uhura wasn't impressed. Let them continue to consider her a dumb female like those of their own species. She would never give them an excuse to call her a coward. When Chuft-Captain turned his baleful gaze away from her and back to the fore port without saying anything else, she felt as if she had won a small but significant victory.

Sulu leaned back against their concave shelter, his

life-support aura compressing to a thin lime-yellow line against his back. Again he examined the Slaver device in great detail. Again he found nothing faintly resembling another toggle switch, hidden button, or any other kind of control that could conceivably activate some unknown setting.

Turning the device once more, in the vague hope he might still somehow have overlooked something, Sulu became conscious of something he had not noticed before. He had had the hand grip in his right hand and the silver sphere in the other. When he'd turned the device this last time, he was certain the sphere had moved slightly. He used his right hand again on the argent globe. Yes, it definitely moved!

Excited, he stood clear of the rock wall. Gripping the sphere firmly this time, he twisted sharply to one side. Nothing. He twisted in the opposite direction. This time the globe not only moved, it turned halfway around on its axis.

The familiar blurring distorted the device. This time, when it coalesced, the sphere was gone. In its place was a cone with its apex facing outward. The cone had a rounded base that blended smoothly into the hand grip. The configuration was so simple that Sulu almost shrugged it off as merely another disguise form and twisted the sphere back. But maybe the thing did something, despite its innocuous appearance.

One small, added shape gave credence to that thought. A tiny, round transparency was emplaced between the cone and the hand grip. A peculiarly arranged series of tiny lines were etched into it. They resembled an asterisk more than anything else.

Spock leaned forward as soon as the sphere shape had given way to the cone. Now he ran a finger over the strangely engraved little lens.

Chuft-Captain, he knew, would also have interpreted that tiny but significant transparency at first glance. "A self-destruct mechanism would not have a gun sight."

"No, it wouldn't," agreed Sulu readily. "Let's see what this setting does." Widening his stance, he raised the device as if it were an old-fashioned pistol. Aiming at a point on the distant horizon, he pulled the trigger.

An intensely blue beam sprang from the point of the cone, crossed into space. Slowly the helmsman lowered his arm until the blue line, which remained constant as long as he held the trigger down, touched the lowest ridge of rock and ice. There was a brilliant flare of pure white light. Sulu shut his eyes, blocking out the powerful radiance, then took his finger off the trigger. The glare vanished slowly, like a dying ember. In its place appeared a thick, rising cloud of dense gas and smoke mixed with vaporized ice and stone.

Sulu opened his eyes, stared in horror at the still growing pillar of boiling gases.

"We can't let them have *that!*"

"Fascinating," was all Spock said immediately. His attention was held by the tower of carbonized solids. "No laboratory in the Federation has ever produced a hand weapon of such power." He squinted into the distance. The cloud was finally beginning to dissipate, and he could see through it a little.

"The entire crest of the ice monolith you fired at appears to have vanished. Total conversion of matter to energy at this distance, and by a simple hand weapon."

"An army of Kzin warriors armed with these would be invincible," Sulu observed in awe, gazing at the simple cone shape he held. "One man could fight off a small ship. The whole galaxy would be their dinner table."

"And it was, Mr. Sulu, it was. I do not imagine they were called Slavers because of their benign dispositions."

"If we . . ." Sulu started to add, but something he saw caused him to pause. A rising wave of ice particles and small gravel was racing toward them like a dark cloud from the region of the destruction, carried on a disturbed wind front by the shock of the vaporization.

"Hit the dirt!" he yelled.

Both men curled up beneath their overhanging boulder, tried to press themselves into the solid stone. But like the power of the Slaver weapon, the shock wave when it arrived was far stronger than either had imagined. Both men were lifted from their places and slung through the atmosphere. Sulu did something to the

Slaver device just before he hit the ground hard. Spock landed nearby, no more gently. A faint reverse shock whistled over them a moment later, stirring both immobile bodies like sawdust on a plate. They did not move.

A few minutes later a slim, flattened shape *thrummed* overhead. In its observation chamber, one seated Kzin let out a snarl of triumph at something just glimpsed below.

"There they are, Chuft-Captain!"

The injured commander leaned forward, recognized the two motionless bipedal shapes. "Peculiar. There must have been a ground-level aftershock. They were too exposed to cope with it." He grinned. "How fortunate for us. Set down as close to them as you can manage, Pilot."

"Yes, honored one." The pilot operated controls and the *Traitor's Claw* began a slow, smooth descent. The "stolen" police vessel touched down only a few meters from where the bodies of Spock and Sulu rested unmoving on the icy surface.

Chuft-Captain glanced over at Flyer. "Bring them in. Carefully."

"Yes, Chuft-Captain." Flyer saluted, turned, and headed for the airlock.

While he was gone the rest of the Kzinti waited anxiously in the observation chamber. Uhura regarded the aliens with interest. She had hopes that Sulu and Spock were feigning unconsciousness, perhaps in a bold attempt to get themselves taken on board the Kzinti ship, where with the aid of the Slaver weapon they might have a chance to overpower her captors. So she received a rude shock when the party of suited Kzinti returned, carrying two limp forms that showed no hint of consciousness.

"They are alive, Chuft-Captain," Flyer reported to his commander as the other Kzinti stood the two former prisoners back on the police web, which had been turned off to allow them to be placed, but which was then quickly switched back on to keep them upright.

"They have sustained some bruising, mostly internal, from what our physician told me," Flyer said. "Their life-support belts cushioned them enough to keep them alive. Without those belts, I am sure they would have been scattered in pieces across the ice."

"Some bruising, yes." Chuft-Captain's right hand rubbed at his cracked ribs, touched gingerly at the bandages wrapped around his chest. Flyer handed him an object and the commander gazed down at it speculatively. "Meanwhile we have the problem of this."

His uncertainty was understandable. Before being knocked unconscious, Sulu had managed to twist the cone shape. It had once more reverted to the maddeningly familiar silver sphere.

Both officers regained their senses together. Sulu saw that the Kzinti had no interest in them for the moment. The whole crew were offering suggestions dealing with the Slaver weapon. Much yelling and growling was evident. Everyone held a different opinion, it seemed. But eventually, simply by fiddling incessantly with the device, one of them discovered the sphere twist. Or rather, *a* sphere twist. Somehow it seemed to Sulu that the globe had been turned in a manner different from the way he had done it.

Expectedly, the silver ball vanished. But the cone shape did not appear. Instead, the sphere was replaced by a smaller, rose-hued globe. A small grid was set into the top of the ball.

None of the formerly talkative Kzinti volunteered an opinion as to the possible function of this new manifestation. The device had proven too many wrong already, and none of them wished to be embarrassed in front of Chuft-Captain with an inaccurate appraisal of the device's capability.

So it was Chuft-Captain who finally had to ask for theories. "What would this be?" He pointed a thick finger at the small, reddish ball.

"I have no idea," Flyer said quickly. He glanced thoughtfully at a gauge set into the side of his armored suit. "Whatever it does, it generates power."

That revelation produced more confused yowling and growls from the assembled Kzinti.

Nor were they the only ones speculating on the device's newest, and most surprising, manifestation.

"There's a grid set into it," Spock said to Uhura and Sulu. "It may be another communications setting. Possibly related in some way to the first communicator shape keyed by the first notch in the toggle slot, but," and he almost frowned slightly, "that would seem redundant, and out of keeping with the Slaver's oft-demonstrated efficiency. Not to mention the economical, many-functions-in-one nature of the device itself. If we—"

A new—startlingly new—voice spoke in the observation chamber. It spoke in Kzinti, or at least something very close to Kzinti. It had the distortions common to an out-of-town rural visiting a large, cosmopolitan metropolis and trying to converse in the local dialect. That meant it was comprehensible, but spiced with a notable yet not quite definable difference.

It was immediately clear that the voice did not emanate from the mouth of any of the assembled warriors; this was confirmed by the manner in which they abruptly ceased all conversation among themselves. The voice sounded again. It had a faint crackle in it, like carbonation in liquid. All at once it became evident to everyone that the voice came from the little grid on top of the Slaver device's newest configuration.

"Whatever it is, it sure has the Kzinti frightened," Sulu observed with satisfaction.

"That's not surprising." Spock's placid expression showed that it wasn't. "The Kzinti, if I recall correctly, have many legends of weapons haunted by their original owners."

Uhura stared, fascinated, at the device. "Could it be a voice-response control, requiring verbal direction?"

The Kzinti had clustered closely around Chuft-Captain and the device, and the muffled sounds of conversation were all the frustrated officers could make out.

"I think not," said Spock. "Somehow it actually appears to be conversing with them." He paused, listening. "Yes. It gives replies to direct questions, and reasons abstractly where appropriate. A reasoning computer so small, capable of independent analysis and reply? Even with the subminiaturization that modern Federation technology has achieved, that is hard to believe. A computer, yes, of any tiny size you want. But one capable of reasoning and decision-making? An incredible accomplishment."

"Are you sure, Mr. Spock?" Sulu asked.

Spock listened for a while longer, then nodded affirmatively. "It is much more than a computer. Its logic circuitry must be infinitely more sophisticated than anything we have yet developed, save for huge reasoning computers such as the main one on board the *Enterprise*. This one appears capable of similar activity, and it is unbelievably smaller."

The crowd of Kzinti, their initial excitement beginning to fade, spread out from one another. So when the voice spoke again, it became loud enough and clear enough for the translators hanging from each of the prisoners' waists to interpret.

"How long," Chuft-Captain was asking the tiny rose sphere, "since you were last turned off?"

"I do not know," the stilted voice of the Slaver device promptly replied. "When I am off I have no sense of passing time."

"Very well." The Kzinti commander opted for another tack. "What is the last thing you remember?"

"We were on a mission." Spock couldn't tell from the awkward inflection in the machine's voice whether it was referring to several Slavers, or the device and a single owner, when it said "We." "I may not tell you of the mission unless you know certain coded terminology."

Flyer spoke up. "If you could describe to us the positions of the stars above the last ship or world you were on, we would be able to guess how much time has passed since then."

"Without certain code words," the computer voice informed them evenly, "I may not describe the location."

Patience was not one of the Kzinti's finer qualities. Chuft-Captain couldn't keep the irritation out of his voice when he next addressed the device. "One of the settings on you was a matter-conversion beam of tremendous power. We know that, having observed it in operation." He glanced back, smiling victoriously at the frozen prisoners. "We all saw what it can do." He turned back to the device. "Tell us how to find that setting on you."

There was a pause, then, "Move the toggle until you reach the original null position."

This affirmative response, without a single reference to code words, produced an excited, anticipatory chattering among the assembled Kzinti, so much so that their yowling drowned out everything else the computer was saying.

"That's the end, then," said the despondent Sulu. "They've succeeded in communicating with the device."

"There must be *something* we can do." Uhura fought against the invisible bonds restraining her, found the police-web field strong as ever. Then she noticed Spock. The first officer was never demonstrative, no matter how serious the situation; but considering the gravity of their present predicament, he appeared even more phlegmatic than usual.

"Mr. Spock, you know what's happened," she called to him. "Don't you have any suggestions?"

Spock apparently did not. He was staring blankly at the excited cluster of milling Kzinti. "Most peculiar," he murmured, and that seemed to constitute his final words on the matter.

Uhura stared back at the Kzinti, but saw nothing to inspire such a comment from her superior.

Chuft-Captain raised the Slaver weapon, brandished it aloft triumphantly. If Uhura had no inkling of why Spock was so fascinated, Sulu did, the moment he set eyes on the weapon again.

It had changed, obviously in response to Chuft-Captain's request. But it had not changed into the matter-conversion configuration. At least, not into the weapons mode Spock and Sulu had used piror to their recent recapture. Not one cone but a pair projected from the hand grip now. Neither apex faced outward. Instead, the two points faced each other. They came close to touching, forming a distorted dumbbell shape.

Still chattering enthusiastically among themselves, the knot of Kzinti trooped from the chamber, moving toward the ship's airlock.

"That was not," Spock said decisively, "the total conversion beam. We must assume the weapon gave them directions for employing still another new setting."

"But if it wasn't the conversion beam . . . ?" Sulu hesitated, glanced anxiously around at the exit taken by the departing Kzinti.

Uhura, meanwhile, was shifting her attention from one officer to the other, their statements only serving to confuse her further instead of providing enlightenment.

Followed by Flyer and the rest of the Kzinti, Chuft-Captain marched outside. The Kzinti commander still walked in pain, leaning to his left and occasionally clutching at his cracked ribs. The party of armor-suited aliens moved a respectable distance from the *Traitor's Claw*. Having already observed the power of the Slaver weapon, Chuft-Captain wanted to be well clear of his ship before activating it again.

Once they had ascended a jumble of shattered ice blocks, he inspected the re-formed weapon. The double-cone arrangement looked little more like a weapon than many of the device's previous manifestations.

"Like the other configurations," he informed his subordinates, who stood below and slightly behind him, "this new one appears to be devoid of a gun sight."

"It may be a broad-beam weapon," Flyer suggested, "for use on distant or rapidly moving or multiple targets. We saw its power. There may be only a need to aim it very generally in a target's direction. It is definitely a weapon. I suggest you fire at a very distant subject."

Chuft-Captain concurred. "Very well." He assumed as formal a marksman's stance as he could manage with his damaged ribs.

"We can't let them have that weapon." Uhura fought the police web frantically. Though she exerted all the energy in her body, shoving in every direction including straight up, she was unable to move a centimeter and remained frozen in place.

Spock's reassuring comment was delivered with an

eerie calm. "They're not about to get it, Lieutenant. I think you are worrying needlessly." She stared at him uncomprehendingly. Sulu did likewise, but the helmsman had a glimmering of what the first officer meant.

"Why aren't they?" she asked.

"Assume you are a Slaver war computer, Lieutenant Uhura. A small one, to be sure, but a war computer nonetheless. You have been deactivated, you do not know for how long, but when you were deactivated there was a war in progress. Assume furthermore that it is likely, as Mr. Sulu has suggested, that you are a secret weapon in the truest sense of the term, on a secret mission of some sort." He paused a moment, continued when Uhura had had time to digest this.

"Now you are abruptly awakened by aliens you have never seen before and retain no memory of. They do not know any of the military passwords. They are certainly not recognizable as belonging to the hierarchy of possible Slaver allies. They ask you so many questions it's obvious they know little about you and are trying to find out a great deal more, particularly anything involving weapons settings. Your true owner is nowhere about." He turned to eye her expectantly.

"What would *you* think?"

Uhura didn't have to consider long before replying. "I'd think that I'd been captured by the enemy. Or at least by a non-ally."

"And when they asked you," Sulu prompted eagerly, "how to find your most powerfully destructive setting, what would you give them?"

Uhura and the helmsman exchanged meaningful glances while Spock merely stood staring thoughtfully out the main port, wishing the Kzinti were in view and yet very glad they weren't.

Chuft-Captain aimed the double-cone arrangement as best he could. Focusing on a distant hilltop, he pulled the trigger on the Slaver weapon.

Chuft-Captain vanished. So did Flyer and the rest of the Kzinti standing with him. So did several tons of ice and stone beneath them, and so did part of the hull of the *Traitor's Claw*.

In fact, everything within a radius of twenty meters of the former Chuft-Captain simply disappeared—including, naturally, the Slaver weapon. As Spock had surmised, the war computer built into the device had reasoned that the Kzinti were not entitled to operate it. Instead of the weapons setting discovered by Spock and Sulu, it had provided Chuft-Captain with its self-destruct setting.

Portions of three rooms on board the Kzinti vessel had been opened to space. The control room, a storage chamber, and the crew common room now looked out onto a near vacuum. Walls, equipment, and the ground they had rested on had completely vanished. The conversion had extended to within half a meter of Spock's left leg.

There were no aftereffects. The self-destruct setting operated much in the manner of normal atmospheric lightning: a million-volt bolt could strike a tree and a man a few meters away might not be harmed. Similarly, though the imprisoned officers had been standing frozen on the very edge of the disruption field, they had not been touched. Within the disruption field, however, everything for a radius of twenty meters from Chuft-Captain had been converted. A violent *whoosh* of air escaping from the *Traitor's Claw* was the only sound produced by the disappearance.

Spock barely had time enough to say clearly, "Activate life-support belts!" Having cut into the control room, the self-destruct field had sliced through the police web and its power supply. The three prisoners found they were able to move. Hands touched controls at their waists. Three lime-yellow auras sprang instantly into existence in the dim light of the powerless observation room.

Uhura was studying the smooth-sided, round-bottomed crater in front of them with interest. "Total-disruptor field." She wasn't worried about an attack from any remaining Kzinti. If any remained aboard, they would be too busy trying to lock themselves into airtight compartments and find alternate sources of atmosphere to bother offering hinderance to escaping prisoners.

"Yes," commented Spock. "Another conventional weapon. It would seem that the total-conversion beam Lieutenant Sulu and I discovered was the only thing the Slavers had that we do not also possess, in one form or another."

Sulu walked to the edge of the sliced-open room. It had been cut, he noted, as neatly as with any industrial phaser. The sides and bottom of the crater were smooth as glass, marred only by a few unbalanced boulders and chunks of ice that had fallen into the pit and gathered at the bottom.

"No sign of the weapon, of course." He stood straight, sighed in disappointment. "It would have looked nice in some museum."

"It would never have remained in a museum long, Lieutenant," Spock observed quietly. "There was too much power in that single unique setting. If not the Kzinti, then the Klingons or some other warlike species would have tried to possess it, to copy it, and to duplicate its destructive potential." His gaze lifted and he stared across the open pit. On the far side of the pit and intervening icefield the shuttlecraft *Copernicus* waited. Only the gaping glassy depression in the ground indicated that anything out of the ordinary had occurred on the barren planet of Beta Lyrae. The depression . . . and a small police vessel sliced as neatly as an apple by the knife of some titan.

"Strange," the first officer of the *Enterprise* mused aloud, "how the past sometimes breaks through into the present. A war a billion years old could have sparked a new conflict between the Federation and the Kzinti." He turned to face his companions.

"I think it's time for us to leave. The weapon is now history, along with the Slaver Empire. We have a conference to attend. But while we don't have the weapon, Lieutenant Sulu, at least we have something that might grace your imagined museum."

He gestured nearby. The stasis box that had contained the Slaver weapon rested near one half of a tilted table in the room. The other half of the table and the Kzinti's own empty stasis box had lain within the self-destruct disruptor field and had vanished.

"The box isn't much," Spock observed, "but even though empty it will excite those who see it. They can fill it with their imaginations."

Uhura nodded, leaned over the table's remains and tucked the box which had caused them so much time and trouble loosely under one arm. Devoid of its contents, it was only an ordinary metal container. An ordinary metal container over a billion years old.

Moving carefully downward, they made their way out of the hulk of the *Traitor's Claw*. They skirted the slick rim of the pit, a technological rabbit hole down which had vanished the belligerent dreams of Kzin. Once more on solid ground, they made their way steadily toward the *Copernicus* and a distant rendezvous with their ship, their friends, and a new race to whom the Slaver Empire was more tall tale than truth . . .

XI

The commander of Starbase 25 greeted them personally when the *Enterprise* had finished docking procedure. "Jarrod Shulda, Captain Kirk," the deceptively ordinary-looking man introduced himself. The two shook hands, turned and stared down the extended docking tube leading into the body of the station.

"We know what your mission is, Captain," Shulda said volubly, "and we've been preparing for your arrival." He checked a wrist chronometer and smiled. "Glad you made it on time."

"Was there any reason to assume we wouldn't?" Kirk wondered aloud as they turned down a corridor.

Scott and M'ress accompanied him. The Caitian communications officer appeared unaffected by her recent unfortunate experience. Soon after the pheraligen had taken effect, she and M'viore and R'leez had resumed their normal duties and shifts. Their mental readjustment was helped by Dr. McCoy's instructions to all personnel to extend sympathy and understanding to their three temporarily deranged shipmates, while mentioning any actual incidents or encounters as little as possible. The order was complied with, even by the security personnel whom the three berserk Caitians had put in Sick Bay.

"No offense, Captain. I wasn't impugning your vessel's efficiency. I'm glad you arrived on time because it will take some of the pressure off us, here at the base." Shulda tried to add some humor to a vitally important, serious situation. "Starfleet Command's mighty nervous about this whole Briamos business. They've been talking our ears off here, asking for confirmation of your arrival. I'm happy I can finally send that. Frankly, Captain, you could have arrived here the day after you received your orders and I suspect we still would have had half a dozen worried inquiries from anxious bureaucrats concerned over your slow pace."

"Well, we're here now," Kirk said easily. They were entering a small conference room and the captain added softly, "Most of us, anyhow."

Now who was worrying needlessly? He was no better than those back at Command, continually thinking about the unknown progress of the three officers on board the shuttlecraft *Copernicus*. Resolutely, he shut all thoughts of Spock, Sulu, and Uhura from his mind.

It was an effort.

A florid, plump little woman with oriental features and the air of a society matron was standing next to a small podium going over a handful of notes when they entered. She turned, saw them, and scurried crablike across the floor to greet them. All her movements were quick, her gestures expansive as a courting blue jay, voice brisk and prying.

"Captain Kirk." She extended a smooth palm, thimble-thick fingers extended. "I'm Chu Leiski, sociologist by trade, diplomatic adviser by necessity."

"So you're the resident expert on our friends-to-be, the Briamosites?" Scott was eyeing the woman uncertainly.

"Lieutenant Commander Montgomery Scott," supplied Kirk, "my acting second-in-command, and Lieutenant M'ress, acting communications chief."

"My, my, Captain, but to a stranger you'd seem to be running a thespianic enterprise. But as they say, all the universe is a stage. Please take some seats, any you like, and we'll get started. I'm please to meet you all. We've a great deal to brief you on."

A little breathless with trying to keep up, Kirk slid slowly into one of the chairs in the conference room. Sociologist Leiski moved to stand behind the podium. She put down her notes and activated the electronic readout set into the podium top.

"None of the information I'm going to impart to you is critical by and of itself, but I've included everything we know on the Briamosites. No telling, no telling when during the conference some obscure chunk of information will become crucial. The Briamosites are a very thorough people, and they admire that thoroughness in others. So that's how these briefings will run—thorough in execution and thorough in content. You have to explore a whole pool in order to find the school of minnows, sometimes."

Shutting out the homilies, Kirk asked, "Just how big is that pool? How much have we been able to learn about the Briamosites, Chu Leiski?"

"Not a great deal, Captain. Certainly not as much as we'd like to before you have to go off to this conference. That's why," and she smiled at Scott, "despite your chief engineer's compliment, I can't pass myself off as the resident expert on the Briamosites. There *are* no experts on Briamos and its people."

She leaned both elbows on the podium. "In fact, we're hoping that you and those of your crew who attend or participate in the conference will learn all they can, so they can come back here and lecture me—and all the other so-called experts." Quite suddenly, she dropped her chatty, informal manner and exchanged it for that of the dignified instructor.

Moving to a large screen, she touched a control. The screen lit up, but no pictures or words appeared on it yet. "My connection with the Briamosites comes from the fact that I was an assistant to Ambassador Laiguer. I was half observer, half adviser to him on personal Briamosite interactions. That was my specialty."

"Since you served as the ambassador's assistant and have spent more time among them than any of us, why aren't you coming with us to the conference?" Scott wanted to know.

She smiled again, briefly. "I'm not an official diplomat, nor a member of Starfleet. Just a civilian technician. I have no diplomatic credentials to present to Briamos. As I said, the Briamosites are a very thorough folk. They're as thorough about protocol as anything else. My presence in the official negotiating party would be considered insulting."

"You don't have to be part of the actual negotiating group." Scott could be persistent. "Why dinna ye just come along to give us on-the-spot information?"

"I have to stay here, much as I'd like to go," Leiski told him. "I've been assigned to relay all information on the progress of the conference from here, as it arrives from Briamos and the *Enterprise* back here to Starbase Twenty-Five. I'm to provide my own comments and analysis to accompany your reports, and in turn I'm to convey back to you any suggestions or orders they might come up with." She ruffled her notes.

"I told them I could comment, albeit a little slower, from Briamos via deep-space beam, but it apparently was considered vital in certain circles to have a knowledgeable intermediary between Starfleet Command and Briamos while the conference was taking place. That's me. Besides," she added convincingly, "in a few days you'll all know as much about the Briamosites as I do."

The lectures proceeded smoothly. Despite her pose of self-deprecation when it came to her professional accomplishments, Chu Leiski proved an adept and efficient teacher. Occasionally Kirk brought other personnel along, from Sciences, or Communications, or other departments, as Leiski's subject matter shifted to bear particularly on one section's specialty. But as the days passed with no communication from the *Copernicus*, Kirk found his attention wandering when it should have been fixed on this or that aspect of Briamosite culture.

Finally, after the last lecture, questions were put to

Chu Leiski by Kirk and other officers. She replied with answers and questions of her own.

As the room was emptying, Leiski drew Kirk aside. "I know you'll do the Federation proud, Captain. I wish I were going with you."

"Obviously Starfleet thinks you're more important to them here," Kirk told her. "I know you'd like to be part of the conference, and you will be, an integral part. You just won't be there in body."

"Oh, it's not that, Captain." Leiski was cleaning the nails of her left hand with a nail on the right and she didn't look up at him. "I hope the conference is a success, naturally, but I don't especially care if I'm a part of it. I just like Briamos and its people, that's all, and I want to make sure I have the chance to go back." She looked up now, smiled fitfully. "Do well, Captain Kirk, so I can go back?" She turned and left.

Alone in the room, Kirk felt confident for the first time. No matter how temperamental and difficult professional diplomats such as Ambassador Laiguer found the Briamosites, they had to be a people worth knowing if they could inspire such affection and interest in a woman like Chu Leiski...

Kirk was resting in the command chair, brooding silently. He and McCoy had been discussing items of no particular importance—a rare luxury for them both—when Kirk suddenly said, "You realize, Bones, that if they're not here by fourteen hundred tomorrow we'll have to leave without them. We can't delay departure."

"I know, Jim. I'm sure Spock, Sulu, and Uhura know it too, wherever they are."

Kirk turned, stared at the blank viewscreen. His hand tightened slightly on the arm of the command chair, but only McCoy noticed.

They should have reported in by now!

M'ress was already at her post when Kirk entered the bridge the following morning. He glanced over at her, framed a wordless question. She shook her head slowly. The message he had hoped for had not arrived.

Almost, he asked for something she could not give.

Then his lips tightened and he took his seat half angrily. "Mr. Arex, Mr. Vedama, prepare for Briamos departure."

"But, Captain," Vedama began, "can't we——?"

"The one thing we can't do, Lieutenant, is be late for that conference. We depart at fourteen hundred. I won't risk traveling at maximum velocity and the chance of an engine malfunction delaying our scheduled arrival, in order to wait any longer. You know the Briamosites' fanatic attitude toward punctuality. You attended many of the lectures yourself."

"Yes, sir. I did." Discouraged, Vedama turned away.

Arex commenced programming their course, frowned his odd Edoan frown, and called back over a shoulder, "Captain Kirk?"

"Yes, what is it?"

"Captain, our detectors show an unidentified shuttlecraft coming in."

"Check with starbase communications, M'ress," Kirk ordered quickly, hardly daring to believe.

"Yes, sirr." A pause, then she said excitedly, "They arre not expecting any shuttles, sirr. And none of theirr own arre out."

"We're too far from any well-populated worlds for easy shuttle transportation," Kirk mused.

"Call coming in, sirr," the Caitian communications officer announced. She added without waiting for an order, "Acknowledging incoming signal."

This one time, Kirk did not reprimand her.

"Shuttlecraft *Copernicus* to *Enterprise*." Spock's lean, relaxed tones gave no hint of anything amiss on board the overdue shuttle. "Request docking."

"M'ress, put me through." He waited while she nudged the necessary controls and then he spoke into the chair pickup. "Spock, this is Kirk here."

"Hello, Captain."

Kirk waited, until it was evident his first officer didn't intend to expand on his greeting. " 'Hello, Captain'? Is that all you have to say, Mr. Spock? You're three days overdue." He tried to sound accusing, but came out appearing worried. "What happened to you in Gruyakin?"

"We had to cope with the fact that the stasis box had been stolen prior to our arrival, Captain."

"Stolen?" Kirk twitched violently.

"Yes, Captain," came Spock's confirmation, calm as ever. "We recovered it only after the stasis box had placed the would-be thief in a stasis field of his own."

"Stasis field of his own?"

"That's correct, Captain. However, that was a minor problem, compared to the trouble the Kzinti caused us."

"Kzinti? Kzinti!"

"It is not like you to respond to every statement with a questioning echo, Captain." The first officer sounded mildly reproving without being outright insubordinate.

"It's not like anyone, Mr. Spock, to go after a stasis box, and then have it stolen, and then run into—" He stopped, took a deep breath. "Mr. Spock, I will expect to see you in my cabin as soon as you've docked and gotten yourselves squared away—and bring that stasis box." A sudden thought moved him to ask quickly, "Lieutenants Sulu and Uhura are all right?"

"Yes, sir," "Yes, Captain," came the almost simultaneous replies from both officers.

"Good. You can both report to me along with Mr. Spock. Maybe the three of you together can come up with one sensible explanation for your delay."

"I'm sure you'll find both the stasis box and our explanation equally intriguing, Captain," Spock assured him.

As usual, Spock understated Kirk's reaction. All four sat in his cabin. Spock was concluding their story. He had related it all, without pausing. Kirk simply sat at his desk, shaking his head in response to one part of the tale, nodding at another, staring in disbelief at still a third. The first officer did most of the talking, while Sulu and Uhura occasionally broke in to provide emotional coloration of their own. The stasis box rested on a table between them.

"And that is how the box has come to be here empty, Captain," Spock finished.

Kirk stared at the metal cube for a long moment.

"My congratulations to all of you. Merely being here is proof of how well you carried out your assignment."

"I beg to differ with you, Captain," said Spock. "We lost the contents of the box, the Slaver weapon."

"That was unavoidable, Mr. Spock. While we don't have it, more importantly neither do the Kzinti. Furthermore, the Federation still has the three of you." He studied the box. Its silvery surface shone metallically in the cabin light. "There ought to be *something* we can—" He broke off, and a slightly mischievous, slightly satanic grin appeared on his face.

"We'll take it to the conference," he announced. "Mr. Spock, you and Chief Engineer Scott can rig a small device to place inside for generating an imitation Slaver field. The box itself," he went on, leaning forward, "is every bit as impressive as any discovered. With an aura surrounding it, no one would know it's been opened. No need to tell the Briamosites, or the Klingons, and I don't think any of them will rush to open it manually, in front of all the others."

"That would be deceitful, Captain," Spock observed disapprovingly.

"Diplomatic, Mr. Spock, simply diplomatic. Remember, the Briamosites will choose between the Klingons and the Federation. I am not going to stick to Marquis of Queensberry rules when something as vital as an interstellar alliance with a race as important as the Briamosites is at stake. And especially not when the matter also involves Klingons."

"Pardon, Captain . . . Marquis of Queensberry rules?" Spock asked.

"They have to do with boxing, Mr. Spock," Sulu informed him.

"Oh yes, boxing. One of the ancient barbarous human martial arts." Sulu bridled and Spock hastened to add, "No offense, Mr. Sulu. I was referring only to the primitive, unrefined techniques of human warfare, not to fencing or the more sophisticated forms of self-defense."

Sulu looked uncertain, but relaxed.

" 'Barbarous' is the right word when negotiating with Klingons, Spock." Kirk had turned grim. "You know the Klingon watch phrase when it comes to diplomacy: 'That which is expedient rather than that which is truthful.' So we'll bend the truth a little bit ourselves. We may not actually have to lie. If no one asks us whether the stasis box has been opened, I see no reason to volunteer the information that it has."

"You are rationalizing, Captain." Spock refused to be argued out of his stance. "But considering the importance of the conference, I find, reluctantly, that I must concur with your methodology. We must show ourselves as adaptable as the Klingons."

The *Enterprise* was well on its way to Briamos from Starbase 25 and approaching the limits of Federation territory, when an unexpected buffeting struck the ship. One moment they were cruising along easily—the next, the ship was shuddering as if afflicted with metallic pneumonia. As suddenly as the disturbance began, it stopped.

"Now what could have caused that?" Kirk wondered, then added more loudly, "Lieutenant Uhura, damage report."

"All stations all decks report no damage and secure, Captain," she reported in a few minutes. "Several sections want to know what happened."

"So do I. Mr. Spock?"

The first officer was bent over his readouts, then looked up. "I am not certain, Captain. It could have been caused by any of several phenomena, external or internal." He touched a control. "Engineering, Mr. Spock here."

"Aye, Mr. Spock," replied Chief Engineer Scott. "What the devil was that?"

"You do not know, Commander?" Spock asked.

"No sir. I was hopin' you'd be able to tell me."

"I am attempting to find out by eliminating possibilities, Commander. Bridge out." Spock made several more fast checks, looked back at Kirk.

"It would appear to be an external problem, Captain." Spock appeared to hesitate. "As far as outside causes—"

Further buffeting, not a repeat of the last but stronger this time, rocked the *Enterprise* again. It had enough force to jolt small objects loose from their places at desk and console. It also lasted slightly longer than the previous shaking, and stopped just as mysteriously.

Uhura relayed the gratifying no-damage reports from each deck and section while Spock worked feverishly now at the science computer.

"I think I have it, Captain." He glanced up finally from his instrumentation. "If the information compiled by our long-range sensors is accurate, we would do well to immediately—"

He never finished the suggestion. A giant hand slapped the *Enterprise* sideways, flung Kirk from the command chair. He barely caught himself in midair to keep from being thrown against the navigation-helm console.

All across the bridge, other crew members were slung from their positions. Only Spock, who was half prepared for the shock because of what the sensors had told him, clung tightly to his seat and absorbed the buffeting. But this time the shaking didn't stop. It fluctuated from dangerous to irritating, but never ceased entirely.

Kirk crawled carefully back into the command chair. "Mr. Sulu, all ahead warp factor eight! Emergency power!"

"I'm trying, Captain," Sulu shouted after a frustrating struggle with the controls. "She's not responding properly. We're caught in something."

"Energy storm," Spock announced loudly, over the noise of the shaking. "Captain, sensors report a variable pulsar in the immediate spatial vicinity. That's what's causing the uneven buffeting. It's rotating at a high rate of speed, throwing out intermittent, unpredictable bursts of tremendous energy. I should have recognized the cause sooner but—" He broke off, concentrated on keeping his seat as a violent *spang* sounded through the fabric of the ship's hull.

Kirk thought of a hammer pounding on a metal pail—and they were inside the pail.

"Captain!"

Kirk instantly recognized the urgent voice shouting over the chair intercom.

"Hang on back there, Scotty."

"What's going on, sir? The strain on the engines tryin' to hold us to a course through this is makin' my stress gauges look drunk. And the hull's showin' strain, too."

"Variable pulsar, Scotty."

"What? But how did we get so close? Shouldn't ... ?"

"I know, Scotty. Let's wonder about that later. Bridge out." He rolled to his right, remembered the sensation so well described in books of sea captains of old. "Mr. Sulu, change course. We can't fight through this. Compute to—" He held on, gritting his teeth, forearm straining as another violent jolt battered the ship. "Compute position of pulsar, utilizing sensor readings, Mr. Sulu. Engage course directly opposite to plotted wavicle flow!"

"Aye, Captain!" A brief pause was long enough for the *Enterprise*'s superfast navigation computer, operated by Lieutenant Arex's skilled three hands. Then Sulu fed it to the helm. Abruptly the *Enterprise* came about, although there was no sensation of turning on the bridge: The curve the ship was making was far too gradual for it to affect the artificial gravity field.

The buffeting gentled, the galactic storm falling to a electromagnetic zephyr, but didn't cease completely.

"How are our shields holding, Mr. Spock?"

The first officer checked his instruments. "Still holding, Captain. I would be surprised if we have not suffered some external damage, though. We were caught utterly unprepared, and our shields are not designed to absorb that kind of intense radiation bombardment anywhere but at different spots at a time, as in a phaser attack. The storm enveloped us completely."

He checked his readouts again. "We absorbed saturation-level bombardment for nearly two minutes." Someone on the bridge whistled in awe. "We are fortunate to still have power."

"I know we've been lucky, Mr. Spock. But if we'd struck that storm at a sharper angle, plunged deeper into it before we realized what was happening, we'd have less than power." Everyone knew what Kirk was implying. A variable pulsar, at close range, could put out more than enough energy to fry the best-shielded vessel in space. The *Enterprise* had barely escaped being turned into a vast, metal coffin.

It was a nervous moment as another tsunami of energetic particles rocked the ship. This was the last one of any kind, powerful or gentle. Seconds later the warp drive had outpaced the wave front assaulting them.

"All right, Mr. Sulu." Kirk discovered half the muscles in his body were still contracted, forced them to relax. "Compute a new course and bring us back toward Briamos . . . and keep a slight curve out on the new heading." That ought to keep them clear of the receding pulsar's most powerful outbursts.

"Damage reports coming in, sir." Uhura listened a moment, then added more quietly, "They're not negative this time."

"I don't doubt it." Kirk readied himself. "Anything of real significance?"

"Several sections on Decks Seven and Eight report external structural damage in their area, sir. Estimate is that a portion of hull plating will have to be replaced."

"Contact Engineering and inform Chief Scott—though he may know about it already. Tell him to put a couple of crews to work on the damage. They'll have to rig something temporary as best they can. We can't afford the time to go back to Starbase Twenty-Five for formal repairs."

"Our appearance when we arrive in orbit around Briamos will not be the best, Captain," Spock pointed out.

"I know, Spock, but I'd rather show up looking a little bruised than not show up on time. According to what I heard during our briefings, if we're late we might as well not show up at all."

"I have already examined a part of the briefing material in detail, Captain, and I concur." The science officer turned his attention to the fore viewscreen, which showed only steadily burning normal stars forward. "A near thing. We should take time to report the hazard."

"That's right." Kirk turned, glanced over his shoulder. "Lieutenant Uhura, give me Starbase Twenty-Five contact."

Uhura worked busily at her console. Kirk waited ... and waited. "Lieutenant, what's the delay?"

"I'm sorry, sir. Apparently some of our external communications facilities were damaged by the energy storm. I've finally gotten through to the base, but I can only receive audio at the moment."

"That'll do, Lieutenant. Inform Engineering and have Scotty get on that damage also."

"Starbase Twenty-Five," came a pleasant, mildly concerned voice over the bridge speakers. "Lieutenant Jorgenson speaking. Go ahead, *Enterprise*."

"Mr. Spock, you have the coordinates?" The first officer nodded. "Tell them, then."

Spock switched on his own pickup. "Lieutenant Jorgenson, are you recording this transmission?"

"Yes, sir."

"Very well. We have just ridden out a violent energy storm, radiation put out in ship-crippling bursts by a variable pulsar of," and he read off several figures, giving galactic position and the pulsar's estimated frequency of critical-intensity outbursts.

There was an unexpected silence at the other end. Kirk and Spock exchanged puzzled glances. "Do you copy, Starbase Twenty-Five?" Uhura finally asked.

"We copy," came the lieutenant's voice, "but ... would you mind giving those figures again please, sir? Especially making certain of the coordinates?"

"The coordinates were correct the first time," replied Spock evenly, "however," and he repeated the entire sequence of identifying numbers.

"But that's impossible," Jorgenson insisted. "Those figures can't be right!"

"I assure you that it is not impossible and that our figures are correct." Spock sounded just the faintest bit peeved. "Are you denying that we just experienced the situation described?"

"No, no ... it's not that, sir. I've counterplotted your figures against the base charts and we have that pulsar clearly marked. There are four beacons of deep-space broadcast capability set well clear and equally spaced around that pulsar to warn approaching ships of the danger well in advance."

Kirk's thoughts tumbled over one another. "This is Captain Kirk speaking, Lieutenant. We certainly weren't warned. We picked up no beacon transmissions." He glanced sharply to his left. "Lieutenant Uhura?"

"No, sir!" She looked shocked. "You can't miss an emergency deep-space beacon. Not even if I wanted to. I didn't pick up as much as a cautionary beep."

Kirk hesitated, but Spock spoke into his chair pickup. "Are you sure about those four beacons, Lieutenant?"

"Positive, sir," came the reply, crackling with static due to the *Enterprise*'s damaged communications network. "It says here in the manual that they're fourth-degree amplitude broadcast, too, and were serviced only two years ago. You should have picked up at least two signals well in advance of any potentially damaging energy surge."

"It seems most unlikely, Captain, that two recently serviced beacons of that type should fail simultaneously." Spock sounded unusually grim.

"True, Mr. Spock." Kirk chewed his lower lip, looked thoughtful. "Still, there can't be many ships passing this way. They *could* have failed."

"Possible, Captain," Spock conceded. "I am not denying that, only saying that the odds are large against it. Deep-space warning beacons are powered and designed to remain operative without inspection for a hundred years. That two of them should fail together in so short a time . . . I find that a difficult concept to accept."

"So do I, Spock. But at that moment that's one of only two possible explanations I can think of. And I don't like thinking of the other one."

"That the beacons were intentionally tampered with?"

"Yes. Although I admit that seems little more reasonable than a simultaneous double failure." He paused, then directed his voice to the chair pickup once more. "Starbase Twenty-Five . . . Are you still there, Lieutenant?"

"Yes, sir."

"Report that at least two of the four beacons and possibly more apparently have become inoperative."

"*Inoperative,* sir? But that's impossible also."

"There's no other explanation, Lieutenant. Not unless all our external sensors and communications equipment has been rendered completely useless." Uhura shook her head violently. "And I'm assured that's not the case.

"Put in a report and have Starfleet maintainance get a repair team out here to check those beacons as soon as possible." He paused, and added even though he knew the answer, "Could those beacons have been destroyed by an energy surge from the pulsar itself, Lieutenant?"

"No, sir. According to the manual here, those four beacons are Class-AA-shielded. Nothing short of a full nova would knock them out. I just don't understand this, sir."

"Neither do we, Lieutenant, although we have a suspicion and it's not pleasant. However"—he took a deep breath—"we are still on course for Briamos and expect to arrive slightly delayed but still within the time parameters set by the Briamosites. You can report that back to Starfleet Command for us."

"Will do, sir. And, sir?"

"Yes, Lieutenant?"

"If there's negligence proven in this case, someone's going to pay for it."

"I have news for you, Lieutenant," Kirk replied. "If there's *no* negligence proven, someone's going to pay for this."

XII

Other than the unexplained incident involving the unbeaconed pulsar, the flight to Briamos was devoid of surprises. That pleased Kirk just fine. One near disaster before the conference had even been convened was quite enough.

Briamos's main system, containing two populated planets including the Briamosites' homeworld, was impressive. And Briamos itself was as beautiful a world as any in the Federation. Its twin world of Niamos, orbiting farther out, was smaller but equally attractive.

Clearly the Briamosites had not squandered the natural opportunities nature had given them. The deep-range scopes and sensors on the *Enterprise* indicated highly developed populations on both planets. With Niamos, an inhabitable world, hanging only seventy-five million kilometers off in space, the ancient Briamosites had been gifted with a natural reason for developing space travel.

While they did not possess warp-drive capability as yet, and journeys between the three close Briamosite solar systems involved—by Federation standards—unconscionably long times, the vessels that Kirk saw when they approached Briamos were superbly designed and very efficient-looking. So much so that Chief Scott was of the opinion that the Briamosite ships could be adapted to warp-drive technology, and therefore fast deep-space flight, with few modifications. No doubt that capability would be one of the first items the bargaining Briamosites would seek in deciding who to ally themselves with. But it would hardly be critical. Both the Federation and Klingon could offer Briamos high-speed FTL technology.

No, the Briamosite decision was likely to hinge on less definable reasons.

Five warships, each nearly as large as the *Enterprise*, drifted out of low orbit to greet them.

"We're being scanned and hailed, Captain," Uhura reported.

"Have a good time but check your weapons first," murmured Kirk as he admired the lines of the approaching ships. "Let's keep in mind that they're likely to be cautious at the same time they're displaying impatience. Put them through, Uhura."

The screen cleared instantly and they saw their first Briamosite. Their first live one, Kirk reminded himself. He had studied those features at lecture session after session. The actual sight, therefore, was expectedly anticlimactic. He now knew Briamosite features as well as those of M'ress, Arex, or any other nonhuman Federation race.

Since the screen proportioned everything, one couldn't tell from the portrait that the alien stood over two meters tall, this being the Briamosite average. Partly, the alien resembled a human being who had walked in front of one of those ancient amusement park fun-house mirrors (the one that made fat women happy by squeezing them to an unnatural thinness while stretching them to Watusi heights). The forehead was high, the head itself long and narrowed. But it was not a hollow-cheeked skull face. The Briamosites were thin, they were not living cadavers.

The one regarding them now did not smile. Neither did he frown. Not much could be told from that, one way or the other. Even sociologist Chu Leiski hadn't been able to learn much about Briamosite expressions during her limited sojourn on their world, and the shy people had been reticent to discuss the meanings of their occasional facial grimaces and twitches.

One thing they did know, Kirk remembered: as long as a Briamosite did not on first greeting show lower canines and groan softly, he or she was at least offering a neutral greeting.

The eyes were stretched like the rest of the gangling body. Ellipsoidal orbs peered out at Kirk, their pupils eerily small. As if to counterbalance the high, narrow skull the ears were wide pleated shapes like the wings of a bat, and roughly that size. They stuck out boldly at right angles to the nearly hairless pate. A three-centimeter-high gray fuzz ran in a straight line from the forehead down below the back collar, much in the fashion once favored by certain primitive Amerinds of Earth.

The figure spoke. Considering the small size of the mouth opening, the words that emerged sounded quite normal in inflection and pitch. Now that he was speaking, the Briamosite gestured freely with one hand or the other, hands which ended not in fingers but in four small, flexible tentacles, each tipped with a pointed claw painted a color different from that of its seven fellows. The ears moved also, in a manner which Kirk recalled from his notes as signifying friendliness. While the two arms were jointed much like human arms, the weaving boneless tentacles gave them a decidedly graceful, supple look.

As the speaker moved, the pins holding his toga to one high shoulder sparkled. Stripes which Kirk recognized as indicating rank ran across the upper folds of the garment. The skin beneath those folds was a light gray-green, hairless but definitely not reptilian in appearance.

"To you greetings, Captain Kirk of the Federation ship *Enterprise*. Am I—I am Colonel-Greeter Pliver here to welcome you to our system home and to conference." His ears swayed in agitation like those of a nervous rabbit. "Worried I was that you might not be here in time. You have arrived barely six vilvits the polite side of deadline."

"We're sorry, but we were delayed," Kirk explained quickly. Then he recalled the view that the Briamosite's portrait had replaced. "That's quite a welcome you've given us—five warships. You, Colonel-Greeter Pliver, make me feel like an honored guest. But all those weapons aimed in our direction kind of counter the effect."

"Apologies are extended," said Pliver.

At first Kirk thought the Briamosite might be struggling with an unfamiliar duty; but that impression had changed swiftly. Already Kirk was coming to regard the alien as a slickly professional diplomat the Federation Diplomatic Corps would have been proud to match wits with.

"We felt it necessary to provide an escort," Pliver continued smoothly, "for your own protection."

"Protection from what?" a new voice wondered. Kirk glanced back, saw McCoy emerge from the turbolift and stride onto the bridge.

"Hello, Bones. I was just going to ask that myself." He returned his attention to the viewscreen. "We can take care of ourselves," he said meaningfully. "Who do we need so much protection from?"

"Why, from mutual enemies yours, the representatives of Klingon. They have been here for," and Kirk thought he detected just a hint of reproach in Pliver's voice, "three days."

"Klingons . . . As I told you," Kirk went on, "we ran into some trouble on our way here. If you take a look at the damaged exterior of our ship you'll have some idea of why we were delayed."

"I have already noticed the damage, during your initial approach from deep space, on our scanners." He didn't sound particularly sympathetic, Kirk noted. "Most unfortunate. Assuming, I am, as little as we know about you of the Federation, that you are telling me a true story, Captain Kirk. I would hate to think that Federation of yours thought so little of us as to send a second-class damaged ship to represent them because it was not needed somewhere more important."

Almost, almost Kirk said the first thing that came into his mind. But he recognized it as a clever ploy, and a test. Pliver had deliberately baited him, testing his patience, his pride, his ability to maneuver mentally in a stressful situation.

Calmly, he replied, "The *Enterprise* represents the finest class of ships in current Starfleet operation, Colonel-Greeter Pliver. I assure you that our damage is as genuine as it was unwished. You may have the opportunity of inspecting it yourself, if you desire."

"Perhaps sometime during the conference," Pliver responded pleasantly, having tried Kirk and not found him wanting.

McCoy leaned close, was careful to keep his voice below pickup range. "They're a handsome people, Jim, if this one's any indication. And sharp operators." He turned, strolled casually toward the science station as Pliver, with an excuse, begged a moment's pause. No doubt to report the results thus far to his superiors.

"Five warships to protect us from the Klingons, eh? Mighty solicitous of our health, wouldn't you say, Spock?"

"I detect a familiar note of sarcasm in your tone, Doctor," the first officer replied. "The Briamosites, in preparing to ally themselves and their future with either the Federation or Klingon, are only exhibiting a cautionary xenophobia natural in such a situation. Clearly the presence of these warships is designed to insure that we do nothing unpleasant, should the conference not proceed in our favor. We would not, of course, but the Briamosites cannot be sure of that in their own minds. I am certain a similar escort surrounds the Klingon ship.

"While they do not possess warp-drive technology, from the appearance of their vessels and from Commander Scott's engineering analysis I would estimate they have ample firepower to blast any unruly visitor from their skies, be it Federation cruiser, Klingon, or both.

"Also, the presence of the warships constitutes an important show of force for Briamos. They naturally wish to impress us with their power and potential so that we will make our most generous offers of alliance and they will be able to obtain the best for their systems." Spock paused a moment, added, "I believe the presence of the five ships is best described by an ancient human saying once employed by the primitive tribes called nations. 'Showing the totem,' I think it was." There was a touch of disgust in the Vulcan's voice.

" 'Showing the flag,' " McCoy corrected him. "What's the matter, Spock? Didn't individual tribes on Vulcan ever show the flag?"

"Perhaps far in our past we did, Doctor," Spock conceded. "However, we disposed of our ritualistic slogans and totems much earlier in our racial history than humanity did."

Pliver returned to the viewscreen. "Your orbital coordinates are as follows, Captain. They have been transcribed for your own instrumentation systemology. You see, we have done our homework, too."

As always, there was no evident movement of the mouth beyond the minimum necessary to form the requisite words. But Kirk was beginning to relate certain significant hand and ear motions to what he had learned during the series of lectures at Starbase 25, and if he was interpreting them correctly now, it meant that

Pliver had, in addition to his sleek diplomatic style, a well-developed sense of humor.

"I'm sure you have," Kirk complimented him. "We've heard a great deal about your energy and abilities." That ought to earn the Federation a diplomatic point or two, he thought. "Mr. Sulu, stand by to receive coordinates."

"Standing ready for input, sir. Standing by, Colonel-Greeter."

Pliver looked pleased and a little startled at being so acknowledged. His expression didn't alter, but he read the coordinates with a definite flourish. "These will place your ship in close proximity to the Klingon vessel, Captain."

"Just a minute," Kirk said hastily. "If we may have any preference as to orbital location—"

"It is preferred," Pliver broke in smoothly but firmly, "that the vessels carrying both ambassadorial staffs remain in the same area. This will simplify," he added reassuringly with a friendly wag of batlike ears, "communications and transfer of personnel from both ships to the place-of-conference. That is located in a small resort community a modest distance from our capital city. It is on the seacoast, which is a region I am told you should find pleasant. The climate may be somewhat warm for you, but not unduly so. It was determined at high levels that it would be best to hold the conference in one of our most desirable, exclusive recreational areas as opposed to a stuffy, formal official structure in some city crowded. Landing coordinates for shuttle or transporter will be provided shortly. Until then, Captain Kirk, a pleasant forward looking-to."

Pliver switched off. Kirk couldn't be sure whether that last twist of ears indicated expectation or downright friendship, but either would be a sign that this first contact had concluded successfully.

"End transmission, Captain," Uhura said formally.

A snicker sounded from close by the science station. McCoy wore a wide, half-sardonic smile. "I like the Briamosites already, Jim. Some of their top politicians have seen a chance for a free vacation, so they're going to hold it on the Riviera instead of in the capital, where their constituents could keep an eye on them—assuming they're ultimately responsible to a constituency, of course."

"I beg your pardon, Doctor. *The* Riviera? That is a generalized human term, an adjective and not a noun."

"It wasn't always, Spock. Long time ago, it referred to one specific site on Earth. Nowadays any coast area on any world that proves especially hospitable to settlement is known as a Riviera site. Putting this conference in the local version of it," McCoy chuckled, "is a sign of the Briamosites' humanness."

"Yes," said Spock, his disappointment evident, "I'm afraid you're right, Doctor."

McCoy responded cheerfully. "Don't worry, Spock. One day soon we'll run across a race that wants to join the Federation and behaves exactly like Vulcans."

"A day I look forward to, Doctor, with great anticipation," the first officer replied. "However," he added in a more analytical tone, "it appears that the Briamosites possess many admirable qualities. I am looking forward with interest to the conference."

"On that, we both agree," finished McCoy.

Under Sulu's direction, following coordinates given by the Briamosites, the *Enterprise* was moving slowly toward the orbital station assigned to it. The five Briamosite warships shadowed the Federation cruiser every kilometer of the way.

"What the Colonel-Greeter Pliver said about placing our ship and that of the Klingons close together in order to facilitate transportation and communication is undoubtedly true, Captain," Spock ventured conversationally. "At the same time, a superficial reason masks the real one."

"Oh, there was never any question in my mind about it, Mr. Spock." Kirk thoughtfully stared at the viewscreen, which showed two Briamosite warships shining between the scanner and the green-blue world farther below. "They want both us and the Klingons together, nice and neat and accessible, so they can keep an eye on us all with a minimum amount of worry."

"Approaching designated position, Captain."

"Thank you, Mr. Sulu. Let's see what our counterparts and fellow arguers look like."

Sulu switched on the forward scanners. A small dot appeared, barely visible against the great cloud-covered bulge of the planet Briamos.

"Increasing forward magnification," Sulu declared.

The dot leaped at them. Sparkling in the viewscreen was a Klingon cruiser, analog to the Federation's *Constitution* class. It was an immaculate technological vision, hanging in space like an abstract jewel. Every centimeter of its surface shone brilliant and mirror-bright. The winged shape looked as if it had rested in a Starbase vacuum dock for months.

McCoy let out an appreciative whistle.

"She really shines, Jim. The Klingons must have polished her hull from bridge to engines."

Spock wasn't impressed. "I apparently have more confidence in the Briamosites than you do, Doctor, judging by your reaction. They seem too intelligent to me to be overawed by such superficialities as mere appearance."

"I tend to agree with you, Spock," Kirk continued grimly. "But you have to admit that with the damage we suffered from that pulsar we don't present a very impressive sight alongside that." He paused, leaned forward in the command chair, and squinted hard at the viewscreen.

"Jim, something the matter?" wondered McCoy.

"The ship." Kirk was lost in some thought of his own and spoke almost inaudibly. "I recognize that ship . . ." Then he sat back, added loudly, "The rogue planet, without a sun. The world of the illusion-masters who tested us—"

"We're being scanned, sir," Uhura interrupted, "by the Klingons this time."

"Yes. If they have a hailing signal out, acknowledge it, Lieutenant."

"They do, sir," she reported immediately. "Making contact."

A face formed on the screen; dignified, impressive, with a very un-Klingon bent toward humor. Most important of all, it was familiar. Dangerously familiar.

"Jim," McCoy whispered, "you're right. I remember the illusion-masters and our contest there. And . . . I remember *him*. Isn't that—?"

"Kumara," Kirk said sharply. "The Klingon I went to the old experimental Interspecies Academy with. Yes, that's him."

"The Klingons have clearly," added Spock, who also recognized the face, "chosen their best to represent them."

About that time the transmission must have cleared on board the Klingon ship, for the Klingon captain's eyebrows lifted in recognition. "Well, James Kirk. A surprise to see you again, Jim. Twice in the same year. A pleasure."

"One we could do without," grumbled McCoy.

Kumara glanced to his right, eyeing something offscreen. "I am just studying my other forward scanners, Jim, as you approach. It seems that these Briamosites trust you no more than they trust us. I'm glad to see their suspicion isn't one-sided. I can tell you, it took quite an effort to stay diplomatic in the face of their arrogant reception for us. There are four warships boxing my ship. Two against nine, then, if anything should go wrong."

"You make alliances as fast as you break them, Kumara," Kirk replied tightly. "It seems to me you talk awfully confidently—and dangerously as well. How do you know they aren't monitoring this frequency?"

"Their vessels and civilization are impressive for a primitive race," Kumara admitted. "But we tested this with a shuttlecraft of our own several days ago. They do not possess the equipment to break in and eavesdrop on this particular frequency." There was a pause as the Klingon captain glanced at something or someone out of view and made a disapproving sound.

"Dear me, Jim," he said when he turned his attention back to the screen pickup, "it appears that your ship has suffered a considerable amount of damage. Not very appealing to look at, I can assure you. What happened?"

"We were caught," Kirk said slowly, seeing no reason to conceal the matter, "in a wavicle barrage from a variable pulsar. A supposedly beaconed variable pulsar. The damage almost was severe enough to keep us from arriving here in time for the conference." He leaned forward again. When he spoke, his voice had assumed a low, threatening undercurrent of accusation. "I don't suppose, Kumara, that you have any idea what caused those beacons to malfunction?"

The Klingon captain looked offended. "Am I expected to know the position and disposition of every petty Federation navigational device? I sympathize with your concern, naturally."

"Of course you do," murmured McCoy sotto voce. "We can see that you're all broken up over it."

"So you had nothing to do with it, then?" Kirk persisted.

"To say that my ship was responsible for the destruction of an interstellar navigation beacon is inflammatory, besides being personally insulting, Jim."

"I could care less how you interpret it," Kirk shot back. "Did you destroy those beacons?"

"We destroyed no navigational beacons," Kumara replied with great dignity. Then he added in a slightly less formal voice, while finding something of extreme interest in the underside of his fingernails: "We were, however, patrolling routinely on our way to this conference through the fringes of the disputed territories. We did encounter a couple of malfunctioning fragments of space debris, hazards to navigation, actually, which we promptly eliminated so as to prevent the possibility of an accident to any vessel of Klingon or Federation."

"Then you *did* blow out those beacons!" Kirk slammed a fist down on one arm of the command chair, glaring furiously at the calm face on the viewscreen.

"Hazards to navigation, Jim," Kumara corrected him.

"Your pardon, Captain."

"Who's that?" Kumara looked to the right on his screen, saw Spock's outline flickering in and out of his view. "Ah, the inimitable Commander Spock."

"I might remind you, Captain," said Spock flatly, "that the destruction of Federation property, in particular something of a nonmilitary nature such as a navigational beacon, is in direct violation of the Klingon–Federation subsidiary articles of peace as appended to the Treaty of Organia."

Kumara shook his head, looked very tired. "I told you and will tell you for the last time, gentlemen, that we destroyed no navigation beacons. We torpedoed several nonfunctional pieces of free-floating metallic debris, that's all."

"The beacons," Spock continued, as if the Klingon captain had said nothing at all, "would not have been broadcasting unless there was something to broadcast about. Specifically, imminent danger from a high-intensity burst of radiation from the pulsar they were placed around. So if you destroyed them at a time when no such outburst was imminent—and there is no other way you could have approached the beacons near enough to do so, without first receiving an all-clear from them—*then* you could say they were nonfunctional.

"Furthermore," the first officer continued, "to say in the first place that an object as small and low in mass as a beacon could present a hazard of any kind in the little-frequented section of space where they were located is absurd. A starship traveling at warp-drive would barely take notice of the impact a beacon-sized object would make against its meteoric shields as it disintegrated. And the chances of such a collision occurring are small enough to border on the infinitesimal."

"Ah," countered Kumara, wagging a cautionary finger, "but they are finite, Commander."

"That may be so," Spock began, "but—"

"And no matter how slight the possibility, we of Klingon always seek ways to improve the space lanes and make them safer for travel by any ship."

"Kumara," said Kirk softly, barely holding his anger in check, "I am reporting your destruction of both beacons to Starfleet Command. An official protest will be registered with the imperial government, and—"

"Oh, come now, Jim," the Klingon captain chided him. "Why waste the power? There's no way you can prove that my ship was responsible for the so-called demise of your precious beacons. In fact, there is no way you can prove we were even in the area, which," he added quickly, "we were not, of course."

"He's right, Captain." Spock looked disappointed. "Our claim is not supported by fact, only by supposition and deduction."

"Good enough for me, Mr. Spock," Kirk snapped, a mite testily.

"True, Captain, and for myself also. However, Starfleet will not regard it so. Certainly not enough to base a protest on, one which could trigger a grave interstellar incident. There would be charges and countercharges, and without proof . . ."

"Spock's right, Jim."

Kirk didn't look around. "I know he's right, Bones. But this is one time I wish he wasn't."

"From what I can overhear of the discussion taking place around you, Jim, involving some of your officers, I would presume, you'd best heed their advice. They are quite correct. You can't do a thing." The Klingon captain sounded very pleased with himself.

"On the other hand, Kumara," Kirk mused dangerously, "I could apply inferential logic of my own regarding the destruction of the beacons and use that as grounds on which to take appropriate retributive action."

Kumara's veneer of good fellowship—never thicker than need be—abruptly vanished. So did his air of affected courtesy. No longer did he resemble some peculiar hybrid. He had turned thoroughly Klingon in expression and manner, although his reply was still more controlled than the average Klingon captain would have managed, considering the implications of the threat Kirk had just made.

"If it's a fight you're looking for, Jim, we'll be most happy to oblige you."

"No." Kirk leaned back in the command chair, satisfied at the result his warning had produced. "I was just getting tired of that oily grin of yours."

As if on cue, the expression in question reappeared. "Which oily grin, Jim? This one?" Kumara had a real sense of humor, a genuine rarity among Klingons, making him all the more dangerous.

Now that Kirk had indicated he had no intention of opening hostilities, the Klingon captain once more relaxed. "No, naturally we cannot fight, Jim. This conference is far too important to interrupt with petty squabbling among ourselves. Of course, once our friends and allies the Briamosites learn firsthand of the natural, ingrained duplicity of the Federation, then with their numerous well-armed ships about to assist us, I might reconsider."

"Don't count on their help in anything, Kumara. They're not your friends and allies yet."

"In good time, Jim. Merely a formality, as you will discover. I have preparations to make. Until the conference, then . . . ?" And without giving Kirk a chance to reply, the transmission from the Klingon cruiser terminated.

"*'In good time,'*" Kirk muttered, mimicking his Klingon counterpart. "In about twenty million years, maybe, but not before."

"I don't believe the Briamosites will be around in twenty million years, Captain," Spock pointed out philosophically. "Most species are—"

Kirk sounded tired. "I don't think they will either, Mr. Spock. I wasn't being serious. I only meant to say that—never mind. Obviously Kumara destroyed those beacons. They have an excellent intelligence service. Undoubtedly they knew we were coming and which direction we were coming from: Starbase Twenty-Five.

"With that in mind, they eliminated the beacons so we wouldn't know when the pulsar was going to emit a dangerous outburst of radiation. All of which was intended to prevent us from attending the conference. They could have canceled the beacons and, traveling at maximum velocity, still have arrived here three days ago as Colonel-Greeter Pliver informed us.

"You saw Kumara's first expression, Bones. He wasn't expecting us to show up at all. Thought the pulsar would finish us." Kirk smiled grimly. "Well, we've a few more surprises we can spring on him."

"The important thing is that we're here," McCoy pointed out. "We'll outmaneuver Kumara at the conference. Klingons have a bulit-in aversion to diplomacy that will eventually undo their standing in the eyes of the Briamosites. That's for sure."

"Not entirely sure, Doctor," Spock cautioned. "One must realize that this Kumara is not a typical Klingon. He appears capable of subtlety and even courtesy. Furthermore, there is the unsightly condition of the *Enterprise*. The damage we have sustained has already given the Klingons the first few points with the Briamosites."

"I still can't buy that, Spock."

"If you have studied the recordings of the lectures given at Starbase Twenty-Five, Doctor, you will recall that the Briamosites attach a good deal of importance to personal appearance." He indicated the main screen, which once again showed a view of the gleaming Klingon cruiser. "A detail to which Captain Kumara and his crew have clearly paid much attention. The contrast between his vessel's appearance and that of our own can only be to his benefit. Remember," he added after a pause, "humans originated the ancient saying about the importance of first impressions."

"Mr. Spock, even the Briamosites will pay most attention to the last impression. That will be the critical one, and we have something very impressive to demonstrate the power of the Federation with. That." He pointed to the corner, where the empty Slaver stasis box rested unobtrusively.

"The artifact, Captain? You still intend to employ trickery to convince the Briamosites that the box is unopened and untouched?"

"I do, Mr. Spock. Toward the Briamosites *and* the Klingons. You know firsthand what a Slaver stasis field looks like. Surely you and Mr. Scott can build a small device which can fit inside the box and simulate such a field?"

"As I mentioned once before, Captain, that should not be too difficult." Spock still didn't appear enthusiastic about the idea.

"No one will test the field," Kirk pointed out, seeking to convince his first officer, "because the only sure way to do that would be to open the box, and none of the Klingon delegation is likely to be lugging a nullifier around."

"You really think the box will be that impressive to the Briamosites, Jim?" a dubious McCoy asked.

"I do. Not just the presence of the box, Bones, but the fact that we would bring it down to an alien world with us, just to demonstrate our friendship. The Briamosites are very sophisticated, remember. We can't risk thinking of them as an inferior race. In straight intelligence they're likely to be the equal of any member race in the Federation. They have everything but warp-drive technology.

"I'm sure they know about Slaver stasis boxes, if only by reputation. So I'm expecting them to react toward our box exactly as we'd react if some strange people came to negotiate with *us*, carrying an unopened stasis box like a loaf of bread, purely for us to admire.

"It'll be even more impressive," he went on enthusiastically, "because we've brought a stasis box knowing that Klingons will be present. That fact should impress the Briamosites more than the presence of the box itself. A lot more than a shiny ship!" He smiled expectantly. "Kumara will be even more impressed and surprised than the Briamosites—just as I would be if he'd brought an unopened stasis box with *him*."

"We have no formal treaty as yet with the Briamosites, Captain," Spock reminded him. "What certainty have we that they will not attempt to take the box for themselves? Revelation of our prevarication when they find the box is empty and its field a fake could drive them into the Klingon orbit permanently."

"If they steal the box, Mr. Spock, I'm not sure they're the type of people the Federation would want as fellow citizens anyway. But I don't see that happening. Too many imponderables. For one thing, I don't think they have enough familiarity with stasis fields to construct a stasis nullifier."

"Klingons do," McCoy observed. "They could simply ask the Klingons for help in opening the box."

Kirk grinned triumphantly. "And there's the catch, Bones. Just because they steal the box from us doesn't mean they'd want an alliance with Klingon. Furthermore, in order to gain Klingon aid in opening the box, the Briamosites would have to trust it to Kumara's care more or less.

"While the Briamosites have a lot of firepower ringing both the *Enterprise* and Kumara's ship, it's still possible that either of us could outrun them before they could seriously damage us. And I don't think the Briamosites are naïve enough to trust Kumara with a stasis box, either stolen or one of their own.

"Besides, theft of a stasis box from us would be tantamount to an excuse for war on the part of the Federation. As advanced as their civilization is, I don't think the Briamosites are ready militarily to take on either Klingon or the Federation, and I believe they're realistic enough to know that.

"No, their best bet is to be truthful and straightforward throughout the entire conference, to play fair with both sides and not risk their whole future on something silly like stealing an archaic alien artifact. They might envy us the stasis box, but I don't see them chancing all their hopes on a single theft."

"Kumara won't feel that way, Jim," McCoy continued.

Kirk shook his head. "Yes he will, Bones. Consider: If he tries stealing the box, he'll have to do so in front of, or at least with the knowledge of, the Briamosites. That would constitute a breach of Briamos's neutrality, not to mention an insult to every high Briamosite official attending the conference. The result would be to drive Briamos into the Federation."

"I see now." McCoy nodded slowly. "You're planning this whole incident with the box, half hoping the Klingons *will* steal it."

"That's the idea, Bones. Of course, once Kumara discovers that the box has long since been opened and emptied, he'll come running back to Briamos squealing in outrage about the treachery of the Federation and its deceitful minions—that's us. But by then it'll be too late, if I read the Briamosites correctly. If I've learned anything about them from all those lectures, it's that they're basically a decent, honorable people. Once offended by the Klingons, I sincerely believe they'd remain firmly allied to the Federation, no matter what Kumara might claim after the fact."

"Which makes it all the more important for us to convince them to join with the Federation, Captain, in the event that Kumara does not try to steal the stasis box," Spock reminded them both.

Kirk turned in the command chair. "I'm not arguing that, Mr. Spock. How long will it take for you and Scotty to concoct something to put inside the stasis box that will simulate a Slaver field?"

"In our spare time, Captain?"

"No, this is a priority assignment, Mr. Spock. You should begin immediately."

"Very well, though the entire idea still strikes me as tending too much to the childish . . ."

"So was the Trojan Horse, Spock."

The first officer didn't reply as he walked over and picked up the box of Slaver metal. After a brief examination to refamiliarize himself, he turned to Kirk and said, "I estimate three hours to plan the device and design the schematics and another three or four to build and install it in the box."

Kirk looked satisfied. "Fine, Spock. Go to it."

Spock headed for the turbolift.

As events developed, it was fortunate that the first officer's estimates about the time required were accurate. Colonel-Greeter Pliver called now to inform them that the first meeting of the conference had been scheduled to take place at 0900 ship-time the following morning.

Later, when the device had been designed and computer-tested, Spock was able to leave the details of construction to Scott and his engineering staff and head for his cabin—to sleep, and with worried thoughts about the critical conference ahead . . .

XIII

The Federation delegation consisted of four smartly dressed officers: Kirk, Spock, Sulu, and Uhura. They met in the main transporter room the following morning.

"This first meeting will probably consist mostly of introductions," Kirk was saying as the four walked toward the transporter alcove. "You know: 'Captain Kirk, meet the esteemed president of Briamos's second stellar system. Esteemed President, First Officer Spock. Captain Kumara, greet Captain Kirk,' and so on. Everyone says much, means little, and generally uses the opportunity to size up his counterparts. But just because no vital issues are likely to be discussed doesn't mean this opening meeting isn't important, Mr. Sulu." The helmsman, who had been sunk partly in his own thoughts, looked startled.

"Your collar is folded in on the left side, Mr. Sulu," Kirk said sharply. "Straighten it."

"Yes, sir." Sulu hastened to do so. "Do you think the Briamosites care enough about appearances to have researched our uniforms so they can check on our individual appearances?"

"I don't know, Mr. Sulu," Kirk said easily. "They might not know a Starfleet dress uniform proper from an engineer's work coveralls. But," he added quietly and meaningfully, "*I* do."

The helmsman double-checked his straightened collar.

All four officers looked splendid in their dress uniforms as they stepped up into the transporter. Spock carried the Slaver stasis box in both arms. The box was bathed in a delicate blue aura; in appearance it was indistinguishable from the cerulean halo the originally unopened box had been enveloped in when Spock had first seen it back on Gruyakin VI.

Second Engineer Dastagir was manning the transporter console. Kirk turned to him. "Engineer, you have the coordinates for setting down which the Briamosites provided for us?"

"Yes, sir," came the ready reply. "Already programmed into the computer, sir. Ready when you are."

Kirk nodded once. The four officers assumed a waiting stance on four separate disks in the alcove. As soon as they were properly positioned, Kirk signaled to Dastagir. The second engineer initiated transport.

Gradually the four stiff figures were replaced by four

pillars of flickering metallic iridescence. The figure-pillars began to fade . . . and coalesce . . . and fade again. And coalesce again.

Startled, Engineer Dastagir hurriedly checked dials and readouts. Everything read normal, all instrumentation reported proper functioning, yet . . . the four columns of energy had still not vanished. There was such a thing as abnormally slow transport, affected sometimes by a surge-delay in the transporter equipment, sometimes by localized planetary effects. But as the seconds slid away, Dastagir could rule out either of those possibilities.

Something sparked from the console. A nervous, crackling sound filled the room. Fragments of multihued energy broke from the four fluctuating pillars and appeared to drift between them, filling the transporter alcove with an illusion of rainbow snow. Pops and snarls filled the room as confused mechanisms growled in frustration at one another.

Within the alcove the four figure shapes were oscillating wildly now. At the strongest point of coalescence the four officers were discernible down to individual characteristics. At the weakest, when they had become amorphous cloud forms, they seemed almost to blend into a single glittering sphere.

Frantically Dastagir threw switches, overrode, backed up, compensated for. Oscillation intensified but transportation did not take place.

Faced with a disaster of frightening proportions, Dastagir did the only remaining thing he could. He threw the emergency control which would freeze energy levels within the transporter alcove in their present mode. Additional power flowed on request into the transporter mechanisms to lock the four fluttering, uncertain figures within the alcove in place, together with the indistinct swirl of energy surrounding them.

Once the control had been cut in, nothing changed. The four figures neither coalesced nor grew any dimmer. Energy levels held suspended. That gave Dastagir time to do what any intelligent engineer in his position should have done: call for help. Sweating, fumbling at the intercom control, he waited anxiously for a reply.

It came promptly, its calmness contrasting violently with his own excited, anxious self. "Bridge here. Commander Scott speaking."

"Commander, sir, this is Dastagir Engineer Second, down in the main transporter room, sir."

"Slow down, Dastagir." Scott had immediately detected something in the usually imperturbable engineer's voice. He sat a little straighter in the command chair. "Trouble?"

"Yes, sir, I've locked them on emergency hold and—"

"Calm down! *Exactly* what's the matter?" A horrible suspicion was forming in the chief's mind. "Did the captain and the others get down yet?"

"No, sir, that's just it. And I don't *know* what's the matter. I've double-checked everything and the transporter insists it's functioning properly and it's not—" Dastagir stopped, caught his breath, rambled on rapidly. "I had the Briamosite coordinates programmed in and was beaming-down Captain Kirk and the other officers when something went haywire."

"Haywire's not an acceptable engineering term, Mr. Dastagir," said Scott sharply. "Elaborate."

"As near as I can make out there's something producing a field distortion in the transporter, sir. I couldn't beam them down and I can't pull them out of it, so I threw in the emergency lock. They're field-frozen now. And there's something else happening I've never seen before, some kind of energy–matter interaction taking place on the transporter itself."

"So you threw the field lock?"

"Yes, sir." Dastagir sounded desperately unhappy. "It was all I could think of to do."

"Don't . . . do . . . anything . . . else," Scott ordered Dastagir, spacing the words out for extra impact. "I'll be right there." The chief engineer hit the off switch on the intercom, spoke toward the navigation-helm console. "Mr. Arex?"

The Edoan looked back at him. "Yes, sir?"

"Assume command. We're experiencin' a malfunction with the transporter the captain's usin'."

"How bad?" asked Arex, worried.

Scott was already racing past communications and a curious M'ress on his way to the turbolift. "It doesn't sound good. I canna tell for certain until I see for myself."

Once inside the lift car, Scott pressed the emergency override. This sent the car directly to the transporter room, bypassing all other demands on the car's service and producing puzzled stares from several waiting crew members scattered about the ship as their anticipated lift went racing past their respective call stations without stopping.

As the chief entered the transporter room his gaze went first to the alcove. He saw the flickering silhouettes of sparkling wavicles fluttering on the four transporter disks, noted the energetic abnormality coloring the air around them.

Those observations were superficial. The real definition of what lay within the alcove would be found in readouts and dials on the instrument console. He was checking them out immediately, balancing their stubborn readings against the impossibilities registering visually within the alcove.

Dastagir stood helpless to one side, watching, ready to assist if he was needed.

"Any sign of any unusual activity in the mechanisms before the trouble became apparent, Mr. Dastagir?"

"No, sir," the distraught engineer replied, hands clenched tightly at his sides. "I tried readjusting the matrix, canceling the initial input—everything I could think of. Nothing worked. They just continued to oscillate." He licked his lower lip, gazed at the alcove. "It's the blurring of the field parameters that has me really worried, sir."

"Probably nothing to get excited about," Scott lied. "Get Dr. McCoy and a medical team up here." He nodded in the direction of the alcove. "They might need some dressin' up when we bring them back."

If we bring them back, he added silently to himself. Better not even consider that.

He took a handful of tools no less intricately formed than McCoy's surgical instruments and dropped to a prone position, on his back. Once the base panel in the console was off, he slid his head inside, reached in and up with boths hands, and set to work on circuitry no less sensitive than the organic variety McCoy operated on.

At Dastagir's request, and explanation, Dr. McCoy, Nurse Chapel, and several meditechs arrived in the transporter room several minutes later. All of them stared dumbfounded at the particulate storm suspended within the alcove.

"Scotty, what happened?" asked an anguished McCoy.

"Don't know for sure, Doctor," Scott told him, his voice tinged with strain. His head did not emerge from the bottom of the console. "I'm tryin' to find out now."

"But Jim, Spock, the others—"

"They're no worse off now than they were when this started, Doctor," replied Scott. "Engineer Dastagir had the sense to throw a lock on the entire system when he couldn't figure out what was happenin'."

McCoy's thoughts were running down predictable paths. "The Klingons," he began furiously. "They've done something to—!"

"I dinna think so, Doctor," Scott's cautious voice broke in. It reverberated faintly inside the console. A couple of moments later he emerged, holding several strange-looking, gleaming tools in his right hand. Both hand and tools looked damp with a transparent fluid thicker than water and McCoy knew the engineer had been adjusting fluid-state switches.

"Damaged wavicle rectification system," Scott said tightly, wiping his wet palm on his pants. "I hope that's all it was. Those switches shouldn't ever bust, but once in a while they do. Our luck these took a bad moment to rupture." He turned to the console, put his tools down, and glanced briefly at Dastagir. "Let's bring 'em back, mister."

"Yes, *sir*." Dastagir moved to stand alongside the chief and assist, while McCoy, Chapel, and the rest of the medical team stood aside and looked on anxiously.

Dastagir threw a switch and Scott's hands moved simultaneously on familiar controls. The wavering, banshee whine of the transporter abruptly softened, steadied, and then strengthened. The background field of waltzing energies vanished, leaving only four cylinders of fire. Crackling and sputtering no longer issued from the console.

The four pillars in the alcove intensified, melded into four recognizable, well-dressed figures. Scott meanwhile kept his attention fixed on one particular gauge. When its luminescent pointer reached a certain number, he threw a large switch.

All four figures solidified. The envelope of energy surrounding them vanished, and the whine from the transporter dropped to nothing. The four collapsed into various, sprawling positions on the alcove disks.

McCoy and the rest of the medical team were at their sides instantly, Scott and Dastagir a few seconds after. Scott leaned over the kneeling form of McCoy. The doctor had rolled Kirk onto his back and was passing a medical tricorder over the motionless form of the captain. Scott saw no visible damage, but he knew that any serious injury the officers might have suffered would probably not be easily noticeable.

McCoy started at the top of Kirk's head, grunted in what sounded like a gratified manner when he had reached Kirk's neck, and continued passing the compact device down the unconscious captain's body until it passed over his feet. A few readjustments to the instrument and McCoy repeated the pass, moving from feet to head this time. Then he relaxed visibly.

"He's all right," he told the expectant Scott, glancing back up and smiling in relief at the engineer. "Heartbeat, brain functions, involuntary muscular activity, everything, all his vital signs read normal—adjusting for his unconscous state, of course."

"Same here, Doctor," reported Nurse Chapel. She was bending over the lanky shape of Spock.

The reports were identical from the technicians examining Sulu and Uhura. "They're okay, then?" asked Scott.

"Looks like." McCoy rose.

Kirk's eyelids were beginning to twitch and his head to move from side to side. A low, tired moan escaped his lips. McCoy knelt again on one side and Scott on the other. Together they helped the groggy captain to his feet. Scott looked briefly at his wrist chronometer.

"If you can certify them all right, Doctor, we'll take them down to the bulk transporter."

"But the Klingons—" McCoy began.

Scott shook him off. "I told you, Doctor, the Klingons had nothing to do with this. Either it was unexpected but plausible equipment failure, or else we suffered some concealed damage from that pulsar outburst we rode out. And the captain has to be down on the surface within the hour, to attend that conference. Remember the Starbase lectures. The Briamosites make a religion of punctuality."

"But surely they'll accept a reasonable explanation for a delay, Scotty?"

"I wouldn't count on it. These people strike me as bein' basically good folk, but they've got their peculiarities. And I canna blame them for bein' nervous about this conference. If the captain and Mr. Spock and the lieutenants can be there on time, they've got to try and make it."

McCoy's reply was hesitant but positive as they supported the swaying Kirk. "I don't see why they can't go . . . so far, Scotty." Looking over a shoulder, he saw that the other three officers had also been helped to stand.

Under the doctor's direction, the four stunned officers were helped stumblingly out of the transporter alcove. Kirk walked like a man drunk, as if he couldn't find his balance. But by the time they had walked-carried him as far as the console, he shrugged off their support. Putting out both hands, he braced himself on the console, then turned, leaned against it, and raised his left hand to his forehead, wincing. His eyes opened, and he seemed to see them for the first time.

"Mr. Scott, Doctor McCoy . . . What happened?" There was an odd lilt to Kirk's otherwise normal voice, as if the captain hadn't yet regained full control of all his faculties. Neither the chief nor McCoy paid much attention to it. After the disturbing experience of being frozen in a transporter field for an abnormal length of time, a few mild side effects were only to be expected.

Scott explained. "There was a malfunction in the transporter, Captain. Maybe due to damage received from that pulsar we encountered. We had put you all in limbo for a while until I could get it fixed. You gave us all a bad scare."

"Oh . . . I guess that explains it." Kirk paused, then frowned and stared at Scott. " 'Captain' . . . you called me 'Captain.' "

Scott and McCoy exchanged glances. "Naturally, sir," said Scott, as gently as possible.

"Are you feeling all right, Jim?" McCoy was watching Kirk closely.

"Jim?" Kirk's voice sounded a touch higher, more tenor, than usual. Part of that could be attributed to shock at his recent experience, but not all of it. "Why are you calling me that?" Now the captain sounded—and looked—a little scared.

"What else should I call you, Jim? What's wrong?" Privately McCoy was thinking: temporary amnesia. But no . . . Kick recognized his name and title, merely wasn't identifying with them. Something else was wrong, then.

The three officers stared at each other as if paralyzed, until a new voice broke in: "Scotty, Bones! What in the name of the seven black holes has happened?"

Both men turned together. Sulu was eyeing them in a most authoritative fashion. The helmsman released himself, started toward Scott and McCoy—and almost fell. Startled, he looked down at his feet, registered surprise and astonishment, and then came toward them again . . . walking carefully as if treading on eggshells.

"Jim? Sulu?" McCoy's dazed gaze switched back and forth between captain and helmsman.

Sulu's eyes traveled over his lower body. He extended both arms out in front of him, rotated them over and back. His hands went to his face, felt the features as would a blind man touching a friend. His eyes widened.

"Oh my god! What's happened to us? What's happened to *me?*" He gestured shakily toward the body of the captain. "If I'm Kirk, in Sulu's body, then who are you?"

"I'm Lieutenant Uhura, of course," replied Kirk's body, in that peculiarly modulated tone that was so like Kirk's normal voice yet wasn't. Then Uhura-kirk looked down at herself. She said nothing for long moments.

"*I'm* here, Scotty, Bones. In Sulu's body." Kirk-sulu eyed them both, amazed and stunned.

"It would appear," put in the voice in Lieutenant Uhura's body very calmly and rationally, "that while we were in the malfunctioning transporter field a part of each of us was switched."

"A most important part," Kirk-sulu agreed, staring over at the now-alien shape of his science chief. "That *is* you, Mr. Spock?"

The first officer spoke to them, from Uhura's body, with Uhura's voice. While the tones were unquestionably those of Lieutenant Uhura, the choice of words and flatness of speech were those of Spock. "It is, Captain." He started toward them, stumbled for one of the few times in his adult life, and moved on much more cautiously.

"It would appear, Captain," Spock-uhura said, addressing himself to Sulu's body, "that I am not quite myself." McCoy did a double-take—he was beginning to wonder who *he* really was—but Spock was serious as ever. The joke was unintentional. "That *is* you in Lieutenant Sulu's body."

"It's beginning to look so." Kirk-sulu still sounded overwhelmed by it all. Turning, he stared across at the stolid form of Mr. Spock, who was carefully inspecting himself, running hands over his body, head, and, most particularly, a pair of unfamiliar ears.

"Since everyone else has been accounted for . . ." There was no need to finish the comment. But the voice in Spock's body finished for him, and confirmed the inevitable. "Yes, it's me, sir," admitted Sulu-spock. "I feel so strange, sir. This body . . . so many subtle differences. I feel different, altered. Not ill, exactly. Just queasy."

"I would sympathize with you, Lieutenant," said

Spock-uhura, "but at least you have ended up in a body of the proper gender. If you wish to compare unnatural feelings," and at that Spock-uhura glanced down meaningfully at its curvilinear form, "I believe mine far exceed yours. Nothing could feel more awkward than this. I find myself in a body of different sex and different race. I believe I can cope sufficiently with the mind, but the rest will take careful work."

"Don't count on being unique, Mr. Spock." Uhura-kirk was experimentally walking in a small circle, testing out a different arrangement of mass and new, more powerful musculature. "I didn't exactly end up in an easy-to-compensate-for container either, you know." She almost stumbled again, caught herself, then grinned.

"No wonder I nearly fell down the first time I tried to take a step, McCoy. The captain uses a longer stride than I'm used to."

"The question remains, what can be done to put us back where we all belong?" Kirk-sulu's attention was focused on the wide-eyed face of the ship's chief engineer.

Instantly, every other eye in the transporter room turned the same way.

Scott collected himself, thought a moment, and started to reply . . . to Uhura-kirk. Correcting himself, he shifted to address the body of Lieutenant Sulu.

"Nothing right away, I'm afraid . . . Captain," he told Kirk-sulu apologetically. Turning, he bent over and reached into the still-open console panel near the floor. He withdrew a small rectangle, about twenty centimeters long, which was filled with microcircuitry. It looked like a piece of metallic turf.

As he spoke, his fingers wove an intangible web over the battered, damp panel. "Everything that's been damaged on this I've either bypassed or replaced. The key to the personality–mind switch you've all experienced is locked in place on this panel.

"To put you all back to your original bodies, I've first got to figure out exactly what went wrong. Then I have to trace the one minuscule portion of the damage that produced the personality switch and change current flows, matching energy levels and duration precisely all the way, mind you, so that when you go back into the transporter the personality changes will reswitch themselves without doing further damage to some other portion of your bodies or minds."

He let the panel dangle carefully from one palm. "It's not," he added meaningfully, "a five-minute job for a maintenance tech to perform with a hammer and chisel."

"Wait a minute," said an excited Sulu-spock. "The transporter computer bank holds memories of all our transporter patterns. Why can't we just go to another transporter, desolidify ourselves, and then have the right patterns punched into the transporter so that when we're recombined it will be in the correct pattern ... and proper bodies?"

"I dinna think it's that easy, Lieutenant," Scott began to explain. "If you'd been completely dematerialized in the transporter and then fully rematerialized elsewhere, I might be willin' to try it. But that didn't happen. Only part of your patterns were switched, and it was before full dematerialization had taken place." He shook his head. "No, I dinna think it's a good idea. It might even make things worse than they are now."

"I don't believe any of us could stand that, Mr. Scott," said Spock-uhura.

"That's for certain," agreed Kirk-sulu. "Things are going to be hard enough to cope with as they stand." He faced Scott again. "I don't expect miracles, Scotty. How long before you can localize and repair the troubled sections?"

Scott glanced down at the tiny panel, which had suddenly assumed enormous significance. "I kinna say for certain, sir. At least a couple of days. I dinna want to take a chance with you all in the transporter until I'm sure as I can be that I've fixed it."

"A couple of days?" Uhura-kirk glanced down at her massive—to her—linear shape. "I don't know if I can handle a couple of days in this body, Mr. Scott."

"I'm afraid you'll have to, Lieutenant," said Kirk-sulu meaningfully. "We'll all have to."

"But what about the conference, sir?" she wondered.

McCoy nodded. "That's right, Jim." He checked his own chronometer. "You're supposed to be down on Briamos for the conference's opening session in two-thirds of an hour."

"They're expecting Mr. Spock and myself," noted Kirk-sulu. He pointed at first Uhura's body, then Sulu's. "That means that the four of us are still going to have to attend. It's too late to change designated envoys, and I don't think the Briamosites would accept anyone below captain's rank as a designated ambassador."

"But how are we going to manage, sir?" wondered Sulu-spock. "It doesn't seem possible."

"It *has* to be possible, Mr. Sulu. We can't ask for a postponement of the conference time without offending the Briamosites, and even if we could there's no guarantee that Scotty will be able to fix the transporter and put us back in our own bodies," and he added hastily, unable to leave so grim a thought without hope, "in a reasonable amount of time."

"What precisely do you propose, Captain?" Spock-uhura looked on with interest.

"Mr. Spock, the captain and first officer of the U.S.S. *Enterprise* will be present at this conference." His gaze wandered to his own body (how strange to be staring at a self that was not a mirror image), now inhabited by the personality of Lieutenant Uhura, and to that of Mr. Spock, in which Lieutenant Sulu was currently residing. "So will Lieutenant Sulu—that's me. And Lieutenant Uhura—that's you, Mr. Spock." Uhura's head nodded once. "What you and I do is not particularly important. We're lower-ranking officers, attending our superiors. We won't be closely watched.

"Mr. Sulu, you and Lieutenant Uhura will be acting as principals in this little play. So your imitations will have to be much more convincing. Mr. Sulu, at least you're in a body of proper gender, one not unlike your own in build and musculature." He turned his attention to his own ghost shape. "The success of this pantomime, Lieutenant Uhura, and of the entire conference, rests on your shoulders—even if they happen to also be mine." His own eyes were staring back at him expectantly. To his surprise, he found he had to repress a slight shiver.

"For one thing," he went on, "you'll be operating under the constant scrutiny of the Briamosites. Now, Captain Kumara knows me, but not intimately. I don't know how much he remembers in the way of personality traits and habits from our time together at the defunct Interspecies Academy. Probably not a great deal. But you'll have hormonal and other physical responses, the normal reactions of a male human body, to cope with. Some of them may surprise you at unexpected moments. Somehow you're going to have to act natural, nonetheless."

"I don't see that I'm going to have it that much easier, sir," objected a concerned Sulu-spock. "At least Uhura's in a human body. Talking about unexpected hormonal reactions, I'm in a Vulcan body. Already I'm feeling, well, itchy."

"It should not be overly difficult, Lieutenant," Spock-uhura insisted quietly. "All you have to do is act sensibly."

"That's easy for you to say, Mr. Spock," countered Sulu-spock testily.

"And you'll have to learn to control your facial expressions," Spock-uhura warned the lieutenant. "Those grotesque distortions of lips and mouth, the unnecessary head gestures must be eliminated if you halfway expect to ... to ..."

Spock-uhura halted in midsentence, staring at nothing in particular. "Most peculiar," the first officer finally murmured in Uhura's bell-like voice. He looked up at Dr. McCoy. "I presume, that my near outburst just then is what might be called an emotional response."

"Possibly, Spock. If so, it was very mild." McCoy considered carefully. "You raised your voice, but that's not necessarily an indication of emotional coloring."

Spock-uhura placed both hands against his forehead, winced at something that was not pain. "I feel most unusual, Doctor. My self appears reluctant to follow directions." Abruptly, the hands dropped and

Spock-uhura looked at Kirk-sulu primly. "This is going to be more difficult than I first assumed, Captain."

"It's not going to be easy for any of us, Mr. Spock." Kirk-sulu sounded firm. "But it has to be tried. Otherwise Briamos will ally itself with Klingon. I'm willing to chance anything to prevent that from happening.

"We have a couple of things going for us, however. Briamosites know very little of human behavior. Our ambassador," he added drily, "didn't strike me as your average human being anyway. So much of our seemingly aberrant behavior can probably be explained away, if we do anything awkward. It will be more difficult to fool the Klingons, but they think all humans are a little crazy in their behavior anyhow."

"That is not entirely a Klingon assessment," noted Spock-uhura pointedly. "The present situation would only tend to reinforce that belief."

"We might stall the Briamosites for an hour or so now, Mr. Spock." Kirk-sulu looked thoughtful. "We have to. We're going to need that hour to give ourselves a crash course in each other. But for several days? No, never." He walked over to confront his own body.

"Lieutenant Uhura?"

"Yes, sir," his own voice, but an oddly higher tenor, responded promptly.

"You are going to have to become me. At least, you're going to have to well enough to fool the Briamosites and the Klingons. At least our voices weren't switched. You're speaking with my vocal cords and my lungs. You've served as acting captain several times. This is another of those times, only you're going to have to be more than just acting captain. You're going to have to be Acting Captain James T. Kirk."

"I'll do my best . . . Lieutenant," she replied. Both of them smiled.

It was good to see himself looking so confident, Kirk thought a little crazily. He still felt as if he were talking in a dream. Any minute now they would all wake up, back in their own bodies, ready for the conference—everything all right again.

Then he realized his exuberance might be due in

part to the fact that he was in a more youthful, responsive body. They would have to watch for subtle as well as blatant differences like that during the conference.

"We're all going to have to exercise some to get used to our new bodies," he went on. "Our strides, as Lieutenant Uhura has pointed out, are different now. So are our reaches. I can't have myself, meaning you, Lieutenant Uhura, reach for a stylus only to miss it and clutch empty air. Enough errors of that sort and sooner or later the Klingons would catch on that something's definitely wrong with us. Once that happened, they would find ways to take advantage of us, to our detriment regarding the Briamosites."

He turned to Spock's watching form. "As for you, Lieutenant Sulu, you're going to have to talk like a Vulcan, think like a Vulcan, act like a Vulcan."

"I'll manage somehow, sir," Sulu-spock replied calmly. "I mean," and he seemed to stand a little straighter, "I will endeavor to execute my assignment to the best of my abilities, Captain."

"There is no need to overdo it, Lieutenant," cautioned Spock-uhura mildly.

"Let's move to the main briefing room," Kirk-sulu instructed them. "We'll work on our individual acclimatizing there." He turned to regard the watching McCoy and Scott. "Scotty, you get to work on that panel." He indicated the tiny board which had caused all the trouble. "Requisition all the technical assistance you need."

"Aye, Captain. Maybe we'll get lucky." There was more enthusiasm in his voice than in his thoughts.

Kirk-sulu's gaze shifted. "Bones?"

"Yes, Jim."

"What kinds of side effects can we expect to encounter from now on?"

"Besides the obvious ones of getting used to a strange body, Jim, of walking easily and reaching normally and other physical activities, there may be mental shifts of the kind Mr. Spock just experienced." He looked helpless. "I can't predict what else might happen."

"I know that, Bones, but speculate the best you can."

The *Enterprise*'s chief physician thought a moment, aware of concerned eyes on him, eyes that were slightly haunted. "You personally shouldn't have too much trouble, Jim. You're in a human male body not greatly different from your own. You might have to concentrate on restraining yourself in certain situations."

"Restraining myself how, Bones?"

"You're operating a considerably . . . well, not considerably," he hurriedly corrected himself, "but younger body than the one you're used to. It will react faster, move more rapidly than your own—as excellently conditioned as that one is.

"You already brought up reaching for something and coming up short. It works both ways. You have to be careful not to reach for something in a hurry. Your hands are liable to get there before your mind thinks they will. You could hurt or at least embarrass yourself."

"What else?"

"Listen. I think you can all cope with the physical changes," McCoy said convincingly. "It's the other problems that worry me. Your mind, Jim. How do you feel mentally? Can you remember everything?"

"Everything I try to," Kirk-sulu informed him.

McCoy looked pleased. "Then the personality transfer extends to full memory as well. That should make things easier. You'll have it easiest of all, Jim."

"What about the others?"

McCoy walked over, confronted Spock's body. "Lieutenant Sulu?"

"Yes, sir?"

"I wish I had some practical advice to give you, but I don't. How do you feel?"

"A little funny, Doctor. But it's not overpowering me. I can handle it." He frowned, then hastily wiped the expression from his face. "I just feel generally . . . well, not depressed, exactly. But dull—as if, as if I can't get excited or sad about anything. It's not that the laughter isn't in me. It's there, in my mind. But . . . for instance, I was trying to think of something funny to say just now, when you spoke about retaining our memories. I thought of an old joke that applies, and it's one that usually breaks me up. I recognized the humor in it, recognized it's as funny as ever, but . . . I couldn't laugh."

"Vulcan control," said McCoy, without a trace of a smile. "Try, Sulu. Think of the joke again. I want to make certain your own mind isn't in danger of being submerged in something alien you can't handle. See if you can consciously override the endocrinal suppression."

Sulu struggled with himself. Then a faint smile appeared on the face of Mr. Spock. It widened slightly, and the first officer laughed. It was a little forced, but a laugh nonetheless.

"Please don't do it again, Lieutenant," Spock-uhura requested. "The unnatural sight makes me ill."

"I don't think he will, Spock," Kirk-sulu told his first officer. "Bones, does that convince you that Sulu will keep control of his thoughts?"

McCoy nodded.

"Good. From now on, Lieutenant Sulu, you're going to be a model Vulcan, aren't you?"

Sulu-spock nodded, once. "As phlegmatic and poker-faced as possible, sir."

Spock said nothing. McCoy turned, walked over to confront Uhura's form. He had to consciously lower his gaze, so used was he to staring *up* at the first officer.

"And what about you, Spock? How are you coping?"

"Adequately, Doctor," came the lilting response from Spock-uhura. "But some of the sensations I am experiencing are truly remarkable. It is an intriguing experience, one filled with ample opportunities for discovery. But I fear I may experience some physical difficulties, contrary to your primary concern over our mental reactions. My thoughts are reasonably lucid, my control over them seems firm. But this physical configuration is sufficiently, radically different from my natural self. I'm afraid I find it a bit clumsy."

"Clumsy?" Uhura-kirk looked upset. "What do you mean, 'clumsy,' Mr. Spock?"

"No offense is intended, Lieutenant. It is clumsy only to me. For example, I find that I must cope with a considerably different and to me not especially efficient distribution of mass. It's a question of leverage and muscular control. I do not think I could ever master it, but I believe I will, with practice, be able to manage it."

"Speaking of distribution of mass . . ." Uhura-kirk began accusingly.

"That's enough, Lieutenant," Kirk-sulu said sharply. "You're not reacting the way I would, are you? You're the captain now. Don't forget it."

Kirk's face assumed an expression of embarrassment. "Sorry, sir. I forgot myself, for a moment."

"If it helps," Kirk-sulu added with a grin, "consider your predicament a temporary promotion."

"If this is what I have to go through to make captain someday," Uhura-kirk replied with a shy little smile, "I think I'd just as soon stay in communications. Don't worry, sir," she finished briskly. "I'll make an efficient you."

"I'm sure you will, Lieutenant. Neither Kumara nor his staff knows us well enough to recognize personal idiosyncrasies, so your imitations won't have to be letter-perfect. The way I sometimes rest my chin on one hand when I'm thinking, for example." Uhura-kirk promptly placed her chin on her right hand and looked pensive. "Or the way Mr. Spock raises his eyebrows when something surprises or especially interests him." Sulu-spock promptly lifted both brows and assumed a distinctly supercilious look.

Kirk sounded pleased. "That's the idea, Lieutenant. Only keep Mr. Spock's comments in mind and don't overdo it. Better to act like a humanlike Vulcan as opposed to a caricature." He hesitated, then went on. "It'll be best all around for us to keep everything—our words, our movements, everything—as simple and brief as possible. That will help to minimize opportunities for error. Opportunities the Klingons can only turn to their advantage. Let's go."

He turned and headed for the turbolift, walking carefully and working to adjust his pace to Sulu's slightly different way of walking.

"Bones," he said, glancing back at McCoy, "if you

can think of anything else we ought to watch for, let us know in the briefing room. And, Scotty, no matter where we are, even if we're down on Briamos and in conference, you get in touch with me—meaning Lieutenant Sulu—the instant you've corrected the transporter and are ready to try switching us back."

"Aye, Captain, you can be sure I'll do that. Even if it means insultin' our sensitive friends the Briamosites."

Moving like a quartet of drunken ensigns on leave, the four officers entered the turbolift. When the doors had closed behind them and the telltale alongside indicated the car was moving on its way, Scott turned his attention from the wavicle rectifier to the introspective Dr. McCoy.

"Did you mean what you said, Doctor, about them being able to handle their transposition?"

"I didn't see any reason to be overly pessimistic, Scotty." He looked concerned. "But I don't know, I just don't know . . . There are several psychology tapes I've got to run through. In case any problems do arise, I want to be prepared to treat them as best I can. Let's just say," and he gestured at the little rectangle of complex circuitry Scott was holding so carefully, "that the best thing for them would be to fix the transporter and put all of them back in their own bodies." He turned, his gaze traveling to the turbolift doors behind which his fellow officers—and friends—had departed. "Dual-personality delusions are easily treatable, Mr. Scott, but when there's a physical as well as mental basis for a psychosis, then I can't help but worry . . ."

Neither officer said another word. McCoy led Chapel and the rest of the murmuring medical team into the returned turbolift. Scott turned to the second engineer standing expectantly nearby. He held the almost-dry circuit panel up to the light, turned it slowly over in his hands, tilting it this way and that. Then he lowered it, and sighed.

"Dastagir, tell Loupas and Krensky we've got a little job to do. Tell them I'll be right there to detail what's got to be done. Tell them to forget about their off-time. No one in Engineering's going off-time until this cursed piece of electronic guts is turned right-side up again."

"Yes, sir." Second Engineer Dastagir moved to the intercom to relay the chief engineer's instructions. Scott moved toward the turbolift doors.

And far below, the anxious Briamosites listened unhappily to the asked-for hour delay and wondered about the courtesy of their maybe-allies of the Federation...

XIV

Nearly an hour later the frenetic discussions filling the main briefing room were interrupted by an apologetic beep from the room intercom. Kirk-sulu moved to the desk, thumbed the receiver switch and acknowledged the call.

"Yes, what is it?"

"Mrr. Sulu, I— Oh, I'm sorry, Captain. We werre told and it was all explained forr us, but—"

"Never mind, Lieutenant M'ress," Kirk-sulu told her. "No need to be embarrassed. Sometimes I get confused myself as to who I am now. It's hard enough for us to cope here." He looked back into the room at the three familiar and yet not familiar forms, all discussing matters of great import among themselves. "I'm not sure any of us are easy at mind. That's our problem, not yours. We have to convince the Klingons and the Briamosites, not our fellow officers."

"That's what I'm calling about, sirr," the communications officer purred. "We just rreceived communication from below. I spoke with that Colonel-Grreeterr Pliverr, the Briamosite liaison? He was concerrned that ourr delegation had not beamed-down yet."

"Concerned or angry, Lieutenant?" Kirk-sulu asked.

"My imprression was of a perrson willing to extend concessions, sirr, but at the point of losing patience."

Kirk checked his, or rather Sulu's, wrist chronometer. "We still have a few minutes, according to the extension the Briamosites granted us, but Pliver has our interests in mind by reminding us, Lieutenant. Contact

Pliver and inform him we're on our way to the transporter room and should be greeting him in person in a very few minutes."

"Yes, sirr. Brridge out."

Kirk clicked off, called for attention. The discussion ceased and the other three looked at him expectantly. "We're out of time. Mr. Spock." Sulu-spock nodded. "Lieutenant Uhura." Spock-uhura smiled . . . weakly. "Captain Kirk?" Uhura-kirk said, "I'm ready, Lieutenant."

Kirk-sulu looked grimly satisfied. "Let's go to the masquerade, then." He led the way to the door and they left the briefing room.

Kirk-sulu and Spock-uhura stopped in the hallway. The other two officers did likewise. There was an uncomfortable pause. Then Uhura-kirk muttered, "Oh," turned down the hall, and started for the turbolift. Sulu-spock fell in alongside her, his stride natural and seemingly unaffected. The two "lieutenants," as was proper, followed.

"That's better, Lieutenant Uhura," Kirk-sulu told her. "How are you handling me?"

"All right so far, sir," Uhura-kirk replied. Kirk still felt he was listening to an echo everytime she spoke with his voice, his lips. "But it seems a little more difficult to concentrate." They entered the turbolift. "It's fighting the tendency of my body to pull me one way, when my mind tells it to behave another. The hormone differences, I think. I keep feeling emotions that I know are unnatural . . . but for this body, they're perfectly natural."

"Your mind," Spock-uhura told her, "is battling the captain's instincts. We will have to be on constant alert against doing anything without thinking first. One of us could be in full mental control over our present bodies, but while thinking of something else that body might react naturally, producing an awkward situation. This is a war with ourselves. We must take care never to let down our vigilance."

The turbolift deposited them near another of the personnel transporters, on the opposite side of the ship from the damaged one. Scott awaited them there. He had left reconstruction of the critical panel to his subordinates long enough to handle the beam-down of the captain and the others personally, this time.

Uhura-kirk marched over to the console, said firmly, "All right, Scotty, we're ready for beam-down."

"Very good, Captain. I—" Scott stopped, startled, to stare in disbelief at the captain's face. "Are you—?"

"No, Scotty, I'm still over here, where you left me." Kirk-sulu gestured with a hand. "You're speaking to Lieutenant Uhura."

"What do *you* think, Mr. Scott?" Uhura-kirk asked hopefully in the captain's familiar voice.

"I think," a dazed Scott muttered, "I'd better get that wavicle rectifier fixed in a hurry or there won't be a sane person left aboard this ship." He waved an arm weakly. "Go ahead, I'm ready."

The four officers moved away from the console and took their places in the transporter alcove.

"Is there a possibility, Mr. Scott," wondered Spock-uhura, "that we could be reintegrated into our proper forms when we emerge on Briamos?"

Scott shook his head slowly. "I seriously doubt it, Lieu—Mr. Spock. There's no question that in order to return you all to your own bodies you have to be reassembled through the altered path of the original rectifier. But if it means anythin'," he added, "I hope I'm wrong, Mr. Spock, and you're right."

"We can hope," Kirk-sulu murmured as the chief engineer energized the transporter.

"I hope you set down in a nice, quiet chamber somewhere where initial observation will be by as few Briamosites as possible, Captain," Scott said. Kirk barely had time to nod Sulu's head as the transporter took effect.

He felt the usual disorientation, the blurring of vision and thought. It was joined by an unexpected sense of fear. But it passed, and along with it Kirk's momentary worry that their experience had given them all a phobia against using transporters.

They rematerialized on the surface of Briamos. Kirk started to slump, caught himself—and stood erect more rapidly than he normally would have. Since he had been learning the past hour to compensate for a strange body, handling the slightly higher gravity of Briamos was easy. He saw the others adjust with equal swiftness.

Sadly, Spock did not get his wish. Unspoken exchanges between him and his companions indicated that they were still firmly ensconced in the wrong bodies.

Nor was the chief engineer's hope fulfilled. Instead of the nice, quiet reception room they had all hoped for, they found themselves standing on a tall reviewing stand covered with a green canopy and lined with pennants and banners, facing four tall, attenuated Briamosites, whose slimness was accentuated by their attire, making them resemble more than ever animated scarecrows.

All four aliens were elegantly clad in bright emerald uniforms. Red striping sliced across the lower third of both jacket and pants legs. They wore, male and female alike, decorative tiara crowns. Each of these was cocked at a different but rakish angle on their high skulls, and sparkled with multicolored cabochons of different stones. Whether the tiaras were a badge of office, a sign of rank, or simply an article of clothing Kirk couldn't decide.

Less attractive by far were the five figures standing on the other side of the Briamosites. Captain Kumara was flanked by four of his own officers. They wore their own dress uniforms and were a blaze of barbaric design and color. Perhaps they were more colorful, Kirk mused, but they were certainly less dignified, even a bit childish. Whether they would appear so to the Briamosites, of course, was another matter.

Kumara made a Klingon sign of greeting, smiled slightly at Uhura-kirk. "Greetings to you, Jim. We were worried that you wouldn't be able to join us."

"Hello, Kumara," Uhura-kirk said, even as Kirk caught himself. He had almost replied to the greeting. The transition from the familiar surroundings of the *Enterprise* to this vast open plain and reviewing stand had been abrupt enough to unbalance his carefully prepared Sulu-image. He had spent so much time helping Uhura learn to act like himself that he'd nearly slipped up. Fortunately, Uhura *was* prepared, and she'd handled herself well already.

"In fact," she added, "I was worried about how depressed you'd become if we didn't arrive. You are sure you're feeling all right?"

Kumara responded with a tight-lipped little smile.

Kirk felt a surge of elation inside. Kumara showed absolutely no suspicion that anything was wrong. They just might carry the incredible impersonations off—if their luck held.

"Greetings to you, Captain Kirk." Kirk recognized the by-now-familiar face of Colonel-Greeter Pliver as the tall Briamosite moved to gesture at Uhura-kirk. "Sorry are we for whatever problem delayed you from arriving at the appointed time, and certain am I that it will not so trouble you again."

This was a veiled warning about punctuality, Kirk knew, which they'd better heed. They had already presumed on the Briamosites' version of courtesy once. Another such request would push them into the poorly understood realm of local insult.

"We had some trouble with one of our transporters," Uhura-kirk explained truthfully, without going into details. "I'm sure it won't happen again. Our delay bothered us as much as it did you, Colonel-Greeter. If there's one thing I can't stand it is people who can't keep their appointments."

A derisive snort sounded. It came from the knot of Klingon officers around Kumara.

"It's not," Uhura-kirk went on, "that we had any desire to minimize the pleasure of your company, you understand. It was only that our transporter operator disobeyed orders. He was reluctant to inflict the distasteful company of certain others on us. The person's intentions were worthy, but his insubordination could not be tolerated." She glanced toward the Klingons and made a face. Kirk was amazed at how disgusted he could look when he wanted to.

Her insinuations struck home. One of the Klingon officers bridled at the hidden insult, but was restrained by a dour Kumara. A tall Briamosite standing behind

Pliver made a small muffled sound that Kirk took to be local laughter. He forced himself to keep from smiling. Uhura's story had not only explained away their hour-long delay, it had apparently made them the first winners in the exchange of greetings. Of such tiny asides were powerful alliances forged.

"This is Sarvus, Leader of all the Briamosite systems, final arbiter of multiple-world decisions." Pliver introduced them to the elegantly appointed, two-and-one-half-meter-tall Briamosite who had stifled his laughter at Uhura-kirk's comment. "And Vice-Leader Chellea," Pliver continued, indicating the tallest member of the naturally towering alien delegation.

Leader Sarvus stepped forward, leaned like a willow to his right. His right arm curved downward to slap lightly against his slim right thigh.

"Pleasure in making your acquaintance," said Uhura-kirk. Kirk watched as his own body imitated the formal Briamosite bow-and-greeting, arm hooking down, back of the hand rapping the thigh. Uhura had gained considerable command of Kirk's musculature by now and she performed the subtly difficult movement with admirable smoothness.

Kirk started to relax just a little. Inspection showed that Kumara and his companions still suspected nothing. He found himself really believing that they just might be able to bring off the masquerade.

Uhura-kirk turned to face him and Kirk forced Sulu's body into an attitude of attention. "My executive officer, Mr. Spock." Sulu-spock stepped forward, nodded slightly in typically perfunctory Vulcan fashion, and said nothing. That was just as well, and in accordance with their plans prior to beam-down.

Uhura, occupying Kirk's body, would be forced to do a lot of talking. But there was no reason why the rest of them couldn't remain as quiet as possible. The less they said, the fewer the opportunities for making a fatal mistake.

"My helmsman, Lieutenant Sulu," Uhura-kirk went on. Kirk stepped forward, felt his strange body bow respectfully. "And communications chief, Lieutenant Uhura." Spock manipulated Uhura's body, stepping forward to bow and in the process nearly falling over. Clearly he still hadn't quite mastered the intricacies of feminine musculature, particularly that of Lieutenant Uhura, which would require more adjustment to handle than the average female form.

He caught himself, dropping to one knee and then rising hastily before falling flat on his face. Kirk forced himself not to move. Instead, he watched for the expected reaction among the Klingons—and got a pleasant surprise. None of them were looking in his direction. They were chattering softly among themselves and hadn't noticed Spock's slip.

But why should they be paying attention? Kirk reminded himself. Uhura and Sulu were only subordinate officers, hardly worthy of notice. Kirk and Spock had already been introduced. Kumara was looking over a shoulder and conversing with one of his aides. Maybe their present situation would have more advantages than disadvantages, Kirk mused. He and Spock could observe the Klingons closely, without being subjected to similar attention. Kumara and his associates would be watching their original bodies, now inhabited by Sulu and Uhura.

He tried to overhear their whispered conversation, and failed. It didn't seem important, though. One of the officers was smiling the particularly unhumorous Klingon smile. Certainly there was no sign they regarded Spock-uhura's slip as anything other than a simple stumble.

Nor did the near fall appear to have bothered the Briamosites. Perhaps they weren't quite as sensitive as Kirk had been led to believe.

"Leader Sarvus will now speak," announced Colonel-Greeter Pliver portentously. This was the signal for Klingon and Federation officers alike to forgo their own conversations and stand attentively.

The Briamosite leader withdrew a small book from one breast pocket, opened it to the first page, and began to read. The speech was long, but the pages turned quickly. It was a carefully worded, thoughtfully prepared speech. It expressed feelings of friendship for both the Federation and Klingon peoples, declared a desire for extensive future relations of mutual benefit, and promised not so much as a grain of sand to either side in return for concessions and benefits the Briamosites were seeking for themselves.

Clearly the local precepts of diplomacy were as fully evolved as Briamosite technology. They were in no hurry to join either the Federation or Klingon, and it would take considerable persuasion to change their minds. Nor could they be fooled. But Kirk knew that the pressures both sides were bringing to bear on Briamos to join one side or the other would eventually force them to do so.

The Leader finished, closed the back of the tiny book. There was silence. The Briamosites appeared to be waiting for something. Uhura-kirk turned, glanced back helplessly at Kirk, which was a mistake, though it would probably have been worse for all of them to continue facing each other quietly, grinning like idiots.

Kirk knew what should be said. "Yes, sir, a wonderful feeling which we would greet our hosts with in kind," he murmured expressionlessly. Uhura recovered quickly, turned and repeated what the captain had just said, in somewhat different words so that it wouldn't smack of an echo.

But the damage had been done. As Uhura-kirk spoke, Kirk saw Kumara eyeing the "captain" uncertainly. Kirk began to sweat, though it did not show.

"And so we thank you for your magnificent welcome, Sarvus of Briamos," Uhura-kirk was saying. Kirk felt the words sounded a little stilted, but he doubted the Briamosites would notice. "We extend to all of Briamos and its sister worlds the best wishes and hopes of the United Federation of Planets. I, too, hope that our future dealings may always be this pleasant, enjoyable, and relaxed, and that together we may continue as equals to extend civilization a bit farther into the galaxy."

Kirk let out an internal sigh. Uhura had remembered all the speech, once he, as Sulu, had jogged her memory. He'd kept the formal reply purposefully short, eliminating many flowery phrases the psychodiplomats at Starfleet Command had thought would appeal to their hosts. The couple of sentences were enough—and Uhura had still almost forgotten them entirely.

The Briamosite officials appeared satisfied, though, despite the brevity of Uhura-kirk's response. As she had recited the speech, Kirk had seen the initially suspicious Kumara relax and lose his puzzled expression. But . . . it had been a near thing.

His worst suspicions were confirmed as soon as Uhura finished. Kumara was always more dangerous when relaxed. "It looks like you're not feeling too well, Jim," he murmured to Uhura-kirk. "A bit nervous, perhaps?"

"As a matter of fact," Uhura-kirk replied quickly, "my big problem is that I might be too relaxed, Kumara. I don't have anything to be nervous about . . . unlike some people I know."

The speed of her response was good, but the wording sounded a touch bitchy to Kirk, and was hardly the way he would have replied. But it seemed to serve where it counted most, among the Briamosites. They sensed strength instead of Kumara's implied uncertainty. Fortunately, Kumara didn't have a chance to follow up his initial accusation, or he might have succeeded in rattling Uhura.

Colonel-Greeter Pliver stepped physically and verbally between Kumara and Uhura-kirk. "We have prepared a parade somewhat. We call them something else, but 'parade' will serve. This is our way of displaying for you, Captain Kirk and Kumara Captain, part of our culture in a way we hope is entertaining to you all." He waggled his ears, and Kirk recognized the Briamosite version of a chuckle.

"If paraders seem they especially happy, is not because they are glad to see you necessarily. For purposes of parading, today was declared local metropolitan holiday so paraders could take off workings to participate. Are being compensated for not working."

Uhura-kirk nodded slightly. That was the correct response. Kirk was permitted the luxury of smiling, although it was with Lieutenant Sulu's face.

Every time the Briamosites hinted at their sense of humor, Kirk was elated. It was one area where the

Klingons couldn't hope to compete, lacking much of any kind of humor other than the sadistic. However, he cautioned himself, the grin fading, it would be better not to count on the aliens reacting in any predictable fashion until the conference got underway and he had a chance to see how their hosts reacted to serious matters.

A great fanfare of brassy but bizarre music rolled across the grassy sward in front of the reviewing stand they stood on. It sounded like violins and organs competing with damp bagpipes. At a signal from Pliver, the visitors followed the Briamosite leaders out from under the concealing canopy. Kirk took in their surroundings.

The metal-and-wood reviewing stand was nothing extraordinary, a simple construction designed to be functional rather than impressive. Across the open green-blue field Kirk saw spires, lofty and attenuated like the Briamosites themselves, rising from the distant resort town where the conference hall was located. A curving slice of deep azure, like a blue plate viewed almost edge-on, showed where the ocean of the northern hemisphere backed onto the town.

The fanfare became a rather dizzy march. Variously dressed ranks and clusters of well-organized Briamosites strode back and forth in front of the parade stand. Their long limbs swung supplely as they walked.

The four Briamosite leaders beamed approvingly as each new group appeared. Uhura, using Kirk's body, dutifully tried to mimic their appreciation. It wasn't easy. Nothing was spectacular about the parade, though the Briamosites appeared to feel otherwise.

After the parade had run for half an hour and there was still no end in sight to the flag-waving, uniformed ranks before them, the inflexible Klingons were beginning to twitch noticeably. Kirk knew that the sight of "inferior" beings passing in seemingly unending waves before them was enough to crack even Klingon self-control. One officer snapped at another who was crowding him too closely, and only a harsh, single word whispered by Kumara kept them from fighting on the stand.

The parade continued for another two hours. By

then Kirk could almost feel sympathy for Kumara, who looked about ready to scream. When the last rank of marchers had faded across the plain, the final banner receded into the distance, Leader Sarvus turned to both visiting captains. He wore a blank expression but his ears fidgeted happily, the Briamosite version of a politician who has just surveyed his constituents and seen a healthy majority of favorable votes.

"Gentlesirs, what think you? You have just seen forty-five (untranslatable noun) representing all the continents of the several worlds of the United Systems of Briamos."

"Very impressive," Kumara lied quickly, always first to flatter.

"Very much so," said Spock-uhura, "I wish only we could see it over again."

The comment produced pleased fluttering from the ears of the four Briamosite officials. It engendered the exact opposite reaction from Kumara and his cohorts. The prospect of sitting through a repeat of the just-endured parade was almost more than they could bear.

Nevertheless, it gave Kumara an opportunity to display his remarkably un-Klingonlike diplomacy. "We also would enjoy a repeat," he said with a perfectly straight face, "but too much pleasure in a single day dulls one's mind for more serious endeavors. Hopefully another day."

"No doubt you are right," an impressed Leader Sarvus admitted. "Until tomorrow, then, at the conference hall within the town, at the appointed time. You will transporter coordinates for the conference place be given."

One of the Klingons stepped forward to huddle with Colonel-Greeter Pliver. After a moment's hesitation, too brief to cause comment, Kirk-sulu moved to join them to record the coordinates.

"These will bring you down by the lakeshore, in the chamber itself within the building," Pliver told them after they had both noted the series of numbers that would tell their respective transporter computers where to set them down. "The structure itself is not an official one, but part of a large recreational complex, so your surroundings may a bit informal seem."

"We are looking forward," Leader Sarvus was saying to Kumara and Uhura-kirk, "to hearing the arguments and persuasions of both your governments." For a moment the supreme leader of the Briamosite peoples looked troubled. "Actually we do not seek an alliance so soon, but external considerations seem to be forcing us inexorably in that direction. I need hardly tell you both," he cautioned more firmly, looking at each captain in turn, "to present the strongest arguments you can muster. The Council of Greater Briamos will base its decision on the evidence you present to us in these coming few days. Once concluded, we of Briamos will abide permanently by that decision."

"All of us are looking forward to the first session," said Sulu-spock.

"Until tomorrow-time, then," murmured Uhura-kirk softly.

"Yes, until tomorrow." Kumara responded now to one of his officers, who called for him to move aside so they could be transported up to their ship. Unable to resist a last stab, Kumara half smiled at Uhura-kirk. "We are in a hurry to return to our ship so that we may supervise maintenance procedures, Jim. That is a function treated with notorious sloppiness in the Federation, a characteristic of most Federation activities—as anyone can tell by looking at the *Enterprise*."

"Our damages would not have been incurred," Uhura-kirk responded loudly, for the benefit of attentive Briamosite officials as much as for Kumara's ears, "*despite* interference with navigational beacons, if we hadn't been so involved with the recent recovery of an interesting artifact. An artifact," she said, directing her words now to the Briamosite leader Sarvus, "which we will present for your edification and inspection during the conference, sir."

Kumara looked dubious and curious all at once. "What sort of artifact?" But Uhura-kirk didn't get the opportunity to reply.

The Leader was speaking. "We not really are interested in archeological matters right now, Captain Kirk.

There are far more important matters to be dealt with."

"I believe you'll be interested in *this* artifact," Uhura-kirk insisted. "It is, in a way, part of our presentation. A means of showing you the thoroughness with which we of the United Federation explore our own worlds and those around us. The artifact will not take up much space, and will be an interesting diversion to all attending the conference." She noticed the Klingons staring at Kirk's body. "*You* should find it interesting also, Captain Kumara."

The Klingon commander looked interested in spite of his attempts to appear otherwise. What sort of trick did Kirk have up his braided sleeves this time? Why haul an old bottle or some such relic into as critically balanced a conference as this one?

Kirk-sulu noted the effect of Uhura's words on the Klingon captain, but didn't smile. They had already gotten something out of the Slaver stasis box, and without even having to display it. Kumara was worried about the mysterious artifact. Good! The more it troubled him, the less ordered his dangerously fertile mind would be, and the fewer opportunities for creating mischief of his own he would have.

"As you say, Jim," the Klingon finally finished lamely.

Kirk-sulu watched with his companions while the four Klingons dissolved, taking with them a Kumara so rattled that he had forgotten that by leaving now, Kirk would have the last word with their hosts.

True to her training, Uhura didn't waste the chance. "You must excuse our friends the Klingons," she said. "Anything new and alien to their own culture makes them uneasy."

There, that was a suitably neutral statement, but one loaded with overtones they would begin to work on the Briamosites' minds after this day was done.

They were ready to beam-up. Kirk almost pulled out his own communicator. Fortunately, Sulu-spock reacted fast and did the same a step ahead of him.

"Mr. Scott?" Sulu-spock said into his pickup.

"Yes . . . Mr. Spock." Scott's response was broken by an infinitesimal pause.

"You may beam us aboard," Sulu-spock informed the distant chief matter-of-factly. "I have new coordinates to program in for our beam-down tomorrow."

"Very good, Mr. Spock. Standing by."

"Tomorrow—with expectations of benign developments," Colonel-Greeter Pliver told them with that odd little sideways bow of the Briamosites. His words and attitude were as warm as official neutrality permitted, but Kirk felt confident that the Greeter was on their side.

However, he reminded himself, it was not Pliver's vote that counted, but those of the three distinguished aliens conversing in low tones behind him.

XV

Somewhere elseness became the norm for a moment or two. Then they were greeted by the familiar surroundings of Transporter Room 3. A smiling chief engineer rushed around toward them from behind the transporter console as soon as the four had fully coalesced.

He went straight toward Kirk's body. "Captain?" His voice was hopeful, hesitant.

"Sorry, Scotty," Kirk had to say. Scott looked over at Sulu's shape, where the words had been generated. "I'm still in Mr. Sulu's body. All four of us are still switched around."

Scott fought hard not to look disappointed. "I tried a couple of little things, sir, with the console levels. As much as I could without risk of makin' things worse." He shrugged. "It was an unreasonable hope."

They stepped down out of the alcove, walked over toward the turbolift doors. Scott stopped to gaze longingly at the transporter.

"We're still workin' on the original damaged rectifier, Captain," he informed them. "I've also been workin' with the computer, on Mr. Sulu's suggestion that we use your original recorded patterns to beam you out and then back in—hopefully back in your proper bodies." He shook his head sadly. "I still don't think it'll work, Mr. Sulu." He directed his words to Spock's watching form, where the helmsman's mind was still housed. "But if the realigned rectifier should fail for some reason, then we'll have no choice but to try it anyway.

"Still, I'm afraid that if I send you all out and bring you back, and you're still not correctly reintegrated, you might never be able to get your own bodies back. Overlapping pattern fixation on the false patterns you're now using would prohibit ever reversin' the situation."

"We'll try it as a last resort only then, Scotty," Kirk-sulu agreed.

"I hope we dinna have to, Captain," the chief engineer told him. "You might all end up frozen in these bodies for the rest of your natural lives."

Spock-uhura glanced down at himself, at the body of the communications chief. "The prospect of remaining forever locked in this form is indeed appalling, Mr. Scott."

"I'm not thrilled about it either, Mr. Spock," Uhura-kirk told him firmly. "I'd like nothing better than to, to repossess my own body." Her hands gestured at herself. "The chemical balance of this male envelope initiates some of the most absurd reactions."

"We'll all be glad when"—he was careful not to say "if"—"we're back where we belong, Lieutenant," Kirk assured her soothingly. "Keep us posted on progress with the rectifier, Scotty. Oh, how's the stasis box coming along? We'll probably take it down with us tomorrow."

Scott was glad of the chance to report some good news. "All ready for you, Captain. It's on the bridge. I couldn't put it in your cabin," he added a mite apologetically, "without forcin' the door seal, and I didn't want to do that."

"It's just as well, Scotty. There's nothing to hide from the crew, and I don't think I can get into my own cabin myself now. The voice and retinal patterns that the door lock would recognize belong to that body," and he pointed at Uhura, "not to Mr. Sulu's, where I'm presently residing. If I need to get into my own cabin, Lieutenant Uhura's going to have to come along."

The four officers took the turbolift to the bridge. Although everyone on board the *Enterprise* had by now been thoroughly apprised of the quadruple body switch—mind switch, rather—it still took personnel encountering it for the first time a few minutes to get used to addressing Captain Kirk as Uhura and Sulu as Captain Kirk, and so on.

As Scott had promised, the stasis box was waiting for them. It rested on a small stand next to the left arm of the command chair. Kirk-sulu walked over to it, and was joined by Spock-uhura. "It certainly looks real enough, Captain," the first officer said.

Kirk had to admit that it did. Using Spock's descriptions of the original box, the engineering department had inserted something into the box which produced an encapsulating blue aura. The top of the box had been resealed by some exotic weldfill technique, as much art as metallurgy, so that with his face only a centimeter away Kirk couldn't see where the box had been opened.

Reaching out, he picked it up, his hands feeling a faint tingle from the false stasis field. "*I'm* convinced, Spock. But will it fool the Klingons?"

"Even sensor equipment will produce information insisting that the aura," and Spock-uhura indicated the box, "is a genuine Slaver field. The Klingons will not be given an opportunity to inspect the box closely. Furthermore, Klingon has encountered only one stasis box in its entire history of stellar exploration, and that was several hundred years ago. They are not as familiar with the artifacts as we are and so are unlikely to know enough to expose the fraud."

With that, the first officer resumed his position at the science station. The ensign he replaced couldn't help staring as he moved aside. He knew Spock was taking over, but all he could see was Uhura.

This caused Kirk to look around the bridge. The

captain was manning communications, and he, as Sulu, was seated in the command chair while Spock was serving as helmsman and Uhura was at the science station. That view of the bridge would be certain to set Kumara thinking. Instead, Kirk decided to give his Klingon counterpart something else to dwell on.

"Lieutenant Uhura."

"Yes, Captain," she replied in his own voice, from her position at communications.

"If you pick up any transmissions from Kumara's ship, or from the surface, acknowledge them but do so mechanically. Under no circumstances provide visual communication. And if the Briamosites or Kumara desire to speak to me, Lieutenant, you'll have to answer."

"I understand, sir," she replied. Kirk didn't think he could ever get used to conversing with himself.

So far everyone had performed admirably under impossible circumstances. Uhura had played Kirk reasonably well. It said something for the camaraderie that normally existed on board that they could imitate each other so efficiently. Kirk had to stay alert constantly, though, to make certain those imitations never degenerated into caricature.

They had succeeded in avoiding any serious psychological problems. Those might still lie ahead, he knew. Give the body's normal endocrine system long enough and it would begin to affect the minds housed in unfamiliar surroundings. The sooner the conference below could be concluded successfully, he knew, the better their chances would be. Meanwhile, they could only remain vigilant and hope Dr. McCoy's worries found no basis in fact.

Spock was walking back to his own cabin, musing on the intriguing but distressing events that had left him imprisoned in this cumbersome, awkward form. Thus far he'd been able to repress anything seriously upsetting. He could imitate—as long as nothing terribly drastic was required—human reactions. But he was still very much himself.

Before leaving for rest and recreation period, until

they beamed-down tomorrow, all four of the officers had gone over their personal needs with that other mind inhabiting their natural bodies. All indication of amusement absent from her voice, Lieutenant Uhura had warned Spock above all not to forget taking the several monthly capsules her system required, which he would find in the dispensers in her cabin. Spock assured her he would not.

It was difficult enough to face the possibility that he might have to live the remainder of his life in this human body. He was not about to risk getting it pregnant. Not that, he had hastened to assure her, his own mind could in its wildest moments conceive of permitting that to happen. But she made him promise to take the supplement capsules nonetheless. Spock could have quarreled with her on personal grounds. But since the communications chief regarded the subject so emotionally, he decided to humor her.

He stopped. Someone was standing in his way. Spock moved to go around him. The man, a tall ensign from organic fabrication whom Spock didn't recognize, moved to block his intended path.

"In a hurry?" the ensign said, grinning in a moronic fashion not becoming to a member of Starfleet forces. He leaned on one hand against the corridor wall.

"If you will kindly let me pass," Spock said with a touch of irritation.

"Hey, now!" The man shifted to block Spock's new attempt to walk around him. "I know you're a superior officer and all, but I didn't think you'd already forget about..."

It suddenly occurred to Spock that possibly all the crew, certainly not all those on long sleep cycles, had learned of the transformation of the four officers into different bodies. This ensign's familiar attitude toward a superior officer was decidedly unbecoming, but that was a matter between him and Lieutenant Uhura, a matter in which Spock had no particular desire to interfere.

Fighting the peculiar hormone reaction all at once surging through the body he inhabited—a fight which required the most vigorous application of mental discipline—he tried to explain. "I am not Lieutenant Uhura, Ensign."

The man stared at Uhura's face, heard Uhura's voice. His initial bravado turned to confusion, puzzlement. When he spoke he sounded a little hurt.

"Now, what's this all about?" the ensign broke into a wide grin. "You didn't always used to stand on rank."

Spock rushed on, hoping to spare this unfortunate individual any further embarrassment. "There was a transporter semifailure. It resulted in the transfer of the minds of your captain, your executive officer, and Lieutenants Sulu and Uhura into the wrong bodies upon reintegration. That is the present disturbing state of affairs. They will remain this way until Engineer Scott can trace and correct the trouble with the damaged transporter."

"Oh, come on, Uhura! What are you feeding me? You're Uhura . . . Lieutenant," he added, a touch accusingly. "Tell me I don't know how to recognize—"

"I happen to be Commander Spock," Uhura's voice informed the ensign frostily. "Presently I am inhabiting Lieutenant Uhura's body. Lieutenant Uhura's mind is located in the body of Captain Kirk. If you will take the time to contact the bridge, or any of your fellow shipmates who doubtless heard the announcement while you did not, you will find that what I am telling you is the truth."

The ensign's face ran through a remarkable gamut of expressions in a short time. "You're joking with me, aren't you? This is some kind of game you're playing." The man didn't sound as positive as before. "Look, if it was something I said—"

"There's an intercom." Spock-uhura indicated the grid-and-panel set into the corridor wall. "Contact whomever you wish and check what I say."

"All right. All right, I will," the ensign responded, with the air of one about to call a bluff. "We'll call this joke off fast." He thumbed the intercom.

"Excuse me, is Yeoman Anderson there?" A pause, during which the ensign smiled faintly and Spock-uhura stood quietly waiting. "Yes, Anderson? This is

Ensign Kearly. Hey, did something go wrong with one of the transporters recently? I heard this hysterical story that the captain, Mr. Spock and—"

A strong female voice at the other end spoke from the grid. "Yes. Don't you know about it, Kearly? Damnedest thing . . . I guess you must have been deep in sleep cycle. Seems that in trying to beam down to Briamos there was some kind of problem with the transporter. Rumor up from Engineering says that it was caused by that pulsar wave we ran through a while ago." The ensign's face, as he listened to this, was drawn.

"Anyway, it seems like everyone trying to beam down got all shifted around, wrong mind in the wrong body. It's hard to believe, I know, but I've personally—"

"Never mind, Yeoman." Ensign Kearly sounded a bit shaky. "I just wanted to confirm it." He clicked off, turned to stare at Uhura's form. He looked, and sounded, as if he were confronting a ghost. "Then . . . you really *are* Commander Spock?"

The first officer replied as gently as he could. Still, he was unable to keep all the irritation out of his voice. "Believe me, Ensign Kearly, this present situation is not more palatable to me than to you, or to anyone else—least of all Lieutenant Uhura."

"Yes, ma'am—I mean, sir." The ensign executed a hurried, harried salute, excused himself, and moved rapidly away. Spock was allowed to continue on uninterrupted, with ample time to consider the peculiarities of human interrelationships.

Spock's comment to the ensign about the unpalatability of the present arrangement was an understatement as far as Uhura was concerned. Presently, the communications chief was resting in her own cabin. A technician with special clearance had had to open it manually for her, since Kirk's face and hands wouldn't key the door seal any more than his tenor would substitute for her higher, more delicate voice.

Although the captain's body she was imprisoned in was in excellent condition, compared to her own she found it awkward, clumsy, and oddly unmobile. Funny, she thought, leaning back on her bed, how one could grow so accustomed to something like a body. After all, what was it but an envelope of flesh to provide mobility for the mind?

Experimenting in the privacy of her cabin, she tried to sing a favorite song, the one she had composed for her grandfather back on Earth. In place of her beautiful, throaty tones the room filled with an excruciatingly harsh, unmelodic gargling noise. It might have passed as a cry for help, but certainly not for music. She sat up in amazement that so grating a sound could issue from her throat.

There were any number of other things about her present body that made her feel uncomfortable. The best thing she could do would be to ignore them and try to relax. She lay back down again. The sooner she had her own body back, the better. The thought of spending the rest of her life in this lumbering masculine shape appalled her at least as much as did the prospect of spending the rest of his life in her body did Mr. Spock.

By the following morning, Engineer Scott could only report that the sensitive work on the damaged rectifier was proceeding as fast as he dared permit.

Kirk-sulu carried the stasis box in a large, unadorned container as the four prepared to beam down for the second day of conference, and the first real negotiating session. To hide their deception, the container had been made large enough to hold both the box and the false field it was generating, since a true Slaver stasis field would have appeared outside the walls of a smaller container.

A familiar but never comfortable instant of not-being, and the four officers found themselves in a modest but impressive domed chamber large enough to hold a hundred people easily. The floor was composed of slabs of irregularly cut stone resembling gold-veined marble. The entire wall on their left was made of long slim panes of some transparent glassy material. Kirk noted that it appeared to lighten and darken to match the changing sunlight pouring into the chamber. There were probably occasional clouds outside today, he thought.

They walked toward the window-wall and he saw that the chamber and the building they were in were set on a hill overlooking a broad swatch of ocean and beach. Towering sandstone cliffs streaked with horizontal bands of brown, orange, and maroon lined an imposing headland in the distance. Small craft of unusual design and construction swarmed like insects within the quiet water of the bay.

Kirk recalled what Colonel-Greeter Pliver had told them about this being a very popular resort area, within reach of the capital city. Trying to imagine himself one of the happy, thin aliens cavorting in sand and water below, he wondered how many of the local honeymooners—assuming Briamosites had honeymoons—partygoers, or ordinary vacationers realized that an interstellar conference was taking place only a couple of kilometers away from them. Or if they cared.

Come to think of it, if a similar work-halting conference were being held on Earth, the average citizen would shrug and wonder if he might squeeze out another day of vacation without offending his boss. After all, the future of the universal civilization was a trifle compared to the travails and adventures of everyday life. Fortunately, Kirk knew, there were those who took the business of civilization somewhat more seriously. They became philosophers or artists.

Or they joined Starfleet.

A long *U*-shaped table was set up near the window-wall, just out of reach of the invading sunlight. The rest of the chamber was empty of furniture, giving it a spaciousness one usually felt in far larger halls. The two prongs of the *U* faced into the room while the curve backed against the window-wall.

Leader Sarvus and Vice-Leader Chellea sat at the apex of the *U*-curve. They were flanked by Colonel-Greeter Pliver, who now rose as the Federation representatives approached, and several other undoubtedly important members of the Briamosite hierarchy whose faces were new to Kirk. One of them sat particularly stiffly. His clothing and manner marked him as a military man. Empty seats, four to a side, lined the outside of both horns of the table.

"Greetings, Captain Kirk, Mr. Spock, and Lieutenants," said Pliver, walking around the table to shake hands human-fashion with each of them. He conducted them to their chairs on the near side of the *U*. The seats were a bit tight and narrow for the human pelvis, but the four officers managed—though Spock, in Uhura's body, had a difficult moment.

Pliver glanced curiously at the large box Kirk was carrying. "What does the lieutenant carry, Captain?" he asked, talking to Kirk's body. "The artifact?"

"Yes," replied Uhura-kirk. "We'll unveil it later." As Pliver seemed satisfied with that and didn't press for details, Uhura wisely kept quiet.

Kumara and his attending officers arrived a few moments later. They took the four seats on the horn of the table opposite their Federation counterparts.

The Briamosites promptly opened the conference by reasserting their humanlike characteristics. Every official present, lips firm and ears wagging like flowers in a strong breeze, delivered a substantial speech, including Sarvus and Chellea. No one intended that his part in this important occasion should fail to be entered into Briamosite history. In addition to a sense of humor, it was clear the inhabitants of Briamos were developed politically. So Kirk, Kumara, and the other guests listened while the officials of Briamos detailed variously the importance of the conference: what they hoped might be achieved by it, their desire to maintain friendly relations with both governments no matter which one they eventually entered into alliance with . . .

The self-important speeches, Kirk knew, were a characteristic common to immature races. Even the member races of the Federation hadn't entirely outgrown the juvenile aspects of government.

"I now declare open this conference," Sarvus declaimed at last. "We of Briamos look forward to hearing from each of you at length." Kirk tensed. The time had come for formal presentations, and serious business.

It was the signal for the opposing executive officers,

in this case Sulu in Spock's body, to rise in turn and deliver long prepared presentations. For Sulu-spock, the words had been constructed by the best Federation psychopoliticos at Starfleet Command and then relayed out to Starbase 25. Sulu-spock read the sentences mechanically, spelling out as clearly and persuasively as possible the advantages which would accrue to Briamos if they aligned themselves with the Federation.

Kirk knew the speech would have been more impressive and had greater impact if it had been delivered half extemporaneously by Spock himself, since Spock had the words fully memorized. But that wasn't possible. Kirk noticed that Spock, in Uhura's body, was following Sulu's recitation closely.

The Briamosites didn't appear offended by Sulu-spock's reading of the prepared statement. As Kirk had hoped, they seemed more interested in content than form. All Sulu had to do was maintain a posture of Vulcan detachment, keep his voice a monotone. That was easy enough. The only problem in rehearsing the speech back aboard ship had been to restrain Sulu during the more emotion-charged sections of the speech. After much practice he had been able to recite the words without overly emphasizing any of them. Just as he was doing now.

If anything, it was even flatter in tone than Spock would have presented it. They had decided to err on the side of reality rather than risk having Sulu reveal anything by trying to drive a particular point home.

From Leader Sarvus and Vice-Leader Chellea down to the lowest-ranking official present (a representative from one of the outlying Briamosite worlds), the assembled alien officials received the address quietly. Occasionally they would nod or jerk their heads in meaningful but indecipherable fashion, or lean over to whisper briefly to some colleague. They did not interrupt, with either applause or boos, or with questions or comments.

When Sulu-spock concluded the speech and sat down, Chellea responded with a short paragraph of thanks, then asked Kumara to present his side. The Klingons' executive officer acknowledged his captain's nod, rose, and loudly proclaimed the Klingons' hopes and intentions.

Kirk bristled at some of the claims and outright falsehoods contained in the speech, but restrained himself. First of all, it wasn't Lieutenant Sulu's place—the body he occupied—to raise objections unless his comments were specifically requested. Secondly, Kirk knew that they would have ample time later to counter the Klingon arguments and make objections of their own.

Looking smug and satisfied, Kumara's first officer concluded his speech in a burst of fiery rhetoric accusing the Federation of intending everything for Briamos from child-stealing to slavery, and resumed his seat. His smile shrank considerably when, much to the surprise of both parties, the Briamosite officials removed tiny devices from beneath their portion of the table. On touching controls, each instrument regurgitated long scroll-like strips of plastic opacity imprinted with dots and dashes and curlicues. Both Kirk and Kumara expected that their words would be somehow preserved, but they hadn't expected each official to make his or her own personal record. It displayed a thoroughness Kirk had not given the Briamosites credit for. He should have.

After thoughtful inspection of their individual scrolls, the officials looked up at their visitors. And the questions began. They favored neither side. The assembled Briamosites fired questions rapidly, almost impatiently, at the respective speechmakers.

Both Kumara's executive officer and Sulu-spock responded as best as they could. Once, another Klingon officer replied to a question from Vice-Leader Chellea when the executive officer seemed at a loss for words. That was what Kirk had been hoping for. When the Briamosites offered no objection to the new speaker, it meant that he, in Sulu's body, and Spock, in Uhura's, could now offer their own expertise during the questioning.

So as the questioning continued relentlessly, when "Spock" or "Kirk" appeared slow to respond or unsure of certain answers, Kirk felt this was more than made up for by the impressive speed with which the two suboffcers, Lieutenants Sulu and Uhura, answered the queries. Indeed, even the Klingons appeared impressed by the literate, thorough responses the two Federation lieutenants provided in response to certain difficult questions posed.

Once, a particularly unsubtle inquiry was made by one of the Briamosite officials in regard to the depth and preparedness of the Federation's armed forces, in reference to something the Klingon executive officer had mentioned in his speech. Everyone was surprised when communications officer Lieutenant Uhura responded. They were more than surprised, they were astonished at the lengthy list of impressive figures, details, and placements—all unclassified—which were provided, seemingly with effortless recall.

Kumara in particular eyed Uhura curiously, wondering at the apparently unrehearsed expertise she had demonstrated in a matter not related to communications.

"Isn't it a fact, Lieutenant," Kumara said quickly, when Spock-uhura had finished reeling off the stunning array of statistics, "that the starship grouping monitoring Starbase Fourteen was removed only two months ago because that section and the races in it weren't thought worth protecting by Federation officials?"

Kirk watched Spock-uhura closely without trying to betray his concern. Kumara had concocted a tricky question. It was true, as the Klingon had claimed, that Starfleet forces had been withdrawn from that sector recently. But that had nothing to do with not wanting to extend protection to federated peoples in that area. However, it did show the extent and efficiency of Klingon intelligence.

Actually, the ships had been transferred to airdock for normal maintenance and overhauling and were scheduled to return to their positions in another two months. But it looked, if one viewed the matter as Kumara did, as if the Federation was guilty of indifference to the people of Sector 14, or at least of gross negligence. Kumara could argue that the reappearance of Starfleet vessels in that sector now would be a Federation attempt to cover their error and curry favor with the Briamosites.

Sometimes, however, when the best-laid plans of mice and men went awry, they could lead to equally efficacious new plans. Such was the case now, as Spock turned a physical disadvantage into an advantage. "I cannot answer you, Captain Kumara," Spock-uhura claimed. "A communications officer is not privy to such detailed information about military maneuvers. Since it doesn't pertain to my specialty, I can't confirm or deny your report. Ship movements are more in the province of navigation."

Kirk promptly picked up his cue. "I'll be glad to check on unclassified movements in Sector Fourteen and report back to this assembly," Kirk-sulu declared. "I do know that ships are often called from duty for standard maintenance." He looked at his own body. "Isn't that true, Captain?"

"I am not permitted to confirm information of such a sensitive military nature," Uhura-kirk replied, fast enough to earn an order of merit.

There! Those multiple responses countered Kumara's accusation while leaving the facts sufficiently ambiguous to forestall the need of a specific reply.

Kumara accepted his semantic defeat with good grace. It was only one of dozens of similar verbal battles that would be contested across the conference table before the day's session drew to an exhausted end.

The session went on into the early Briamosite evening, which was later in arriving than that of a normal twenty-four-hour human day. The setting sun of Briamos was turning the sandstone parapets across the bay to ribbons of grainy flame, and lights were winking on on the pleasure craft circling beneath them, by the time the questioning finally came to an end.

Uhura-kirk rose. "If there are no more questions from our hosts—"

Kirk-sulu broke in hurriedly, "One more item on today's agenda . . . Captain."

Uhura-kirk recovered quickly. "I was about to bring

it up, Lieutenant." She remained standing, gestured toward him. "The presentation and display."

Kirk-sulu felt relief he didn't show. Standing and picking up the crate they had brought from the ship, he moved between the table horns.

"A stand or small pedestal of some sort will be helpful, sirs," he told the Council, directing his voice toward Pliver.

The Colonel-Greeter wagged his left ear, touched a switch set into the table before him. A section of seamless wall slid aside, revealing a pair of huge, armed Briamosite soldiers. The Colonel-Greeter barked instructions at them. They vanished into the wall, reappeared moments later with a single-stemmed pedestal-table.

Kirk wasn't surprised by the presence of the armed troops. Such grim visages were present to insure that in the event the conference didn't continue in an atmosphere of sweetness and light, the Briamosite hosts would be protected from Klingon–Federation belligerence. Automatic weaponry would have been more efficient, but the presence of live troops would be effective enough, he knew.

"You can show it at any time, Lieutenant Sulu," Uhura-kirk told him.

"Yes, sir."

Picking up the container, he placed it on the pedestal and began unsnapping the side and top panels. When the last latch had been flipped, he touched a switch in the base of the container. Dramatically, the top and all four sides fell away simultaneously, revealing the glowing stasis box.

Expressions of amazement filled the chamber. They came not from the phlegmatic Briamosites, but from Kumara and his officers.

"What is this artifact you have brought to show us?" Leader Sarvus inquired, eyeing the box intently.

Kirk-sulu went on to explain about the ancient, extinct civilization of the Slavers and the isolated relics of their culture, the stasis boxes, which were occasionally discovered in scattered parts of the galaxy. As the story continued, several of the Briamosite officials wagged their ears in recognition and appeared more and more impressed. That meant that the wonders of the stasis boxes were at least known to the people of Briamos.

"As you can see," Kirk concluded, gesturing with Sulu's hand at the softly glowing cube of Slaver metal, "this stasis box has not yet been opened. It could contain an ultimate weapon, any kind of valuable device, or nothing at all. But to show you our good faith and our confidence in the people of Briamos, we've brought it here for you to see."

"Even though," Uhura-kirk added meaningfully, "we knew there would be Klingons present."

"It's a fake!" Kumara rose angrily, trying to divide his attention between Kirk-sulu, the box, and Leader Sarvus. "They wouldn't dare bring a real, unopened stasis box here to display on an unallied world. Especially," he added with a loaded grin of his own, "knowing that there would be representatives of Klingon present."

When neither Sulu-spock, Spock-uhura, or Uhura-kirk elected to respond to Kumara's accusation, Kirk decided to risk appearing a bit authoritative.

"If one of your officers has at his waist a standard-issue imperial science 'corder, you can see for yourselves."

Kumara stared curiously at Sulu's form for a moment, then shrugged, his mind too busy with more important matters to follow up the impossible suspicion that had briefly occurred to him. He eyed one of his subordinates. "Kaldin. Let him use yours." He looked at Sulu. "I assume you'd prefer to run the analysis yourself, Lieutenant, rather than let one of my men near your precious 'stasis' box?"

Kirk-sulu nodded, walked over to the Klingons, and took the compact instrument from the glaring officer who proffered it. Carefully he passed the device over the box, making certain the setting on the instrument was not set too deep, where it could pick up traces of the metal within, modern metals which Scott had used in constructing the Slaver-field falsifier. He also avoided the edges around the top of the box, where Scott had resealed it.

Then he turned and handed it back to the Klingon officer, walked back to stand next to the pedestal, and waited. There *was* a chance he might have mispassed the 'corder, that it might have detected a hint of the chief engineer's handiwork.

Apparently he hadn't. The Klingon officer read the readouts on the device, performed a few hasty calculations with a separate instrument, conferred with the other subofficer on his left, and turned a grim, solemn gaze on his captain.

"Sir, the box is Slaver metal."

"You're certain of that, Kaldin?" Kumara asked tensely.

"There can be no mistake with these readings, Captain," Kaldin insisted, gesturing with the 'corder. He extended the hand holding the device. "Slaver metal cannot be faked. Even if it could, the metal readings translate according to their nuclear bonds as being over a billion years old, and that *certainly* cannot be faked. To last until now, any metal would have to have been encased in a Slaver stasis field. Check the readouts for yourself, sir."

Kumara wrenched the small instrument away from the officer, glanced briefly at the readings and handed it back. When he looked up at Kirk-sulu again his expression was more speculative than anything else. "Very well. So you do dare. But how can I be certain that it is a real unopened stasis box? Simply because it's Slaver metal is not proof enough."

The conversation was beginning to revolve around Kumara and Kirk-sulu, a dangerous development. Uhura-kirk recognized the danger, spoke quickly to the captain. "Mr. Sulu, Captain Kumara is doubtful that we're telling the truth. Why don't we produce some facts he can't argue with. Let's open the box for all to see—right here, right now."

"Yes, sir," Kirk-sulu acknowledged. Turning, he took a small cutter from his waist and extended it into the field. Evidently he was going to use the thumb-sized flamer on the box's upper rim.

The reaction was uncertainty among the Briamosites. Among the Klingons, who were familiar with stasis boxes and their properties, the reaction was much more predictable. They were on their feet, staring in disbelief, except for one officer who was hunting frantically for a place to hide.

All of Kumara's usual poise temporarily deserted him. He was waving both hands wildly, his gaze switching nervously from Uhura-kirk to the ready Kirk-sulu. "Wait . . . ! Jim, have you gone mad?"

Kirk-sulu activated the miniature cutter and moved the high-intensity, dark blue flame closer to the metal of the box.

Desperately Kumara whirled to face Leader Sarvus. "Sir, I beseech you, stop this! The humans have gone crazy. You can't just open a Slaver stasis box with some crude tool. It could set off a disruptor bomb or some other ingenious Slaver trap within the box. A special device is required to open the box safely." He turned disbelieving eyes back to Kirk-sulu and the threatening little flame. "We could all be killed!"

"You want proof, we're going to give it to you," said Uhura-kirk indifferently. "Existence is a game of chances. We're not afraid."

"Just the same, Captain Kirk," urged Leader Sarvus, a mite shakily, "we would prefer that if there is any truth in what Captain Kumara says, you do not demonstrate your courage so recklessly. There is no need." He indicated the box with a long, graceful arm. "*I* believe you."

"As you wish, sir." Uhura-kirk looked toward the box. "Never mind, Lieutenant Sulu."

"Yes, sir." Kirk-sulu flicked off the cutter, replaced it at his waist. He fought to keep from grinning at the look of relief that appeared on Kumara's face. Well, he could hardly blame him. If their positions had been reversed, he doubted he would have been crazy enough to try and call the box bluff.

"It is true, honored leader," Uhura-kirk was telling Sarvus, "that a Slaver stasis box must be opened carefully. But there is no need to be concerned when the openers have confidence in their abilities. A stasis box is nothing more than a simple technological toy. Its age doesn't imbue it with any mystic properties. It's all a matter of basic physics." She glanced back at Kirk-sulu. "Isn't that right, Lieutenant?"

Kirk-sulu nodded, then reached out and gave the stasis box an impressive little shove. The box and aura fell to the hard, polished floor. This was a calculated risk, designed to demonstrate beyond argument for the benefit of the Briamosites how courageous and self-assured the representatives of the Federation were.

Of course, if Scott's aura-simulator should break loose inside the metal container, and the aura vanish without any other sign of disruption, Kumara and his colleagues could turn from frightened to threatening. But Kirk was worrying needlessly. Mindful of the captain's pre-set plans, the ship's chief engineer had secured the box's fake components tightly. The box bounced, but its blue halo continued to glow steadily.

The two Klingon subofficers yelped despairingly and dove behind their seats. Kumara's executive officer winced visibly, but held his position. Kumara did likewise, but his hands tightened on the edge of the table.

Kirk-sulu approached the box. He gave it a short kick. It went bumping and bouncing toward the Federation side of the table, while a couple of Klingon officers orchestrated each bounce and tumble with appropriate moans.

"I do wish," Kumara finally felt compelled to request, "that you wouldn't let him do that, Jim."

"All right." Uhura-kirk smiled. "I think we've amply demonstrated relative values of, well, not courage, but confidence."

"Insanity, you mean," Kumara whispered by way of reply, his eyes still fixed to the box.

"Lieutenant?"

Kirk-sulu picked up the stasis box, placed it on the table in front of his chair, and sat down.

Glowering furiously but helpless to do anything, the Klingon officers resumed their seats.

Leader Sarvus rose, placed both hands and long, limber fingers on the table before him as he regarded Kirk and Kumara. "The Council will retire for private discussion of today's session, gentlebeings. We must debate among ourselves all that has been told and . . . shown to us. Everything will be considered. If you desire them, refreshments will be brought to you. Since we may require additional information or elaboration of material already put to us, we request that you do not leave until we formally adjourn this meeting."

"That's fine with us," said Uhura-kirk pleasantly, after a rapid and unnoticed glance over at Kirk-sulu, who nodded confirmation of the Leader's request.

"And to us," rumbled Kumara, still eyeing the stasis box as if he expected it to leap across the open space between them and blow up in his face.

"We will return in," and the leader named a figure that corresponded to about two Federation hours. If Kirk's suspicions regarding Briamosite politics were even partly correct, the figure Sarvus mentioned was decidedly optimistic. He didn't expect the Briamosite council to conclude their deliberations in double the indicated time.

Not that that bothered him. He was prepared to wait. Events had proceeded well for the Federation. A glance at Spock-uhura showed that his first officer was also optimistic about the outcome of the conference.

There was a rustling of soft-legged chairs as the various Briamosite officials slid away from the conference table. A panel in the curving wall slid aside and the officials disappeared into an unsuspected chamber. That left the four Klingons and four Federation officers seated quietly facing each other.

Kumara had turned and was huddled with his subordinates. They conversed in whispers. Kirk and his companions did likewise, glad of the opportunity to drop their mimicry for even a few minutes.

"Captain, I've never been so terrified in my whole life," Uhura confessed in Kirk's own voice. "I never used to know what stage fright was. Now I do."

"You were terrific, Uhura," Kirk assured her. "And you, Mr. Sulu. You make a very convincing Vulcan."

"Thank you, sir. I had an excellent instructor."

"I must add my own congratulations, Lieutenant," said Spock in Uhura's mellifluous tones. "You've imitated me quite convincingly. I must say it is a strange sensation to attend a conference and watch while one's own self replies to arguments, answers questions, and moves about independent of one's own thoughts. It is very much like a dream."

Kirk's estimate of Briamosite decision-making ability was correct. At least four hours had passed before the assembled knot of gangly aliens filed back into the conference chamber and resumed their seats. They looked exhausted, mentally worn, but satisfied. Clearly they had reached agreement on one or more points.

Leader Sarvus alone did not sit down. Instead, he made a complex gesture with both hands, his amazingly flexible hearing organs dancing like the sails of toy boats in a spring breeze. "The Council of Briamos has decided."

Kirk leaned forward in surprise. So did Kumara. Neither captain had expected a final dispensation this quickly.

Sarvus noticed their heightened attentiveness, smiled with his ears. "We of Briamos do not do things in haste, but we like to do them without of time being wasteful. We do not feel further information is warranted or necessary. Enough has been presented, combined with what we already have learned, for a lasting decision to be handed down.

"Toward the unsuccessful side, we wish no animosity." Kirk tensed in spite of himself. "We wish to remain friends with all. But it has been determined that it is in the best interests of the United Systems of Briamos to ally itself with the United Federation of Planets."

Kirk began to smile broadly. He glanced to his right—and what he saw killed the smile instantly. Fortunately, the Klingons were so outraged and excited at the Briamosites' announcement that they didn't notice Spock was also smiling. If they had noticed that inexplicable anomaly...

"*Ssst!* Mr. Sulu!"

Sulu-spock looked down at the insistent whisper, the smile fading curiously. Kirk grinned back, hugely, grotesquely, and pointed casually to the "science officer's" mouth. Sulu-spock looked blank for a moment, then shocked, as he realized what had happened. The smile vanished instantly from his face and he resumed the dour expression more suited to a Vulcan executive officer.

Kirk returned his attention to the rest of the chamber. No one had seen the unnatural smile. Certainly none of the Klingons had, or they wouldn't be raving with such single-mindedness at their Briamosite hosts.

"Sorry I am," Leader Sarvus declared in a firm, no-nonsense voice. "But Council its decision has made. We have all the factors considered and balanced in objective fashion. We see no reason to change that decision. Nor can you present any additional evidence which would lead us to do so." He paused to let the Klingons absorb that. "Until tomorrow when we will an official leave-taking have for both sides, is suggested strongly we—"

"I have some suggestions of my own," a furious Kumara broke in. He was wholly Klingon now, his veneer of carefully cultivated gentility obliterated by the brusque finality of the Briamosite decision. "Since you have chosen to display the irrational obstinacy of so many of the more primitive races, you leave me no choice now but to—!"

Kirk had his communicator out and was in the process of activating it. He was too late. Kumara had come to the conference prepared to deal with any eventuality, including the Briamosites' announced decision. The Klingon did not bother with a communicator, with orders or directions, but simply touched a switch at his waist.

A vast humming filled the chamber, the heartbeat of a huge yellow glow that enveloped various sections of the room. Members of the Briamosite council scattered in confused panic. At their cries, wall panels slid aside and armed, alert Briamosite guards rushed into the chamber. But there was nothing for them to do, no one for them to arrest, no antagonists for them to subdue.

The Klingons, the four Federation representatives, and Leader Sarvus of the United Systems of Briamos had vanished with the glow.

Kirk realized what was happening before they rematerialized on board the Klingon cruiser. So incensed was he at Kumara's action that he nearly spoke out of turn—and out of character. Luckily, his companions were as furious as he was.

Sulu, carefully maintaining his Vulcan pose, spoke first as waiting Klingon guards herded the prisoners out of the transporter alcove. His angry but controlled comments reminded the others that they were still imprisoned in the bodies of their friends and shipmates. "This is a direct violation of the Federation–Klingon treaty," Sulu-spock declaimed. "Such an action is tantamount to a declaration of war."

"I would hardly go that far," countered Kumara thoughtfully. There was no humor in his words, but he seemed less apoplectic now that he was safely aboard his own ship and once more in control of events.

The prisoners were escorted down a corridor and into an elevator shaft. "The Federation–Imperial treaties have power only within Federation—Imperial space," Kumara declared pleasantly. Kirk badly wanted to respond to that statement, but forced himself not to. It wasn't his place.

Uhura-kirk had to speak for him. "The systems of Briamos lie within the areas covered by treaty."

"That's so," conceded Kumara as the elevator moved. "However, within an inhabited, intelligence-dominated, technologically advanced system such as Briamos, the treaties have no force. Briamosite independence takes precedence over outside agreements. If we were acting outside the region claimed by Briamos, then all treaties would be in effect. Within their system, Briamosite jurisdiction has precedence," he added smugly. "We're prepared to argue the point with the Briamosites, not the Federation."

"You're basing this kidnapping on a legal technicallity," Spock-uhura risked adding. "Submitting your specious argument to jurisprudence will reveal holes in it large enough to drive a starship through, Captain Kumara."

Kumara eyed Uhura's form curiously. "You dabble

in interstellar law in addition to handling communications, Lieutenant?"

"A hobby only," replied Spock-uhura, promptly shutting up. It was exceedingly painful, but Spock was going to have to force himself not to reply to the Klingon commander's continued perversions of logic. Lieutenant Uhura wasn't supposed to know about interstellar law.

"Don't talk to me of technicalities," Kumara countered.

"Technicalities!" Uhura-kirk exclaimed in disblief. "You call the abduction by force from a treaty conference of your counterparts a technicality? Not to mention the kidnapping of the leader of an independent system."

"By force?" Kumara's lips curled in a Klingon grin. "No one has touched anyone. As for the other, we'll argue about it later. I have no more time to waste on subtleties."

That casual comment was far more chilling than any direct threat could have been.

The elevator doors slid aside and they were ushered onto the bridge of Kumara's ship. Several Klingon officers looked back briefly from their respective stations. One called out urgently, "Honored Captain, the Briamosite security vessels are converging on your position."

"They have received word then that we've invited their Leader to be our guest," Kumara murmured.

A curt alien sound, midway between a cough and a grunt, came from the vicinity of the Briamosite leader. Translation was not necessary. Its meaning was abundantly clear.

Kumara made a gesture and two of the Klingon soldiers prodded the tall leader. He moved forward reluctantly. Kirk watched, thinking frantically, cradling the stasis box under one arm. It had been beamed aboard with him, and there was nothing more he could do beyond grabbing it before some Klingon plucked it from its resting place in the transporter alcove. He wondered how much longer it would be before Kumara's attention switched from the viewscreen forward and the closing Briamosite ships, to the softly pulsing box Kirk held tightly next to his left side.

"Give me an open channel," the Klingon commander instructed his communications operator, "to the Briamosite ships."

A few adjustments to his instrumentation and the Klingon nodded to his captain. Kumara indicated that the Briamosite leader was to come forward, where he would be within range of the bridge visual pickup. When the leader refused, he was "assisted." Not especially gently, Kirk noted tight-lipped.

"They're your ships," Kumara said, indicating the converging shapes on the main viewscreen. "Tell them that you're in good health and that as long as they keep their weapons quieted you will not be harmed."

"Why to my people should I lie?" The Leader stared over Kumara's head, entwined his flexible fingers in resignation.

"If you insist on playing the martyr, then naturally I can't stop you," said Kumara shrewdly. "You can always be one later. I think we can resolve our present situation, if you don't find our hospitality pleasing. So let's discuss before we come to any final, fatal decisions, shall we?" He indicated the viewscreen again.

"They can attack any time. Why rush your death?"

Leader Sarvus looked uncertain. He glanced back at Kirk-uhura for advice.

Uhura grew frantic, tried to look at Kirk-sulu without looking at him. But they had several simple, prearranged signals for communicating in emergencies without giving their altered identities away. One tap on the floor would indicate a negative, two taps positive. Kirk-sulu's boot stamped twice, nervously it seemed to any onlooker, and Uhura hurried her reply.

"Go ahead and tell your ships to hold back, sir. Let's see what Kumara has in mind, first."

The Leader's ears twitched sharply. "It shall be as you say, Captain Kirk." He turned back toward the screen, his gaze passing over and utterly ignoring Kumara. "As we have little experience in dealing with the things of Klingon, we must rely on the advice of those who know them better."

Leaning forward over the pickup, he gave the order not to attack. There was a wait. A report came from the Klingon science station.

"Scanners show that all alien vessels continue to maintain their positions, Honored Captain."

Kumara looked up warningly at Sarvus. "Tell them to pull back. They can keep us within range if they like, but they're close enough to make me nervous."

The Briamosite leader spoke into the pickup once more. Then the viewscreen showed the warships, now numbering an impressive dozen, moving away from the Klingon cruiser.

Kumara appeared satisfied, and turned his attention to Uhura-kirk. "Now it's your turn, Jim. You'd better talk to your own people. As soon as they discover you're not down on the surface, and learn what happened, they're liable to panic instead of reacting sensibly."

"That'd be hard on you, wouldn't it?" a bitter Kirk-sulu said. Kumara ignored the lieutenant.

"Any attack would of course result in your death, Jim, and that of your companions. Needlessly, as you'll soon see. Either that or we'd destroy the *Enterprise*. Neither possibility can be to your liking." He barked an order at the communications officer, who promptly switched to standard Starfleet intership frequency.

Kirk-sulu's foot struck the deck twice again. Uhura-kirk didn't even look in his direction this time as she absorbed the instruction. *"Enterprise?"* she said into the aural pickup.

"Scott here. Is that you, Captain?" The chief engineer's worried voice gave no sign that he knew he was speaking to Lieutenant Uhura and not Kirk himself.

"Yes, Mr. Scott. We have been kidnapped by the Klingons."

Scott started to reply, sputtering, but Uhura-kirk cut him off quickly. "Remain calm, Mr. Scott." (How fortunate, Kirk mused, that Kumara wasn't aware Kirk commonly called his chief engineer Scotty.) "We have not been harmed. So far, it seems we are not going to be. We are going to . . . discuss the situation soon.

"Leader Sarvus of the United Systems of Briamos

has been abducted with us." She added, for good measure and for Kumara's edification, "If it was only myself involved I'd have you arm all weapons and engage, Mr. Scott. However," and she looked back at Sarvus, "with the Leader of our new allies on board, we cannot risk a confrontation."

Kirk mentally wrote out a commendation for Uhura. She had managed to confirm officially that the Briamosites had now formally joined themselves to the Federation.

"Are you certain, Captain?" Scott inquired, emphasizing the "Captain."

"Mr. Scott," Uhura-kirk replied, "Mr. Spock, Lieutenant Sulu, and Lieutenant Uhura are all here with me. If any of them could speak, I can assure you they would give exactly the same orders."

That satisfied Scott that Uhura was acting with Kirk's approval. "Verra well, sir. But tell the Klingons not to try movin' a single planetary diameter farther out than they are now. If they do, we're goin' to open their ship up like a pre-stressed package of carbonated beverage."

Kumara chuckled. "Such belligerence!" The amusement didn't last but a couple of seconds. "That's enough," he instructed his communications officer. "Keep monitoring both *Enterprise* and local frequencies. I want to know if and when any of the involved parties contemplates aggressive action."

"Yes, Honored Captain," the communications chief replied efficiently.

Another officer called out. "The *Enterprise* is raising defensive screens, sir. Energy readings indicate that she is activating her phasers!"

"Calm down, Kivord," the Klingon commander said. "They're just warning us not to do anything without informing them first of our intent." His gaze traveled to Uhura-kirk and Leader Sarvus. "We have no intentions of trying anything without your knowledge . . . and consent."

Leader Sarvus recognized a negotiating cue when it was offered to him. "You mentioned we might to an arrangement come," he murmured resignedly. "What sort of arrangement? You must know there is nothing I, a single individual, can do concerning the decision of the Council."

Kumara took his time, walked away from them and sat down in the command chair. "I realize that we cannot force Briamos to rescind its verbal agreement with the Federation, no matter how much more beneficial an alliance with Klingon would be."

This time Sarvus didn't bother to sneer. "Whatever chance the Klingon Empire might have retained for future assignations with Briamos has been obliterated forever by your actions this day of," the Leader said woodenly.

"I'm aware of that." Kumara sounded disgusted. "Those who are foolish enough to join themselves to the Federation rarely manage to extricate themselves from their entrapment. The Federation has numerous exceedingly devious methods for insuring that captive peoples never regain their independence of action. Once snared by Federation lies, a race can never free itself from that efficient network of agents, lies, and deceptions.

"However, we can do something else. If we cannot convince Briamos of the efficacy of aligning itself with the Empire, at least we can prevent you from making the fatal error of joining the Federation. You, Leader Sarvus, will sign treaty forms declaring yourselves to be permanent neutrals. You will make no alliance, mutual agreement of cooperation, or material exchange of any official sort with either the Federation *or* Klingon." Kumara leaned forward intently.

"Furthermore, Jim," he told Uhura-kirk, "you and your executive officer Spock will acknowledge witnessing this treaty. You will sign, in your official capacity as ambassadors-designate, treaty forms to the effect that the Federation will not violate Briamosite neutrality or attempt in any way to induce the Briamosites to ally themselves with the Federation any time in the future." He sat back in the command chair.

"I think that's a reasonable request, considering your present situation, Jim. If you consent to do this, then upon the signing and registering with relay stations of the treaty articles, you will all be permitted to return to your ship and you, Leader Sarvus, to your world, free and unharmed."

"I . . . I don't know what to do." Sarvus looked hopefully at Uhura-kirk.

She responded, staring straight at Kumara, with the same words she thought her captain would use. "You expect us to give in to political blackmail, Kumara? If you kill us, the *Enterprise* will take you apart deck by deck. If the *Enterprise* fails, the Briamosite fleet surely won't. The Briamosites will know what you've done because you'll have to kill Leader Sarvus also. Once that's done, their alliance with the Federation will become stronger than ever. And there will be trouble on a scale you can't begin to imagine."

"Oh, I can imagine it," Kumara responded, unperturbed by Uhura-kirk's stormy reply. "I just don't think what you postulate could happen."

"You seem to place a great deal of confidence in the Federation's unwillingness to go to war."

Kumara executed the Klingon equivalent of a shrug. "A few officers lost here, a couple kidnapped there. That's not sufficient grounds for intergalactic war. Besides," he continued, smiling humorlessly at each of them in turn, "future political possibilities and the legality of the treaties you sign need not overly concern us here. What is actually at stake, now, here, this moment, is far simpler to grasp and balance: your lives. But there's no need," he added more easily, "to consider such extreme possibilities." The smile returned. "I can see that in order to convince you to see clearly, some persuasion beyond mere logic is going to be necessary . . ."

XVI

The Klingon bridge was silent save for the steady thrumming of instruments as the prisoners considered that first direct, ominous threat.

"This is the so-called civilization you considered allying yourselves with," Uhura-kirk said sadly to the towering Briamosite leader.

"Forgive us," Sarvus replied. "We were ignorant of true facts. That has now changed."

"One of our respective moral codes is not necessarily better than the other," Kumara observed, "simply different." He turned his gaze on Uhura's form. Spock regarded the Klingon commander calmly out of Uhura's eyes.

"Say what you mean," snapped Uhura-kirk. "Your attempts at rationalizing criminal behavior aren't fooling anyone."

Kumara ignored her, glanced at the Briamosite leader. "I think we can demonstrate the sniveling sentimentality of the Federation races in the face of danger, Leader Sarvus. It will serve to illustrate the undependability of the Federation in difficult situations. For example, it is enlightening to know," he went on, his attention returning to Spock-uhura, "that humans are absurdly irrational when it comes to threats to females of their species. All I need to do is threaten one of them. That one," and he pointed suddenly at Spock-uhura, "with bodily harm, and they will rapidly capitulate to the most unreasonable demands. Are those the kind of people you wish as allies?"

Kumara looked around the bridge, beckoned to one of the guards standing near the elevator doors. "Kora. Present yourself."

A massive Klingon ensign left his station and marched over. He was a young, hugely muscled specimen and stood nearly as high as Leader Sarvus's shoulders, towering over everyone else on the bridge.

"A little demonstration can be entertaining as well as instructive," Kumara said easily.

Uhura-kirk looked outraged. "This is barbaric, Kumara!"

"Perhaps. Sometimes old methods are best, however." Kumara glanced up at the waiting, silent ensign, then pointed across the bridge. "That one, the female."

Kora nodded, grinning wickedly.

"Not too fast, mind you," Kumara instructed the

bulky soldier. "I have to give our guests plenty of time to change their minds about my proposal."

Sulu-spock took a step in front of Uhura's body. "You can't let this go further."

"Why not?" Kumara appeared to be enjoying himself thoroughly. "I see no one who is going to stop me."

Several other guards now focused their weapons on the other three officers.

"It's all right, sir," insisted Spock with Uhura's voice, as he stepped out to confront the Klingon fighter. He looked at Kumara. "Let us proceed."

"Brave lady," the Klingon commander said. Privately, he was disappointed. She should be cowering in terror, as obviously outmatched as she was. Well, Kora would change her attitude fast enough, and perhaps her face as well.

"Don't try to interfere, Captain," said Spock-uhura to the real owner of the body he was using. "I'll . . . take care of things."

Kumara stepped down out of the command chair, gave further instructions to his fighter. "Remember," he whispered, "I don't want her killed. Rearranged convincingly, yes, but not killed."

"I will be careful, Honored Captain," the soldier insisted. Kumara nodded, then stepped out of the way. The huge Klingon advanced on Uhura's body, arms outstretched.

"You can stop this any time you wish, Jim," he told Uhura-kirk, "by agreeing to my requests."

Uhura-kirk looked agonized over the situation. Actually, it was a cover to allow Uhura a covert glance at Kirk-sulu. When the captain appeared content to let events take their course, she wiped the concern from her/his face and watched the open space in the middle of the bridge.

The Klingon reached out with a long, thick arm. Spock-uhura's leg whirled up and around in a peculiarly forceful kick that battered the grasping arm violently to one side. The kick was followed by a hand that thrust straight at the Klingon's solar plexus. Even with Uhura's lighter musculature behind it, the well-directed strike carried plenty of impact.

Kora *whooshed*, looked surprised, and backed away clutching at his middle.

"Don't fool around, Ensign," ordered an irritated Kumara.

"I was not, Honored Captain," Kora growled. Glowering ferociously at Uhura's form, he approached more cautiously. The combatants warily circled each other.

This time the Klingon feinted with a kick of his own. Before he could withdraw the feint, Spock-uhura's hands came up in a strange way and caught the leg. They twisted, applying leverage as well as force. With a crash the Klingon fighter tumbled to the deck. Several of the other Klingon crew members murmured in confusion among themselves.

Breathing hard, Spock-uhura stepped back as the ensign slowly climbed to his feet. If Spock had been using his own body, Kora would not be getting off the deck. He was trying to compensate for lack of strength with skill.

"Watch him, Uhura," Uhura-kirk warned.

It was a deserved warning. Doubly embarrassed now in front of his crewmates and captain, the ensign had turned an apparently routine assignment into a personal vendetta. He advanced carefully, giving Spock-uhura all the respect he would a Klingon male.

Spock-uhura thrust with an arm. A Vulcan arm would not have been blocked, but Kora just barely managed to deflect Uhura's slimmer limb. Forsaking any hint of subtlety, the much bigger, heavier Klingon rushed past the extended arm, charging blindly into the communications officer's body.

They fell to the deck. Powerful arms locked around Spock-uhura's waist and began to tighten. Spock knew he would have to do something fast or the body he was inhabiting would soon pass out.

Bending and moaning as if in dire distress, he reached back with one hand concealed beneath the two entwined bodies. It came up behind the Klingon soldier, caught at his neck in the difficult-to-duplicate fashion which only a born Vulcan could truly master, and pinched.

The massive shape of the ensign went suddenly limp. Spock extricated himself from beneath the Klingon bulk, stood up panting, and looked around.

Puzzled and angry mutterings came from the Klingon crew members. One, another guard, bent over the unconscious Kora's body, threw a bewildered look at Captain Kumara and an even more uncertain one at the retreating form of Spock-uhura, who had moved to stand alongside his companions.

"Well?" an angry yet confused Kumara said.

"Ensign Kora is alive but unmoving, Honored Captain," the inspecting guard declared. "If I did not know better, I would say he has been somehow paralyzed."

"Impossible!" Kumara gazed in disbelief at Spock-uhura. "He must have struck his head on the deck."

"Face up to it, Kumara," said Uhura-kirk, "our Lieutenant Uhura defeated your chosen fighter fairly by Klingon standards, and by Klingon law you can't force her to fight again."

"Yes, yes, I know." Kumara was desperately trying to salvage something of the disastrous situation. A glance at the Briamosite clearly showed that the honor of Klingon had suffered in the eyes of an inferior alien race. That was embarrassing.

Then he brightened, having thought of a way to turn a defeat into victory. "I have done what I really intended, Leader Sarvus, which was to fool these representatives of a heartless government into displaying their true inclinations. They are dedicated only to the arts of war, as their attitude just now proves."

"How can *you* say that?" interjected Sulu-spock, stepping forward. "You who are of Klingon, one of the most militaristic societies in galactic history. You have no room for honest feelings, for the good things of civilization such as art and poetry and song!"

This wholly impossible emotional outburst from the *Enterprise*'s executive officer left Kumara without words. "Poetry . . . Ah, you mean the coldly logical mathematical precision of rhymes."

"Oh no, no!" Sulu-spock protested vehemently.

"Members of all Federation races are sensitive to all aspects of creative endeavor. Myself, I often prefer free verse."

Spock-uhura shuddered at that, but no one noticed.

"From the heartrending strains of Szygenic music," Sulu-spock was saying passionately, "to the loose mind-stanzas of M'radd of Cait. Some of those sonnets are so . . . so . . ." Sulu-spock wiped away a tear. The unfamiliar precipitation burned, but Sulu bore it stoically. "You'll have to excuse me," he said, the tears flowing freely now. "The mere thought of his poetry causes me to lose all control."

If Kumara had been flabbergasted by the diminutive Lieutenant Uhura's prowess at hand-to-hand combat, the sight of a sobbing Vulcan was unreal enough to paralyze him almost as completely as was the still-unconscious Ensign Kora.

Uhura-kirk jumped into the silence. "You see, Kumara, you can't win. You can't threaten us into signing those treaty forms, and now you'll never convince this gentlebeing," and she indicated the Briamosite leader, "that everything you say isn't a lie."

"No doubt there is to that," Sarvus declared with finality.

No one could tell if Kumara heard any of this. He was in a state of shock, first from seeing one of his most powerful warriors knocked silly by a delicate human female, and second by the sight of an emotionally upset Vulcan.

Finally he blinked, seemed to see them clearly again. "There are a great many things in this universe I do not pretend to understand," he declared softly, with more modesty than the average Klingon fighter, "and today's events are among them."

He turned to face Uhura-kirk. "I concede this conference to you, Jim. I cannot continue playing the game while I doubt the evidence of my own eyes. You have won a round, not a war. But while I do not know how you have done what you have done here, I still can win a greater victory. You may return to the surface of Briamos," and he smiled mirthlessly, "but *that* remains aboard." He gestured at the glowing cube beneath Kirk-sulu's arm.

"That's not possible," insisted Uhura-kirk, playing her part to the hilt. "You know what the Federation's reaction would be if we turned over an unopened stasis box to you."

"My dear Jim, how outraged you can be. You have no choice in the matter. I am not a believer in useless causes, so I will not kill you when there is no benefit to it. Briamos has married itself, sadly for them, to the Federation. Similarly, it is useless for you to insist on retaining the stasis box. It is allied to no one. It remains here, with me. I would rather have it than Briamos anyway." He threw Sarvus a contemptuous look. The dignified Briamosite leader was not affected.

Uhura-kirk turned to Sulu-spock. "Mr. Spock, your opinion?"

"It is a risk, Captain. The box hopefully contains nothing dangerous to the Federation. Captain Kumara is correct when he says we have no choice. He risks a major diplomatic incident over the theft, but that is his problem. We can do nothing except refuse transport. By moving within the field, we could conceivably kill ourselves, thus inviting attack by the *Enterprise* and Briamosite ships. But we have someone besides ourselves to consider." He indicated the watching Leader. "We cannot ask him to risk his life."

"Don't for me worry, gentlebeings," Sarvus said. "If you believe that box would be so valuable to these . . . creatures"—and he gestured at Kumara, who bristled but did not reply—"then I am here quite prepared to die."

"No. It would be useless," Uhura-kirk said, seemingly despondent but actually trying hard not to laugh. "Kumara would still have the box." She composed herself, faced the Klingon commander.

"We accept your offer because we have no choice. I'm betting the box contains nothing the Empire can use."

"A wise choice, Jim." Kumara was feeling progressively better about things. What matter a few systems? They had gained a Slaver stasis box! "Naturally, the box may be empty. Who knows?" He waved at the guards. "Escort them all back to the transporter room and have them beamed down to their previous positions."

The four Federation officers and Sarvus were herded from the room, Kumara's attention turned to the box. Walking over to where Kirk-sulu had placed it on the deck, he picked it up. Turning it over and over in his hands he finally placed it on the floor next to the command chair, basking in its strong azure glow.

"Klaythia," he called to his chief science officer, "set up a field nullifier."

"Immediately, Honored Captain."

"Perhaps this will contain the final weapon," Kumara murmured as he stared at the metal cube. "The device which will enable us to achieve our destiny and wipe the decadent Federation from this part of the galaxy, so that we may expand as was intended for us in the Great Scheme of Things." He walked around the box, inspecting it from all sides.

"And even if it is empty," he concluded with delight, "Kirk will have no way of knowing that. It will always prey on his thoughts that he might have given us an all-powerful discovery. At least, if nothing else, I will gain personal satisfaction from this unfortunate conference!"

The instant the five former prisoners had rematerialized on the surface of Briamos, before the startled gaze of two guards in the otherwise empty conference chamber, Uhura-kirk turned to the Briamosite leader.

"I hope you'll excuse us if we depart quickly, sir. There are reasons to think Captain Kumara might try to go back on his decision letting us go. We'll be safely out of the grip of the Klingon transporters back on the *Enterprise*. And some simple adjustments in your own communications equipment will prevent him from beaming you aboard also."

"No need to worry about that." Sarvus's reply was calm, but his ears were semaphoring like leaves in a hurricane. Other excited Briamosites were entering the room, having been called by the two guards. Several turned as soon as they entered, departing on the run. "I have just given orders for our ships to attack, assuming the Klingon beast has been foolish enough to linger within range of our weapons." He sounded curious now. "But why should the Klingon risk waiting here to try and recapture you? He has gained the valuable box. Surely he should be speeding away from this spatial vicinity to avoid pursuit by your ship."

"He might try to come back," Uhura-kirk told the Leader.

"We'll beam a complete explanation to you, sir," Kirk-sulu said, unable to restrain himself any longer. Ignoring Leader Sarvus's increasingly confused expression, he flipped open his communicator. "Kirk to *Enterprise*."

"*Enterprise* here," came the prompt response. "Engineer Scott spea—" There was a pause, then Scott added excitedly, "Captain! You're back on the surface. What—?"

"Tell you soon, Scotty. Beam us up immediately and prepare to get underway."

"But I . . . Aye, Captain. Stand by."

Kirk flipped off the communicator. While he didn't think Kumara would return on discovering that the stasis box had been opened previously and that the instrument generating its "stasis field" was a fake of Federation manufacture, he did not want to linger around Briamos to find out. The Briamosites could take care of themselves. While he didn't necessarily relish the thought of someone else destroying Kumara, diplomatically it would be better if the Federation wasn't involved.

Four pillars of multicolored energy filled the conference chamber. Beyond, tall pleasure-seekers enjoyed the warm waters of the cliff-cupped bay and the white gypsum sands, ignorant of the drama that had been played out during their vacation times.

Before his vision faded, Kirk saw the Leader of the United Systems of Briamos waving to them. His perpetually frozen expression had finally shattered, and he was smiling with his face as well as his ears, as if to insure beyond a doubt that Briamos and its sister worlds would remain a staunch and valuable addition to the Federation civilization for many centuries to come.

Kirk was no more disoriented than usual when he rematerialized back on board the *Enterprise*. Scott was manning the transporter console himself. When Kirk took a step toward the engineer, out of the alcove, he nearly stumbled awkwardly. It was an awkwardness, however, born of renewed familiarity. At the same instant he was looking down at himself, there came a startled exclamation from behind him.

"Captain!"

The voice and form were those of his helmsman, Lieutenant Sulu. But *he* had been occupying Sulu's body! And if Sulu was standing there, healthy and composed *behind* him, that meant that he—

Sulu finished the thought for him. "Captain, we're back in our own bodies!"

"So it would appear, Lieutenant." Spock stepped out of the alcove, looking expectantly toward the transporter console.

Scott trotted around to greet them, beaming with personal as well as professional satisfaction. "I tried to tell you, Captain, but you told me to beam you up *fast*. I figured that explanations weren't necessary anyhow. Besides, there was a *chance* it wouldn't work, that I hadn't made the repairs completely or properly."

"Unlikely, Mr. Scott, if you felt confident enough to beam us back up without warning us first."

Spock's comment was delivered with his usual seeming indifference, but Scott knew the first officer well enough to recognize a supreme compliment when he heard one. Spock's seemingly unconcerned statement meant more to the chief engineer than a fistful of written commendations.

He accepted it as matter-of-factly, however, as it had been given—one professional, high-ranking officer to another.

"I don't know about the rest of you," Sulu said, "but I feel like I'd been wearing the same set of clothes for twenty years and just had them cleaned for the first time."

"It's strange," Kirk agreed, "to be back in something you never imagined being without." He smiled tightly at his chief engineer. "Thanks, Scotty. Ship's status?"

"Ready to leave Briamos orbit, Captain. All stations alerted and waiting."

"Then we'd better get underway." He moved to the nearest intercom, flipped it to open mode.

"Bridge, this is the captain speaking," he said forcefully, thoroughly enjoying the sound of his own voice inside his head.

"Is it really the captain?" came the uncertain reply. Kirk recognized the gentle voice of Lieutenant Arex.

"It is, Lieutenant. We're all back in our own homes again. Warp-factor three, set course for Starbase Twenty-Five. I'll be up in a second."

"Very good, sir. And sir?"

"Yes, Lieutenant?"

"It's great to have you back where you belong."

"Thanks, Mr. Arex." Kirk grinned at the ancient snatch of song. "We feel the same. Kirk out."

Uhura stepped down out of the alcove, still a little dizzy from reintegration, in more sense than one. "You can go now, Mr. Scott."

The chief eyed her oddly. "I beg your pardon, Lieutenant?"

She looked abruptly embarrassed. "I'm sorry, sir. I was still playing the captain."

"And you did a conference-saving job of it, too, Lieutenant Uhura." Kirk eyed each one of them in turn. "That's something which will go into everyone's records. Let's go."

As they stepped into the waiting turbolift car, Kirk noticed that the communications officer was limping. Old fears came back. Perhaps Scott's rectifier hadn't been one hundred percent corrected. "What's the trouble, Lieutenant?" he inquired uneasily.

"I've got a bruise that feels like it covers the whole back of my right leg, sir," she replied feelingly, "and both my arms weigh about twice normal."

"I am sorry about that, Lieutenant Uhura." Spock sounded apologetic. "It was difficult enough for me to counter the size and strength of the Klingon soldier

Captain Kumara pitted against me. I'm afraid I was forced to employ muscular arrangements which your body is not familiar with, as well as blocking off certain neural responses in order to shut off pain so I could remain functioning."

Uhura winced, rubbed at the back of her injured leg. "I wish you'd been a little more careful, Mr. Spock. I'm pretty proud of this body myself and I don't like having it banged up."

"Truly, I'm sorry, Lieutenant. If there had been another way of avoiding the damage, I assure you I would have employed it."

They emerged on the bridge to be greeted by a number of uncertain stares. As soon as it was made abundantly clear to all that the four officers were back in their original selves, the bridge personnel relaxed.

One who was waiting to greet them on their return strolled over to the command chair as soon as Kirk had seated himself.

"If you've no objection, Jim, there's something I'd like to request of you." McCoy indicated Uhura, Sulu, and Spock. "Of all of you."

"What is it, Bones?"

"When we're well on our way, I'd like to interview you four and record the interviews. I think the results would make an excellent monograph, one I'd like to submit for publication in the *Journal of Starfleet Physicians*. Mind-to-body transposition has been accomplished surgically, via transplant, but never before by transporter. If we could determine how to do it safely and repeatedly, there could be enormous potential benefits for—"

Sulu glanced back over a shoulder from his position at the helm-navigation console. "Just as long as I don't have to go through it again, Doctor."

"Nor I, Lieutenant," added Spock from behind the science console, in a tone that was not truly emotion-laden but that carried plenty of impact.

Kirk checked the main viewscreen. Stars showed brilliant against the velvet blanket of space where Briamos had recently rode. They were well on their way.

"The Klingons should be opening the stasis box about now. Don't you think so, Mr. Spock?"

"Yes, Captain."

Kirk was unable to suppress a sly smile. "Wonder what they're going to say when they find nothing inside except a small generator projecting a simulated stasis field?"

Spock sounded unexpectedly uncertain. "The scenario you envision is not entirely in keeping with the facts, Captain."

Frowning in puzzlement, Kirk turned in the command chair, stared at his first officer. "What do you mean, Spock?"

"It was not my idea, Captain." Spock almost sounded embarrassed. "It was done at Chief Scott's insistence. I remonstrated with him, insisting that it was a juvenile notion, but the chief can be difficult to dissuade when he fixes on a particular idea. Also, he has less tolerance for the Klingons than most of us. I could, despite my personal position, see no harm in allowing him to proceed."

"Proceed? Proceed with what? Spock, what are you talking about?" Kirk didn't know whether to be upset or consoling. Here he was sure the entire Briamos incident was behind him, and now Spock seemed to be hinting that something had been done without his, Kirk's, knowledge. The first officer's comment about Scotty's well-known dislike for the Klingons only made him more nervous. They had escaped Briamos with a solid commitment from its inhabitants, while avoiding any dangerous encounter with the Klingons. But now—

What had Scott done . . . ?

Kumara and his science staff had adjourned to a sealed, double-walled room. They stood behind a portable shield, watching through the superdense but transparent plate as the field nullifier continued to hum at the stasis box.

"Something's wrong," Kumara muttered uneasily. The nullifier had been operating for several long moments, yet the blue aura surrounding the box had not disappeared as it should have.

"I do not understand, Honored Captain," his equally concerned science chief said. "All settings and power levels are correct. The instrumentation is not complex and follows precisely the schematics set down in the manuals for such a nullifier. The aura should vanish. It should have vanished long before now."

"Try successively lower power settings, Klaythia," the Klingon commander suggested.

"I will try, sir." Klaythia adjusted controls on the remote he held. The third setting he tried produced an audible click. The blue halo vanished instantly. Everyone in the room was satisfied, except Klaythia.

"I don't understand, sir," he murmured uncertainly. "This stasis-field generator is operating at a much lower output than any previously recorded level for a Slaver box.

"There's a first time even for stasis boxes, Klaythia. Since the box itself generates the field, anything is possible. Maybe this box is especially old and its power has failed." He sounded pleased. "It may contain a particularly valuable device, to have been sealed for so long."

He was leading the assembled science officers toward the box, which sat on a low table in the center of the otherwise empty room. This was a great moment for the Empire!

A low whine sounded from within the box, rising rapidly in volume to a dangerous howling. The party of Klingons froze.

"Is that normal, Honored Captain?" asked one of the lower-ranking specialists.

"No. No, I've never heard of it happening before," declared Kumara, taking a cautious step backward.

The whining increased. Powerful lights began to glow, pulsing unevenly from the slowly opening top of the box. The whine became a scream and the box started to quiver and bounce on the table.

Kumara and the other Klingons continued their steady retreat, eyes glued in fascination to the dancing box. "Something went wrong with the nullifier, Klaythia. We've set off some kind of previously unknown type of Slaver self-protection device."

"No . . . Honored Captain." Even now Klaythia was more afraid of his commander's wrath than of what the increasingly energetic box might do. "I assure you, all was checked and rechecked before the nullifier was activated. It is operating properly. I admit I cannot account for the way the top of the box is opening without manual assistance but—"

There was a loud *bang* from within the box and several howls of despair from the assembled officers and specialists. The box jumped several meters, hit the right-side wall, leaped to the ceiling, then fell to the deck again, while the Klingons scrambled to open the sealed door.

The box lay still. Two officers paused, half in, half out the opened doorway.

A violent explosion blew the top of the box roofward. Most of the Klingons broke and ran in terror, shoving each other aside in their haste to escape. More colored lights shone from the box's interior. Flashes of bright, colored smoke appeared, formed glowing symbols in the smoky air of the chamber.

Kumara squinted, coughing in the haze. He discovered he recognized the symbols. They were Federation script and spelled out:

FEDERATION FOREVER!

And below that:

DOWN KLINGON!

Now the noises from inside the box organized themselves into a coherent pattern. Klaythia, who had flattened himself to the deck at the initial violent explosion, looked up thoughtfully. Kumara lay next to him and was climbing to his feet.

"I believe, Honored Captain, that those sounds are an electronic rendition of the Federation Interstellar Anthem."

"Imbecile!" Kumara belted his science chief hard

across the mouth, even as he was drawing his sidearm. "I am all too familiar with the insulting propaganda contained in that wailing that passes for music among humans!"

Aiming the sidearm at the cheerfully tooting box, he fired. There was a small *ke-rummp* as the box blew apart. The music died out slowly and rather pitiably. Kumara fired again, at the glowing words floating in the atmosphere of the chamber. The burst passed through the letters, blew a smoking hole in the far wall. He could only hope the infuriating words would fade before anyone else saw them. He turned away, confronted the face of a security officer who had gathered enough courage to peek back into the room.

"No one," he said angrily to the soldier, "is to enter this room until those obscene symbols have been cleansed from the air, and this debris disposed of. Is that understood?"

"Yes, Honored Captain." The security officer withdrew hurriedly.

Walking back into the room, he holstered his sidearm and kicked contemptuously at the shattered rubble of the box. Most of the container had been vaporized or melted by his weapon.

"Let this remain always in your memory, Klaythia," he told his science chief, "as an indication of the fiendish way in which the human mind works."

"It will, sir," said the subdued Klaythia. He stared mournfully at the remnants of the box. "What a shame, sir. . . . All that valuable Slaver metal, gone."

Kumara let those words sink home. Realization filled him.

Kirk was just a light-minute too far away to hear the stream of curses that filled the chamber on board the Klingon cruiser.